Praise for Norman

"A grand, sweeping historical r ... ration and development of the A... esting and engaging book for fans of the real history of the West."
541-258-7151—The Lincoln Journal Star

"Norman Zollinger is one of America's literary gifts to the future. . . . *Meridian* is a beautiful saga that makes one aware of his past and proud to be an American. It is a book that forges from America's history a reminiscence of the indomitable spirit that makes one proud to say, 'This is my land and these were my people.'"
—*El Paso Herald-Post*

"Zollinger's seventh novel is a richly detailed and colorful tapestry of history, adventure, discovery, romance, and suspense."
—*Publishers Weekly*

"[A] fine historical novel. . . . As one might expect of a Zollinger novel, the characterization is superb. . . . Once more Zollinger brings his formidable storytelling talents to bear on a subject about which there is much to say, but little has yet been said. *Meridian* is a magnificent novel, as close to being a true epic as has been written of this era." —*Roundup* magazine

"Zollinger brings his characters—especially the estimable Carson and charismatic Frémont—to vivid life in a historical setting suffused in violence and romance. A fine tale of Americans along their way toward Manifest Destiny." —*Kirkus Reviews*

"In *Meridian*, Norman Zollinger captures the spirit and the characters of one of America's most historically significant eras—the unveiling of the complicated geography of the West and the expansion of the nation's boundaries to the Pacific. Key players in the drama were John C. Frémont and Kit Carson. Zollinger brings these men and their comrades to life and leads them from St. Louis to California in sweeping drama packed with action and interest. This is not only an exciting story well told but a glimpse into a pivotal three years of America's past."
—Robert M. Utley, award-winning historian and author of *The Lance and the Shield: The Life and Times of Sitting Bull*

Forge Books by Norman Zollinger

Chapultepec
Cory Lane
Meridian: A Novel of Kit Carson's West
Not of War Only
Passage to Quivira
Rage in Chupadera
Riders to Cibola

MERIDIAN

A Novel of
Kit Carson's West

NORMAN ZOLLINGER

A TOM DOHERTY ASSOCIATES BOOK
New York

NOTE: If you purchased this book without a cover you should be aware that this book is stolen property. It was reported as "unsold and destroyed" to the publisher, and neither the author nor the publisher has received any payment for this "stripped book."

This is a work of fiction. All of the characters and events portrayed in this novel are either fictitious or are used fictitiously.

MERIDIAN

Copyright © 1997 by Norman Zollinger

All rights reserved, including the right to reproduce this book, or portions thereof, in any form.

Interior illustrations and map by Wendy Zollinger

A Forge Book
Published by Tom Doherty Associates, Inc.
175 Fifth Avenue
New York, NY 10010

Forge® is a registered trademark of Tom Doherty Associates, Inc.

ISBN: 0-812-54287-8
Library of Congress Card Catalog Number: 96-53955

First edition: June 1997
First mass market edition: October 1998

Printed in the United States of America

0 9 8 7 6 5 4 3 2 1

For the crew of the ONE–EYED JACK

Acknowledgments

Thanks are due to so many people the author is not sure he can list them all.

First to my wife, Dr. Virginia Malone, without whose patience, listening, reading, support, love, and advice *Meridian* might never have been written.

To Jim Crutchfield, who so generously contributed the background for the Bent Rebellion section of the book. His own fine book, *Tragedy at Taos,* proved to be a gold mine for me.

To my publisher, Tom Doherty, who redirected my attention to Kit Carson to begin with.

To my friend and agent, Stuart Krichevsky.

To my much-esteemed fellow writer Richard S. Wheeler for his continuing help and encouragement.

To Gil Jaramillo, the good friend who vetted my execrable Spanish.

To Jim Traver, "the Front Stuffer," who taught me about the Hawken gun.

And above all to my editor, Dale Walker, without whose sage comments and contributions *Meridian* would not be half the book it is.

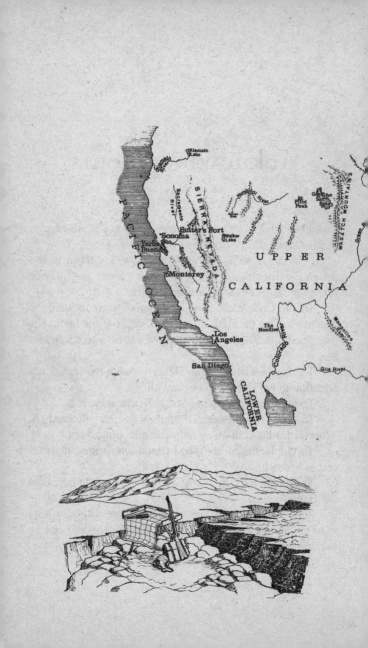

THE WEST 1845

Missouri Intelligencer—October 6, 1826

Notice to whome it may concern:

That Christopher Carson, a boy about sixteen years old, small of his age, but thickset, light hair, ran away from the subscriber, living in Howard Co., Mo., to whome he had been bound to learn the saddler's trade on or about the first day of September last. He is supposed to have made his way toward the upper part of the state. All persons are notified not to harbor, support, or subsist said boy under penalty of the law. One-cent reward will be given to any person who will bring back said boy.

(signed) DAVID WORKMAN

Franklin, Missouri

Part One

THE SCOUT

1

Encounter

No one could have made a more ridiculous, embarrassing beginning to a new career than Bradford Ogden Stone made when he first met Kit Carson at Bent's Fort on the Arkansas River that first day of July 1845.

The day marked Stone's twenty-third birthday, the first he had ever spent away from his home in Groverton, Illinois.

To blunder so badly with a man who had been his hero since childhood, and to do so in front of other men whose good opinion he desired, almost made him turn tail and run back to Groverton with the first wagon train leaving for the East.

But, to use the words he would hear Kit shout into the cold dawn in those frost-covered mountain camps, when he roused the men of the expedition from their bedrolls: *"It's time to catch up!"*

2

Bradford Stone had not had more than two dozen words with his new employer, Brevet Captain John C. Frémont, when the captain accosted him in the courtyard of the fort. Stone was headed to still another round of the salt pork, beans, and peculiarly leaden biscuits the Bent's Fort cooks had dished up for breakfast every day of the week he had already spent there.

"You will doubtless be pleased to know that Mr. Carson's

here at last, Mr. Stone," Frémont said. "He came in from Taos in the middle of the night."

"Where is he, sir?" Stone did not fail to notice the captain's faintly patronizing smile.

"He's in Charlie Bent's dining hall. He's almost through eating. Go on in and introduce yourself. I have things I must attend to."

Stone tried to stay calm as he moved toward the fort's great dining hall, but after half a dozen careful steps he broke into a run, slowing only when he reached the door, but not soon enough to avoid crashing headlong into the diminutive man in buckskin just emerging.

The little man took the force of Stone's hundred seventy-five pounds full-on and sprawled backward into the smoky air of the dining hall, flat on his back in the grease-mottled sawdust that covered the dirt floor.

Stone bent over him and stammered an apology, hoping that wherever Carson was seated in the hall he and its other occupants had not witnessed his clumsiness. From the hooted laughter issuing from the nearest trestle tables, this was clearly not to be.

His first wish was to get around the prostrate figure and find Kit, wherever he was, but a lifetime of family drilling in the demands of decency stopped him. He offered both hands and helped the buckskin-clad little fellow to his feet. The man's hands, clasped in Stone's, seemed almost delicate—and of a size with the rest of him. Flat as a pine plank, he nonetheless had good, broad shoulders for his height, which Stone guessed to be five feet two, an inch more at most, and a weight of no more than a hundred twenty pounds.

Stone thanked heaven that even though the small man was not smiling as he brushed himself off, there was a twinkle in his eyes. "Are you all right, sir?" he asked.

"Just fine. I reckon I've been handled a sight rougher a time or two in my life." He peered hard at Stone. "Say . . .

ain't you the new mapping feller from Illinois Captain Frémont just told me is coming with us?" Small as he was, he blocked the door, and did not seem in any particular hurry to step aside.

"Yes, sir," Stone said. "But may I get past you, sir? I'm looking for someone, and from here I could never see him through the smoke."

"I expect I know most everybody in there. Who is it you want to see?"

Well . . . even though he should recognize Kit Carson from pictures he had seen of him, it would not hurt to have him pointed out, and perhaps this friendly, harmless little fellow, who had taken what amounted to an assault on his person with high good humor, could make the introduction Captain Frémont should have made himself.

"I'm looking for Mr. Carson."

The man in buckskin smiled. "Well, you don't have to look another inch, friend. I'm Kit."

Stone's mouth dropped open. Then he added insult to near injury. "No!" he said. "You *can't* be Kit Carson! Why . . . you're just a little bit of a . . ."

"I sure am that." The tiny man smiled again. "But I am Kit Carson. Don't it beat all hell?"

3

For all the bizarre, bewildering, absorbing sights which had caught Bradford Stone's greenhorn eye at Charles and William Bent's massive adobe trading post in the last week in June of 1845, before the calamitous meeting with Carson, he had still turned his most frequent gazes on the distant southwestern mountain wall that leaned toward the plain. He had peered for hours through the glare and haze for his first glimpse of the famous mountain man and guide.

While he had looked for Carson all through that sometimes perplexing week, he almost forgot the exasperating sessions with his new employer, the equally famous Captain John C. Frémont.

Frémont had ridden through Bent's wide gate two weeks before he had, and had assured Stone, his new mapmaker, on *his* arrival that Carson would any day drift down through Raton Pass, one of the hazy trails Stone thought he could discern in the distance as he peered through Bent's big telescope.

In his eagerness to see Kit, and in his admiration of him, he discovered he was far from alone. The great scout had already cast long shadows into every corner of the fort a full week before he got there. Hunters, wranglers, wheelwrights, carpenters, traders, the unimaginative cooks—and even the ordinarily mute Arapahos who wandered through the compound—had talked about Kit's impending arrival as if it were a Second Coming. Many of them had known him before; some were seeking their first real sight of him as Stone sought his; all seemed every bit as excited as he was at the prospect.

Among Frémont's men the words *"when Kit arrives"* seemed an every-morning litany. By the time the week had run out Stone just knew Carson would *"bestride this narrow world like a Colossus"* when he rode in—not that Bent's Fort in those first days had appeared such a narrow world to him.

He had hoped from the outset that Carson would reach the fort for his birthday, but he had given up on that until he met Captain Frémont in the courtyard.

But meeting Carson *had* become the birthday present he wanted to give himself.

Even without either of the two men knowing about it, it could have been a far more rewarding birthday than it turned out to be.

He had missed Carson's actual arrival.

Kit had finally hailed the fort's gate in the middle of the high-plains night when Stone was sound asleep. Stone had become confident by that time that he had put his best foot forward with Frémont, after a shaky start.

Stone's congressman from the Second District of Illinois, Jakob Myers, the longtime family friend who had secured for him the surveyor-cartographer job with "the Pathfinder"—as the newspapers were already calling Frémont—had given him ample warning about the captain, and good advice about how to comport himself with the great explorer.

"Be a little circumspect with Johnny Frémont, Bradford my boy," Congressman Myers had told Stone when he put him on the St. Louis–bound train in Chicago for the first leg of his journey west, more than two months ago. "He's a brilliant man, and decent enough at bottom, I suppose, but arrogant and volatile. Quick to likes and dislikes. Chances are that you are a more skilled topographer than he is, certainly more up-to-date in the arts of your profession, but I would not let him discover all your talents until you have worked for him awhile. He is inordinately proud of his own abilities, and he doesn't care much for rivals. I would be particularly careful about all the painting you propose to do along with your mapping duties. He's an artist of some accomplishment himself, you know."

"Should I abandon my plans in that regard, sir?"

"Not at all; just be as delicate with Johnny Frémont as you can."

In all modesty, he knew Myers was probably right about his mapmaking being more "up-to-date" than Frémont's. He had studied the published maps the Pathfinder had produced on his journeys of the past three years, and he had persuaded himself that as excellent as the work *seemed* at first glance, Frémont still worked primarily as a traditional "plane method" surveyor, and obviously had little knowledge of the newer geodetic disciplines Professor Wendell Strike of Harvard College had just begun to teach when Bradford Stone studied with him back in Cambridge.

As for Frémont's artistic skills, Stone knew nothing of his abilities in oils or watercolors, except that some distinguished botanists in America and Europe, none of whom had ever set foot in the far West, had praised the Pathfinder's renderings of Rocky Mountain flora unreservedly.

"And Carson, sir?" Stone, with his tearful mother and his sister Carrie looking on, had asked the congressman on the windy Illinois Central platform before boarding his train.

"I won't claim to know Christopher Carson at all, Bradford, although I met him briefly when Frémont brought him to St. Louis once. There has been an enormous amount written about him, of course, but except for Johnny Frémont and his wife Jessie, and Senator Benton, I suppose, I don't think any easterner *really* knows him."

If Congressman Myers did not know Carson that day, in his sublime ignorance Stone felt sure *he* did.

He had read every word about Kit Carson he found in print, and as Jake Myers had just said, there had been a lot of words, all glowing, some defying credibility. A good many of the stories about the mountain-man-now-turned-explorer's-guide had been related by Frémont himself in the reports to Washington which the congressman made available to Stone. More accounts of Carson's exploits had been read into the Congressional Record by Myers' good friend and political ally, the Pathfinder's father-in-law, Thomas Hart Benton, the powerful U.S. senator from Missouri, who was called "the Thunderer" by friend and foe alike for his booming speeches in the United States Senate on behalf of westward expansion.

But most of the stories of Carson's exploits Stone had found himself: articles in *Century Magazine* that Frémont's gifted wife had written, and the stirring tale called *Outnum-*

bered: Kit Carson and the Cheyenne Hundred, which purported to tell the story of a typical single-handed Carson triumph over a horde of bloody redskins. This lurid ten-cent
novel had been penned by one Horace Trevelyan, a New
York writer of adventure stories. The book rested now in
Stone's baggage, awaiting still another reading, his third
since he'd found it in a Boston bookstore.

All the works on Carson had made him the most famous
westerner in the country in this first half of the nineteenth
century.

Yes, Brad Stone felt sure he knew Kit Carson long before
he met him.

He did not make his first small revision of that supposed knowledge of the great mountain man until he
reached St. Louis, where an overnight stay was made
more pleasant by a letter Congressman Myers had sent
weeks before. The letter introduced him to Senator Benton
and his reportedly handsome, formidably intelligent
daughter, Jessie Frémont.

No sooner had Stone settled into a room at the Planter's
House near the riverfront than a message from Mrs. Frémont
came by runner, inviting him to dine with her and her father
at the Frontenac.

4

He met them in the old hotel's candlelit, mahogany-paneled
dining room, flattered that they would make time for him.

He enjoyed the wine, the marvelous *filet de boeuf,* and
their company, Mrs. Frémont's particularly. She reminded
him of his older sister Carrie, who had always understood
him better than anyone else in the family. He was still grateful to Carrie for the way she had stood between him and his
mother's daily entreaties not to go out into "that savage

wilderness," right up to the moment they said good-bye to him with Jakob Myers looking on. "You still don't understand, Mother," Carrie had said. "Brad owes this to himself. Going west and meeting Mr. Carson has been his dream as long as I can remember."

He would have enjoyed Benton and his daughter even more had he not been so apprehensive and nervous, sitting at dinner with such an important, cosmopolitan pair, and had he known it was the last civilized dining—by eastern standards—he would do for more than half a year, and the last good piece of beef he would eat for three long months.

Over sherry before they ate, Benton made an impassioned harangue—in lofty rhetoric which brought to mind some of the senator's campaign speeches Stone had read—about the importance of the opening of the West to "the manifest destiny of our great nation." Benton was a big man, with the head of a lion and a trumpet voice. He went on with what amounted to another marathon speech throughout dinner, talking first about the "significant part you will play in that destiny, young man." He spoke about his son-in-law's western exploits and future political prospects at great (and by the time coffee arrived, almost boring) length—when all Stone really wanted to hear was more about Kit Carson.

After all, the senator and Mrs. Frémont were the only people he had ever met who were actually intimately acquainted with the former trapper and Indian fighter.

He hung on the senator's words—Mrs. Frémont's, too, when her overpowering father permitted her more than one—listening for any chance scrap about the westerner who had become his secret hero. None came. When they reached dessert and the time neared to take his leave, Stone had learned little about Carson he had not already known, but he dared not voice his disappointment.

He had brought two of Jessie Frémont's *Century* articles on Carson to the Frontenac to get them signed, and when he

pulled them from his new Moroccan-leather dispatch case—
a farewell present from Carrie to her "explorer" brother—
his dog-eared copy of *Outnumbered* slipped out of the case
as well.

Mrs. Frémont pointed to the book and laughed. "I'm not
sure I would show that to Mr. Carson when you reach him,
Mr. Stone."

"I don't understand, ma'am. It's certainly not critical of
him. On the contrary . . ."

"That's just it. The author has praised Kit more than he
likes—and for things Kit says never actually happened. He
says he is not the hero Mr. Trevelyan pictures in his book,
and that in the scene where the hundred-odd Cheyenne
chase him down that mountainside, he would have kept right
on riding, instead of stopping to kill thirty of them." She
laughed again. Her laugh warmed him, but he thought he
detected some pain in it, too. "But then he's demurred at
some of *my* literary efforts on his behalf as well, and as far
as I know I've always been scrupulously faithful to the facts
of his experiences with the Indians as he related them to
me—very reluctantly, I might add. Getting Kit to talk about
himself at all is like pulling teeth. I think he would be happier if no one ever wrote a word about him. Wait and see."

That surprised Stone a little. Trevelyan and the other eastern chroniclers of Kit and his adventures had painted him as
a towering Arthurian paladin who frequently recounted his
prowess in bardic tones at the Round Table of popular opinion, a man possessed of an astonishing amount of sophisti-
cation. It had not put him off, but he delighted in learning
now of his hero's becoming modesty from someone who
actually knew him.

And Mrs. Frémont had just said, "Wait and see." Wait?
Stone had no notion of how long that wait would be.

"Jake Myers says that mapmaking is only one of your
gifts, Mr. Stone," Senator Benton said now. "He informs us

that you are a talented portrait and landscape painter as well. Oils, I believe Jake said."

"I . . . dabble, sir." He felt as if he were confessing a dirty little secret. All through his boyhood, his young chums had teased him about the time he spent sketching and painting instead of playing One Old Cat or hunting possum in the bottomlands of Salt Creek, the brackish stream that meandered through the low thornwood forest northeast of his home in Groverton.

"Is it your intention to make a pictorial record of Johnny's expedition," Benton asked, "and perhaps capture the West the way Inness and Cole recorded the eastern wilderness before we tamed *it?*"

"Some such idea has crossed my mind, Senator. But I could never place myself in the company of the artists you just mentioned . . ." Congressman Myers' warning suddenly leaped to mind and he almost stammered, ". . . or in that of Captain Frémont."

"Mr. Stone," Jessie Frémont broke in, "could you please do at least one small sketch of Johnny the moment you join him at Bent's Fort—and send it back to me? He only spent a few days with us here in St. Louis before he left for the Arkansas again with the new orders he got from President Polk. It will be dreadfully long before I see him."

"I would be delighted, Mrs. Frémont—if the captain will consent to sit for me."

"Yes . . . getting Johnny to sit, for anything, can be difficult." She smiled good-humoredly. "Thank you, Mr. Stone." The smile suddenly went into hiding. "And please do other sketches from time to time. Men change when they face danger almost every day for months on end." Strong woman though she might be, an almost palpable fear and concern for her husband emerged as plainly as if she had spoken of it. It struck Stone then how much the lonely life of an explorer's wife when he is off on his adventures must resemble the temporary widowhood of a woman a seafaring captain has left behind. That accounted for the small pain he had heard in her laugh.

And perhaps her sudden plunge into gravity—and the remark about men and danger—made him wonder as suddenly if he would ever see Senator Benton and his daughter again, considering the hazards he was sure to face when he set off into the wilderness with John Frémont and his legendary scout Kit Carson.

Making maps for the Pathfinder in the high dark forests of the West, perhaps under the watchful eyes of hostile savages, would be quite a different exercise from surveying town building lots and mapping farmlands in settled northeastern Illinois, as he had done since leaving Harvard College. The deadliest perils he had faced in his brief professional career had been a balky horse, a broken buggy wheel, and a miserable bout with poison ivy. Well, he had known genuine danger once, in a Gloucesterman schooner during a storm off Martha's Vineyard on a holiday outing with Harvard classmates, but he could not claim to ever have looked on death close-up.

But he felt no fear when he bade the senator and Jessie Frémont farewell in the staid tranquillity of the Frontenac's dining room, but that look on her face in those last moments before he left sent a prickle of apprehension racing across his scalp, making it tingle as it sometimes does in that highly charged second just before lightning strikes.

5

Early next morning he proceeded to the St. Louis coaching station to catch the stage for Independence. The late night with the senator and Mrs. Frémont had caused him to sleep in, and even though he passed up breakfast, he arrived none too early. Two other passengers occupied the open-sided coach: a tall, gaunt, leathery older man—in a homespun coat and high-water pants, whose face was spiky from a hit-or-miss shave, and who held what Stone took to be a Kentucky squirrel rifle between his legs—sat with a plain-looking woman in a faded calico bonnet and a soiled man's duster.

An impatient, scowling driver who said his name was Sam helped Stone load the rattletrap conveyance with the gear a Negro boy from the Planter's House had carted to the station for him. Stone's tardiness doubtless had provoked Sam's scowl, as well as did the mountain of luggage Stone was taking west: a treasured, brand-new transit theodolite; the polished-pine plane table and its calibrated scope inherited from Uncle Tom Ogden; his drafting kit holding the French aledade; two priceless jeweled-bearing Thaxter compasses; the sixty-six-foot, weighty length of surveyor's Gunter chain; his tubes of oils; brushes; a bulky stock of canvas together with its stretchers; and two floral patterned carpetbags stuffed with his extra clothes and books—including, naturally, and in spite of Jessie Frémont's gentle dismissal of it, the Trevelyan.

"Where's your raffle?" the sour driver asked when he and the boy had stacked everything on board.

"My what, sir?"

"Your raffle!"

The tall male passenger in the coach chuckled. "Sam means your rifle, mister," he said. He patted the long gun between his legs. In spite of the "mister," Stone thought he heard a faint touch of French in the tall man's accent.

He turned back to the driver. "I don't own a rifle, sir."

Sam's eyes went wide and he shook his head. "You fixing to go out on the prairie without a raffle? Suffering Christ! You got a *handgun*, then?"

Stone shook his head.

The driver heaved a sigh of magnificent disgust. "Ain't a wagon boss in Independence will let you join his train without no weapon, partner. You best fix yourself up with a firearm soon as we hit Fort Osage. It'll cost you. You should have gotten one here in St. Louie, but now we ain't got time. I'm rolling this here rig in one more minute."

Stone instantly resolved not to let Sam know that in addition to never having owned a gun, he had never even fired one. For the first time he regretted not joining his boyhood companions on those abortive hunts in the scrubby Salt Creek woods.

The bonneted woman amazed him by sleeping through the entire initial half-day of the long, spine-jarring journey through Missouri's hilly woodlands, and although the gaunt man stayed awake, it appeared as if he would never speak another word. Not too surprising. Unless he had yelled at the top of his voice he could never have made himself heard above the racket the ironbound wheels of the coach made on the pitiful roads.

They stopped at noon at a pleasant stream in rolling wooded country. The driver clambered down from his high seat and wandered into the thickets of sumac bristling on the roadside embankment to relieve himself, and in a moment the gaunt man followed him. They had taken one other such break at about ten, but as Stone recalled, their lady companion had not availed herself of the midmorning opportunity. He felt no particular urgency himself, but he thought it courteous to give her a chance to find a secure place of her own without being directly under his masculine scrutiny as she sought it. He joined the other two.

By the time the three men finished their business and returned to the coach, the woman in the bonnet had perched herself on the stage's fender, opened a huge wicker hamper, and was taking jars and packets from it. The gaunt man hurried toward her as the driver hoisted himself back into his seat, reached behind him and pulled an oilskin pouch from somewhere under one of Stone's carpetbags.

Food!

In his rush to leave the Planter's House and get to the coach stop, he had forgone breakfast, and had forgotten all about provisioning himself. Until that moment he had not given a solitary thought to any need to eat, and in his excitement had felt no pangs in his empty stomach, but now . . .

He wandered down to the stream, chagrined at his tender-foot's lack of foresight, trying his best to look casual and disinterested, and praying in silence that wherever they stopped for the night it would be possible to buy a meal. Fort Osage still lay uncounted miles and another full day ahead.

"Mister!"

It was the man's voice calling him while the woman beside him beckoned with what looked to be a shank of mutton.

"Emmy has here more than enough for three," the tall man said next. The slight accent was more noticeable now.

The woman called Emmy scooped hardtack and some suspiciously glutinous-looking grits onto a flimsy slab of bark she had evidently ripped from one of the birches at streamside while the three men were taking care of matters in the sumac thicket. No eating utensils were anywhere in sight; Emmy's less-than-immaculately-clean fingers had just raked the grits onto the bark. Stone took a deep breath and dug in with his own.

The woman still had not uttered a peep, and something about the way she repeatedly glanced at the tall man told Stone that without his express permission she would not do so for the entire trip. He had begun to think they would make the journey in total silence, but when the other man finished stoking a mouth that looked as if it had been slashed into his face with a knife, he belched and pushed a greasy hand at Brad.

"I am called Legrand, mister . . . Baptiste Legrand," he said. "This woman here is *ma femme,* Emmy. I ordered her from a farm in Pennsylvania. How does one call *you?*"

"Bradford Stone, sir." Legrand had *ordered* her? Stone had heard of such barbarous arrangements, but had never really thought he would examine one as close as this. "May I pay you or Mrs. Legrand for the food?"

"No, no, no!" The refusal was so vehement Stone thought perhaps he had offended him, until the man continued. "You will do as much for someone else many times before all your journeys end. Sam says you voyage as far as Bent's."

"Yes, sir."

"And what will one do at Bent's? Is one a trader?"

"No. I will leave from there to map the route through the mountains to Oregon."

"It will be one's first time to the far Northwest?"

"Yes."

Legrand laughed, then turned his gash of a mouth into the grin of a gargoyle.

"Excusez-moi," Legrand said. "One did not mean to laugh, Mr. Stone, but this is a strange turn, *vraiment.* On your very first trip through the mountains you will open the way for Emmy and me to go to Oregon when they let the next wagon trains leave for the Northwest next spring. Five years ago it would have been me leading *you* through the Rockies."

"You are experienced in the mountains, Mr. Legrand?"

"I hunted beaver there for thirty-two years. Three more years than I should have. Beaver is all gone now, but, *sacrebleu,* so is the market. Emmy will teach me to become a farmer. It is a trade I do not know."

Stone thought that Baptiste Legrand, in his homespun

jacket, too tight for even his spare frame, already looked like a farmer, one dressed to go to town. Then he pictured Legrand in buckskins and furs, and it made all the difference in the world. There *was* something about him of what Stone imagined a lean, mountain wolf to be.

That he had been a mountain man accounted for his being French, or more likely, French Canadian. Since the beaver trade exploded in the first forty years of the century, the West had filled with men like Baptiste Legrand, hunting fur alone or in the Hudson's Bay Company's Canadian brigades. Most often they competed with Americans, but not infrequently they trapped the same streams side by side with men like Jed Smith, Jim Bridger, Beckwourth—and Kit Carson.

Stone *had* to ask.

"Mr. Legrand, are you by any chance acquainted with Kit Carson?"

"One has known Kit for more than fifteen years. Trapped with him for ten of them."

"Could you tell me about him, sir?"

It was the last question Stone had to ask.

While Emmy packed away her supply of victuals, stories of Kit Carson rolled from Legrand's thin lips like water over a spillway, and once back on the road—fortunately an easier, smoother one now, permitting conversation—the flow continued.

Yes, Legrand knew Kit.

Stone sat entranced as they rolled through glades that suddenly took on a wilder look, and he decided that if he had become a prisoner of hero worship, Baptiste Legrand had, for a far longer time, been a victim of a similar—and to him every bit as acceptable—imprisonment. Until then, Stone had not realized what an almost proprietary interest in Christopher Houston Carson he had developed. Kit belonged to Bradford Stone, and now this former comrade of Carson's was validating every thought Stone had ever had about the courage, strength, animal cunning, and stamina of the giant Frémont had called "the Nestor of the West" in one of his reports.

Legrand had witnessed Kit's celebrated duel in '35 with the gargantuan French Canadian bully Chouinard—or Shunar, according to most reports.

The Frenchman had been terrorizing his own countrymen in the Hudson's Bay Company brigade which bivouacked with Carson's camp, horsewhipping them or beating them with his mammoth fists for little or no reason. When he turned his brutality loose on the Americans to similar effect, Carson confronted him, told him that even though he, Carson, was "the worst American here," if Shunar did not mind his manners he would "rip his guts." The Frenchman went for his horse and his rifle, and Kit, armed only with a pistol, no match for the long gun, Legrand said, mounted and rode toward Shunar before an entire camp which fully expected to see him killed.

"Kit surprised Shunar by riding right up to him before he could get the rifle raised," Legrand said. "They both fired, so close together we only heard one report. Shunar fell with a ball that went through his wrist and arm and Kit took powder burns on his neck. We had no more trouble with that *bête* of a Frenchman from there on out. Kit *était merveilleux,* let me tell you, Mr. Stone."

It was as if Legrand, in speaking of Shunar as "that *bête* of a Frenchman," had abandoned his *own* blood origins and identified totally with Carson the American—a tiny, but to Stone, telling, revelation. It squared with everything else he had heard about Kit's ability to inspire loyalty, even from former enemies.

Legrand confirmed that, too. "Some of *les sauvages,* the Indians he has fought, have much respect for him, even some of them whose people he has killed and whose hair he has lifted. One can say this much about Indians: they admire a brave man even if he is an enemy, and *le bon Dieu* knows Kit is the bravest of men."

Stone's fellow passenger had been present, too, in the bloody "island fight" against the Blackfeet, also in 1835, when Kit took his only reported wound, a fusil ball in his shoulder, and Legrand had taken part in an even earlier and more deadly Carson battle in 1833.

After Carson and his companions had recaptured some horses stolen by a band of Crow warriors with a vast superiority in numbers on their side, his satisfied fellow trappers had indicated their willingness to break off the engagement, just take their reclaimed animals and run for it. Carson, to teach the Crows a lesson, by Legrand's account, had persuaded his men to continue the combat until a dozen Indians were shot and scalped.

Perhaps that particular recounting should have shown Stone a new facet of the man he would soon meet, but it did not. The Carson he wanted was embodied in what Legrand said next.

"In all my time with Kit one never saw him afraid. I do not think he has ever known fear."

Would Bradford Ogden Stone ever belong in the company of such a man?

There was more, lots more, by the time they reached Fort Osage on the second night, and if Stone had already heard some of it at least in miniature, and would hear all of it again over the years, it was not enough. Eager as he was to reach Independence and push off from there for the great American desert and his new life with John C. Frémont and, above all, Kit Carson, he said a reluctant good-bye to Baptiste Legrand at Fort Osage, where the French Canadian said he would remain with Emmy until the next fall's trains for Oregon formed.

"Give Kit my regards, Mr. Stone," he said. "And fix yourself up with a rifle before you leave Independence. I would procure a Hawken gun if I were you, the model they call the Plains. It may be the best all around fusil made. Kit carries one, if he has not changed."

2

Beyond the Great Meridian

At Fort Osage Bradford Stone picked up his travel voucher for the next available wagon train for Bent's Fort, and was crushed when told it would not leave Independence for another fortnight.

As it turned out, he was able to put the time to pretty fair use.

He moved on to Independence and decent quarters at Smallwood Noland's hotel, a surprisingly accommodating and well-appointed hostelry for this far from the amenities of civilized life. With Noland's help he bought a horse and a mule to trail behind the wagon the freight company assigned him to, that of a Caleb Miller of St. Louis, a sundries trader on his way to Santa Fe.

It rained most of his first week in Independence, but between thundershowers he found the sooty shop of a gunsmith named Adolph Diefenbach, who brought out a used Hawken Plains for Stone's inspection.

When he hefted the Hawken in the dark little gun shop, its weight amazed him. He exclaimed about it to Diefenbach, a sour-looking man who peered at him through narrowed eyes.

"Weighs twelve pounds," Diefenbach said. Something about Stone must have told the gunsmith of his ignorance; he proceeded to show Stone how to load and cock it. "Sorry

I can't test-fire this piece for you—the rain and all." He lowered the hammer from full cock and handed the weapon back. "Might as well leave it loaded, mister. Never know when you'll have to use it. Keep it bone-dry."

Stone wondered why they could not fire in the rain. Carson had to shoot in downpours as well as blizzards. He tried holding it out in one hand and at arm's length, and sighted down the top of the hexagonal barrel in the manner Horace Trevelyan had described in the running battle Carson fought with the Cheyenne dog warriors in *Outnumbered*. Stone was not a small man, and his outdoor work as a surveyor had kept him fit and fairly strong, but in a few seconds his arm shook as if he had the ague.

Kit Carson must have the arm size and strength of Mr. P. T. Barnum's circus strongman.

"It's all right to keep it loaded, Mr. Diefenbach?"

"Long as you don't get it wet."

Stone checked the brass name plate on the rifle's stock.

S. HAWKEN
ST. LOUIS

It seemed the genuine article, all right, but he had to ask. "Tell me, Mr. Diefenbach, is this the same kind of rifle Mr. Kit Carson uses?"

"Not only the same *kind*, sonny." The narrowed eyes turned positively shifty. "I bought that fusil from Kit himself last time we seen him here in Independence."

This sharpster did not fool Stone for a moment. Diefenbach had probably already sold gullible emigrants "the same gun Kit fires" a score of times. But Stone said nothing, and left the shop with the weapon, together with a powder horn, a 100-grain measure, wire brushes, cleaning oil, and enough caps, balls, patches, and black powder that he felt he should be ready to engage the entire Cheyenne Nation himself—at least that portion of it Kit had not already dispatched to the Happy Hunting Grounds in Trevelyan's story.

More rain and two severe thunderstorms kept him in his own room or in the small public room at Noland's for the better part of the second week. With the Hawken in plain view he read *Outnumbered* from cover to cover one more time.

Jessie Frémont had been right. Mr. Trevelyan knew even less about guns and fighting Indians than Stone did. From watching Diefenbach load the Hawken, and even allowing for Carson's undoubted swiftness in handling weapons, he knew Kit could not have shot thirty howling Cheyenne warriors unless they marched up singly and patiently waited for him to fire, reload, fire, reload, and fire again.

He vowed to take the gun to some secluded place and practice what Diefenbach had shown him, but he never got the chance.

Word came to Noland's Hotel that Ben Shales, the wagon master, would call "Wagons west . . . ho!" the next morning, the eleventh day of May.

2

Ten o'clock on the second morning out from Independence—Stone sat alongside trader-merchant Caleb Miller in his big Murphy wagon.

Miller had filled the Murphy with hardware, yard goods, and patent medicines whose efficacy Stone doubted, with all Stone's baggage and equipment piled in, too, and his still-loaded Hawken right under Caleb's in a wooden rack behind the seat, wrapped in a finely meshed, oiled cloth Miller insisted on providing. The rifle was protected further from the weather by the wagon's canvas top.

They cleared the last of the patchy woodlands bordering

the turgid river Miller called "the Big Muddy," and Stone got his first clear, unobstructed view of the Great Plains.

Until that moment he thought he knew something about prairies; he had surveyed half a dozen fairly sizable ones in Illinois, acreage as extensive as a quarter section, hemmed in by hardwood forests on every side, some with chest-high grasses thick enough to stop his horse. The wiry, matted fronds he hacked his way through, lugging his transit and chain, would soon disappear, yielding to plows that would almost race each other across newborn farmland as soon as Stone's work was finished.

After one look to the West from Caleb Miller's Murphy wagon, the prairies he had mapped suddenly became garden plots, hardly bigger than the blanket on his bed at home in Groverton.

He stared openmouthed at a horizon-to-horizon, seemingly boundless, green vista of breeze-rippled grass, a scene totally different in kind, not merely in degree, from anything he had ever looked on.

What happened next certainly must have resulted from the small wind causing the grass to sway, from the shadows of the wild, dark clouds lowering far ahead of them, and from the pitch and roll of the heavy wagon—but the whole earth heaved and billowed as he watched. He knew then why the great, lumbering wheeled vehicles in this train were called "prairie schooners." They were setting sail across an uncharted ocean of grass, with the wind snapping at the canvas top of the wagon—puffing it out like the mainsail of that Gloucesterman off Martha's Vineyard and whistling through the ox team's harness and the wagon's guy ropes, and with the giant wheels creaking as does a ship's deck in a gale.

The tiny world of Bradford Ogden Stone had suddenly expanded, beckoning to him as if there were no one else in the entire wagon train.

He had loved his Illinois country since childhood, but he realized then that he had only loved it in the way a tradesman loves a nap after lunch. Awestruck by the lonely splendor and magnificent openness of what lay ahead of him, and lured by its seductive if unarticulated promises, he became in an instant a lover of quite a different order and magnitude.

That feeling would never leave him.

The "swelling scene" had become old hat, of course, to Caleb Miller, a decent, affable sort in upper middle age who had already demonstrated the patience of a saint in dealing with a rank beginner such as Stone; he was making his third trading trip to Santa Fe. Even in their relatively brief time together he revealed himself as a storehouse of knowledge about the trail they traveled, but he also turned out to be a slight disappointment in one significant regard. He had never met Kit Carson personally, although their paths had crossed a time or two.

Compared to that initial, staggering look at the plains, the rest of the six-week-long, grueling journey receded into the distant banks of memory.

The names of the places where they camped stayed with him, whether because he actually remembered them so well or because he was to hear them again so many times over the intervening years: Lone Elm and Council Grove—beyond which they would have to stay alert for possible Indian attacks, Miller told him as the hairs on the back of his neck tingled—were followed by Diamond Spring and Lost Spring. The "creeks"—Cottonwood, Little Cow, Pawnee, and Big Coon—came next.

"Actually," Miller said once, "the worst attacks along the trail don't come from Kiowas or Comanches. These trains got a lot of firepower. The Texians can be the most dangerous, and they ain't even Indians, but mostly they take out after the Mexicans coming up from Santa Fe. Now that

Texas came into the Union five months ago I can't figure out why Washington don't put a stop to it. The Texians will get us into war with Mexico yet, mark my words."

Stone had no feelings about this, no opinions. There had been war talk back East for years, but for so long now he discounted it, as did most people he knew. But he did store Miller's remarks away.

Alternating with the gentle zephyrs that cooled their sunburned faces, fierce west winds pummeled them, and once a full day of torrential downpours matted the grass as if nature had run a monstrous flatiron across the land. Only minutes after the storm passed the grass sprang upright again into glorious firm waves. And the heat and dust returned.

They saw herds of antelope, their leaps at a distance looking like more ripples in the grass, and once, just west of Pawnee Creek, after Stone heard what seemed distant thunder coming out of an absolutely cloudless sky, what appeared at first to be a dark river rolled across the plain in front of them.

Buffalo! Heading north.

Stone spotted Ben Shales, the wagon boss, and five more men with rifles at the ready, riding out after the pounding buffalo.

"Ben must have decided these here critters ain't got no redskins chasing them," Miller said. "Lakota lodges must be already filled with meat this year. By gar, *we'll* eat well the next week or so. Ever tasted buff, *amigo?* Hump is better than any steak you ever had, once you get used to the gamy smell. We'll have to pay Ben and the boys, of course, but he ain't no highbinder. He'll probably just ask enough to cover his powder, caps, and balls—and maybe two bits an hour or so for his time."

Stone glanced back at his untried Hawken in the rack. A brief daydream.

It took an hour for the herd to cross their trail and leave it open again. The dust from their passage hung in the air for another hour.

"I had no idea there were so many of them," Stone said to Miller.

Miller laughed. "*That* ain't many, friend Brad. Trip before last—my first—we had to circle the wagons for three days before one herd cleared out. Must have been fifty or more Sioux riding with them that there time. Minneconjou, I recollect. Turned out they was more hungry than spoiling for a fight. Wasn't even wearing paint."

"Were you attacked on either of your other two trips, Caleb?"

"Once. Kiowa. Hit us from out of a little scrub draw so damned quick we didn't have no time to circle. They was after horses. Funny thing, though. Hardly even much noticed the attack myself. They hit the front of the train where the *caballada* was that day, and I was near fifteen wagons back. Could have happened in a whole different country. But two of the Mex wranglers got themselves killed. We'll pass their graves long about tomorrow. One other lost his hair, but lived to tell about it."

Then, two days out from Little Cow Creek a band of nine or ten nearly naked horsemen appeared half a mile off to the left of them and rode parallel to the caravan for an hour. The tingle in his scalp this time was real enough, and nasty. It began at his hairline and crept backward pretty fast when the mounted men veered toward them and Miller reached back for his rifle. Stone grabbed the Hawken and cradled it in his lap as the trader did his.

"Brulé Sioux, it appears like," Miller said as the riders neared. "This bunch ain't going to be no trouble. Beggars." He turned and put his rifle back in the rack.

Stone held on to his.

He did feel disappointment at the appearance of the first Plains Indians he had seen.

These were not the "noble savages" of Jean-Jacques Rousseau, or even of the now suspect Horace Trevelyan. They looked dirty and destitute in their skimpy breechclouts, with greasy, lank hair devoid of feathers, and displaying cringing and furtive looks. None of them were armed.

They worked the length of the train, begging tobacco, powder, food, whiskey, or anything else the traders were willing to part with. When Stone put his Hawken away, he clambered back into the wagon bed and found his sketch-pad. He regained his seat just as the Indians rode up on Miller's side of the wagon, but with this closer look he returned the pad to the wagon bed behind him without a single stroke from his charcoal on it. He could not bring himself to sketch these pitiful derelicts.

"By the look of them," Miller said, "I reckon their own people run them off. Took their guns, too, I notice. The Brulé are proud folk. They don't cotton much to braves who let themselves go to hell the way this bunch has. Don't judge redskins by this lot, Brad. They been hanging around white men too damned long."

The remark baffled Stone. Should not an association with white Americans have elevated these primitive creatures, instead of turning them into mendicants?

"There's a length of calico back there I don't mind parting with," Miller said. "It's red and yellow. See if you can find it, would you?"

That night Stone made a sketch of Miller by firelight and gave it to him. The trader stared at it for five minutes and then grinned like sunrise.

3

Caleb Miller and Brad Stone parted company at the beginning of the new trail called the Cimarron Cutoff, where

Miller would slant down to Santa Fe with a dozen of the other traders and their wagons, forgoing a stop at Bent's. He offered to talk to another of the wagoneers heading for the fort on the Arkansas about taking Stone on as a passenger, but Stone had no objection to making the rest of his journey on horseback, although he worried a bit that the mule he would trail might cause him trouble.

He and Miller piled his gear on its back, lacing it on the stubborn animal with what Miller called a "diamond hitch," an ingenious web of ropes Stone was sure he could never duplicate.

He had failed to buy a saddle scabbard for the Hawken while at Diefenbach's, and Miller pressed one on him, protesting when Stone tried to pay him for it.

"That picture you done of me is pay enough." Miller climbed up into his wagon seat. "See you around, *amigo*." He turned his face to the southwest, cracked his long whip over the oxen's backs—and the huge Murphy wagon rolled away. He did not look back.

They had traveled together for more than a month, and although Stone was sure he had made in Caleb Miller another friend such as Baptiste Legrand, it seemed a casual, offhand farewell. It was too early in his life in the West for him to know how typical a good-bye it was.

4

When he caught his first sight of Bent's Fort on the twenty-third of June, he thought he was looking at another of the many mirages which had delighted him on the trek so far, and which, during the last week on the trail, he had tried in vain to sketch before they faded.

To his painter's eye, the huge, blocky building with its incredibly thick walls of adobe had no business spoiling the

otherwise unbroken sweep of the grassy Indian Territory
prairie. It looked far more primitive-Gothic than American:
a grim, dark castle-in-abstract, as improbable as any riverside mansion on the Hudson.

Squarish, but narrowing toward the east, the fort's
immense walls, thirty feet high it appeared, and perhaps a
hundred yards or so on a side, were blank and featureless,
save for the wide eastern gate, the only ground-level break
in its facade Stone could see, and a row of openings just
below the parapets. Rifle ports, he presumed. The southeast
and northwest corners were closed off by round watchtow-
ers, also adobe, complete with crude crenellations and soaring fifteen or twenty feet above what he took to be the
roofline when the wagon train neared the gate. From the
windy heights of the latter of these towers he would, in just
another day, take up his watch for Carson.

Since they left Miller and the other traders back at the
start of the Cimarron Cutoff he had ridden up near the front
of the train with Ben Shales, but not so close as to encroach
upon the busy wagon master. Shales now reined his horse
over to Stone's.

"We'll take the wagons clear around to the walled yard on
the western side of the fort, Mr. Stone," Shales said. "You
can head right on through the gate. One of Charlie Bent's
Mex navvies will take your horse and mule to the corral
once you get unloaded."

It pleased him no end to ride through the gate at Bent's all
by himself, with his Hawken in its scabbard.

Whether Frémont saw him ride through the gate or not he
never did learn, but the explorer captain came to his room on
the ground floor of the fort a mere five minutes after he'd
settled into it, bursting through the door without so much as
a knock.

"Welcome to Bent's, Mr. Stone! You will dine with me in
Charlie Bent's living quarters. He has come up from Taos to

take charge here while his brother and partner, William, is in St. Louis on business. We meet at six."

He left without another word—and without waiting for one from Stone.

5

Perhaps because of a slight uneasiness over Frémont's peremptory treatment of him, Stone, as they shared a preprandial sherry with Charles Bent, worried about what the Pathfinder's reaction would be when he asked him to pose for the picture he had promised his wife.

His nervousness proved unnecessary; Frémont fairly bubbled as he exclaimed, "Yes!"

There seemed little sign of the possibly jealous rival Congressman Myers had warned Stone he might find. The captain was far too confident a man, he decided, to envy anyone else's talents.

Mr. Bent revealed himself as a grave but friendly man. He was a stout man, and with his full but neat gray hair, his keen eyes, and in his black frock coat and boiled shirt, he looked more a Boston banker than the tough, shrewd boss of a frontier trading empire.

In spite of Frémont's enthusiasm when Stone asked him to pose, the dinner promised to be strained when compared to his being wined and dined by Jessie Frémont and her father at the Frontenac. The captain ignored him, exhibited toward him an almost massive indifference, directing all his remarks to Mr. Bent. Reserved as he was with Stone, he was voluble with the co-owner of the fort.

Even with the soft southern accent which came from his birth and rearing in Savannah, Georgia, Frémont's every word was forceful.

"We can't set off for the mountains for another month,

Charlie, because of the president's personal orders to me. But if we can't leave here by first September, we'll have to cross the mountains to the coast in the dead of winter. Little as I relish the prospect, it will have to be done. Even with the delay he insists on, the president wants us in northern California in the spring."

California! For the first time Stone realized the full extent of Frémont's projected explorations. When he'd signed on for the expedition with the help of Jakob Myers, he had thought that all the mapping would be done on the trail to Oregon, over the new cutoff route a man named Lansford Hastings had been promoting over the past year. In truth, Stone, in his preoccupation with meeting Carson, had given little thought to the principal reason for his being here at Bent's at all. He wondered what exactly President Polk's orders to the Pathfinder were, and why he would hold off their departure for a month—but of course he did not ask.

Mr. Bent eased some of the strain by getting Stone to tell him of his antecedents and background—and of what he expected in and from the West. He seemed genuinely interested. Stone could not tell if Frémont paid heed to any of it. Trying not to talk too much about himself, Stone feared Carson's name came out half a dozen times.

"Kit and I are related now by marriage," Bent said. "We married sisters down in Taos. I live there most of the time, you know."

At one point Charles Bent turned the subject to what people in the East might be thinking about the troubles with Mexico.

"Is there talk of war?" he asked.

"A little, sir. I did hear some on the trail. I hope it won't come."

"It won't," Frémont broke in. "I deplore the whole idea."

Stone tried to put the thought away from him, but he was sure he heard a slightly false note in the captain's voice. He took himself to task silently for doubting his new employer even for a second.

By the time his dinner companions turned their attention to cognac and cigars—which Stone declined, drawing a quizzical look from the captain—he had not spoken five more words, and decided Frémont had forgotten about their sketching session, but before they left Bent's table the captain said he would meet Stone in the courtyard at nine in the morning. "I hope you're good, Mr. Stone," he said.

6

Ordinarily he did sketches with his pad in his lap, but in his desire to do justice to his subject for the sake of Jessie Frémont, and to satisfy whatever demands the Pathfinder might make himself, Stone brought out the smaller of his two easels.

He set it up in the courtyard at about five minutes short of nine. It attracted a crowd immediately: buffalo hunters; trappers in greasy, fringed buckskin; a few Mexican traders out of Chihuahua—just an exotic name to him—and more from Santa Fe; an officer of the First Dragoons, come to Bent's from Leavenworth to buy horses. All manner of civilians from a variety of occupations crowded in on him, including one who claimed to be a doctor and who reeked of whiskey. A silent group of Indians, Arapaho hunters and trappers in the employ of Mr. Bent, and who presented a marginally better appearance than had the wretched visitors on the trail, made a circle around the others. Most of the Indians had wrapped themselves in brightly colored blankets, even though the late June day promised to be a scorcher, but a few wore the same canvas or woolen trousers and checked flannel shirts as did the white men who had gathered closer to him. Several had stuck what he guessed to be eagle feathers in their hair, but they still were not the "wild" red men of his boyhood dreams.

He wished he could capture some of *them* in charcoal, too, but he knew he must keep his drawing hand and his mind intent on rendering Frémont with as much fidelity as his skill and the distraction of his audience allowed. He would have much preferred to do the likeness indoors, but Frémont had insisted on meeting him outside, in the fort's immense inner courtyard.

At nine on the dot the door to Frémont's ground-level room, which opened directly on the yard as did his, swung wide, and the great man strode into the sunlight, his gait free and easy, that of a man brimming with an acute sense of his own worth.

John C. Frémont was of a height with Stone, who unless he bent his neck could not pass under a six-foot lintel without it clipping the top inch of his head.

"Let's get started, Mr. Stone," Frémont said as he took the chair Stone had hauled from his room for the sitting. "I can allow you exactly twenty minutes."

Frémont had dressed himself in buckskin, smooth, supple-looking, and spotless—unlike the soiled outfits Stone saw around him—and he wore a broad-brimmed, flat-crowned hat much like those of the Mexicans nearby, except that it had a narrow band of Indian beadwork around the crown.

Just as Stone began to work, Frémont looked up at one of the blanket-clad Arapahos who had settled in to watch what to them must have appeared some strange paleface rite.

"Lend me a feather, Sleeping Bear."

The Indian grunted and pulled one from his jet black hair and handed it to Frémont, who jammed it in the beaded hatband. Stone knew then that he looked at a man with a sure sense of style and dash; the effect of the feather was electric.

Stone had to work at greater speed than he would have

liked, interrupted as he was by a stream of some of the men on the rolls of the expedition who wanted to talk with their commander. His subject introduced most of them, but so hurriedly Stone knew he would not remember a single name. He had to stop completely for five or six minutes once as Frémont broke the pose to examine a string of horses paraded for his inspection against possible purchase for his exploration team.

In Stone's nervousness the night before he had not directly asked the captain about Carson. He did so now—but as casually as he could.

"Kit has been down in Taos, spending time with his new wife, Josefa, and her family, Mr. Stone," the captain said. As with the night before, it was not yet "Bradford," much less "Brad."

Frémont went on. "Kit's been trying to farm on the Little Cimarron. Damn it! He's no farmer. I need him. My expedition cannot get under way without him! Not to despair, however; I do expect him any day."

As he talked he bobbed his head with too much vigor for Stone's drawing hand to do its absolute best work, but Stone certainly could not tell his new commander to hold still for him as he would a hired model in a life class.

What had Jessie Frémont said? . . . *"Getting Johnny to sit, for anything, can be difficult."*

Frémont's mild impatience with the thought of a Kit Carson wasted as a farmer and a family man only served to enlarge the image of the great scout already in Stone's mind—not that it needed any such enlargement.

He did wonder about Frémont's insistence on his second-in-command rushing to his side. Had he not told Mr. Bent at dinner last night that the expedition could not leave for another month at the earliest? Obviously, Frémont wanted his people to wait on him, not the other way around.

Bradford Stone got to know the face of John C. Frémont

that morning. He supposed the only way to characterize it was as "noble." As he worked, clear, piercing, cobalt blue eyes stared straight at him from under brows as thick as Osage hedges and a high forehead framed in wavy dark hair. Above a firm jaw whose jut of aggression his full black beard could not quite hide, a wide mouth bent into a slight smile, a mouth used to giving orders and having them obeyed. But steady as he was when not talking, there seemed to be an air of tension, of nervousness, about him.

Even after the lengthy dinner, the man behind the face still remained a stranger. With those intense eyes fixed on him, Stone had the uneasy feeling that he was not quite measuring up, without even knowing what he was being measured for. Not one thing in their two brief conversations had turned on Stone's professional credentials, and only the one slightly threatening remark the night before—"I hope you're good, Mr. Stone"—had addressed itself to what Stone was engaged in at the moment.

When he finished and leaned back, Frémont left his chair and moved around behind Stone with startling swiftness and grace. He peered down over Stone's shoulder, close enough that Stone got a whiff of bay rum.

"Hmmm . . . ," was the Pathfinder's only comment.

Stone did not see him the rest of that morning.

7

Stone wolfed down a hasty noontime meal of cornmeal mush and beef jerky in the dining hall and set out to explore the fort. He wandered through the entire sprawling adobe complex, resisting with a herculean effort urges to poke his nose into places where he had no business poking it.

In another large, hall-like room piled to the ceiling beams with flour and bean sacks, saddles, traps, wagon parts, and all manner of implements and gear he did not recognize, he found Mr. Bent behind a counter doing sums in a mammoth ledger. In his green eyeshade and ink cuffs, he looked this afternoon more clerk than *either* banker or frontier entrepreneur. Bent looked up and smiled.

"I watched you as you drew Captain Frémont's picture, Mr. Stone. I sure don't know how you do it."

"I didn't see you there, sir."

"Kept well to the back. Sometimes a man can see more that way." The smile faded into a look of slight discomfort. "Mr. Stone . . . I may be speaking out of turn, but . . ."

"I don't see how you could be speaking out of turn with me, Mr. Bent."

"Well, I've kind of gotten the feeling Johnny Frémont's been pulling the cinch a mite tight on you, but of course it ain't my business to say . . ." He drew a breath. "Oh, hell!" He drew another breath. "All right . . . Brad, isn't it? I'll be as frank and honest as I can, then. Be a little patient with Captain Frémont. I got the feeling you was wondering what was wrong with you last night at dinner, and again this morning while you worked. It's not you, son. There is more than meets the eye at stake in the expedition you will soon go on with Frémont and Kit. The captain is feeling considerable pressure from Washington at the same time they are making what he's got to do a hell of a lot harder. For one thing, his father-in-law has set up such high hopes for this trip with President Polk it almost invites failure."

"He doesn't look the sort of man to accept failure, Mr. Bent."

. Bent laughed. "No, he don't. But the strain on Johnny comes out in some funny ways. He wasn't exaggerating when he said he could not get going without Kit. Oh, there are other scouts he could use, good ones like Fitzpatrick, who went out with him before, but none of them have the settling effect on him that Kit does. Things will turn a sight better all the way around when Kit arrives."

Again—"*. . . When Kit arrives.*"

8

That talk with Charlie Bent had taken place four days earlier, and now Kit *had* arrived.

Fat lot of good it would do Bradford Ogden Stone.

3
Taos Lightning

"When you come to dinner tonight, Brad, bring that Hawken gun I saw you ride in with," Charles Bent said when Stone found him in the commissary again three mornings after Kit's arrival and the collision only Stone did not think comic. "You'll want to join in the general hullabaloo and noisemaking we'll use to celebrate the Fourth."

"Will Mr. Carson be there, sir?"

"You bet. Kit's big on the patriotic stuff." He peered closely at Stone. "Better show up, Brad. You'll have to talk to him *sometime*, you know."

Perceptive man, Mr. Bent. Stone had not gotten over his chagrin at the meeting with Carson to any great extent, and he still had not recovered to the point where he was in any mood to celebrate. Certainly not in the great scout's company.

He had given Carson a wide berth since his disastrous debut, but now he would have to face the man in nine hours at Mr. Bent's dinner.

When he returned to his room after talking with Bent, he found a note from Captain Frémont commanding his presence at an expedition meeting in the dining hall at two that afternoon. He would not have the nine hours' respite after all.

2

Men in buckskin suits—but not one of them the immaculate outfit worn by John Frémont—jammed the hall. The captain sat by himself behind one of the trestle tables at the far end of the room. He waved Stone to a chair at its side, next to one occupied by Bent. Carson sat cross-legged on the floor in the center of a row of other men—almost directly in front of Stone.

He kept his eyes away from Carson for most of the meeting, but he could not help stealing a glance at him from time to time as the captain roughed out the path they would take, barely touching northernmost California on their way to Oregon country. Frémont ran his hand in broad sweeps across a map pinned to the wall behind him.

Stone suddenly remembered something the skipper of the Gloucesterman had told them tongue-in-cheek that stormy day in the Atlantic. *"You can tell the worth of a navigator by the size of his hand. Ask him to show you where you are on the chart. When he slams his hand down flat—the bigger that hand is, the more accurate he's apt to be."*

Frémont's map did not appear too trustworthy, but the hand he brushed across it seemed large enough.

Carson looked attentive all through the captain's rapid-fire discourse.

It was still difficult for Stone to believe that this slight man was the stalwart fighter and wilderness leader whom Baptiste Legrand, Jessie Frémont, Senator Benton, Frémont himself, and half a dozen Horace Trevelyans had pictured for him. If Carson had looked tiny while flat on his back in the doorway, he looked even tinier now in the company of the other mountain men of Frémont's expedition. Stone wondered how much his *size* might have shaped his life. Back home, five-foot Shorty Draper's stature had made him withdrawn and painfully shy, but frighteningly combative when aroused. Here Kit was sandwiched between two of the tallest and bulkiest of Frémont's sizable crew, identified for Stone by Mr. Bent in a whisper as Dick Owens and Basil Lajeunesse—"Old friends of Kit's," Bent said. "Two of the best. Maybe as good as Alexis Godey or Joe Walker there." He nodded toward two more sizable men in that front row. "I reckon I never seen such a collection of savvy old mountain hands in one place before, except maybe at some Green River rendezvous."

Stone found himself the object of a good many curious stares, at least from those in the gathering who had not attended his sketching session with Frémont.

He thanked heaven Carson did not look his way.

Nineteen or twenty men clustered at the front of Charles Bent's fairly large dining hall. That number, according to what Captain Frémont was saying now, only amounted to about a third of what the entire expeditionary force would total by the time it left for the mountains.

"Some of our splendid company are not here yet," Frémont said, "but that need not concern us for the moment. We shall on no account leave here before first September at the earliest, anyway. So if some of you have any urgent, personal business to look after, you have almost two months in which to do it, gentlemen."

Bent chuckled. "Urgent business, hah!" He drew a stern look from Frémont, but the affable merchant went on all the same. "Not that I don't set great store by every one of them, but the only urgent business this bunch has got is drinking whiskey and bedding their Indian wives—in that order. And calling them 'gentlemen'? Ask their wives about that. Maybe Johnny ought to ask the Blackfeet or the Crow they've killed and scalped if these mean old coots are gentlemen. And I can see three or four swatches of Lakota hair from here, too."

It appeared there would be sixty or more of these veterans in the band when they finally took the trail for Oregon. Why did the government, and more particularly Captain Frémont himself, see the need for sixty armed and capable, experienced fighters? Threescore constituted a small army. Stone had not heard that there had been any increase of hostile activity among the tribes of the eastern slope, the Great Basin, or the northern forests. Could it have anything to do with the possible war with Mexico lurking on the horizon? The government and the captain knew things he did not. The expedition could be heading into a small Indian war beyond the mountains. He had shuddered at Bent's invocation of "Lakota hair" when he saw the filthy black tresses dangling from several belts.

Well . . . with the celebration planned for tonight in the courtyard after dinner, he would apparently have his chance to test his rifle, if he took the Hawken with him.

3

Eight men gathered at Charles Bent's table for dinner: Frémont in a brocade smoking jacket; the mountain men Joe Walker, Alexis Godey, and Dick Owens; Carson; and a small, swarthy, quiet man in his early thirties Bent introduced to Stone as Señor Luis Aragón, a Mexican trader out of Santa Fe.

Rifles were stacked in a corner, and Stone leaned his Hawken alongside the others, glad to put it down before anyone remarked on it.

"I think you and Mr. Stone have met, Kit," Frémont said as they sat down.

"Yes, Captain," Carson said. "We did sort of run into each other the other day."

Frémont roared with laughter. So did two or three of the others. Stone might have winced, but he had long since disabused himself of any hope that he had heard the last echoes from the fiasco at the entrance to the dining hall.

"Is that your Hawken there, Mr. Stone?" Carson said.

"Yes, sir."

"Fine-looking weapon. Is it loaded?"

"Yes, sir."

"Name's Kit. We best get to that right off. We'll be spending a lot of time together—starting pretty quick."

Stone hesitated. "And I'd like it if you could call me Brad, sir."

"That can be done, too."

An Indian girl dished up slabs of venison and a steaming bowl of vegetables resembling the succotash of Stone's mother's own Illinois kitchen. The three veteran trappers bent to their plates and put the food literally under attack, until Stone saw nothing but elbows and the tops of shaggy heads—in Walker's case, the top of the fur cap he showed no inclination to remove.

An immense brown earthen jug of what Stone presumed to be whiskey or corn liquor sat in the center of the long plank table. After Charles Bent's comments of the afternoon he fully expected one of the mountain men to reach for it without delay, but none did.

While they ate, Stone learned something new about Kit Carson, something neither Jessie Frémont nor any of his other chroniclers had passed along.

The Mexican trader Aragón engaged the scout in conversation—in Spanish. Stone had some Harvard-acquired French, but he was totally ignorant of the language of Cervantes. The exchanges were not limited to just a word or two, and the length of the remarks, by Carson in particular, surprised him. From the looks of Aragón and his ready laugh at some of Kit's sallies, it seemed the scout possessed considerable fluency in the Mexican's native tongue.

Aragón appeared to be a man of refinement, at odds with the others at the table, except for the stylish Frémont and possibly the man named Godey, a handsome fellow a little younger than most of the others. Stone could not place Carson in either group.

As the Mexican trader and Carson conversed, Aragón looked around him, and Stone could almost determine the very second the trader must have decided that he was being a bit discourteous by only speaking Spanish. It did not strike Stone that way, nor, from the earnest way they were diving into their food, did it appear to offend any of the others.

Sure enough, for the rest of the meal Aragón confined himself mostly to English, heavily accented, true, but flawless in grammar. That attentiveness to the feelings of others in this subtle way was Stone's first experience with what he would someday hear Spanish speakers call *la cortesía,* a trait he would find time and again in his country's southern neighbors.

"Señor Bent tells me you have just come up from Taos, Señor Carson," Aragón said to the scout while the Indian girl deposited a giant black enamel coffeepot and eight matching cups in the center of the table.

"That I have, Don Luis," Carson said. "Only four days ago."

"One trusts Doña Josefa is well, *señor.*"

"She is indeed. She will be mighty pleased to hear you asked about her."

The Mexican started to say something more, then, composed and suave as he had been to that moment, he suddenly seemed unsure of himself.

"If one may be so . . . indelicate . . . , Señor Carson—may one make respectful inquiry about Doña Ana, the most delightful cousin of Doña Josefa?"

"Ana Barragán?"

"*Sí, señor.* Señorita Barragán. She is still a *señorita,* no? She has not become espoused or affianced since I visited in Taos in the spring?" His voice seemed suddenly fearful and hopeful at the same time.

"Married or engaged, *amigo?* The answer's no—unless it's happened in the two weeks I been gone." Carson looked highly amused. The relief appearing on Aragón's face was remarkable.

Ana . . . Barragán, was it? Pretty Spanish name, Stone mused. Probably belonged to a pretty woman; Aragón was a decidedly handsome man.

With the meal finished, tough, scarred hands across the table from Stone reached for the brown jug. The Indian girl—Stone by now had learned her name was the not-very-Indian-like Lucy—had brought out no glassware of any kind. The jug made its way around the table from man to man, and each drinker hooked the handle with the first two fingers of his left hand and tipped the neck of the jug to his mouth while the heavy vessel rested on his shoulder. Joe Walker spewed a gob of chewing tobacco on the floor before he took his turn. After Godey and Owens drank, the jug would come to Stone, and he squirmed a little at the prospect. He took a drink from time to time—he had after all attended his share of beer parties while in Cambridge, had occasionally tasted a sherry as he had with Frémont and Charles Bent the night before, and now and again sipped the odd dram or two of Scotch whiskey—but he had no particular liking for strong spirits.

He wished that the passing of the ominous jug had proceeded in the opposite direction so he could see how Frémont, Kit, Señor Aragón, and Charles Bent handled the situation.

Remembering Frémont's look when he turned down the cognac at the previous dinner, he decided he had better drink, and that he could not just sneak a sip. He would have to take an honest draught and make a fearless swallow as the first three had.

So when Owens handed him the jug he did just that.

The mouthful seared his gullet until he thought his eyes would pop from his head, and even the substantial amount of venison and succotash he had eaten could not mask the burn when the concoction reached his stomach. Tears filled his eyes. This was no ordinary whiskey. To make matters worse, in trying to steady the jug on his shoulder as Owens, Godey, and Walker had done with such practiced ease, a stream of the liquid had leaked from the side of his mouth and soaked his shoulder. He feared it would eat a hole in his jacket.

"Careful with that good stuff, sonny!" Joe Walker shouted. "Unless Charlie has another jug, there ain't hardly enough to go around. It ain't every day we get a crack at Taos Lightning."

The fire in his stomach seemed to be nothing when compared to the one in his face, and in his agitated state he did not notice whether Carson, Frémont, Aragón, or Bent took a drink at all. He had to force himself to look and see how Carson had taken his pitiful try for acceptance.

The scout gave Stone a flicker of a smile.

Charles Bent rose from the table. "Let's get out on the balcony, gents. Time to fire off a few rounds for Old Glory."

Stone followed the others to the corner that held the rifles and picked up his Hawken.

He walked out into a far different Independence Day celebration from any he had ever known as a boy in Groverton, or later in Chicago and Boston with their dignified, almost liturgical Fourth of July parades.

Darkness had fallen, but the courtyard beneath them blazed with the light from a dozen bonfires whose flames leaped as high as the balcony. More light bloomed at the ends of crackling torches. On the mud-and-stone platform of the watchtower where he had trained the telescope on the southwestern mountain wall in his weeklong vigil for Carson, more bonfires illuminated the Stars and Stripes, run up on a twenty-foot wooden pole and rippling toward the heavens in the updraft from the flames.

It looked as if every denizen of the fort and even the Arapahos and the wagon crews camped beyond its northern wall had turned out, and all were armed. Brown jugs like the one they had moments earlier passed around the table were making the rounds from group to group, and must have been doing so all the while the men on the balcony sat at dinner. The drinkers staggered against each other. Some fell, but bobbed up again as quickly. Shouts, snatches of songs, and wild cries and whoops rose in a crescendo above the sound of stamping feet. In the center of the throng, three buckskin-clad figures with fiddles were sawing away with manic industry while five pairs of men danced a mountain reel, their shadows weaving and waving on the firelit walls.

Stone glanced at the men who had just left Charles Bent's table with him.

Frémont, hands clasped behind him, gazed at the scene below with a look Stone could only characterize as one of aloof superiority. Charles Bent beamed like a jack-o'-lantern. Luis Aragón, his thoughts perhaps still dwelling on the "most delightful" Ana Barragán, did not seem part of the gathering at all.

But Kit and the other three mountain men . . .

The burning gleams in their eyes were more than just reflections of the fires in the yard.

"Kit's big on the patriotic stuff," Charles Bent had said, and the fervor gripped not only Carson.

Godey, Walker, and Owens were thumping each other's shoulders and yipping out over the unruly mob churning up dust in the throbbing courtyard under the balcony. Dick Owens's great voice boomed, "Long Live the U.S. of A.!" followed at once by, "Three cheers for our Uncle Sam!" from Joe Walker—both echoed by Godey and Carson. Shouts and bloodcurdling yells conveying the same sentiments rose from the mob in the yard in a powerful answering chorus straight out of Bedlam.

It struck Stone as strange that men who had deliberately exiled themselves to the wilderness should evince such unbridled, ecstatic patriotism. These were men who had broken with friends and families often before they had been old enough to put razors to their cheeks. Carson had run away from home at sixteen, he remembered reading. They truly could no longer know the country they had left behind; some of them could probably not remember it.

Down in the yard two of the navvies from among those who had tended the *caballada* on the long trek across the plains were trundling a small keg away from a barrel upended in the center of the courtyard, and around which half a dozen of the mountain men had gathered. The navvies zigged and zagged as they rolled the smaller one, and a powdery dust as black as Illinois topsoil trickled from the container and stained the earthen courtyard. When they reached a point about fifty yards straightaway from the barrel, but at least twice that distance along the erratic course of the trail of powder, a third navvy stepped forward and thrust the blazing brand he carried into the earth beside the keg. Sparks sputtered from the streak of black and then it began to burn, flames licking it from the ground, turning the streak into a raceway where a ball of Greek fire bounded through the zigzags toward the larger keg.

The six men at the barrel were now gripping the top of it, but turned from it as if to begin a race.

Charles Bent chuckled. "Kit!" he shouted. "A little bet?"

"If I get my pick, Charlie," Kit said, "I'll take Crip Jones. Five dollars?"

"Done," Bent said. "My man is Billy Burroughs."

"What are you wagering on, Mr. Bent?" Stone said.

"The last one down there to break and run for it is the winner, Brad," Bent said. "I think the boys raised more than fifty dollars for a purse tonight. Of course, the gent who hangs in the longest might not live to spend his winnings. Some of them get pretty stubborn—Jones and Billy in particular. That's why Kit and I put our money on them."

It *was* a race, a race with death—or rather *from* it. The larger barrel was a bomb, and the powdery black trail was a fuse.

The great mob below had fallen silent, and Stone could hear the furious hissing of the lighted powder train from his place on the balcony. By his reckoning the fire would reach the barrel in about twenty or thirty seconds.

Then three of the men touching the barrel tore themselves away and the silence was shattered by jeers, laughter, and catcalls, some from the end of the balcony where Godey, Walker, and Owens stood. A derisive snort issued from Frémont. Stone heard Carson chuckle softly.

A few seconds later, another of the contestants rushed off toward the shadows, just as the fireball on the train of black powder made its last turn and shot toward the barrel, and a sigh of satisfaction heaved from the crowd. Stone could not tell if it was due to appreciation of this loner's courage, or to the prospect of the showdown that would follow.

The last two men stared at the streaking fire as if transfixed, their hands hard on the barrel in a death grip. Had Charles Bent said "stubborn"?

One of them only an eyeblink before the other, they

bolted. The second one did not quite outdistance the blast that shattered the barrel; it knocked him to the ground, and when he arose, with a splintered half-stave from the barrel stuck in his left shoulder and dripping blood, he limped away through billows of white smoke, to be thumped on the back and glad-handed all around. The shadows swallowed the loser.

"Good old Crip," Carson muttered. "Five, Charlie, *por favor.*"

"He seems badly hurt, Kit," Stone said.

"He'll be just fine. Ain't but a scratch."

"but the limp . . . ?"

"He's had that limp nigh on fifteen years. 'Crip' is short for 'cripple.' Caught a Bannock arrow in his thigh on the upper Snake in '29 or '30. Point's still in him somewheres. Crip don't move so good no more. He can ride all right, but he can't walk fifty feet without going to his knees."

Stone marveled that a man with such an infirmity would enter a contest where only nerve could win, and where only speed and agility could save him.

"Time, gents," Charles Bent said. He stepped to the rail of the balcony and Carson, Frémont, and the three veteran mountain men moved forward with him.

Stone hesitated for a moment before he joined them. Every face in the yard had turned up to the balcony, rifle barrels spiked upward. Out of the corner of his eye he saw that even Captain Frémont had produced a pistol.

Stone cocked his Hawken and raised it above his head as the others had.

"*Let her rip!*" Bent called.

Stone took a breath and pulled the trigger.

He had never known any fusillade to equal the one with which the mountain men of John C. Frémont saluted Independence Day, 1845.

The reports of the hundred or more rifles in the yard and

from those on the balcony were stupendous, but the loudest report of all to his beginner's ears was the one that had not even sounded.

His Hawken had failed to fire.

As a pall of white smoke drifted level with the balcony he felt a small hand settle on his shoulder. "I heard you say it was loaded, Brad," Carson said.

"It is, sir."

"When did you load it?"

"The man who sold it to me loaded it . . . in Independence."

"You didn't load it your own self?"

"No, sir."

"You kept it dry?"

"Yes, sir."

"Let me have it. Let's slip in another cap for starters."

Carson cocked the Hawken, and with a small knife that appeared like magic, flipped the percussion cap away from the breech and inserted a new one fished from his pocket. He raised the rifle and pulled the trigger. Again, only a click. Then he slipped the ramrod from the underside of the rifle and ran it down the barrel. About two inches of the rod protruded from the muzzle. "Appears like it's loaded, all right," he said. "If it was empty the rod would have gone almost home. I think you got a bad mainspring, Brad. It ain't got enough left in it to touch off the cap." He smiled. "Adolph Diefenbach sold you this Hawken, didn't he?"

"Yes, sir . . . Kit."

"Rapscallion ought to be taken out and hung."

He cocked the gun once more and turned to Basil Lajeunesse, who was taking another pull at Charles Bent's liquor. "Bring that jug over here, Bass," he said. "Bang it on the nipple of this Hawken for me when I hold it up."

"Sure thing, Kit. Mainspring?"

"Appears so."

Kit lifted the Hawken into the air and Lajeunesse swung the bottom of the jug against it.

The report seemed louder than had all the massed firing of just half a minute earlier. Every eye on the balcony turned toward them.

Kit fiddled with the cocking mechanism. "You never fired this rifle, Brad?"

"No, sir." He knew he could not lie to this man. "I've never fired any gun."

Carson studied Stone for a moment.

"You figure on going into the mountains with us without knowing how to shoot?" He paused. It seemed he was turning something over in his mind. Would the scout now pass this along to Captain Frémont? Brad Stone's great adventure might have ended right this moment. Then Carson said softly, "Meet me in front of the dining hall at seven in the morning. I'll bring a Hawken just like yours, except it fires when you want it to. We got work to do."

4

The Rifle Lesson

At Harvard College Bradford Stone had studied under some of the finest professors in the world; none of them possessed the teaching art and skill Kit Carson revealed for him in the next three days.

While his own Hawken spent time for repairs with the fort's gunsmith, Kit and he rode out each morning to a dry riverbed some six or seven miles east of Bent's and well away from the wagon trail. Carson did not say so, but Stone knew he was taking him this far from chance onlookers to save him more embarrassment of the sort that had beset him on the balcony. This consideration of the feelings of a fellow human gave Stone his first real look into the *character* of this self-contained little man.

2

They must have fired off two or three hundred rounds in the three days they spent under the scorching sun of that dusty, bone-dry tributary of the Arkansas. At the end of it, Stone's right shoulder felt as if a mule had trampled on it, he feared powder smoke had permanently blackened his face, and his hands were blistered from grasping the over-heated metal of the Hawken which Kit brought along for him to use. Carson offered soft-spoken admonitions to "*squeeze* the trigger, don't pull it, and for the Lord's sake never *jerk* it," spoken in that light, persuasive voice of his. The frontiersman spent almost no time on Stone's actual marksmanship, so execrable that first hot morning the balls struck the earth yards wide of his mark for at least twenty rounds, and did not come a great deal closer the entire day. Stone asked about it.

"Nobody can teach a man how to aim. Sooner or later something inside him will take care of it. It's got more to do with the heart than the eye. There *are* a few fine points an old rifleman can help with, and we'll get to them later. But shooting has to be natural to begin with."

There came a keen lesson in just watching Kit handle his weapon.

As Carson fired, loaded, and fired again, one easy motion flowed into the next, his slim arms and tiny hands swinging the Hawken up against his shoulder with the breechblock almost touching his cheek, his index finger closing on the trigger simultaneously. It was rifle up . . . cock . . . fire . . .

rifle butt-down in the earth . . . powder horn out . . . powder, patch, ball, and ramrod in . . . rifle up . . . cock . . . fire—not one part of the drill distinct and separate from any other, all done swiftly, but with nothing hurried.

After half a dozen shots, Kit had Brad stand beside him and try to match his movements when he loaded and fired.

"Don't really *aim* before firing, Brad," he said. "Just *think* the ball into the target. Now . . . let's load, both at the same time." Stone heard him counting, "One-second-one . . . one-second-two . . . one-second-three . . ." as they began.

It seemed almost too easy, until Stone realized they were not performing the operations at anything like the speed he had blinked at when Kit fired by himself. The first time Stone performed the sequence he heard Kit reach the count of ninety before they fired. The scout made no comment whatsoever. As the morning went by Kit picked up the pace so gradually Stone hardly noticed. They had to stop repeatedly, of course, to clean the rifles, but except for another pause for a quick lunch of jerky and a pull at their water bottles, they stayed hard at it until midafternoon. By that time the count was down to forty-five, and just before they mounted up to return to the fort late on day three, they were firing regularly at intervals of less than thirty seconds, once or twice reaching a low of twenty.

"Good work," Kit said. "Reloading fast is a heap more important than dead-eye shooting."

And it dumbfounded Stone to discover that throughout that last afternoon he was actually hitting the targets—a number of dried-up buffalo sun pies fifty paces off—four times out of five. He had been so intent on mirroring his patient tutor's moves he had given no thought at all to aiming. His shots did not all strike the targets squarely, as did Kit's; most of the balls just kicked gray-brown shards off the edges of the chips before singing away from the rocky riverbed. But they were hits.

"Good shooting," Carson said as they headed into the sunset.

"Good enough?"

"Well . . . not quite. Not yet. You'll have to stretch yourself some for the longer shots. But like I said the other day, it'll come. Funny how quick a man's shooting gets really good when his belly's been empty for a week and he's sighted in a deer at two or three hundred yards—or when he's leveling on a Blackfoot he figures wants his hair."

3

John C. Frémont remained an enigma.

Congressman Myers, who had met Frémont only in the company of his good friend Senator Benton, had filled Stone in as best he could on the captain, and his counsel had been of great value. Stone had pictured the Pathfinder as a difficult man to deal with at best and he had prepared himself for that, but the captain's cavalier attitude toward a man who was, after all, supposed to be a trusted member of the team, hurt nonetheless. Then, as Charles Bent had forecast, the captain's edgy demeanor softened somewhat when Carson, with his longtime comrade Dick Owens in tow, arrived at the fort—a clear indication of Frémont's reliance on the mountain man. Whatever remained of that edginess, Stone decided, was caused by Washington politicians holding this impulsive adventurer in check for some undisclosed reason.

Stone had come west expecting they would be en route to their exploration and mapping within a week after he reported to Bent's Fort. It now appeared as if at least two months would go by before they left the mammoth trading post for the mountains. He had wanted to plunge straight into the great adventure, but meeting Kit Carson and absorbing the sights, sounds, and smells of the new world he had

entered, especially his three-day shooting lesson, had at
least kept him occupied and free from too much disappointment. He did chafe from time to time, and it struck him that
this relative inactivity must be doubly frustrating for a man
of Frémont's pantherlike restlessness. Charles Bent ratified
that.

"Johnny itches to head out for the tall timber," he said.
"He's not one for sitting around."

"What's holding us up, Mr. Bent?"

"He ain't exactly putting me in the picture. I've speculated some, of course, since your first night at dinner with
us, when he talked about his orders from President Polk. I
suspect you won't move out until he gets new ones, and I got
a notion it's got something to do with Washington's
all-of-a-sudden, heated-up interest in California. But everybody here is thinking something like that, too. Must be
something big. Maybe it's that talk of war coming up the
trail. Johnny's recruited a hell of a large party for just a mapping jaunt. I know it pays to be on the safe side, but on his
first two trips—in '42 and again last year—his outfit was a
fraction of the size this one is shaping up to be. *You* got any
idea why, Brad? You work for him."

"I understand we're to be out much longer this time, Mr.
Bent." It sounded lame, and Stone decided frankness would
serve him best in the long run. "I probably know less than
you do, sir. Captain Frémont hardly talks to me."

Bent regarded him for a moment before going on.
"Thanks for trusting me with your openness," he said at last.
"I guess it's time for me to open up a little, too. I've grown
fond of you in the ten days you've been here. By the way, so
has Kit—if you haven't noticed. As for Johnny . . . well,
the truth of the matter is that he likes to run his own show,
top to bottom. The fact that some Illinois congressman and
his own father-in-law insisted he put you on sticks in his
craw. He'll get over it, but it might take awhile." He laughed.

"If I was you—and if you can square it with your conscience—I'd make sure Johnny shows up in a lot of those pictures you're making. He softened some toward you right after that first time you sketched him."

5

Catamount!

"That gap up there southeast of the Spanish Peaks is Raton Pass," Kit said. "Just beyond it lies New Mexico." He motioned toward the break in the mountain barrier. "If we run into trouble, it will only come sometime after we ease down the other side. We won't mount a night guard until we leave the summit. Not that I really expect trouble."

Kit's evocation of possible "trouble" did not alarm Stone as it might have a few weeks ago. Perhaps he was making a small start on becoming a veteran. He had already begun to look on this trip from Bent's to Santa Fe and Taos as a windfall, a chance to measure himself for the upcoming, larger expedition to Oregon shaping up under Frémont's planning back at the trading post on the Arkansas.

The Santa Fe trader, Luis Aragón, riding beside Stone and Carson, had prompted this unexpected journey. The engaging Mexican had sought Kit out in the dining hall, where the scout and Stone were eating supper the night after the third and last day of rifle practice. It turned out they knew each other much better than had been apparent that night at dinner with Bent, Frémont, and the mountain men.

"Señor Carson, I have a great favor to ask of you."

"Name it, Don Luis," Carson said.

"It is my understanding that Capitán Frémont will not require your services for many weeks."

"That's true, far as I can tell."

"Would it be possible for you, along with perhaps another of your men, to escort a friend of mine from here to Santa Fe? This friend is the trader Don Pablo Espinosa, whom I believe you know."

"*Sí*, Don Luis. He freights goods up Taos way from time to time. A good, honest trader."

"I would not ask, *señor*, but word has come up the trail from San Miguel that there is Comanche activity on the upper Río Pecos, and Don Pablo has with him his wife and *dos niños*, a boy of five and a girl of seven. He would postpone his departure until things are quiet, but his wife Doña Olivera is *embarazada*, very far along with child, and he wishes to take her to her midwife in Santa Fe for the birth."

"Can't they go down the western slope of the Sangres, and steer clear of the Pecos? I don't think the Comanches are ranging that far up from the Staked Plains right now."

"Ah, *sí, señor*, but as you know, that route is not a wagon road, and Don Pablo has with him a small *caballada* of half-wild mustangs and a heavy ox-drawn *galera*—containing the proceeds of his entire trading season. It is necessary for him to use the big *camino* all the way to Santa Fe. It is, *de veras*, impossible to take a wagon over the Sangre de Cristo trails. I would, of course, accompany you myself. You should be back with Capitán Frémont in two or three weeks, I should think."

Carson pushed his tin plate of beans away from him and placed the tips of his slender fingers together. "Be glad to do it, Don Luis—if Captain Frémont will allow it."

"*Gracias, señor, muchas gracias.* I have already spoken to *el capitán*. I am pleased to say he approves."

"It's done, then. If we can leave tomorrow."

Stone's heart sank. He had hoped to spend a lot of time

with Kit before Frémont's expedition pushed off. There was much more to learn from him than how to use a Hawken. Without him, Bent's would become a dreary place.

Aragón, despite Kit's quick agreement, suddenly looked tentative. Articulate as he had been so far, he nearly stammered as he went on. "Will you return to Bent's by way of Taos after delivering Don Pablo and his family to Santa Fe and safety, *señor?*"

"*Sí.* I would admire very much to see *my* family."

"May I ride with you?"

"Sure enough." Kit grinned widely. "Does Doña Ana Barragán figure in your asking, *mi amigo?*"

There rose a flush of deep red in Aragón's face. "*Sí, señor.*"

"Well . . . I never could stand in the way of true love. Josefa would never forgive me. Come on along, Don Luis."

Stone had heard the name Ana Barragán for the second time, but he had little time to consider it as Carson turned to him.

"How about it, Brad? Would you care to make this jaunt with Don Luis and me?"

Stone's heart raced. "Why, yes!" he said excitedly.

He scarcely slept a wink that night.

2

The next morning they set out for Santa Fe, the fabled city at the end of the trail that bore its name.

Only when they were well down that trail, and Bent's Fort had disappeared in the shimmering high-plains haze behind them, did Stone begin to speculate on why Kit had asked him to go along. He could have recruited any one of the dozen old mountain men who had chosen to lounge around Bent's rather than take Frémont's offered leave of absence before the survey team headed for the coast. From what Stone had learned, not one of these old veterans ever turned down any request of Kit's, no matter how demanding or hazardous.

Kit must truly be expecting no real trouble, as he had said. With Stone's new and still-minimal skills with the Hawken, he doubted the nonpareil scout of the Great West would think him anywhere near ready to fight Indians, should it come to that. Had there been such a prospect in the offing, he would have taken someone like Joe Walker, Owens, or Alexis Godey.

On the trail now, Stone asked about it.

"You'll do just fine, *amigo*. When Ewing Young first took me out from Taos to hunt beaver in '29, I hardly knew a thing more than you do now. If I can break you in even half as well as Ewing did me, Captain Frémont will be mighty pleased. I was a worse tenderfoot back then than you are." He grinned. "'Course, I had been a navvy and a teamster by that time, and I could throw a diamond hitch on a mule or a horse that didn't look like a cat's cradle missing half its strings."

In addition to the Espinosa family, Luis Aragón, Kit, and Stone, the caravan held a *caballada* of nine loose mustangs. A second yoke of oxen were to spell the ones pulling the Santa Féan's heavily loaded wagon. Two mixed-breed dogs with a predominance of wolfhound in their makeup raced alongside the wagon, where hung three crates of White Leghorn fowl with a skinny, drooping rooster that nevertheless trumpeted at the morning sun in the loudest cock's crow Stone had ever heard. The Indian navvy tending the *caballada*, a painfully shy boy of twelve or so, with jet black hair reaching to his waist and a bronze mask of a face, fascinated Stone.

"Diego—one forgets his Indian name," Don Pablo Espinosa, a short, jovial, fat man, said, "comes from San

Ildefonso Pueblo. His last name is the same as mine, of course—Espinosa. Diego is Tewa."

"San Ildefonso Pueblo" and *"Diego is Tewa"* meant absolutely nothing to Stone. Shy or not, riding bareback on a frisky paint horse and wearing only a headband and a breechclout, Diego unleashed a whirlwind of energy as he herded his unruly charges along the hot road well in front of the Espinosa wagon—using a cattle prod to goad them along. Stone dug out his sketchpad and drew Diego at their first stop for a meal.

"Diego must think he smells home already," Carson said, nodding toward the Indian lad. "Going to be hard keeping up with him when we start down the other side with Don Pablo's wagon."

Although the two Espinosa children, Pepe and Concepción—bright-eyed, nervously active youngsters both of them—skipped about gleefully at their first evening camp, and showed tremendous stamina the following day as they ran alongside the wagon for what seemed miles, Stone saw little of Señora Espinosa, that is, he did not see her *frequently,* as she spent almost all her time bumping along in a rough bed in the bottom of the wagon. But he saw *a lot* of her on the few occasions when he did. There was an extraordinary lot of her to see. Taller than her husband by an inch or two, in her present delicate condition her girth had reached twice his—even as rotund as Don Pablo was. Aragón had said in his plea to Kit to serve as the party's guide and escort that Doña Olivera Espinosa was "very far along with child." The lady indeed appeared so—at least to Stone's unpracticed eye.

Other things claimed his mind and eyes as they rode. Through Charles Bent's telescope he had stared for hours at the range that arched away from either side of Raton Pass, but this would be the first time he had ever ventured into real mountains. The "mountains" of Missouri he had coached through with Baptiste and Emmy Legrand had been mere hints of the peaks he now saw.

His professional equipment rode on the back of the pack-horse he trailed, and when they left Bent's he fully intended—Carson's schedule for them permitting—to get in some practice mapping mountains before doing so under Frémont's critical eye in the much more significant survey-ing tasks to come. An hour into the pass he knew that par-ticular good intention could turn out to be one of the cobbles with which the Road to Hell is said to be paved. The new sights on either hand fascinated him too much for him to work.

Low scrub covered the northeastern approach to the pass, but once they began the slow ascent from the plain it gave way to stands of small coniferous trees Carson called piños, and then, as they neared the summit, to sentinel pines so lofty that from Stone's angle of perspective their bristling green tops seemed to run together like the groined vault stones of a cathedral. Some squawking, jaylike birds flashed slate-gray through their branches. It was a wonderland of golden yellow rocks, greenery, and wild water, all under a sky such as none he could possibly have imagined—one as dark as the Prussian blue nestled among his oils.

The vistas on either side of their route took his breath.

The wagon road skirted gorges so deep and narrow that even the rays of the afternoon sun—still almost straight above their heads—failed to reach their bottoms, and with the sound of swift, unseen streams rising from the depths, it was as if the road itself floated in converging rivers of semi-darkness.

He soon realized all he could reasonably hope to do on this trip down to Santa Fe was to take it all in as best he could, and accustom his flatlander's widened eyes and newly alerted ears to sights and sounds they had never feasted on or heard before. Perhaps by the time Kit, Aragón, and he took the road north to Taos he could absorb this splendor with more equanimity and commit part of it to paper. Oil on canvas, of course, would be the more promising medium, but although he had brought his surveying tools, his painting gear remained at Bent's. In his excitement about leaving on this first intimate journey with Kit he had even left his largest sketchpad in his room at the fort.

Near the top of the pass, far across the canyon, something tawny moved against the rocks, and for a moment he thought one of them had come to life.

A mountain lion bounded up the steep slope.

He was riding almost in tandem with Kit, and the scout must have heard his gasp and seen where he was looking. "You're shot with luck, Brad," he said. "Beginner's luck. And some of it must have rubbed off on me. I been riding these mountains for near twenty years now, and while I've seen *parts* of catamounts in the brush a hundred times or more, I ain't never seen one whole mountain cat except for *dead* ones, until this minute. Ain't it free and fine, though?"

The animal remained in sight only a few seconds before it disappeared beyond the rimrock, but its sleek form and the image of its lustrous grace and power as it leaped upward from ledge to boulder to a still-higher ledge, burned itself into Stone's brain.

"You ain't going to forget seeing that feller ever, Brad, mark my words," Kit said. "Except that I got Josefa to think about now, I'd trade places with that critter anytime."

"Kit . . ." Stone said. "I don't think I could ever leave this country now that I've seen it. I belong here." Exactly why the fleeting glimpse of a dumb animal should produce such a profound effect on him, Brad Stone had not the faintest notion, but it did.

"I know how you feel," Kit said. "Felt that way myself when I first came out. Always will. Now look. But life ain't always jim-dandy in the West. It can get rough. Hate to give advice about something so personal, but someday, when you feel like throwing it all away, and when things are at rock bottom, think about that lion and how you felt today. Amazing how a little thing like that can see you through."

It must have embarrassed the scout a little to make that clearly deeply felt speech; he suddenly lashed his horse's flank and shouted, "Time to catch up!"

3

Carson called a halt at the barren summit of the pass. The sun had dropped behind the western mountain wall, but the sky still remained aglow, iridescent amethyst. Off to the west, under the first, early evening winking light of Venus, a thin, horizon-to-horizon bank of clouds caught the sun's last low-angled rays and turned a vibrant red. It stayed full light for twenty minutes perhaps, but when darkness finally fell, it fell suddenly and almost audibly. The air turned sharp and bracing.

"We can have a fire tonight and tomorrow morning," Kit said, "but we'll make cold camps from the southern foot of the pass until we reach San Miguel and swing back northwest into Santa Fe."

Diego, on his splashy pinto pony, had taken the horse herd two or three hundred yards down the wagon trace, where the big trees began again, and the young Indian had strung a picket line between a pair of them. Obviously he intended eating apart from the rest of the party, but he had no pack, bag, or packhorse. Stone did not trouble himself about it; back at the fort Carson had told him not to bother with provender, as Espinosa would furnish all the food, coffee, and good *cigarros,* and then Don Pablo announced he would not only open his larder to them, but cook for all of them as well. The Mexican had a fire going in short order.

The first night out from Bent's, Espinosa had served them the usual beans and jerky, and Stone expected the same tonight, wondering a little about the condition of even dried meat after it had spent two days in the superheated air under the sun-hammered canvas of the wagon. Taking a cue from Kit, he lounged against his saddle a dozen feet from the fire and watched as Aragón pulled a pack of playing cards from his pocket and began laying them out on his blanket in some Mexican version of Patience, while Espinosa busied himself with pots, pans, and ladles. He had laid flat patties of some sort on the tin mess plates lined up beside the fire, and several jars gaped open beside the plates. The meal would be a bit more complicated than Stone thought.

Doña Olivera struggled from her pallet inside the wagon to sink heavily onto the seat with Pepe and Concepción beside her, the pair stilled for once—by their hunger, probably. Stone's hunger, too, had sharpened in the crisp night air.

In no time the lid of Espinosa's largest kettle was clattering, popping up and emitting vapors that when they reached Stone seemed as sulfurous and fiery as the winds of Hell.

If Don Pablo had not served the señora, the children, Kit, Luis Aragón, and him in that order, he might not have eaten, but when each of them fell to it when the plates reached them, and when none of them collapsed or doubled over with cramps, he decided that while the food might be unappetizing in the extreme, and even mildly toxic, it probably was not lethal.

"*Es caldo,* Señor Stone," the trader said as he handed Stone a bowl filled to overflowing with what looked like stew. "*Es muy bueno, señor. Verdad.*" Stone understood the "*bueno*" all right, but he would have to wait and see how damned *bueno* it actually was.

He brought a small spoonful to his mouth.

He could swear the food began to burn his lips before the spoon even reached them.

Compared to this blistering concoction, he recalled Charles Bent's raw whiskey the night of the Fourth as a gentle, soothing syrup. Tears streamed down his cheeks, and in an instant the top of his head was bathed in sweat. He tried manfully to swallow, but his throat muscles simply would not work. Surely this seething, acid mixture would eat suppurating holes in the lining of his stomach. He spit it out.

A burst of laughter from Carson served to fan the flames from his mouth to his cheeks, and the heat increased when courteous Luis Aragón permitted himself a tiny smile. Espinosa looked stricken.

"Give Señor Stone some salt, *pronto,* Don Pablo!" Carson called to him. He turned to Stone. "It's the only thing I've ever found that will even begin to put the fire out in a hurry. You'll get used to hot food in these parts. You'll have to. This is the kind of vittles we eat every day in Taos."

The salt did calm things down—a little. With grim determination he finished up his plate, discovering in the process that the rest of it did not burn nearly as much as that first mouthful had. And to his amazement it tasted good.

By the time he swallowed the last morsel, Kit had gotten to his feet, refilled his plate, and had set off with it down the dark roadway toward Diego's horse camp. The rest of the party seemed to have forgotten the young Indian navvy.

Don Pablo refused Stone's offer to help clean up the pots and pans and the litter around the fire, and when he finished these chores by himself, disappeared inside his wagon, returning in a moment carrying a guitar.

The Santa Fe trader began to strum a plaintive air. From her place on the seat of the wagon Doña Olivera sang along with the notes of the guitar in a lovely lilting mezzo. Stone had no need to understand Spanish to know the song concerned itself with love, and from its mournful notes, unrequited love—and loss. Luis Aragón seemed to know the song. He did not sing along with Señora Espinosa, but he mouthed every word. Stone wondered if his thoughts were running to the lady he had now mentioned twice, Doña Ana Barragán.

Pepe and Concepción had disappeared, surprising Stone a little; the night before their father had to threaten them—in Spanish that would likely translate to the direst of punishments—to get them bedded down in the wagon a full hour after Señora Espinosa herself retired.

Their whereabouts became apparent in a moment.

The two children walked into the circle of firelight just as the song ended. Between them, holding a tiny brown hand in each of his own, Kit Carson beamed.

"A fandango, Don Pablo, *por favor!*" Kit cried, and Espinosa began to play again. This time the music soared with great thumping rhythms that underscored the tinkling of a tambourine Doña Olivera produced out of nowhere. Carson and the two youngsters whirled into a dance.

The mountain man and the Espinosa children danced for at least half an hour without a rest. More than reflected firelight gleamed in the three pairs of eyes as they linked arms, broke apart, circled each other, and jigged across the rocky ground.

Done at last, Kit lifted each of them into their father's arms at the rear opening of the wagon. Then he walked to the fire, stared into its embers for a moment, and settled down beside his saddle, pulling his blanket to his chin. Luis Aragón, too, wrapped himself in his, and was soon fast asleep. Somewhere an owl hooted.

Stone knew there was no point in trying for sleep just yet, so he gazed up at the sky until Ursa Minor made a ten-degree start on its nightly turn around Polaris. The stars in the handle and the Dipper bowl emitted a wild glitter even though a full moon tried to sponge them out.

He thought about the high mountain views of the afternoon, the love song, and then the joyous dance of Kit, Pepe, and Concepción.

Mostly, he thought about the lion . . . and Kit's words about it.

". . . When you feel like throwing it all away, and when things are at rock bottom, think about that lion and how you felt today."

He relaxed then into the warm cloud of camaraderie that still hovered over the tiny, sleeping camp, and he even smiled at the memory of the exotic food that had seared his mouth and gullet, but which left a mellow aftertaste.

He could not remember a grander day.

6

Comanche!

He awoke into darkness when Kit roused the camp next morning with the shout Brad Stone had heard the afternoon before and would hear scores of times before that year and the next were out.

"It's time to catch up!"

Coming out of the fog of sleep, he had not the faintest notion about what Kit wanted them to "catch up" to or with this morning.

The words were, as he would learn over the next few months, Carson's own peculiar, longtime locution, used to shake a band of mountain men out of their bedrolls to begin a tough day on the trap lines.

As they breakfasted in the dark on biscuits, beans, and a strong, aromatic Mexican coffee, it soon became clear something was troubling the veteran scout. When dawn broke Stone found Carson staring intently down the road at the first needles of golden light piercing the darkness in the timberline, right where Diego had bedded down with his mustangs.

"Damn that boy!" he said. "He's started down the pass without us."

Sure enough, when Stone looked, he saw no sign of the Indian boy or his nine-horse *caballada*.

Kit broke into a light-footed run, and in seconds reached the spot where he had taken Diego his supper the night before. Within half a minute he was back at the Espinosa wagon.

"From the look of things, Diego must have left more than an hour ago." He turned to Pablo Espinosa. "I sure am sorry to put Doña Olivera to any pains, Don Pablo, but we'll have to push pretty hard this morning. We can't even slow down for washouts or too many of the deadfalls we come across. I don't want the boy to get too far ahead of us. We'll be lucky to get within sight of him by nightfall as it is. But he'll stop to graze and water them *caballos* when he reaches a meadow lower down the pass. We won't, and maybe we can make up some ground that way."

"*Sí, Señor Carson, yo sé,*" Espinosa said. "Do not worry about Señora Espinosa. *Mi esposa* has traveled hard roads many times before this."

"And keep *los niños* in the wagon. We can't have them running loose today."

"*Sí, señor.*"

Kit turned back to where Luis Aragón had joined Stone.

"Don Luis . . . Brad . . . from here to San Miguel we ride with our rifles loaded. If you ain't taken care of that little chore already, do it now."

To this point Kit's face had worn a look of irritation; now it appeared as cold as black ice—and as hard. Stone failed to understand his concern. Surely the fact that Diego had started the descent without them did not cause this darkening of his features. Was this one of those uncanny inner warnings of impending danger that had kept Kit Carson a step ahead of his enemies all his life in the wilderness?

2

It did not take them until nightfall to catch up with Diego after all.

Just as Kit predicted, the navvy *had* stopped to graze his *caballada* in a flower-scented mountain meadow three hours down the southern side of the pass. He had not left it, although his horses had.

They found him lying faceup in the meadow, in the center of a circle of columbine and other alpine blooms and grasses that had been beaten flat and trampled into chaff by his horses and by those of his attackers. The shaft of an arrow protruded from his naked chest, just under the sternum, and another had pierced his side. A canyon of a wound split his bronze face all the way from a wide-open right eye to his chin, and the top of his head was a swamp of drying blood where the longest strands of his black hair had been ripped away. The goad he had used to herd the mustangs still hung from his wrist by its braided leather thong.

Luis Aragón looked as if he might vomit; Stone felt he might himself. Pablo Espinosa had stopped the wagon fifty yards short of them, and Stone silently blessed him for it.

Carson dropped to his knees beside the body. He slipped the cattle prod from the dead boy's wrist and held it up to Don Luis and Stone. Blood had congealed on the iron point.

"Comanches, sure enough. Diego made what fight he could," Kit said. "They just used arrows and the hatchet. It don't appear they have rifles. If they did they most likely would have shot him when he made his fight. We can't count on their not having firearms; they might just have been saving powder, although I ain't never found Comanches very thrifty when they got hold of guns." His voice came out dead level, with no intonations. He could have been assessing a battle fought a century before. Standing behind him as he examined Diego's body, Stone could not see his face as he talked. Carson stood up, tossed the goad into the blood-stained grass at Diego's side, and began walking toward the edge of the circle of flattened turf, inspecting every foot of it, bending to the ground, and once picking up a horse dropping and squeezing it.

"Nine or ten of them," he muttered, his words drifting lightly to where Aragón and Stone waited, "Maybe an even dozen. Must have been waiting for Diego. Gone about that same hour we lost to him this morning, I expect. They hardly spent any time here at all. Good at their work, Comanches."

"Do you suppose they are still close by, Señor Carson?" Aragón asked. His voice held an echo of Stone's own inner trembling.

"I doubt it. They hightailed it for the plains as soon as they rounded up the horses. But it makes no difference, Don Luis. *They will not get away.*" Even with the slight emphasis on the last of it, there was no passion in the promise, no sound of anger. "We will find them, *amigo,* if we have to hunt them all the way to Texas. With the horses they took, they won't travel as fast as we will."

Surely Kit had no intention of going after as many as twelve armed killers with just himself and three other men—or two actually, since he could not take Espinosa from his wife and children. And one of the two a rank beginner. No. Not even the great Kit Carson would think of chasing out after a dozen dangerous Comanches under such circumstances.

"*¡Bueno!*" Don Luis said.

Don Pablo handed the ox-team reins to his wife, stepped down from the wagon, and began to walk toward them. Pepe and Concepción jumped from the seat and tried to follow him. He herded them back to Doña Olivera.

When Espinosa reached them, he stared down at the Indian navvy's prostrate form. "*Pobrecito.* One dreads telling his mother and father. They have worked for *la familia* Espinosa nearly twenty years."

"Sorry, Don Pablo," Carson said. "We ain't got time to grieve. I want you to get back on the trail and push as hard as you can for San Miguel. I think you'll be safe as long as you keep moving. There likely ain't two Comanche parties raiding between here and San Miguel in the same week, but they might just get another one on the way if we don't track this one down and punish it."

"*Sí, Señor Carson.*"

Kit had said "we." Was he including Stone?

The answer came quickly. "Yoke your spare oxen up front with the team pulling your wagon now, Don Pablo," Carson continued. "You'll have to trail my packhorse, and Don Luis's and Señor Stone's, behind you. They would only hold us up if we took them with us. The three of us will have to travel light and fast."

"You do not wish me to accompany you then, Señor Carson? *Mi esposa* can drive a wagon."

"No. You'll have your hands full getting the lady and *los niños* to San Miguel and then Santa Fe, my friend. But I'd sure appreciate it if you could fix us some grub to tote along. Nothing much. We'll eat light—if we find time to eat at all."

"It is as good as done, *señor.*"

."And will you bury Diego?"

"*Sí.* I regret there is no *padre* with us. I will do what little I can, and say a *súplica* for his Indian soul."

"*Muchas gracias, Don Pablo.* One thing more. Do you know the little box canyon at Piedras Negras?"

"*Sí.* Half a day from here, no?"

"Right. Leave our three baggage critters there so as we can pick them up when we finish what we have to do. Cut some brush and pull it across the mouth of the *cañon* to keep them there. No need to fuss about closing it up too tight. If we don't get to them in two days' time, we won't never get to them."

Espinosa had already begun to dig the grave by the time Kit, Aragón, and Stone had climbed into their saddles once again.

3

They rode down the mountain through the ponderosa forest to the east, and as totally without experience as Brad Stone was, even he could easily have followed the broad trail left by the Comanches and the stolen mustangs; but when they left the towering pines, the trail thinned out, and after two more miles faded away to nothing.

It did not look to Stone as if a single human soul had passed this way in a thousand years. Kit, with only an occasional glance at the ground, rode with stern purpose, though, seeing signs hidden from Stone, and from Aragón, too, from the look of him.

"Let me lead," Kit had said when they left the broad, marked trail through the trees. "I don't want either of you messing up sign, so stay at least a dozen yards behind me, no matter how eager you are to lift Comanche hair."

The three of them still rode some distance up on the slope overlooking the plain, and Carson soon sighted their quarry. Or said he did. He reined in his horse and ordered Stone and Aragón to dismount. Stone could not pick out a thing in the sun and heat and haze.

"Don't strain your eyes, Brad," Carson said. "They're

crossing hardpan about five miles from here right now, but you'll see their dust any minute. Can you make out that deep wrinkle in the prairie? That's the upper Cimarron. They're heading for a bosque about ten or twelve miles down from where they are right now. We'll ride easy for a while ourselves, so we don't raise much dust, and then we'll catch them in the bosque after dark. We'll be upstream so as we can water our horses and get a bite to eat before moving to the attack. We'll have that same full moon that looked so pretty last night, but we'll have to wait until they build a fire so we can really get them in our sights. We can only get off two, maybe three shots apiece. Make them count."

Stone's face must have signaled some doubt. "We can do this," Carson added. Nothing in his soft, sure voice said this was guesswork or mere hope. "We'll walk our horses downstream and hitch them a quarter mile or so from the Comanche camp. We want them quiet, and we don't want them all used up if we have to skedaddle fast. If we don't get most of them killers with our first two volleys, and if I've missed a sign or two and there are more of them than I figure, we'll have to make a run for our horses. They'll have all the fresh mounts they need to chase us down, what with their own and those they stole when they butchered poor Diego."

Memories of the shooting and loading training in the riverbed came rushing back. No matter how adept they were, there would be no way they could reload their rifles in the saddle and at a gallop, with well-mounted, howling savages on their heels.

Rifle drills were one thing; actual combat would be quite another.

"One thing in our favor," Kit said next, "is that they ain't expecting us—else they would have pushed along a lot faster than they have."

4

In the dark bosque Stone lay on his belly, his Hawken poked around the trunk of a cottonwood. At their stop upstream he had gulped down what seemed gallons of water, but his mouth was dry again and his tongue swollen. Aragón hid behind a companion tree, and Carson crouched between them, looking even smaller than he had the day Stone met him.

Below them, not twenty short yards away, nine half-naked Indians lay about a small fire in various states of wakefulness, some rolled into blankets, three sitting up and staring at the fire. It gave Stone a strange turn when he thought that Carson, Aragón, and he might have looked much the same to casual eyes the night before, perhaps those of this same band.

He could see two or three bows, quivers of arrows, a scattering of fur-and-leather garments, and a pair of long, wicked-looking lances with iron points. Beside the fire lay the carcass of a large animal, cut into two sides from which whoever cooked it had hacked large chunks. The mammoth roast, if he could call it that, must have been pulled from the fire much earlier; the smell rising to the top of the slope where the men lay hidden already carried the heavy, sickly odor of congealing fat.

"We may not get back all Don Pablo's horses," Carson whispered. "Look there. They already killed and started to eat one of them, or one of their own, more likely. One or two of them must be looking after the rest of the herd. They probably ain't got enough rope for a picket line and just got the critters hobbled down by the stream."

One of the Indians got to his feet. He looked no taller than Carson, but without the trim hardness of the scout. Bare to the waist, his sloppy stomach—distended as if it were the result of longtime malnutrition—hung over the beltline of a pair of grass-stained buckskin trousers worn through at the knees. He waddled off into the dark shadows well across the fire from Carson, Aragón and Stone.

Kit whispered again. "We'll wait until he comes back or another of them comes into the light. He's probably gone to piss, but he might just be taking his turn guarding the horses. Either way, I won't be with you at the start of it."

Stone had a question, but Carson spoke before he could get it out, as if he had known what the question was.

"Not to worry, Brad. I'll slip to the other side of their camp to put them in a crossfire. When you hear an owl hoot—let her rip. Now for your targets. Don Luis will work from the left and you, Brad, from the right. Go for the ones who ain't sleeping first. You'll have all the time you need for the second shot, the third might take some doing. Move before you fire the third one if you can. Aim a mite low. Shooting down you tend to miss on the high side. Don't try nothing fancy. Aim for what you're sure you can hit. We can finish them later if we have to."

Without another word he was gone.

Even with Luis Aragón lying beside him Stone felt desperately alone.

Another Comanche, a skinny, hideously ugly creature with a flat nose that spread from cheek to cheek struggled to his feet. He stretched, looked to the left of the camp, started that way, but when the man who had left earlier suddenly strode into the light of the fire, the thin man muttered something and turned back to the right. He stopped. If Kit's hooted signal to fire came now, this would be the one Stone would have to kill. Stone should not miss; the Comanche was big enough. Stone would have to will himself to pull the trigger when the time came.

Squeeze . . . squeeze . . . do not pull! He moved a little to get the barrel of the Hawken well clear of the bole of the cottonwood. The firelight played across his target, and he trembled in fear that the Indian might move just as Carson hooted. None of the shots he had fired in practice above the Arkansas had been at a moving target.

Then he felt Luis Aragón get to his feet.

Of course! He had to stand as well, to reload quickly. He stood, moving as quietly as he could, feeling more naked and exposed than before, even though the tree still sheltered him. He framed the bare chest of the skinny Comanche deep in the V of his Hawken's sights. The Hawken seemed even heavier than during the shooting lesson. He laid the barrel across a branch.

Nothing to do now but wait.

Stone had never been a particularly devout man, but in the next few seconds he winged a fervent prayer heavenward to whoever might be listening.

"Whoo-ooo . . ."

The owl hoot drifted to his ears and right on through to the bones of his skull. The crash of rifle fire—his own a part of it—followed almost at once. The three of them had fired off their rounds within the same fraction of a second.

Stone's Comanche slipped to his knees as if he were doing it calmly and deliberately. Just before he folded forward into the dirt Stone saw the gleaming star of blood streak its crimson points across the Indian's chest.

Aragón had brought his man down, too.

And somewhere in the middle of it all, Carson's man had fallen. Stone would never know for sure how he registered any of the hits; the flash from Kit's rifle blossoming in the blackness straight across the Indian camp blinded him, or so it seemed. And yet he would forever after have this crystal recollection of the scout striding out of the cottonwoods and into the camp itself as he reloaded. He had his rifle to his shoulder. How had he rammed in powder, patch, ball, and the long, unwieldy rod so quickly? Stone's own reload had been far from his slowest—he was up and aiming well before Luis Aragón—but there was Kit, firing again.

The small Comanche camp burst apart; there had only been nine Indians and now three of the nine were gone, but it seemed as if a full score were racing for their weapons. Stone swung his Hawken to a shadowy figure making for the stream, and pulled the trigger. This time his target was not as stationary as the first. The Indian staggered, put a hand down, lurched and fell face forward only to regain his footing and turn back. His shoulder gushed blood. Aragón's rifle boomed, and Kit fired again, too. Stone heard a shriek off to his left and saw Kit's man knocked backward.

Stone looked at his man and froze. The Comanche lifted a rifle and took aim.

"Reload!" Kit shouted. "I'll take him."

The Indian spun about at the sound of Kit's voice. Carson, his rifle at his feet, drew one of the pistols from his belt. Both weapons cracked at once. Smoke had begun to fill the Comanche camp, but even before it lifted, Stone could see Kit standing, his opponent now stretched out like a deadfall log. Aragón proved as successful with his shot. A Comanche thrashed on the ground in such agony his convulsions rolled him right into the fire. His writhing stopped even as flames licked at his head and naked shoulder.

Stone frantically reloaded his Hawken and looked for another target. He saw the four they had not brought down running for the stream, shafts of moonlight turning them to ghosts. One fell even as Brad watched, victim of Carson's second pistol shot.

"Don't let them reach the horses!" Carson yelled.

Kit ran past, holding one of the long lances Brad had seen earlier. Stone heard Aragón fire again just as Kit reached a terrified Comanche, and plunged the lance deep into his back. Stone's Hawken was ready to fire now, and he settled himself for another shot. In the moonlight he could not aim with certainty. *"Just* think *the ball into the target,"* Kit had said when he trained him. It *worked!* Another Comanche was down. If Aragón's last shot had found a home, only one remained, excepting any who might still be with the horses. Carson had disappeared, but through the dark grove another shot shattered the sudden quiet. Kit must have somehow reloaded a pistol. Carson had not carried his old Plains as he sped past Stone with the lance. But he must now be fully exposed and with no ready round to fire. Stone ran toward the sound of the voice.

He heard the horses whinnying and neighing in terror now, felt the ground shake from what seemed a thousand hooves, and when Aragón and he reached the stream they found Carson, both pistols in hand, one still smoking, with the last of the Comanches sprawled in front of him.

Not quite the last. Another cowered by the frantic herd, this one a scrawny, quivering fellow, a boy not much older than Diego, his eyes wide and white in the moonlight as he stared at the pistols trained on him.

"Don Luis, look to the horses, *por favor.*" Kit's voice had reverted to its customary, easy lightness. Aragón looked completely composed, almost as elegant as he had at Charles Bent's dinner. He started for the horses as Kit turned to Stone. "Reload your Hawken, and keep this critter covered until I fix my pistols and decide just how we'll get shut of him. Don't want to use up no more powder."

"You're not going to kill *him,* are you, Kit? He looks like he's surrendered."

"He's toting Diego's hair. The others must have let him do the honors; he's about the age to be on the lookout for a wife, and Comanche females set great score on scalps."

Stone got a glimpse of the long black tresses and the ugly patch of shriveled scalp. He turned away, busied himself with his reloading. It took as much time as did his first try on the Arkansas. Had he been this slow only moments earlier he would have died.

"No . . . I ain't about to kill him," Kit said. "This is his lucky day. We'll turn him loose, but first we'll scare him good. I want him to carry the news of this fight down to wherever the bigger Comanche raiding parties are, someplace on the *llano,* I expect. We want them to know how three white men punished this bunch for what they did." When Kit finished talking he jammed the reloaded pistols into his belt, drew a knife from the sheath at his side, stepped close to the Indian youth, and placed the point on the boy's Adam's apple. The boy did not move, even when Carson pushed the knife forward and a trickle of blood ran down his throat. In the moonlight the blood looked black. Kit said something more in the strange tongue, but at the end Stone caught one word he knew: *"Carson!"*

"Don Luis!" Kit shouted then. "Bring this varmint a horse. Not a good one."

In moments the Comanche was on the bare back of a pony, moving it through the cottonwoods, beating its flanks with the free end of a rope tied to a sort of crude hackamore Aragón must have rigged for it. He did not look back.

"Don't know if I've done the right thing after all," Kit said. "He'll have a time of it explaining just how he got away, but he'll make out there was at least a hundred of us, if I know Comanches. That might help some." He turned to me. "Let's give Don Luis a hand rounding up these horses, Brad. Then while he makes something like a *caballada* out of them, you and I can sashay back through the camp and tidy up. I'm pretty sure we done a good job. I don't think we left one still breathing, but if any of them are, we'll have to finish him—and do what else we have to do."

Stone helped Kit and Aragón restore some semblance of order to the horse herd. Contrary to Carson's conjecture, the Indians had roped Diego's mustangs on a picket line, and even after the frenzy of the gunfire, they gave little trouble. But the Comanches had only hobbled their own mounts. Two had already broken free of their restraints in their panic, and had wandered away from streamside and through the trees. A few more had bolted across the shallow water of the stream, and were galloping out of sight.

"Let them go," Kit said. "We could hunt them clear to Council Grove without catching one of them. As it is, we made a little profit with the three it seems we got."

Aragón proved himself a wizard at handling horses. Stone hoped he might be called to help the Mexican, but Carson put a quick end to the hope.

"Come on, Brad," Kit said. "Let's backtrack to the camp and see if any of our red *amigos* are still twitching."

He walked to the spot where the last of the Comanches lay on the soft ground near the stream. This Indian would require no more killing. Moonlight made his wide, staring dead eyes pure white marble.

Kit knelt beside him, and drew his big Bowie. He drew the blade swiftly and deeply across the dead man's upper forehead, grasped the hair and yanked it to the back of the head with a vicious snap of the wrist. Another stroke of the knife and the scalp came free. The hair and skin dripped blood as Kit rose and started toward the Comanche camp.

The seven there were also dead, and Carson stripped the hair from all of them. He stuffed each bloody mess into his fringed buckskin shoulder bag. The clearing still smelled of rancid grease—and now a coppery stink on top of it.

Stone had forgotten the Indian that Luis Aragón's second shot had sent rolling into the cooking fire.

"We can pull that haunch onto the coals as soon as we get that dead Comanche out of them. Too bad the fire took *his* hair," Kit said. "When Don Luis gets done with them horses we can eat the animal they started on."

Eat?

Stone ran toward the trees, dropped his Hawken at his feet, thrust his arms into the darkness, found and leaned against the trunk of a cottonwood. He heaved until his stomach knotted.

5

He felt no better when Carson announced they would bed down right there in the Indian camp until sunrise. He felt grateful Kit made no mention of burying the dead Comanches, but the thought of sleeping so close to the mutilated bodies added to his queasiness.

"We need rest," Kit said. "We'll have to ride hard when the sun comes up. It won't be easy herding a dozen horses back to the Santa Fe wagon road, but I want to catch up with Don Pablo and his *galera* as fast as we can. I think this was the only raiding party on the prowl today, but it won't pay to take any more chances than we already have."

Carson slept. Perhaps Luis Aragón slept as well. Stone did not.

If the day before had been one of the best if not *the* best of his life to date, the one just concluded had easily been the worst.

He tried to persuade himself that this should not be so. Three men defeating ten Comanches, killing nine of them. In truth, the fight had only required one of them—Kit. If Aragón and Stone had not been there when they found Diego, Carson would have come to this cottonwood grove alone, and the result would have been the same. Don Luis and Stone had pulled their own triggers, true, but Kit had stationed them and aimed them. They had been mere added weapons in the fight, supplements to Kit's Hawken, the U.S. 1836s, the long lance, and the scalping knife.

7

The Voyageurs

They caught up with Pablo Espinosa long before they reached the box canyon at Piedras Negras.

"Something's up," Kit said. "Don Pablo should have made better time than this. I didn't expect to see him until we were halfway to San Miguel."

The trader had parked his wagon at one side of the high woodland trace in the shade of a juniper a bit taller and bushier than most along this stretch. He had staked his livestock in a meadow hauntingly like the one where they had discovered Diego, except that this one was cut almost exactly in two by a mountain stream.

Stone could see no sign of Espinosa or either of the children, and for a dark moment he was sure Indians had attacked again, even though the grazing oxen and horses told him this was unlikely.

Then the trader stood up on the driver's seat and looked back over the wagon top at them as they rode up with their herd. He gripped the brace that held the canvas so hard his hands were white. His brown face had turned even whiter.

"*Señor Carson!*" he called. "*Ven acá, con presteza, por favor.*"

Stone thought something had happened to the children, but then the heads of Concepción and Pepe, with their tousled, jet black hair and enormous eyes, popped up. They looked as frightened as their father did.

Sharp little cries and deep groans came from inside the wagon.

Doña Olivera was having her baby.

Kit dismounted, tossed his reins to Stone, and ran to the front of the wagon. Espinosa and the children had already ducked back inside, and the scout climbed up over the seat and followed him. In a few seconds Carson shouted.

"Brad! Don Luis! Come here, quick!"

Aragón began to move the *caballada* into the meadow with Don Pablo's stock. He seemed in an awful hurry.

"Don Luis," Stone called to the Mexican. "Did you not hear? Señor Carson wants our help."

Aragón shook his head. "One does not wish to appear unfeeling, Señor Stone," he said, "but this . . . frightens me more than fighting the Comanches. I would only be in the way. And I would become ill, *también*. You will have to serve for both of us. *Muchas gracias*."

Stone tied his horse and Kit's to the rear wheel of the wagon, and went to the large opening at the rear and peered inside.

Doña Olivera lay with her head toward him, with Carson between her legs, doing something Stone had no wish to discover. The children and Don Pablo looked over the mountain man's shoulders, their faces three brown moons of worry.

"There you are, Brad," Kit said. "Good. Tell you what you can do. Come to the front of the wagon and get Don Pablo and *los niños* out of here. Doña Olivera and I got work to do. I can take care of her and this baby that's due any minute now without no trouble, but I won't be able to deal with them if it turns awkward."

"You don't need my help in there, Kit?" Stone held his breath for the answer.

"No, but thanks. This ain't something I ain't never done before. Brought Adaline into the world myself. In a blizzard. This one looks easy. Get Don Pablo to fixing grub. Doña Olivera will likely be a mite hungry when this is over."

"She's all right?"

"Fit as a fiddle. This lady done this twice before, too, remember?"

Adaline? Somewhere in his reading about Kit, perhaps in one of Jessie Frémont's *Century Magazine* articles, Stone had come across the name, but the particulars eluded him. At any rate, he had no time to think about it. He stepped to the front of the wagon and called the trader and the children out.

Twenty minutes later, as he kept the frantic Espinosa at his cooking chores almost by main force, and tried with small success to teach two eager youngsters with whom he did not share a language how to play hopscotch, another cry, a lusty bawl this time, issued from the wagon.

"It's a boy!" Carson shouted.

2

"Señor Carson is so gentle, *tan dócil,* Señor Stone," Doña Olivera Espinosa said as she nursed crimson-faced Cristóbal José Jesús Esteban Espinosa by the fire that night. "Such soft kind hands. No *comadrón* could have done it better. I will be proud to have *mi niño pequeño* carry the name of the great *señor.*"

Luis Aragón must have seen his puzzlement. "Cristóbal is Christopher in English, Señor Stone. Don Pablo has named his *hijo* for Señor Carson. Cristóbal is how his Mexican friends address the *señor.* And a *comadrón* is what I think you would call a male midwife in your language."

Carson announced they would not begin their journey again until morning, in order to give the mother and infant a chance to rest.

"Besides," he said, "I want to see if I can bring in some game. When we come completely down out of the mountains, hunting won't be near as promising."

He was gone from their camp for most of the rest of the

day, returning just after sundown, the carcass of a small antelope draped across his horse's neck. He rescinded his earlier rule about making "cold camps."

"I scouted out all the approaches to where we're at while I hunted. I cut no sign at all of any more Comanches. I think we got clear sailing into San Miguel, so tonight we can have a fire."

Kit got in another round of dancing with Pepe and Concepción after the trader cleared away the remains of dinner. As Kit spun the children about to Don Pablo's guitar accompaniment, Stone kept seeing him flitting like a wraith through the Comanche camp as he went about his deadly business, and Stone saw the hands which now held those of the children, Pepe and Concepción—the same hands that had eased the baby from Doña Olivera with the gentleness she described—as still dripping with Comanche blood after he scalped his fallen enemies.

The dance done, but with the children still clamoring for more, the Espinosas retired to the wagon, and Aragón set out to inspect the animals in the meadow. It left Kit and Stone sitting by the fire.

"Kit," Stone said, "could I ask you something?"

"Fire away."

"You mentioned delivering someone named Adaline."

There came a space of silence, then . . .

"My daughter. Her mother was an Arapaho named Wa'anibe who's dead now."

"I'm sorry . . ."

"No need; it was a long time ago." The scout's voice quavered. "I put Adaline in the Howard School in Fayette, Missouri, a few years back. I see her from time to time. Not near as much as I'd like." A knot cracked in the fire, sounding much like the report of one of the pistols in the bloody bosque. When Carson spoke again his voice had lightened, as if he had willed it. "I remarried. *Her* name was Making-Out-

Road. She was an Indian, too, a Ute. I *say* I married her, but now that I'm a Catholic, maybe that ain't rightly so. Leastways I don't think Padre Martínez up in Taos would look at it that way. He never would have married me and Josefa otherwise, I figure."

"And the Ute lady . . . ?"

"Oh, she's alive somewheres." He laughed. "She threw me out. We fought a lot. About money mostly. She ran up some ungodly bills on my account at Bent's whenever I was on the trap lines. Fancy clothes and liquor. When I took her to task about it she just tossed my duds and gear out of her lodge while I was away on a beaver hunt. That's a Ute divorce. I ain't seen her since."

Stone felt a little uneasy that he had asked such personal questions the way he had, and he changed the subject.

"Luis Aragón seems intent on a certain lady in Taos."

"Sure is. Ana Barragán has that effect on young *hombres*. You'll see when we get to Taos. Ana has lots of *caballeros* paying court to her, but I think her daddy, Don Bernardo, would kind of like Luis for a son-in-law."

Ana Barragán. Her name had come up for the third time. Stone had thought it pretty enough the first time he heard it. Now it rang in the mountain silence like a crystal bell.

8

City of the Holy Faith

They reached La Villa Real de la Santa Fe de San Francisco—the full Spanish name of the capital of the province of Nuevo Méjico—in the middle of one of the heavy rainy-season downpours that often pelt the upper valley of the

Río Grande without mercy in the late spring and early summer.

The streets leading to the plaza—*calles,* Don Luis called them—were foot-deep rivers of sucking mud.

Fortunately, Don Pablo had situated his home and trading center on a good, hardpan-and-stone road at the far southeastern edge of the village, and they had little trouble getting his heavy wagon settled in its stockaded compound.

As happy as the elder Espinosas were to be home at last with the brand-new baby, Concepción and Pepe shed copious tears when they said good-bye to Carson.

Aragón left Kit and Stone shortly after they parted company with the Espinosas, and headed straight for his family home somewhere down near the river, El Río del Norte. He would join them in the morning for the ride north to Taos— and his Ana Barragán. "And, of course, I will come to Casa Tules tonight, Señor Carson."

"*¡Bueno!*" Kit said.

"Casa Tules?" Stone asked.

"You'll see."

From the time they were fifty yards away from the Espinosa home in the driving, slate-gray rain, Stone did not spy another soul before they arrived in the center of the town.

They slogged their way there through narrow, empty streets that seemed to Stone no better thoroughfares than the back alleys of the seamier sections of Boston or Chicago. The adobe walls of the buildings on either hand were soaked to a dull shine by the torrential rain.

This legendary little city that lent its name to the great trail leading all the way from Independence fell in those first minutes so far below Brad Stone's expectations he wished he were back at Bent's, readying himself to set off for the mountains with Captain Frémont.

"We'll see if Fabiano Minjárez can put us up at La Fonda on the plaza," Carson said.

Stone studied his famed companion. The rain had wet Carson through to the bone, leaving him bedraggled, hunched into the saddle, dripping water in small cascades from the fringes on his buckskin shirt and trousers. The brim of his leather hat bent down almost into ruffles and ran as freely as did his other garments. Stone, knowing he looked the same, wondered if even the most tolerant of hoteliers would offer lodging to such a disgraceful pair of mendicants.

He had not counted on Kit's universal renown and the respect in which the denizens of this strange small city held him. It surfaced quickly, beginning with the innkeeper himself. A swarthy, mustachioed, portly Mexican wearing a white apron carried two wooden buckets and placed them at his feet as they came through the door.

"*¡Hola! ¿Cómo estás, Don Cristóbal?*" the man cried, stepping behind a small desk in the tiny foyer. Stone was at a loss to determine how he even recognized the scout in his disheveled state.

"*¿Cómo estás, Don Fabiano?*"

"How may I be of service, Señor Carson?"

"*Dos cuartos para pasar la noche, por favor, mi amigo,*" Kit said.

"*Sí, señor. ¡Con mucho gusto!* Don Cristóbal will dine with us at La Fonda tonight, one hopes?"

"*Sí, amigo.* But first I want to show Santa Fe to my young friend here when the rain stops."

When the rain stops? It did not look to Stone as if it would ever stop. If anything it was coming down even harder than it had when they entered town. He saw the reason for Minjárez's two buckets. The roof of this "passably good inn . . . the best in Santa Fe" leaked like a sieve. Puddles were making small lakes on a packed-earth floor in this miniature lobby where beetles scurried in manic desperation to escape the swirling little floods.

Carson continued. "I kind of thought on making a visit to Casa Tules sometime this evening."

"La Tules will be happy to see you, Señor Carson." Minjárez smiled. "Even if you win from her."

Kit laughed. "She should. The old girl took me for a hundred fifty-seven *reales* last time I played her tables. One other thing, Don Fabiano: we hitched our ponies and pack animals at your rail. Could you have a *peón* put them in your stable and get our stuff inside?"

"It is done, Don Cristóbal."

"And I'm pretty sure *mi amigo*, Señor Stone, will want a bath."

2

The mirror in Stone's room, the first he had seen since leaving Bent's, showed him a face he did not know, even after shaving off five days' growth of beard.

The difference did not lie in the sunburned forehead, nor in the brown hair that had grown nearly as long as Kit's. The eyes had changed. He might have expected it. They had seen too much these past few days.

He immersed himself in the tin tub a Mexican boy clad in white cotton filled for him, and scrubbed away the grime and sweaty dust, dressed in the driest clothes he could find in the packs the same youngster ferried in from the mud of some corral, and walked to the cubbyhole that served La Fonda as a lobby. While he waited for Kit, brilliant sunlight suddenly streamed through the inn's front door.

He stepped outside to take his first real look at the fabled little city that had so far been such a dismal disappointment. From somewhere church bells tolled. They gave off dissonant, tinny notes. Vespers? He lamented his ignorance. It was not a sound he had ever heard on weekdays in solidly Protestant Groverton, Illinois.

The plaza, which an hour earlier had been a clutching sea of gumbo as black as sin, had dried rock hard as if by magic. In Illinois or Massachusetts a bright sun coming after a heavy rain would have filled the air with steam for hours; here, in the desiccated atmosphere of something over seven thousand feet of altitude, it was as dry and crisp as if it had gone months without a drop of moisture. The light seemed to issue not only from the sky, but from the very earth.

And the people!

Every one of the Santa Féans who had kept themselves so hidden during Kit's and his sodden ride through the *calles* leading to the plaza and La Fonda appeared to have gathered in the open space in front of him especially for his perusal. There must have been two hundred of them. He gazed open-mouthed at the most astonishingly varied assortment of exotic human beings he had ever seen. Tall, thin, short, fat, and of almost every possible configuration and shade of skin, their garments looked like costumes, their headgear alone so variegated it was as if he had walked into the middle of a mad milliners' convention.

The fur hats and sombreros he saw now were familiar from Bent's, of course, and there had been feathers and feathered caps galore on the Arapahos in the compound of the trading post on the Arkansas. But here he saw even more of them, one to his utter delight the full-feathered warbonnet he had lusted to see since leaving Illinois, plus beaded headbands and top hats of the beaver Kit had once hunted, military caps cocked above gaudy, gold-braided uniforms—Mexican, he surmised, and as tight as a second skin—together with the occasional honest-to-God burnished helmet straight out of one of his early history books. Bonnets of the poke variety such as the one Emmy Legrand had worn back in Missouri, and blanket hoods that almost concealed their owners' bronzed Indian faces, floated past him in a seemingly endless parade, interspersed with felt fedoras and flat-brimmed, leather mountain hats in considerably better shape than the soggy ones in which Kit and he had made their entrance at La Fonda.

But in that kaleidoscope of humanity, the women caught and held his eye.

Except for a few ancient crones with faces like old leather purses, the females in the crowd had daubed their cheeks with some sort of chromatic paste from just beneath the eyes almost to the jaw line—a few were yellow, some blue, now and then a hideous, thick patch of lumpy white, but most an incendiary, cherry red. Willowy as most of these younger women were, and no matter that many of them looked as modishly turned out as any he had seen in Boston, the garish smears made them look like the clowns under Mr. Barnum's big top. Two of the yellows had coated their faces so heavily they appeared diseased.

As a painter, it revolted him that they would hide the God-given rich, golden hues of their natural complexions.

"Ugly, ain't it?" Kit had appeared at his side. "Sure glad the habit ain't reached Taos yet."

"Why do they do it? Is it some kind of Mexican fashion?"

"Partly. Mostly, though, they lard themselves up with that colored grease to keep their skin looking and feeling young. I guess they think the colors make it look a little better. Sometimes they won't wash it off for a month, and then only when they're going to a fancy party. It don't work worth a damn on their skin as far as I can tell. And it don't smell so good, to boot."

Sure enough, when one of the señoritas sailed by fairly close to them, Stone got a faint whiff of rotten eggs.

But other, more delectable odors had begun to reach him. They had neared the dinner hour, and the smell of corn and

onions cooking, reminiscent of the odors escaping Don
Pablo Espinosa's kettle at the top of Raton Pass—thought by
him so hellish at the time, but now in his hunger remembered fondly—began to fill the plaza.

Carson sniffed the air, too. "Let's grab a bite with Don
Fabiano," he said, "and then mosey over to Casa Tules and
see if we can't take the lady of the house for a few of her
reales."

3

"That's the Palacio across the way, the Palace of the Governors," Kit said when they sauntered into the plaza after a
meal Stone enjoyed since Don Pablo's fiery feast had made
him ready for it. "We won't go there. Minjárez told me that
Manuel Armijo—he's governor of Nuevo Méjico—is in
town and living there right now. Don Manuel don't care
much for me, and I guess I feel the same about him."

That came as a surprise. Without anyone having told him
as much, Stone had assumed there was no one in the entire
Southwest Kit disliked, or the other way around. Of course,
out-and-out enemies like the Comanches they had killed in
the bosque on the upper Cimarron were another matter.

Indians. Santa Fe seemed filled with them. As they
crossed the plaza they neared a group of eight or ten squatting in the dirt. All men, they wore outfits markedly different from those of the Arapaho at Bent's or any native
garments Stone had seen earlier today: each was dressed in
a white blouse of sorts with a full skirt; solid-colored head
bands; trousers under the kirtles or whatever the skirts were
called.

"Navajo," Kit said. "'Dineh,' they call themselves.
They're hostages—kind of. Being held here while the Mexicans parley a treaty with the tribe."

"No one guards them?"

"Ain't necessary."

"They won't try to escape?"

"Won't even *think* of making a run for it until they been here at least a month, and this bunch looks like they just been brought in. They like white man's food, and believe it or not, they just plain like to see the city sights. Human as any of us, I reckon, and sure as hell as curious. Good people, even if my Ute friends don't cotton to them much."

He nodded affably at one of the older Navajos as they veered their course to pass them, and got as affable a nod in return, and a warm smile. The old man raised his dark brown hand palm outward, and Kit did the same, stopped then, leaned over, and touched his palm to the other's.

"Viejo," Kit whispered.

"Jefito," the old Indian replied.

"Viejo" Stone already knew, but *"Jefito"*? He asked.

Kit blushed. "Means 'Little Chief.' Don't know as I deserve it, but some of the Navajo call me that."

As they continued their stroll across the plaza Stone tried to take in the "city sights" himself.

The buildings of Santa Fe he observed on that walk with Carson looked at first glance crude and lumpy, misshapen even, their rounded corners slanted ridiculously out of plumb. Their walls and buttresses struck him as far too massive for their function. To his untutored outlander's eye they appeared as if they might at any moment sag back into the earth from which they had been gently molded, as opposed to being truly constructed. He had not yet learned that gentleness and strength could exist, not only side by side, but *within* the selfsame entities—whether they be hovels, palaces . . . or people.

But even then the *color* of adobe reached deep inside him and brought a warm response. The painter in him, he supposed.

A walk of about three minutes brought them to a long adobe wall, this one distinguished from its neighbors by a coat of whitewash, holding a small, low-linteled doorway, and an intricately carved door in the center of it.

At a hitch rail in the *calle* a dozen horses nodded, some of the finest riding stock Stone had ever seen. Fine as the animals looked, their accoutrements were even more resplendent. Silver-mounted saddles glittered in the last of the sun. The saddles were slung over intricately embroidered black blankets of such a gleaming, smooth, tight weave that for a moment Stone took them to be silk, and the bridles were studded with multifaceted chunks of ornamental glass that winked merrily in that dying sun.

"Casa Tules," Kit said. "Are you a betting man, Brad?"

"No, sir."

"Pity. This is the best place to put down a wager west of the Mississippi. I think you'll find La Tules, Doña Gertrudes Barceló, the woman who owns this establishment, interesting, to say the least. She's a great lady now. Welcome in the finest circles in Santa Fe, and even at the Palacio. It ain't always been that way. Some years back she earned her living with something a little more questionable than gambling, but all that's been forgot. She's been generous with the money she's made here. Hell of a lot of orphans can thank La Tules for a pretty good life nowadays. Incidentally, *las tules* means 'the veils,' although she never hides anything. She's about the most honest soul I've ever known. Every bank in her house is arrow-straight. Let's go on in."

He pushed his way through the small door. Stone had to bend his back to negotiate the opening, something which would always prove a bit of a bother for him in Taos and Santa Fe.

He found himself in a small vestibule where a long hardwood table, snugged against the wall opposite the door, held a number of partly filled cut-glass decanters and a score of drinking glasses, no two alike. The tiny room reeked of liquor.

A man dressed in a tight, black-and-silver suit was pouring drinks for himself and another man who wore the long frock coat of a banker. They glanced at Carson and Stone just once and turned back to each other.

Since no servant seemed in attendance, Stone assumed the drinks were either the compliments of Casa Tules, or that the bar operated on some sort of honor system. The smell of liquor was so overpowering, and the quarters so confining, he feared that if they lingered he would not have to actually put a glass to his mouth to feel the effects of alcohol. Fortunately, Kit had no intention of lingering. He beckoned for Stone to follow him, and they went through another tiny doorway straight into a scene of low-level tumult.

A narrow, windowless room stretched out for twenty-five or thirty yards. As was the case with La Fonda, it had a packed-earth floor, but unlike the hotel, Casa Tules must have had a serviceable roof; there was no sign that the early afternoon rain had made any incursions here. The crosswise ceiling beams were stained a deep, dirty brown, apparently from years of the oily tobacco smoke such as that now curling up around them.

Lamplight streaming from sconces set in the walls played over thirty or forty men and perhaps half as many women, all bending over gaming tables with high rails. Almost every player in the room seemed to be talking, in low, discreet tones, but with the cumulative effect something like the sound of the rolling Atlantic surf Stone had listened to on Martha's Vineyard.

"The big game here is monte," Kit said. "Ever play it?"

"No."

"Maybe it's best you don't start tonight, then. These are high-stakes banks. I ain't got no idea what Captain Frémont pays you, but your *dinero* won't last long with La Tules if you ain't smack on top of things. If you want *I* can stand in for you. Or you can try that French wheel thing. Forget what they call it."

"Roulette?"

"That's it. Damned thing don't take no particular amount of brains."

"I'll just watch."

"Smart man. Before *I* play, though, I want you to meet the lady of the house."

He led Stone toward the far end of the room, threading his way through knots of elegantly dressed men and past women of stunning Latin beauty, none of whom looked up from their play or took any notice of them. As relatively dark as the casino was—if one could call this adobe cavern a casino—the long room was not totally without its brighter spots. The walls were hung with Spanish tapestries such as Stone had only seen in art museums in Boston and New York.

At the far end of the *sala* one table was placed at right angles to all the others, and behind it a huge, maroon mohair-upholstered armchair with a high scrolled back, gilded as might be the throne of some minor Balkan principality, held the most remarkable looking woman Stone had ever seen. Dealing cards to a table ringed by patrons, she had not noticed them as they approached.

La Tules did not affect the peculiar smears of supposedly curative cosmetics Stone had seen on the women in the plaza, even though in her case it might have been worth a try. Deep seams lined her brown face, and a few gray strands streaked her dark hair, but nothing about her actually indicated age. Nothing indicated youth, either. Around her neck, possibly as much to hide more wrinkles as for mere show, she had twisted three heavy gold chains, from one of which hung a crucifix almost six inches in length, and fashioned of what Stone was certain was solid gold.

Even with the tiny pits in her forehead that suggested smallpox sometime in the past, anyone with the most idle eye for these things would judge La Tules a formidable beauty. For Stone's part, he wanted to paint her. She wore a lavender brocade gown with a dramatic V of décolletage, daringly exposing a magnificent bosom from which not even the gold cross would draw the eye of the viewer. Rings, all gold as well, and each mounted with a mammoth stone of some kind—a diamond, two rubies, an amethyst, and others he did not know—encircled every one of her brown fingers and both thumbs. On anyone else he would have found the display vulgar. Not so with La Tules. Amazingly, they did not seem to hamper her manipulation of the playing cards she dealt, even though the rings held her fingers wide apart. The cards flew from the deck, and with darting swiftness her black eyes followed each one as it fluttered to the table. He stared at her spellbound.

"Handsome critter, ain't she?" Carson whispered.

Then she looked up.

"Cristóbal!" Her voice boomed. *"¿Cómo estás, mi amor?"* She glanced imperiously around the table. *"Perdón, mis amigos.* Play at the bank of La Tules is stopped *por el momento.* We shall resume after we have a talk with Señor Carson. If you cannot wait, find a place at another of the tables, *por favor."* Faces turned toward the scout. Two of the men nodded, and one stepped up and thumped him on the back.

La Tules smiled at Kit, cast Stone one brief glance of candid curiosity that left him feeling naked, and went on. "Let me come out of my playground, Kitito, and we shall have a drink together. How long has it been since I have seen you? Six months? Far too long!"

"Just four months, *querida,*" Kit said, smiling. "Makes me feel good you think it's six."

"Doña Josefa? She is well and prospering?"

"Far as I know. I been up at Bent's with Captain Frémont. I ride north to Taos in the morning."

"*¡Bueno!* La Tules hopes you will find time to get that sweet child *embarazada*. But perhaps you already have. No?" This was greeted with laughter from the others at the table. Friendly laughter.

"I'll do my very best, *mi doña*," Kit said.

La Tules stood then, rising like a full, golden, voluptuous moon, moved out from behind the table, *floated* to Kit, and embraced him as if she would squeeze the life from him. A dizzying scent of powerful cologne reached Stone. She was not much taller than Kit was; seated, she had appeared at least as tall as Stone.

When at last she released him, Kit turned.

"Brad," he said, "this lady is Doña Gertrudes Barceló, La Tules. Doña Gertrudes, meet my young friend Bradford Stone."

Even during that disturbing flick of her eyes when La Tules first spied Kit and him, and again as Stone followed them as she dealt her last round of monte, he had not really seen those eyes. She turned them on him now. Black as onyx, deep as dark pools, a man could have drowned in them. She kept them hard on Stone as she continued. "*Encantada, Señor Stone,*" she said. "Stone? As in *la piedra, señor?*"

Carson laughed. "Exactly, *mi doña*. And he looks about as *talkative* as a rock right now, don't he?"

All Stone could do by way of acknowledging the introduction was to nod feebly, hoping the blood he felt rise to his cheeks had not resulted in a noticeable blush. Whether La Tules saw a red face or not, she favored him with a smile of such hot intensity it would have melted stones in any language.

Then she turned and led them from the table to an alcove

just off the *sala.* A man in a short black jacket stood by a massive, carved Spanish table that held a graceful lamp.

"*¡Aguardiente, Carlos, por favor!*" La Tules said. Stone looked a question at Kit.

"Mexican brandy. Good stuff. A lot smoother than the Taos Lightning you choked on at Charlie Bent's, but it kicks every bit as hard. We got a long ride ahead of us tomorrow. So I'd watch myself, if I was you."

Stone drank sparingly when Carlos brought not a decanter, but a squat, dusty bottle, and genuine cognac glasses, not tumblers from the odd assortment in the vestibule.

"Your young friend here is a fine-looking *hombre,* Kitito," La Tules said as she held her glass out first toward Stone and then toward Carson. "Perhaps he would like to meet a talented, cooperative *señorita* while he is in Santa Fe. I can arrange that, you know. You, of course, have not benefited from one of my arrangements since you met and courted Doña Josefa. Señor Stone is not similarly occupied with some young *mujer* is he?"

"*Are* you, Brad?" Carson asked.

"No, sir."

La Tules arched a dark eyebrow. "*Would* you like the assistance of La Tules in that respect, *señor?*"

Something had happened. Stone knew he should have found himself shocked to the marrow, but he did not. He had never judged himself a great hand with the ladies, and not a bit practiced in the badinage they seemed to crave as the price of an encouraging smile. But something *had* happened.

Not that he was smitten with Doña Gertrudes Barceló in any romantic way, but he suddenly felt an urge to devilishness and bravado he had never felt before.

"Yes, Doña Gertrudes," he said, "I would like your help

very much. But only if it should include the person and charms of the lady called La Tules." He held his breath.

The alcove shook with La Tules' laughter, and the flames of the lamp on the table danced and wavered with the force of her breath. Carson's laugh echoed hers.

"*¡Magnífico!*" She turned to Kit. "Your friend will do well with *las mujeres* over the course of his life, Kitito, if he has not done so already." She sighed deeply and turned back to Stone. Again those deep, luminous eyes held him fast. "Ah . . . if La Tules were only twenty years younger . . . Hmmm . . . perhaps ten would do it." She roared with laughter again. "We must stop this. La Tules might soon reduce the years to five, then two, then none at all. *¡La juventud!* Youth! No one ever receives nearly enough of that commodity. Enjoy it while you have it, Señor Piedra."

Then her joyous face darkened as she turned to Kit again.

"I am truly sorry to tell you this, Cristóbal, but all of Casa Tules' banks are closed to you."

"Why, *mi amiga?*"

"Don Manuel is coming here tonight."

"Armijo?"

"*Sí.* A runner arrived just before you did, demanding La Tules reserve a whole bank for the governor and his party."

"But why do I have to leave?"

"I don't want Don Manuel to see you."

"He's seen me plenty of times before. We don't care much for each other, true—but you know I would never give him any trouble. Leastways not here in Casa Tules."

"It is different tonight, Cristóbal," she said. "And things are a little different here in Santa Fe from what they were when you were here last."

"How so?

"The talk of war that has come up the Camino Real in recent weeks."

"But it has for years. I've heard some come over the trail from Independence, too. Don't mean a thing."

"This time I think it does, Cristóbal."

"Maybe. It makes me heart sorry to think about it. But even if it's true, what's that got to do with me and Manuel Armijo?"

"*El gobernador* has become a frightened man."

"Always was."

"He is much more so now, Kit. Frightened men do foolish things. Already he talks of placing Americans in Santa Fe under arrest. He does not dare arrest them all; it would ruin us here and Don Manuel knows it, but he might be happy to start with you as an example and a warning. No American in Nuevo Méjico is nearly as well known as you, and it would put fear in all the others."

"So you would like Brad and me to leave?"

"*Por favor.*" It sounded a genuinely heartfelt plea. "I cannot bear the thought of you behind bars in *el juzgado, mi querido.*"

"It probably wouldn't come to that, Doña Gertrudes," Kit said, "but as a personal favor to you, Brad and me will be on our way right quick. Sure hate to go without taking some of your *dinero,* though. *Muchas gracias y adios, amiga.*"

She looked over Stone's shoulder and he turned to see Luis Aragón. "*¿Cómo estás, Don Luis?*"

"*Muy bien, mi doña,*" the trader said.

"You know Señor Carson, of course, Don Luis, but have you met his friend Señor Stone?"

Aragón smiled. "*Sí.* We have just completed a joint venture, *doña mía,* in the course of which we have become excellent *amigos.*"

"*¡Excelente!* La Tules likes her friends to be friends with each other." She turned to Stone. "Don Luis is another who turns down the help I offered you. He is in pursuit of a *paloma linda* in the north." She turned back to Luis. "How goes it between you and Ana Barragán these days?"

Aragón shrugged. "*¿Quién sabe?* Perhaps I will learn when we reach Taos. Señores Carson, Stone, and I ride there tomorrow."

4

The sun had not quite disappeared when Kit and Stone emerged from Casa Tules, but the street with the splendid horses still nodding at the rail was filling with purple shadows.

Carson fell silent as they walked back through the twisted *calles* of Santa Fe and across the now empty plaza to La Fonda; it gave Stone more than enough time to think about what he had found in this little city at the foot of the southern outrunners of the Sangre de Cristo Mountains, and what he had found in himself.

The tiny swallow he had taken of the *aguardiente* could not account for his sudden attack of boldness with La Tules.

He thought perhaps he knew what had happened.

He must have changed considerably since the fight with the Comanches.

He had Kit Carson to thank for this as much as he had him to thank for saving him. His utter confidence in Kit had somehow come winging back to him as confidence in himself. "La Tules spoke of war, Kit," Stone said as they neared La Fonda.

"Yes."

"But you said it meant nothing."

"I ain't exactly sure, though. Guess I just wanted to put the old girl at ease. Maybe it was to put me at ease, too. In some ways I'm as Mexican as she is now, but I can't forget I was born and bred American. If war does come I might have to take Josefa away from Taos. And I might have to fight my neighbors. I don't want to even *think* about war."

5

Stone lay awake in his room.

Fabiano Minjárez would be knocking on his door at five in the morning, but that prospect only seemed to make falling asleep more difficult. He got up, pulled on a pair of trousers and a shirt and wandered out to the plaza.

The scarred rock of a moon which had lighted the bosque where they fought the Comanches was now a few days past full, but it still emitted enough light to bathe the plaza in silver. Across the square from La Fonda glimmers of yellow flickered in the few barred windows of the Palacio.

Perhaps Governor Armijo had returned from Casa Tules, perhaps the palace household staff still awaited him. Some raucous cries issued from the saloon section of the hotel behind him but soon everything subsided into silence.

But dead as Santa Fe seemed to be at that moment, he could feel a ferment of life seething just beneath the surface. Something at once sane and savage. It had been there when he rode in with Kit, but he had not noticed it.

He had not wanted to think of war—but he did.

9

The Blue Light of Taos

"That there monster deep gash down below us is the *upper* gorge of the Río," Carson said, pointing to a great rift cleaving the valley floor, its depths black with the shadows cast by the morning sun.

The chasm lay perhaps a thousand feet beneath where Carson, Aragón, and Stone had reined up on a piñon-dotted promontory to let their horses cool. His surveyor's eye told him it must still be another thousand feet from the canyon's rim to the bottom of the gorge. They had just climbed from the churning whitewater of the Río Grande del Norte, losing the river for five miles or more, finding it again north of where it had hidden itself behind this high, rocky hill.

Even on the trip over Raton Pass he had not seen terrain as breathtaking as this upper gorge. It looked as though the land had cracked itself in half. Dark and dead as the depths appeared, he would not have been surprised had the flames of Hell suddenly leaped above the rim's knife edge.

"Where's Taos?" he asked.

Aragón laughed. "One cannot see the village from here, Señor Stone. It is still almost *cuatros leguas*—four Spanish leagues—away. More than fifteen of your English miles."

"Distances is almost always more than they seem in this country, Brad," Kit said. "Let your eye roam from the top of the gorge way up toward the big blue mountain on the right. Taos lies almost at the foot of the range there, under that thin blanket of smoke from last night's cooking fires. We'll make good time this morning; it's downhill all the way from here."

"And we shall ride right by the eastern gate of the *estancia* of Don Bernardo Barragán," Aragón said, something almost reverential in his voice, "halfway down the trail to Taos."

"Will you leave us there, Don Luis?" Carson asked.

"No, *señor*, I will go straight on into town with you, secure the room I always take at La Posada, and send my calling card to Don Bernardo. I must wait and see if he will permit me to pay my respects at *la hacienda*. He insists on strict adherence to the proper forms. Although I believe him to be a friend, I am not at all sure he will even permit me to see Doña Ana on this trip."

"Don Bernardo is a tartar, sure enough," Carson said. "But I guess you think Ana Barragán is worth any amount of trouble. I know I thought Josefa was when I was courting. Didn't take as much guts on my part, though, as it will for you."

"Aragón blushed, squirmed in his saddle as if it burned him.

"Well now, gents," Carson said, "speaking of Mrs. Carson, I ain't getting one inch closer to her sitting here on this hilltop like a statue. Let's catch up!"

Carson dug in his spurs, and he and his two horses fairly flew from the top of the hill.

Aragón lashed his horse into motion, too, and Stone made a poor third in the little cavalcade, but he was the only one of the three riding down the slope with no other purpose than to see new sights.

He had never seen more glorious sweeps of sagebrush than he did on that morning ride down into Taos. On either side of the trail it made tufted, blue-gray quilts of the sloping plains that rolled away for miles on either side of the trail, curling up at the base of the wooded mountains to the east as if they had been pulled over banks of giant pillows.

They dropped from the crest of the hill in minutes, and the gorge disappeared, but such had been its impact he remained conscious of it long after it had vanished.

The larger clumps of sage brushed against his pants and his horse's flanks where the trail narrowed, sometimes to invisibility; the sagebrush was stiffer and tougher than its feathery look from the hilltop had led him to believe. This entire western landscape was something like that, had been that way in some respects ever since Independence. From a distance it seemed as welcoming and pastoral as this thick carpet had looked from the hilltop; but seen close up, harsh . . . even cruel, as cruel as that dark bosque on the Cimarron.

After they had pushed along for the better part of an hour, they came upon two gigantic pillars of laid-up and mortared fieldstone well to the left of the trail through the scrub and sage.

Arching across the columns and limned against a sky of indelible blue, some artisan had worked wrought iron into an enormous sign bearing a name whose letters were at least a yard in height: BARRAGÁN.

A broad road of crushed white stone in a much better state of repair than the trace they traveled led off to the west over a slight rise in the blanket of sagebrush. The pillars, the road, and the bold letters of the name silhouetted against the morning western sky somehow seemed an affront to this natural setting, and the twin columns brought to Stone's mind Shelley's *"vast and trunkless legs of stone. . . ."* As with old dead Ozymandias's warning to *". . . look on my works, ye mighty, and despair,"* it seemed a statement of demanding arrogance.

A small sigh escaped Aragón.

About a hundred yards inside this mammoth gate, and a few Gunter chain–lengths off the drive to the north, the sage had been rooted out into a grassy square Stone estimated a hundred feet on a side. Pockmarked gravestones and weathered wooden crosses filled the area, as did asters and giant daisies. In three places, small, fenced enclosures held more splintery wooden crosses gray with age and bunched together like a giant's jackstraws. At the far northwest corner, a flimsy, open-sided wooden shed leaned away from what must be the prevailing westerly wind, only the faintest of breezes this bright morning.

"That field is the burial ground of *la familia* Barragán," Aragón said. He crossed himself. "Doña Ana's ancestors and many of the people who have ridden the Barragán range for the family or worked in the *hacienda* have rested there for nearly two hundred years. Her one brother lies there. And her mother, *también*. Doña Ana is Don Bernardo's only remaining child. That is why he guards her so strictly."

"They live over there toward the river?" Stone asked.

"*Sí*. But one cannot see the *hacienda* from here. Don Bernardo's land runs from the gate all the way to the lip of the gorge—*tres leguas*—and from that hill where we started down, all the way across the slope ahead of us to Ranchos de Taos, two kilometers ahead."

"Sure you ain't changed your mind, Don Luis?" Carson said. "Your *señorita* might be waiting for you on *el portal* right now. You could pick her a nosegay of them daisies on the way in."

Aragón shook his head. "No, *señor*. One could not possibly pay a call on Doña Ana without the express permission of Don Bernardo."

They rode on. The Mexican cast a wistful glance back at the gate and the country to the west of it—toward that unseen *hacienda*, Stone supposed.

A wave of affection for this shy, courteous, now suddenly unsure man, who this past ten confusing days had become a friend, and then a comrade-in-arms, swept over him. Aragón's longing seemed a thing Stone could touch and feel. He wished him well.

Another half hour's ride brought them to a small hamlet, perched on the far side of a cottonwood-choked, shallow gully. The treetops had kept its low buildings hidden until they were almost on top of them.

"Taos?" Stone asked.

"Not yet." Carson laughed. "You seem as het-up about getting there as I do. Taos is another five miles. This is Ranchos de Taos that Don Luis spoke about. Taos itself is pretty small, but it ain't this small."

Not everything about the place was small.

As they rode up out of the cottonwood bosque in the bottom of the gully, a huge adobe church blocked the sky.

"San Francisco de Asis," Kit said. "Padre Antonio Martínez married me and Josefa here. Place was packed. There are more Jaramillos in this valley than you can shake a stick at, and Josefa is a Jaramillo. So was Ana Barragán's mother, by the way."

The church, more massive than anything he had seen in Santa Fe, dominated the land beyond the gully.

They had come upon it from the side that enclosed the nave, and ungainly as its great, widespread buttresses and bulging rooftop appeared at first, something about it spoke of an immense weight of faith. It had taken an incredible amount of devoted labor to build this marvel, and a long, long time. The two square towers with arched belfries peeping above the roof held barrel-sized bronze bells.

Stone tried to picture the diminutive Kit Carson taking a bride in this overpowering setting.

2

To Stone, Taos itself presented an even less prepossessing aspect at first sight than had Santa Fe, but the village itself did not disappoint him nearly as much.

For one thing, they rode into it in full, bright sun instead of through a blinding rainstorm, and then, too, he had not pitched his expectations nearly as high for this northern outpost of Mexico as he had for the more famous city down the river.

Except for its area and population, a fraction of Santa Fe's, Taos at first glance looked much the same: dirt streets, low, flat-roofed adobe buildings. Dogs ran loose everywhere. Spring lambs nosed through flocks of sheep grazing unattended in the pastures south of town, and some of the sparse grassland held tiny herds of cattle with calves still romping on unsteady legs.

In the town itself, black-and-white long-haired goats wandered through the *calles*. Scrawnier pigs than he remembered from farms he had surveyed in Illinois rooted noisily through trash and jettisoned foodstuffs piled outside those low-linteled doors, and squawking chickens fluttered away from their horses' hooves. Except for some low scrub along a creek they splashed through, he did not see a single tree.

The few people who came in view bore little resemblance to those he had seen in Santa Fe. For one thing, they moved at a slower pace than the energetic throngs that had scurried through the streets of the provincial capital, and their dress—white cotton for the most part, but now and then with a homespun, ankle-length gown or rough jacket—appeared far more sober. Three of them, faces alight with smiles, waved to Carson. There were Indians, too, but here they all affected the same costume, men and women: light blue blankets draped over their heads and shoulders, some with a fold of the soft woolen fabric pulled across their faces, only dark eyes showing.

"Taoseños, Taos Indians," Carson said when they rode past one such group. "Their pueblo is just two miles up the road. Been in these parts maybe half a thousand years, they say. The pueblo itself is a hell of a thing to see, *amigo*. Even bigger buildings than you can find in St. Louis, bigger than San Francisco de Asis we just now passed. Unless I miss my guess, you'll want to paint it someday."

At the plaza, much smaller than that of Santa Fe, but with a skeletal, weathered, wooden gazebo rising in the center of it, Aragón left them, saying he would see about his room in La Posada, the inn at the west end of the square.

"I'll go with him and get me a place to stay, too, Kit," Stone said. He did not really want to. He wanted to see the scout by his own fireside.

"No need, Brad," Carson said. "You'll live with me and Josefa until we start back to Bent's. *Hasta la vista, Don Luis.*"

The Mexican rode off.

"I expect he wants to go to church, light a candle, and do a hell of a lot of praying before he beards Don Bernardo," Carson said. "I know I would if I had to face that tough old stallion. Actually, Luis ain't got a lot to fret about. He comes from money and a damned good family, and I know Bernardo Barragán already thinks our *amigo* is a pretty good catch, even if Luis doesn't. Mexican girls like Ana most often don't have much say in these matters, anyways. On the other hand, she's a strong-minded young woman. She's fought the old Don all her life, according to Josefa. Hot-tempered and every bit as proud as he is. Might damned well pick her *own* man when she's ready. Josefa did."

"Does the lady return Don Luis's affection?"

"Hard to tell with Ana. She flirts a lot, and teases. You tell *me,* if you see them together this trip. Never was much of a judge about stuff like that, and I've never been any kind of hand with the ladies."

"Nor have I."

Carson snorted. "Couldn't tell that with the way you got on with our friend La Tules."

"Believe me, that was but an aberration."

"A what?"

"Something out of character for me. I'm usually not like that at all."

"Sure!" Kit grinned.

3

They turned form the northeast corner of the plaza into a street that looked marginally better than the one which had brought them into town from the south, and after a ride of only four hundred yards or so Carson pulled up in front of a rambling adobe house built in a U, with the open side toward the roadway. Whitewashed rocks decorated the yard, a flagstone walk ran from a hitchrail to the door of the house, and a few pink and yellow blossoms tossed their heads in the slight breeze. It was the first thing approaching a flower garden Stone had seen since Council Grove on the wagon trail from Independence. At Bent's there had been no evidence of attempts to raise anything hungry mountain men and the fort's workers could not put in their stomachs.

"*¡Mi casa!*" Kit exclaimed as he slid from the saddle.

The hitchrail partly closed off the open space. Someone had already tied a fine-looking, jet black horse to it. The animal and its leather-and-silver trappings called to mind the ones Stone had marveled at outside Casa Tules.

Carson peered at it, slapped its glossy rump, and chuckled. "We might have saved our friend Don Luis the trouble of sending his card out to Estancia Barragán."

"How so, Kit?"

"He could have gotten his courting under way right here at Casa Carson. That critter there is Soberano Negro, the horse Doña Ana Barragán's daddy gave her for her birthday just this last April. Her seventeenth, if I remember right. Ana must be paying Josefa a visit. Her and Mrs. Carson are by way of being cousins, you know. Her mother was Josefa's aunt, but I guess I already told you that."

They tied off their horses, and in an instant the door at the deepest part of the U flew open and banged against the adobe wall.

"*¡Querido!*"

The cry had come from a trim, tiny woman in a neat, cotton print dress who now raced toward them. She hurled herself into Kit's arms and buried herself there before Stone could get a good look at her.

Just then another figure appeared in the open doorway that Josefa Jaramillo Carson had burst through to greet her husband.

Stone did not take in how Ana Barragán was dressed. His eyes were drawn to her face, one of the loveliest he had ever seen. The young woman's eyes were locked on his.

Her face formed almost a perfect oval, the smooth dip beneath her cheekbones the only break in its contours, its shape faintly Oriental and exquisitely framed by the way she had raked her black hair back from her forehead.

Her skin glowed darkly. Nothing on his painter's palette, nor any mixture of its pigments, could possibly have matched its tones: light brown, but golden, too, and of a quality and texture he had never known. But above all else, the dark eyes—whose exact color he could only guess at with thirty feet of sunlit garden separating them—gripped him as if something physical had actually roped the two of them together.

"Brad! Wake up, *amigo!*"

He turned. Kit's smile was as broad as he had ever seen it.

"I think I know what happened to you just now," Kit said. "I seen it often enough before, but I *would* like you to meet Josefa. This is *mi esposa,* Brad."

"*¿Cómo estás, señor?*" Josefa Carson's smile was amazingly like her husband's.

Kit grinned. "No hand with the ladies? Josefa likes you enough with one look to say '*estás*' instead of '*está.*' Ain't never heard her do that before with somebody new."

Stone himself did not know which term to use. He settled for answering her smile with his own. Kit must have told Josefa something about him, but in his near trance he had not been conscious of a single word passing between the Carsons.

Even embarrassed as he suddenly became at his behavior, he flicked his eyes back to the doorway. Ana Barragán had vanished. He forced himself to turn his full attention on the Carsons.

Kit and Josefa held hands. She was a small woman, and in her own way as much of a beauty as the one he had just seen, although not of the same striking, dramatic kind. A quiet woman, he felt sure. She looked to be about the same age as the young woman who had appeared in the doorway.

Josefa Carson's hair, done up in a sedate bun, looked a shade lighter under the morning sun than had Ana Barragán's. Her skin showed none of the deep, dark glow of Ana's, either, but it was every bit as smooth. He saw straight, even features, and a high, pale forehead.

If Stone's memory of Jessie Frémont's *Century* articles about Kit was correct, he must be about thirty-six years old now, but standing with his hand clasping Josefa's, he looked not a day older than she. At this first sight of them together they seemed little more than children.

This could hardly be the Kit Carson whom Stone rode with from Bent's Fort. Where was the tough, capable scout, the diamond-hard frontiersman who had twice guided Johnny Frémont through the wilderness? The smiling, winsome, tiny man he looked at now almost seemed an impostor, not the Indian fighter Jessie Frémont—and Horace Trevelyan, too—had written about . . . or the one Brad Stone had seen on the Cimarron . . . except that he had slung over his shoulder the buckskin bag he had stuffed with Comanche scalps that night in the bosque.

Surely he would not bring those disgusting trophies into his own home.

Then Kit released Josefa's hand and began to undo the flap of the shoulder bag. Stone recoiled.

"I brought you something, *mi amor*," Kit said.

The bag gaped open. A strong aroma filled the air around them with something far different from that Stone had expected.

The odor of perfume reached him like a reprieve.

"The damned stopper's worked loose," Kit said. "Thank God the bottle ain't broke." He pulled a small amber vial from the bag and handed it to Josefa. "Bought it from Luis Aragón. Part of the goods he and Pablo Espinosa were taking back to Santa Fe."

"Muchas gracias, mi querido," Josefa said. "You never forget me. But . . . we must . . . show Señor Stone to his *cuarto*—his room—and then I will have Ana help me with *un desayuno*. You must be hungry. Ana will stay to eat with us."

She curtsied to him, turned, and started up the path. No one had appeared in the doorway again.

"Kit . . . ," Stone whispered when he thought Josefa out of earshot. He pointed to the buckskin bag. "What happened to the . . ."

"Scalps? I dumped them just before we reached San Miguel. I had no use for the ugly things."

"Then why did you take them at all?"

"I want them Comanches to think they're hanging in some white man's lodge. That will bother them a whole lot more than if they could bury them with the bodies when they get around to doing that."

With relief Stone turned his thoughts back to the young woman he had seen, and then he followed Kit up the path, to step into the first home he had entered since leaving Groverton.

4

Ana Barragán had had no intention of lingering in the doorway even as long as she had, but the sight of the big stranger standing alongside Don Cristóbal as Cousin Josefa rushed into her husband's arms held her fast.

She took a firm grip on herself and broke away from the doorway, but not so quickly that he did not see her. Their eyes met. There had been no deliberate search on her part to find his eyes, as there had been with other new men so many times in the past. But it did not seem to be a chance meeting, either. Her eyes had been drawn to his, and his to hers.

As she passed through the sitting room on her way to the kitchen, she made a quick detour to the window that opened on the small front patio. She slipped behind the drawn curtain in time to hear Josefa say, "We must . . . show Señor Stone to his *cuarto* . . ."

If they must show the tall man—a *yanqui* by the look of him, *sí*—to a room, *his* room, as Cousin Josefa had said, he would be a guest at Casa Carson for at least one night.

Cousin Josefa, Don Cristóbal, and the *yanqui* stranger were talking now, but she paid little heed to their words as she looked the new man over.

She told herself that except for those compelling eyes, nothing particularly or immediately appealing marked this newcomer: he had not shaved for a day or more; his light brown hair poking from under the brim of his leather mountain hat looked lusterless, at least until he removed the hat when he bowed slightly to Cousin Josefa. His jacket and *pantalones* looked as if he had worn them every day for a month. As he mumbled something in *inglés* she did not catch at all, he appeared unsure of himself. Shy? . . . Perhaps. When he smiled at Cousin Josefa and tipped his head a little uncertainly to one side she decided that was it. She smiled herself. She had dealt with shy young men before, flirted with a few, brought them out of their shells. Most of them, though, like poor Luis Aragón, she had left exactly as she found them.

The *yanqui*'s face, whether he was shy or not, looked strong and pleasant, and he certainly was satisfactorily tall; standing beside him, Don Cristóbal seemed a midget. Not many men in Taos would be of a height with him. Only Papá. *¡Nombre de Dios!* Why did she have to think of Papá every time a new man caught her eye?

But there was no more time to think of that. Cousin Josefa had started up the walk. It would not do to have her cousin find her here, peering secretly at this stranger as if she were a schoolgirl. She raced for the kitchen. Josefa would need help.

5

Stone hardly took notice of the small, tidy room Josefa Carson ushered him to, except that when she left him, he discovered someone had placed an enameled tin basin, a pitcher of water, a cake of aromatic yellow soap, and fresh towels on a carved wooden chest. He had detected no sign of servants. Ana Barragán must have been here just seconds earlier, must have assigned herself the task of seeing to the needs of the Carsons' unexpected guest. Josefa had not had time to do it or to tell her to.

He washed, hurrying the process, wishing he had time to pull his pack apart, find his toilet stuff and shave, longing momentarily for the tin tub at La Fonda and a change of clothing. But he had no time.

He walked the hall Kit had pointed out as leading to the sitting room where they were to meet when he was settled.

When he entered he found Ana Barragán.

Alone.

6

"*¿Cómo está, señor?*"

She sat in one of those Spanish chairs with the legs curved

like an hourglass, seeming entirely at her ease, but with her upper body straight as a young tree, shoulders back and pressing her bosom against the leather vest she wore, her head tilted high, one small foot encased in a black riding boot placed slightly ahead of the other.

"I am quite well . . . *muchas gracias, señorita* . . . and you?"

She did not answer. He thought she probably had not understood his English. But she smiled.

"*¿Habla español, señor?*"

He shook his head. "I'm sorry, no." He waited for some sign of understanding. "And you, *señorita*—do you speak English?"

"*Un poquito.*"

He hoped it meant what he thought it did.

"My name is Bradford Stone," he said. "I really regret not speaking Spanish. I am new to Mexico."

"*Sí. Yo sé. Y me llamo* . . . excuse me, *señor* . . . I will try to speak *inglés,* however badly. I am called Ana Barragán."

"I know."

"*¿Cómo?* How does one know what I am called, Señor Stone?"

"Kit . . . Señor Carson . . . has spoken of you."

"Can one hope Don Cristóbal says nice things about one?"

"Indeed you can, *señorita.* He speaks very highly of you."

Her face showed no response to this. Remembering the huge gate bearing the name Barragán, he wondered for a second if she simply accepted it as her due. Kit had called her headstrong. Yes, her eyes—which Stone now discovered were a dark brown—flashed a little.

Then they lapsed into awkward silence—awkward, but not a total loss.

She leaned forward a little, turned her face from him, and gazed out the small window that overlooked the street, giving him a chance to study her even more closely than when she had looked at him.

Dressed for riding, he supposed, she wore what he took at first to be a long skirt, black as the gleaming boots, but which on closer examination proved to be pleated pantalettes such as those he had seen on two of the younger Mexican women at Casa Tules. A heavy belt of linked silver medallions crowned with turquoise held these skirtlike trousers at her slim waist. Over a dazzling white silk blouse fastened at the neck with a silver pin of what he guessed to be an Indian design, the leather vest she wore looked as soft and supple as the silk.

A black leather hat with a flat brim and a pillbox crown rested on the table at her elbow, and a silver-and-turquoise band, smaller but much like the belt, encircled its crown. He tried to picture it on that full head of long hair that had been casually gathered and then bound at the back with another piece of silver. The light streaming through the window caught her hair and made it look as if *it* was flecked with silver, too.

It required some moments to take this inventory, and while she still gazed through the window her expression began to change. In seconds it became one of outright amusement.

She turned to him. The flash of her eyes was brighter. "Have you not seen enough now, *señor?* May I take *my* turn?"

"Certainly, *señorita,*" he managed to blurt out. "May I sit down while you look?"

"*Sí . . . por favor.*"

When he found a chair opposite her and virtually collapsed into it, he did not turn his head as she had. She had asked him if he had seen enough and he had not.

Never had he undergone a franker gaze from a woman. La Tules' inquisitive scrutiny of him had, by comparison, been but a glance of idle curiosity. He could not read her smile as she looked at him.

He fidgeted. He regretted his unshaven face, the dirty trail clothes he still wore, and he hoped that the reek of the last two days' sweaty ride from Santa Fe did not reach across the room to her. He itched, damn it, and he could not scratch, not while she looked at him.

Somehow he found enough courage to return look for look. Looking turned out to be a good deal easier than talking. Just two nights earlier he had spoken with an exceedingly worldly woman with a fair amount of confidence, if not boldness— and now he had become tongue-tied with a mere girl.

Carson had said she had just reached seventeen a shade more than three months ago. Stone had an unmarried sister four years older than Ana Barragán.

He suddenly remembered that Carson, his hero, had taken a wife half his age, perhaps less than half, if he could believe his eyes.

"Señor Carson says you have met *mi amigo* Don Luis Aragón, *señor.* That you traveled to Taos with him."

He had totally forgotten that his friend and comrade had come up from Santa Fe for the sole purpose of courting this same young woman. Had this lapse of memory been deliberate? Before he could give himself an answer, someone spoke behind him.

"Glad to see you two are getting to know each other."

Kit had entered the sitting room with Josefa.

Ana looked at Josefa. Her eyes sparkled . . . a bit wickedly, perhaps?

"Este señor es muy caballeroso, mi prima. ¿Es guapo, no?"

"¡Verdad!" Josefa said. But then her face took on an air of concern as she went on in Spanish, rapidly. Stone heard the name of Luis Aragón and felt another stab of something like guilt.

Ana looked at him twice, once when Josefa made another reference to Luis Aragón, the second time when Stone heard "Estancia Barragán" and then "Don Bernardo," with what he was sure was a warning in her voice. A fierce little spark blazed in Ana's eyes. Then her pretty mouth twisted and she almost spat out a word.

"¡Cuál idea!"

With that she rose, and left the room in a rush.

Josefa Carson followed her.

"I guess I better translate for you," Carson said. "Ana thinks you're something special as an *hombre*, but Josefa reminded her of the way Don Bernardo feels about men in general and Americans in particular. That's what caused that fuss. Josefa pointed out that the old hawk probably won't allow any *yanqui* anywhere near Estancia Barragán. Ana kind of took exception, for all the good it will do her. Fiery little thing, ain't she?"

"She certainly does seem a young lady of spirit." What a pompous ass he sounded. "Weren't there also some words about Luis Aragón?"

"Yes, but if you're worrying that you might find the handle of that knife he carries sticking out from between your shoulder blades, don't. Luis is too damned fine a man for that kind of thing. Sometimes I think he's too damned fine in general. People tend to take advantage of him."

"I see no reason for Luis to think me a threat to him, anyway."

"Uh-huh." Kit grinned. "Well, if things go the way I think they *could* go in the next week or so, our *amigo* will just plain die of heartbreak . . . quietlike. Come on, let's join the ladies and get some grub. Josefa and her cousin are damn good cooks, but even if they wasn't, right now I could eat a raw skunk that ain't even been gutted." He paused. "One more thing—you'll be interested to know that Ana also asked Josefa if she could spend the night. Hope it don't get her in trouble with her daddy." He grinned again, even more broadly than before. "I can see by your face that Ana staying here don't sit too bad with you."

10

Firelight

In the week following his arrival in Taos, Brad Stone forgot a lot of things: his eagerness to begin his work with Johnny Frémont; the fight with the Comanches on the Cimarron; the brief sojourn in Santa Fe; even his continuing close examination of his friend Kit Carson.

Such was his fascination with Ana Barragán he could hold little else in mind.

His preoccupation with her continued when they faced each other across the small table at the combined breakfast and lunch the two young women laid out, the *desayuno,* as Josefa had called the meal.

He had come to the table from the sitting room every bit as hungry as Kit had said *he* was, but although it smelled delicious, he scarcely touched his food. He barely heard the few words the two Carsons uttered, most in Spanish, and he certainly contributed little to what English conversation took place. To his surprise, Ana was not one bit more talkative than he. He became vaguely conscious of smiles and something like half-restrained giggles on the part of his hosts as they sat together, and he tried not to stare at the girl across the table from him. In a ridiculous attempt to avoid her eyes he inspected every corner of the kitchen, every nook and cranny, every open cupboard. Over the years he would come to know that kitchen well, but he would forever remain at a loss to describe it as he saw it that first bright day in Taos with Ana Barragán facing him.

He never remembered what they ate, either.

As they finished, Ana, who had not avoided looking at him for more than a fraction of a second, turned to Josefa. *"¿Hay un fandango en la plaza esta noche, no, prima?"*

He caught that well enough. A dance in the plaza tonight.

At the balls and cotillions arranged by the wives of his professors back at Harvard College he had been an adequate dancer, but only adequate. He must have crushed a hundred different sets of slippered toes in his four years in Cambridge. And he and his schoolfellows almost never saw the same young lady twice—the faculty wives discouraged any "intimacy" whatsoever between students and their partners.

A "fandango," as Ana had called it, would be an entirely different experience. He remembered the wild, abandoned steps of Kit and the two Espinosa children as they spun around the fire at the top of Raton Pass. Ana had probably whirled through dances like that since childhood, too.

As they neared the end of the meal, a round of chatter in Spanish began between the two women. Stone caught none of it, but smiles wreathed Carson's face. When Ana and Josefa suddenly left the table and disappeared in the hall leading to the sleeping quarters at the back of the house, the scout burst into laughter.

"Don't rightly know if I'm supposed to let this out, *amigo,* but the old problem of female finery just came up. I guess Ana had the right of it this one time, at least, when she complained to Josefa that she didn't have 'a thing to wear.' She said there was no way in hell she would go to the plaza tonight in riding clothes, and she ain't got time for a trip to the *estancia* and back. In about five seconds Josefa's wardrobe closet is going to look like a Rocky Mountain blizzard hit it. Good thing for Ana our two ladies are of a size."

"What am *I* going to wear, Kit? All I have with me are trail clothes and the odd jacket I wore to Casa Tules."

"Well, with your size, you sure as hell can't borrow any of mine. I wouldn't worry, though. From the way Ana's been acting, you could show up with her in the plaza in a gunny sack."

Stone grinned, and then said quickly, "I feel as if I'm intruding; no one actually asked me to come tonight."

"If you ain't been asked, I got a hunch you sure will be." Carson pushed his chair from the table. "Now . . . if you're finished eating, I'd like for us to get on over to Charlie Bent's. Josefa told me Charlie blew in from the Arkansas last night. He lives here when he ain't running the fort for his brother William. William Bent came in from St. Louis the day after we left with Aragón. That let Charlie come back home for a spell. Charlie's wife is Josefa's older sister. He might have brought us a message from Captain Frémont. Hope so. We got to get moving toward the mountains soon if we're to get to Oregon and California while the weather holds."

That last had an immediate effect on Stone. Surely a part of him wanted to get back to Bent's Fort to begin the adventure with Kit and Frémont; a bigger part wanted to stay right here in Taos for a while.

"We'll walk to Charlie's," Carson said. "Don't fret, *amigo*. Plenty of time to get ready for tonight."

2

Bent was already entertaining company when Carson and Stone arrived, a Mr. Ceran St. Vrain, who turned out to be the "well-to-do Taos trader" Frémont had mentioned, the man who had staked Kit and Dick Owens in their farm and sheep ranch on the Cimarron, the embryo venture Kit had left to join the expedition.

St. Vrain—"Cerrie," Bent called him—seemed a highly agreeable gentleman with a round, jolly face, and possessed of an obvious affection for Kit that rivaled Mr. Bent's. Stone liked him immediately.

The visit began with a round of back thumping and hearty handshakes all around, which to Stone's great pleasure included him. Charles Bent had brought no specific message from Frémont, but he did carry news. The captain had enlarged the expedition team by the addition of fourteen new members.

"Johnny's put on a dozen Delawares, Kit, including that tough old brute Segundai. They're listed on the expedition rolls as 'hunters,' but I think I know what he really wants them for. The only critters Segundai has hunted in recent years are the two-legged kind."

"I suppose you're right," Carson said. "Don't know what particular two-legged critters the captain might want them to hunt, though. We shouldn't meet any real trouble where this outfit's heading. The Great Basin tribes and almost all the Oregons are pretty friendly, leastwise they was last time I was in either place."

"Delawares?" Stone asked. "Aren't Delawares Eastern Seaboard Indians?"

"They *was*," Kit said. "They been living somewheres north of the Nations since they was 'removed' some years back. About the best trackers I ever seen. We had a bunch of them with us the last time I went out with the captain." He turned to Bent. "You said fourteen new recruits, Charlie. Twelve Delawares. Who are the other two *hombres?*"

"Fellows from back East. A Ted Talbot and an Ed Kern." Bent glanced at Stone, and Stone thought he caught a flush of embarrassment before he turned back to Carson. "Kern's from Philadelphia, a topographer-surveyor just like Brad here." He coughed. "Paints pictures just like Brad, too. Don't know why Johnny hired Talbot. He comes from Washington and strikes me as a politician."

A topographer-surveyor? Stone wondered if he still had his job with Frémont. Had he made a mistake by coming south with Carson instead of staying at Bent's and mending fences with the captain? Could Kern be his replacement?

As much as meeting Ana Barragán had made him want to stay here in Taos, he longed now to return to the Arkansas; he knew he would not rest easy until he asked his employer for a straight answer about his future.

Remembering Bent's kindness and openness when they discussed his situation with Frémont back on the Arkansas, he thought of pursuing the matter, but Bent, Kit, and St. Vrain had switched their conversation away from Frémont and his expedition.

"What do *you* think, Kit?" Bent said, turning to the scout. "Will there be war between us and Mexico? It will be a bad time for you and me if it comes to that. With our homes here in New Mexico . . . and our wives . . ."

"I got no opinions on the subject, Charlie," Carson said. "I won't let myself have opinions. You know why. I sure as hell could never bring myself to shoot at my neighbors here in Taos. On the other hand, there ain't no way I could ever unlimber my Hawken against the Stars and Stripes."

"Kind of echoes my sentiments. Suppose we could just sit a war out if it comes?"

"Don't know. I guess we could start out that way. But how long could it last? Well . . . I just take life a day at a time myself."

Bent laughed. "More often you take it just a *second* at a time."

Stone told himself that all this had nothing to do with him.

Even a large war here in the Southwest would hardly trouble Frémont's expedition. Most of the planned exploration was to take place well north of the Mexican border, starting in the Great Basin. There would be the dip into California before starting north for Oregon—and California was still Mexican territory, in name at least, if not by reported inclination. But from what the Pathfinder had said, they would hardly be there overnight. Oregon headed the list of the unmapped areas Frémont intended visiting, and the expedition should be able to get there before war came—if it was coming. Frémont and his men—Stone among them, if either this Ed Kern or Ted Talbot had not actually pushed him out of the picture—could do their work with impunity. They would be a thousand miles away from the scene of any probable conflict.

War. The idea of it alone should have frightened or at least alarmed him. But in Charles Bent's pleasant sitting room, he listened to the talk of these three experienced southwesterners with amazing indifference. He wondered if the fight with the Comanches had actually seasoned him a little.

"Mexico's losing its grip on California," St. Vrain said. "The Californios in the north don't pay one hell of a lot more heed to Mexico City than the Mexicans here in Taos do."

"You're sure right, Cerrie," Kit said. "Leastways that was my feeling when I stayed at Sutter's Fort with the captain early last year. 'Course, that don't mean they'd welcome *us* with open arms, either. Even Sutter, for all that he's been a good friend to Americans, has taken out Mexican citizenship, and he'd probably go right along with his Mexican neighbors, whatever they decide to do if push came to shove. I got the idea they want their own country last time the captain and me was there in '43."

"So did the Texians, for a while," St. Vrain said. "Sooner or later, though, anybody on this continent with any brains wants to be American."

"Let me change the subject," Bent said. "How things been going with the Navajo while I been away, Cerrie?"

"Quiet." St. Vrain looked thoughtful. "Oh, there always are some depredations, but they been raiding the Pueblos for the most part, not the ones here at Taos, but farther down the river, Cochiti and Sandía. They ran off every head of sheep the San Juans own last month, and a week ago they killed three young Pueblos at Cochiti. If Kit was staying in Taos I'd ask him to take out after them, particularly if they get close to town."

"Hold it, fellows," Bent broke in. "Here comes Señora Bent with the coffee and *bizcochitos.* No more war talk, *por favor,* and for God's sake, no more talk about hostiles."

"*¡Hola, Doña Ignacia!*" Carson said to the woman who had just entered the room with a straw tray filled with mugs, biscuits still steaming from the oven, and an enamel coffeepot.

"*¿Cómo estás, Don Cristóbal?*"

Ignacia Bent was a few years older then her sister Josefa Carson. She stood no taller than either her sister or Ana Barragán, but was not as slim as they were. Unlike the dusky gold Stone had seen in Ana's face, Doña Ignacia's complexion had Josefa's paleness, with skin tones a good deal lighter than those of almost all the Mexicans he had seen close up, including Doña Olivera Espinosa and La Tules. She had done her black hair in the same neat, homely bun as her sister, too.

Still holding the tray, she curtsied when Bent introduced them. "*¿Cómo estás, Señor Stone?*" A wonderful twinkle brightened her coal black eyes. She placed the tray on a low table and turned to her husband and said something in lyrical Spanish.

Once again Kit leaped to Stone's aid as an interpreter, but to his embarrassment as well.

"Ignacia says that Josefa and Ana are exactly right. That you're a fine-looking *hombre, amigo.*"

Stone did somehow stumble his way through a request to the scout that he thank her for him, adding a clumsy *"muchas gracias"* to the lady himself. Then he puzzled over how word of his arrival with Kit had reached Casa Bent so speedily. As far as he remembered, neither Mrs. Carson nor Ana Barragán had left Kit's home before he and Kit did. He determined to learn Spanish as quickly as he could. Things promised to go on around him that he better begin to comprehend. There were things he would want to say in that language, too. He did not know what things they would be, but he already knew to whom he wished to say some of them.

"I think we better mosey back to my place, Brad," Kit said. "We got tonight's party to get ready for."

3

Carson had dressed for the dance in the plaza in something like one of the full dress suits Stone's classmates and he had worn to those faculty affairs at Harvard College, and it made Stone feel like a seedy tramp in his battered jacket and soiled, unpressed trousers. He had shaved and bathed, of course, and splashed himself with the bay rum Kit brought to his room, but these were the only improvements in his appearance or his grooming from what they had been at the *desayuno.*

Kit and Stone waited for the two women in the sitting room, and when they finally joined them, the look of Ana took Stone's breath away, but not before he got a hint of the scent she wore, a light, fresh fragrance—lilies of the valley.

Ana's rummaging in Josefa's wardrobe had yielded spectacular results. The long dress she had borrowed from Kit's wife clung to the subtle curves of her young figure far more revealingly than had her black riding habit. White as the snow, it plunged from her shoulders to a deep V between her breasts and clung to her hips closely enough that every step she took as she entered the sitting room became a marvel of silky motion. She still wore the silver belt, and three strands of delicate silver beads circled her neck, one looping well down into the shadows of the V. The lace shawl, the *mantilla,* also white, hung from her shoulders halfway to her knees.

She had done her hair much as it had been before, gathered at the back with the silver fastening, but she had lifted it to a full round wave above each of her temples, and it framed the oval of her face like the setting for some precious gem.

"This is Josefa's wedding dress," she said. "Josefa says it will bring me *buena fortuna.*"

"You'll scare Brad half to death, Ana," Carson said.

"*¡Basta, Don Cristóbal!*" Ana cried. "Does Señor Stone think he is the only good fortune that might come Ana's way tonight?" Her voice buzzed with spirit, but of the teasing rather than the waspish kind. Her eyes danced.

They walked to the plaza as the sun began to set, and just before they reached it, Ana hooked her arm in his. When her hand worked its way between his side and his upper arm his whole body tingled. He looked down to see her face turned up toward him.

"You do not object to Ana's touch, Don Bradford?"

He smiled; answer enough, he felt. In any event she could not have heard an answer had he voiced one; the plaza throbbed with the sound of horns, fiddles, and pounding feet. At the corner where they entered, a small boy, all in white, paraded back and forth, beating a red tin drum. Huge bonfires blazed at the corners of the plaza, and someone had jammed lighted torches into the ground at intervals of a dozen feet or so around its entire perimeter.

The roof and platform of the old gazebo, where three fiddlers, two trumpeters, and a guitarist played, had been decked with Bengal lights, the ingenious rice-paper lanterns Stone had seen line the banks of the Charles in Boston at a twilight regatta during the spring of his senior year in college.

The sun had disappeared now, and all across the plaza, laughing, singing men and women whirled and twirled, bright-colored skirts floating in perfect circles above the flash of the women's dusky legs. The jingle of spurs kept time to the lively rhythms. The open space, bathed in the orange from the fires and the torches and with its splashes of reds, greens, blues, and yellows from the suits and dresses on the dancers, had become a kaleidoscope.

"You must dance first with Ana, Don Bradford," Ana said, "and you must save the last dance for her, *también*—and as many others as you wish."

"I do not dance at all well, Doña Ana," he said. "You might not want any more of me after our first attempt."

"Then we will sit together, sip some wine, and talk."

The two Carsons had heard this, and they beamed.

Before they could dance he discovered there were greetings to be made. Kit hailed Ceran St. Vrain and a buxom, motherly woman Stone presumed to be Señora St. Vrain. She looked more Mexican than Josefa Carson. The big, kind face of Charles Bent loomed over St. Vrain's shoulder.

Ignacia Jaramillo Bent folded her sister Josefa into her arms, a powerful hug to unite two women who probably gossiped together every day. St. Vrain's wife advanced on them and swung two massive bare arms around the still-embracing sisters.

He felt grateful that Ana did not remove her arm from his and join them.

When he turned from watching the Señoras Bent, Carson, and St. Vrain weld themselves into a small, affectionate

mountain of flesh and silk, he discovered that Don Luis
Aragón had come to stand in front of Ana.

On the trail from Bent's Fort, Don Luis had always
affected more sartorial elegance than had Carson and Stone,
with his buckskins cleaner, trimmer, and better fitting, and
the linen he wore spotless, but tonight he had outdone himself.

His suit, as black as Ana's riding costume earlier in the
day, bore silver braid on the short jacket and down the outer
seam of skintight trousers. The ruffles of his shirt looked
like the petals of a white rose. Stone half expected to catch
a scent of attar. A broad-brimmed black hat, not atop his
head, but held on his back by a silver cord around his neck,
and polished black boots with heels like spikes, completed
his stunning outfit. He had trimmed his hair and mustache,
and had combed a sweet, aromatic oil through his ebony
hair.

Looking at Aragón, Stone felt himself a derelict.

"Doña Ana . . ." Aragón bowed, and breathed the name in
tones of worship.

"¿Cómo estás, Luis?"

"Espléndido, now that I have seen you, Doña Ana."

Brad had no trouble deciphering espléndido, but aside
from his clothes, the Santa Féan certainly did not appear
splendid; he looked ill. Frozen-faced, he had not smiled at
Ana as he greeted her, nor did he smile when he turned to
Stone.

"Señor Stone."

"Glad to see you, Don Luis." Stone feared his voice
betrayed his true feelings, but Aragón did not seem to notice.
His eyes looked glazed and lifeless even in the winking
plaza lights. He turned to Ana.

"Would it be possible for Doña Ana to honor her poor servant Luis by dancing with him?"

"Lo siento, Don Luis," Ana said. "I am sorry, but I have

already promised every dance tonight to Don Bradford here."

Silence blanketed even the music and the gaiety. Aragón looked as if he had just taken a mortal wound. Stone felt a moment of pain himself at his friend's utterly crushed look, but it quickly gave way to a surge of joy.

He really did not see Aragón leave them; he was too occupied looking down at Ana.

Her hand slipped from his arm and took his, and she led him by it into the happy maelstrom of spinning couples.

While he did not know a single one of the complicated steps she guided him through with a sinuous, soft but insistent pressure from her lithe body, he had never danced so well.

He forgot poor Luis Aragón until that first dance ended and she took him to a long table at the plaza's edge. He never did learn the name of the wine they drank. Although it was headier stuff by far than any he had ever tasted, water might well have produced the same effect.

"Luis Aragón is a nice *hombre,* but he can be *un taladro,* what I think you *yanquis* call a bore," Ana said. "My father likes him, and of course I do, too, but I do not want a man who thinks I am a goddess. I am a woman, Don Bradford. Do not forget that—ever—*por favor.*" With that, and without any guilt, he stopped worrying about his friend Don Luis.

The rest of the evening flew by. They did not talk much. The Bents, the Carsons, and the St. Vrains joined them too frequently for that. They did not dance every dance, but Aragón did not appear again to make a claim. Then, when they left the plaza with the Carsons and St. Vrains to go to a late supper at the Bents', Ana tugged at his sleeve and held him back. She turned her face up to him.

He kissed her.

11

The Quiet Courier

Ana María Barragán had not even tried to write in her diary since she met Bradford Stone at Cousin Josefa's three days ago.

Perhaps it was just as well. The things she wished to put on paper should never be seen by any eyes but hers. His worst enemies would never call Papá a snoop, but the way things stood between Don Bernardo Barragán and his daughter at the moment, he might decide to become one any day. He knew she kept the diary; he had given it to her just last Christmas.

Old Galinda—on Papá's orders she was sure—had not allowed her a moment alone since she returned to the *estancia* early Saturday afternoon to get a change of clothes. Ana had planned to ride straight back to Cousin Josefa's when she gathered things together. For a day and a half Don Cristóbal had been cooking a *cabrito* in the pit he had dug behind the Carson casa, and Josefa had invited the St. Vrains and the Bents and some other villagers, Señor and Señora Simeon Turley probably, for dinner. Bradford said he had never tasted ". . . what did you say it was, Doña Ana?"

"*Cabrito,* Don Bradford—a spring kid."

"A baby *goat?*" He had looked a little appalled, and they had all teased him, Don Cristóbal in particular. She could not wait to ride into Taos tonight and see his face when he took his first bite of *cabrito*. And, of course, more important reasons would hurry her return to Cousin Josefa's. She had spent three evenings and the better part of two days with Bradford, but now it seemed like seconds. By comparison, the ride out to the *estancia,* which was to take her away from him for a mere three hours, became an eternity.

Then her plan to return to Taos crumbled to dust. She had found Papá's note on the writing table in her sitting room.

> You will not leave the hacienda for any reason unless I expressly permit it. This is an order.
>
> Don Bernardo Barragán

His full name—instead of "Papá"? And written in imperious, half-inch-high letters, every stroke a lash. If she had not shaken with anger as she looked at that signature leaping from the page, she would have laughed at it.

There had been no laughter at Estancia Barragán all that long Saturday afternoon and evening. The two days that followed dragged out even longer.

Without once explaining the reason for this confinement, this humiliating *imprisonment,* Papá had watched her like a hawk for two days now, but only from a distance. He did not go near her diary, but he must be in the grip of one of his more terrible rages to have written that note instead of talking to her. Nor had he taken a single meal with her since she'd returned from Taos Saturday afternoon, and for the first time in years had not taken her to Mass at San Francisco de Asis in Ranchos de Taos on Sunday morning. It must have cost him more than a few *centavos* to bring Padre Antonio Martínez out from Ranchos Sunday afternoon to hear her confession and give her communion. Padre Martínez had said Mass for her all by herself in Mamá's little chapel adjoining the *hacienda,* where the same Padre Martínez had baptized her a month after Mamá died. She had gone to Mass and communion in Mamá's chapel a few other times as she grew, when some childhood illness confined her to her bed, or when summer storms or winter snows made travel into Ranchos de Taos impossible.

2

"Don Bernardo has heard about the foreign *hombre* who stays with Doña Josefa and Don Cristóbal," Galinda explained when Ana asked the old Navajo *dueña* about the note. More often than not Galinda took Ana's side in arguments with her father, usually with remarkably softening results, but there were limits to his patience when men paid any attention to her, even if the man was Luis Aragón, whom he had always seemed to like. This promised to be one of the times Papá had reached such limits, and from his black looks, it might turn out to be the worst.

Galinda would respect his commands where men were concerned.

"This man staying with *la familia* Carson is a *yanqui?*" the *dueña* asked.

"*Sí.*"

The old woman frowned. "Not good, *niña,* not good at all."

No, it was not good. Growing up at Estancia Barragán, Ana had never thought too much about her father's dislike of Americans, had simply accepted it as another fact of life. Americans had not visited the *hacienda* twice in the past three years, and before that she would not have been able to tell a hairy *yanqui* in dirty buckskins from the French trappers who occasionally ròde through the Barragán gate to beg a supper or lodging for the night. For some reason Papá even despised nice Señor Bent, choosing to forget they were related by the important American's marriage to a Jaramillo. Papá *did* admit to a grudging regard for Don Cristóbal Carson, but he did not so much as speak to the other Americans who had settled in Taos after the fur trade had expired and the French disappeared. That must have happened when she was nine or ten. By that time Papá was taking her with him on his trips to Cañon de Chelly every spring and fall.

The stern note indicated Papá had probably not only heard about Bradford, but about everything else that happened in the plaza Wednesday night. Three of Estancia Barragán's *vaqueros* had danced right by her and the American, and any of them could have made a full report to him. One, Mario Ruiz, had smiled at her—and looked hard and hatefully at Bradford. Mario had a *boca muy grande,* the biggest mouth of any of the riders on the *estancia,* and a wagging tongue run by a brain no larger than a pea.

But most of the fault was hers. She certainly had not displayed much wisdom in devoting herself to the American for the entire evening as she had, with all of Taos looking on. And the kiss that she permitted him in front of the Bents, the St. Vrains, and the Carsons . . . *permitted* him? *¡Ana María Barragán!* She should tell the truth and shame the Devil. It was more *her* doing than his—an act of impulsive idiocy.

Pero—she regretted neither the dancing nor the kiss. Particularly the kiss.

After the way she'd treated Luis Aragón when the Carsons, Bradford, and she reached the plaza Wednesday night, she could not have blamed Luis if he had run straight to Papá with the story himself. He had paid a call at the *hacienda* an hour after her return on Saturday. She had not seen him then, but Galinda told her that Papá had invited him to stay. Perhaps it was an admission on Papá's part that she was growing up, that if Luis was around she would forget the *yanqui.* He had lived as a guest here at the *hacienda* for two days now, but she knew in her heart Luis had not said a word about Bradford to Papá, and would not. Even the mournful calf he had become since the dance would never let anything slip he thought might cause her trouble, no matter how much

her behavior Wednesday night had wounded him. The
wound must have been a deep one. He had stayed even farther away from her than Papá had since he arrived at the
hacienda. She smiled ruefully. Falling in love with Luis
instead of what she had allowed to happen would have made
life with Papá a good deal easier to manage.

So far not one word about Bradford had passed between
Papá's hard, tight lips, but his dark eyes had flamed every
time he looked at her; it would be folly to think he did not
know. It would be worse than folly to storm at him and try
to argue him out of whatever he felt about the American. She
did not lack the courage, had flown at him scores of times
when she really wanted something, but since Papá never
shrank from or yielded to any *man*, she knew a woman's
anger, even hers, would have even less effect on him. Tears,
which had sometimes brought results in the past, would not
work this time, either.

But some of those stolen kisses—shameless thefts in full
view of neighbors as well as relatives as they had been—
went to the very heart of her being. That it had all come
about so quickly did not trouble her a bit. Although Galinda
disagreed with her, she had always known that when love
came it would come without warning, the way a summer
storm crosses the mesa.

She had one other regret. She had not made confession
Sunday. But that public kiss at the dance and the regrettably
too few others of the next two dreamlike days and nights did
not really call for a confession, did they? They could not
count even as venal sins. And if they did? *Que será, será.*
Penance could be attended to later if it came to that.

If she did manage to see Bradford again before he left
with Don Cristóbal, it would only be at Cousin Josefa's or
here at the *hacienda*, and nothing could happen in either
place.

Men, boys rather, had kissed her before. Papá had never

known of it, thank Heaven. Her riding teacher, a young *vaquero* up from Chihauhua who rode for the *estancia* for a month two years ago, and whose name and face she could not now recall, had given her a fierce, fevered kiss once when they had stopped for lunch in a *barranca* at the north edge of the Barragán range. She had not told Papá about it, of course, nor even old Galinda. The rider might not have lived to see Chihuahua again had Papá learned of it, and in fairness to the *vaquero,* it had not been done entirely against her will. It began with curiosity. She had felt a pleasant tingle, had even pressed back a little, but she had not allowed the second kiss he tried for. Within two days she had forgotten it completely, and she had given no thought at all to taking the episode into Padre Martínez's confessional with her.

Then, a year ago, on the fall trading trip with Papá to Cañon de Chelly, there had been a slightly more serious kiss from Galinda's nephew Manuel when his aunt and the rest of his people were away from the family hogan at a medicine sing. There had been more than one that time, and she felt much more than a mere tingle when Manuel's lips found her mouth and then the hollow in her neck. But in spite of a burning that swept over her and set her hands to trembling, she had called a halt when he tried to unbutton her *blusa* with hands that trembled even more than hers. She also kept this adventure from her father, and from Galinda, too. Had the old Navajo known of it, she would have been taken ill with shame that a member of her own Dineh clan could have forced himself on a girl Galinda looked on almost as a granddaughter.

But Ana duly and fearfully reported this second adventure in her first confession after they returned to Taos.

She had not been sure, but she thought she heard a chuckle from the darkness behind the grille. Padre Martínez did not even mention penance.

Bradford's kisses promised to bring something different.

In truth, judged only by that first one in the plaza, he did not seem to know as much about kissing as did Manuel or the stupid *vaquero*, perhaps not as much as she did herself, even if she had only learned about it in her imagination.

But even Bradford's very first kiss filled her with unexpected warmth; it was at once light and deeply satisfying. He did not attack her mouth with his as the Barragán rider had, nor did he press his body against hers with the fervor Manuel had shown. This was not the kiss she had secretly looked forward to someday experiencing, but she knew as they left the plaza that she wanted his kisses again, no matter how unskilled they were.

If that first kiss had left a little something to be desired, the embrace that went with it did not. When he took her in his arms he gave no sign that he wanted to imprison her. This was not a man who would ever make demands on her. It was a new feeling. Even Papá's far too rare hugs had always had about them a hint of capture and confinement.

3

Back at the Carsons' after the dance that night, Josefa and Don Cristóbal had quickly gone to bed, leaving the two of them alone in the sitting room.

"Tell me about yourself, Don Bradford," Ana said when they settled in to face each other in the lamplight.

"I would like it if you would just call me Brad."

"I do not know if I could do that. Bradford sounds funny . . . strange to one who knows only Spanish and Indian names, but Brad is even funnier. It sounds like an *explosión. Brrahtt!*"

¡Dios mío! Had she hurt or insulted him with that? It was not a good beginning, but things would never go well

between them if he had no sense of humor. To her relief he smiled.

"Then Bradford it is. Actually, you may call me anything you like . . . Ana."

She could not resist her sudden impulse to tease. "One has not yet granted permission for you to forget the 'Doña.'"

The crestfallen look he gave her was exactly the reaction she wanted, but she knew she had better erase it in the next instant. Galinda had said times without number that she might pay heavily for her willful teasing someday. "You have that permission now, Bradford. In fact, you have one's insistence on it." His face lifted and his look lightened. "Tell me about yourself, *por favor.*"

"Ladies first, Ana," he had said, grinning boyishly.

"I was born here on Estancia Barragán," she began. "I think you already know that my mother . . ." She crossed herself. ". . . was a Jaramillo. She died giving birth to me . . ."

She went on at a rapid pace, eager to get her tale over with so she could hear his. She told him a little of how it had been for her, growing up in an enormous *hacienda* perched almost on the eastern lip of the gorge of the Río Grande. It pleased her when his eyes widened as she spoke of herding cattle with her father as a girl of eight, and of shearing sheep with *los pastores,* the shepherds of Estancia Barragán, and of the years when she was often the only female in the huge Barragán home except for faithful old Galinda. She did not tell him of her loneliness.

"Galinda and her people at Cañon de Chelly taught me almost everything I know, except how to read, write, cipher—and pray. I learned those things from the *monjas* in the convent school at La Familia Sagrada in Chihuahua—mean old *buistras,* every one of them."

"*Monjas* would be nuns, but what are *buistras?*"

"I think in English they are buzzards. You catch things in Spanish quickly, Bradford. Your *oreja* is very good."

"*¿Oreja?* Ear!" He laughed. "*Muchas gracias.* Galinda is an Indian?"

"*Sí.* Navajo or, as she would say, 'Dineh.' I have gone to her home country with Papá and her every year for as long as I can remember, often *twice* a year. Papá trades with the Dineh. The *estancia* is not his only business."

"Where is Galinda's home country?"

"Four days' ride west of here. Cañon de Chelly. The most beautiful place on earth. Perhaps someday I can show it to you, Bradford."

"When can I meet your father, Ana?"

That brought the only chill of the evening. She had deliberately avoided thinking of how Papá would react to a *yanqui* entering her life. "Let us not talk of that yet. *¡Ahora!* Now, back to what we were talking about. Do not put me off any longer, *querido.* Speak to me of your life." She wondered if her face had betrayed anything. She wondered if he had grasped the meaning of *"querido."*

Of course, his meeting Papá would have to be faced eventually. She did not look forward to it. Perhaps Cousin Josefa could be of help. Papá liked Josefa, and she in turn liked Bradford. It took no second sight—such as Galinda claimed—for her to determine that.

While her thoughts had been running helter-skelter, Bradford had finally begun to talk.

". . . in a small town called Groverton. It lies just west of a big city called Chicago. Lots of trees. I built a house in the branches of one of them when I was just a boy. . . ."

Now he told her, haltingly, of his childhood, of his father, mother, and sister, of the affection he bore for someplace where he had gone to school in the eastern part of his own country, of the job making maps which had brought him to Señor Bent's great trading post on the Río Arkansas. And how he, above all else, wanted someday to be an artist, a painter.

He talked a great deal about Don Cristóbal. It became plain that Bradford worshiped him, and it became slightly maddening. She liked Cousin Josefa's husband well enough herself, but she really wanted to hear only about Bradford Stone tonight.

But she would not hear it all, or nearly enough of it to suit her, for without warning, as if he could not help himself, he reached out and took her hands in his and drew her toward him.

That second kiss was a stunning improvement on the first, and she forgot all about listening to anything but her heart. Bradford was quick at other things than Spanish. His hands moved to the small of her back. He drew her to him. Another kiss followed, then so many she could not count them, nor did she want to.

Perhaps, although it made her heart ache at the thought of losing him even for a moment, it was just as well he was leaving for the north so soon, and that he would not see her again for . . . What had he said, a year?

But now, even with the shackles Papá had placed on her, the time had come to stop living in the memories of the last hours with Bradford at Cousin Josefa's. She *had* to see him.

But how? She could not get a horse to ride to town. Papá had ordered the stables barred to her. Even if she could secure one of the loose burros or a mule, she was unsure if she yet had reached the point of open defiance of her father. Reason had to be tried with him for a day or two, at least: Rebellion remained a last resort, and probably doomed to failure, too. She vowed to do or say nothing that would stir him to more anger or suspicion than he had already shown.

4

Then, after three days back at the *hacienda,* Papá found her on the patio. Without a word he handed her what looked to be a letter, turned and left.

> Dear Don Bernardo—
>
> We have not yet met, sir, but I am sure you will agree with me that we should. I intend coming to Estancia Barragán tomorrow at the latest. I realize it would be more courteous of me were I to wait until I receive your permission, but I could be leaving Taos with Mr. Kit Carson on a moment's notice. If you do not wish to see me I will understand if I am turned away at your door. It is my sincere hope that this does not happen.
>
> This is solely my idea, sir. Doña Ana does not have any knowledge of this letter.
>
> > Respectfully,
> > Bradford Stone

12

Through the Barragán Gate

Stone had not seen Ana for more than three days now, and until this visit to Estancia Barragán he had no idea how closely a Mexican father could sequester and virtually imprison even the most willful, determined daughter. But he also had no idea until this moment *how* determined Ana Barragán could be.

He was excited by the prospect of returning to Frémont's expedition with Kit, but the thought of possibly not seeing Ana before they left for the north had plunged him into despair, but a despair not without its uses. It had steeled him against most of the uneasiness he knew he would feel at facing the elder Barragán.

He would never have had the temerity to ride uninvited to the *estancia* and demand to see Don Bernardo the way he intended doing today, but Carson had announced a few nights before that they could leave for Bent's Fort to rejoin Frémont in as little as a week. That had given him a sudden overwhelming sense of urgency. Even if he would not be seeing Ana for a long time after his return with Kit to Bent's Fort, he wanted to get things straight with the Don before he left.

There had been no answer to his letter.

Ana had come the three miles to the gate to greet him and ride with him to the *hacienda*. She did not dismount when they met near the graveyard, but she moved her black horse next to his and leaned toward him for an embrace and a hurried kiss.

On the trip up the white stone road she told him of the effort required to talk one of the Barragán stable's Indian *peónes* into saddling El Soberano for her, and how she had ignored the warnings of her old Navajo *dueña*.

"Galinda is even more frightened of Papá than I am, Bradford," Ana said, just as they reached the *portal* of the *hacienda*, "and *Dios* knows I am frightened enough myself."

2

Bernardo Barragán stared at Bradford Ogden Stone over the immaculate top of his gigantic mahogany desk. He looked as cold as any man Stone had ever known, but there was nonetheless a hint of a burning inner rage.

The few other Mexicans Stone had met—at Bent's, at Santa Fe, and here in Taos—had not prepared him for his first sight of the lord of Estancia Barragán.

He was taller than most of them—Stone's height easily— and looked even taller with the rigid way he held himself. Under a wreath of iron gray hair and behind the guards mustache his face gleamed as white as that of any Englishman. But there was an unmistakable Iberian cast to his features, most prominent in the aquiline, slightly beaked nose. Fierce, almost predatory jet black eyes held Stone fast. He could see why his neighbors called Don Bernardo Barragán "El Gavilán"—the hawk.

"You, *señor*," Barragán said, "have come to Estancia Barragán without permission or invitation. Can you think of one reason why I should not set the dogs on you?" He spoke each word in English with no trace of accent whatsoever.

"No, sir. I think you would be entirely within your rights. I do hope, as much for Señorita Barragán's sake as mine, that it does not come to that."

Stone and Ana had entered the austere, bone-white study to find Luis Aragón seated at the side of the room. Stone started at the sight of him. The Santa Féan looked uncomfortable and embarrassed. He nodded awkwardly to Stone.

But the look he turned on Ana carried so much agony that Brad Stone felt it nearly as much as if it were his own.

"What is Don Luis doing here, Papá?" Ana said. Her eyes flashed.

"He is here because I asked him," Don Bernardo said. "I have my reasons. Do not concern yourself with them. Be silent . . . and notice that I do not even say '*por favor.*'" He turned to Stone. "Your attentions to my daughter are not wanted, *señor*, either by me or by her! And they will not be tolerated."

"*¡Pero, Papá . . . !*" Ana's cry throbbed in the study's close air.

"*¡Silencio, mija!* Do not speak when men are speaking."

Well, at least it did seem some sort of an admission on Don Bernardo's part that Brad Stone might be a man. To that point the Don had appeared to look upon Stone as an insect crawling across his path that could not be allowed to break his stride.

"I believe," Don Bernardo continued, "that as brief as this conversation has been, we have talked long enough. The time has now come for you to leave, *señor.*"

"Of course I will leave. if you insist, Don Bernardo," Stone said. "I must also leave Taos soon, but when the work I leave to do is completed, I will come back to Estancia Barragán, and I will keep on coming back as long as Señorita Ana wants me to."

His words staggered Don Bernardo. It became instantly plain he had never before been talked to in quite this manner.

"I warn you, *señor.*" Barragán's dark brows bristled. "If you come here again, it will not only be dogs I turn loose on you. My *vaqueros* will be under orders to shoot you on sight from this day forward if you are found on Barragán land again. *¡Le prometo!*"

A frightened gasp came from Ana.

Stone's mouth had dried up, but he swallowed and managed to talk.

"Don Bernardo," he said, "please do not threaten me, sir. My feelings for your daughter are such that I will gladly risk anything to see her." He took a breath. ". . . And if I am not mistaken, she shares that feeling."

"*¡Sí!*" Ana cried. "I do. *En el nombre de Dios,* I do, Papá. *¡Es verdad!*"

At this there came another gasp. No, it sounded more sigh than gasp. And it did not come from Ana, but from Luis

Aragón. Stone had wondered Friday night if he had lost a friend, now he became sure he had.

The small sound from Aragón had caused Don Bernardo to turn toward the trader.

"I should think *you* would concern yourself with this, Señor Aragón! Not five minutes ago you asked my permission to marry my daughter." Barragán's voice had suddenly lost its ice and turned to pure flame. "I cannot understand why you have not thrown down the gauntlet and called this *yanqui puerco* out. Have *all* the men of my race lost their honor . . . and their *cojones?* Why do you think I asked you to sit in on this distasteful meeting?"

Even as Stone focused on his own emotions he felt a stab of sympathy for the forlorn little Mexican whose brown face had now reddened, probably with shame.

Don Bernardo turned back to Ana. "And now, *mija,* you will go at once to your rooms, and you will stay there until I send for you. Galinda can bring you what food and drink you may require." He turned back to Stone. Perhaps turned *on* him would have been the better word. "Leave Estancia Barragán at once, *señor!*"

He placed his hands on the desktop and fixed Stone with a steely, unblinking eye.

"Don Bernardo!" Stone said. "Do not for one moment—"
Ana broke in. "Please, Bradford, do as Papá says!"

3

Stone left the *hacienda* wondering where he had found the courage to speak as he did, and if it had deserted him at the end. It did little good to tell himself he had only made his retreat because of Ana's *"Please, Bradford, do as Papá says,"* and the fear in her voice as she said it, even if it was the truth.

Almost to the gate, and for no reason he could explain, he turned his horse into the Barragán burial ground.

He rode into a strange, dead landscape. Most of the stone markers slanted away from the vertical in varying degrees, victims of God-knew-how-many years of frost heave and burning, baking sun. Some of the wooden crosses sprouting up through clumps of wiry grass had splintered, a few fractured beyond repair, or with their crossbars missing. However much care the Indian and Mexican workers at Estancia Barragán lavished on the great, fortresslike *hacienda* or the outbuildings closest to it, the little cemetery looked as if no one had visited it for years. What he had thought pliant grasses when seen from the sage-lined trail were only tough but stunted weeds.

One path into the far northwest corner, worn into a trough in the glass-hard caliche, looked as if someone had traveled it fairly regularly, and perhaps in the last month or two, if the broken vegetation at the edges of the trough meant anything.

He turned toward the path, dismounted, tied his horse off on one of the timbers of a shed at the edge of the little graveyard, and wandered among the stones. Aragón had said that many of the men and women who had worked this land for Don Bernardo and his forebears lay buried here, but along this particular path every single marker bore the name Barragán. The scouring winds of countless decades had rounded almost every corner, pitted the surfaces of the slabs, and filled the strokes and serifs of the lettering with dust. He stopped at one of them.

Francisco Antonio Jesús Manuel Barragán
A.D. 1609–A.D. 1643
Requiescat in Pace

Two centuries, had Luis said? Time had no boundaries in this old land.

A few feet farther along the path he found a stone with marginally sharper edges and of a slightly lighter shade of gray. Bouquets as dry as old bones, and with the colors of the blossoms faded, lay atop the mound. Someone, though, and probably within the last year or so, had placed a fresher, brighter bunch on the others. He had no trouble reading this gravestone.

> Ana María Jaramillo y Barragán
> Esposa y Madre
> Niña del Dios
> A.D. 1810–A.D. 1828

For a brief moment it frightened him to see Ana's name above a grave.

He shook the fright away.

Her mother's name had been Ana, too, apparently, and from the dates, she had died when she was but a year older than Ana was right now. Had not Aragón said there had also been a brother who died? He should find another stone close by. Yes, there was an even newer one twenty feet down the path.

But before he could take a step toward it, the soft silence was shattered by a rifle shot.

Now *genuine* fright hit him hard. He dropped to his knees in the sage and looked back up the road toward the *hacienda.*

The slanting sun had half-silhouetted three mounted men, one of them holding a smoking rifle above his head. Another of the horsemen gestured toward the gate. The rider's clenched fist seemed to shout, *"¿Vamos, yanqui!"* The shot had been a warning.

He waved and stepped back on the path, trying his damnedest not to hurry as he walked to his horse, which had torn itself free of its tether at the crack of the rifle, but luckily had not bolted.

He mounted and rode back to the road and on through the mammoth gate.

13

La Cayuda

Two mornings after Bradford's frightening visit, Papá sent her word by Roberto, the *mayordomo* of Estancia Barragán, that she was to breakfast with him on the patio. She expected to find Luis Aragón with him, but the table had only been set for two.

"I have been called to Santa Fe to confer with Governor Armijo," he said when Roberto brought their coffee. "I will leave within the hour, and I will be gone the better part of a week. While I am gone, my orders will remain unalterably in force, and you will obey them. You are not to leave the *estancia.* Since the *vaqueros* will be making a sweep of the northwest *llano* to prepare for the early branding, and are consequently unable to guard you here at the *hacienda* while they do their work, you will accompany them."

"Are you not afraid of what I might do with so many *men?* I might take every one of them to bed."

"*¡Basta!* Do not utter such obscenities at my table!" For a moment she thought he would strike her for the first time in her life. He looked as if he was making a terrible effort to control himself. "You will not be within three kilometers of the *vaqueros.* And Galinda will go with you. You will stay with her at La Casita de la Cayuda at the old sheep camp by the Río Gorge until I return or send for you. The *vaqueros* will take your horses after they leave you at La Cayuda. This *sucio yanqui* will not be able to find you there."

No, he would not, but . . . someone else could.

Don Cristóbal knew the trail down the gorge of the río to the one that led to the mesa top and the very door of La Casita de la Cayuda. If he would, he could guide Bradford or tell him how to get there. A mapmaker should surely be able to find his way.

She had to get a message to him. The year before she would see him again would be an eternity of misery. Galinda doubtless could find a dozen men and possibly a few women—either on the staff of the *hacienda* or among the itinerant workers or passing peddlers—who would take a letter into Taos and Casa Cárson. Even the few among them who might not like the daughter of the *hacendado* for some real or imagined reason were fond of the old Navajo woman. Anything she wrote to Bradford could be couched in innocuous words and phrases, and in English. But it could also be read somewhere along the line by someone who understood it, and who might then think to curry favor by telling someone else, who would rush to Santa Fe to report to Don Bernardo.

If there were only some way to send Galinda herself. She spoke more than enough English to report what Bradford said, and the old *dueña* still rode well enough—but her absence from the *hacienda* for a full day would arouse Papá's suspicion, too, if someone saw her and sent the word down to the capital. He would ride back like the wind, and head straight for the shepherd's cabin with a pistol in his hand.

Then it dawned on her.

She *could* trust one person living here at the *hacienda*. Someone who was free to come and go, without being under Papá's or Roberto's or the *vaqueros'* watchful eyes. She knew how cruel and heartless it would be, but it had to be done. There was no one else.

She found him in the library.

"Don Luis," she said. "Would it be possible, *señor,* for you to come to my assistance on a matter of some delicacy?"

"*¡Por supuesto, Doña Ana! ¿Qué pasa . . . ?*"

2

Two more days remained before they were to leave for Bent's. The journey could not begin nearly soon enough for Stone, and yet part of him wished it never would.

The last three days and nights here in Taos without seeing Ana—and with no message—had plagued him terribly.

He almost talked to Carson about it, but knew he could not. The scout had planted deep roots in Taos, and had tied himself to virtually every corner of the community. There could be no way he could help Stone, even if he agreed to, without the knowledge of such help becoming common currency even at the *estancia.* No, he could not put Kit at risk.

He would not even tell him how much he was suffering.

Then Aragón, more mournful and wounded-looking than ever, rode in from the *estancia* with a letter from Ana, and everything changed for both of them.

Don Luis had proven himself a true friend after all by bringing Stone the message, feeling as he did about her. Certainly the sad-eyed Santa Féan did it for *her* and not for Stone, but Stone feared *he* might not have done any such selfless thing himself were he in Luis's place.

3

"Please, Kit," Stone told the scout when he and Aragón went to him for help. "Do not involve yourself personally in this. Sketch a map for me and let me go alone."

"*¡Ni modo, Señor Stone!*" Aragón broke in. "You will

lose your way. Doña Ana will be devastated. She might even try to find you."

"He's right, Brad." Kit shook his head. "The trail up to the mesa and La Cayuda is a mite hard to find even in daylight, and it will be pretty near dark in the bottom of the gorge long before the sun goes down. You could miss it easy and have to ride clear down to Pilar. Captain Frémont would have my hide if you got lost and I showed up at Bent's without you."

"I'm not too sure of that. He may no longer want me, Kit."

"Because of that new mapping fellow he's put on?"

"Yes." He had never mentioned his concern about his job with the expedition to Carson, but Kit had the instincts of a crystal-gazer.

"Let's worry about that when we get to Bent's. We better think about the work at hand. We'll head west an hour before sunset, and I'll have you at the road leading up to the *casita* just before dark. We'll part company there. You can't get lost on the ride up from the river. But I don't want you arriving on the mesa until the Don's *vaqueros* are in their bedrolls, even if they ain't close by the cabin. No trick getting back to Taos once you've seen the way there. One word of advice, though. Day after tomorrow, you'll have to leave La Cayuda well before daybreak. Don Bernardo's riders will be in the saddle pretty early, and you'll have to start back down into the gorge before they spot you. You ain't going to have much time for sleep." He grinned. "But I guess you hadn't really planned on sleep, anyways. 'Course, I could have gotten the reason for this little trek all wrong."

Luis Aragón looked even sicker than he had when he arrived at the Carson home and had politely refused the late lunch Josefa offered him, claiming, "Something wrong with *mi estómago*, Doña Josefa—*está muy caliente*."

Then Aragón staggered Stone again.

"*Con permiso*, Don Bradford. May I ride to the mesa top

with you? I could watch for Don Bernardo's men in the event that things go wrong."

It did make a certain amount of sense, but it would be the height of cruelty to have the earnest, decent trader so close at hand if . . .

"No, Don Luis. You can ride as far as the trail Señor Carson spoke of. The rest of the trip I must make all by myself. I will have to take my chances with the Barragán *vaqueros. Pero, muchísimas gracias.*"

"*De nada. Buena suerte . . . mi amigo.*"

God bless Luis Aragón. Stone did not doubt for a second that he meant "*mi amigo.*"

Carson broke in. "You'll have two nights at La Cayuda, Brad. It's as long as I can hold off heading north."

4

Would Galinda never go to bed? Ana came close to screaming at her a dozen times after they had eaten, only to finally realize it was still long before she usually retired. The sun had not even neared the rim of the gorge, and Bradford, if he came, would not clear the trail leading up from the river until darkness fell.

The *dueña* had her own separate sleeping chamber with a door of its own and a thick adobe wall between the tiny room and the quarters Ana occupied herself. Some longtime Barragán shepherd had built the *casita* for his wife and children well back in the last century, before *los pastores* had become the hermits so many were today, woman-fearing bachelors for the most part. This old shepherd had raised two generations here before the place had fallen into disuse. That was a long time ago. Ana remembered living here for a short time herself when she was a child, but she could not remember when or why.

A *portal* looked out over the rim of the gorge, half a kilometer away, and when Galinda had carried their bags inside, she settled in a high-backed wicker chair and gazed into the western sky. The sun still hung a hand or two above the horizon, but it would plummet soon.

The long-dead shepherd had added a room as a *casa de abuela* for the grandmother of the family. It seemed tonight's arrangement would not be much different. One thing had gone well. After the *vaqueros* had escorted them to La Cayuda and ridden off, she had not so much as glimpsed one of them.

She had not told Galinda that Bradford might come to her tonight—she would not think "might"; he *would* come—but when the Navajo came out of her room she stood in front of Ana, blocking her view of the setting sun.

"This *yanqui* will come to the *casita* tonight, no, *mi niña?*"

"*Sí, vieja.* How did you know?"

"You have acted like a heifer in the spring since we left the *hacienda*. Galinda has seen young *mujeres* like you before. This is nothing new in her long life. If what Galinda thinks will happen while she sleeps does happen, and Don Bernardo learns of it, he may decide to send you back to the convent in Mexico. And if he finds out the *yanqui* has been here tonight, and if the *yanqui* does not leave Taos as he plans and go somewhere far away, the Don will kill him. Knowing this, do you still think a night or two is worth it?"

"Papá will be in Santa Fe a week. Bradford leaves Taos in only two more days. Papá will not hear of this."

"Do not count on that."

"Who would tell him? You?"

"Galinda did not tell him of her own *sobrino* Manuel. And she did not tell Don Bernardo of that young rider from Chihuahua."

"You *knew?* About both of them?"

"I saw both of them kiss *mi niña* in a dream."

"In a *dream?* That's nonsense, Galinda."

"Dreams are not nonsense when you have the gift. . . . All right, those times I guessed. It was not hard."

"Men are not as good at making guesses about this kind of thing as women are, Galinda."

"But Don Bernardo might guess *this* time, if only because he has feared this ever since you began to have the times that make a girl a woman. He will look for signs."

"Help me, then."

"I cannot. You must guard yourself when he looks at you, and now that he has met the *yanqui* he will be looking hard all the time. And you know, of course, that you must guard against something else. The one thing Don Bernardo would not have to guess about. You can take care, can you not?"

"I . . . am not really sure. I think I . . ."

"Thinking is not enough. Maybe Galinda can help with that. Her ways do not always work, but I think they must be tried."

"You do not think what I might do tonight is right, do you?"

"For Galinda there is no right or wrong in things like this. You will do what you feel you must. It was that way with me when I was young. Do you love this *yanqui?*"

"*¡Sí!* Of course I do! You don't for a moment think I would be—"

"Perhaps you do love him. But . . . you do not do this partly to wound Don Bernardo?"

"No! Let's get back to what you think you should teach me. *¡Pronto!* We do not have a great deal of time."

The old Navajo woman fixed her black eyes hard on Ana for a long moment, then went to her room and brought out a saddlebag.

Ana thought about Galinda's question: *"You do not do this partly to wound Don Bernardo?"*

How much truth did it contain?

Galinda pulled a small clay pot from her saddlebag. She untied the thong around the circle of deerskin covering it and peeled it back. "You must put this salve inside you, *mi niña.* Use a lot of it."

The reek of the salve reached Ana's nostrils, a rank and fishy smell.

"*¡Los cielos!* How long have you had this awful stuff?"

"It is not old. Galinda only made it up when she saw how you would be with the *yanqui.*"

"*¡Dios!* I could not possibly use anything so revolting with Bradford."

The old woman shrugged. "The choice is yours, *mi niña.* You no longer need me now. I will not leave my room until the *yanqui* has gone away."

5

A full moon would have been more romantic, but she blessed the protection of the velvet dark.

She had not brought the lantern through the sage that led to the rim of the gorge, and she heard his horse long before she saw it, almost cried out once, but decided to wait until she was sure. There was always the slight chance that Papá had ordered one of his *vaqueros* to roam the rim at night. It did not seem likely, but she did not want any questions, now or when Papá returned next week, about what she was doing under the stars, on foot, this far from La Cayuda.

Then she saw his face in the starlight.

"Bradford," she breathed. "*¡Mi amor!*"

Part Two

THE
PATHFINDER

14

Time to Catch Up!

The Upper Arkansas
August 1845

Brad Stone, after more than five weeks on the trail from Bent's Fort, still wondered if things would ever turn easy between him and John C. Frémont.

The captain's mercurial changes of mood baffled him. There had been times since the expedition left Bent's Fort on the sixteenth of August and climbed the eastern slope when Frémont seemed ready to accept him as a full-fledged member of the team, only to resume treating him like a flunky, and still calling him "Mr. Stone" the very next instant.

In the latter maddening moments, Stone would gladly have tendered his notice had it not been for Carson, not that the scout and he had ever discussed his relationship with Frémont in so many words. He prized the relationship with Kit above all others in his life—except one. It seemed better for the moment not to dwell too much on that one.

He could apparently put one worry firmly behind him. He had been mildly surprised and pleased to find that the addition of the new topographer, Edward Kern, to the rolls of the Pathfinder's expedition, had not, after all, put him out of work. Adventure and comradeship notwithstanding, he needed the job. When he had said good-bye to Congressman Myers and boarded the train in Chicago there had not been much in the way of savings left from the surveying work he had done in Illinois since college. It was already past time for him to begin repaying his father for the loan the elder Stone had made him for this journey of discovery, and he would need an income and a chance to accumulate some capital were he to stay in the West. And staying in the West was more important to him than ever since that night of wonder at La Cayuda.

2

When he left Don Bernardo's study after that first visit to Estancia Barragán, Ana had somehow escaped her room and was waiting for him at the front door with his horse. They had fallen into an embrace at once warmly affectionate and chilled by the anguish of parting. Her face looked particularly downcast when he told her that Carson had decided on their departure date. There would be no delay.

"So soon?"

"I'm sorry. Can we see each other at Kit and Josefa's before I leave?"

"You saw Papá. He will not let me out of his sight until you are gone."

"I will come back, Ana."

"*¿Cuándo?* When, *querido?*"

"I don't really know. Captain Frémont will keep us out as much as a year, I'm afraid."

"I will be here. Papá cannot hide me from you when you return. Please write to me, but send your letters to Josefa. Once Papá knows you have left Taos he will let me come to town again."

She held her arms out to him.

They kissed. She smiled when they leaned back and looked at each other. "Your kisses get better all the time, but that will only make me miss them more."

He had not known then that he would see her one more

time before he left with Kit, and his heart turned as heavy as a rock.

He could still feel that kiss on his lips, and all the ones of the night above the gorge. Her desperate, fierce yet feathery touch when they made love for the last time before day broke over La Cayuda had stayed with him through every one of the long, hot days and piercingly cold nights of the march from Bent's.

3

His worry about his job left him shortly after he and Kit reached Bent's Fort and the expedition started up the Arkansas, but the confused state of things with the Pathfinder continued in the weeks that followed.

He had had little to do with the other new man, Ted Talbot, since leaving Bent's, and it did not seem likely that he would. Talbot had served as Frémont's chief administrative officer to this point, and except for Stone drawing supplies from him, their paths seldom crossed.

As for Ed Kern, whether the new topographer would eventually replace him or not, he liked the man.

He found Kern as modern in his approach to mapmaking as he was himself, and a skilled artist as well, particularly in watercolor painting and pen-and-ink sketches. He apparently had made a thorough study of plant life at some eastern botanical institute; his accurate, painstaking but vibrant renderings of the flora of the mountains they had already crossed, and the spiny scrub that dotted the desert they were now traversing, captured the tiniest early autumn leaves and needles faithfully enough to make them fairly leap from the drawing paper.

Frémont, a fair botanist and artist of flora himself, went ecstatic over Ed Kern's work.

Stone had never felt himself impelled toward this sort of art; he could do it passably well, but larger canvases and oil portraits in particular had always interested him more. He now wanted to do one particular portrait enough to taste it, even though he might fail to do its subject justice.

He *would,* someday, paint Ana. He already had the beginnings of several portraits of her in the sketches, one a nude, which he had done at La Cayuda.

Kit, of all people, had some thoughts about art and artists.

"There's been a regular river of you picture fellows out in this country. Everybody back East by this time must know pretty much what it looks like. Guess that's part of the reason why there's such a stream of immigrants the last year or so."

"Does that bother you, Kit?" Stone asked.

"Not much. Oh, I'd hate like hell to see this country change *too* much, but I reckon I'll be dead before that happens, anyway."

"Then you'll forgive us painters?"

"Sure. Especially if they're like you and this new fellow Kern."

No surprise sprang from the fact that Carson had taken a liking to Kern. Stone might have felt a little jealous of the new topographer, a blond, blue-eyed, well-set-up, high-spirited, and monumentally vigorous man from Philadelphia, ten or twelve years older than Stone, but Kern seemed closer to Frémont then he did to Kit. Stone disliked accusing his commander of snobbishness even in his private thoughts, but there was no avoiding the suspicion that Frémont looked on Kern—who came from a wealthy Main Line family—as someone of his own class. Obviously he did not intend to widen that view enough to include Bradford Stone.

Kern himself, Stone was delighted to discover, harbored no such pompous or autocratic attitudes. He deferred to Stone in countless little ways, asking his opinion on the gear he had brought with him, and listening attentively when Stone told him of the work he had done in the prairies around Bent's Fort when he had kept his watch on the Spanish Peaks for Kit's appearance. It relieved Stone to find that Kern, who had hunted deer in the Alleghenies as a boy in Pennsylvania, would need little or no instruction in how to best endure the rough life of the expedition's camps, or in the use of firearms.

But perhaps Ed Kern felt otherwise.

"I can sure learn more from you, Brad, than I can from anybody else I've met since I came out here, with the possible exception of Carson and the captain. The other older hands here don't really understand the extent of my ignorance and offer advice reluctantly, if at all," he said in the first extended talk they had together after Frémont introduced them brusquely and then strode off. "You got to the West long before I did, and Mr. Carson speaks highly of you."

"A month's time hardly counts as 'long before,' Ed. I'm still a greenhorn myself."

"It's more a matter of experience than time, I guess. You at least have been blooded. I've never once heard a shot fired in anger. Every last soul in the party knows about the fight Carson, you, and that Mexican fellow made down on the Cimarron. Scared me half to death just to hear about it. Mr. Carson says he never could have carried off that affair with the Comanches without you."

Hearing this brought Stone a small thrill of pride, together with a twinge of disappointment. Although a number of the old mountain men, Alexis Godey, Owens, Walker, and the largest man in camp, affable, friendly Basil Lajeunesse, had gone out of their way to clap him on the back and exclaim over his part in the events on the Cimarron, the captain had never once mentioned the bloody little battle. Stone was sure the account of the fracas would never find its way into the journal everyone in camp knew Frémont was keeping.

But it brought a wave of gratitude that Carson himself had spread the word. It took no brainwork to figure out that Kit had related the bosque episode solely to elevate Stone in the eyes of his fellow members of the expedition.

"One bit of advice," Stone said to Kern, "not that I have any particular right to give it, but I think you could start calling Mr. Carson 'Kit.'"

"He won't mind?"

"Mind? I'm pretty sure he'd like it."

"Thanks. This is quite a crew Captain Frémont has put together. If I didn't know most of their pedigrees, I'd take them for a flock of cutthroats. They are good men, though, aren't they?"

"They're like Kit—most of them are, to some extent, at least. There's only one Kit Carson, though."

"True enough. Impressive man. But I was bowled over when I saw how *small* he is."

"So was I when I met him. Well . . . *someone* was bowled over—but that's another story."

In subsequent conversations he found Kern to be a mild, refreshing cynic. Although he said he found Kit "impressive," he did not stand in the same awe of the former trapper to nearly the extent Stone did. "I think Carson's big reputation in the East is due at least as much to the way it has been bruited about by Frémont, his wife Jessie, and Frémont's blustering father-in-law, as by anything of note he's done himself," he said. It might have put Stone off the Philadelphian had Kern not been every bit as amused by the postures Frémont himself affected, the splendid garments, the haughty bearing, and the look the Pathfinder sometimes had of listening to distant voices not heard by the mere mortals of the party. "Our commander can be a strange piece of work, Brad."

4

As Kern had said, it was indeed "quite a crew" that had resolutely turned its back on Bent's that summer of 1845.

The sixty-odd mountain men made up the most terrifying looking group of human beings one could have found outside of nightmares. Almost all of them wore beards of varying lengths and of every condition of tidiness, but with most as wild and tangled as the coats of the shaggier forest animals. Nearly every one of them chewed tobacco—not too neatly, either—and the grayer beards were stained from gobs of brown spit and dribble, the beards matted, and with dirty yellow streaks running through them. Weapons sprouted from the belts of their greasy buckskins like the quills of porcupines: knives, pistols, hatchets, English half-axes with thin blades better suited for cleaving a skull than for splitting any stick of firewood thicker than a wrist, and—belted to the waist of Lucien Maxwell—a saber.

The ex-trappers and the muleteers smelled like rancid butter. Stone could not remember one of them ever removing his soiled shirt or trousers for sleep, and certainly not for hygiene. As far as bathing was concerned, he was fast forgetting that any such thing was even possible anymore himself.

In the last of the high plains they crossed every drop of water was a priceless pearl. But even when they reached the mountains at the headwaters of the Arkansas, there had not been much inclination for the most fastidious of them—Frémont, Carson, Alexis Godey, Kern, and Stone—to scrub away the trail dust.

Although the summer had not yet run out its string of glorious, warm afternoons, the water in the mountain streams and springs seemed only a scant degree above freezing.

After three days on the forest trails that laced the flanks of the larger peaks, he and Kern did make one sincere but foolhardy attempt at a morning bath in a shallow, frothy, swift-running creek, to the howling laughter of a dozen or more of the old hands.

The water barely covered their ankles, but they could stand no more than thirty seconds of it. They scarcely had time to do more than merely splash their naked upper bodies before the cold drove them hopping to the stream's stony bank. The bones in Stone's feet suddenly turned to painful icicles he feared might snap at every step. It must have felt like that for Ed Kern as well, but neither of them let a peep escape through their chattering teeth for fear it would set their audience to jeering even more boisterously than they already were.

He began to wonder how badly he smelled himself, but ultimately decided he did not care.

The twelve Delaware Indians Frémont had recruited for the expedition fascinated him, particularly the tall, splendid-looking Segundai, whom Carson said held the rank of chief, adding, ". . . whatever that means to Delawares. 'Chief' is a peculiar title with Indians of any kind. As often as not it's only a temporary thing. The leader of a war party, for instance, might be a chief only until he and his raiders get back to the women in their lodges. And then again it could be a religious handle. Sometimes 'chief' and 'medicine man' are one and the same."

"Are these Delawares as capable as they look, Kit?"

"You bet. Segundai and the ugly little one called Crane, and a half a dozen of the others, was out with the captain and me last year. I figure myself a pretty damned good tracker, but I ain't a patch on Segundai—or *any* of the men with him, far as that goes. They could trail a grasshopper across slickrock like it was an elk in mud."

"And they're good fighting men?"

"They sure are that, Lord knows. All good shots," Carson said. "I think Segundai has taken a couple dozen scalps himself over the years, and none of his warriors is far behind." He laughed. "But if we're lucky, Brad, we won't see that side of them on this trip."

"You don't think we'll have trouble with hostiles, then?"

"No. But remember, I said something like that before you, Luis, and me started down for Santa Fe. I got more to go on this time. This is far and away the largest party of armed men I ever been with. Even Digger Indians ain't stupid. We're likely to get an easy passage."

The side of Segundai and his warriors they had seen so far was a grim, stoic, brooding, almost gloomy one. But each of the silent Delawares wore a look of dignity Stone admired. Tall—remarkably clean considering the rigors of the journey which had reduced almost all the white men of the expedition to slovenliness—they were, in varying degrees, handsome. The only exception was little Crane, on whose ugliness Carson had remarked. They bore little resemblance to the nondescript Brulé Sioux he and Caleb Miller had encountered on the wagon trip across the Great Plains.

The mountain men, by contrast with Segundai's and Crane's gravity, presented for the most part a rambunctious, often jolly aspect. But from the first day on the trail a ferment of belligerence bubbled just beneath the surface.

Fights brought on by things as petty as a borrowed sewing needle the borrower had not returned broke out with clockwork regularity. Dismayed at first, Stone finally grew accustomed to such disturbances. After all, these strange, tough, wild men had never been noted for nor hired on for their social graces.

Most often the combatants savaged each other with their fists with no more damage than a flattened, bleeding nose or a broken tooth.

But one night, after a particularly long and arduous day's

ride through the barrens along the eastern shore of the Great Salt Lake, one of these frays turned ugly. Carson had limited the use of drinking water to half a canteen a man, with warnings that except for his smile verged close to threats. It had drawn nerves taut across the camp.

A teamster and a gargantuan French Canadian former trapper named Jean Dumonde each claimed a cut of venison for himself, and a fight broke out between the two at the campfire to which Carson had assigned himself, Stone, and Alexis Godey.

It began with the usual round of curses. Then, without warning, knives glinted in the light of the cooking fire into which the disputed chunk of meat had fallen. The two men leaped at each other. In seconds blood flowed. Stone, sitting with Godey and Carson twenty feet away, was sure one of the two men—perhaps both—would die before the struggle ended.

Carson, half the size of either of them, rose, shot toward the pair, hurled his diminutive body between the antagonists, and stopped the fight just as Dumonde readied himself to draw his blade across the teamster's throat. Godey reached the three of them a half second later.

Kit whispered something to the two men, but how the scout actually put a halt to the expected carnage Stone could not tell from where he sat. Both Dumonde and the teamster dropped their knives. In moments they were hugging one another as if they were long-lost brothers.

"What did you say to them, Kit?" Stone asked when Carson and Godey returned.

"I don't rightly recollect."

"Hah!" Godey exploded. "*I* do. Kit told them he would kill the winner. He meant it, too."

It would take a band of Indians courageous beyond belief to even think of attacking these fierce men and their Delaware tracker-warriors, thought Stone. And the prevailing question remained unanswered. As Charles Bent and some others had speculated, why did Brevet Captain John C. Frémont of the U.S. Army's Corps of Topographical Engineers—not by experience a commander of combat troops—need what was in effect a small army just to make maps? Protection from hostile Indians? It did not seem likely from what Kit had said. On the record, Frémont had felt no such necessity on his two previous excursions in the Northwest. The question, and some of Stone's thoughts, had apparently occurred to Ed Kern, too.

"Last I heard," he said, "the British are giving up their argument about the northern Oregon border, and I sure wouldn't expect the Russians to press very hard on their claims. Hard to tell what our captain's intentions are. He doesn't give much away. Maybe he's quietly working on his father-in-law's expansionist agenda. You realize, don't you, Brad, that we've actually been in Mexican territory for the last week?"

"Technically I guess that's true, but I suppose there would be a pretty good-sized argument about the exact borderline. Back at Bent's I thought perhaps part of our mission was to establish it once and for all." Even though nothing Kern said came as news to him, it all reminded him just how out of touch he had become with his own country.

Kern went on. "Senator Benton has lined up a lot of support for his notions in Washington—in the Congress *and* the White House. A lot of it depends on whether or not we can avoid war with Mexico. War looked likely when I left Philadelphia. I hate to think it, but maybe it's the only way we can, as you put it, 'establish' a legitimate border in the long run, men and nations being what they are."

While recognizing the importance of what Kern said, particularly about the likelihood of war, it did not seem the sort of thing Bradford Stone should concern himself with. His problems with Frémont were smaller—but much closer at hand.

15

The Ghosts of Pilot Peak

The Great Salt Lake
September 1845

"With all respect, Captain," Stone said to the man at the camp desk in front of the tent flying the American flag and the pennant of the expedition, "when will you assign me useful work? I've hardly had my transit out of its case since we left Bent's Fort." He did not add that Ed Kern had been out with all *his* equipment and a crew of helpers every day for the past week, surveying the eastern shore of the lake. The Philadelphian had returned to camp each night utterly fatigued, but recounting his day's exertions in a voice as happy as the song of a lark. Stone had grown more envious and morose with each recital.

"You'll find employment soon enough, Mr. Stone." Frémont's cold tone seemed to indicate he intended to say no more on the subject. But suddenly he brightened. "Glorious country we've passed through, is it not?" For this last, his voice had turned lively, vibrant, almost warm, much as it had at dinner at Bent's when Stone first proposed sketching him. He wondered if he would ever get used to these lightning reversals of mood on the part of his commander.

"Yes, sir," he said. "Although I must confess I'll be glad to put this desert behind us."

"And so will I. But we had a splendid outing yesterday."

"Yes, sir."

"We must be the only white men ever to go there, unless

Jedediah Smith visited it in the late twenties or early thirties."

Indeed, the ride in the bright, cool air out to the peninsula-
island at the southern end of the lake the day before had
afforded a few of the party—Frémont, Carson, Joe Walker,
and Stone among them—a marvelous experience.

2

The level of the lake had dropped significantly in what the
older hands said was an unusually dry year, making it possible to gain the shore of the island on horseback. Even so, the
saltwater still rose to the animals' chests, and their hooves
sank to the fetlocks in the wet salt of the bottom of the submerged isthmus. The salt that formed the shores of the lake
and the island, exposed as it was to the powerful, drying
September sun, created wide swaths of pure white crystals,
but once the horsemen reached the island's interior they
found a different sort of terrain from anything they had seen
for days. Freshwater pooled in the dips and sinks on every
hand. Yellow and pale green grasses two and three feet high
waved and trembled in the swales they traveled through, giving off a pleasing scent. And wild sunflowers and delicate,
winking purple asters dotted the small hillocks rippling the
island as far as the eye could see. To their amazement game
abounded—antelope. There had been little red meat in camp
for days and the mountain men went wild with glee as they
hunted the graceful beasts. Three fell to Walker's Hawken
and Carson added two more to the day's bag, one with an
incredible shot of more than three hundred yards and with
the target at a dead run. To yips and shouts Stone got one
himself, his mouth falling open in astonishment that he had
actually hit it. Five others in the party brought down animals
as well.

They spent the night on "Antelope Island," as Frémont decreed they would name this unexpected, quiet, sequestered paradise on the expedition's new maps, without the captain even posting a guard. They left it the next day with bittersweet reluctance.

When they reached the mainland a peculiar little incident occurred.

Standing on the shore, as rigid and erect as any statue, a wrinkled, gray-haired Indian, dressed from head to leathery bare feet in shabby skins, barred their way. He had drawn a bow, and had fixed his aim squarely on the captain's chest. Frémont raised his arm and stopped the column. The old savage growled something in a string of unintelligible words. The guttural little speech stretched to a minute or more.

"Kit?" Frémont said to the scout, who had pulled his horse up beside him. The point of the arrow did not waver, but it did not escape Stone that his employer did not waver, either. For all the cracks in Frémont's character which seemed to Stone to be opening with alarming frequency these days, none of them ever exposed cowardice.

"He says we've stolen his antelope, Captain," Kit said. "Says everybody in these parts knows all the game out on the island belongs to him. Claims he's some kind of Bannock king."

"Shall we simply shoot this antique fool out of hand and have done with it, Mr. Carson? The hour grows late."

"We could, Captain. Sure would be the easiest thing to do. But I kind of admire the old coot. Takes some strong innards to face the bunch of us the way he's doing. He's probably seen a lot of his Bannock kin killed by whites on pure spite. If the captain won't think it's knuckling under, I suggest we buy him off."

"What with? We have nothing in the way of trade goods with us."

"A knife or a few plugs of tobacco might satisfy him. Since he probably has all the game he needs, I don't think one of our kills would do the trick." He urged his horse toward the old warrior and said something to him in what Stone presumed was Bannock. The Indian lowered the bow.

Alexis Godey produced a bright red bandanna, and Kit fished a Bowie knife from his belt.

"Giving him a chew is just dandy, Kit," Joe Walker said, "but a swig of firewater might make him happier. I got a drop of Taos Lightning left in my skin."

The gifts fell at the old man's bare feet. Without so much as looking at them, he stepped back and waved them on with the bow, now relaxed, the sweep of his arm as regal a gesture as Stone could remember seeing. Even the gale of laughter that broke from the mountain men as they rode past him did nothing to erase the dignity from that weathered face.

Yes, it had been a splendid outing, and that encounter with the old Bannock chief had been the most splendid part of it for Brad Stone. But he forgot the incident in the noisy feast that night in the bivouac in the salt flats, with the mountain men stuffing themselves with meat and then dancing until they sagged into heaps by the fire. Frémont, while he did not take part in any of the wild firelit dances, seemed as gay as any of them. The resulting feeling of bonhomie had prompted Stone to seek him out this morning.

3

"When do we actually start across the desert, Captain?"

"I'm sending Carson across tonight with five other men." Frémont turned and gazed off toward the west. "Can you see the faint bulge of a mountain on the horizon, Mr. Stone? The farthest one, well beyond those low north-south ranges. I estimate it to be seventy-five miles or more from here."

"Yes, sir." The mountain loomed in a gap between the ranges, rising from the hazy flats like a pyramid.

"Carson, Lucien Maxwell, Basil Lajeunesse, Auguste Archambeault, and the Delaware Segundai will start for it as soon as the moon is high enough for them to see, and ride hell-for-leather until they reach it. It will be an arduous undertaking, perhaps fraught with peril. If they find game, water, and firewood, they will light signal fires to guide us to them. I have already given Mr. Carson his orders. I hate to part with him even for so short a time, but he is the only scout we have with the moral authority to hold men together on such a forced crossing."

Stone stared hard at the distant mountain. He refrained from asking what Kit and his five men were to do if they did *not* find game and water after crossing "seventy-five miles or more" of bone-dry salt desert on horses that by the time they reached the peak would be at the point of exhaustion if not death.

"You only named four men in addition to Mr. Carson, captain," Stone said. "May I ask who the fifth will be?" He stoically resigned himself to hear the name of Ed Kern.

"Against my better judgment, considering your lack of experience, Mr. Stone, you will be Mr. Carson's fifth man."

"Thank you, sir."

"Don't thank *me*. I'll make no secret of the fact that Kit *asked* that you accompany him, otherwise you would be remaining here in camp." Stone hardly heard the next. "The rest of us shall march out tomorrow and come along at a more leisurely pace to accommodate the baggage animals. We shall make one camp halfway to that peak and signal Mr. Carson with fires of our own tomorrow night when we bed down. If we do not see any light or smoke from the advance party we shall return here to the lake and proceed by the more usual northern route."

Stone knew he should think more about what the captain's

last words meant. If Carson and the men with him, including Stone, failed to find water at the peak, they would probably not make it back to Frémont. The thought sobered him, but . . .

Kit had *asked* for him!—and for a mission that surely would demand more skill and reliability than the escort of Pablo Espinosa and his family had seemed to require when they left Bent's Fort for Santa Fe.

"Shall I be using my equipment, sir?"

Frémont snorted. "You will have no time for mapping, Mr. Stone! You won't even be trailing a packhorse, consequently you will have no equipment with you. Your party will take one mule, to carry water barrels. On this trip survival will be the order of the day, or rather of the night. You may take a compass and a notebook. I believe you will find enough work in this little jaunt to satisfy even you for a while. Now, you don't have the luxury of a lot of time to get ready, so I suggest you find Mr. Carson and place yourself at his disposal. You are dismissed, *sirrah!*"

Stone's cheeks flamed at the curt dismissal and the *"sirrah,"* but he said nothing, only saluted as stiffly as he imagined any drill ground recruit might salute, and strode off to find Kit. His anger drained away with every step he took. All in all, his brief encounter with Frémont had turned out better than he really had dared to hope.

4

The night ride through the Great Salt Lake Desert with Kit Carson, Segundai, Lajeunesse, Gus Archambeault, and Lucien Maxwell uncovered still another America for Bradford Stone.

He had gazed long and hard at the wasteland to the west ever since they reached the salt-whitened shores of the great lake. But that had been during the daylight hours, when the heat shimmer created above the flats by the never-failing sun clouded the vision of the keenest eyes.

Under a full moon the desert became something else. Seemingly lifeless in the daytime, the salt and alkali barrens stretching out ahead of them had now come to eerie silver life, but to a life that had not completely cut its ties with death. As the temperature plunged and the humidity moved upward through the night, the low, sparse, prickly vegetation crushed by the horses' hooves, most of it odorless under a blazing, desiccating sun, now gave off odors alternately pungent and aromatic, and sometimes darkly rank. At the first whiff of the latter Stone felt a sudden malaise that refused to leave him for several minutes and the better part of a mile. The smell reminded him a little of that of the bosque on the Cimarron the morning Kit, Luis, and he left the already festering bodies of the dead Comanches.

About every hour Carson ordered them down from their horses. "We'll lead them for about a mile," he said. He turned to Stone. "Don't know if you know this, Brad, but horses ain't got near the stamina in this kind of country us poor human critters have."

Night lizards, some as white as the desert floor nearly to the point of invisibility, skittered away from the passage they or their horses made. The six riders' long shadows—dancing, long black spikes at the outset of the journey—grew shorter as the moon rose higher behind them. From time to time they rode past the bleached skulls of horned animals gleaming almost incandescently in the moonlight, often with a trail of scattered bones, and once an entire rib cage with a grotesque, thorny plant growing through and around it. Stone's eye trailed away from the skulls themselves as if he could still find the track of the ghostly predator responsible for these small ossuaries. He did spy a faint trail once. The alkali had frozen an improbable pug mark into the alabaster path. From the size of the imprint it could only be that of a lion, and a sharp shock of memory took him back to the catamount he had pointed out to Kit on Raton Pass.

Strangely, he did not tire, nor did he drowse, although by the time they were three hours into the journey he had gone nearly twenty-four hours without sleep. Carson and Segundai, at the head of the small column, seemed every bit as awake and alert, but the three others let their chins fall to their chests from time to time. Basil Lajeunesse, a great, hairy bear of a man, even snored once in a titanic, rumbling eruption that caused Carson and the Delaware to turn in the saddle and look at him, Kit with amused awe, Segundai with a slow shake of his fine head.

Other noises broke the silence. The metallic clip-clop the horses' hooves made on the white hardpan had echoed every foot of the journey, but by now Stone's awareness of it had diminished, allowing other sounds to invade his consciousness. When they walked and led the horses he discovered he was more aware of his own much softer footfalls than he was of the hoofbeats. Off to the north a coyote howled . . . another . . . and yet another, solo singers every one of them. The howls did not seem to call for answers, either. Once, when Carson halted them to rest the horses and allow a sparing pull at the canteens, he even detected the whisperlike scratching of the lizards as they scurried out of sight.

Sometime in the small hours, Kit brought the little caravan to a full halt and ordered all of them except Segundai to dismount.

"We'll have the Chief trail our horses and the mule and go on ahead of us. He'll keep riding for maybe half a dozen miles and then pull them up. We'll tag along on shank's mare. If we don't give these critters a real blow of more than two shakes of a lamb's tail pretty soon, they ain't going to make it. And if they don't make it *we* sure as hell won't."

Just before they all slipped from their saddles, Carson eased his mount toward Stone's. "Just take two swallows from your canteen this time, Brad. Except for one jug apiece we're sending all the water with the Delaware for him to stoke the animals with while he waits for us. We won't drink again until we reach him. There's no telling how long it will take us to find water when we get to the mountain," he said, adding with nonchalance, "if there's any there to find."

Until then Stone had felt no thirst, but on the walk across the flats with his three silent companions it was all he could do to restrain himself from reaching for his canteen again. At first his throat only tickled, but after twenty minutes or so it became more and more parched, and when he ran his tongue across the roof of his mouth it felt like sandpaper. Then his tongue thickened, and once his head turned so light with vertigo he feared he might fall. He could not let that happen, not with these hard, capable men looking on. He tried not to think about what a horrible death thirst could bring, but decided that hell, there could never be a good one, anyway. Easy to see why no talk broke out. Like the others, he kept his cracked lips compressed to keep from breathing through his mouth to save what little moisture had not already left it.

Carson allowed two more sips when they caught up with Segundai and the horses. They remounted in total silence and headed west again. After another hour's ride they repeated the drill. This time Basil Lajeunesse—who had staggered as if drunk on the last half mile of the previous hike—went on ahead on horseback with the tiny *caballada* after a grateful look at Carson for being allowed to ride.

Through the rest of the long night, the moonlit mountain they trudged and rode toward had not changed in size or shape, but when dawn broke behind them it suddenly loomed much larger, as if someone had just run another and quite different picture into a magic lantern, bringing every feature of the peak into sharp relief.

Under the full moon the mountain had been an opaque, silver-gray, unrelieved mass, as featureless as a child's chalk drawing. Now Stone could make out canyons, and narrow, walled valleys on its face and flanks, and a blanket of thick, emerald green forest on its northeastern side. Whinnies and snorts broke from the horses.

Carson's raised right hand brought them to a stop.

"Drink up, gents," he announced to Stone and the others. "You can even drain a whole canteen this time if you're of a mind to. My pony just let me know he smells water up there somewhere. He'll find it for us, if your nags don't—and pretty quick. We'll find wood and game, too, from the look of those green slopes."

To Brad, although none of the ride had been exactly easy, it suddenly all seemed that way.

Carson had not finished. "Trouble is, it appears likely that ain't all we'll find." He pointed to the mountain's lower eastern slope, the one closest to them.

Three separate, thin wisps of smoke spiraled into the air, catching the rays of the early sun. "Looks like we'll have company. And with them three cooking fires going, there might be a hell of a lot of it. Must be a good-sized camp."

"Indians or Mexicans?" Lucien Maxwell asked.

"I'd guess Indians, Lucy. Mexicans almost never get this far north in the Basin." Kit nodded to the others. "Look to your rifle and pistol loads, but keep your weapons in their scabbards. Ain't no point in trying to avoid whoever's up there—or get them riled up by flashing weapons—if they ain't already hostile. They sure as hell will have spotted us by now. We'll ride straight for the camp like we've just been invited for a meal, if I don't hear no objections."

All but Segundai—who remained as mute as he had since

leaving the expedition camp at the lake last night—indicated assent with grunts, and even the Delaware nodded.

"Time to catch up!" Kit said. He dug his spurs into his pony's flanks. "Let's get a move on and pay our respects, *amigos.*"

5

Another hour's ride found them bunched up against the lower eastern slope of the mountain. A scree-littered incline swept upward half a mile by Stone's surveyor's estimate to a rocky shelf where gigantic boulders looked almost deliberately set in place to make the wall of a stronghold. One rock, far taller than the others, guarded an opening large enough for horses to ride through single-file. Behind the boulders the three columns of smoke still climbed lazily toward the heavens. Not a single sound reached Stone's ears after they halted, and except for the smoke, nothing moved, nor could he see any evidence of humans at the huge rocks on the shelf.

High above the rocks a hawk hung motionless on a morning updraft as if it had been pinned in the sky like a butterfly to a collector's board. The morning sun began to heat their backs and bounce from the rocks as a blinding glare.

"Maybe they *ain't* seen us yet, Kit. There ain't no lookouts on them rocks," Lucien Maxwell whispered. In the silence his breathy words sounded like so many rifle shots. "And maybe there ain't even nobody up there, anyways." Until now Maxwell had remained almost as soundless as Segundai.

"You know a sight better than that, Lucy," Kit said. "Lightning didn't set them fires. Ain't no trees or pine duff behind them rocks. There's somebody up there, sure enough."

"Yeah, I expect you're right as usual," Maxwell said. "A feller can always hope, though, can't he?"

"What do you think, Kit?" Basil Lajeunesse asked. "Shoshone? Utes? Bannock?"

"Could be any of them, Bass. Could even be Navajo, but I kind of doubt it. They hate to get this far from their herds, and if they had herds traveling with them they'd be down here in the flats. It probably ain't Diggers, either. They don't often move around in bunches large enough to need three fires. Hell, I ain't going to make any more guesses, not when we'll find out dead sure soon enough." He peered intently up the slope, then glanced up to where the hawk had begun to move in great circles, its wings spread black against the sky. "We'll give them five minutes to show themselves and then I'll mosey up there and have a look."

"Want company, Kit?" Maxwell said.

"It would be kind of nice, Lucy, but no. No sense in all of us losing our scalps with the captain coming along behind us. If whoever's up there ain't kindly disposed toward us, I'll try to get a shot off. If you hear me fire, I want you five to skirt the mountain to the first water you find north of here. Let Brad mark its location so as you can find it again. Fill your canteens and skins, and then start back across the flats to meet the captain and let him know what he might be facing when he gets here." He turned to Stone. "Fish out that timepiece you carry, *amigo*. If you don't see me or hear my shot ten minutes after I reach them rocks, don't wait for me a second longer. Keep everybody together so as there's no missing your signal to leave. You'll have to take Gus, Lucy, Basil, and the Chief out of here fast. If I find trouble, I'll be with you as quick as I can make it. Don't go straight back the way we just come. Head north first. We plain got to have water before we hit the desert again."

Stone wanted to think about the fact that Kit had just put him in charge of four seasoned veterans, all of them far more knowledgeable than he, but it concerned him more that the scout intended going up there by himself.

Carson tapped his horse lightly with the free end of his reins and the animal tossed its head and moved up the talus slope, stepping carefully through the loose stone. It looked to be heavy going for the tired animal.

This lone, struggling excursion up the mountain in full sunlight was far different from the nighttime advance on the Comanches on the Cimarron. Dangerous as that affair had been, Carson had two other not entirely useless men with him then, both on rested horses, and the elements of surprise and darkness had been working for the three of them. Now the scout rode alone. With Stone and the others waiting at the foot of the slope, there was no way they could ride up to aid him in time to do him any good.

Stone, squinting against the glare, watched him make the unhurried climb.

The hawk broke off its circular, soaring flight, flapped its wings slowly a time or two, and then coasted off in a shallow hunting stoop down toward the forested northern shoulder of the mountain.

Then Stone saw the other birds on the boulders.

Buzzards. Five of them in all, two had perched atop the sentinel-like, tall rock Kit headed for. These scavengers high above Stone now sat too deathly still to have caught his eye earlier through the glare coming off the rocks. But now, with the sun angling higher by the second, the glare had diminished, almost bringing the beaks and feathers into sharp focus even at a distance of half a mile. Their heads hunched down between their shoulders gave them a look of intense concentration. What possible gluttonous expectations could the disgusting creatures be entertaining?

Kit and his mount disappeared in the opening in the rock wall. As if the light had dimmed, a veil of silence dropped over the slope. Stone checked his watch, 8:05. Ten minutes, Kit had said.

Stone looked at the other four. Aside from Maxwell's offhand query as to whether Kit wanted company or not, there seemed no particular concern for their friend on any of their faces. Would they ultimately show resentment at Stone, or were they in fact showing it now, their silence a comment on the fact that Carson had draped his mantle of command, however temporarily, around the shoulders of a greenhorn? Probably not Segundai, who always seemed to be listening for orders from deep inside himself. Stone decided he could not worry about any possible injured feelings on the part of Archambeault, Lajeunesse, and Maxwell now. Somehow he would find the will to do everything Kit wanted him to do, if anything needed doing.

The hawk came winging back, closer to the slope this time. He forced himself to ignore the bird's peregrinations and pulled his eyes back to the opening in the rocks.

8:11. Four more minutes and he would have to order them out of here, shot or no shot. The first six minutes had passed in the winking of an eye.

Warm before, the air had turned oven-hot in an instant.

8:13.

He slipped his watch back into his pocket. For his purposes he could gauge the passage of the next two minutes well enough by guess alone.

Then Carson appeared in the opening, stood in the stirrups and waved, urging the four of them up the slope.

They climbed the scree faster than Carson had, but with the horses laboring as if each step upward would be their last, it still took nearly ten minutes to reach him.

6

"We ain't in any particular danger," Kit said, "but we sure got troubles."

"No water?" Gus asked.

"Plenty of water. There's a good, cold spring on the other side of these rocks. Not more than two hundred yards away. The trouble's something else. There's a big Ute village in there behind them big rocks, but it ain't a regular one. Must be near a hundred Indians in it. They only been here two days, and they ain't even put up lodges yet. They got mauled bad in a fight with the Navajo a week ago, and they got fifteen to twenty wounded warriors . . . but that ain't the worst of it."

"What's up?"

"They had to leave their own village south of here."

"How come?"

"Spotted fever."

"Goddamn!" The color drained from Maxwell's face.

"Pretty near the whole village is down with it. Those that ain't are damn near as bad off. There's practically nobody fit to hunt and the ones that ain't felt the full force of the fever yet are already as weak as water."

"Jesus!" Maxwell said. "Let's get our asses out of here *pronto,* Kit."

"Where do you figure on going?"

"Don't give a shit. I seen what this spotted stuff can do to a man a time or two. Bad way to go."

"Well . . . think about this, *amigo:* I just now learned from one of the Utes in there that the nearest other water is eighteen or twenty miles north of here, clear around the mountain. Don't know if our horses can make it there from the look of them."

"Utes will lie with the best of them. They're just trying to get shut of us. I say let them have their way."

"I know this band of Utahs. Tall Elk, the man who told me about the water, is an old friend from trapping days. Knew my first wife. I figure I can trust him."

"But, Kit—*spotted goddamned* fever?"

"Look . . . we just got to use their spring, and I reckon the only Christian way we can pay them for it is by helping them with their sick the best we can." He turned to Lajeunesse and Segundai. "How do you two feel about it?"

The Delaware merely nodded.

"I'm with you," Basil said, "but like Lucy, I don't care a hell of a lot for the idea."

"Hey!" Maxwell broke in. "I never said I wouldn't *stay*."

Kit smiled. "You didn't fool me for a second, Lucy."

Stone thought of assuring Kit of his willingness, but he realized then that the scout had not so much as asked him. He must have taken the assurance for granted.

Carson turned his horse and led them through the opening.

Stone had thought the smells during the night a little like those of the Cimarron with its freight of death. The stench filled his nostrils and almost made him retch.

7

"The rash starts at the wrists," Carson said. "Then it spreads up over the chest and head like with this one." He pointed to an Indian boy of about nine or so, who lay on his back and stared straight up into the sun. "The fever sets in something fierce then. You ache like a mule kicked you, and you can't keep a morsel of food in your stomach. It don't take long after that. Maybe the worst is that you die in a pile of your own shit."

"How many will it kill?" Stone asked.

"Six out of ten. Their only hope is if you can break the fever in time. That's where we come in. Let me have your canteen, Brad. I emptied mine when I rode in here before, and I ain't had a chance to get to the spring." He poured the water right on the youngster's flushed face. The staring eyes did not so much as blink, and as they watched a glaze covered the whites and pupils. "Better if we can soak their buckskins," Carson continued. "Too late for this lad."

"Is it contagious?" Stone asked.

"If you mean by that can you just plain catch it out of the air or something, I don't rightly know," Carson said. "Neither does anyone else, I expect. I seen it hit one or two in a village and skip every one of the rest. Most of these Utes here are down with it, though. They came here because this mountain is one of their sacred places. But there's one mighty peculiar thing. None of the warriors who fought the Navajo show any sign of the fever, not even the wounded. It must have started in their old village while the fighting men was away tangling with the Dineh. Don't know what to make of that."

The Ute named Tall Elk, a distinguished-looking old man who wore a single feather drooping from hair as white as snow, had accompanied them on their first tour of the village and Carson turned now and spoke with him. The old man nodded and left them.

"I told him I'm sending Segundai and Maxwell out to hunt," he said to Stone. "His people need food pretty bad. Ain't been able to look for game much themselves. The Chief and Lucy will have to borrow some Ute ponies. Our own horses are just about done in." He turned to Basil Lajeunesse. "I want you to scour this side of the mountain for firewood, Bass. Tall Elk will find you a couple of men or boys who ain't in too bad shape to lend a hand. Their cooking fires is all but out of fuel. The sick are burning up right now, of course, but they'll need to keep warm when the desert freeze sets in tonight. Besides, we'll need a lot of wood for the signal fire we'll set for the captain. Brad and me will keep ourselves busy playing nursemaid."

8

The rest of the morning and the whole afternoon that followed produced the most grueling and frustrating hours Bradford Stone had known since coming west.

He carried water skinful by dripping skinful from the spring until he thought he would drop in his tracks. Carson, half his size, carried every bit as much. Stone copied as best he could every move the scout made, marveling again at those gentle, small hands, the same hands which had delivered Olivera Espinosa's baby on the road to Santa Fe—in what seemed now another age, another country—and the same hands, he could not forget, which had torn the hair from the dead Comanches in the bitter dark of the bosque.

They must have sloshed water over the prostrate forms of at least forty Utes, drenching them from head to toe, scavenging rags and hides wherever they could and wetting them through to aid the process of cooling down the victims of the disease.

"It will be tomorrow before we can be sure if we done these poor devils any good," Kit said during one of the two short rests they allowed themselves.

"That boy who died was Tall Elk's grandson," Kit went on. "Would have been chief of this village someday. His mother and father, Elk's son, died yesterday, before we got here."

Stone could not have guessed any such tragedy by looking at the old man. His face remained as expressionless as the rocks.

They did not stop to eat, but Stone did not give it much thought. The pervasive stink of vomit and excrement in the camp overpowered appetite.

His ignorance of the Ute language did not hamper his

efforts to help. The fever-wracked victims he tended either lacked the strength to make a sound or were not inclined to talk, even with Carson. As he had seen Kit do, he patted the cheeks of children, squeezed the shoulders of their elders, and forced himself to smile—a lot. His smile could have been no more encouraging than that of a gargoyle; it met blank, stone stares everywhere.

Carson ordered their second, and presumably last, break of the afternoon near sunset, after they had looked at the wounds, some still festering, on the warriors who had fought the Navajo. As far as Stone could see it was futile; they had to redress the lacerations with the same filthy rags and patches they removed.

"Must have been a hell of a fight," Kit said. "More than a hundred on each side according to Tall Elk."

"Why were they fighting? Since they're all Indians, and since this country is so big, I would think . . ."

"All *Indians?* No offense, Brad, but that's kind of an eastern idea. They don't think of themselves as 'Indians.' They're Comanche, Bannock, Arapaho, or whatever. There's as much difference between a Navajo and a Ute as there is between you and me and Canadian Frenchmen like Lajeunesse. They just look alike to us, not to each other. The Dineh and the Utah tribes been enemies ever since they settled in this country."

"What I don't understand is how they don't seem to fight back the way most white people do when they're faced with death. As if they have no will to live. The wounded here seem to have given up like those down with the fever."

"They ain't like us."

"I realize that, but . . ."

"It's all tied up with their religion. Utes is tough as saddle leather. They think they've already fought this thing as hard as they can just by coming here."

"What?"

"This mountain is sacred. There's something else, too. If I've got it straight, they probably feel they got this sickness coming. It's something they share with the people they just fought. The Navajo have a word. *Hozho*. We ain't got one like it in English. Maybe 'harmony' comes close. If a Navajo lives his life in harmony his gods see to it that no harm comes to him."

"That's a pretty primitive notion."

"Works for them, I guess. Maybe we ought to try it some."

Strange thought from a pragmatic frontiersman.

"My first wife was a Ute," Carson said next. "That's how I know something about the way Utes just plain 'give up,' as you called it."

With sunset nearing, the village caught in its glow assumed a somewhat less appalling look than it had worn in the harsh light earlier in the day. The temperature of the air was dropping, but heat still oozed from the sunbaked, sheltering stones that walled the camp.

Working his way through the scattered Utes who had sought the shade on the north side of the larger rocks Stone came upon a group of four, a family by the look of them. A man, lean, fit, clearly untouched by the fever, and not wounded as far as Stone could see, stood over the others, all lying on their backs. He held a long lance with a wicked steel head, its butt against the hard ground.

Stone bent over the smallest of the three supine figures, another boy, and about the same age as the one he had seen when they first entered the village. Not much chance for this one, either. It seemed cruel, but he decided he would have to save his remaining water for the other two, if *they* could profit from it. It was almost half a mile back to the spring.

Only minutes after Stone first looked at him the boy uttered a low, breathy rattle, and at his side the Ute mother gave out a hollow groan that filled Stone with dread and sorrow.

The woman herself looked somewhat better, but thin and weak. Beyond her the third victim, a girl nearing full womanhood, caught his eye and chilled him.

Even though wasted, her face a violent red, her long black hair in disarray, and even with her lips cracked and swollen, the girl could have been the twin of Ana Barragán.

The dread he had felt when the boy died was nothing compared to what he felt now.

He ignored the woman, sluiced the girl from head to toe with the entire contents of his water skin, and went to his knees beside her. She wore a string of trade beads around her neck, and it looked as if they were strangling her. He ripped them away.

The standing man lowered the tip of his lance and took a step toward Stone with an animal growl. He braced himself.

Then, out of the corner of his eye he saw the older woman raise her hand palm outward. The Ute man stepped back.

Stone pulled the girl's head into his lap.

As he brought his face close to hers, the raging heat that was burning her away seared him, too.

Yes, she could have been Ana.

He would have held her in silence until she died and the heat radiating from her slim body had ebbed away, but Carson appeared in front of him.

"You can't keep her alive, Brad. Do what you can for the mother and let's move on and look to those we *can* do something for."

9

Basil Lajeunesse and his two young helpers had long since returned with the firewood, rebuilt the Ute fires, and when Maxwell and Segundai rode in with a string of ponies sagging under the carcasses of antelope and deer, Basil went to work dressing them out for the evening meal. He actually looked cheerful as he issued orders to the three healthy Ute women Tall Elk found to assist him. One of them hauled an enormous iron pot to the fire and suspended it from a tripod, three of the stouter sticks of wood lashed together with lengths of rawhide thong.

While Basil cooked, Carson set Stone, Segundai, and Lucien Maxwell to another task.

"Strip all the wet buckskin from the sick, and every soaked blanket and scrap of cloth. Lucy, rig some racks around the other fires so we can dry them. Cold as we had to get these poor devils today, we'll have to keep them just as warm and dry tonight. I think we did some good this afternoon, and we can't let that go to waste."

As he worked alongside Maxwell and Segundai, Stone's mind kept returning to the girl he had held.

By the time Maxwell finished setting up the drying racks Carson had asked for, Basil had butchered a deer and three of the antelope and had brewed a hearty stew. He watered some of it down for the seriously ill. Stone, the Delaware, and the two mountain men pulled every pan and vessel from their saddlebags to begin feeding the village. The Ute women furnished twenty or so earthen pots and filled them with Basil's concoction.

Stone had finally, or so he thought, forced the image of the Ute girl from his mind, but now he collected two containers of the stew and set off for the rocks at the south end of the village. As he walked her face seemed to appear in the darkness in front of him, or *was* it hers? Half the time the vision became Ana in the flesh: the same straight nose, the same seductively sharp, challenging cheekbones, the same jet black eyes and full dark lips set in the same lustrous skin— and the same faintly impish smile. His steps quickened.

When he reached the rocks, the family was gone.

The darkness had become almost complete now, with

only the distant beams from the last Ute fire he had passed barely lighting the space beneath the rocks. He set his two pots on the ground. Something in the gravelly earth glinted in the dim light. He put his hand out and grasped the string of beads he had torn from the Ute girl's neck.

The Ute girl, wherever she and her family had gone, might well die, most likely would, perhaps already had, but Ana lived. Ana . . . Ana . . .

The slight weight of a small hand rested on his shoulder. "Best get back with the others, *amigo*," Kit said. "We got to lay out the work for tonight and tomorrow. Time for us to put something in our bellies, too."

As he and Carson walked back to the center of the camp the scout reached up and placed his hand on Stone's shoulder again.

"I reckon I know what's running through your mind, *amigo*," he said. "That girl could sure enough be Ana's sister."

10

"We've got to keep the signal fire for the captain burning through the night, and I expect we ought to light it pretty quick now," Kit said. "We'll take turns. An hour for each of us. Will you take the first shift, Bass?"

Lajeunesse, who had just finished devouring what amounted to a whole haunch of venison, lumbered to his feet. He looked as if pain were wracking him. His huge hand wiped the venison's juices from his face, but the drippings still made his beard shine in the firelight. He lurched off toward the opening in the rocks the way Stone imagined a bear might look coming out of hibernation.

"Bass's arthritis is kicking up again," Kit said. "That night air will get to him. Take the second turn a little early, Brad."

He turned to Maxwell. "You and Segundai can turn in now, Lucy. We'll still have a lot of work facing us tomorrow before the captain comes in sight. Brad, Bass, and I will have more nursing to do, and by rights you and the Chief ought to make another hunt. The main party with the captain might not get here until near dark or maybe even after it, and they'll be ready to eat the ass out of a skunk. They'll have plenty of beans and coffee, of course, but I reckon they'll welcome a little fresh meat."

Stone stood up, but Carson waved him back down. "Don't go, Brad. You won't have time for any real shut-eye before you have to spell old Bass. Let's chin a little."

But long moments of silence, broken only by the coughs issuing from the sick Utes scattered through the compound, and once by the thin, eerie howl of a coyote, settled in after the mountain man and the Delaware disappeared in the darkness away from the fire.

"Kit," Stone said at last. "There are two or three things I need to ask you. Please tell me if any of them are none of my damned business."

"Fire away."

"First—the way you worked today among these pitiful, sick people is so different from what happened on the Cimarron. How do you really feel about Indians?"

Carson's gray eyes turned to Stone. "Funny question. I like a lot of them. I married two of them, you know, before I met Josefa. And I got Indian friends all across the plains and in the mountains. In every tribe—Lakota, Cheyenne, Ute, Navajo, all of them. Oh, I will admit I have a little trouble holding on to a friendly feeling for Comanches; ain't had much luck with Comanches. *I respect* Indians. I more or less require that they respect me, too."

"On the record you've killed a good number of them in your time."

"I got to admit that's true. I didn't set out to do that. I do get kind of riled if an Indian robs my traps, tries to steal my meat, or tries to kill me or my friends, but I'd feel the same about white men."

"Back East there is a growing body of opinion that says this is *their* land, that they've every right to resist what Captain Frémont and you and I and our companions are trying to do out here."

"I agree with some of that. But mostly I feel this is everybody's land. I came out from Missouri to make a living in this country, not to move anybody out. Indians hunt and fish this country, but they don't really *use* it. Except for the Pueblos they never grow stuff. And how about the people living on top of each other in your cities? Ain't they got a right to a little piece of this land, too? Look now, I don't want to see every valley out here crawling with people, either. But I can't stop it. And hell, it just ain't going to come to that, anyway, not in your life or in mine, and not for a couple of hundred years or more. Things out here ain't going to change one hell of a lot."

"I'm not at all sure about that, Kit. It didn't take that long east of the Mississippi. Those cities you spoke about, remember?"

"Can't argue with that, I guess. This is a different kind of country, though. Was there something else, Brad?"

"Yes. But this is even a little more personal." Stone took in a breath. Had he already gone too far with this? "I watched you ride up to this village this morning alone, and I tell you my heart was in my mouth. If Comanches, say, had been lurking behind these rocks, you wouldn't have had a chance. Aren't you *ever* afraid, Kit?"

Carson snorted laughter with a touch of embarrassment in it. "That's an even funnier question than the first one you asked." Another small silence dropped over the two of them. "I guess I've never thought about it. Couple of times not being afraid *enough* damned near did me in. Fear can be mighty useful."

There was time for no more talk before Stone left to spell
Basil Lajeunesse at the signal fire.

11

Three more of Tall Elk's Utes had died during the night.
Stone heard some of the keening and wailing at his post by
the signal fire, and by noon one other had died, but the worst
was over.

He did not return to the south end of the village, nor did
he make inquiries concerning the whereabouts of the vanished Ute family. He wanted to persuade himself that he had
never seen them.

With less work to do with the sick and wounded, Carson
stationed Basil Lajeunesse outside the opening in the rocks
again to keep a watch for Frémont, and a minute or two after
three in the afternoon the big mountain man rode back into
the village.

"They're here!" he shouted. "Leastways they're down in
the flats, maybe three or four miles away. Be more than an
hour before they're even within hailing distance."

This gave Stone ample time to dig his drawing equipment
out of his saddlebags and start on that long overdue field
sketch which would some day lead to a full oil portrait of his
friend Kit Carson. It turned out to be a good idea. He posed
the smiling, mildly protesting scout against a tawny, deeply
grained rock under the peerless western sky. None of the trials of the past two days showed in Kit's seamless face.

Carson fidgeted some during the sitting, and Stone knew
again how good an idea the sketching was; he would have
hell's own time getting this restless little man to hold still for
the much longer time an oil would take. When he finished,
he flattered himself that he had done a marvelous likeness,
and perhaps his best work with a drawing pencil ever.

"Do I really look like that?" Kit said.

"It's as honest a rendering of a subject as I have ever done, Kit."

He wondered how it would compare with the sketches of Frémont he had shipped back to St. Louis and Jessie after that first week at Bent's Fort. Had those renderings been as honest?

12

A broad, flat ribbon of dust curled up behind the expedition.

When Basil Lajeunesse reported sighting them at the foot of the slope, Kit had sent the old mountain man down into the desert to guide them in.

Even though a mile still separated the train of wagons and riders from the watchers at the opening in the mountain wall, Stone could begin to pick out individual men and animals. Bullwhips darted over the backs of the mules and oxen like the tongues of snakes, and now and again the shouts of the wagoneers soared to the heights and echoed from the rocks behind him. As the column neared the foot of the talus slope he heard the grinding of iron-clad wheels. The mountain men in the flats with Frémont raised their rifles above their heads, and half a dozen fired off shots, some aimed apparently at the rocks to the right and left of Carson and his party. Ricochets screamed from either side of them.

When the long column of horsemen, carts, wagons, and the three mountain howitzers came to a halt at the bottom of the slope, three mounted men detached themselves from the main body and began the ascent through the scree: Frémont, Ed Kern, and Lajeunesse.

Frémont rode in the lead, neck-reining his animal deftly through the broken terrain, with Kern and Basil two lengths behind him.

The Pathfinder had chosen to rejoin his chief scout and advisor astride the magnificent black stallion Sacramento, which had arrived from Independence the day before the expedition left Bent's Fort.

Frémont had decked himself out in a new suit of bone-white buckskin with the fringes dyed coal black, and he looked as if he had just stepped from the fort's tailor shop. An eagle feather decorated his white hat.

Stone glanced at Carson; the scout was grinning at the spectacle.

"Well met, Kit!" Frémont said when he reined up. His gloved hand went to the brim of his elegant white hat in salute. "You have found us an acceptable campsite, have you not?"

"Yes, sir," Kit replied. "It's a mite shy on shade, but it's got the only good water for twenty miles in any direction. Plenty of game no more than an hour's ride away and all the wood we're apt to need for as long as we bivouac here."

"Fine work," Frémont said. "Why don't you and your men show Mr. Kern and me around? We'll bring what we can of the expedition up out of those flats as soon as I've made my inspection. I've no doubt at all that the place you have chosen will be more than acceptable." He looked at Stone and smiled. "You look fit, Mr. Stone. Did you enjoy your trip across the desert?"

"It was an illuminating experience, sir," Stone said. There was a hint of genuine friendliness in Frémont's voice and manner.

Kit led the way through the rocks into the village.

Once inside the opening, Frémont reined in the black horse. A look of pain and black disgust passed across his handsome, bearded face.

Until that moment Stone had not realized how accustomed he had become to the foul odor of the Ute camp.

They had now reached the first small group of stricken

Indians. A Ute man and woman were returning to the main camp from the spring.

"Who are those miserable creatures and what are they doing here, Kit?" Frémont said.

"Utes, Captain. It's actually the campground for their village. They've got a number of wounded with them, and they've been hit hard by fever. Poor critters lost twenty-five or thirty people just this past week. This mountainside is one of their sacred places. They came here thinking they could heal."

"Get them out of here!"

"But, sir . . . the spring is the only freshwater within—"

"I said get them out of here. This is an outpost of the U.S. Army, sir. I and my command will not share this ground with diseased savages for a solitary moment. *Get them out of here . . . Mr. Carson—now!*"

"Yes, Captain."

Brad Stone saw the dark gray of defeat flicker across Kit's face.

16

The Good Soldier

Carson, Stone, and Basil Lajeunesse stood by the northwest opening in the rocks near the spring, and watched the Utes leave what had been their village.

Some hobbled out under their own power, one wounded warrior using a crude crutch fashioned from what at one time might have been a lance. Mothers carried children out in rake-thin arms. The more able men pulled those older

Indians still suffering from the fever along in drags meant to be harnessed to ponies.

Frémont had ordered all riding stock in the village confiscated and placed at the disposal of Ted Talbot for reassignment to members of the expedition. Actually, the Ute animals were a sorry-looking lot, and Stone wondered why the Pathfinder had even bothered with them. It seemed like theft, without any genuine benefit to the thieves.

None of the departing Indians made any real protest, although a pair hung back, only to be prodded along by Segundai's rifle. Lucien Maxwell shared the duty at the opening in the rocks with the Delaware, the point of his nicked old saber stuck in the rocky ground, his hands resting on the hilt.

Frémont had allowed the Utes to fill their waterskins, bottles, and pots at the spring, and Lajeunesse detached himself from Stone and Carson to help one feeble old woman draw her supply. He placed one of his big hands on the small of her back and guided her through the stone exit with marvelous gentleness.

Tall Elk was the last to leave. He stopped in front of Carson and peered at him for several seconds, his expression indistinguishable from the look of the rocky wall behind him. Kit gazed back, but he said nothing, even when the superb old Ute shook his head and then disappeared through the rocks.

"Where will they go?" Stone asked.

"North, I expect. They've got to get to that water on the other side of the mountain, and make a camp there. When they're well enough they'll head south again for their old hunting grounds. It will be a long walk."

It took the rest of the day for the new occupants to get their gear into the high basin, hauling it up the talus slope by hand and doing it on foot. Hot work in their heavy furs. The wagons, carts, and the mountain guns had to be left down in the desert flats, with some of the larger draft animals staked out in picket lines in the middle of a stretch of wiry grasses.

2

Frémont himself did not dismount once during all the after-noon's activity. He rode the stallion from one end of the vil-lage to the other, almost never stopping. Stone had to admit his captain cut a splendid figure.

Dick Owens told Stone that Frémont had detailed six of the mountain men, with Joe Walker in charge, to ride herd on the Utes until they were too far from their deserted vil-lage to even think about trying to return.

"Ridiculous," Owens said. "Does he think they'll attack us? Them poor critters ain't in no kind of shape to take on an outfit the size of this one. They'll be lucky to find that other water Kit talked about."

Ed Kern found Stone at the dinner hour, and they sat down together at a fire where Basil Lajeunesse was cooking once again. Frémont had Lajeunesse bring him his meal in his tent, but Carson settled in across the fire from Stone and the Philadelphian, well out of earshot. He sat as silent as the stones, hunched over his food, but barely touching it. None of the other mountain men approached him as they usually did at meals. Lajeunesse must have already spread the word about Kit and Frémont's painful exchange earlier in the day.

"That," Kern whispered to Stone, "is a deeply troubled man." Stone did not respond, and Kern continued in the same hushed whisper. "I've seen this before when subordinates are overruled by their superiors on matters they feel strongly about. Funny thing, if Kit had held his ground about the Utes, I think our captain would have deferred to him. Frémont can't afford to get on the outs with a man who means as much to the success of this mission as Carson does."

Stone said, in a tone of mild disapproval, "You think Kit was afraid?"

"No one in his right mind would ever think that. There's something else at work here. . . ."

"What?"

"Well, although I doubt that Kit has ever worn the uniform, I have a notion that he is the prototypical 'good soldier.'"

"Kit a soldier? Nonsense!"

"Hear me out. I don't mean he's some rifle-company lieutenant, but I do think that at times he's like some faithful subaltern who obeys orders on reflex, without ever giving thought to questioning them. Johnny Frémont bet on that this afternoon—and won."

Carson rose, walked to the fire and dumped almost a full plate of meat into it. He walked off into the darkness before Stone could get a look at his face.

"Even supposing what you say is true, Ed, if Kit is the reflexively obedient soldier you describe, is that *bad?*"

"Not in an army. This is supposed to be a scientific expedition, remember. No one has actually told me otherwise."

"I've got to bed down. I'm about to fall apart."

Kern followed him to their bivouac area and in moments they were in their bedrolls. Stone had nearly fallen asleep when it became apparent Ed had not yet talked himself completely out.

"Speaking of soldiers . . . if you're not willing to concede that Carson is one, there is someone else in this outfit who most certainly is."

"You mean our captain?"

"Yes. I got to know him a little better the last two days, when we were catching up to you and Carson."

"So?"

"Although he trained solely as a topographer, I think he lusts to lead men in combat. His saddlebags are stuffed with army tactical manuals, and he spends more time on them—and *Caesar's Commentaries*—than he does on the explorations of his hero, the sainted explorer Humboldt. Makes me wonder what he has in mind when we reach California."

"California's the last of our objectives," Stone said. "And anyway, we will only see a small part of it, maybe none, before we head north to Oregon. We won't even get as far south as Sutter's Fort until long after we explore the new northwestern emigrant route."

Kern propped himself on his elbow. "I know that's the original plan. I'll bet it doesn't turn out that way. And there's something else."

"What now?"

"I think Johnny Frémont sees himself as president of the United States some day," Kern said.

"What?"

"Think about it. He's damned well known in the East, celebrated even, thanks to his wife, Jessie, and her articles in *Century*—and thanks in large measure to what Carson did for him on his other expeditions. With his father-in-law's support he could make it."

"I thought Senator Benton had a lot of opposition."

"It will fade from sight if we go to war with Mexico, and I think that's likely."

"What's that got to do with us and our expedition?"

"Well . . . if Johnny should parlay that kind of backing into a run for the highest office somewhere down the line, a successful military career—particularly if he could somehow win a small battle or two, say in California—could take him right into the presidency someday."

"I can't believe the captain would look for something that dangerous just to satisfy some possible political ambition."

"You don't? I do. I think he's got the killer instinct necessary for it. Knowing what I now know of him, the turnpike to the White House could be cobbled with friend and foe alike."

No question about it, Ed Kern had indeed gotten closer to their commander than Stone had.

"Lord knows, he doesn't consider *me* a friend," Stone said. "Not that I haven't tried to be one. Why doesn't he like me, Ed? Except for the sketches I did of him, things haven't been good between us since the very first day at Bent's." He could have bitten his tongue. In the tough company he was keeping nowadays complainers found little favor. But, now that he had started, he might as well go on with it. "Does he resent the pressure my congressman put on him to get him to take me on? Charlie Bent thought that might be what put him off. Jake Myers called in some fairly hefty IOUs to wangle my appointment."

"I suppose that's part of it."

"Why didn't Frémont just send me packing, then?"

"Oh, he might not like being pressured. He might have some worries about Myers' interest in you, but in your case I think the trouble between the two of you is something else . . . something more."

"What then, in God's name? I've worked like a dog, when he lets me."

"Actually, you just put your finger on it. It has to do with your professional abilities. He knows he doesn't even begin to rank with you as a mapmaker."

"How would he *know* that? He's hardly looked at what little stuff he's let me do. For that matter, he's nowhere near as good as *you*, Ed, and he does know what you can do. Most of the important assignments have gone your way."

"Thanks for the compliment, Brad, but come *on!* I'm not in your class, either, although you're too damned modest to admit it."

"Even supposing what you say is true, which I doubt, how on earth would he *know* about my capabilities? Jake Myers' recommendation of me went solely to my character, such as it is. Old Jake wouldn't know a transit from a teacup."

"You studied under Professor Wendell Strike at Harvard, didn't you?"

"Yes."

"Didn't you see that piece Strike published in the June issue of *Century*?"

"I haven't seen a copy of *Century* since I left St. Louis. If there's a newsstand west of there, I failed to find it."

"Well . . . our Johnny has a copy. I saw it stuffed in with his army manuals. You've been walking in front of him ever since Bent's with what amounts to a target on your back."

"What did the article say?"

"Strike took Johnny to task for the topographical products of last year's expedition. Came damned close to calling them sloppy."

"But for Pete's sake, Ed, that was my professor, not me! The captain can't blame a student for a criticism his teacher made. I've been out of Harvard for more than two years now."

"Well, if Strike had only ended his article right there, that would be exactly right, and probably the end of it. The commander probably sees himself as too big to joust with a schoolteacher who's never been west of the Hudson. But the good professor went on to say that Frémont and the country were fortunate that this year's expedition would have the services of the most brilliant student he ever taught—one Bradford Ogden Stone."

3

The expedition rested for four days on the flanks of the mountain which Frémont decided would go on the maps and into the record as Pilot Peak.

Not all of its members rested. Kit left the camp before daybreak every morning on hunts for game that did not end until well after dark. He took no one with him. Sometimes the faint, distant reports of his Hawken reached the rocks above the camp.

From the numbers of antelope, deer, and smaller animals he trailed into camp on the sagging backs of sometimes as many as three packhorses, he must have engaged in a prodigious orgy of killing. Even Stone realized that some of the meat would spoil in the never-failing sun before a hundred men, each with the cavernous appetite of a Basil Lajeunesse, could eat it all. Kit spoke to no one before bedding down at night or before he left again before the first sliver of sun showed above the horizon.

On the afternoon of the third day at Pilot Peak a rider appeared on the desert east of the lone mountain.

When he'd made the exhausting climb to the camp, and Frémont, Stone, Kern, and a few others gathered around him, Stone recognized him as Cal Johnson, a courier who worked for Charles Bent. He carried a leather briefcase and handed it to Frémont even before asking for food and water.

"I got a letter in my pouch for Brad Stone, too, Captain," Johnson said. Frémont pointed to Stone and disappeared with the case inside his tent.

Could the letter be from Ana?

But the return address on the envelope bore the great seal of the United States of America and read, "Foreign Relations Committee, United States House of Representatives, Office of the Chairman, Jakob Q. Myers."

Myers began with the obligatory inquiry about Stone's health, a report on the visit the congressman had made to Groverton in October, the news that Stone's parents and sister Carrie were all well—but anxious about him, naturally ("*Write to them, my boy!*")—and a request that he also keep Jake himself informed about his adventures with "the fabled

Mr. Christopher Carson" and Brevet Captain John C. Frémont.

> ". . . and of course I am still concerned about how
> things have gone between you and the latter gen-
> tleman. As I pointed out to you the day we parted
> in Chicago, he is not the easiest of men to get close
> to. Here in Washington a great number of influen-
> tial men feel the captain is a shade too precipitate,
> too eager to go beyond the parameters of his mis-
> sion. I am a good friend—and sometime close
> political ally—of his father-in-law, Senator Benton.
> We have both cautioned him to that effect in a joint
> letter that should arrive in the same post as this one
> to you. You, of course, must not involve yourself in
> this matter. All that is required of you is that you do
> your job."

There was a bit more. Myers wrote that he had again com-
mended Bradford Stone to Frémont in the letter from him
and Benton. A postscript said that Jessie Frémont sent her
best to Stone and Carson.

4

Frémont emerged from his tent for the dinner hour. After the
meal he called a meeting for eight o'clock for Talbot, Kern,
Carson, Walker, Owens, Lajeunesse, and Stone.

He had put aside the white buckskin and now had dressed
himself in his regular trail clothes, but he looked at the pin-
nacle of form when they all gathered at the fire in front of
his tent.

"Unfortunately, gentlemen," he said as they settled into
place, "Mr. Carson has not yet returned to camp. We shall

have to proceed without him." He turned to Stone. "Mr. Stone, I want you to make a written record of this meeting. I wish this record to go out with the courier from Bent's when he starts back to the Arkansas the day after tomorrow. It is important that what transpires here tonight be reported by someone other than your captain. I want an objective observer's view of what takes place, everything that is said. Mr. Stone . . . please." He handed a monogrammed leather writing case to Stone. His gaze swept over the group just as a pine knot flared in the fire, lighting his face dramatically.

Stone wondered why Frémont was having him act as recording secretary when Ted Talbot, his putative administrative officer, was sitting with Kern and the mountain men. Talbot had maintained all the other records of the expedition save for Stone's surveying notes and the journal Frémont kept himself. Maybe the letter from Myers and Benton that Jake had mentioned had something to do with it, but there was no time now for speculation; the captain had begun to speak again.

". . . and the courier carried with him dispatches for me directly from the president of the United States." He clearly took great enjoyment in saying that. After a deep, satisfied breath he continued. "I am not at this moment at liberty to tell you precisely what their nature is, but the president's new orders to me will change my plans for this expedition drastically. . . .

"We shall not go up to Oregon so soon as I had planned."

There was some muttering, but it subsided quickly. Kern caught Stone's eye and smiled knowingly. It struck Stone that there must indeed have been something quite out of the ordinary in that dispatch case. Ordinarily, the Frémont he had come to know would have bridled at any interference from any quarter with his plans, and he would normally have kept to his tent in that fine dudgeon Stone had seen before.

The captain readied himself to speak again after a sharp glance at Stone, who bent to the pad he had extracted from the case.

"Be very painstaking, Mr. Stone. Your report will go directly from Bent's to Washington—straight to the desk of President Polk himself."

Stone looked up at that. Frémont smiled at the effect of his words. "Do not despair, Mr. Stone. You'll have time to revise your notes tomorrow. You can take the entire day." He turned to the others. "We shall leave Pilot Peak the day after tomorrow. I am splitting the expedition into two sections. One party, much the larger of the two, will follow the Humboldt River to what I named the Carson Sink in '43. The other will proceed straight west to the lake Mr. Carson, Mr. Walker, and I found and mapped last year. The two sections will rendezvous there, but only for a day or two."

Frémont looked across the fire. His eyes had suddenly narrowed and some of the gleam had faded. Stone turned and saw that Kit had appeared at the outer edge of the circle of light. The Pathfinder kept his eyes on the scout for several seconds, and then went on.

"Both parties will map as they go, of course, since there is still much work of that nature to be done here in the Great Basin. The one heading straight for the lake will arrive there first. After the two parties exchange their information they will go their separate ways. The Humboldt River detachment will head south, seeking the lower passes farther down the Sierra Nevada and crossing into California at about the level of the Lake Fork of the Tulare."

This last bit of news obviously came as a surprise to every one of his listeners. Well, Ed Kern did not look quite as surprised as the rest.

Frémont continued, gaining speed and assertiveness. "They will be taking with them all of the heavy equipment: the wagons, oxen, and the howitzers, all the mules except two—which I will take with my party to transport surveying and mapping gear—and most of the provisions and supplies. The smaller group will travel light, each man trailing only one packhorse. They will strike out swiftly for the North- west, cross the mountains before the first snowfall, presum- ing it can make good time, and follow the American River down to Sutter's Fort. This detachment will refit and resup- ply at the fort, and then move south again to meet the Hum- boldt River party. That should occur by the end of January. Only then will we move on to Oregon.

"Now . . . as to the makeup of the two sections . . ."

Stone could make a pretty good guess about one or two features of the "makeup" even before Frémont said another word. First, he would find himself consigned to the larger, slower-moving unit, buried in it, the only consolation being that he might be able to map a new, southern route into Cal- ifornia. And Frémont would lead the team making the more challenging journey to the Northwest—with Ed Kern as *his* topographer.

Worse yet, Frémont would also take Kit with him.

Frémont continued. "Mr. Talbot will command the Hum- boldt River explorations, with Mr. Kern as his topographer. Joe Walker will serve as chief scout for Mr. Talbot. I will lead the smaller party myself, with Mr. Carson scouting for me. I will also take with me Alexis Godey, Dick Owens, Lucien Maxwell, Segundai, and six or seven of his Dela- wares, and of course Basil Lajeunesse, if the old brute thinks he can stand the pace. It will be the more arduous journey of the two. Basil?"

"I would not let you go without Basil, Captain!" La- jeunesse roared. "I can stand any pace you and Kit can set!"

There came a round of good-natured laughter at the huge bear's earnest protest.

"I think you've just remembered how well Captain Sutter feeds his guests," Frémont said. He turned to Stone. "Pay close attention to what I say next, Mr. Stone." He looked out over the assemblage. "Mr. Kern, where are you?"

"Here, sir."

"When Mr. Stone does his final draft of this report and signs it, I would appreciate it if you would witness it." He fell silent for a moment, then, "Now we come to the very heart of this meeting. . . . Bear in mind that ours is a mission of peace. I want that clearly understood by every man in this command. Both parties will be entering the territory of another sovereign nation—Mexico. We will be guests in California, and we must remember that every single moment we are there. Under no conditions are we to seek conflict with the native Californios. We will not reply with a show of force to any real or imagined provocation. Is that clear?"

Dead silence covered the gathering until someone at the rear spoke up. "It ain't quite clear to *me*, Captain!" Joe Walker had gotten to his feet.

"What is your problem with these instructions, Mr. Walker?"

"Well . . . last I heard, things ain't exactly peaceful in California. In the north there's a whole passel of Californios who been riled at their government for years. When we was there last year, if the captain remembers, there were already two or three little ruckuses underway. Mostly it was talk, I guess, but going in way to the south the way Ed Kern, Mr. Talbot, and me will be going, we could get caught in a nasty little cross fire if talk turns to something more serious—both sides thinking we was with the other. Them howitzers won't look too damned peaceful to Mexican lancers, I can tell you. Not only that, but even if the Californios have patched up all their local squabbles, I hear tell the U.S. of A. could be at war with Mexico easy by the time we get there. You could change your mind about how peaceful we was to behave without word ever reaching us, Captain. We could be riding smack into a battle we didn't even know we was all of a sudden supposed to fight. You mean to tell me that we ain't allowed to shoot back if somebody starts to shoot at *us?*"

"Your orders are that you are not to fight, Mr. Walker. Make sure you got that, Mr. Stone."

A buzz of conversation came from the Pathfinder's listeners and he stiffened. He looked down and spoke to Stone again. "You may stop taking notes now, Mr. Stone. Anything else said here tonight will be strictly off the record." He looked out at Walker and the others. "I do expect anyone under my command to demonstrate initiative in a crisis, but your *official* orders at this time forbid your engaging in combat with . . . *any person or persons you encounter.*"

"Does that go for Indians, too, Captain?" Walker said. "The western slope of the Sierras is thick with some pretty testy red varmints, in particular them mission renegades the Californios call the Horsethieves."

"You *are* permitted to defend yourself against attacks from savages. The Mexican government and the native Californians will welcome help with stopping the Horsethieves' depredations, I am fully confident. I am sure the American settlers now living in California will feel that way, too."

"Well, that makes things a mite more reasonable," Walker said. "But I got to be honest with you, Captain. It don't satisfy me all that much. I got half a mind to hightail it back to Bent's and look for other work."

An ominous silence fell.

Then, to Stone's astonishment, Frémont smiled as if he had just remembered something, or as if he had just been awarded a prize and was now ready to claim it.

"Mr. Carson!"

Every eye turned to Kit.

"Yes, Captain Frémont?"

"Will *you* have any difficulty following my orders?"

Not even half a second went by before Kit answered.

"Never had, Captain. Don't expect I ever will."

"Thank you. Now, gentlemen, you are all dismissed."

The mountain men and Talbot, Kern, and Carson—deep in conversation with Joe Walker—drifted out of sight. Stone stayed behind. Frémont looked a question at him.

"May I have one word, Captain?" Stone asked.

"What is it, Stone?" No "Mr." this time.

"You did not assign me to either team, sir."

"No, I did not. I will inform you of my decision late tomorrow. That will be all, Stone."

Back at their bedrolls, Stone let Kern read Jake Myers' letter.

"I'm not sure whether this will help or hurt you in the long run," Kern said, "but it does explain why Johnny had you write that report instead of Talbot. You're the 'objective observer' he feels he has to have. Ted's an old protégé of Senator Benton's and everyone in Washington is aware of that."

Stone worked on the report by firelight half the night.

5

"Is that contrived apologia for our commander ready for me to witness?" Kern asked the following afternoon when he found Stone putting the finishing touches to his report of the meeting.

"Just a second. I'm almost done."

"Take your time. I'm not going to read every word. At that, the pen might jump out of my hand when I try to sign the damned thing. No matter how honest you've tried to be, it's bound to be an extraordinary piece of fiction."

"You're a consummate cynic, Ed."

"He's using you, Brad. He's using me, too, but he's really wearing *you* out."

"How so?"

"It should not have escaped you that this piece of self-puffery is intended as much for the eyes of Congressman Myers, his House Foreign Relations Committee, and people who read newspapers, as it is for President Polk. Benton needs favorable public opinion and he needs Myers' influence in the House."

"How can a private report to the president sway the public?"

"I doubt if the president himself will ever read your report. Secretary of the Navy Bancroft will. If war breaks out it will be the navy that runs the show in California. Bancroft will see that the press gets a copy. Myers, too. Carrying your signature it will go some distance in persuading Myers that Johnny is making some decent use of you, but mostly Captain Johnny is covering himself. Count your blessings. I have a notion our captain is going to treat you a whole hell of a lot better from here on out."

"Maybe."

"Count on it. He'll need you even more now that you've made him look like some kind of diplomat. By the by, that was an interesting performance last night. It was a stroke of genius on Captain Johnny's part to ask Kit that question. His answer took the wind right out of Joe Walker's sails."

"That at least didn't surprise me. Walker relies on Kit's judgment more than any man in the expedition does except Dick Owens. But dissembling? You think Frémont was lying?"

"'Lying' is pretty strong," Kern said. "He did flirt with falsehood a little, but I have come to expect that from our captain. He talked a lot about peace, but I'd bet my last dollar he went right into that tent afterward and hung his lantern up where he could study those army tactical manuals."

"You don't like him much, do you?"

"Actually, I do, most of the time. He's an engaging, cosmopolitan man, erudite, and with an encyclopedic memory. My only trouble with him is the way he swings from high to low in his moods. When he's in a high frame of mind I doubt if there's a finer companion in the West. When he's depressed it's all I can do to keep from running from him. It can be like a ride on a scenic railway. I blow hot and cold about him. I'm kind of glad I'm going with Talbot. Which party has he assigned you to?"

"He hasn't told me yet," Stone said. "I expect he'll send me south with you, just to get me out of his sight."

"Maybe. I'm not surprised he's taking Carson, though. With our numbers, and trailing those howitzers that suddenly worry Joe, we've been pretty safe from Indian attacks so far, but the party heading for Sutter's is small enough it could be asking for trouble. He'll sure as hell need Kit then. You noticed that he's taking along the best fighters in the expedition."

"Yes." Stone signed the report and handed it to Kern, who leafed through all seven pages. When he finished, he took the pen from Stone's hand. "You're good at this, too. Johnny couldn't have gotten more of what he wanted if he'd written this himself. I wonder . . ." He broke off, and then affixed his signature to the bottom of the last page.

Frémont suddenly loomed in front of them. Stone wondered if he had heard Kern's last remark.

"May I see that, Mr. Kern?" Frémont said.

Kern handed him the report and the captain looked at Stone. "Come to my tent in half an hour to discuss this, Stone."

As Frémont walked off, Kern shook his head. "Yes, I guess he'll still be a tough nut for you to crack, no matter what Benton and Myers told him in their letter." He paused, then went on. "I'm not one to give a lot of advice, my friend, but there is something more I want to say. I know you came

west to map the country, but you have more important work
to do than mapping before you head back East."

"What? Writing more reports for our captain?"

"No. I'm talking about your painting. I've seen your
sketches. If your oils come anywhere near that level, you'll
someday be regarded as one of the most important graphic
chroniclers the West has known."

6

He found Frémont perched on a campstool in front of his
tent, still reading the report. At last the captain looked up.

"This is fine work. You have a talent for this sort of thing.
You must do more of it for me."

"Thank you, sir. May I inquire of the captain . . ."

"Yes, Stone?"

"Nothing, sir. It wasn't important. Will that be all?"

He had never seen Frémont's eyes more piercing. "Not
quite. We have one more matter to settle." Frémont smiled.
"Would you like"—Frémont said then—"to make the trek to
Sutter's along with Kit and me?"

7

By the time the evening meal ended, the euphoria brought
on by Frémont's invitation to join him and Kit had almost
driven from his mind something he needed to do—finish the
letter to Ana he had begun on the shores of the Great Salt
Lake. Back then there had been no hurry for either the letter
to Ana or the one to his parents that Jake Myers now more
or less demanded. He thought at that time that he might have
to wait until they reached Oregon, and find a packet vessel
that served a West Coast port, and send them off from there.

But Charlie Bent's courier would be returning to the fort on the Arkansas in the morning at about the same time the two sections of the expedition left Pilot Peak. The letter to his parents could go in the next post from there to Independence and the East. As for Ana's, the Bent brothers regularly sent mail on down to Santa Fe, and sometimes directly down the Sangre de Cristo forest trails to Taos. Charlie might even be traveling between the fort and his home himself and would deliver his letter by hand to Josefa Carson. With luck Ana could be reading it by Christmas Day.

Frémont had called another meeting, this time exclusively for the members of the Humboldt River party; and with Ed Kern attending it, the area around the fire they shared was deserted.

He built the fire to a happy blaze to give him light to write by, and settled beside it with his pad and pencil.

Beginning the letter at the lake had proven difficult enough; finishing it here at Pilot Peak did not promise to be easier. Although he had improved what little Spanish he had picked up from Kit by stumbling through conversations with Tomás Luna, one of the Mexican teamsters in the expedition, he had to compose the thoughts he would send to Ana in his own language. It put severe constraints on what he could say to her. She might even have to have someone read it to her, perhaps Charlie Bent, Ceran St. Vrain, or that taciturn fellow Turley who had been at Josefa Carson's dinner.

He would just have to rely on Ana reading between the lines.

How he missed her!

All he could do in his letter was to recount the events of his journey with Carson and Frémont. When he reached that part of his chronicle telling her of the horrible two days with the fevered, dying Utes here on Pilot Peak, he shaded the truth about the experience a little, only hinting at the horrors he, Kit, Lajeunesse, and the others had witnessed in that two-day, despairing fight against the disease.

But he found he could not refrain from telling her about the death of the Ute girl who bore her such a striking resemblance.

He had written about half of the account of the girl's death in his arms when someone spoke, startling him.

"I'm sure glad as all get-out that you'll be riding out with me and the captain tomorrow, *amigo*." Kit had come up behind him unseen. Now the scout stepped out of the darkness into the firelight. He glanced down at the pad in Stone's lap. "I reckon I don't have to guess who you're writing to, do I?"

"I thought I'd send it off to Ana in the morning, by way of Charlie's courier."

"Good idea. Be a hell of a long time before we get another chance to send any word to the folk back home, either of us."

"How about you, Kit? Do you want to send a note to Mrs. Carson? I've got plenty of paper here."

"I guess you don't know."

"What?"

Kit stared into the fire. "I can't write a lick. Can't read, either. All I can do is kind of scratch my name, and I only learned to do that since I met the captain. Most of my life all I could do was make my mark."

Brad looked away. It had never occurred to him that a man who possessed in so many ways a truly formidable intellect could neither read nor write.

What difference did it really make out here?

A Hawken gun, a mustang, a wild deer, or a Comanche did not give two hoots in hell if a man turned out to be illiterate.

"Would you like me to write a letter to Josefa *for* you?" he said at length.

A smile wreathed Carson's face.

"I'd appreciate it a lot, *amigo*," he said.

Writing Kit's letter presented much the same problem as the one he had almost finished composing for Ana.

At first he half expected to be embarrassed, writing Kit's letter, a husband writing to a wife.

But he need not have worried.

Poor Kit labored under the same difficulties Stone had faced himself. Writing it in English meant someone would have to translate for Carson's lady as they would for Ana.

But an embarrassment did arise halfway through Kit's dictation.

> ". . . and now I got to say a few words about my young friend Brad Stone. You already know about how he helped Luis and me fight them Comanches on the Cimarron. He has done even better since we left Charlie's fort on the Ark. He's now come close to being a real mountain man. The way he helped with them poor, sick Utes had to be seen to be believed. He never complains, even when things is going bad. If Dōna Ana Barragán ain't settled on Luis, she could do a lot worse than my friend Brad, and you can tell her so for me. He's among the finest men I ever met, and that takes in our old *amigo* Dick Owens, who also sends his—"

"Kit!" Stone broke in. "I can't write *that!*"

"Why not? It's the gospel truth."

"People other than Josefa will read this. They'll know I wrote it for you, won't they? It would make me look a self-serving, conceited fool."

"Put it in."

Stone managed a feeble, imploring grin. "Suppose I just

tell you I put it in—and then didn't. You wouldn't even know until you . . . we . . . got back to Taos—if then."

"If you tell me you put it in, I'll know you did. I trust you, Brad."

"But . . ."

"Put it in."

It seemed as if only moments intervened between the time Stone closed his eyes in sleep and Carson's cry of *"Time to catch up!"* echoed through the camp on Pilot Peak.

The ride to the High Sierras and Sutter's Fort got under way.

17

The Crossing

"California!" Kit shouted.

He pointed down a long valley still amazingly lush and verdant for this late in the year. At this first sight of it, Stone wondered if winter ever really visited this land. It looked from this high pass as if the growing season here was twelve months long.

Back in Illinois the fields would now be lying fallow, sere and brown, if they were not already buried under a foot of snow, and with only brittle, skeletal cornstalks poking above the drifts here and there and the maples and elms in the forests bordering the pastures all stripped naked. The trees in the valley below him were all evergreens, it appeared from here, even the towering oak hardwoods in the river bottom.

He had seen snow in the last week, but all of it capped only the higher peaks of the Sierras. The trails had been remarkably clear for December, by the accounts of Carson and the older hands in Frémont's small party, accounts based on memories of a score of other winters in the mountains. The bulk of the expected snow had not yet fallen, and the pathway to and through the high passes of the Sierras had been bare and dry almost every mile since the Sutter's Fort section of the expedition started up the eastern slope.

The Sierra crossing had not been all that easy, though. The division of supplies had left the smaller party well fixed for staples such as corn, beans, coffee, and salt, but meat of any kind had begun to run out just a few days after Frémont's group left Talbot, Kern, Walker, and the others' party on the shores of what the Pathfinder named Walker Lake.

Lajeunesse, Maxwell, and Archambeault had dried huge amounts of the meat Carson had brought into the camp at Pilot Peak, but not all of it. Great piles of the carcasses of antelope and deer were left rotting in the sun the day the expedition's two sections rumbled down into the flats and struck out for the lake by their different routes.

At the lake, when the two parties made their last rendezvous before moving on to California, Frémont decided that almost all of the dried or salt-cured venison would go with Talbot's much larger section when it headed south. "They have vehicles to carry it," he said. "My party doesn't. It cannot burden itself with luxuries," he said.

Stone failed to see how the sinewy, scaly slabs of dried deer, elk, and antelope hauled to the lake from Pilot Peak could possibly be called "luxuries." Some of the chunks and strips already showed signs of mold, although the greenish white growth had done nothing to suppress the appetite of Basil Lajeunesse, who greeted the captain's new order with a sigh and groan. The big former trapper would never criticize Frémont any more than Kit would, but his wistful look spoke volumes. "We won't find much game in them mountains up ahead, not with everything so dry," he said.

Since their shared experience during the Utes' ordeal with the spotted fever, Stone had grown close to Lajeunesse, close enough to feel comfortable calling him "Bass" as Carson and the others did.

The French Canadian must have tipped the scales at something over twenty stone; his ready smile, and genuine good nature and concern for everyone, convinced Stone that ninety percent of that great weight consisted of heart.

And when Basil smiled, everybody smiled. Frémont himself seemed friendlier, more outgoing, and fairly overflowing with good cheer whenever he spent any length of time in Lajeunesse's company. At times the mere presence of the giant seemed able to lift the captain out of the troughs Ed Kern had depicted.

2

One moonless night when they camped on the desert between Pilot Peak and the lake, an ancient Digger Indian woman burst into the light of their fire like a demonic wraith, long white hair streaming behind her, her pitifully thin arms flailing like the blades of a windmill.

A few of the party were still at supper, but most of the mountain men had already climbed into their bedrolls. It seemed impossible that the intruder could have slipped past the night guard undetected, but somehow she had.

Naked to the waist, her sagging, leathery breasts flapping, and wearing a shredded buckskin kirtle, she looked around her crazily, and then screeched the sleepers in the entire camp to wide-eyed wakefulness, even bringing Frémont on the run from his tent.

Only Carson understood her. "She says her people turned her out to die on account of she can't even find bugs to feed herself no more," the scout said when she calmed a little.

"She's going blind, and when she saw our fire, she thought we was Diggers, too, and she came in here to beg us to take her back. It scared all hell out of her when she saw what she'd stumbled into. We're maybe the first white men she's ever seen. Says she ain't eaten in five or six days; she really can't remember the last time."

The cold that clamps the desert in minutes after the sun goes down had been particularly penetrating that November night, and the old woman shook and shivered uncontrollably. Lajeunesse stepped toward her quickly, holding the buffalo robe he covered himself with at night, and although she shrank from him in terror, he draped it around her shoulders with as much tenderness as a doting mother might wrap a child. She turned a toothless smile on him, but her eyes remained twin white pools of fear. The giant former trapper went to the fire then, drew his long skinning knife, and hacked apart most of a joint of venison, from a spit that one of the Delawares had still been turning when the old woman exploded on them. The Delaware put out his hand, but drew it back at a look from Lajeunesse that could have cracked stone. The mountain man turned from the fire with the meat and held it out to her.

From the look of the joint, Stone judged it to be the better part of fifteen pounds. Surely this hunger-weakened old woman would collapse under the weight of it if she tried to take it from him. Amazingly, the spindly arms did not even droop when Basil laid it in them. She clutched it to her withered bosom as if it were a baby, and sizzling juice streamed down her belly. Surely that hot meat would raise hideous blisters on the naked chest! She did not wince.

Then she turned on her unshod feet and raced into the desert night.

Frémont had watched the whole bizarre affair in such utter silence Stone had forgotten he was there. Now he shouted, "After her, Bass! Bring her back. She can trail along with us until we find a band of Diggers, or some other Indians who will take her in."

For ten minutes the sound of Lajeunesse crashing through the yucca and sagebrush in the pitch black desért beyond the fire's beams sounded like a heavily loaded freight train receding in the distance. Gradually the noise diminished, while Stone looked at Frémont and pondered the real character of a man who could send sick Indians off to near starvation with a casual wave of his gloved hand, and then, in less than a week, make room for a superannuated derelict who had not long to live by any reckoning. Stone came to the conclusion that Bass's abiding attributes of human decency must be a sight more contagious than any spotted fever.

Sometime during the night Lajeunesse returned to the camp for his horse and then disappeared again. They saw no sign of him until they were on the march in the morning.

"Never found a trace of the poor old ugly critter," Lajeunesse said as he wedged his mount between those of Stone and Carson, "and I ain't the worst tracker in this outfit. Even half blind she knows her way in this desert a hell of lot better than I ever will. She'll die in some arroyo soon, if I'm any judge, and if she don't just dry up and blow away, the buzzards will get whatever's left of her."

3

As Ed Kern had predicted, there now seemed little question that things had taken an upward turn in at least the working relationship between Frémont and Brad Stone.

The route Frémont had laid out since the expedition left the Great Salt Lake—to Pilot Peak, Walker Lake, and then to near the foothills of the Sierra Nevada—had been first suggested by a man named Lansford Hastings as an alternative to the northwestern route generally known as the Oregon Trail. But there existed no reliable maps of the Great Basin west of the Salt Lake itself, the stretch consisting mostly of desert and alkali flats, with a faint trace now beginning to be called the Hastings Cutoff. To Stone's knowledge none had even been made by Frémont in his two earlier topographical expeditions, or at least no good ones.

"You and I will plot a new, easier pathway for the stream of our compatriots, the American emigrants who will come to settle the Great Northwest, and the principal burden of the work will fall on you, Bradford," the captain said the day they left Walker Lake. "Your skills," Frémont went on, "and the new techniques you studied under Professor what's-his-name at Harvard, will be eminently suitable for this undertaking."

It amused Stone that Frémont could so subtly dismiss his old professor. The captain knew Wendell Strike's name as well as he did his own; no professional in the country could have remained totally ignorant of the esteemed Harvardian.

Stone's mapping duties began in earnest the second day out from Walker Lake. He and Frémont still did not work in tandem, and while Stone would have liked to observe the Pathfinder in the field, doing things on his own as he had been trained to do brought him great personal satisfaction.

He would rise long before any of the others—save Carson, of course—when his surveys actively engaged him, gather his crew and the scout assigned to guard him as he worked, and ride out well ahead of Frémont and the rest of the party. During the day the party would pass him, hooting and hollering from a distance. As dusk fell he would finish the day's chores and rejoin them at the forward camp. It worked well. It reminded him of Carson's sending one man ahead with the horses and mules, while the rest of them walked, that night they made the desert crossing between the Salt Lake and Pilot Peak. He missed those mules, though.

Frémont's gear already overburdened the two the party had taken with it. His packhorse turned balky most mornings when he loaded it with some of Frémont's equipment in addition to his own.

The captain assigned Alexis Godey to assist and guard him. It came as an initial disappointment—Stone had hoped for Kit, or failing him, Lajeunesse—but he had to admit that in this particular, the Pathfinder knew what he was doing.

Stone had not gotten to know Alexis Godey well since they met at Bent's, even though they had been thrown together some on the night trip to Pilot Peak and in the two days they had all worked among the Utes.

Godey's handsome appearance set him completely aside from the other mountain men. Dark, slim, not as tall as Stone, graceful and athletic when he moved, he trimmed his hair and beard regularly. Stone suspected he was the only member of the party aside from Kit, the captain, and himself who owned a mirror. His speech seemed exquisitely refined when contrasted with the coarse oaths and often nearly animal sounds his fellows directed at him, a lot of it dealing with Alexis's reputed dalliances with Indian women over the years.

But Frémont had not assigned Alexis to Stone on the basis of his looks alone.

Unlike Carson and Lajeunesse, Godey could read and write. He also possessed a smattering of mathematics or at least arithmetic, could handle long division, and had a fair acquaintance with the decimal system. He took meticulous notes for Stone and followed instructions to the letter.

They got along well, made good if inconsequential talk during breaks in the work and during the brief lunches Stone permitted in the first two days they spent in the field together. Alexis, he discovered, was midway between Kit and him in age, and twenty years younger than Lajeunesse. He had a lively mind and a facile, fluent tongue. He resembled Ed Kern a bit in that regard, and many of this younger, very untypical mountain man's comments put Stone in mind of Kern's often comical irreverence. Godey's cynicism differed from that of Kern in one important respect, however. He almost idolized John C. Frémont. Stone decided the captain *needed* Carson, Lajeunesse, and Godey in the circumscribed internal world in which he found himself.

Godey hailed from St. Louis. On their third day together he surprised Stone when he revealed that he not only had spent time with Frémont in his home city, but was acquainted with Jessie and her father. He had even attended the opera with them and had dined with them at the old Frontenac. Stone could easily picture his new assistant in evening dress.

"Jessie Frémont is not only a beautiful lady," Alexis confided, "but she's one of the smartest people I've ever met, even smarter than her husband or the senator, and that's saying something."

Learning about Godey's close connection to the Frémonts and Benton, it now pleased Stone about the St. Louisan no end that never once on the trek had this unusual mountain man—fur trapper, *coureur du bois*, or whatever he chose to call himself—ever presumed on his special relationship with the Pathfinder and his family.

"What brought you west, Alexis?" he asked one noon after Carson, Frémont, and the party passed their mapping site.

"I thought I had a chance to make a fortune in the fur trade. But just when it seemed to be working out for me, the trade died."

"What kept you here?"

"Adventure. Excitement. Mostly it was being with men like Kit and Captain Frémont."

"Will you stay out here when this present expedition finishes its work?"

"Don't think so. I'm still a city man. Before my blood slows down too much I'll head back to the banks of the Mississippi." He raised a knowing eyebrow. "From what the others say, I'm sure you already know how much I like women. Mostly city women. And I like them for more than what a man usually likes them for. But I confess I've done a little thinking about meeting Californio ladies ever since Bent's, when I found out we will go as far south as Monterey. I am not in a *hurry* to get back to St. Louis, you understand."

As far south as Monterey? How did Godey know this? Monterey was even farther south than Sutter's, and on the coast. There could be no real need to make maps there. There could only be one source for Godey's early knowledge of such a move—Frémont himself. The captain must all along have intended exploring a lot more of California than he had maintained at the outset. But even so, there had been no mention of Monterey.

4

Stone gave his commander high marks for one thing; he made some significant additions to the rough-draft maps Stone turned in to him every night. If a mountain man or a Delaware in the party made a discovery of a terrain feature that seemed important as a landmark on this new route to Oregon, he would eventually be able to find his name on the maps when they were published. It had apparently been Frémont's practice in his two earlier expeditions, and he continued it on this one. Carson Sink on the Humboldt River followed Walker Lake. Segundai Spring came a day north of the lake when the Delaware tracker chief, ranging far ahead of the party, found water just when canteens and water skins were showing signs of running low. Under the captain's eye Stone penciled in a Basil Lake, a Crane Creek, another lake named for Dick Owens, and . . . a Stone Mountain, even though five others in the group had sighted the lone mountain east of and well apart from the principal massifs of the Sierras at precisely the same moment he did.

But Frémont's habit of bestowing names the way Napoléon had liberally distributed his storied leather medals on campaign—often for something no more meritorious than keeping a musket clean—did do a little something for morale at a time when it was beginning to need a boost.

The farther up the eastern slope they climbed the scarcer became the game. Because of the dry weather the herds had deserted the high pastures even earlier in the year than usual. The party would not starve if it could cross the pass Kit described before snow clogged it, and that now seemed probable. Ample supplies of beans and cracked corn still remained in the saddlebags, but the men grumbled at every meal at the absence of meat. Although the daytime temperatures rose to the sixties, the thermometer plunged most of the way to zero every night; the ponds and most of the streams remained frozen tight even in the noonday sun, making fishing an impossibility. They might have chopped holes in the ice to run down a line, but Frémont kept them moving too steadily for the time that would require.

"When we cross the pass I will ride without stopping all the way to Sutter's," Lajeunesse said at dinner one night. "Captain Sutter will feed us real, grass-fed beef when we get there. I will eat a whole fat cow myself, hide, tail, udder, teats, and all." Stone believed him.

"We can't kill and eat a horse," Kit said. "We need every one of them to get us over the pass and down to Sutter's. It's a fair ride yet. And we need both mules. You mapping gents sure tote a lot of heavy stuff."

Lajeunesse was not the only one anxious to reach the fort of the famous Swiss. The cry of *"When we get to Sutter's . . ."* and the talk of the feasts they would find there,

became a universal litany among the men as the remaining
food dwindled and stomachs growled.

Lucien Maxwell complained louder than any of the rest.

"I just plain get sick," he said one night at dinner, "when
I think about all them good vittles rotting away back on Pilot
Peak. What's more, no fur-brigade leader would never have
sent all the dried stuff off with Talbot and the other team,
either. I just can't see Captain Johnny being the great commander he's cracked up to be."

5

The summits that loomed above Stone now were loftier by
far than the Spanish Peaks northwest of Raton Pass on that
first trip to Taos with Kit, and as high as anything he had
seen when they breached the Rockies above the Arkansas.
The desert scrub gave way to thick stands of piñon, which in
turn yielded to stunted pine and fir on the northern sides of
the valleys they rode through. The slopes opposite, shielded
from the direct sun every day of the year except those just
before and after the summer solstice, and consequently able
to hold moisture better, sprouted larger trees, taller and
heavier by far than anything he had ever seen before. If any
one of the giants they passed were run through a sawmill, he
figured, it would produce enough board feet of lumber to
frame and side the mayor's big white house in Groverton.

Although the year was well along, wildflowers in abundance decorated the trailside, an astonishing number of them
still in bloom. Frémont seemed to know every one of them,
and took great delight in trilling their Latin pedigrees off his
tongue.

They passed three Indian villages, two deserted ones
tucked away in the forest, a third only a quarter of a mile off
the trail in a grassy timberline meadow with a thin stream

running through it, and where smoke shrouded stick, bark, and skin huts.

"They've moved down the valleys to stay as close to the game as they can," Kit said. "This one will get under way like the other two right quick. Even though there's been no snow to speak of, it probably will be a long, hungry winter."

Silent Indian men, women, and children stared vacantly at them. None of the inhabitants, who also appeared to be dressed in bark and skins, approached, hailed them, or so much as waved.

"Are we in any danger, Kit?" Stone asked as he pulled his Hawken from the saddle holster after seeing the scout do the same.

"Don't think so. We must look pretty fearsome to them. This is probably a pretty peaceful tribe, anyways. They sure don't look much like Blackfeet or Flatheads. I reckon they live this high in the mountains most of the year just to stay out of the reach of their neighbors down in the desert. Still, a man can't be too careful. That's why we ride with our weapons loaded."

Lucien Maxwell rode next to Stone and Kit that day. "I smell meat in that smoke, Kit," he said. "Won't the captain let us take half an hour off the trail to at least see if we can barter?"

"You can ask him, Lucy," Kit said. "I sure wouldn't. You been out with him before, and you know how fierce he is when he's hell-bent on getting someplace."

Maxwell did not ask, and they did not stop.

They did find meat of a sort when they rode through a rocky defile near the top of the pass.

Perched on a stone shelf no more than thirty feet off the trail, they found a row of squirrel-like animals, but each a yard in height, much larger than any squirrels Stone had ever seen. They sat as upright as fence posts, their front paws curled on their chests as if they were resting them on a rail, looking for all the world like little old men sitting on the porch of a country store and surveying the passing scene. They gazed at the column with more curiosity than the Indians in the smoky village had shown, but they did not blink, twitch, or stir.

"Marmots," Kit said.

"Why don't they run?" Stone asked. "Aren't they afraid?"

"No. I think the little varmints know how awful they taste. They think that puts them right smack in God's hip pocket. Well, with the way things are going for us for meat, they sure got a surprise in store for them today." He unlimbered his Hawken. "Bass!" he called. "Just watch," he said to Stone. "This will be mighty interesting, I expect."

They shot seven of the stolid little creatures. None of them moved or tried to run as Kit and Basil fired and reloaded and picked them off one by one.

"Never shot marmot before," Basil said to Stone as they dismounted to collect the kill. "It is like the first time I met Assiniboine up in Manitoba when I was just a young one. I had never seen Assiniboine before and they had never seen white men, I guess. I was all alone, and I tethered my horses and walked down a steep slope to a stream about two hundred yards away to lay out a line of traps. Lucky for me I took my rifle with me. Three of them red killers came out of nowheres and tried to steal my whole damned outfit, and I ran up toward them yelling like a banshee."

"You were all alone and you went after them—yelling?" Stone asked.

"Why not? Man can't let himself get robbed. I just wanted to scare them off. I didn't. They started shooting arrows at me, but they was too far out of range to do them any good. I stopped and plugged one and the other two just stood there. I reloaded and thought about it a bit. Then I brought down another. I guess they'd never seen a firearm in action and they couldn't dope out that it was my rifle doing something to them. I could have taken all day to reload again and get the last one. He stayed as planted as a post until I got him, too. . . ."

"I wouldn't count on that with Assiniboine nowadays," Kit said. "They've learned all about rifles over the years since then."

Stone shuddered. What had Kit said about him in his letter to Josefa? "He's now come close to being a real mountain man." Not close enough, he decided.

In their last camp on the eastern side of the pass that night, Stone came to the conclusion that shooting the marmots had not been worth the bullets. The little animals looked pathetically small without their pelts, and chewing the tough, rubbery chunk Basil handed him made him queasy. The meat smelled foul and tasted worse.

Midway through the meal Lucien Maxwell jumped to his feet. "God*damn* Frémont!" He hurled a chunk of gristly meat into the fire and loosed a heavy gob of viscous brown spit in its wake, where it hissed as if echoing his angry outburst.

6

The crossing over the summit of the pass and the descent through the tawny, sunlit canyons of the western slope pulled aside a curtain to reveal a whole new world.

Once they dipped below the rocky heights, vistas of pure emerald stretched away ahead of the column and on either side of it. The party made its way down through switchbacks so severe and sharp that Stone's eyes were often level with the stirrups and boots of the riders at the party's rear, still on the tier above him. Great waterfalls leaped from the deep Vs between the snowcapped peaks, vaulting from ledge to ledge to crash into unseen rivers deep in the shadowed canyons. They rode so close to one of the more turbulent cascades the sound of the roaring water deafened him. Some of the falls—those with the smaller flow—fell from such staggering heights the water turned to mist that even in the lightest of winds drifted down the canyons before it reached the river bottoms.

Stone mused that this spectacle of beauty must be old-hat to the men he rode with, but the party moved along in such complete silence he began to wonder if it affected their case-hardened hearts as well.

He wished with all his heart that Ana Barragán could be riding these magic valleys with him.

Once they stopped to eat at a bend where the trail made a sweeping curve around a mountain shoulder. The vantage point overlooked the greenest valley he had ever seen.

It was not the first time he had come to a high place with Kit and looked down at a land that made promises.

"California," Kit said again.

18

The Guardian

On the American River
December 10, 1845

They camped in a bend of the American about four miles north of Sutter's Fort. Long, sweet grasses carpeted the grove Frémont selected for their bivouac area, and enormous long-acorn oaks—which Stone had seen from the high trail yesterday and which had become more plentiful with every hundred-foot drop in elevation—arched their branches over them, creating a cathedral-like vault of deep, shadowed green.

Darkness fell half an hour after they settled in, taking away any chance of making a hunt, even for the myriad squirrels they had seen during the last few hours of the ride. With the prospect of making contact with the fort the very next morning, no one complained, not even that perennial grouch, Lucien Maxwell.

Some of the mountain men who had traveled to California before with Frémont set about gathering the long acorns that littered the ground. Dick Owens kindled a small fire and when it had died to embers the men heaped their acorns into the glowing coals.

"They're pretty good eating when they're roasted," Kit said. "Try one, Brad."

He found they were delicious.

"This California is full of such wonders," Frémont said. "It only needs the Americans who will soon be on their way here to exploit its riches."

2

The next morning at ten Frémont called the entire party together.

"I am leaving shortly to pay our first call on Captain Sutter. I shall take Mr. Carson, Mr. Stone, and Mr. Maxwell with me. The rest of you will remain in camp—no hunting, no shooting. But be ready to ride. So soon as I receive Sutter's invitation to the fort, I shall send Mr. Maxwell back to bring you all along. This may yet prove to be an historic day."

A great cheer rose from men who but two nights earlier

would not have cheered the Second Coming unless it promised several sides of beef.

"Meat!" Lajeunesse called out. "Meat at last."

"I should expect so, Bass," Frémont said. "All the meat even you can eat."

If the men were of sudden good cheer, their spirits reflected only palely the soaring mood of Brevet Captain John C. Frémont. He had dressed in the white buckskin outfit he had worn when he rode into the Ute village on Pilot Peak, and he now had Gus Archambeault saddle and trot out the stallion Sacramento for him. He quite literally leaped on the spirited horse's back, lifted the hat with the eagle feather, and waved it like a cavalier.

The four of them rode through country that rolled gently away from the meadows at the riverbank and lifted into small, grassy, friendly hills. Frémont in the lead set a lively pace, but one not so rapid that Stone was unable to take in the pastoral look of the tilled and well-tended fields they presently passed. These stretches had all the civilized, settled aspect of Massachusetts farmlands, and a much more cared for, finished appearance than the ones that surrounded Taos.

They rode past several acres of vineyards whose extent he could not determine since they rolled out of sight over the crest of one of the rounded hills. Pickers had long since relieved the vines of their fruit, and here and there they showed the marks of recent pruning. At the southern end of the vineyard a huge stone winery, snugged against the flank of the hill behind it and seeming almost a part of it, filled the morning air with the sharp aroma of fermenting grapes.

South of the winery, a fenced section of grassland held a herd of cows, black, tan, white, and mixes of all three, placid creatures with pendulous udders and teats like sausages. These were not the beef cattle Lajeunesse was probably fantasizing about back at camp at this very instant, but dairy

animals—Mexican breeds Stone guessed, not the Guern-
seys, Holsteins, and Jerseys of Illinois, but much like them
in color and conformation.

Next to a large barn at the far end of the pasture stood a
small shedlike structure. It must be the creamery. Hallelu-
jah!

Of course there would be dairy products at the fort—in
plenty. Johann Sutter was, after all, a Swiss.

Stone had known about Sutter and his celebrated establishment at New Helvetia for a long time, since Cambridge,
actually, when he had read a *New England Historical
Review* article on California written by George Bancroft, the
Secretary of the Navy, now serving in President Polk's cab-
inet. Back then the story of Sutter, the man who by repute
had become the wealthiest man in California, certainly the
wealthiest nonnative Californio, had been but an evening's
interesting reading. Now he was about to meet the intrepid
margrave of northern California in the flesh.

Sutter, the tale went, had been born in Germany, but had
spent most of his early life in Switzerland, and always rep-
resented himself as hailing from that clockwork little alpine
country. He had arrived penniless in New York, had somehow made his way to Oregon, and then down to Monterey.
A glib, shrewd self-promoter, he had talked Mexican authorities into granting him eleven square leagues of land near the
junction of the American and Sacramento Rivers, just ahead
of Frémont's little party now.

Stone had learned from Bancroft's piece in the *Review*
that this part of the California territory had fallen into desue-
tude and virtual anarchy after Mexico achieved independence from Spain in the 1820s. Bands of murderous
brigands roamed the countryside, and Californio ranchers
and farmers fell under almost continuous attacks by these
outlaws, as well as by numerous bands of renegade Indians
who had once worked as *peónes* for the missions and who

descended again into savagery when the mission system more or less fell apart.

Fighting off Indian raids and assaults from the bandits, Sutter had carved out a small empire. His first rude fort became the heart and brain of it. The earliest American settlers clustered around the fort and the new mill that soon joined it on the riverbank. Although Mexico City looked on these Americans with suspicion, when Sutter became a Mexican national the capital bestowed on him the title "Guardian of the Northern Frontier" with the rank of captain. The appointment enabled him to stand between the new arrivals from the eastern United States and a good deal of official heat.

The Swiss must have been on Frémont's mind as well as they approached the center of his domain.

"Herr Sutter will strike you as the complete Old World gentleman, Bradford. You will find New Helvetia more Switzerland than California, I assure you. I doubt if there exists a more generous or genial host on the entire North American continent."

The cow pasture yielded to a section of garden plots, neat rectangles of beans, corn, and a wide variety of other vegetable plants, some of which Stone did not recognize, the stalks often bent to the ground with the weight of their produce.

And here Stone caught his first sight of the inhabitants of New Helvetia.

Men, women, and a number of children—all in the white clothing remembered from Taos—worked the garden rows with hoes and mattocks. A few spotted the four riders and waved, bowed, or smiled.

They rode past a giant corral where perhaps two dozen handsome horses grazed, and then on through a constellation of small adobe houses, all with red tile roofs and all gleaming with whitewash. At the far south end of this village area they passed the immense open door of a smithy, the largest building they had seen, where sparks lit the cavernous interior and threw fantastic shadows against the inside walls.

"We'll need to use that smithy ourselves before we leave New Helvetia, Bradford," Frémont said. "Captain Sutter even has a foundry somewhere hereabouts, and when Kit and I were here last year he had just begun building a manufactory for the construction of agricultural implements. Perhaps you already know that his grinding mill and sawmill are the largest in all of upper California."

"I had heard that somewhere, sir."

The Pathfinder touched his spurs to the flanks of the stallion and moved out well ahead of the three of them.

"The captain is in a hell of a good mood this morning," Maxwell said to Stone and Kit.

Frémont reached the top of a slight rise to the south of the village, where he reined in the stallion to wait for them.

In moments Stone, Carson, and Maxwell reached the top of the rise. Stone looked down and got his first glimpse of Sutter's Fort.

"Fabulous!" he whispered to Kit.

"It sure is something, ain't it?" Kit said.

An immense adobe-and-fieldstone wall, whitewashed to the same dazzling brilliance of the small ones they had seen, enclosed a number of buildings, each one as mammoth as Charlie and William Bent's main structure on the Arkansas. The wall itself held a huge gate facing them, and its parapet was notched with cannon ports. Stone could see the muzzles of six large-bore pieces.

The flag of Mexico flew from a staff atop the largest of the interior buildings.

"Let us pay our respects and allow Herr Sutter to welcome us," Frémont said.

As they rode down the slope toward the gate, a man

appeared atop the wall. He wore a Mexican suit much like that worn by Don Bernardo Barragán, but with none of Barragán's elegance.

The man cradled in his arms a fine-looking rifle with a black stock, its metalwork chased with silver. He was swarthy, with a jet black beard and mustache, and Stone marked him for typically Mexican—until he spoke.

"What can I do for you gents?" His accent was as distinctively Middle West American as Stone's.

"To begin with, you can open your gate for me, my good man," Frémont said.

"And who the hell would I be opening it to?" the man said.

"I am Captain John C. Frémont of the United States Army Corps of Topographical Engineers."

The man smiled. "Sounds mighty important, mister. Exactly what do you and your three *amigos* want at Sutter's?"

"I wish to speak with Captain Sutter. Kindly inform the captain."

"Well now . . . I'd be glad to do that, except that the captain ain't here. He's on a business trip down Monterey way. My name's Bidwell. I got the running of the fort until he gets back. You're camping with that trail bunch up at Oak Bend, ain't you?"

"When will Captain Sutter return?"

"Don't rightly know."

"Will you open your gate to us, fellow, in order that we might continue this discussion in a more amicable fashion?"

"My, my . . ." Bidwell's smile had turned to a faintly nasty, sardonic grin. "You sure got a fancy way of talking, mister."

"Please be good enough to address me as 'Captain,' Mr. Bidwell! Will you now open the gate to me and my companions?"

"No. I got orders to let nobody inside this wall until Captain Sutter says so in person—and that ain't going to happen for a bit. But why don't you straight-out tell me what you want? That shouldn't be too damned hard, even for a fancy talker."

Frémont looked ready to break things off, then apparently thought better of it. "We need horses, mules, the use of your blacksmith's shop, food. We are prepared to pay, in American money, of course."

"Captain Sutter's got all the American money he can use. Maybe we could spare half a dozen mules. Help yourself at the smith's. No horses, though. We're kind of short of riding stock ourselves right now."

Stone remembered the corral with the good-looking horses.

Bidwell went on. "That's a fair-looking critter you're on, mister . . . Captain. I'll buy it from you myself."

"Don't be impertinent, man!"

"As for food, I will lay on a meal for you and your men, roast beef and all the fixings—free."

"By God, that's great!" Lucien Maxwell yelled out.

Frémont's voice cracked like a rifle shot. "Mr. Maxwell!" He turned to Bidwell. "The United States Army does not accept charity, sirrah!"

"Beggars can't be choosers. You're living on acorns up at Oak Bend, ain't you?"

"Enough!" Frémont said. He turned the stallion and faced Kit. "We will return to camp at once, Mr. Carson. I will not listen to this insulting, condescending oaf a moment longer." With that he lashed Sacramento with his reins and the big animal bounded off toward the rise. The others fell in behind him.

"Hey!" Bidwell shouted from the wall. "Wait a damned old second! You just said 'Carson.' Is that *Kit* Carson with you? Hey . . . come on back here . . . hey . . ." There was a bit more, but it got lost in the drumming of the hooves.

3

Once back at camp, Stone and Carson rode out to look for game.

"That Bidwell seemed to know a lot about us," Stone said.

"I expect we been watched ever since we left the western foot of the pass. Captain Sutter likes to know everything that goes on in his own backyard. Things must be a mite touchy in California nowadays."

"But how did our men learn that the captain turned down Bidwell's offer of a meal?"

"I guess Lucy Maxwell told them. He's as hungry as Bass and the rest of us."

Kit found deer droppings, and they followed other sign he picked up. Stone could not have read a thing from the bent grass the scout showed him. They caught the tantalizing flash of a white rump disappearing in the undergrowth near the river once, but that was all. By the end of the afternoon they had to settle for three squirrels and one scrawny rabbit.

"Captain still in his tent, Bass?" Kit asked Lajeunesse when they returned to camp and turned their pitiful kill over to him.

"Ain't seen him once. Lucy's been waiting on him while you and Brad was gone."

"I'll see if I can find him. If he ain't going to let that *hombre* Bidwell at Sutter's give us some help in the way of vittles, some of us ought to make tracks out of here tomorrow, head for the hills, and find some game. Maybe not the whole bunch, but some of us, anyways."

"Guess we're down to the acorns again, and them measly little squirrels. We won't starve."

"Not much different from the last time the captain and me rode down this valley," Carson said. "We'd been living on piñon nuts and dog stew for near three weeks when we limped into Sutter's."

4

By dinner Frémont still had not left his tent.

Several other of the mountain men and two of the Delawares had also bagged squirrels. December's early dark had settled a gloomy blanket over the camp, and even the flickering light of the fire did little to lift spirits.

The squirrel stew Basil concocted did not taste nearly as bad as Stone expected. The giant had thrown some wild greens into the cooking pot and had laced it with the camp's last few drops of whiskey. He found the meat tough, but palatable. With the sweet long acorns it was not the worst of meals.

One man did not agree with him.

Without warning Lucien Maxwell hurled his plate straight into the fire, spraying juices over Kit and Stone in the process.

"Goddamned Frémont!" he shouted.

The captain's tent was only fifty or sixty feet away. There had been no night noises until Lucy's outburst; the Pathfinder must have heard it.

Maxwell got to his feet. He was not carrying his old saber tonight, but he drew his Colt Paterson from his belt.

"I'm going to that goddamned hideout tent of his and have it out with him," he announced. He took one step around the fire.

The earth did not actually shake when Lajeunesse rose to his feet across the fire from Maxwell, but Brad Stone would always swear it had. The old trapper spread his tree-limb arms wide, turning himself into a giant, hairy cruciform. In his right hand he held the long skinning knife. Behind him his shadow ran out to Frémont's tent, climbed its sides, and covered it like a protective cloak. Basil did not utter a sound, did not seem to breathe. Neither did any of the others around the fire.

Maxwell stopped in his tracks.

Then Stone felt rather than saw Carson stand. The scout moved like a cat to Maxwell, took the pistol from him gently, and jammed it back in Lucy's belt and patted him on the shoulder.

Maxwell turned and left the fire, striding off in the opposite direction from Frémont's tent. The mountain men and the Delawares finished eating, and one by one wandered off to their bedrolls. None of them said a word. Stone, Carson, and Lajeunesse were the only ones at the fire now. Then the French Canadian turned and walked to the space in front of the tent, sank to his haunches fifteen feet in front of it, and sat with his arms crossed. The wicked knife had found its way to his belt again.

"Kit . . . ," Stone whispered. "Did I just see what I think I saw? I know Lucy's no coward, and he had that pistol . . ."

Kit chuckled. "No," he said. "Lucy ain't a coward. Hopping mad as he was, I think he sudden-like remembered that rendezvous on the Green in '39. A fur man from Ohio, every bit as big as Bass, had been bothering a Shoshone girl Bass had taken a shine to like she was his daughter. Bass warned him off, nice as you please. This Ohio trapper whipped a pistol out just like Lucy did just now. Had two other men backing him. Bass buried his knife right to the bone handle in that big hog's chest before he could even think of firing. Man lived, but he weren't much good after that. Bass laid the other two low with his fists."

"Will Lucy persist in this . . . troublemaking?" Stone had been at the point of saying "mutiny."

"Naw. Lucy's a hothead, but he ain't stupid. When he thinks it over he'll simmer down."

Still, as Stone discovered when he awoke in the morning, Lajeunesse did not leave his post in front of Frémont's tent all night long.

5

Captain Johann August Sutter rode into the oak-grove camp of Brevet Captain John C. Frémont on the American River at ten o'clock on the eleventh of December 1845.

Captain Sutter, mounted on a palomino with an astonishing white-gold mane and a long, flowing tail that almost brushed the ground, led a parade of high-wheeled wooden carts, unsaddled horses, and a string of glossy black mules.

Two little brown-faced girls, dressed in white outfits like the confirmation dresses Stone had seen on Irish girls in South Boston, rode in the first cart, holding bouquets of flowers so fat they could hardly keep their arms around them. Behind them in the cart Stone saw sacks of flour, sides of bacon, flagons of wine, jugs of brandy and cognac, and canisters of milk. Foodstuffs, much of it already cooked, and now wafting delicious aromas through the grove, bulged over the siderails of the second cart in line: roasts of beef encased in an inch of rich, glistening fat, salmon steaks, a bewildering number of pots of vegetables ready for a fire, and gigantic loaves of bread that smelled as if they had been baked this morning.

The other carts held what appeared to be Indian servants and workers, and knocked-down trestle tables.

The mountain men flew to Sutter's horse like noisy, swarming bees.

The famous Swiss slipped from the saddle and Dick Owens stepped forward and took the palomino's bridle.

Dressed in a Mexican outfit much like that of the man Bidwell yesterday, Sutter wore a wide-brimmed straw hat which he now removed, revealing a fringe of blond hair circling a tanned bald pate. Though short—not much taller than Carson—he looked to be a block of strength. He was smiling, blue eyes dancing, but Stone took him immediately for a man of habitually serious purpose; his face appeared as square as some of the plottings on Stone's desert maps, all hard, straight lines behind the genial smile.

"Grützi!" he shouted. A chorus of answering shouts reverberated through the oak grove.

Another voice came from behind Stone. *"Wie geht es Ihnen, Herr Sutter?"* Frémont had come out of the tent to join the cluster of men gathered around the Swiss. The greeting sounded cool; the captain looked gray.

"Grützi, Captain Frémont," Sutter said. "I am delighted to see you again, old friend. You have had a good journey to New Helvetia?"

"Until yesterday, sir. I had expected to be more welcome at Sutter's Fort."

"I regret that, sir," Sutter said. He looked at the mountain men milling around him, turned back to Frémont. "But may we defer discussing that until we have a private meeting? At the moment I must give my people their last instructions on preparing a feast for you and your companions . . . with your permission. You and your men are honored guests here at New Helvetia. May I get things under way?"

"Very well, Captain Sutter," Frémont said. "Proceed. I will await you at my tent." He had set his mouth so hard his lips were a thin line. He turned to Stone. "When Captain Sutter is free, Mr. Stone, please escort him to me. And I want you to remain with us make a record of our conversation."

"Now . . . ," Sutter said, "John Bidwell tells me that another old friend has come to New Helvetia with you, Captain." He swept his blue eyes swiftly across the faces turned toward him. "Where is Herr Carson?"

"Right here, Captain."

"Welcome, Kit. It honors us that you have come to visit us again. Every time you ride down our valley it seems you are more celebrated. You have become a giant."

Kit grinned. "Ain't growed an inch since I saw you last, sir. What was it you called me when we first met?"

"Kitzli, It means 'Little Kit,' of course. I meant no offense."

"I took none, Captain. The moniker still fits, I reckon."

Sutter roared with laughter. "You are a sizable man in every respect that matters. Let us spend some time together after we finish eating."

Frémont broke in. "Mr. Carson will join us, Captain Sutter, *before* we eat."

He strode off toward the tent, his back rigid. For a fraction of a second Stone imagined he heard the rattling beat of snare drums. While they talked, the Indian servants had unloaded and set up the tables. Women hauled platters and pots to them in relays. When Stone looked at Sutter again, he found the Swiss regarding him with open curiosity.

"I shall not be longer than a moment, gentlemen. It will take just a word or two," he said. He bowed to Kit and Stone then, and moved toward the tables.

6

"I may speak freely, Captain Frémont?" Sutter asked when they had settled on camp stools at the tent. "I know Kit, of course, and trust him implicitly, but—"

"Mr. Stone, who originally signed on with me as a topographer," Frémont broke in, "is well connected in Washington. He has become invaluable in the accomplishment of my mission, and has proven himself a man of utmost probity, and of many talents. You may place every bit as much trust in him as you do in Kit, I assure you."

"Sehr gut," Sutter said. "Now, Captain, let me begin by apologizing for John Bidwell's behavior yesterday. He acted under orders, my orders."

"But why?" Frémont said. "I have never known anything but warm hospitality at New Helvetia."

"General Castro had a squadron of cavalry posted at New Helvetia most of the summer—to guard us, he said, although I tried to tell him we needed no such protection. His soldiers are gone now, but I think he has a spy or spies inside my fort."

"Castro seems uncommonly nervous. Why, do you suppose?"

"Things have become extremely tense in Upper California since you were here last year."

"Is he concerned about the possibility of war between our countries?"

"I think not. If it should come to that, he knows it will not reach Upper California or have any great effect on our future. This is almost a separate province from the south. For all practical purposes Pío Pico's authority, and that of Mexico City, too, does not reach as far north as Monterey, although of course the governor at Los Angeles wishes that it did."

"Then does the general fear revolt here?"

"Mortally. And not entirely without reason."

"I still fail to see what this might have to do with me or my expedition. We shall not be here long. We are mapping a new route to Oregon. Since its independence Mexico has always tacitly permitted such passage. We will move north in a day or two at most. General Castro has nothing to fear from us, even if he knows about us."

Stone listened intently. What Frémont had just said did not square at all with his previously announced plans. They could not possibly leave for Oregon until they linked up with Talbot, Kern, and Walker. And had the Pathfinder not made it crystal-clear at Pilot Peak and again at Walker Lake that the two detachments of the expedition would meet somewhere *south* of Sutter's Fort—and in the *spring?* Today was only the eleventh of December. Apparently Frémont planned a long stay in California before they left for Oregon, no matter what he had just told Sutter.

"Although most of the disaffected men in this valley are native Californios or Mexican immigrants," Sutter said, "there are several hundred of your countrymen living and working here, almost none of whom have ever become citizens of Mexico, as I have. *You* are Americans—and armed. It may be that the governor fears you might be looked on as a man to rally around."

A total stranger would have known that Frémont's mood soared after he absorbed Sutter's last words.

"That's preposterous," he said. "I am a scientist, not a revolutionary. I am not even a fighting man."

"Ah, but Kit here, and the other men in your party, are renowned as fighting men."

"They came with me as scouts, and to protect me from Indians. If this were intended as a military adventure, I assure you my party would be much larger, and would be accompanied by uniformed men and much heavier ordinance than Hawken guns and hunting knives. There are only a few of us, hardly enough to foment rebellion."

But there *was* a larger party. Had Frémont no intention of telling the Swiss about Talbot, Walker, Kern, and the fifty armed men riding with them—or the mountain howitzers they had by now trundled over some pass in the Sierra Nevada south of here?

Stone glanced at Kit. Carson's face looked utterly passive, but it seemed impossible the same thoughts had not crossed the scout's mind.

"I am greatly relieved that you intend to depart this valley promptly," Sutter said. "Monterey has not entirely trusted me since I supported former governor Micheltorena last February. And although he has little power here in the north, Pico is as rabidly anti-American as is General Castro. He will not be pleased when he learns I have afforded you even this modest hospitality." He waved his arm in the direction of the tables. "But please accept the horses and mules I brought with me today. And please stop at New Helvetia again if you're forced to come back this way when your work in Oregon is done. General Castro may be in a different frame of mind by then." His pink face turned a shade pinker. "Incidentally, returning to the United States by some other route than through California is something you should consider very carefully."

"How so?"

"My sources at Monterey tell me that General Castro is at the point of issuing a proclamation banishing all Americans now in California who have not sworn fealty to Mexico, and forbidding any from the United States from traveling here. That, of course, would include your party. I would hate being put in the position of having to enforce this proposed edict. It almost seems as if Castro knew you were already in the province. I doubt that, of course; I did not learn of your presence myself until three days ago, and my intelligence in Upper California is far more reliable than Castro's."

"Will the American settlers here abide by the general's edict?"

"If Castro does make the proclamation, I fear there will be bloodshed. You and your men might be blamed for it, at least in part, even if you had no hand in it. You have no intentions in that direction, do you?"

Frémont took a second before answering. Then he smiled as he said, "No, Johann. I repeat . . . my expedition is purely a—"

Sutter smiled. "—scientific one. Now, gentlemen . . . you must be hungry. Be my guests."

7

They left the grove called Oak Bend three days later, heading south.

The mountain men had run the horses down to Sutter's blacksmith's in relays for shoeing, and more mules had arrived at camp, together with supplies of food, powder and balls for the rifles, and even more boots and shoes for those men who had not been able to find their size in the loaded cart the day of the great feast. Sutter also sent a dozen head of beef cattle along with the mules.

Stone, Carson, Frémont, and Godey dined with Captain Sutter in his surprisingly spartan quarters at the fort the night before they broke camp, and after a wonderful meal the Pathfinder and their host closeted themselves in Sutter's office for an hour, while Godey busied himself with flirting with the Californio maidservants who had served the meal. It did not appear that the St. Louisan made much headway. The two pretty young things huddled together as if in mutual protection whenever Alexis approached them.

Apparently Kit, the consummate outdoorsman, could not stay in a house for any length of time. He excused himself for a stroll on the fort's grounds while the two captains had their meeting. Stone might have tagged along, but he had spotted Johann Sutter's library through an open door.

The leatherbound works of Goethe, Schiller, and Heine did not surprise him, nor did those in German on agricultural science and animal husbandry—there was one hefty treatise in French, dealing with oenology and viticulture—but what appeared to be German translations of Locke and Hobbes did. So did the Milton—this in English. Bookmarks peeped from most of them.

As they returned to camp in the soft darkness Frémont

held his horse well to the rear, and he signaled Stone to drop back and ride with him.

"I saw your look when we met with Johann in the grove the other day, Bradford. I did not lie to him in any ordinary sense, as you probably thought. He will be telling the absolute truth if he is required to report our conversation to General Castro and he says that as far as he knows we are bound for Oregon. The truth is, of course, that Johann knows precisely what my intentions are—as I am sure you, Kit, and most of the others do."

Stone reflected that despite Frémont's stated assumption of what the others knew, it still remained a mystery to him. And if Sutter was playing some sort of game with the Pathfinder, he was playing it well. Everything he had said at dinner, and every gesture he made, spoke of his relief that the expedition would soon quit the province.

With the next day's early start looming, Stone never got the chance to ask Carson about his feelings, and by the time the scout's morning cry shivered the air, he had more or less forgotten all about it.

19

A Little Bit of Trouble

The Lake Fork of the Tulare
January 1846

"Alex and Basil scouted thirty miles south of here, Captain," Kit said. "Didn't even cut sign of Joe and Mr. Talbot and the rest of our outfit."

They were beginning the third week of the search for the

Humboldt River party, a search that had taken them far down the great mountain wall to the east.

"What could have held them up, Mr. Carson?" Frémont asked. He pulled his telescope from his eye and snapped it closed. "They should have been here by now."

Stone wondered if the captain might slide into one of his emotional ruts again. He had often enough in the past, when things did not go according to plan, especially if it was one of his devising.

"When they crossed the Sierras they might have gotten the snow we didn't get up north," Kit said. "And they could have just plain moseyed along easy-like."

"Damn! Mr. Talbot knows I will need his party soon, even if Mr. Walker and Mr. Kern don't."

"Well, for one thing, Captain, there's plenty of game the way they came. They wasn't heading for a cozy place like Sutter's the way we was, and they just might have wanted to stock up. There's one other possibility. Kind of hate to mention it. Joe's a good guide, but he ain't all that familiar with this part of California, and he could have mistook some other river for the Lake Fork. If that's so, we could have passed them on the way down. With Segundai and Crane looking to the east of us the past two days, and with Lucy and Dick keeping an eye out on the west, it's fairly certain they ain't close by."

"Your advice, Mr. Carson?"

Stone breathed easier. If Frémont asked for advice, it indicated he was still in one of his better moods.

"I say let's settle in to kind of a permanent camp here. They'll show up sooner or later whether we cross tracks with them or not. Joe will put flankers out on the watch for us. I say stay right here, unless the captain's in a hurry."

"As a matter of fact I am in a hurry. I'm anxious to get back to Sutter's and see if General Castro has issued that insulting proclamation Sutter spoke about. There's no point in lingering here in the south . . . unless you can honestly tell me Mr. Talbot has run into difficulties he cannot cope with."

"No, sir, I can't honestly tell you that. I sure wouldn't worry none about them. With their numbers and firepower, it ain't likely they ran into any trouble they can't handle— not even the little bit we did."

A "little bit" of trouble? Stone was willing to concede that the two skirmishes with the Horsethief Indians during the last two weeks were minor affairs compared to the adventure with Kit and Luis Aragón on the Cimarron. But it was still hard for him to think of situations where men were shooting at him as "little."

2

A few days before they had reached the Lake Fork, near the headwaters of what Frémont said was the Mariposa River, Stone had gone ahead to do some mapping as he had in the desert and on the eastern slope. Kit had sent Godey on the first of the hunts for Talbot by then, and the Pathfinder had assigned Maxwell and Owens to accompany and assist him, along with two of the Delawares, Crane and Charlie.

They rode toward the smaller, closer, and barer of two rocky hills Stone determined would make good fix points for the first sightings of his morning's work, when a band of mounted Indians streamed out of the timber on the larger hill. They seemed to be about a half mile off, but when Stone jammed the working notes he had been studying back in his saddlebag and looked at the oncoming Indians a second time, they had narrowed the gap to half that. There were at least a couple dozen of them. Behind the Indian riders a number of others were moving toward them on foot. These were mostly women.

"Horsethieves!" Owens shouted. "Drop the lead of that

mule, Mr. Stone! Make for that bare little knob up ahead, *pronto!*"

"My gear!" Stone shouted back.

"Forget it! Think about your hide—and your hair. You can buy more gear."

Stone might have argued, but a spurt of dust in front of his horse, and the rifle report that followed close on, changed his mind in a hurry.

By the time they reached the hill the Indians were only three or four hundred yards away, and although there had been no more shots, the hackneyed old words "'howling savages" took on a new reality. The screeching was unbelievable.

Owens reined up at the foot of the hill.

"Let's get off these ponies," he said. "Maybe if they get them they'll be satisfied. We'll get in behind those rocks on top."

Two more shots ricocheted off nearby stones as the five of them clambered up the hillside on foot. When they reached the top, fifty or sixty vertical feet above the horde that had indeed seized their mounts, he was relieved to find there a natural little fort. Two- and three foot high boulders enclosed a sandy, craterlike basin, bare of vegetation, but littered with bones. As he jumped inside he tripped over something. A human skull grinned up at him.

Someone else must have fought from this hilltop once—without success.

Lucy Maxwell pushed the barrel of his Plains through an opening in the rocks and fired.

"Goddamn it!" Owens roared. "You know better than that. Wait until I lay out a firing plan and give a signal."

Stone felt a hand on his shoulder. "Hold your fire, Mr. Stone, until we set up a shooting order," Dick Owens said. It was a different tone than he had used with Maxwell. "I don't think they'll try to rush us. Not right away. But if they do, I want somebody primed and ready to shoot all the time." He turned to the Delaware, Charlie. "Take the other side, Charlie. They'll start to ride around this hill pretty quick. If you see them start up the back, give a yell."

Screams and whoops rolled up the stony hillside to the five men huddled in the sandy crater. As Owens had predicted, the mounted band beneath them now began to circle the base of the hill. Their ride, made at a full gallop, had an air of madness about it. These Indians did not look at all like any Stone had seen since coming west; some of them wore the same white cotton clothing he had seen at Taos and again at Sutter's Fort, and most of them wore sombreros.

What had Caleb Miller said about the ragged Brulé Sioux they'd encountered on the trip across the prairie? *"Don't judge redskins by this lot, Brad. They been hanging around white men too damned long."* He also remembered what Frémont—or was it Kit?—had said about these Indians being runaways from the missions.

"I'll shoot next, gents," Owens said, "but only when one of them breaks out of that circle and starts up our way. If more than one does, you take him, Mr. Stone. If the whole bunch comes loose, it's every man for himself and try to take some of these red devils with you."

In the distance Stone could see that the mule loaded with his precious equipment had found a patch of grass or something just as appealing, and the dumb brute munched away, totally unmindful of the clamor around the hill. Apparently their attackers or their women had not spied the animal yet.

He saw Owens put his rifle to his shoulder. He looked down the slope. A pall of frenzied dust rose from the circle of riders now, and one of them had turned his horse away from it and in toward the hill. Owens' rifle cracked, and for a second Stone thought it a clean miss, but in a second a red blotch spread across the Indian's white blouse. The man slipped from the saddle almost as if he were dismounting, but then he crumpled to a lifeless heap, like a waterskin suddenly drained of its contents.

Stone would be the next to fire. He decided then that if his target were on the move he would try for the horse and not the rider.

Behind him he heard the report of Charlie's rifle, followed by a yip of triumph followed by another of clear alarm. Out of the corner of his eye he saw Owens, still reloading, hurry across the basin to take a look.

"Lucy! Crane! Get over here! We got half a dozen of them riding up! Stay where you are, Mr. Stone. Hold any fire until you're dead sure you'll hit something. Keep your eyes on that slope. Don't look at us."

Stone wanted desperately to join the others. They could all die behind him without him even knowing it. The savages could then break like an unseen wave across the stone breastwork in back of him, and he suddenly wanted the small consolation of *facing* whatever fate held for him.

Two more shots rang out from the men behind him on the little hilltop fort and were answered by one from far down the back of the hill. As ordered, he kept his eye on the slope in front of him.

One rider moved to where the body of the Indian Owens had brought down lay motionless—and stopped. *Now, Brad Stone, now . . . squeeze, do not pull . . .*

But he did not fire.

A great, raucous, thunderous laugh from Owens broke across the hilltop, and Stone could not keep from turning this time. He found the mountain man standing on top of one of the boulders and brandishing his rifle maniacally. Was he taunting or tempting their attackers?

"Yah-eee!" he hooted. "Didn't think old Kit could stay out of any fight he heard going on!"

Stone turned and looked out beyond the still-grazing mule to where a column of horsemen raced toward the small hill.

Under the dirty, yellow dust plume he made out the rest of the Sutter's Fort party—with Frémont and Carson riding neck and neck in the lead, neither of them yielding an inch to the other.

The Indians must have seen them as soon as he had; the mad whirl below him broke into fragments, most of the armed horsemen galloping toward the larger of the two hills, the Horsethief women fleeing in panic in front of them. A few pulled up before they reached the hill to fire at Carson and Frémont, but with absolutely no effect, although the dust splashes came dangerously close to the front hooves of both the Pathfinder's and the scout's horses. Neither of the riders wavered.

The battle of the rocky hilltop became history in a few more minutes.

Five or six more shots were fired by the retiring Indians—most of whom had disappeared into the wooded side of the larger hill—but from a hopeless distance. Then there erupted from the woods a cacophony of screaming and yelling.

"They sure do talk tough for critters who won't stay and fight," Owens said. "Filthy talk, too. Cussing like that, you'd think they was mountain men."

Down in the flats again, Stone saw Lajeunesse had the mule in tow.

Carson wanted to go up the larger hill and recapture the five horses the Indians had taken, but Frémont overruled him.

3

Kit sought Stone out that night when they made camp again about seven miles south of the Horsethieves' wooded hill.

"Dick Owens had some nice things to say about the way you fought today, Brad."

"Oh."

"Said you was as cool as any old Indian fighter this morning, and Dick ain't much given to praising people that way."

"But I didn't actually do anything, Kit. I didn't so much as fire a shot."

"Not firing is sometimes even better than firing. Dick said he was mighty impressed that although you actually outrank him in this party, you didn't make any fuss when he took charge."

"That was only common sense."

"He says you followed his orders to the letter. That's important—following orders. In the kind of world we live in out here, somebody's got to give them, somebody else has just got to follow them without no questions—even sometimes when they don't exactly square with common sense."

Carson spoke with the conviction of a man enunciating an article of personal faith, bringing back Ed Kern's remarks at Pilot Peak.

4

A little sequel to the first brush with the Horsethieves occurred the following morning.

Frémont had sent Maxwell and two of the Delawares, Charlie and Crane, out to ride point. "We won't let you get as far ahead of us as we did when you went out with Mr. Stone yesterday, Mr. Maxwell."

But when six of the spare horses escaped the control of the men herding them, and the party wasted an hour chasing them down through the ponderosa, Lucy and the two Delawares had gotten completely out of sight and sound.

They found them at the far side of an immense grassy clearing in the pines, still too far off to hail.

As they watched, an Indian, perhaps from the band they

had struggled with the day before, emerged from the woods and began riding toward the threesome. He had no weapon in his hands that Stone could see, but he *was,* after all, a considerable distance from them.

"Let's get over there fast, Mr. Carson!" Frémont shouted. "You know how precipitate Mr. Maxwell can be. I would like to take that savage prisoner. He might have knowledge of Mr. Talbot's party. Come along, Mr. Stone."

Carson and the Pathfinder set out at a brisk canter, and Stone spurred his mount in behind them, but before they covered half the distance he saw Maxwell raise his rifle.

A puff of white smoke blossomed against the piney background. The Indian fell. The report of Lucy's rifle came faintly across the broad meadow—almost as an afterthought.

"I recognized the son of a bitch from yesterday, Captain," Lucy said when the three of them reined up beside him. "He's the one who took my horse. That pitiful critter he was on ain't it, of course. Him and his squaw and the ten papooses they probably have most likely ate mine already. Dumb bastards don't know good horseflesh when they see it."

Now, here on the Lake Fork of the Tulare, Brad Stone waited for Frémont to come to a decision. He knew that when the captain's spirits were up like this, it would come swiftly.

"Turn the men about in the morning, Kit," Frémont said. "We're going back to Sutter's. We'll wait for Mr. Talbot there."

20

Rumors of War

If Johann August Sutter felt surprise that Frémont had returned to his comfortable kingdom in such short order instead of leading his men north to Oregon, he did not show it.

Apparently the expected edict banning noncitizens of Mexico had not come up from General Castro at Monterey as yet. But Sutter seemed tentative when he agreed to Frémont's request that they be permitted an extended stay while they waited for the rest of the expedition to show up. Although neither Frémont's nor Sutter had ever mentioned the Talbot party in his hearing, it seemed to Stone that the proprietor of New Helvetia had known of its presence somewhere in California all along.

"Captain Sutter is a worried man," Alexis Godey said. "Hospitable as he is trying to be, I think he'll rejoice when we're on our way north."

They camped again in the same oak grove on the American, north of the fort and village which they had used before. Pleasant enough on that earlier visit, their surroundings this time struck Stone and the rest of the men as idyllic. Sutter invited Frémont to stay with him in the fort.

"If you want my opinion, Mr. Stone," Godey said, "I think our host wants to keep his eye on the captain. I detect something strange and evasive in his attitude."

Reluctantly, Stone agreed. Although he could not put his finger on why he thought so, this did not seem to be the same Johann Sutter they had sojourned with the first time.

Stone spent his time mapping the juncture of the two rivers and the rolling country around it, making sketches of the fort, the village, and the inhabitants of both, and writing a letter to Ana several times the length of the one he had composed and sent from Pilot Peak. He still labored under the same difficulty—having always to remind himself that someone else might read the words he wrote her—and the task brought him moments of alternating joy and melancholy.

He tried to tell himself that as a practical man with a strict academic and scientific background he should not be traduced by the romantic notions running through him as he wrote, that he really and truly did not know Ana well enough to build the dream future he was mapping out in his heart for the two of them. But he had fallen deeply in love with her, and he could never again fight that after their last night together.

He had little notion of how he could send the letter to her. Perhaps Captain Sutter could suggest a way. One of those American vessels Frémont said were monitoring the California coast? By their third day in camp the letter had run to fourteen pages. If he could not be intimate, he could at least tell her in detail of everything that had happened to them on the long trip since his last letter from Pilot Peak.

These had become halcyon days for the mountain men, as well.

They staged shooting matches where he marveled at their deadly marksmanship at distances that would defy belief back East. And while he knew he had gotten passably good with the Hawken, he despaired of ever attaining anything like the skill of Lajeunesse, Maxwell, Owens, and, of course, Carson. He entered one of the contests after some good-natured ragging from the big French Canadian, and finished tenth in a field of ten.

The Mexicans and Indians from the village turned out for

these affairs, and if Stone was amazed at the performances, they were awestruck. One elderly Californio who stood beside him at one of the contests confided, "How could one ever fight such *hombres, señor? ¡Es magnífico!*"

Two out of three nights the mountain men, with Kit the one exception, turned out for a dance in the center of the camp, as they had on some of those firelit evenings on the headwaters of the Arkansas. Again Sutter's villagers stared goggled-eyed at the fur-clad monsters from beyond the eastern mountains, the younger women in the crowd giggling from behind fans, or with their *rebozos* drawn partially across their faces, at the sight of men in each other's arms gyrating wildly around the fire, linking and unlinking brawny forearms, their shadows leaping to the tops of the encircling oaks. Lajeunesse, the arthritis that plagued him from time to time apparently forgotten, astonished the onlookers with his nimbleness and lumbering grace as he jigged and skipped to the music from Gus Archambeault's fiddle.

Godey took no part in these festivities. In sublime disregard of his rebuff at the hands of the two serving girls when they dined with Sutter, he set off in hot pursuit of several of the young women in *mantillas* attending these galas. He tried to be discreet, but Stone felt certain from the winks and wise looks from Godey's old companions that handsome Alexis's pursuit succeeded with one of them at least. She was a stunning black-haired, willowy, sloe-eyed creature Stone decided would compare favorably in beguiling looks to all the women he had ever met—save one.

He wondered next if Alexis might be courting danger, for himself and for the rest of them as well, by exercising his wiles on a local woman, perhaps the wife or daughter of one of the Californios who wandered unchallenged through the camp on a daily basis. None of these men appeared to be armed, but Stone remembered the wicked stiletto Luis Aragón carried in his sleeve.

He cautiously mentioned his concern to Kit.

"Good thinking," the scout said. "This kind of thing can be touchy, but I already looked into it. The lady is a widow, which gives her some leeway to begin with, and she ain't got any other man in tow at the moment. Besides, I was told Señora Seguín's reputation in this kind of thing ain't none too good, anyways. Her nickname in the village is La Barracuda. The other women are probably tickled pink that Alexis has taken her out of circulation for a spell at least."

Kit Carson was more than just a scout for John C. Frémont.

2

On the eighteenth of January, Lajeunesse had found Stone sketching at the bank of the river and told him that Frémont had sent an Indian runner from the fort and wished to see him there immediately.

"Bradford, my boy!" Frémont greeted him. "Are you amenable to a small adventure? I am leaving tomorrow to pay a visit to Mr. Tom Larkin, our country's consul at Yerba Buena on San Francisco Bay. I would like you to accompany me."

"I would be delighted, sir. Should I pack my equipment?"

"No. We won't be riding. Captain Sutter has generously offered the use of his launch for us to go down the Sacramento to the bay. There will not be room for your equipment."

"Will Mr. Carson be going with us, sir?"

"No. I want Kit to stay and keep order among the men. And someone has to receive Mr. Talbot and his detachment should they arrive here while you and I are gone. And if General Castro issues that ridiculous proclamation when we are absent from the camp, Kit will lead the expedition north and out of California. If that should happen, you and I shall have to rely on the passports Captain Sutter will issue us to get us from Yerba Buena to rejoin Kit in Oregon. . . .

"Mind you, this is a request for your company and not an order, Bradford. There is some chance that with things in such a parlous state between our two nations the Mexican authorities might detain or—in the extreme—place us under arrest and confine us. It might well amount to something more than a mere inconvenience. Knowing that, will you still be willing to go with me?"

"Absolutely, sir!"

He could hardly contain his excitement as he rode back to Oak Bend. Even if Frémont wanted him along only as clerk and secretary, it loomed as another of the adventures he had longed for since leaving Groverton.

And it promised a good chance to get his letter on its way to Ana. Dispatch cases must leave the consul's office at Yerba Buena for the United States every week.

3

After a glorious three-day trip down the river and into broad San Pablo Bay, and from there into the even larger body of water that opened through two striking headlands onto the Pacific Ocean, they found that Consul Larkin was paying a duty call on General Castro at Monterey, and was not expected back for a week.

The consul's assistant, William Leidesdorff, a friendly, considerate man, accommodated them as best he could, apologizing for the dreary little *posada* in which he quartered them.

Frémont, clearly piqued at the outset by the absence of the

consul, told Stone they would spend three nights in Yerba Buena and then go back up the river.

Yerba Buena presented itself as a dismal, dirty little port and fishing village of mud huts dotting a number of hills on the south side of the bay. With its rickety wharves and docks, and the dense fog that rolled in every one of the mornings they spent there, it appeared a step below "sleepy," and very near comatose.

"Leidesdorff tells me that the Californios who grub out a living in this pitiful hamlet have asked the government to change its name," Frémont said. "They want to call it San Francisco, after the bay itself. Perhaps the wish for something grander will be father to the thought. It does lie deep within a splendid, natural harbor. However, I cannot see it ever replacing Monterey as California's principal seaport."

The third morning the assistant consul provided news of another and more serious nature, from the State Department in Washington this time. A two-month-old copy of *The New York Times* came with the dispatches, and Frémont hurriedly perused it.

"Our ambassador in Mexico City, Mr. Slidell," he told Stone, "has asked for his mission's passports, and there is another story that says General Taylor has moved his division from the Nueces River in Texas into a position on the Río Grande."

"Zachary Taylor? Old Rough and Ready himself?" Stone asked.

"Yes." The captain pursed his lips and gave out a low whistle. "War. No question about it. Only a matter of time. That settles it, Bradford. We shall not go directly back to New Helvetia. I feel now it is imperative we leave immediately for Monterey to confer with Tom Larkin."

"Would you take these new dispatches along to Consul Larkin, sir?" Leidesdorff asked.

"With pleasure, Mr. Leidesdorff. Bradford, take charge of them."

Leidesdorff loaned them horses from the consulate's stables, and they set out within the hour. Frémont told Stone to leave his Hawken with the orderly the assistant consul had assigned them when they arrived.

"Firearms would do us little good, Bradford, and I want to create the impression we are men of peace."

Stone admired the captain's sangfroid. They would be riding through country that could become enemy territory at any moment, carrying Lord-knew-what in the way of probably secret, even dangerous messages to the American official, without any real standing as legitimate couriers.

Leidesdorff had also promised to get Stone's letter to Ana aboard the American ship leaving Yerba Buena in only three days' time.

"It will go north to Oregon first, Mr. Stone, and then by wagon train or express coach back down to Bent's."

For the letter to get to Taos by that route would require considerably less than half the time necessary for it to make it around the Horn. With any luck it could be in Ana's hands in weeks.

4

Monterey gleamed as Frémont and Stone rode in.

The contrast between this sparkling gem of a seacoast city and Yerba Buena was stark.

To the east of the town, which lay in the bight of a fishhook of tidy land green with gardens and alive with flowers, all well protected from tides and storms by the hills on the ocean side of the cape, a stone fort on a bluff stood guard. But other than that, the scene that greeted the two travelers was one of peace and civility. Buildings reminiscent of those at New Helvetia lined three or four irregular but immaculate cobbled streets. The houses, the shops, and even what he assumed were the public buildings, had been whitewashed to the same brilliance as those in Captain Sutter's village, and roofed with the same bloodred tile. The harbor of Monterey looked as lively with commerce as Yerba Buena's had been derelict.

With Frémont's excellent Spanish, and the name of the consul's inn to guide them, it took them no time at all to locate him.

They found Tom Larkin—Frémont had told Stone on the ride down he had come to California as a trader and was well on his way to becoming a millionaire—dining in the patio of his *posada,* an area completely enclosed by interior walls of fitted stone. The branches of a lemon tree arched over the American consul's table.

Stone liked the square-jawed Larkin from the moment the American consul rose, shook hands with them warmly, took the dispatch case from him, and insisted they sit and eat with him, and he felt Frémont liked Larkin, too, although he sensed a tickle of irritation in the captain when the consul proceeded to chat about a variety of things other than what Stone guessed Frémont wanted to discuss.

"Mr. Larkin," Frémont said, disregarding a question about the health of his wife, Jessie, whose magazine articles the consul had apparently read and admired, "could you arrange for me to meet with General Castro? If not today, then tomorrow?"

Larkin looked dumbfounded, struck into silence.

When he at last found his voice, Larkin said, "You'd be walking right into the lion's den, Captain. Do you think that wise? Castro probably doesn't know you're in Monterey, and I wouldn't disabuse him of his ignorance if I were you. May I ask what you want to see him about?"

"I think it behooves a commander to personally take the measure of a possible opponent."

"You have no other reason?"

"None, sir."

"You will make no attempt to secure agreements with Castro which could jeopardize my mission at Yerba Buena?"

"Have no fear of that."

Larkin leaned back in his wicker chair, placed the tips of his fingers together, and smiled warily. "All right, Captain. It's too late this evening, but I'll send a note around to the *presidio* first thing in the morning. Would you like me to accompany you to the meeting if it can be arranged?"

"That won't be necessary, Mr. Larkin, but of course you're welcome. I harbor no secrets."

"Be that as it may, Captain, I must caution you about something."

"Yes?"

"General Castor is not, in my opinion, a very stable officer to begin with, and these days he is under severe pressure. California could blow up at any moment, and he is very jumpy. He might look upon you and your expedition as a threat to his control over the northern part of the state. Are you aware that he knows of your party's stay with Captain Sutter?"

"I am, sir. We did not hide when we entered California. We are only sixteen men all told. That surely can constitute no threat to General Castro's authority."

"True. But are you also aware that he knows you expect to be joined by another fifty armed men coming up from the south?"

Stone detected the surprise that flashed on Frémont's face before he could hide it. It certainly was startling that the American consul—and Castro—knew about the Talbot detachment, particularly when Frémont, and Kit back up at

New Helvetia, had absolutely no knowledge of their own at the moment of the whereabouts of their companions.

On the trip south along the Sierras, Frémont's smaller party had passed through three remote, somnolent Californio villages, but their inhabitants had paid their little party no mind at all. The villagers had been seeing American mountain men for more than thirty years. It seemed doubtful that they would think even Talbot's party sufficiently important to report it to Monterey if Joe Walker led them north that way.

"You have my word of honor," Frémont said, "that I will make no attempt to hide even the tiniest detail of the truth from the general, Mr. Larkin."

Stone wondered if one of the "details" his commander would not hide concerned the three mountain howitzers bumping along in the baggage train of the southern section of the expedition.

"Incidentally," Frémont said, "have there been any messages from Washington, perhaps from the Department of the Navy, that someone was coming out to see me?"

"Not to my knowledge, sir," Larkin said, "but you might check again with Bill Leidesdorff on your way back to Sutter's. We're getting a ton of dispatches from State and the Navy every week, as you might imagine. The confrontation between the U.S. and Mexico is only a paper war at the moment, but it's a war nonetheless."

It seemed strange to Stone that neither the consul nor Frémont mentioned the alarming news about Zachary Taylor's move to the Río Grande.

5

"General Castro says he will see you in about a week, Captain." Larkin shrugged in apparent helplessness. "I protested on your behalf, but to no avail."

After a glance at Frémont's face, Stone did not look forward to that week. But whatever it was he dreaded, it never came to pass. Frémont spent a lot of time with Larkin, and Stone amused himself by practicing his Spanish on shopkeepers, cantina owners, and the servants at the inn. None asked him what he was doing in Monterey. *La cortesía. Sí.*

6

A week later they walked across the parade ground of the *presidio* perched on the bluff east of Monterey, their horses already led off by a murderous-looking groom in uniform. Stone wondered if they would ever come out of the fort again. The place, even in brilliant morning sunlight, looked far more forbidding than it had from the town. Riflemen with fixed bayonets drilled in a far corner of the grounds.

Frémont seemed not to notice them, or the sentries posted behind the crenellated parapets above. He strode across the packed gravel as if he owned the place and was on parade himself.

A crisp Mexican officer met them on broad flagstone steps leading to an arched stone doorway.

"Follow me, *señores, por favor,*" the officer said. "General Castro is waiting for you. He will not wait long." No smile of greeting came. He turned and led them down a long corridor so deep into the dark interior of the stone fort that torches jammed in wall sconces had been set alight.

The officer stopped at a massive, ornate wooden door carved into shapes like amaranthus leaves. He pushed it open and stepped back. "*¡Aquí!*" he said abruptly.

Immediately upon entering the Mexican general's office, Stone saw that Don José Castro was not a "clean desk" man; papers littered every corner of the carved mahogany table he sat behind. He wore a resplendent, dark blue uniform from which yards of gold braid drooped, and the ribbons and medals pinned to his tunic would have shamed a sunburst. Stone wondered if he dressed in this manner every day, or if he had donned the gaudy attire this morning to impress his American visitors. Stone hoped so. A man who desires to impress is usually less dangerous.

Castro was small in stature, but he looked strong and supple, and despite a droop to his eyelids, fully alert. A fit man, obviously. Except that his slicked-back, heavily pomaded hair was jet black, and that he had waxed the ends of his full mustache to rapier points, he put Stone in mind of Don Bernardo Barragán.

Castro looked young to hold such an important post, Frémont's age perhaps. He did not rise. He was toying with a quill pen.

"To what may I attribute the honor of this visit, *señores?*" Castro said as he waved Stone and Frémont into chairs in front of the desk with a flutter of the pen. His dark eyes looked shrewd, suspicious. "Would you care for wine or *aguardiente,* perhaps?"

"None for me, *muchísimas gracias,* Your Excellency," Frémont said.

"No thank you, sir," Stone said.

"*We* are honored," Frémont said now, "that you were kind enough to receive us, *mi general.*"

"What may a general of the Army of Mexico do for you, Capitán Frémont? It *is* 'Capitán,' is it not?" Castro's lips curled in a faint, almost undetectable sneer.

Although Frémont's bland face betrayed nothing, Stone remembered how the captain's temper had flared at a good deal less at other times.

"Actually, I only hold the rank of *brevet* captain, *General Castro,*" Frémont said. Stone wondered if the Mexican had heard the tiny grating breath on the words "brevet" and "general." Frémont continued. "And in answer to your first question, Señor Stone and I have merely come to pay our respects. We desire nothing from you but your goodwill, Don José."

"You have no questions of me?"

"None, sir."

"Señor Stone there, looks as if he could be a soldier, *también. Es un hombre bastante grande.* Does he hold military rank as you do, Capitán Frémont?"

"No, sir, he does not. Mr. Stone serves as a civilian employee of the United States Army Corps of Topographical Engineers, the same branch of my country's service in which I hold my American commission. He is a cartographer, as I am. Mapping is the sole purpose of our explorations in your province, General. Our endeavors will someday benefit our two nations enormously."

"Interesting." Castro played with the quill pen again, this time stroking his cheek with the feathered end. "Perhaps Señor Stone could map out for me your intended movements in northern California. Where do you intend going, Capitán, and just exactly what do you intend to map? Did you come to my fort this morning to make a map of it?"

"We are not spies. I am a man of science, and my expedition is a scientific one."

"Ah, *sí.* But you are a military man as well, *señor.*"

"That is the way things are ordered in my country, *mi general.* The United States Army has many scientific interests that have little or nothing to do with the art of war."

"Strange. Science in Mexico is the domain of scholars. Soldiers only concern themselves with war. Why does not Señor Stone, the civilian, command your 'scientific' expedition instead of you? All your other men are civilians, are they not?"

"They are indeed. My compliments that you know that, sir. Mr. Stone is gifted in his profession. I do not believe he has any desire to command."

"And you, on the other hand, do. *¿Es verdad, no . . . Capitán?*"

Frémont stiffened. "I do not believe that calls for an answer, General."

Stone was sure Frémont had been at the point of using his old, scathing "sirrah."

"In that case," Castro said, "I believe we do not have any more to say to each other." The Mexican smiled as if he had just won this small exchange. He dropped the pen on the desktop and Stone knew it for a signal of dismissal.

Had they come this far just for this brief meeting?

Frémont rose. "I suppose not, sir." Stone could see the effort he made to control his emotions in the rigid way he held himself. "But may I take it," he continued, his voice icy, "that we have your permission to continue our topographical work in the province of California as we move north to American territory in Oregon?"

"For the moment—*sí.* However, take some well-meant advice, *por favor.* I would not linger in California if I were you."

Stone and Frémont started for the door, only to stop when Castro spoke again. "*Perdón, Capitán.* I have just one more question." His voice dripped sarcasm. "Are the three pieces of *artillería* your Mr. Talbot has with him instruments to be used in what you call 'topographical work'? Does Señor Stone take his sightings through a cannon?"

7

They stayed at Tom Larkin's *posada* in Monterey for a few more days. Frémont made a great show of himself around the town, spending an inordinate amount of time trading for leather goods, tents, and supplies for the expedition, to be shipped upcountry to Sutter's, and in purchasing some gifts of tobacco and soap, chores that could easily have been done in half an afternoon. Stone knew the captain wanted to show Castro he could not be run off, even after the Mexican general's threat-tinged voice that Frémont and his men should not "linger in California."

They finally began the ninety-mile ride back to Yerba Buena with the intention of an overnight stay at the ranch of an American settler named Fisher to whom Tom Larkin directed them. "Fisher's *rancho* is about thirteen or fourteen miles southeast of San José Pueblo, Captain Frémont. Look it over. I think it has everything you need if things turn out the way you think they will. Bill Fisher can be relied on."

Larkin's remark baffled Stone, and no explanation of it came from Frémont. It must have referred to something he had discussed with Larkin in the private sessions he had with him before they met with Castro.

Some strange things were going on. Since Walker Lake Frémont had kept Stone next to him as tight as a tick—part of the time at least. He had been, for most of the trip down from Sutter's, a model of forthright openness. Why the captain had taken Stone with him to the fort seemed obvious enough. He had asked him to prepare a report on the audience with the Mexican general to leave with Leidesdorff at Yerba Buena for the assistant consul to send on to Washington. But it seemed every bit as obvious that there were some things he did not particularly want Stone in on.

During the journey north, Frémont spoke only when absolutely necessary, and Stone could not tell if he had slipped into one of those depressed moods again. It did not seem so when they arrived at William Fisher's ranch.

Stone actually saw little of Fisher. Frémont and the rancher huddled together immediately after their arrival, and it seemed their stay would be a reprise of the week in Monterey before the conference with Castro, when the Pathfinder locked himself in with Tom Larkin and left Stone to his own devices.

But the first morning at Fisher's, Frémont surprised him.

"I want you to continue on to Yerba Buena alone, Bradford. Mr. Leidesdorff surely must have messages for me from Washington by now. I shall wait here for your return. Mr. Fisher and I have many things to discuss."

8

Leidesdorff had indeed received a message for Frémont, but not from Washington. One had come down the river from Sutter, sealed and marked *Confidential,* but there was no mystery about its contents when Stone read the one on New Helvetia vellum addressed to him—from Carson. Apparently Kit had gotten Johann Sutter to write it for him.

Kit and Dick Owens had found the Talbot detachment poking along northward toward New Helvetia. As the scout had surmised, Joe Walker had gotten lost. Kit's note said Joe was suffering mightily from the teasing given him by the other mountain men. Exactly as Carson had guessed, Walker had mistaken another unknown river for the Lake Fork of the Tulare and must have passed the Sutter's Fort group well to the west, at about the same time Stone, Owens, and Maxwell were fighting the Horsethief Indians from their hilltop. Stone was still musing about how good it would be to see Ed Kern again, when Leidesdorff handed him another letter. Stone detected a faint trace of lilies of the valley.

The return address read, "Casa Carson—Taos—Provincia de Nuevo Méjico."

Ana! He ripped it open with such force a piece of the wax seal flew all the way to the corner of the consulate's small office. Leidesdorff smiled, and excused himself. He must have smelled the perfume, too.

Bradford, *mi amor*—

Señor Charles Bent is writing this for me, so do not think my English has improved so very much. He said I should not tell you this, that I *speak* English very well, and he has no trouble, but I insisted he put it in.

(Charlie here, Bradford. I made very little change in Doña Ana's actual words, believe me, my boy.)

It makes me very angry that I must make this letter such a secret thing. Everything I say in it I wish to shout from the top of Taos Mountain, but you know, of course, how Papá is about you and me. Today is the first time he has let me come to Taos from the *estancia* to visit Cousin Josefa, so it is only today I have read the letter you sent to me from the place you call Pilot Peak. Josefa says to thank you for helping Don Cristóbal write to her. Josefa says it is the first letter she ever got from him. Señor Bent is helping her send him a letter, too. It will go to him along with this one to you.

I have always been happy at Estancia Barragán, but I fear I will never be happy there again— unless you are with me. I cried hard all day every day for three days after you rode away with Don Cristóbal to Señor Bent's fort on the Río Arkansas, and I will cry again when this letter leaves.

In the truth of God, I cry a little every day, but I do not cry at night when I sleep, because you are with me then. You hold me in your arms and you kiss me. You kiss me and hold me all through the long night. It is more than a dream.

My face gets red and hot when I think I must make Señor Bent put this in this letter.

Your letter brought me great joy, but I did not read in it everything I wanted so very much to read.

I am very sorry for the Ute girl you told me about. It is too bad she had to die, but I am jealous of her. She died with her head in your lap. I think I would almost be glad to die myself that way.

Write again—and quickly. And this time tell me that you love me. I feel you do. But I must see the words themselves. I love *you*, Bradford—*con todo mi corazón.*

Ana

In a postscript Charlie Bent sent his best to Kit and Captain Frémont, and assured Stone that the contents of the letter had left his mind as soon as he had Ana sign it. Stone despaired that Ana had the courage to put her heart on paper, and that he had not, and so he penned another letter to her before he left the little office. In it he told her a dozen times he loved her.

21

Omen on Gavilán

When Stone returned to the Fisher ranch from Yerba Buena and told Frémont he had still not received word from Washington, the Pathfinder fumed in irritation and impatience.

Stone handed him Sutter's carefully sealed envelope and watched as he read it with William Fisher also looking on.

It clearly contained the same news as did Kit's to Stone, that the scout and Owens had found Talbot, Walker, Kern, and the rest of the expedition wandering the foothills of the

Sierras, but at eight or more pages the letter looked far too long to carry only this one piece of information.

Indeed, Frémont exclaimed, "Kit's found Mr. Talbot!" after he could have scanned no more than the first few lines, and returned then to read for the better part of five minutes, emitting angry little grunts, and with his face flashing a series of small storms.

Frémont did not divulge anything else the Swiss had to say, but when he finished the letter he handed it to Fisher, a dour, gray-haired Vermont Yankee whom Stone had not yet seen without a pistol strapped to his side, and then asked if he could have a few words in private with the rancher.

Frémont and Bill Fisher sequestered themselves in Fisher's ranch office for the better part of an hour, and when they emerged Frémont said, "Bradford, I must ask you to make another trip to Yerba Buena for me. We must get word to Mr. Carson at New Helvetia that now that he's found Mr. Talbot and the others I wish him to bring the entire contingent down here to Mr. Fisher's ranch. Mr. Leidesdorff will accommodate us by sending an express courier up the river, I am sure. Time is not only of the essence, it has become everything. While you are at Yerba Buena, ask again for messages from Washington. And discover if you can if General Taylor has met the enemy on the Río Grande."

The last instruction seemed casual, as if it were a matter of indifference to Frémont whether or not Taylor was anywhere near the northern border of Mexico.

Stone left for the small port on San Francisco Bay thirty minutes later.

2

Kit and the whole expedition, howitzers and all, arrived within the week, and Stone wondered what sort of trouble bringing the three guns so close to Monterey could generate.

He wasted no time in getting together with Ed Kern, bringing Kern up to date on everything that had happened to the smaller party while they were separated from the Talbot detachment, with particular emphasis on Frémont's meetings with Tom Larkin and General Castro. He told the Philadelphian how Frémont had pointedly excluded him from his meetings with Larkin and the rancher Fisher.

"It's as I said back at Pilot Peak, Brad," Kern said. "He's using you. Still, that might work to your advantage, as it did then."

"What possible use can I be to him if he won't place any trust in me?"

"I don't claim to know everything, but I do know he's using you."

"All right, that's enough about me," Stone said. "Tell me about *your* trip, Ed."

"Well . . . until Joe got us lost, it was a promenade. Oh, we did have hell's own time getting those damned howitzers across a couple of mountain streams that had left their banks. Those guns . . . I thought our good friend Sutter would faint when he saw them. I had the feeling he couldn't wait to get rid of us. His demeanor sure didn't square with what I'd heard about what a genial host he is. I think all this milling around California that Captain Johnny's had us doing is beginning to trouble him."

"Sutter *has* been a little nervous lately. Have you told Frémont of his reaction to the guns?"

"Yes, but he just shrugged it off, said Sutter would have to get used to things like that."

Stone told him then about Castro's knowledge of the three cannons.

"Doesn't surprise me," Ed said. "Joe might have lost his way, and Basil and Godey's remarks are making the poor devil pay for that, but he's got a keen sense of what goes on around him in the wilderness. Couple of times he swore we were being scouted when nobody else saw a thing. He wanted to take out after whoever it might be, but Talbot and I talked him out of it. What you and our captain learned in Monterey sure makes it look as if Joe was right, though. What's the latest about what's going on down on the Río Grande?"

"No war yet. At least Larkin at Monterey and Leidesdorff at Yerba Buena have had no word about it, but they do think it's getting close."

"What does Captain Johnny say about that?"

"Virtually nothing." He told Ed then of Frémont's one casual bit of interest in Zachary Taylor's whereabouts.

"Hmmm . . . I would think he'd be occupied with little else at the moment. He's taking a big chance, moving us down here even deeper into California when there's every likelihood of a war breaking out before we could ever start north for Oregon . . . if we're really going there. We might have to fight here in California whether we want to or not." He paused. "But maybe that's exactly why he brought us all down here."

"Captain Frémont talked of nothing but peace when we met with General Castro—pretty persuasively, too. He told Castro we're on our way to Oregon, and he sounded as if he meant it. It was the same when we met Larkin."

"What's the mood of our friend Carson? He was still down in the dumps after we parted company at Walker Lake. Did he cheer up at least a little?"

"He's revived some. Kit never stays down long."

"Back to our Johnny. Maybe he intended that peace talk for *your* ears as much as for the Mexican's. I'll believe we're on our way to Oregon only when we actually cross the border."

3

The time spent at Fisher's ranch turned out to be much like the good days at Sutter's for the members of the expedition, with the possible exception of Alexis Godey. No supple, seductive women such as La Barracuda appeared on Godey's horizon. The glum look on his face brought round after round of ribald remarks from his fellows, and Stone laughed uproariously even at some of the coarsest of them.

The mountain men danced to Gus Archambeault's wild fiddling some of the nights at Fisher's as they had at New Helvetia, but to an audience that only consisted this time of the half dozen Californios who worked Fisher's ranch, *vaqueros* who put on a dazzling show of horsemanship after watching the shooting contests the Americans staged.

The Californians rode as if they were centaurs, and their spinning *reatas* as they chased down calves circled magically through the bright spring air.

In one other stunning display they planted a meadow with several dozen wooden pegs hardly larger than a man's hand, galloped their horses across the grass at full tilt, and with long, slim, needle-pointed lances plucked the pegs from the earth without a miss. Stone's thoughts ran back to Kit running the much heavier lance through the back of the Comanche on the Cimarron.

But Kit seemed diffident these days, and at times uneasy, particularly after one of his few private meetings with Frémont. Stone wondered if the Pathfinder was taking his chief scout into his confidence.

After two weeks at Fisher's *rancho,* Frémont, at a hastily convened meeting in the ranch house with Bill Fisher at his side, announced another move for the expedition. More groans came from Joe Walker, who was still suffering from the gibes of his comrades for getting Talbot lost on the Tulare. "I had some notion we was going to fight somebody soon. I know you've never said so, Captain, but why did we haul them guns all across hell's widest goddamned stretches?"

Frémont ignored Walker's outburst. "Mr. Fisher says that he has found a better campground for us a few leagues from here," he told Kern, Talbot, Carson, Godey, Walker, and Stone. "Our host regrets turning us out, but it is plain to me that we are exhausting his resources and we do not wish to outstay our welcome."

The "few leagues" turned out to be a few leagues closer not to Sutter's or Oregon, but to Monterey and the coast.

"He's *looking* for trouble now," Kern whispered to Brad when the meeting ended.

4

The expedition made a fine camp in the corner of a mile square, level field of new spring oats near the headquarters buildings of the *rancho,* one considerably larger than Fisher's, owned by a William E. Hartnell, a somewhat shy, almost painfully reserved Englishman who had come to California after a lengthy stint in the cattle business in South America. Hartnell might have agreed to the Américans descending on him en masse the way they had, but he seemed, to Stone, at their one and only meeting soon after the arrival, to be somewhat discomfited by the expedition's presence now that it actually occupied his land. He stared at the howitzers warily, as if he thought they might spout flame and shot at any moment.

"I can't blame the man if he's a little nervous," Kern said. "If this General Castro that you and Frémont met knew about our mountain guns, he sure as hell will know about our move here. He won't stay convinced of our peaceable intentions now that we're moving cannons closer to him. I expect we'll be hearing from him fairly soon. Hartnell probably expects to hear something from the general, too, and he figures that for his personal well-being and that of his operation here, none of it will be good. Even if Hartnell's become a Mexican citizen now, as Sutter has, he can't afford to get on the outs with Monterey."

"Sutter must be worried about Castro, too," Stone said.

"Well, the Swiss at least has the luxury of being at a much greater distance from the seat of power than Hartnell does."

Frémont for his part looked serene as he rode the camp every day.

5

As Kern predicted, they heard from General Don José Castro.

At high noon on the Wednesday of their second week at Hartnell's, visitors arrived, just when Lajeunesse was fixing lunch.

Three men, all in the blue-and-white uniform of the Mexican army, rode into the American camp. One of the mounted men carried a silver trumpet; one held aloft a staff with the flag of Mexico fluttering in the breeze the brisk canter created; the third wore a saber with jewels on the scabbard and rode a length or two ahead of the others. His uniform carried as much braid as General Castro's and nearly as many decorations.

"Three extra mouths to feed, Bass!" Kit called out.

When the three riders pulled their horses up and the

mountain men swarmed to them, the rider with the trumpet loosed a few clear but off-key blasts from his instrument.

The men broke into laughter, and then, led by Lajeunesse, cheered. Some tossed their fur caps in the air. Gus Archambeault fired off his rifle, causing two of the visitors' horses to stamp nervously.

"¡Bárbaros!" the bemedaled officer screamed. "¡Basta!" Then, in a calmer tone, said, "Soy Lugarteniente José Antonio Chávez. ¿Donde está el capitán Juan Frémont?" He glared at each man in the circle around him, finally fixing his eyes hard on Kit. "¿No habla español, bufón? Do not you or one of these other clowns speak Spanish?"

No one spoke for seconds.

Kit gave the young officer a look that verged on being a sneer. "¿El español de tu madre, o el de tu patrio? ¡Es su preferencia, caballero!"

Lajeunesse guffawed, quaked with laughter, and several of the other men joined him. Stone turned to Godey. "What did Kit say that's so damned funny, Alexis?"

"Kit just insulted this peacock pretty good. It's like he more or less called him a bastard. Very subtle. Hard to explain if you don't know some of the finer points of Spanish."

The officer had turned absolutely livid.

Carson continued. "Sure we speak Spanish, mister, and some of us every bit as good as you do. But we only speak it to Mexican gents as mind their manners. Now why don't you ask your question again? In English this time, since you just let on you got at least some of our lingo. And don't forget the one English word we want to hear. It's pronounced 'please,' in case you don't know."

Carson's cool words did little to assuage the temper of the young officer. Chávez's nostrils flared. "Do not try my patience, you dirty little bandit. In the name of Don José

Castro, Commanding General of Upper California, I demand to see Captain John Frémont—at once!"

"You *demand* . . . ? Demanding ain't exactly the kind of thing us Americans like to hear." Kit was containing wondrously the anger he must now be feeling. "I'm still waiting for that 'please.'"

Another voice came from somewhere outside the circle. "That's enough, Kit. Thank you. I will deal with this officer." Frémont had ridden up on Sacramento.

The captain was wearing his everyday homespun and cotton, and he wore his battered old trail hat, and he had not trimmed his dark hair and beard. He drew a look of contempt from the immaculately outfitted young Mexican.

"I am Captain John C. Frémont, young man. You hold the rank of lieutenant, I presume?"

"*Lugarteniente, sí.*"

"And you are called?"

"Don José Antonio Chávez."

"State your business, Lieutenant Chávez—briefly and to the point."

Chávez reached down into his saddlebag, pulled out a parchment packet sealed with wax, and handed it to Frémont. "This comes from General Don José Castro, *yanqui!*" Frémont shot him a sharp look, but the lieutenant, undaunted, continued. "There is no need for you to open it, *señor.* The document it contains is merely for your records. General Castro has ordered me to tell you what it says. In English." Chávez swelled his chest. He put his hand to the hilt of the saber and pushed down until the scabbard cocked up behind him. "As military governor and commanding officer of all the northern districts of the Department of California, I, Don José Castro . . . ," he began. His stilted delivery told Stone he had learned this speech by heart, had probably rehearsed it.

"'. . . order you, Brevet Captain John C. Frémont, United States Corps of Topographical Engineers, and all of those serving under you, to quit the said province of California within one week of the date of this decree. You are commanded to retire with all speed possible beyond the mountains which form the border between our nations. Failure on your part to obey this order will result in immediate confinement for you and your band of criminals, and then transportation in shackles to Mexico City, where you will be held for trial as armed enemies of the Republic of Mexico. Do not for a moment doubt that I, General Don José Castro, have more than sufficient military strength at my disposal to enforce this order, nor that I will hesitate to employ that strength with all the vigor I possess.'"

Not a sound came from anyone in the gathering, but every one of the mountain men, including Kit, now turned their eyes to Frémont.

One of the Mexicans' horses whinnied.

Then Lajeunesse, a whip coiled in his meaty hand, stepped out of the circle and took one huge step in Chávez's direction.

"Stand fast, Bass!" Frémont shouted. He urged Sacramento even closer to Chávez's sorrel, until his eyes were no more than a foot or so from those of the Mexican officer.

"You insufferable young puppy!" the Pathfinder exclaimed in a voice all could hear. "'Band of criminals,' did I hear you say? Do you have any idea at all of the nature of the insult you and your boorish general have just offered the United States of America in the person of one of its serving officers?"

Stone had seen Frémont hot with anger before, but this was heat of an entirely different magnitude, and when he looked at Chávez again he found the young officer's face had undergone a remarkable change. Even serving under Don José Castro, the foppish young man had clearly never before encountered anyone quite as terrifying as the man he faced at the moment. Chávez began to wilt.

"Now . . . *Lugarteniente* Chávez . . . ," Frémont continued, "go back to Don José Castro and give him this reply to his ill-advised and thoroughly offensive decree. First, express to him my disgust that he is breaking the word he gave me when I met with him in Monterey, that I and my companions would be permitted to go about our business in the province he commands. Tell him of my anger, and tell him of my unyielding refusal to obey his ridiculous order. Band of criminals indeed! I should by rights allow Mr. Lajeunesse there, one of my 'criminals,' to take his whip to you."

In the twinkling of an eye *Lugarteniente* José Antonio Chávez became a mere boy. His hand moved from the hilt of his saber and the scabbard dropped. Frémont's gaze turned down toward it. "You may quit my camp now, Lieutenant, and do not ever wear a sword again to a place where I command—unless that sword is drawn!"

A throaty roar of approval rose from the men of the expedition.

As Chávez and his two companions turned their horses about and rode off, Frémont faced his men, lifted his sweat-stained old hat, and waved it.

"Excuse me, gentlemen," he said, smiling, "I must tidy up for dinner." He turned Sacramento in a full circle and set his spurs into the stallion's flanks.

"Magnificent," Kern whispered to Stone as the Pathfinder rode off toward Hartnell's *hacienda*. "Now mind you—we should recognize that this Mexican general is well within his legal rights to order us out of his backyard, but I'll be the first to admit my heart was pumping pretty fast at our Johnny's performance."

6

A day and a half later found the expedition perched on the flat top of a small mountain in the nearby eastern range. A check of one of Frémont's 1844 maps gave its name as Gavilán Peak. It rose abruptly from the far side of a great foothill meadow split by an arroyo whose banks sprouted a thick mat of brush.

It looked a good defensible position, but, Stone wondered, could sixty men, no matter how skilled at fighting they might be, stand against a modern army? Well, he could hope Frémont would find some advice about what he should do next in one of those tactical manuals. But even if he did not, that general in Monterey would soon discover he had Christopher Carson to contend with, as well as John C. Frémont.

Ted Talbot, with whom Stone had had so little to do since leaving Bent's, proved to be a pretty fair engineer for the log fortification Frémont ordered him to build with the help of ten Californios recruited from Hartnell's ranch. A crude but substantial redoubt sprang up on the mountaintop in no time at all, a log embrasure with a solid five-foot-high wall broken only where the three mountain guns poked their surly muzzles through the breeches.

With deep, rocky gullies behind the position and to the right and left of it, there now remained only one possible direction from which an attack could come. And it would have to come from across a broad plain that stretched away to a skimpy forest half a mile away.

"They will have to be brave men to try to charge us," Godey said. "Unless they come up here in great numbers, not enough lancers could reach the top to worry us."

"I hope they're brave," Dick Owens said. "If they're only

smart, and just sit down there and try to starve us out, I sure don't want to spend any amount of time in Bass Lajeunesse's company if the old bear can't get enough to eat."

Once the crews had finished the fort to Talbot's satisfaction near sundown, Kit, a hatchet in his hand, walked to a grove of skinny aspen saplings growing on the rim of one of the gullies behind them, cut and trimmed one out to a length of about twenty feet. Then he carried it as he might a lance to the center of the log breastwork, where Frémont was conferring with Walker and Talbot.

"This one do, Captain?"

"Admirably, Kit." Frémont held a packet of cloth out to the scout, and Carson shook out the folded Stars and Stripes. He ran a length of rawhide through the two brass grommets at the banner's corners and lashed it to the slimmer end of the tall sapling. By now about twenty of the men had gathered.

Then the captain and Kit bent their backs to the task of driving the thicker, pointed end of the pole into the hard ground, piling stones around it when they finished. The early evening breeze caught the flag's folds and whipped the stripes and dancing stars out to catch the last rays of the setting sun. A great, echoing cheer from the mountain men greeted the sight, reminding Stone of the Fourth of July celebration at Bent's.

"This is probably the first time Old Glory has ever flown over any part of California," Frémont said when the cheer died at last. "It will not be the last. I want a fire here, Mr. Carson, and I want it absolutely blazing—night and day! Our flag must be seen clearly at all times."

There seemed to be no question in the mind of anyone on Gavilán Peak that Castro and the Mexicans would come against them in force; there was only a conjecture about when. Guesses flew across the top of the mountain like the swallows that filled the copper sky at twilight. Joe Walker did not guess; he hoped. "After that insulting bastard that Castro sent, I can't wait to get a Mexican in my sights."

7

All the guessing ended next morning when half a dozen blue-uniformed riders, one of them holding the Mexican flag on a long, piked staff, ventured cautiously out of the woods across the plain from Gavilán Peak, just as the sun rose behind the little mountain and flooded the western meadow. The officer leading the detachment looked as if he could be Lieutenant Chávez, but even when Stone, peering over the breastwork with a number of the others, put Ed Kern's telescope on the group, he could not be sure. Behind them mules pulled gun carriages to the edge of the grass, while men on foot hurried along beside the caissons, carrying canisters and tamping rods.

"We're even in cannons," Kit said. "They've got three and we've got three. It will come down to men with rifles in the end. It most always does."

Joe Walker fidgeted happily.

As the groups at the breastwork watched, some of the men tending the distant guns unharnessed the mules and led the animals back toward the forest, while others piled up cannonballs in neat, black pyramids.

"I'm no expert in artillery," Kern said, "but if that's where they're going to position their guns, we're *way* out of range. I have a hunch we'll stay that way."

"Do you suppose," Alexis Godey broke in, "that they think we will ride down to the meadow and make a charge? Ridiculous! I have no desire to be out in the open with those lancers. Remember those *vaqueros* at the Fisher ranch? I'm content to wait for them up here with my Hawken and my patience. What do you think, Kit?"

"Mainly you're right," Carson said. "On the other hand, it might not be a bad idea to try to take those guns before the Mexicans move cavalry and riflemen up to protect them."

"You bet!" Joe Walker said. "I don't relish facing lancers any more than Alexis does, but I ain't too keen on cannon fire, either. And I just pure hate sitting on my ass doing nothing. I say let's get down there right quick."

"I can't see any men in the woods yet," Kit said, "but I expect they'll show up soon."

The Pathfinder had come up behind the group unnoticed. He must have been there for several minutes. "We'll wait, Mr. Carson," he said. "If there is to be a battle, General Castro must begin it. We have not come to California to start a war."

"Yes, sir," Kit said.

As Frémont walked off, Ed Kern cast a glance at Stone that looked like *"I told you so. . . ."*

"Damn it, Kit!" Walker said when Frémont had moved well out of earshot. "Can't the captain see it? We ought to get down there and get those guns while we still have a chance. You should have put up an argument."

Kit shrugged, but said nothing.

Through the rest of the morning hours Stone and Kern took turns with the telescope, and by the time the sun had reached its zenith, Kit's idea of making a quick seizure of the Mexican guns had become academic.

The forest across the meadow had by this time filled with soldiery, almost all of it on foot. Beyond nosing a few feet from the woods to take a look even as Stone and his companions were doing from the log wall, none of the men they saw left the cover of the trees, but Kern and Stone made out a good deal of movement in the shadows behind the forest's edge.

"There must be at least a hundred men down there now," Stone said at two in the afternoon.

"More like two hundred," Kern said. He swung the telescope to the south, where the road from Monterey snaked through some low hills and into the forest. "And a hell of a lot more are moving up." He handed the glass to Stone. "But take a look yourself while I hop to it and tell the captain what we've seen."

Sure enough, at least two squadrons of cavalry were entering the woods. But once the forest swallowed the body of riders, all movement inside it seemed to stop.

Stone kept the telescope on the gun positions. The blue-clad gunners had moved away from their three high-wheeled, ugly weapons and were now squatting behind them in a semicircle halfway between them and the nearest trees. It looked as if they had settled into a game of cards.

It remained much the same until late afternoon, when a body of cavalry, twenty-five or thirty strong, perhaps the same mounted men Kern had spied earlier, moved out of the woods, their horses held to a walk, but with their lances leveled. When they reached a point in the meadow considerably closer than the half dozen riders had yesterday, Stone saw through the glass that the leader was indeed Lieutenant José Antonio Chávez. He had slanted his naked saber over his shoulder.

The mountaintop shivered in a frenzy of activity. Cries and orders—Frémont's voice trumpeting above all the others—echoed through the little fort. In less than three minutes forty men of the expedition on horseback, with Carson out in front of them, thundered out of the breastworks and down the rocky slope, without Brad Stone and Ed Kern.

"Assist Mr. Talbot with bringing the howitzers to bear if they overrun us down in the meadow, Mr. Kern," Frémont yelled just before jumping the stallion over the log wall to race after Carson and the others, "and you, Mr. Stone, make a full and accurate record of what transpires here today. A battle sketch or two or three would be quite in order, too."

Stone tried to content himself with the thought that he occupied the finest seat in the house for viewing what promised to be a harrowing spectacle.

But the great Battle of Gavilán Peak fizzled out even before it began—and without a single shot being fired.

8

By the time the expedition's forty-man force reached the arroyo and its matted thicket, dismounting there to form a skirmish line, the Mexican cavalry had turned about and scampered for the cover of the forest. The sudden retreat puzzled Stone. He had no firsthand experience of war or warriors, but it certainly had not seemed to him at the meeting in Monterey that Don José Castro was afraid to fight, surely not when the odds were stacked as distinctly in his favor as they were today.

The Mexicans did not emerge from the woods for the rest of the afternoon, and after an hour on the banks of the arroyo, Frémont, Carson, and their companions returned to the mountaintop.

At a late supper Frémont mounted the carriage of the howitzer closest to the flag and faced the mountain men, the silent Delawares, and the ten Californios who had remained with the Americans after the breastworks had been built.

"Gentlemen! As you know, the affair today came as a bitter disappointment to me, as it must have to you. Nonetheless, you acquitted yourselves well, and I am proud of you. Apparently General Castro has not as much stomach for a fight as he claimed in the message Lieutenant Chávez delivered two days ago. That does not mean, of course, that he will not find it. It is only fair that I tell you what my intentions are. I will not be driven from this position! You are all aware that despite what happened today we are still vastly outnumbered, and cannot in the long run prevail against the superior force we face. But even if they roll their guns forward and finally come at us, on horseback or on foot, we can make it very costly for our enemy. If there are those among you who do not share my feelings, you are free to leave. It should not present any great difficulties once darkness covers us." He paused. Then he pointed at the Stars and Stripes, now hanging limp above them. "I will not dishonor my country's flag!"

There had been roars of approval and cheers in plenty in the past, but nothing to equal the ones that followed the captain's oratory.

When Frémont raised his arms and finally hushed the crowd, he said, "I do not think we need fear that General Castro will attack tonight, but he most likely will tomorrow. Have someone build up the fire lighting Old Glory, Mr. Carson."

Stone wondered if Frémont's stirring if somewhat pompous little speech had just deluded these men, and perhaps him as well, into thinking they had tasted victory with the aborted foray of the afternoon.

Before most of the expedition bedded down, Lucien Maxwell, on early night guard, broke the silence with a shout that brought the mountain men on the run and woke the few in camp already sleeping.

"Rider coming up!"

The man on horseback, whom Lucy stopped fifty yards or so below the breastworks, identified himself as a courier with a message from Tom Larkin, back at the consulate in Yerba Buena.

Frémont met him at one of the gun breaks in the log wall, took a dispatch case from him, and directed Lajeunesse to feed the man. Then the Pathfinder opened the case as he walked to his tent and disappeared behind the flap. "Damn!" Stone heard him shout from inside.

Stone sought out the courier and learned he would not return to Yerba Buena until the next night. It afforded plenty of time to scribble a short note to Ana.

9

Except that Frémont ordered no sally from the fort, the next day turned out to be pretty much an echo of the second. They could see Mexican soldiers flitting back and forth in the shadows of the trees, but with the exception of two who obviously were scouts, none ventured out of the woods, and the position of the guns did not change. Stone and Kern took turns keeping the telescope on the road, but other than three wagons filled with what they took to be foodstuffs, nothing else came from the direction of Monterey. No additional troops moved in. If the siege—if it could be called that—had not lifted, it had not gotten more threatening. Kit had located a fine spring in one of the gullies on the back side of the small mountain, and the supply of food and fuel would last easily for another week or ten days.

Some of the men groused a little at the inactivity. Joe Walker for one, and Lucy Maxwell for another, came out loudly for taking the fight to the Mexicans without delay, even if it meant riding right into the woods itself. Walker called for an immediate battle with the Mexicans at the top of his voice, apparently unconcerned if Frémont heard him.

"It ain't exactly like chasing ten or twelve Shoshones with stolen horses, Joe," Carson said. "We're likely to get more fighting than we want before we're out of here as it is. I don't cotton to the notion of riding down there where we ain't got no chance."

From time to time during the long day Frémont visited the section of the wall where Kern and Stone kept their watch and stared out across the grassy plain toward the forest. Beyond a nod, he greeted neither of them.

Stone told Kern of the explosive *"Damn!"* that had issued from the tent the night before, presumably right after Frémont read the message from Consul Larkin.

"That's probably got a lot to do with his present state of mind. Something sure put Captain Johnny down again. He was still in fairly fine fettle after he and Kit came back up the mountain after their great 'attack.' Maybe it was something in that dispatch he got."

10

Stone awoke unaccountably early next morning when it was still full dark, and left his bedroll to discover a strange, disturbing sight.

The long pole to which Kit Carson had fastened the American flag had fallen over during the night, and the flag itself had dropped directly into the fire meant to illuminate it, burning it to blackened shreds.

Frémont stared down at its remains, and Stone could not decide whether flag or man looked more burned out.

Although there had been no sound to alert them, the men whom Stone knew best gathered around Frémont one by one—Lajeunesse, Carson, Owens, Godey, Archambeault, Maxwell, and Kern, but none of them edged too closely to the captain.

Frémont seemed totally unaware of them, and when he spoke, it was to himself, although they all heard him clearly.

"An omen . . . ," he said, his voice sepulchral.

Dead silence covered the mountaintop.

Then Kit stepped to Frémont's side.

"Captain . . . ," he whispered.

At last Frémont turned to him. It was as if his eyes were too dead to truly see the scout.

"Yes, Kit?"

"Does the captain have any special orders for the day?"

"Orders? Why should I have . . ." Then his eyes flickered, but perhaps it was only the reflection from the fire's glowing coals. "Ah yes . . . orders. I must have orders. That is my function, isn't it? And yours is to obey them, is it not, Mr. Carson?"

"Yes, sir."

Frémont looked at the ashes of the flag again and then back at Kit. "Prepare the entire expedition for a march, Mr. Carson. We will quit this place within the hour."

Stone's heart picked up its pace. Did Frémont mean they would move to attack?

"We are going to Oregon to complete our tasks in the Great Northwest," Frémont said.

"Well . . . ," Kern said to Stone, "I for one am fully inclined to feel that honor has been served. And frankly, I'm damned relieved that Captain Johnny seems to feel the same."

"Time to catch up!" Carson cried.

Oregon!

The thought of terminating his contract with the Pathfinder at the Columbia River settlements set Brad Stone's heart dancing.

He would join the first party going back down the trail to Bent's, and from there head down to Taos.

Ana!

22

Travelers in the Dark

Klamath Lake, Oregon
May 1846

The expedition's journey to the rainy camp at the north end
of Klamath Lake had been colored gray by the depressed
mood of its commander. Although Frémont's spirits lifted to
a degree at odd times during the tortuous trip—principally
when he devoted himself to his botanical studies—his everyday demeanor could at best be described as listless.

"I think he feels he failed his country at Gavilán," Kern
said once, long before they reached the lake, "that he cut and
ran, when he should have stayed and fought. Nonsense!
Even *he* should realize we stood no chance with Castro in
the long run, and that no one in their right mind will call it a
failure."

Stone agreed. So did some others. Word of Frémont's
challenge to Castro seemed to have spread the length and
breadth of Upper California. At the American farms and
ranches they passed on the road north, the owners had been
universal in their praise of what had happened at Gavilán
Peak. So, too, had been the travelers who attached themselves to the column for a day or two for protection in
Horsethief country. Little by little they learned that the
Americans in California, and even some of the Californios,
now looked on Frémont as some sort of savior for standing
up to Don José Castro at all. One or two hinted that if Frémont and his famous wilderness fighters turned back and

marched on Monterey, armed and well-mounted men by the hundreds would rally to whatever flag Frémont hoisted—be it the Stars and Stripes or a wispy guidon of his own devising.

One, a man named William Hargrave, rode all the way from his ranch in the Napa Valley and caught the expedition on the trail south of Sutter's. Stone thought him a virtual twin of Frémont, full black beard, high style, and with an imperious manner more than just a faint imitation of the Pathfinder's.

"If you turn about and march immediately for my ranch, Captain," Hargrave said, "I can have a hundred armed, determined men in the saddle and waiting for your orders in as little as twelve hours."

"Thank you, Mr. Hargrave, but I am not in California to make war. General Castro forced the incident at Gavilán Peak on me."

Hargrave could not contain his disappointment.

"Perhaps in a few more weeks, then?"

"I am on my way out of California."

"I see. May I ask one favor, sir?"

"Certainly."

"Please do not tell Captain Sutter that I called on you."

"Why not? Do you not trust him?"

"Just ordinary caution, Captain."

They had made another stop at Sutter's on the way up, and Carson, Kern, Stone, Talbot, and Godey dined with the Swiss, but Frémont declined the invitation and kept to his tent up at Oak Bend. Sutter appeared more circumspect and guarded than on their previous visits.

Then began a weird, aimless journey to the north.

Frémont would start them off in one direction in the mornings, and often turn the column ninety degrees right or left at noon for no discernible reason. Once they back-tracked almost a dozen miles in a day that brought angry curses from the mountain men, and doleful looks from Segundai and his Delawares. They wandered. Kit had estimated they would arrive in Oregon in no more than a week, but after almost a month they were still meandering through northern California.

They almost reached the border of Oregon once, but then Frémont turned them maddeningly south again to spend almost two weeks in the vicinity of the ranch of Peter Lassen, a Dane who was doing some interesting experiments with new crops on his remote holdings. When Frémont learned Lassen was even trying to raise cotton, he perked up to some extent. Perhaps he was hearkening back to his Deep South beginnings. The captain ordered Kern and Stone to name the mountain visible from the ranch Lassen Peak on the maps they were formulating.

He issued the two cartographers no other instructions about their topographical work, and Stone found it pleasant for them to be left alone. This was the first time he had worked with the Philadelphian since the upper Arkansas, right after leaving Bent's more than half a year before.

Kern nagged Stone teasingly about his art, and the two of them now found time to work on that together, too. Kern paid most attention to rendering the mountain flora, but he also revealed great gifts as a landscape painter, and Stone learned much from watching him do a watercolor. Cynical as Kern could be, he demonstrated no such trait as he applied his brush to paper with loving delicacy.

Transporting their heavy surveying gear to the sites they mapped precluded Stone taking along his easel, and he mostly did charcoal sketches with his pad in his lap, but he managed one small oil on canvas, a portrait of Kern. And in doing it he made a discovery.

Portraiture had always been his paramount love in painting, but the works he had done in Cambridge and Groverton had been mostly second-rate reflections of the masters he admired, classically formal and stiff, the backgrounds the dark monochromes of Gainsborough or Rembrandt, with an occasional failed attempt to capture in the subject's face and figure the chiaroscuro of the immortal Dutchman.

On one of the few bright days of this northern journey, when they'd finished a heavy morning with the chain, transit, and plane table, and had stopped to eat, he posed Kern on a log which had been dragged into a meadow in the shadow of newly named Lassen Peak. Kern was wearing drab expedition woolens, now badly stained, but with a bright red-and-yellow bandanna cast loosely around his neck. The April sun and their exertions had brought beads of sweat to his brow.

Stone intended at first just to forget about the composition and framing of his subject, and do Ed's fine face with its chiseled features in some detail, delaying the comparative drudgery of brushing in the background until he found time back in camp.

He had always worked fairly quickly and freely, never bothering to sketch out a charcoal pattern, going directly to the underpainting. He began this way this time.

Something strange happened. He found his brush—a slightly flexible, favorite "bright"—working almost with a mind of its own. He brushed in the stark outline of the peak and a lone, twisted pine he could see in the middle distance, blocked in the doughy clouds which had gathered around the lofty head of Lassen and the rolls and dips of the vast meadow, alive with gigantic daisies—all as if another hand were doing it. When he turned his mind's eye to Kern's face, he found he would either have to scrub out the landscape work or position the Philadelphian's actual portrait well left of the center of the canvas. He chose the latter course. Kern, a good critic, would doubtless laugh at such a departure from orthodoxy.

But something happened. In the bright sunlight, the

"leans" of the underpainting dried in no time at all, and he set to work on the "fat" passages with the brush in a fever brought on by something other than the sun.

He leaned back on his camp stool and looked at his work. He did not know quite what to make of it, but he felt sure he had captured the Ed Kern he knew. Too bad it would appear so strange to other eyes that it would have no artistic value.

Kern meantime, realizing Stone had finished, broke his pose and walked around behind him.

"Great Scott!" he said. "Have you any idea what you've done? You've just eclipsed three centuries of studio portrait painting. You've taken it back to those marvelous things that came out of northern Italy during the Renaissance. And you've set it in the American West. You've discovered yourself, my friend. It's as fine as any portrait work being done today. Pity you didn't have a better subject."

Kern had pinned down the strangeness of it, all right.

Stone suddenly recalled an obscure old portrait by Giovanni Bellini, where a lean, hard-featured man, a Florentine or Venetian doge, gazed right at the painter, oblivious to the Tuscan landscape spread out behind him. With the ancient, crumbled ruins also visible in the painting, as Stone remembered it, the Bellini oil made a felicitous blend of softness and severity.

Ed's assessment of the portrait, if a trifle excessive, basically was correct. He had to get Carson—and Frémont, Lajeunesse, Godey, and even Sutter and Don José Castro—into just such portrayals. They were all as much part and parcel of the American West as the lean Italian had been of Tuscany. He might be laughed right out of the courts of criticism, but this was the way he would have to do it.

2

In another confusing move that brought more complaints from the mountain men, Frémont uprooted the expedition from Lassen's ranch and replanted it at another—that of an American named Samuel Neal—long miles to the south of Lassen's and once again farther *away* from Oregon. There seemed no reason for this countermarch. They had mapped the area around Neal's thoroughly on the way up. Stone found himself as disgruntled as the others; the baffling move would delay him in completing his contract with Frémont and postpone his start for Taos.

Kit, when Stone asked the reason for the turnabout, could not provide an answer. "He ain't told me nothing. It's like he's marking time, but I got no idea why."

He told Kit then of his plan to return to Taos and the scout commiserated with him.

"Now I see the reason for the long face you been wearing since we left Lassen's," he said. "Wish I could put a bug in the captain's ear about the fix you're in, but he ain't listening to nobody nowadays. He's always kind of ducked way inside himself from time to time, but I ain't never seen him go in hiding quite like this."

Sam Neal, a bluff, hearty former blacksmith, seemed to Stone a full-blooded brother of the mountain men. He had accompanied Frémont on an earlier trip west, had cut all his ties with his own country, stayed in California to work for Johann Sutter for a while, and had then struck out on his own to develop a stock ranch on Butte Creek, a swift-running branch of the Sacramento.

Perhaps, as Kit had said, the captain was not "listening to nobody nowadays," but he spent a great deal of time conferring with the rancher.

"They look almost like conspirators," Kern said. "Neal's sent two different riders south with messages from our illustrious leader to Tom Larkin since we got here. Captain Johnny's pretty closemouthed these days, but he did let that much slip."

Then, after three enervating days at Neal's, Frémont, in another surprising and almost offhand order, led them out again.

This time it looked as if he really meant to take the expedition all the way to Oregon. They headed due north from Neal's and, compared to the milling around and dillydallying before Lassen's, they made good time. Frémont, to Stone's satisfaction, left the planning of the route and all decisions about starts and stops up to Carson.

Before leaving, Kit had his own session with Neal, and reported to the others that the rancher had warned him there would be the distinct possibility of encounters with hostile Indians as they paralleled the Cascades, on the left, and until they cleared the northern shore of Klamath Lake.

They did see a few Indians at a distance and, Lajeunesse and Maxwell riding point, cut sign of others every day of the journey, but none threatened trouble, and not one approached the column, even to beg. There seemed to be no danger of attack. Still, it was a relief—even though they were pelted all the last day of the trek by a cold, driving rain—when they reached the lake and settled into a bivouac on the northern shore.

Wet and miserable as the weather continued to be, nothing could dampen Stone's spirits. They were in Oregon at last. Then, only minutes after they made their soggy camp, Frémont gathered the men and told them they would start for the Columbia and the American settlements at dawn.

As they began to eat the supper Lajeunesse had prepared, the rain stopped, if only for the moment. It seemed to Brad Stone a more reliable omen, certainly a happier one for his immediate personal future, than Frémont's fallen flag had been. Although the earlier rain had thinned Lajeunesse's stew to soup, it was pure ambrosia.

But before he finished eating it, a cry rang out from the darkness beyond the fire's beams.

"Hello the camp! It's Sam Neal here. Can me and my partner ride in without getting our heads blowed off?"

"Come on in, Mr. Neal," Kit yelled back. "You're just in time for supper."

Sam and one of his Californio hired hands rode into the firelight, water streaming down their slickers. They looked utterly exhausted.

"I got to see Captain Frémont, *pronto*," Neal said, as he slid from the saddle and let Dick Owens take the reins of his horse. "I got a real urgent message for him."

"I'm right here, Sam." The captain strode into the light. "What's the message?"

"Actually, *I* ain't got the message. Feller I got bedded down back at my ranch does. He's been on your trail for weeks, and the silly son of a bitch thought he would ride up here alone through hostile Indian country like he was sashaying down a city street somewheres in the East. Couldn't let him do that, of course, but he acted so god-damned upset I thought I'd better come up myself."

"Who is he?"

"Man named Archibald Gillespie. For God's sake, don't call him Archie. I did and he like to bit my head off. He says he's a U.S. Marine, out of Washington in the D. of C. He's carrying a message for you straight from the president of the United States, if he can be believed. I told him to go back to Yerba Buena and send it on to the Columbia and he pretty near went crazy. I went as far as Pete Lassen's with him and told him to stay put until I found you."

Then Frémont, suddenly bubbling with energy, an-nounced that he was selecting a small crew to start a hard, fast ride back to Lassen's ranch first thing in the morning, with Archambeault and Talbot to take the rest of the expedition straight on down to Neal's. The smaller party was pretty much the same team that had left Walker Lake together: Frémont, Carson, Lajeunesse, Maxwell, Owens, Godey, Segundai, and six of the other Delawares, including Crane, Delaware Charlie, Denny, and tall, silent Swanok, the one closest to Segundai of all of them save Crane. Ed Kern would go with Frémont this time, and Stone resigned himself to being dropped in favor of the Philadelphian until the captain turned to him. "You will ride with us as well, Bradford. I may need your services more than ever now."

He clapped Stone on the back. The change from the Frémont who had left Gavilán Peak in such a dudgeon was nothing short of miraculous.

3

The expedition broke camp at dawn as planned, except that no dawn broke. The rain, even heavier now than that of the last week, began again as they mounted up.

A day's march in the punishing wetness found the forward party at the southern end of the lake, where a surprise awaited them in the person of Lieutenant Archibald H. Gillespie himself. The marine had tired of waiting for Frémont at Lassen's, and over the entirely reasonable objections of the rancher had foolishly headed north on his own. Lassen himself and two Americans had given chase. When they caught up with Gillespie he refused to return to the safety of the ranch with them, and the trio, as fearful for the marine as Neal had been, had accompanied him north through this stretch of Klamath Indian country.

Neal voiced his disgust to Frémont in Gillespie's hearing. "I told you he was a silly son of a bitch, Captain. He don't seem to savvy we could have missed him and Pete here just as easy as we found them. He's lucky Pete rode north with him." Sam's sharp words were met with an icy stare from the marine.

As foolish as this self-important young officer might be, after Stone heard Gillespie tell the captain the details of his circuitous journey from Washington to Klamath Lake, he admitted grudgingly that Washington's messenger was most certainly a man of courage. The lieutenant, carrying dispatches to Ambassador Slidell in Mexico City and to Consul Larkin and the naval commanders suddenly operating in California waters, had landed first at Vera Cruz in a Mexico poised for war with America, traveled its bandit-infested highroads unarmed, made his scheduled stop in its nervous capital on his way to the Pacific Coast, and had taken ship at Mazatlán for Honolulu in the Sandwich Islands and there caught another bound for Yerba Buena—alone.

Frémont took Gillespie to his tent for a private meeting, and when the two of them emerged after an hour, Frémont told Kit that they would head south for Lassen's ranch again. "Sam will go straight back to his own place and wait for Gus there, with instructions for Gus and the expedition to proceed to Sutter's. We shall all meet there."

They arrived at Lassen's in a day, and Frémont conducted another round of meetings with Neal, Peter Lassen, and Lieutenant Gillespie. Gillespie's dispatch case, recently emptied into Frémont's lap at Klamath Lake, now bulged with what Stone was sure were messages for Consul Larkin. Stone had half expected he would be dragooned into writing them, but Frémont did not seem to require any help this time.

He mentioned it to Kern.

"The game's afoot," Kern said. "We're going back to take another crack at General Castro after Gillespie leaves us, mark my words. I don't suppose anyone in California really knows yet, but I'll make a small wager we're already at war with Mexico. Whatever . . . Our Captain Johnny is 'up' again—and in full flight."

Stone's heart sank. Ed's hunch about war was bad enough in itself, but it also probably destroyed any chance Stone had of getting back to Taos before the summer had run its course.

The raging vernal storms continued unabated as they rode south.

4

Then tragedy struck the Pathfinder and his suddenly luckless companions two nights out from Lassen's.

Perhaps it was the heavy going through forests which had become swamps that dulled the usual razor-keen alertness of every member of the small party, even that of Kit.

Perhaps it was at least in part the new, manic excitement Stone saw in the eyes of John C. Frémont every time he looked at him.

Perhaps it was the way the captain drove them. . . .

. . . And perhaps fate had simply taken charge.

<h1 style="text-align:center">23</h1>

<h1 style="text-align:center">The Klamath Ax</h1>

"It's every bit as much my fault as it is the captain's, Brad," Carson said when it was over.

"But Kit, you and Lucy didn't come back in from riding point until long after everyone had gone to bed. It's not your fault! The captain has always made the assignment of the night guard his responsibility. He's never let anyone else do it."

"I should have known!"

"How could you?"

"When nobody challenged Lucy and me when we rode in, I should have figured out the captain hadn't posted any guard. Didn't even think of it. I . . . just went to sleep. It's the first time he forgot about a guard since Antelope Island back at the Salt Lake, and maybe only the second time ever—in all the time I've knowed him. But that ain't no excuse for me."

Brad Stone grieved for the man. Unlike the scout, he could not lift the blame entirely from the shoulders of their commander. If Frémont had not driven them almost to the point of collapse before they made camp, someone might have been awake enough to sound an alarm when the savages burst in on them.

The Klamaths, as Kit would later identify their assailants when all the bloody work was done, had come upon them in the middle of the night, and with the swiftness of a bolt of lightning.

The first anyone in the expedition knew anything had gone wrong was when Kit cried out from his bedroll.

"Wake up! Grab your rifles!"

As silently as the marauders had moved through the rain-soaked glade, wild screams and truly blood-curdling whoops followed close on Kit's warning shout. Stone awoke from a dreamless sleep into a howling, dark nightmare.

Mexicans? He reached for his Hawken blindly, found it, leaped to his feet. *No time to think. Find a target!* Blackness everywhere, with only ghostly shadows moving through the weak gleams of the dying fire. Then one flash of lightning. *Indians!* Crazed shouts, strangled cries. The deafening cracks of rifles. Animal grunts. How would he

tell friend from foe? Only two yards away a figure looming, drawing a bow. Not hard to tell with this one. A naked
body and a black topknot caught in the failing firelight.
Burning eyes.

Fire!

A great, shuddering exhalation as his target sagged to the
sodden earth. *Do not look at him! Reload.* Butt of rifle slam-
ming down hard, but slipping away in the mud. *Damn!*

*Easy now . . . easy! Hold off panic, somehow. By the num-
bers, then. . . .* Rod stripped from the stock, up and ready . . .
powder horn to the muzzle. *Don't let the charge be wet . . .
dear God, don't let it be wet! . . .*

All he heard then were the crashes of bodies hurtling
through the underbrush.

And silence.

Then Kit's voice, shouting, "Somebody build up that fire,
pronto! We need light. . . . It's over . . . they've gone."

It all could not have taken thirty seconds.

Another streak of lightning flooded the figures in the
glade, making them glow as if they were lit from within,
keeping them in Stone's retina for a full deep breath after it
had gone. Once the white images faded, it turned even
blacker.

Then, closer to him, he saw Lucy Maxwell at the fire—at
first only dimly. He was piling a skeletal tower of squaw
wood atop the coals. The thin, spindly, dead pine branches,
wet almost through, steamed for a moment before flaming
when the heat burned away the wetness.

Things were still happening.

"They're not *all* gone, Kit!" someone shouted, words
fractured, breath coming hard. "I've got ahold of one of
them!"

Alexis Godey. Stone had not seen him in the brief flash of
lightning, but now Godey's voice, although it seemed to
come from some faraway, dark country, jerked Stone's eyes

to where two shapeless gray shadows struggled with each other against the deeper blackness.

The light from Maxwell's fire now flooded the bivouac, and in it Alexis still grappled with the shadow . . . no longer a shadow now, but an Indian, naked except for a breech clout dripping rain—and something else. The lower bodies and legs of both Godey and his enemy were awash in blood, but it turned out the blood was Indian. A great hole in his chest gouted it. Godey had taken hold of him from behind, but the Indian, writhing and straining, was swinging a wicked half-ax back over first one shoulder then the other, trying to get at the head of the St. Louisan.

Then Kit's small figure appeared in the light.

He wrested the half-ax from the Indian's grip, and swung it with calm deliberation into the warrior's skull. Godey let go as more blood spurted out and spattered him. The Indian fell . . .

. . . across the body of Basil Lajeunesse.

At last the fire blazed like a beacon, revealing a scene Stone hoped and prayed he could someday forget.

Six . . . seven bodies lay stretched on the wet ground, three of them in lakes of blood with more still streaming from them. He shuddered with even more horror than he had that night on the Cimarron, when he had first known armed conflict and had looked for the first time on the obscene, sickening detritus of violent death.

This was different—worse.

The dead were not all enemies. Three of them were comrades—and one was even more—a friend. . . .

He could not see the face of Basil Lajeunesse, but there was no mistaking the mountain man's enormous, lifeless body.

Near him on the ground lay the inert figures of the grotesque, likeable little Delaware, Crane, and his friend Denny. The shafts of four arrows stuck out at odd, crazed angles from Denny's back and chest. Crane's throat had been cut—not cleanly, but torn, ripped—and his bear-claw necklace had somehow slipped into the wound and lodged there, giving him another red mouth, twisted into a hideous imitation of a toothy grin.

One of the other Delawares had fallen, too—Charlie. But as Stone watched, he struggled to his feet. An arrow had found the soft flesh above his left armpit and had run right through it. The point stuck straight out in back of him.

Stone exulted when he determined the three other bodies he saw were those of attackers, not friends, one of the fallen the victim of his own still-smoking rifle.

"Kit!" Frémont had moved into the widening circle of light as well.

"Sir?"

He pointed to the dead man lying across Basil's body. "I wish you hadn't done that. I would like to have interrogated that savage as to why he and his hellions mounted this attack."

"Well, Captain . . ." For the first time Stone thought he heard a hint of exasperation with Frémont creep into the scout's voice. "Even if we beat him half to death I got real doubts this critter would have told you his name, let alone why they done it. And if he did decide to talk, he wouldn't have lasted long enough to tell you, anyway. Don't know how he kept fighting with that hole in him. He was still trying to part Alexis's hair when I took his weapon. I'll need Alexis when we go after them."

Kit went to his knees beside the bodies, pushed the Indian away from Lajeunesse, and rolled Basil over on his back.

Stone gasped, and heard a sob escape Frémont at the same instant.

Bass Lajeunesse's great bear's head lay opened wide, split from the forehead to the right cheek into two unequal pieces. Thick ribbons of blood had spilled down into the old mountain man's beard, and pieces of his brain bulged from the wound as if they were chunks of a pinkish gray sponge. Kit rocked back on his heels and pulled what had become of the huge head into his lap.

"This is what woke me up," Kit said. "I actually heard the ax hit Bass. That buck there"—he nodded toward the body of the Indian he had killed—"must be the one what done it. Bass probably didn't even feel a thing, thank God."

Sam Neal looked down at Lajeunesse and turned to Archibald Gillespie, who had come from his bedroll to stand beside the rider. "That could have been you if Pete Lassen hadn't taken you in tow, Lieutenant, and if we hadn't found the four of you. Think about that . . . Archie!"

Then a new sound came—one more terrible than any Brad Stone had ever heard.

At the edge of the circle of light Segundai stood over the body of little Crane.

The Delaware chief's face seemed as stoic as ever, but he was moaning, some sorrow far beyond words rising from deep within him, but as Stone listened, the sound changed to one of anger, and then to an inhuman rage that he knew at once he would never find words to describe to someone who had not heard it.

The rain fell heavily again.

"Brad . . . ," Kit had left Basil's body, and now stood over him staring at his leg, "take down your pants!"

"What?"

"You've been hit, *amigo*."

Stone looked down. A six-inch rent between his right knee and hip lay open in his trouser leg as neatly as if a razor had slit it. Now he realized that the stickiness he had felt was not from the rain soaking through his buckskins. Blood. And immediately after that discovery he felt the sear of pain. He undid his belt and pulled his pants down to his knees.

Something had split his flesh from front to back on the

outer side of his lower thigh. The Indian must have loosed an arrow before he died. Blood oozed from the wound.

"Just a scratch."

"No it ain't. It ain't going to kill you, but it's a hell of a lot more than a scratch. You sit right there. I'll be right back to do a little doctoring."

He watched Kit move off through the trees toward where they had picketed the horses and mules when they made camp earlier.

While the scout was gone, he watched Dick Owens do some doctoring of his own on Charlie, as Segundai, stoic as stone again, looked on. Dick snapped off the head of the arrow that had gone through the Delaware's shoulder and pulled the feathered shaft free. Then he led Charlie to the fire. He pulled a burning stick from the fire.

"I'm going to burn where it went in and where it came out, Charlie," Dick said. "It may not do the job, but I can't pour whiskey into a wound like that. It's too narrow. I'm going to have to stick this in on both sides, you know that, don't you?"

The Delaware nodded.

"All right. Take a good hold of yourself."

Smoke rose from Charlie's shoulder in ugly puffs as Owens probed, pushing the stick in an inch or more, jamming it back in the fire twice and repeating the process front and back. Even from twenty feet away Stone smelled the sweet but nauseating stink of burning flesh.

The Delaware did not utter a sound.

"Don't worry none about what Dick is doing with Charlie, Brad," Carson said, appearing suddenly with a bottle and a handful of wadded cotton rags. "This won't hurt near as bad. As open as that cut looks, whiskey will work well enough on you. Ready?"

"Go ahead, Kit."

Stone tried his level best to remain as silent as Charlie had during his ordeal—but could not. He held it to a whimper, and tears rolled down his cheeks.

When he could at last draw an easy breath again, he said to Carson, "Did I hear you say you're going after them?"

"You sure did."

"You'll take me with you, won't you?"

"Nope."

"Why not? I want revenge for Basil and Crane as much as any of you."

"So do I, but right now this ain't got much to do with revenge, *amigo*."

"Then why . . . ?"

"Looking for revenge sometimes only muddies up good sense. When I went out for the whiskey I saw they'd gotten to our picket line. We only got nine horses and two mules left. We got to get the rest of our animals back. And of course we got to learn the Indians as attacked us tonight a thing or two. After they settle back into their village some- wheres and eat the mules they took, they'll get to thinking they got away with this, and they'll be back."

The scout inspected his handiwork. "That ought to do it once I get a bandage on it."

"Take me along," Stone implored. "Please, Kit. I know I'm not the best shot in the world, but won't you need my rifle?"

"I'd admire to have you with us, but that leg of yours will stiffen up pretty bad. A hard ride and you wouldn't be nowhere fit to fight. You'll do the captain and me a lot more good by staying here and looking after Charlie. There are other good fighters I can't take with me, either, on account of we're short of horses." He bent to the task of binding up the wound. "I ain't got nothing to stitch this up with, even if I was any good at it. I sure am sorry. You're going to have a pretty nasty scar."

As Kit worked, a shadow fell across the two of them. Fré- mont.

"How are you doing, Bradford?" Frémont asked.

"Fine, sir."

"Good man!" The captain looked down at Carson. "When do you advise we set out to even the score for this atrocity, Kit?" He had kept his voice low, but a strange ferment seemed to be working in him.

"Soon as we can, Captain. I'd like to get moving before the rain makes it too hard to cut decent sign. I'd like to catch them before they're back with their women and children so we don't have them to worry us, too. I'd like to catch them in the open, but if that don't work out, we shouldn't have no trouble locating their village."

"Splendid. I want to kill ten of those monsters for each of the three men we lost, forty if Charlie dies. My only fear is that we will not find enough of them to slake my thirst for vengeance."

"We'll find enough of them, Captain. Might even find a few more than we want."

Frémont looked down at Stone again. "I heard what Kit said about you not coming with us, Bradford, and I am in full agreement. Pity. I can see you want revenge for our fallen comrades every bit as much as I do."

2

Carson and Frémont took Ed Kern, Dick Owens, Godey, Segundai, and three of the other Delawares with them when they rode from camp at a faint daybreak that promised an end to the rain.

Lucy Maxwell, who had suffered no wound in the attack, but who had wrenched a knee racing after the Klamaths as they fled with the stolen mules and horses, remained in camp with Stone.

Maxwell set the other mountain men to digging graves for

Bass and Crane, voicing in bitter tones the same sentiments Stone felt at being left behind. He had no luck trying to get the Delawares to help. They sat silently by the fire, their faces smudged black with charcoal and their heads bowed. Maxwell finally persuaded a pair of them to drag the bodies of the dead Klamaths off into the woods to become carrion. The Delawares scalped both of them before they moved them through the trees. Perhaps, as Carson had told Josefa in the letter Stone had written for him, he really had *"come close to being a real mountain man,"* but he knew he would never be able to view that savage operation without his stomach turning.

"Poor old Bass," Maxwell said. "Wish to hell he could watch the buzzards tear that Klamath bastard that killed him to shreds. One thing ought to comfort him, though, wherever he is. Even if a redskin finally did get him, he'd have been damned proud of one thing. . . ."

"I know, Lucy. He kept his hair . . . ," Stone said.

The brief, deadly struggle had left Klamath arrows scattered throughout the camp, a section of ground near the fire bristling with them like the back of a porcupine. The arrows fascinated him. They all had long, true shafts and steel points, some of them as broad as spearheads and sharpened to a fine edge on both sides, none nearly as crude as the Comanche lance on the Cimarron. It must have been one of these that had sliced through his pants and leg.

"Hudson's Bay Company trade goods," Maxwell said.

From the number of them, the raiding party had been a large one. He wondered aloud if Frémont, Carson, and the few men they had taken with them knew this.

"Can't worry none about them, Brad. At least they're mounted. We ain't. We won't even be able to run for it if them Klamaths come to call again."

After they had disposed of the corpses, the black-faced Delawares settled in by the fire again. Swanok called

Maxwell to one side. "You leave now Joe. Go down trail for two–three miles. Delaware all sick. Catch up when feel better."

Stone was surprised to see Maxwell nod. "You can't leave them here alone! There are only four of them. As you said yourself, the Klamaths could come back."

"I know. But I think Swanok and his Delaware *amigos* want to moan a little, and they don't cotton to us seeing or hearing it. Let's cut you a stick to lean on. Without no horses until Kit gets back to us, we'll have to hoof it."

Maxwell called a halt after a nightmarish, painful mile, and while resting they heard the sound of rifle fire emanating from the camp they had left—three . . . four shots, then silence for half a minute, then two more shots.

"Klamaths?"

"Reckon," Maxwell said. "Swanok was counting on it." The mountain man looked marvelously unworried.

In no more than half an hour, Swanok and his three companions joined them. The tall Delaware held out two fresh scalps.

"Delawares not sick so bad now," he said.

3

Carson, Frémont and the small punitive expedition returned two days later, intact—the raiding party larger in fact than it had been. They had intercepted the main party on its journey south to Neal's, reinforced themselves with another two dozen mounted men, and set off on a hard ride for the Indian villages at Klamath Lake.

"We had all our luck at the first one we reached," Kern told Stone. "Took them completely by surprise. I'm not sure—didn't count them myself—but I think we killed thirty or forty of them. You know, I spoke a couple of times about how I think Captain Johnny lusts to lead men into battle, but it's our friend Carson who's got the makings of a general. The way he deployed us, we didn't get a man scratched. He's a wonder . . . but a truly cold-blooded man if I've ever seen one—scary. . . ."

"I went through that with him once myself, Ed."

"Anyway, after the fight we burned the village to the ground. The Klamaths in the other two villages we found must have gotten the wind up pretty bad. Their huts were deserted when we reached them, so we had to content ourselves with torching them as well."

"Maybe it will go some distance in satisfying our commander's desire for revenge."

"I will say one thing about our commander, Brad. He's as brave as any of our men. Carson was cut off from the rest of us once at the first village, and Johnny rode straight to his rescue all alone, took on two Klamaths who were after Kit—shot one of them, and jumped Sacramento all over the other and ran him off. I think he just might have saved Kit's life."

24

Pathway to Power

The reunited expedition reached New Helvetia in the dead of night and camped again at Oak Bend, but this time no invitation awaited Frémont for him to stay in Sutter's quarters at the fort. The Swiss, however, did host a dinner for the captain and his principal lieutenants, Stone among them.

This time Frémont revealed no reluctance to attend, even though he had been in an extended period of gloom since the death of Basil Lajeunesse, as had all of them.

The deadly slope into war, not between the United States and Mexico—already a forgone conclusion in Stone's mind, and indeed in the minds of Kern, Carson, and presumably that of Frémont as well—but war right here in Upper California, had steepened precipitously since the last time they tucked their feet under Johann August Sutter's table.

Sutter seemed even more guarded about discussing politics than he had been on any of the other occasions Stone had seen him.

Over brandy Sutter let slip that two different, incipient, purely local wars had almost reached the ignition point.

Trouble had been brewing for almost two years between Governor Pío Pico in Los Angeles and the general in Monterey, Don José Castro. "Neither of these gentlemen are actually any more loyal or even attentive to Mexico City than circumstances force them to be," he said. "They are vying with each other for personal autocratic control of the entire province. Pico, my sources tell me, has already begun negotiations with the British for military help and possible annexation, with him as some sort of viceroy, I suppose, and with Castro recognizing Paredes, the new president of Mexico, he may feel it a good time to break away. Don José, for his part, probably thinks there is some temporary advantage in reestablishing California's bonds with the mother country, which he can break when it suits him. I am of the impression that the general, like the governor, truly wishes power for himself. I have no wish to be quoted on any of this, Captain Frémont . . . *bitte.*"

Some perilous incidents, minor armed clashes between the forces at Monterey and Los Angeles, had already occurred, he added, but no really large conflicts had broken out yet. He expected them, he said, with genuine regret in his voice.

"And there is something even more immediate and serious at work in California, Captain," the Swiss went on.

"Since we met last, Don José has issued another edict." He hesitated, as if reluctant to go on.

"So?" Frémont said.

"The general has ordered all noncitizens of Mexico in Upper California—a euphemism for you Americans, of course—to leave the province by year's end, and he has barred entry to any new emigrants from the United States. He vows to turn the wagon trains back at the border, with force if necessary."

"Outrageous, sir!" Frémont had come to full alert.

"*Ja.* Well . . . I suppose he is within his legal rights as far as the new arrivals are concerned, but my heart goes out to them all the same. Many are already rolling their wagons through the Great Basin even as we sit here. As the guardian I might have to take a part in—"

"Captain Sutter!" Frémont broke in. "I am even more concerned about the American settlers who have been living here for years. Even if the general has the legal right to evict them, he does not have the moral right. He has already victimized them quite enough. While I realize the Americans in California do not have written contracts with Mexico, they invested their time, lives, and treasure on the clear understanding that they were welcome here. They have right on their side."

"Unfortunately, that does not seem to count for much with Don José."

Frémont nodded—too artfully, too sagely, in Stone's view, as if something had suddenly gratified him.

"Captain," Sutter said, "I take it you still have work to do in Oregon?"

"It can wait, Johann."

"But you will obey the general's command to leave the province?" Clearly, it was a plea.

Frémont looked away and did not answer.

Genial Johann Sutter looked as though Frémont had dealt him a blow.

Stone felt relieved when they left Sutter's table. He wanted desperately to return to Oak Bend and his bedroll. And only partly because his leg had begun to hurt again.

2

A night later, just as dinner was almost over, nine men rode into the Oak Bend camp from the north, instead of coming by way of the road up from Sutter's Fort.

The man who appeared to be the leader of the band turned out to be the same William Hargrave who had ridden from his Napa Valley ranch to meet with—and all but worship at the feet of—the Pathfinder the month before, after the affair at Gavilán Peak. Two others identified themselves as American settlers in the Sonoma and Sacramento Valleys: a John Fowler and a man named Ide whose first name Stone did not catch. Ide, a lanky six-and-a-half-footer, had a gaunt look and a messianic burn in his eyes. Fowler looked as short and solid as Johann Sutter. The others in the group seemed to be trying to keep their distance from the mountain men. Only Hargrave, Ide, and Fowler dismounted and approached the fire where Stone, Kern, Carson, Godey, and Owens were finishing their last cup of coffee.

Hargrave declined the cup Owens offered him, and asked for Frémont. Godey went to the tent and the captain came to the fire in seconds.

"To what do we owe the honor of this visit, Mr. Hargrave?" he asked.

"Before I answer, Captain, may I have your assurance that you will not tell Captain Sutter of it? We should be gone within the hour."

Frémont took his time before answering.

"Very well," he said.

"May we speak in private?"

Frémont stroked his beard. "I think not, Mr. Hargrave. I suspect that what you wish to speak of will affect the men of my command. I desire them to be privy to anything we say here tonight. I have never kept secrets from them."

Hargrave looked at the man named Ide, then turned to Frémont again. "I know and trust you, of course, Captain," Hargrave said next. "Mr. Carson I would have confidence in on reputation alone." Hargrave looked pointedly at the others. "I do not know these men. However, Captain, if you are willing to vouch for them . . ."

"I most certainly am, sir . . . unreservedly."

Hargrave seemed to think that over. "I have been told," he said then, "that you are now even more in sympathy with our cause than when we met south of here last month."

"And by whom were you told that, sir?"

Hargrave looked at Ide again before answering. "Mr. Lassen and Mr. Neal have apprised me of their recent conversations with you, sir."

"I have never lacked sympathy for your cause, Mr. Hargrave," Frémont said. "I have it in abundance, but at the moment sympathy is all I have to offer."

"You have no desire to lead us, then," Hargrave said, "should we take up arms in defense of our homes and rights?"

"Mr. Hargrave . . . ," the Pathfinder said. "My desires are of no consequence. My government sent me to California to conduct a scientific survey of the West, and to blaze peaceful trails—principally a new route to Oregon for American settlers to take. Nothing in my portfolio includes making war. I will obey my government's orders."

Stone looked at Carson. The scout probably knew more about obeying orders than did any of the men standing around this fire—including John C. Frémont.

But Hargrave had begun to speak again. "You seemed ready enough to go to war at Gavilán Peak, Captain. That is the reason I made that trip to see you last month with my offer to raise a fighting force for you—and why I have made this visit. I had hopes."

"That was a different thing entirely, sir. My nation and its flag were insulted by Don José Castro before we took up our position on Gavilán Peak. I could not tolerate that insult even in a time of peace. My government does expect initiative from its officers in such circumstances, and I would have defended the honor of our flag even if such action resulted in my court-martial. But tell me—are you and your fellow Americans planning overt action?"

Ed Kern leaned toward Stone and whispered. "The hunt is on, Bradford, my boy. Captain Johnny wants this bucolic firebrand to beg a little more."

"*Are* you planning action, Mr. Hargrave?" Frémont asked the Napa man again.

Hargrave examined Frémont with searching, troubled eyes. "I can't answer that, Captain. Not here. Not now . . . since you have turned us down." He took one more look at Ide, who shook his head, then he turned back to Frémont. "Perhaps my friends and I had better leave. This meeting has been a grievous disappointment to our hopes."

3

"All right, all right!" Ed Kern said just before he and Brad turned in. "So I was wrong. We were treated to a ridiculous display of indifference on Johnny's part tonight. It might be that Hargrave is too much like him, Brad. In my opinion the captain should have turned his attention to that fellow Ide."

"Why?"

"He appeared to me to be the real force in that crowd. Did you notice how Hargrave kept looking at him before he spoke? Captain Johnny ignored Ide completely. The man

looks shrewd, a bit wild, but a leader. Frémont wants the settlers to rise against Castro, but without a promise to help."

"I don't see how he could make a promise."

"I suppose he couldn't, but Johnny might have gotten
everything he wanted from Ide if he'd played his cards right.
It may be that I don't know our commander nearly as well
as I thought I did. But I *can* tell you with a fair amount of
certainty that his flair for high drama and intrigue will bring
him down someday."

Stone had no doubt now that Frémont had intended to mix
in the political affairs of California from the very start, ever
since they met at Bent's, and perhaps long before that. All
the talk of Oregon, and the one brief excursion to the north
shore of Klamath Lake, had been part of a subterfuge—or at
best the planning of a secure line of retreat if things did not
go well.

But, was the Pathfinder acting under orders from Washington, possibly from James Polk himself, or was he edging
ever closer to armed conflict on his own initiative? A good
case could be made either way. There was always the ominous presence of the three mountain howitzers.

And Stone at last suspected he knew the reason for Frémont's erratic, sometimes vacillating leadership of the expedition the past two months, the aimless peregrinations
through Upper California that seemed to serve no purpose.

The Pathfinder was awaiting news that war had broken
out between the United States and Mexico.

The very fact that Frémont had talked of the probability
of war a good deal less than anyone near the center of the
expedition strengthened Stone's suspicion. It defied credibility that the only U.S. Army officer presently in California
would not concern himself with the crisis between the two
nations every waking moment. He had even discounted the
chances of war being imminent when Stone and he met with
Consul Larkin in Monterey, and Stone had remarked to him-

self at the time how strange it was that neither the Pathfinder nor the consul had talked of General Taylor's advance to the Río Grande beyond the barest mention.

The mountain men of the expedition did not remain silent about it, though. Joe Walker's pronouncements rang the loudest. He still rankled because Frémont had not made an attack on the Mexicans in the woods back at Gavilán Peak.

Walker dug out a small American flag from somewhere in his baggage and fixed it to the barrel of his Hawken.

"This one won't fall over in no fire," he said with a sharp edge to his voice. He made a great show of the brave little banner whenever Frémont rode up to Oak Bend from the fort, but the captain never once commented on it.

4

Then the expedition began to grow.

One by one, sometimes in pairs, American settlers armed to the teeth drifted into camp. Now and then a native Californio joined them. The mountain men fed them all, and if Frémont was in camp rather than down with Sutter at the fort, he talked at length with each of them. Some stayed no longer than it took to eat a meal, but more found permanent places for their bedrolls and their horses. Within a week the expedition numbered almost a hundred men. The newcomers, while not as savage in appearance as the old hands who had come west from Bent's, were all hard, tough men who looked as if they were spoiling for a fight. To a man they expressed contempt for Mexicans.

More than one brought alarming news, some of it hard to credit. Don José Castro was on the move, one said. Mexican cavalry by the hundreds were about to enter the Sacramento Valley, with permission from the general to rob and rape. "He says they can have their way with any American women they can get their hands on." No, said another, no Mexican troops were headed north, but Don José was hiring Indians to attack the ranches while hordes of others were being paid to set fire to the spring crops as far north as Lassen's. Ranchers and their employees had been murdered in their beds in the Napa and Sonoma Valleys and in their homes across the San Joaquín. The Americans in the province had made attempts to overthrow Mexican sovereignty and there had already been a number of small battles with casualties among the ranchers and farmers all the way down to San Jose.

Frémont's eyes lit up at two last bits of supposed intelligence. A British frigate, H.M.S. *Collingwood,* eighty guns, had sailed into San Francisco Bay and was putting Royal Marines ashore at Yerba Buena. And with the situation so volatile, even the Russians were said to be contemplating a move back to their old colonial settlements near the Oregon border.

Kern put it all down to fear-driven, baseless rumor. "All except that about the *Collingwood* and the Russians," he said. "That could be true, in part at least. I wouldn't put it past the British, or the czar, to try to steal a march on the United States here in California if we're already at war with Mexico. Remember what Sutter said about Pío Pico cozying up to Her Majesty's government? I kind of doubt that they would try to take Yerba Buena, though. It hasn't that much strategic value. Monterey? Possibly."

Stone decided his friend was probably right again. "Damn it!" Kern went on. "If we are at war, it would be nice if somebody would let us know about it. Taylor's dragoons could be a couple of hundred miles into Mexico by now, and Castro could get orders from his government to march on us any day. This lack of news is one thing we can't lay at the feet of Captain Johnny."

"Larkin can't have heard anything about full-scale hostilities as yet," Stone said. "Gillespie was supposed to stay at

Yerba Buena for another month at least. From my impression of him at Klamath Lake, if there were any news, nothing could stop him from bringing it upriver to the captain if he had to swim."

But if Kern discounted the story about Castro's troops moving within striking distance of Oak Bend, or about the Mexican general paying the Indians to terrify the American settlers, one of the men of the contingent at Oak Bend did not—Joe Walker.

Walker clamored for an attack on Monterey without any more delay, talking about such a move to any of the mountain men who would listen, and to a lot of those, Carson for one, who would not. He raged at each tiny fragment of purported intelligence, treating it as gospel no matter how improbable it seemed, particularly the one that said the settlers had already taken up arms against Castro. "The least we could do is help these people. Goddamn it! Most of them are Americans. They're *ours!* Leaving them to fight the Mexes by themselves is even more gutless than the way we ran away from Gavilán." It made no difference to Joe when that report, at least, proved false. There had been no rising.

In any event, Frémont gave no orders.

From the Pathfinder's conversations with the new arrivals that Stone or Kern overheard, it became more difficult every day to tell anything about what the captain might be thinking. Although his words to all the settlers seemed much the same, his tone and gestures made his message to each of them subtly different. Without putting it in hard, clear language, he persuaded some of them—or so it seemed to Stone—that he would rally immediately with all the guns he commanded to any genuine rebellion against Mexican authority they made. Others were just as sure that he would do absolutely nothing.

It troubled Stone that the captain was sending these earnest men such contradictory and confusing signals.

The man William Ide, who had so impressed Ed Kern, came to call again at night, one of the few nights when the captain had decided to stay at Oak Bend instead of returning to the fort.

Ide rode in this time without William Hargrave, but with another American settler from the Sonoma Valley in tow, one Ezekiel Merritt. Merritt, although a head shorter than Stone, must have weighed nearly three hundred pounds. The extremely tall, almost emaciated Ide and the fat man with him made a strange pair.

The same loose ad hoc council of Frémont's men that had attended the earlier session with Hargrave—Kern, Stone, Carson, Owens, and Godey—sat in at the fireside talk the Pathfinder held with Ide and Merritt, again at Frémont's insistence.

This time Joe Walker, who had been the first to greet the pair, and who had engaged them in a short conversation before they joined Frémont, shouldered his way into the gathering, carrying his Hawken flying the Stars and Stripes across his chest. He propped it between his knees when he took a place directly across the fire from Frémont.

"Mr. Hargrave did not accompany you this time, Mr. Ide?" Frémont asked.

"No, Captain. I hate to say this, but I don't think you'll have much truck with him from here on out. No offense, but I got a hunch you know why."

"Yes. I suspect he was dissatisfied with our last meeting."

"Ain't hardly the word for it." Ide's fierce smile matched the hot eyes Stone had seen on the previous occasion.

Walker grunted and spat into the fire.

"Were you not dissatisfied too, Mr. Ide?" Frémont asked.

"Ain't got time to be one way or the other, sir. I ain't looking for satisfaction, anyways."

"You're not here to try to get me to change my mind?"

"Wouldn't even think of it."

"What is the purpose of this visit, then?"

"Zeke here has got something to tell you. I guess I could have told you myself, but I wanted you to hear it firsthand, straight from him." Ide waved at his hefty companion, who had not yet uttered a word, even when Ide introduced him.

Frémont waited ten or fifteen seconds in silence. "Well, Mr. Merritt?"

Merritt cleared his throat. "I'm going to take the Mexican fort and barracks at Sonoma, Captain Frémont."

"You're *what?*"

"I'm going to take the fort at Sonoma."

"And just how do you propose to carry out such an ambitious undertaking, Mr. Merritt?"

"I got fifty, maybe sixty good men who'll help me do it."

"Are any one of them, and more to the point are you, a military man?"

"No, sir."

"The fort at Sonoma, it is my understanding, is garrisoned by regular troops of the Mexican army. Disabuse me if this is not so, Mr. Merritt."

"I reckon that's so, Captain." Merritt fell silent for a moment. "I see what you're driving at. But my men will all be fighting for their lives and homes. And they're almost all Americans."

A happy explosion came from Joe Walker. "That's telling him, mister!" He began waving the Hawken with the flag. "This outfit's behind you to a man! Just point us at them damned Mexicans! Tell him we're ready to ride, Captain."

Frémont shot Joe a withering look. He turned back to Merritt. "Don't be carried away by Mr. Walker's impetuosity, sir. Of course we're behind you, but only in the moral sense. We are not in any position to offer military assistance—at the moment."

"I told you so, Zeke," Ide broke in. "Coming here was almost a waste of time. I don't much like it, either, but I do understand the fix Captain Frémont's in. He's a U.S. Army officer, and it ain't like it would be if we was at war with Mexico."

"Thank you, Mr. Ide," Frémont said.

"Don't thank me yet, Captain. It ain't like I'm letting you off the hook entirely. I said coming here was *almost* a waste of time. I wanted you to hear firsthand just how serious Zeke and the Sonoma Valley men are. And there's one other thing. Those three howitzers you been parading up and down California—since you ain't going to be using them yourself to help us, can we have them on loan? It would make things a mite easier for Zeke when he attacks Sonoma."

"Impossible, sir! My guns are the property of the United States government. I cannot let them out of my control even for such a worthy cause."

With that Joe Walker leaped to his feet.

"Goddamn it, Johnny! That's it. I've had enough. I quit! I won't spend one more night in any camp where you're in command." He started to leave, stopped. "Send what money you owe me care of William Bent. I hope I never see your weasel face again." He turned and stamped off into the darkness.

Kit had risen at Walker's tirade, and now started after him.

"Stop where you are, Mr. Carson," Frémont said. "I want you here for the rest of our discussion with these gentlemen. Mr. Walker will come to his senses without your help." As Kit sank to his place by the fire again, the captain faced the two Sonoma Valley men. "Please forgive this petty annoyance. I am truly sorry if my decisions do not sit well with you and Mr. Walker, but I have made them, and you and he will have to abide by them, as painful as that might be." The Pathfinder, proud as Stone knew him to be, was keeping amazing control of himself. And he actually did sound sorry. "Having said that, I believe it is no dereliction of my duty to wish you well if you decide to attack the fort at Sonoma. If, before that happens, General Castro should come against the northern ranches and settlements, well . . . we shall have to see."

Merritt looked uncomfortable, but Ide's thin lips curved into that hot smile again. "What you're saying, Captain, is that we ought to go ahead with our plans, right?"

"You will have to make that decision on your own, sir. As I said, I wish you well. You are brave men."

No matter what the words, Stone felt the Pathfinder had just urged the two men from Sonoma along a one-way road to war.

"Now," Frémont said, "we have heard troubling and alarming things these past few weeks. I think your reports on conditions in Upper California might be more reliable then mere gossip, Mr. Ide. I have a question."

"What do you want to know?"

"First—do you think that Mr. Merritt here can really take the fort at Sonoma?"

Ide shrugged. "Taking it won't be no problem. Holding it? Your guess is as good as mine. I only know that Zeke and his people feel they got to try. I'll be right there trying with them. We'll sure be sorry you and Kit and your mountain men won't be with us."

Frémont seemed to absorb that, and continued. "There's something else I'd like to talk about now, Mr. Ide. How much credence should we give the tales we have heard that General Castro is inciting renegade Indians to violence against the settlers . . . murder, pillage, burning crops, and the like?"

There was no mistaking the look of astonishment on Ide's face. "Forget that crazy stuff, Captain. I ain't an Indian lover or an admirer of Castro, and I won't shed a tear for him when he goes down, but I got no reason to believe he's up to any such shenanigans. No, none of that is true. And I think I'd know if it was. Even if the general tried to get them on the warpath, I don't think he'd have much luck. Them red-skins ain't exactly angels, but it's been years since they made war against any white men in this country."

"We had plenty of trouble with the Horsethieves along the San Joaquín."

"They ain't a bit like the Horsethieves. The Sacramento and American River tribes are really pretty peaceful, not a bit different from the ones Sutter's got working for him. Matter of fact, even the ones in the backcountry villages have worked some on the ranches and *estancias* in northern California for the better part of twenty years . . . when they had a mind to work. They're mostly too damned lazy to even think of causing a whole hell of a lot of trouble."

Frémont seemed disappointed by Ide's words, but he recovered quickly. "Thank you, Mr. Ide," he said. "Now . . . please accept such hospitality as we are in a position to offer. Stay the night. Stay longer, if you wish."

"Thanks, Captain, but it makes sense for the two of us to hightail it back to the valley before any unfriendly soul sees us. And we ain't as likely to run into a Castro patrol at night."

"Let me ride a mile or so with you, gentlemen," Frémont said. "Even if I'm in no position to help, I am in full accord with your intentions."

No sooner had the meeting broken up than Kit left the fire, in search of Joe Walker, Stone felt sure.

And just as he expected, Ed Kern had thoughts about the meeting he showed no reluctance to share.

"Joe quitting as he did presents a big problem for Captain Johnny, if Kit can't talk the damned fool out of it. Walker's not the only disaffected member of this expedition, but he's easily the most influential. You must have heard the grous-ing around camp."

"But, Ed, we've heard that sort of thing ever since we left Bent's."

"Yes, but this is different. I don't think most of it has anything to do with some supposed lofty principle as it does in the case of Joe. Mountain men, I've learned, are a nervous, energetic bunch, not given much to examining their navels or their consciences. They're always ready for a fight, and sometimes for the flimsiest of reasons. If our commander doesn't do something pretty damned soon to end their inactivity, he'll have *more* Joe Walkers to contend with."

5

Walker, even after a long talk with Carson, the substance of which Kit did not reveal to anyone, left camp in the middle of the night, roaring out to the north at a gallop.

"I think Joe is heading for the Basin and straight on to Bent's," Kit said. "He shouldn't have gone off this way. He's been with the captain a long time."

6

In the morning, the grumbling on the part of the mountain men that Ed had commented on, augmented by that of some of the expedition's new enlistees, reached a higher pitch. Walker's leaving, and his stated reasons for it, became the talk of the camp. Most of the men Stone listened to approved. Carson prowled the grove, buttonholing every mountain man who raised his voice, and to Stone's relief no others left.

"Kit's just saved Johnny's bacon again," Ed Kern said. "He sure must worship him."

Frémont called another meeting—not just of his lieutenants, but of the entire camp, newcomers, navvies, Delawares, and all—after the noon meal.

"Men!" He began in a voice that Stone was surprised did not shake the acorns from the lofty oaks of the grove. "Unsettling news about the intentions of General Castro has reached me. I believe each of you has heard some of it. Word has it that this unspeakable tyrant down in Monterey plans to turn the savages of the Sacramento and American River Valleys loose on the American settlers living in Upper California. These same settlers are already engaged in defending their homes and families against the depredations of Castro's cutthroat Mexican soldiery. They consequently will be in no position to turn and fend off the attacks of the murderous Indian ingrates they have clothed and fed for years. . . ."

Stone gulped. Frémont was not actually lying. Such reports about Castro and the Indians had reached him, of course, but according to what Ide had said no one should put any faith in them.

"Now," Frémont continued, "we have not come to California to begin a war with Mexico. The charter under which we operate expressly forbids such action. . . ." He paused theatrically.

"But there is nothing in the present situation to prevent a preemptive punitive campaign against the savages. They are not Mexicans, or citizens of that country. I propose to set out from here at Oak Bend—with all the forces at my disposal— to burn the Indian villages along the two rivers. . . ." Again the pregnant second, and then the shout.

"Are you with me?"

After the roar of approval, Frémont let his gaze sweep across the crowd of men in front of him. "Mr. Carson!" he called. "Can you have the expedition ready to move out by tomorrow morning?"

"Sure, Captain," Kit said, "but—"

"I am not interested in hearing any 'buts,' Mr. Carson. Can you have the men ready?"

"Yes, sir."

7

Ed Kern had one observation on the captain's speech. "Turning the men's attention to the Indians to keep them with him was a clever ploy. They'll forget Joe Walker once we spy a single Indian they think needs killing."

Stone did not discuss with Kern his own troubled feelings at Carson's acceptance of Frémont's plan to wage war against the Indian villages on the San Joaquín. Kit had heard with all the rest of them William Ide's astonished denial last night that Castro had ordered the Indians—or paid them—to commit atrocities against the settlers.

The scout must have felt as appalled as Stone at Frémont's almost casual decision to mount raids against a probably peaceful people. Kit had made no protest beyond that one feeble "but," and Stone could no longer avoid thinking about Kern's proposition that Kit obeyed orders blindly.

But Brad Stone was no different. He knew he would go with the expedition if ordered to when it left tomorrow. And he would take a full part in whatever action Frémont and Carson led them into.

His wound had healed; it still pained him some when arising in the cold of morning, but once the unfailing California sun had warmed the air and he had moved around a little, he could ride and walk again with no difficulty.

He could fight, would fight.

The niceties of the willful course Johnny Frémont had just set them on would have to be considered only at some later, more tranquil time.

For the moment, and for the foreseeable future, he owed Frémont his complete, unquestioning—blind?—obedience.

8

"When I left Philadelphia," Kern said, as he and Stone rode a dozen yards behind Kit and Frémont through the smoky wreckage of the last Indian village the men of the expedition had burned, "I could never have guessed that I would get tired of fighting Indians."

"We haven't really done much of it, Ed," Stone said.

"Depends on how you look at it. It's enough for me. Since I never once got an Indian in my sights, the only thing that has engaged my attention fully the past two days is watching our friend Carson. Other than that, I'm bored."

"Bored?" Stone said. "It was hard for me to feel bored when I was as scared as I was yesterday."

"Don't get the idea that I wasn't scared enough. I think I only contained myself as well as I did because I have such faith in Carson. His tactical methods ought to be written into those manuals Captain Johnny reads. This work is almost an exact repetition of the raid on the Klamaths."

"I didn't go along on that one."

"The number of dead Indians is much greater, but the way Carson planned the attacks to protect us while we did our job was the same. I'm glad I didn't personally kill any of these pitiful wretches. What the hell kind of Indians are these poor devils, anyway?"

"Kit told me they're a mix of five or six California tribes. They're more or less grouped together, or were, as 'Mission Indians.' They've lived close to whites so long they've more or less lost their old tribal identity."

"I can believe it," Kern said. "These villages have all looked more like Mexican towns than they do like Indian camps." He pointed to the smoking ruin of an adobe not too unlike ones Stone had seen in Taos. One village yesterday even had a small church.

It had been a chaotic two days since they left Oak Bend, except when Kit ran the show, something that Frémont, to his credit, did nothing to prevent. Without actually saying it in so many words, Frémont encouraged the scout to take command.

Well, no one, least of all Brad Stone, would accuse John C. Frémont of being stupid. Arrogant, stubborn, rash, elitist, pompous as a pontiff, often quixotic, autocratic, impulsive but at rare times disappointingly indecisive, yes . . . but stupid, no. And no one could ever question his courage, either.

One of the Indian village mongrels was yapping at Stone, dashing up from time to time to try to nip at his horses's fetlocks. The small, mangy animal and the less aggressive members of the pack it apparently ran with were the only living things left in or around the fire-blackened mud-and-stick lodges. He saw no Indian bodies here, though. As had been the case with every village since the first one, early yesterday, where the surprise of Carson's attack had been complete, the news of their coming had outrun them, and they had found no enemy. Only at the second did they catch so much as a glimpse of the inhabitants, fleeing into the woods or breaking across the river. As with this ruined village, none had died there, either.

But in that first village, the raiding party, forty strong, had killed dozens of Indians in the very first frontal onslaught, more than a hundred, Dick Owens guessed, and a dozen more had run directly into the deadly rifle fire from the first flank attack of Lucien Walker's group, made from the high ground well back from the river's eastern edge. Stone could not recall seeing one of the villagers carrying a weapon of any kind—no rifles, bows, or lances—but perhaps he had not been close enough to Kit and Frémont's charge. By day's end, not one man of Frémont's force had taken the smallest wound.

A day ago Stone and Kern had forded the river from the west with the party led by Dick Owens, ten mounted men whose horses kicked up great sprays and splashes. Owens, no crazed killer as Maxwell sometimes appeared to be, had not signaled for a fusillade. For all the carnage created by Carson's and Maxwell's front and side attacks, neither Stone nor Kern had been called on to fire once. As was the case with Kern, Stone felt no disappointment.

They torched the second, third, and fourth empty villages, rode half a mile beyond the fourth as the lodges blazed, then turned about.

"Do you want to look for more villages farther up the river, Captain?" Kit asked Frémont.

"No, Mr. Carson. I believe we've made our point with these savages."

"Then I'll turn the party around and start back for Oak Bend, sir."

"Carry on, Mr. Carson. And, Mr. Carson, you did see war paint on the warriors of that first village yesterday, did you not?"

"No, sir."

"Hmmm. I swear I did. No matter, the very least that will come of this enterprise is that it will give heart to our American friends in the Sonoma Valley, and all across Upper California. We've saved lives the last two days."

"Yes, sir. I expect we saved *a lot* of lives," Kit said.

25
Flag of the Bear

At ten o'clock in the morning on the fifteenth of June, a distraught Johann Sutter rode up from the fort to the camp at Oak Bend. When he slipped from the saddle he did not even look for someone to take his horse's reins before he raced for Frémont's tent.

The Swiss drew the usual crowd of mountain men, with Brad Stone among them. The "founder of the feast" had lost none of his popularity with the men of the expedition, but he seemed to Stone to be preoccupied this morning, too troubled to do more than nod absently to Kit, Owens, Talbot, and the rest of those who had trailed him to Frémont's tent quarters.

"Captain!" he called out. Even before the Pathfinder had time to emerge from his tent Sutter went on. "I have just received dreadful news."

Frémont came through the flap, not yet fully clothed, still in his underwear and buckskin trousers. Sleep still clouded his eyes, but he came completely awake and alert in an instant at the sight and sound of Sutter. Perhaps the agitation in Sutter's voice, whatever the cause, had an element of racing contagion about it; Frémont seemed suddenly every bit as excited as the owner of New Helvetia, as if he had already sensed exactly what was troubling the Swiss. "What is it, Johann?"

"A band of your fellow Americans have seized the fort and barracks at Sonoma, John! They have taken possession of the entire town!" He had to stop for breath. "If that were not alarming enough, they also have made a prisoner of my good friend General Mariano Vallejo and his family. These miscreants have incarcerated him and his wife and children in their home. Don Mariano serves as deputy *comandante* for General Castro in the Sonoma and Napa Valleys, but I cannot think why your Americans should think him an enemy. He is one of the finest gentlemen in the province, and he has always been friendly to their cause, even while remaining loyal to Mexico."

"When exactly did this happen?"

"Early yesterday morning."

"Were there casualties?"

"Blessedly . . . no. The soldiers of the garrison put up virtually no resistance. The report I received said they could not believe what was happening. In any event, Don Mariano commanded only a tiny, token force. General Castro has never completely trusted General Vallejo."

"Who led this . . . attack?"

"Ezekiel Merritt, a settler, in league with a troublesome rancher by the name of William Ide. . . ." The Swiss paused, as if uncertain about going on, but at last he spoke again. "I believe you know them, John. They visited your camp here at Oak Bend some time back. At night. In secret. They did not stop at the fort. I would have thought you would have dissuaded them from . . ." He stopped.

So much for the supposed secrecy of Ide and Merritt's nighttime mission, Stone thought.

"Forgive me, Johann," Frémont said now, "but you sound as if you think I had something to do with this revolt . . . or whatever it purports to be. I assure you I did not. I was neither consulted nor advised about it. This insurrection is as much of a surprise to me as it is to you."

Stone had heard John C. Frémont toy with the truth often enough, but this was his first bald-faced lie, the first Stone had heard, at least.

"I make no accusations, Captain." Sutter had reddened noticeably. "But I do believe you are now in a position to nip in the bud something that could have tragic consequences. When this news reaches Monterey, General Castro will have no choice but to march north with every soldier he commands. The Americans in possession of Sonoma cannot possibly hope to stand against him. Counting auxiliaries, he has nearly a thousand troops at his disposal. If the Americans do not leave Sonoma without offering resistance, he will not be merciful."

"Just what do you propose I do about it?"

Sutter hesitated a moment. "You could go to Sonoma yourself, John. If you leave tomorrow morning there might still be time to avert a bloody conflict. Castro cannot turn out his troops and get there for a week. Talk to Merritt and Ide. Get them to abandon this rash enterprise before disaster overtakes them. They will listen to you as the ranking United States officer in California. As I said, Vallejo is a friend, and as magnanimous a man as I have ever met. If they free him now as they should, and return his town to him, I am sure he will take no action, since no one was injured. You can call on me to help you persuade him. I hope you will try at least. Surely it cannot be too late to—"

"Say no more, Johann. Of course I will go to Sonoma, my friend. I will leave this afternoon and ride through the night, if necessary."

A grateful, beaming Sutter thanked Frémont, pled urgent business at the fort, mounted, and said good-bye. He saluted as he rode off.

Frémont then turned to Stone.

"Bradford! Get your writing case and we will draft a message to Consul Larkin and Lieutenant Gillespie at Yerba Buena, and one more to be dispatched to Washington at our earliest opportunity. I want you to append a note to the latter dispatch describing every single detail of this meeting with Captain Sutter. Make sure that it is quite explicit on one particular point. Captain Johann August Sutter—an official of the Mexican government, as evidenced by his title 'the Guardian of the Northern Frontier'—has specifically asked me to go to Sonoma. As a matter of indisputable fact he has *begged* me to go there, as I am sure all present will acknowledge. I want everyone within the sound of my voice to sign this note or make his mark.

"Mr. Carson . . . have the entire expedition ready to march within two hours . . . and Mr. Talbot, see that your howitzers are in shape to travel and that they will be ready for action whenever I give the word!"

2

On the move again, and during the last morning's ride into the Sonoma Valley, Bradford Ogden Stone had more time to think about his present circumstances.

He had now kept company with Frémont and Carson for almost exactly a year. One would have thought him fairly well adjusted to his new life in the West after such a length of time, and in many ways that seemed to be the case. He had undergone long months of rough outdoor life, made far more strenuous journeys than the one they were now completing, and had acquired countless new skills, some of which, such as learning to shoot his Hawken, had even led to survival.

He still could not throw a diamond hitch on a mule on a cold morning without hearing a peal of laughter from one or more of his companions, but by and large he felt a modest sense of accomplishment when he considered his new abilities as "a man of the western wilderness."

He had contained fear, looked death in the face. He had taken a wound. He had killed two men.

The memory of the killing on the Cimarron still haunted him from time to time, and he wondered if that was only because it had been the first. If he still squirmed a little at the remembered sight of that Comanche he'd brought down in the shadows, he certainly felt no pangs of conscience at all about the death of the Klamath warrior who had wounded him; the recollection of Basil Lajeunesse's ruined head, and of the mutilated bodies of Crane and Denny, remained too strong for that. Perhaps, as seemed true of Carson and the other men of the expedition who had killed for years, it got easier. Sobering, that.

He had made good friends this year, and of two or three different sorts. Kit would forever occupy a special place. Stone felt the scout had truly become a friend, and there remained still that strong pulse of hero worship. His awe of Carson had grown over the last year rather than diminished.

And when he left Groverton he had never known what it was like to have a brother. In Ed Kern, riding alongside him, he had one now. Alexis Godey, too, while Stone could not share intimacies with him to anything near the same extent he did with Ed, had become a friend. Basil Lajeunesse—bless the good old mountain man in his grave in the forest overlooking Klamath Lake—had been one, too.

There had been a time earlier in the adventure when he would have lamented the fact that he would probably never be able to count John C. Frémont among his friends.

And there was another friend: quiet, self-sacrificing Luis Aragón.

With all his experiences since leaving Bent's Fort he should have a better grasp of what was going on around him.

He had come west as a mapmaker, a twenty-three-year-old, more or less bookish man who had never fired a gun or skinned a squirrel, one who did not know a Comanche from a catamount nor an *alcalde* from a long-acorn oak. He had had no forewarning back then that he would become embroiled in a war.

He had never been close to a war, had not the remotest knowledge of one; his country had not been at war since ten years before he had been born. But even in his ignorance he knew there was something strange about the events leading up to this one.

The expedition, even with the three mute field guns bumping along at the rear of the column, and with heavily armed recruits swelling its ranks by the day as they crossed the green, spring ridges between Oak Bend and Sonoma, hardly constituted an army. It seemed to him that the sharply disciplined men he saw drilling in the *presidio* at Monterey should be able to crush Frémont's ragtag force without too much danger or difficulty anytime their commander chose.

He still wondered why General Castro had not pressed his advantage in numbers in what had turned out to be the utterly farcical "battle" at Gavilán Peak.

He wondered even more at the erratic behavior of Frémont. By now the mountain men had marched and countermarched a thousand miles and more within California's boundaries, without once taking the fight to this supposed enemy. The Klamaths had taken their own vicious fight to the expedition and brought the mountain men and the relentless Delawares down on their heads, and Frémont had last week bloodied the villages of largely unarmed and virtually helpless Indians. But no one in the expedition, mountain man or Indian tracker, had fired a single shot at one solitary Mexican soldier or hostile Californio.

Perhaps that would change now that Merritt and Ide had begun their revolt at Sonoma. Frémont could not straddle this particular fence much longer, and it did seem as if he were ready to jump from it directly into the settlers' camp. The route they were taking to the Napa and Sonoma Valleys would put them smack into any of several paths Castro's forces could be using as they moved up from Monterey to crush the rebellion north of San Pablo Bay.

With the possible exception of Carson and Ed Kern, every rider in the column seemed eager to go into battle. "Not one of them," Kern said, "has the faintest idea of what's involved here. It's just the fundamental nature of these brutes, I suppose. The Americans who've joined us for this march I can understand. They have a stake in this. But men who can't even remember their own homes back East? Mind you, I don't mean to imply they're barbarians. I've seen too many instances of their decency, even kindliness, for that. But I don't think any of them, even the Delawares, who must be completely in the dark where the behavior of white men is concerned, seem to have ever come upon a fight they didn't like. Carson, of course, I don't know about. I don't think he approves of what we're up to, but he simply will not criticize Captain Johnny."

If Kit did not approve, and that seemed likely, Stone thought he knew why. The scout's reasons were probably much the same as his. Memories of Yerba Buena and Monterey, and the looks of the tiny hamlets they passed through on the way to Sonoma, kept crowding him. The inhabitants all had something of the look of the Mexicans of Santa Fe and Taos. Kit's own people.

Too many of the men Stone saw, even if they had in their workaday whites little of the quiet young trader's elegance, reminded him of Luis Aragón.

And the women?

Well, the less he thought about that, the better. . . .

Kit, riding alongside the Pathfinder with his Hawken cradled in his arms, must be thinking every bit as hard about Josefa and that sage-blanketed valley running down to the great gorge of the Río and filled with Jaramillos. Had he not said once that he sometimes thought he had become almost as Mexican as he was American?

For Kit the prospect of taking up arms against people of his wife's and his Taos neighbors' heritage and religion must be hanging him on the needle horns of a terrible dilemma.

For this last morning's ride into the town of Sonoma itself, the Pathfinder had chosen to wear his army uniform, the first time Stone had seen him in it.

On this last stretch of road leading to Sonoma, Kern asked a question to which Brad Stone, for this one time at least, seemed to have the answer.

"I wonder why Johnny didn't bring his friend Sutter with us?"

"I think he feared Sutter might talk Merritt and Ide out of this. And I guess that's why Frémont had all of us come along. He doesn't want them talked out of this revolt. He wants to get in on it himself."

3

After immaculate Monterey, and to a lesser extent even unprepossessing Yerba Buena, Sonoma—the heart of the town at least—presented a disgusting aspect.

It seemed a shame, the more so since its builders had placed their village in as lovely a setting as any Stone had seen on his western journeys. It lay in the center of a flat-bottomed, verdant valley flanked by pleasant green hills, actually low, rounded, age-old mountains covered with live oak and juniper. With such a setting the town should have sparkled like a gem.

But in Sonoma's plaza the sights and smells sickened him. Apparently the villagers did all their slaughtering in this public square, not bothering to remove unwanted bones, horns, tails, and hooves from either the sight of the populace or the ravagings of the town's stray dogs. This boneyard slaughterhouse was no temporary aberration; the aged condition of many of the cow skulls littering the plaza told Stone it had been used for this purpose for a long, long time, years perhaps. It was an abattoir and a gigantic ossuary all in one.

The mountain men, Delawares, and settler recruits had not been in the plaza more than a minute before the head of the column was beset by all manner of flying insects, clouds of gnats together with ghastly, unseen, swarming rivers of fleas, all doubtless drawn here by that immense sprawl of sun-festered, stinking carnage.

The barracks Ezekiel Merritt, William Ide, and their fellow rebels had taken the week before closed the northern side of the square. From the top of a thirty- or forty-foot pole in the middle of the stacks of bones, a crude banner of unbleached muslin or some such rough fabric, possibly four feet by six, caught a slight, foul-smelling, hot breeze. In the center of the flag its designer had drawn a passable image of a grizzly bear for a device, and a giant star filled the upper corner. A legend on the rough cloth, in berry juice or paint, read: CALIFORNIA REPUBLIC.

Frémont and Carson had reined in their horses, while Kern and Stone, forming the next two-rider rank, pulled up behind them. The captain and Carson stared up at the muslin flag.

"Interesting, Kit," Frémont said. "Of course . . . that defiant, gallant little banner will have to give way to the Stars and Stripes in fairly short order . . . but it would not be prudent to mention that to our hosts for a bit."

"Yes, sir." The scout seemed puzzled as he gazed upward.

Then Stone remembered Carson could not read. He would recognize the grizzly bear, his old Rocky Mountain nemesis, well enough from his years on the trap lines, but the words CALIFORNIA REPUBLIC might as well have been written in Sanskrit for all his ability to decipher them.

"Well, our hosts—and allies," Frémont said. He pointed to the main carriage door of the barracks, a brass cannon in place on each side of it. There a number of curious men, all Americans by the look of them, had laid down weapons they had been cleaning to turn their full attention on the column. Three men left the group and strode toward Frémont: Merritt, Ide, and lagging a couple of paces behind the other two, a sullen-looking William Hargrave.

"Welcome to Sonoma, Captain," Ide said. "You've brought your whole command?"

"Indeed I have, sir."

"Good. We may need them fairly quick."

"Are things in secure order here, Mr. Ide?" the captain said. He merely nodded at Hargrave and Merritt.

"You can damn well bet they are," Ide said. There was no mistaking the pride in his voice.

"Congratulations." Frémont slid from Sacramento's back and waved gnats away from his face before he went on. "Has there been any report of General Castro's troops moving north? I presume you have sent out reconnaissance patrols. I must confess that I was a trifle disconcerted that we were not met and challenged somewhere along our line of march since we left the vicinity of Sutter's Fort."

Ide gave no sign that he had taken offense at the implied criticism. "Actually, we ain't had to patrol, Captain. Some U.S. Marine fellow, name of Gillespie, who's staying down at Yerba Buena with Bill Leidesdorff, the assistant American consul, has been sending riders up to us just about every day. Castro ain't made a move yet. Kind of funny. It ain't like he ain't heard we took this town. If word reached Yerba Buena it sure as hell reached Monterey."

Again Frémont batted at barely seen insects. "I have no wish to complain, Mr. Ide, but could we not continue our discussions where these pests can't get at me?"

"Sure, Captain. I guess we're more or less used to them.

We've got an office and command post set up inside the barracks. We can talk there."

"Where can my men bivouac?"

"There's an open field just a few hundred yards northwest of here. It has a well and some decent grazing right nearby. I'll have one of Zeke's men lead the way. We'll lay on some grub as soon as you're settled in. We're having a little gathering in the plaza tonight to make some proclamations and the like. Maybe you and your men could join us. We'll throw a dance right after the speechifying is over with."

"Splendid!" Frémont turned to Carson. "Turn the column over to Gus Archambeault, Mr. Carson, and relay Mr. Ide's invitation. Tell him that when our camp is in order I want our American flag flying proudly from my tent." Ide opened his mouth to say something at this, apparently thought better of it. "Once you have given my orders to Gus, Mr. Carson," Frémont continued, "please find Mr. Godey, Mr. Talbot, and Mr. Owens, and have them join Mr. Kern, Mr. Stone, and myself in Mr. Ide's office in the barracks." He faced Ide and his two silent companions again. "We are at your complete disposal, gentlemen. Lead on."

He signaled to the mounted men directly behind him in the column, and Stone and Kern dismounted and handed the reins of their animals to the men following on their heels. Kit turned his horse about and rode back down the line to find Talbot and the others Frémont had named.

As Stone, Kern, and Frémont followed the three Sonomans toward the wide gate leading to what looked like a drill ground at the rear of the adobe barracks, the captain turned back to the two of them. "I cannot understand why Lieutenant Gillespie did not send his dispatches straight to me. I am not at all sure I want reports getting to Captain Sutter before I read them. His behavior has been a touch unsettling lately."

"With respect, sir," Stone said, "the lieutenant would have

no knowledge of our trip here until he received the messages we sent from Oak Bend. He probably thought us still in camp at New Helvetia. If he did, I imagine he forwarded everything to the fort. He could not, of course, be aware of your present feelings about Captain Sutter."

"Good thinking, Bradford!" His face above the dark beard brightened. "Thank you, my boy. But that brings something else to mind, something we must deal with directly and immediately when we convene in Mr. Ide's command post."

Ide shot the Pathfinder a sharp look, but said nothing.

4

From the look of the barracks Stone could pretty well imagine what Ide's office would be like, and when they entered it through a door opening in the wall of the passageway that led to the drill ground the tiny cubicle brought an instant of déjà vu. Windowless, it seemed scarcely larger than the anteroom at Casa Tules in Santa Fe. The table in the room held piles of paper, maps in wild disarray, pens, inkwells, and four pistols—cocked, Stone noted—right in the middle of the small space. Four Spanish chairs nestled under the table's top.

Remembering the flag flying in the plaza, the crowded office—with only a slightly smaller concentration of insects buzzing about—appeared to Stone an unlikely setting to be the nerve center, probably the capital, of anything as grand as that CALIFORNIA REPUBLIC the legend on the homemade banner promised.

Moments after they had all entered, Carson appeared in the doorway with Owens and Godey, just as Frémont, without waiting for an invitation, seated himself at what looked to be the head of the table. The chair the Pathfinder took, at the far end from the door, had arms and a high, carved back.

Ide settled in across from him. Then Merritt and Hargrave, who had hung back until Ide took his place, fairly leaped to the two empty chairs at the sides, as if they had determined well in advance not to be excluded or pushed aside by any of the expedition's men.

Frémont slapped at something crawling across his cheek. Ide apparently noticed and smiled. "Sorry about all these bugs, Captain," he said. "We've had a lot of rain this past week and it ain't going to be a whole lot better until things dry out. It ain't much different where we had your men camp. You said something about your tent. No need to even pitch it. We'll set you up at the Vallejo place by dinnertime. That far from the plaza the bugs shouldn't bother you none. And maybe by that time you won't pay them no more mind than we do."

"One can hope. Will there be room at the residence for my staff, too, Mr. Ide?" He waved airily at Stone and the others.

Staff? When had the handful of rough-and-ready adventurers lining the walls of the room and turning the air close become a staff? Stone and Talbot—and on rare occasions Ed Kern—were the only ones who had ever served the Pathfinder in anything remotely resembling a "staff" capacity, and there had never been enough of that kind of work for any of them to be called staff officers.

Kit's functions as the chief scout of the expedition had been of an entirely different nature from any supposed staff work. And so had the jobs of Dick Owens and Alexis Godey and the few others with the column now moving out of the plaza—guards, hunters, and scouts who had been close to Frémont from time to time in their long journey from Bent's Fort to Sonoma. Perhaps the army manuals were having a much stronger effect on the captain than even bemused Ed Kern might suppose.

"Don't rightly think we can put up anybody but you at Don Mariano's, Captain," Ide said now. "You'll have to share the mansion with the don and his kinfolk until we decide what to do with them."

"General Vallejo? Your prisoner?"

"Yes, sir. We kind of got him under house arrest. Actually, it was his idea. He offered us his parole. I think you'll enjoy his company. He's an educated man like you, and he's traveled a lot in the United States. Stocks the best wines in California, and lays out the best table in Sonoma."

"You mean I am expected to share quarters with the enemy?"

"Well . . . we kind of thought . . ."

"Are you telling me, Mr. Ide, that General Vallejo still enjoys the freedom—and what appears to be the luxury—of his home? This seems to me to be a very lackadaisical attitude toward a prisoner of war. Why don't you have him in close confinement in the guardhouse here?"

"For God's sake, Captain! We couldn't do that to a real gent like Don Mariano. He's been a damned good friend to every American in this valley. We weren't rebelling against *him* when we took Sonoma. Besides, he gave us his word of honor he ain't about to run away."

In the doorway Carson cleared his throat. "I reckon I can vouch for General Vallejo, too, Captain. I've known him for years. He made a trip to Taos once, and is a good friend of Charlie Bent's. He's a genuine first-class *hombre,* sure enough. He'll keep his word."

Frémont stiffened. "Forgive me, Mr. Carson, but in my opinion you and Mr. Ide are both somewhat too naive and trusting. If General Vallejo chooses to break his parole—something an American officer would never do, of course—he could rally those Californios who do not approve of this . . . 'republic,' and at almost the same moment General Castro takes the field against it." He turned to Ide again. "I would like you to take Vallejo and his people into custody—at once. Bring them here to the barracks and lock them up."

William Hargrave, absolutely silent until now, stood up swiftly, knocking his chair over in back of him. The disgust with Frémont he had exhibited at Oak Bend was now even plainer. "No, goddamn it! I'm going on record here and now that I'm against it, and I'm sure Zeke and Bill Ide feel the same. We're trying to give birth to a decent, honorable new country here. This would be a hell of a bad way to start. We sure as hell aren't going to lock Don Mariano up in our flea-bitten jail. If you want that done, Captain, you'll damn well have to do the job yourself."

"Very well, Mr. Hargrave, I will do it myself, or have it done." If Frémont had stiffened before, he now became unyieldingly rigid. He turned back to Kit. "Mr. Carson, when we finish here, pick a squad of twelve men, have one of these gentlemen or someone they appoint, guide you and your squad to the Vallejo residence, and take the general and the members of his entourage in hand."

"Women and kids, too, Captain?"

"Yes. We'll make permanent arrangements for them later. If the general or any other man you find there protests—shackle him. Put them in a cell or cells here in the barracks and mount a guard. Remember at all times that they are the enemy."

"Yes, sir," Kit said. To Stone's eyes his friend looked sick. He could make a good guess at what was running through Kit's mind, or at least hoped he could. "Captain . . . ," Kit went on, "I won't need no twelve men to bring in Don Mariano."

"Probably not, but I want the general to come to a clear understanding of how we intend doing business now that I have taken command in Upper California."

A strangled cry came from Hargrave. Frémont sent the Napa man a withering look, then turned back to Ide, whose eyes glowed even hotter than they had at Oak Bend. "Once Mr. Carson does his duty, will there then be a sufficiency of quarters in General Vallejo's home for my staff officers as well, Mr. Ide?"

"Sure. I just hope you and your so-called 'staff officers' don't break nothing or dirty the place up. Casa Vallejo is maybe the most beautiful house in Upper California, including Johann Sutter's, and even with the Don a prisoner and away from it, your men damned well better remember that Sonoma takes pride in it."

Frémont put his hands on the table and pushed himself back. His face had turned to ice. "I and my men will be as circumspect as the situation warrants, sirrah! I will not press the point, but I do not take too kindly to the suggestion that my most trusted lieutenants comprise a band of vandals."

More than the wings of insects were making the air hum. The tension had turned it electric. Surely Frémont could hear and feel it, too.

Hargrave had said they were trying to give birth to a new country. Stone had never before, of course, witnessed the birth of a nation, or even the lying-in, if indeed either was happening here today. If it was a birth, he hoped against hope the infant had not entered this threatening world stillborn.

"Now, gentlemen, it is time to assess our strategic situation. How many men do you have under arms, Mr. Ide?" Frémont asked. If any doubts lingered on the part of the captain about the effect of his words on his listeners, none showed. The Sonoma men, and Hargrave from the Napa Valley, were not as easy for Stone to read.

"Hard to *tell* how many men we got, Captain," Ide said. His preacher's voice had weakened. "It damned near changes by the minute. Almost every man in the valley's got a lot of work to do this time of year. They come and go so much it's hard to make a tally. We did take a rough count two days ago. Had a hundred and thirty then—give or take a dozen."

"Give or take a dozen? Just what sort of military planning is this? How on earth did you ever manage to take this town? And why do your men come and go? Can't you keep them in line?"

"Hard to keep farmers in line during the growing season." Ide suddenly had turned beaten and humble. "Look, Captain, I . . . don't really care how many men we got. With yours we got enough for what we have to do. . . ." The hot burn had left his eyes. Stone supposed that even stronger men might have wilted under Frémont's domineering arrogance.

"I can see you need me for more than just my men," Frémont said. From the even more confident tone of his voice, he had discerned the advantage Ide's new demeanor had given him. "Now, let us discuss arms, ammunition, and supplies."

"Zeke here knows a hell of a lot more about that stuff than I do."

"Mr. Merritt?" Frémont said.

The fat man started as if he had been rudely awakened from a nap. "W-well . . . ," he stammered. He must have been mesmerized by Frémont's performance to this point. "We all got rifles and pistols, of course. And plenty of powder and balls of our own. Each of our men feeds himself here in town. We're a sight better fixed than we were before we took the barracks. When we captured it we also collected a lot of the garrison's munitions: over a hundredweight of black powder easy, more than two hundred muskets, and nine brass cannons. We'd sure hold still for somebody teaching us how to use them."

"Very good, Mr. Merritt, very good indeed. Our Mr. Talbot is an accomplished cannoneer. Your willingness to learn is admirable, but we won't require it. There are a number of gunners in our ranks. Turn the cannons and everything but your own personal arms and ammunition over to Mr. Talbot. From this moment on he will serve as our quartermaster as well as our artillerist." Frémont looked at Kit now. "I am going to adjourn these proceedings now, Mr. Carson. Take your men and fetch the enemy general at once—twelve men, remember?"

"Yes, sir."

Stone glanced at Ed Kern, wondering if the wry Philadelphian was thinking what he was thinking. Ed wore the same sly smile he had worn through so many similar moments in the past.

Carson left his place against the wall and stepped toward the door. Dick Owens started to follow him.

"Wait, Mr. Owens!" Frémont called out. "Mr. Carson can manage quite well without you. I want you to check with Mr. Talbot and see what sort of order he has brought our bivouac. Tell him he will reside in General Vallejo's house with Mr. Stone, Mr. Kern, Mr. Carson, Mr. Godey—and you and me." He turned to the others. "You are all dismissed. We shall meet here again tonight after Mr. Ide finishes his affair in the plaza. Incidentally, Mr. Ide, I may wish to address the good citizens of Sonoma at that time myself."

With that he stood abruptly, nodded curtly, but not unpleasantly to Hargrave, Ide, and Merritt, and strode through the small door. He ducked, but the eagle feather angling from his hat brushed the lintel.

Stone and Kern left the office last, just behind Ide and Hargrave, who said to his companion, "The son of a bitch could have *asked* to talk to our people tonight."

"Ain't important, William," Ide said. "I know he sticks in your craw like he does in mine. But keep in mind we need him. Let's ride to the Vallejo *casa* with him, and see that Stebbi treats the captain the way he thinks is right, although I expect Stebbi will. He loves Don Mariano and the *casa* more than he does his wife, but he ain't no fool."

5

Once outside and separated from the others as they began the search for their horses, Kern tugged at Stone's sleeve.

"Captain Johnny doesn't realize or doesn't give a damn that he's appropriating their revolution."

"You're right. A junior U.S. Army officer can't just declare war on his own account. And it sure sounds to me as if that's exactly what the captain has just done."

"He might have heard we're already at war, and for some reason of his own is keeping it from the rest of us."

"Come on, Ed."

"I was only referring to the high-handed way he's treated Ide and the two others. We haven't fired a solitary shot at the Mexicans, while these poor devils have actually begun the war and have already taken an important objective, even though their action here wasn't what you could call a battle of Titans. I can't for the life of me understand why Ide and Merritt, to say nothing of Hargrave—whose nose is even more out of joint than those of the other two—haven't gotten their backs up about our noble commander and told him to just mind his own business."

"They want his help."

"He turned them down back at Oak Bend. They don't look like weaklings, and it took a lot of courage for them to do what they did against what I have to presume was a trained garrison. . . . " He laughed. "Well, my friend, it may be small, but our Johnny has found his war. And speaking of war and armies, how does it strike you to be a 'staff officer' now?"

Stone could only grunt sourly at that last bit. "Well at least it has one advantage, Ed. We won't be sleeping under the stars and attacked by every insect in California."

By the time they found and mounted their horses, caught up with Frémont, Ide, Hargrave, and Merritt, and neared the bivouac area, they met Carson's men and their prisoners on their way back toward the plaza.

A raven-haired middle-aged man whom Stone took at once for General Mariano Vallejo, despite his civilian attire, rode at the front of the procession with Carson. Clean-shaven except for muttonchop side whiskers that reached almost to the corners of a smiling mouth, there seemed little of the military man about Don Mariano Vallejo. From his smile when he sighted Frémont, there seemed even less of the prisoner about him.

A buxom young Californio woman in a *rebozo*, pretty, but with a distraught, tear-stained face, followed in a small, open-topped buggy she drove herself, squeezed between two children whose large black eyes were alive with fright. The trio put Stone in mind of Doña Olivera Espinosa and her two tots the morning they found the Tewa navvy Diego butchered in the meadow at the southern foot of Raton Pass.

Two very sober, mustachioed men in uniforms much like those of Don José Castro and Lieutenant José Antonio Chávez rode behind the buggy.

None of the three Californio men, Stone was relieved to see, wore shackles. Mountain men, all of whom had been with the expedition ever since Bent's, composed the entire guard detail bringing up the rear. Kit, surely as sensitive to the nuances of the situation as Stone was, had no doubt picked his guard detail for this unpleasant task from Frémont's most tried and true veterans. He would not risk a mutiny if he chose any of the American settlers who had ridden with them from Oak Bend or joined the column as it crossed the ridges between New Helvetia and Sonoma. He, too, must have remembered William Hargrave's short-lived and imperiously quenched objections to Frémont's order to bring the Vallejos to the guardhouse. The ranchers and farmers who had attached themselves to the column since leaving Sutter's could well feel much as the Napa man did about Vallejo.

Unlike the affable, chatting Mexican general, Carson looked uncharacteristically grim.

"God!" Kern whispered. "Surely Johnny's not going to lock those kids up in that pesthole of a guardhouse."

"I hope not," Stone said. "I can't believe an American officer would subject women and children to anything like that. The captain, for all his faults, is not a monster."

The man Stone had decided was Vallejo reined in his horse when he neared Frémont, and Kit pulled his up, too. Frémont set the spurs to Sacramento, and when he reached Kit and Vallejo, halted the big stallion. Stone, Kern, and the two mountain men behind them bunched up ten yards short of the captain.

Frémont cast his eye over Kit's prisoner, the shivering threesome in the buggy, and the two unknown prisoners riding behind the little vehicle, and set his back even more rigidly than usual. The early afternoon sunlight caught clouds of insects in its rays. Vallejo urged his mount a pace or two closer to Frémont.

"I take it you are Brevet Captain John Frémont, *señor,*" he said.

The words—in completely unaccented English—came out in a warm, rich, musical voice that went well with the handsome face. It certainly failed to reflect the speaker's present humiliating circumstances. Nothing in Vallejo's look revealed any particular discomfort either.

"I *am* John C. Frémont, General," Frémont said. "But you are mistaken about my rank, sir. Just this morning I became a colonel."

Stone stared in wonderment. By what authority had the captain so suddenly become a colonel? A stunned silence fell over Frémont's men. Alexis Godey, just behind Stone, drew his breath in sharply. Dick Owens gasped.

"That explains something," Ed Kern muttered. "I guess a colonel does need a staff. At least those I've met have seemed to. But how . . ."

"My thought, too."

"Maybe he's somehow learned we're finally at war, and that as the only U.S. officer on the scene he's been promoted. He could have let his command in on it, though."

"I can't tell you why, but I get the feeling it came about just this moment."

The Mexican general saluted Frémont smartly. He smiled. "Please accept my apologies, Colonel Frémont, that I cannot offer you my sword. I tendered that totally useless plaything to Señor Merritt the day he so skillfully took my barracks without putting my garrison or his own men in any danger."

"Thank you, sir," Frémont said. "I would argue with you about an officer's sword being a useless plaything, but tendering it to me is of no importance, I assure you."

"Señor Carson here, who is an old friend," Vallejo said, "tells me that I and my family, including *mis dos hermanos*—my two brothers back there behind the *calesín* holding my wife and children—are to be imprisoned in the barracks guardhouse by your orders. We only agreed to accompany Señor Carson until we heard this directly from you, Colonel. Is this disturbing news true?"

"Unfortunately, yes, General. I regret I must take this action, but . . . such are the fortunes of war . . . for the vanquished."

"Ah . . . perhaps you are privy to information I do not have, *señor*. I am not aware of a war existing between our countries. The taking of Sonoma by Señor Merritt, Señor Ide, and their friends is *puramente* a local matter, and one to which I am at least partly sympathetic. I see very little in the way of pressing military reasons—if this is indeed a military situation—for my and my brothers' incarceration, since we gave Señor Merritt our parole . . . and I see no reason at all for the arrest of my wife and children."

"I am sorry, sir. When my staff and I move in, there will not be room for them in our new quarters."

"I have not talked personally with Don José Castro, my superior in Monterey, for some months; but it has been my understanding that you and your men, Colonel Frémont, have been guests of the Republic of Mexico during your stay in La Provincia de California. Should you, upon serious reflection, decide to allow me and *mi familia* to return to our home and remain in the custody of Mr. Merritt, to whom I volunteered my parole, you have my word that your embarrassing detention of us will be forgotten. You may go about your business as before, leaving Señores Ide, Merritt, and their people to resolve their differences with my government without any outside interference. Please forgive my characterizing your presence in Sonoma in such terms." Vallejo was showing supreme—but by no means high-handed—confidence. "*También,* tell me, *por favor,* that it is *not* true as Señor Carson says, that you intend keeping Señora Vallejo and her children under lock-and-key as well. I told Señor Carson he surely must be mistaken. He agreed that he may very well have been. He speaks highly of your generosity and *cortesía.*"

"Mr. Carson is too modest, General. And too quick to assume blame. He does not make such mistakes. My orders were explicit, and he relayed them to you accurately."

"Well then . . . will the colonel not . . . reconsider?" The confidence, although not quite gone, had ebbed. "My children . . ."

Frémont tugged at his beard. He held Vallejo in his gaze. Even across the thirty feet or so separating Frémont from Stone and Ed Kern, that gaze seemed to harden by the second.

"Johnny won't back down," Kern whispered. "He can't. Not in front of us. Talk about a Rubicon. . . . 'Hail Caesar!'"

"No, he's not like that. . . ." Stone broke off when Frémont began to speak again.

"I am sorry the terms I am insisting upon seem harsh, General, but a commander who yields to an enemy without putting up any more resistance than you did, sir, cannot legitimately expect more generous treatment. It embarrasses me to have to point this out." If the acid of contempt in Frémont's voice burned Vallejo, he gave no outward sign of it. Frémont continued, ". . . and I am doubly sorry, General, that in this matter I cannot countermand my orders to Mr. Carson. As a military commander of some rather peculiar sort yourself, you surely must understand."

Vallejo did not just speak now, he cried out, indignation and agony striving for the upper hand. *"Para mi no es cosa, señor. ¿Pero mi esposa y mis niños? ¡Es un desenfrenado, se lo juro!"*

There was a good deal more, all in an anguished Spanish Stone did not quite get. Vallejo's sudden outburst in his own tongue signaled the Mexican general had totally abandoned his calm reserve. Although he had seemed entirely at his ease throughout the early part of this confrontation, he must have been holding only a slippery grip on his emotions.

Stone's heart went out to him.

"Take hold of yourself, man!" Frémont snapped. "Comport yourself like an officer." He turned Sacramento away from the Mexican, looked back. "My staff and I must move along without further delay to occupy our new quarters."

If Mariano Vallejo's good nature had prevented him until now from sensing the scorn with which Frémont had addressed him from the outset, the Pathfinder's next utterance would have driven it home for him. "I must now bid you good day, *General!*" The last word dripped sarcasm.

The captain—colonel now?—lifted Sacramento's reins and let the big horse carry him up the road.

"*¡No soy cobardo!*" Vallejo screamed at Frémont's back. "I am not a coward!"

The Pathfinder did not look back.

6

Sutter's Fort, for all its imposing facade, had been just that, a fort, and so in its way had been the austere Estancia Barragán.

Casa Vallejo, on the other hand, now beckoned with warmth and welcome from half a mile away. Big trees in full, glossy leaf lined the crushed-stone drive to the old mansion. The Vallejo house may not have actually been old, but it appeared so in the russet-and-rose glow of late afternoon, and shrubs and plants flowered everywhere Stone looked. A tinkling fountain with a marble angel hovering over it spurted water turned golden by the sunlight into an oval pool in a garden to the right of their line of march. With the scent of blossoms filling the air, and the hordes of insects now far behind them, it struck Stone as the promise of some "Paradise Regained" before he chided himself that his expectations had only been generated by someone else's tragic loss.

When they reached the house itself, seven shy women and six men holding sombreros across their chests, had lined up in front of the wide steps leading to a veranda and a double door. The entrance was decorated with fancifully carved jambs and lintels and bright glass panels which some artisan had etched with intricate renderings of mammoth lilies.

A slim, stooped man of middle years, with a wan countenance, and wearing a short black jacket with scarlet piping and mother-of-pearl buttons, stepped from the silent line and placed himself squarely in front of Sacramento as if he knew instinctively that Frémont was the most important personage in the small cavalcade.

William Ide spoke out. "This is Don Mariano's man, Stebbi, Colonel, he runs the *casa* for the general. Stebbi does speak a little English."

The man bowed to Frémont. *"Bienvenidos, señor. Me llama Esteban Muñoz. Soy el mayordomo de Casa Vallejo."*

"Muchísimas gracias, Esteban, ¿Cómo estás?" Frémont said.

"Muy bien, señor. Before he left, Don Mariano instructed his poor servant Esteban to inform Your Excellency that *suya casa es su casa. ¡Bienvenidos a la Casa Vallejo!"*

"I take it that you will serve me with the same diligence and loyalty you served Don Mariano?"

Muñoz did not hesitate before replying. *"¡Sí, señor!"* The words rang with something approaching genuine sincerity, as had the welcome.

Without further conversation the Frémont members of the party dismounted and three of the five other men still waiting in the silent receiving line, these in the *paisano* white of field hands, stepped forward to lead their horses off. Ide, Hargrave, and Merritt stayed in the saddle.

"Stebbi will take good care of you and your people, Captain," Ide said. He fidgeted a bit. "Sorry . . . *Colonel.* Guess I ain't quite used to that yet." He hesitated for a moment before going on, as if he wanted to see the effect of his apology. "They feed right good here at Casa Vallejo, Colonel. Serafina López is the best cook in the valley, and if I don't care a whole hell of a lot for weak stuff like wine, Don Mariano keeps the best there is. I suppose William, Zeke, and I ought to get back down to the barracks now; we still got recruits coming in about every hour that we got to swear in and outfit. I expect we'll see you later in the plaza. . . . Is eight o'clock all right?"

"Perfectly, Mr. Ide. We'll be there. You are dismissed until then, sir."

When the Sonoman and his two companions turned their mounts and rode off, Frémont started up the broad steps.

"Esteban!" he said. "We will dine at six. I will meet with you at a quarter to the dinner hour to select the wines." He had not so much as favored the *mayordomo* with a glance, merely tossed the words over his shoulder as he walked through the double doors one of the women servants leaped to open for him.

Stone would have thought the Pathfinder had been the master at Casa Vallejo for sixty years, not sixty seconds.

"Come along, gentlemen!" he shouted back through the open doorway.

7

Ed Kern, still in his boots, bounced on the four-poster bed, laughing fit to be tied. "My only regret is that I have to share it with *you,* you smelly wretch. Did you see the way that fellow Muñoz sniffed at you? Take a bath, for the sake of our country's and Captain Johnny's reputation."

Esteban Muñoz, after leading Frémont to the master bedroom, had assigned the two of them to the quarters vacated earlier in the afternoon by Señora Vallejo. He had merely waved them through the door without a word and disappeared.

"Snooty SOB, isn't he?" Kern said.

Stone figured he knew the reason for the *mayordomo*'s aloof attitude when he showed them to their room. If Muñoz, despite his warm welcome to Frémont, felt any resentment or enmity about this new occupancy he did not intend to show it. But the pained look on his face—and the speed with which two of the younger women in the servants' lineup appeared now, first with a copper tub heavy enough that it took the two of them to carry it, and then with buckets of steaming water, soap and towels—betrayed how he felt about the way they looked and smelled.

Stone, although he had practically no experience with domestic servants, hazarded a guess that Muñoz took far more offense at the thought of two uncouth, filthy, and probably disreputable *norteamericanos* sullying what he regarded as *his* immaculate premises than he did that such brutes had displaced his mistress and her family.

Somehow, while Frémont and the others were touring the first floor of Casa Vallejo and awaiting Kit's return from escorting its rightful owners to the barracks guardhouse, Esteban had sorted out what gear went with which of his new householders, and had his suddenly fleet-footed minions, men and women, install the stuff in the proper chambers.

Even before Stone and Kern reached the room, servants had already laid out their razors, combs, and their few other grooming articles on Señora Vallejo's dressing table. They must have brought in the bottle of bay rum Stone found on the table, too; it was hardly the kind of thing the señora would have used in *her* toilette.

Stone stripped to the skin and stepped into the tub, hopping then from one foot to the other to keep from scalding them, and was still performing this ridiculous dance to Ed Kern's tuneful laughter when the door popped open.

One of the younger and prettier maidservants appeared with a stack of what appeared to be freshly laundered male undergarments in her arms. *"Para ustedes, señores. Stebbi . . ."*

Then she stopped in her tracks, stared at him for a split second before averting her eyes, and a small smile played across her face.

Stone froze. Kern hooted, and it was enough to jolt Stone

out of his shock. He dropped straight down into the tub and let its high sides conceal him, causing the soapy water to surge over the copper rim and onto the carpeting. Mortification burned him so he did not even feel the water's heat. The girl hurried to a chest in the window bay, unburdened herself, turned, and raced for the door—but not before sending one more furtive glance his way.

She giggled as she fled down the hall.

"You've made a conquest, Bradford, my boy." Kern rolled on the bed, laughter almost choking him now. When it subsided he sat up and looked at Stone. "You should have asked her to scrub your back. Seriously, she's an uncommonly pretty girl."

"I was too embarrassed to notice."

Stone washed hurriedly and left the tub. He dried himself as Kern began his bath. He pulled on a suit of underwear he found in the pile the girl had brought. The suit was pure silk. He stretched out on the bed. "Since you think her so pretty, shall I call her back to scrub *your* back, Kern?"

"No thanks."

"Not interested in that sort of thing?"

"One of the reasons I signed on with Captain Johnny and came west was to forget about women—or at least *a* woman—for a while." Had Ed's voice turned bitter? Whatever obscure regret Kern was thinking had faded away by the time he emerged, his face cheerfully sardonic again. "That young lady who just surveyed your attributes—we should probably leave her to Alexis Godey."

Had Kern expected him to ask about the woman he wanted to forget? Stone decided his friend had not.

He decided, too, that Kern knew nothing of Ana Barragán.

Would he *ever* tell his good friend about her?

It made him think that for all their deep and genuine camaraderie, he and the Philadelphian knew precious little about each other.

When this great adventure ended they would probably go their separate ways. Kern had talked frequently and fervently of his desire to get back to Philadelphia as soon as he had satisfied his contract with Frémont. Did the woman he had hinted at have anything to do with that?

They would remain friends, keep in touch for a while, think back on each other with fondness, perhaps even meet again and reminisce on the glory of these days, but then . . .

Did it differ with Kit? Carson had had a fully-fleshed history for Bradford Stone long before they met a year ago. It had its beginnings long before he watched through Charlie Bent's telescope for Carson to ride down the north slope of Raton Pass to the sandy banks of the Arkansas and into the life of Brad Stone. Nothing of the reality of the year-long association had diminished that history an iota. With Stone's intention to stay in the West as firm as it was, he would stay close to the scout for years—if Kit let him.

He owed Kit, owed him for the giant steps in the general direction of his maturity, owed him for the discovery of the place he wanted most to be.

And he owed him above all for the biggest discovery of his life . . . Ana Barragán. . . .

"Wake up, Brad! Get dressed."

"What's the matter, Ed?" Had he really fallen asleep or had he just been trance-deep in his thoughts about the two very different men and the even more different women?

"It's five minutes to six. Get a load of those smells, and I don't mean the flora. Ide sure as hell was right. Somebody here really knows how to cook."

8

At the affair in the plaza, Ide and Merritt recovered much of their confidence and zeal when the crowd cheered their

appearance and then their words. The townsfolk greeted Frémont, too, with a wild and largely approving display after
the surprisingly short speech he made in which he praised
Ide and Merritt to the skies for their triumph the week
before.

Even Hargrave, caught fast in the spirit of the moment
apparently, seemed to have lost at least a little of his antipa-
thy toward the Pathfinder. By the time the fiddlers, drum-
mers, and trumpeters made their appearance in the light of a
dozen bonfires, the entire throng, and the eager, rambunctious mountain men in particular, were ready for a party. That
it would be a party in a boneyard seemed to bother no one.

Stone viewed the prospect with badly mixed feelings. He
had delighted in watching his friends indulge themselves at
Bent's and ever since, but the thought of watching more of
these festivities, in a small Mexican town reminiscent in so
many ways of the Taos of his very first night there, made
him lonely. The first man and woman he saw dancing
together would make him long for Ana, and he had done
more than enough of that without any prompting.

But for Frémont's "staff," as well as Ide and his fellow
Sonomans, there was to be no party.

The self-proclaimed colonel ordered all the men who had
attended the meeting in the barracks in the afternoon into the
small office, lighted now by oil lamps that attracted a new
and different army of insects.

Frémont took the same chair again, and opened the dispatch case he had brought to the plaza with him.

"The first order of business," he said, "is to announce the
formation of a new and expanded fighting force to prepare
for battle against our enemy, General Castro."

"Beg pardon, Colonel," Ide said, "but ain't Zeke done
well enough with his little force? An expanded one will cost
money, and we plain ain't got it. With you and your mountaineers with us now, we should . . ."

"Bear with me, Mr. Ide. Mr. Merritt has carried out a splendid action, true, but against virtually no opposition, due in large measure to the reluctance of this so-called general, Vallejo, to resist him. The soldiery Mr. Stone and I saw on a visit to Monterey some time ago has yet to take the field. They will present us with much more in the way of military problems than we have yet been required to solve." He fished in the papers in the case. "I have here a table of organization for a new force to be called the California Battalion. It will be the principal armed service of your republic."

"It won't be part of the U.S. Army?" Ide said.

"Not yet."

"Who's going to command it?"

"I am, sir, but only if I have the approval and sworn loyalty of you and your fellow American-Californians. If I do not get that approval, of course, I will have no choice but to take my men north to Oregon, thence back to the United States . . . and wash my hands of matters here."

In the silence that followed, Stone thought back on Kern's conviction that Frémont had, like a snake-oil peddler, fomented this rebellion—without a genuine commitment to it—and was now taking de facto control of it. For all the new colonel's avowal that this proposed "California Battalion" would be solely an instrument of Ide's brand-new little country, it seemed more that the Frémont tail sooner or later would wag the California Republic dog.

The *"Not yet"* in answer to Ide's question had been the tipoff.

Ide looked at Merritt and Hargrave, both of whom nodded . . . nods of resignation, not of enthusiasm.

"You've got us, Colonel," Ide said.

"Splendid!" It came close to being a shout of triumph. "I was absolutely certain men of your intelligence and determination would see things my way. That, gentlemen, is why I became emboldened to appoint myself Colonel-in-Chief of the California Republic just this morning." Frémont lifted the papers he held. "Now . . . we have work to do. I have already commissioned officers for the Battalion. I will administer an oath before we leave.

"Mr. Carson, Mr. Owens, and Mr. Ide will serve as captains and company commanders. Mr. Godey, Mr. Hargrave, and Mr. Merritt will serve under them as first lieutenants. Mr. Talbot, as quartermaster, will hold the rank of major. Mr. Stone, as adjutant, is also commissioned as a first lieutenant. The staff assignments of Major Talbot and Lieutenant Stone will by no means keep them out of combat. Every officer in the Battalion will be a fighting man."

He looked at Kern before he resumed. "Don't be disappointed, Mr. Kern. You will be given a captaincy—and a special, critical assignment."

"Yes, sir. May I ask what my special, critical assignment will be . . . Colonel?"

"First thing tomorrow morning," Frémont answered, allowing no more than a split second to pass, "you will select a party of twenty men, including two of the expedition's Delawares, and remove the Vallejo party from the guardhouse, take them to Sutter's Fort, and confine them there. Afford Señora Vallejo, with her children, the accommodations due a lady. Give her husband and his brothers the minimal comforts their rank requires, and keep them under armed guard at all times. Once that is accomplished, you will then place Captain Johann Sutter under house arrest and take command of all of New Helvetia in the name of the California Republic."

At this there came a collective murmur from the group. Frémont continued. "You will see to it that no foodstuffs, arms, munitions, wheeled vehicles, or other supplies leave Sutter's Fort without a requisition from Lieutenant Stone, countersigned by me."

Then the only sound in the office was the dusty whir of the moths as they circled the smoking lamps.

9

"To paraphrase good old Will," Kern said when they were back in their room at Casa Vallejo, "'What a piece of work is John Charles Frémont.' Damned if I didn't think for a moment there I might be listening to Napoleon or Alexander. No question about it, our Johnny was born to command. How did that little séance strike you, Lieutenant Stone?"

"I'm taking piggyback rides on the things you figured out long ago, Ed," Stone said. "It seems to me the cap . . . colonel . . . got everything he was after; Ide and the people here are sworn to follow him now, and it looks as if he will get that little war you speculated might someday help him politically. But above all, once you get Vallejo to the Sacramento and place Sutter under arrest, he will have neutralized and isolated the only two men in Upper California who could possibly mount any sort of a challenge to him, not that I'm sure Sutter ever would. He's taking no chances, though. He sure didn't vacillate today."

"Go to the head of the class, Lieutenant."

"Damn it! Don't call me that."

His angry protest at Kern's calling him "lieutenant" notwithstanding, Stone had to admit something about it pleased him.

He had been caught, to extract another quote from the Bard as Kern had done, in the infectious excitement of an *"enterprise of great pith and moment"* just as the others had.

He had regrets, though. He regretted that he had not been assigned as Kit's junior officer, and he regretted having to think about how much longer this new turn of events would delay his return to Taos . . . and Ana.

26

The Rosary

Estancia Barragán
May 1846

Ana Barragán's pregnancy began with exquisite happiness
but the joy she felt changed to concern for Bradford's safety,
and after five months, to a recurring nightmare terror, awake
or asleep. She feared nothing for herself, but everything for
Bradford—and the child.

She could fool Papá about her condition for only a few
more days now, until he returned on the fourth of May from
his latest trip down to Santa Fe.

When he discovered her secret he would turn volcanic. As
insane as he might become at his first sight of her new girth,
and the realization of what it meant, even he would know it
was too late. Too late to send her to that *curandera* in Santa
Fe who was said to "take care" of some of the girls in Taos
who got themselves in trouble, but who managed to keep it
secret from their families and Padre Martínez. Even if he
had discovered it early enough, she would have fought like
a cat if Papá ordered her *abortar.* Dios willing, she would
bear Bradford's child if she died in the process.

There had been many trips to the capital for Papá this past
six months. The meetings with Governor Armijo must have
been serious and important; some had lasted as long as three
weeks.

Since Christmas, when he had finally, with stubborn
reluctance, permitted her to go into Taos, and raised no

objections to the long stays she made with Cousin Josefa and Cousin Ignacia, she had been able to avoid him when she first began to show, and to make matters even easier for a while, he seemed to have forgotten Bradford Stone.

Not surprising. He had a new crop of Americans to hate since war broke out three weeks ago, not that it was much of a war where New Mexico was concerned . . . yet. Rumors she had heard at the Carsons' and the Bents' said some American general named Stephen Kearny was moving along the great overland trail to Santa Fe with a big army, and that Governor Armijo was calling out his militia to meet the Americans. Perhaps that was the reason for Papá's talks with the governor in Santa Fe. A war, as much as the prospect of it disturbed her, might keep his mind off her and Bradford. She took herself to task briefly for looking on something as horrible as a war, where her friends, neighbors, and relatives might die, as a convenient device for the solution of her and Bradford's problems with her father. But she need not feel too much guilt. The villagers she had talked with the last month had not concerned themselves about any conflict. The generally held opinion said that Taos itself would not be involved, or affected.

This war might affect Bradford much more dramatically. It could turn into a much bloodier affair in California than it ever would be here, but she determined it best not to think about that with everything else that plagued her at the moment.

She had not been able to fool *herself* about her condition for almost four months now, and she had not fooled her Taos cousins for the last two. They did not talk about it, but as the bright black eyes under arched brows strayed more and more often to her waist when they met, she knew they knew. Nor did they doubt for a moment who the father was.

Forlorn Luis Aragón must know now, too. He no longer stayed at the *hacienda*, but he still made frequent trips up the valley to Taos, and he called once at Cousin Josefa's when Ana was there having lunch. After catching sight of her he reddened and averted his eyes. He had never before been able to take them away from her for a second.

She had been unable to fool Galinda from the beginning.

A mere three weeks after the night at La Cayuda, the *dueña* had looked at her intently one morning when she helped her with her bath. "Galinda warned you, *mi niña*. You should have at least tried her ointment. You are going to bear a child."

"That's ridiculous, *vieja*. I feel too good. I haven't been sick once."

"The sickness will come soon, unless you are very lucky. White women are not like Dineh women. They scare themselves into being sick."

"Nonsense. I am as strong as any red woman, you conceited old *bruja*. But I am not *embarazada*. How could you tell this early anyway, even supposing you were right? My belly is still as flat as a *tortilla*."

"Galinda does not have to look at your belly. It will not swell for months. Galinda sees the child that is coming in your *eyes*."

"My eyes? What's in my eyes?"

"See for yourself, *niña*." She held a hand mirror in front of Ana's face. "There is a special look."

"I see no 'special look.'"

"Look harder. They gleam. Your Mamá had that same gleam in her eyes when you were on your way."

Galinda was wrong about one thing: Ana went right on feeling good, more alive than she ever had. Not a single episode of the "morning sickness" she had heard about visited her. But when she missed three of her times, she finally had to admit that her Navajo nurse and friend was right. Even if her belly still remained flat, something stirred inside her, and her first feeling when she knew at last was one of soaring rapture.

She had to write and tell Bradford! When she wrote him last, she had not been totally sure.

Her rapture lasted all of thirty seconds.

Was she going *loco?* She could not even think of telling him! If Bradford did not believe Papá's cruel threats the day he left the *estancia,* half a week before the night at La Cayuda—she did. And Papá had said a dozen times since that if Bradford ever again rode so much as a quarter of a kilometer inside the gate, the *vaqueros* would ride him down on the smoking, white road and kill him before he could turn his horse . . . if Papá did not arrive in time to do it himself. Frail old Roberto had told Galinda that "the Great Don" had announced that "there will be a sack of gold as big as a man's head for the Barragán rider who puts the first rifle ball in the heart of the *yanqui puerco.*" Any of five of Don Bernardo Barragán's most faithful *vaqueros* would have done it for considerably less. According to Galinda, who laughed at the idea—as if anything about it could be funny—Roberto said he might even try himself were word to come from town that Bradford Stone had returned to Taos.

If her father's hatred had reached such a peak merely because Bradford wanted to pay court to her, what pinnacles of fury would it ascend once he *knew?*

And if she never suffered from more than the mildest nausea, it sickened her that everyone at the *estancia,* except Galinda and herself, looked on the killing of the man she loved as some kind of blood sport such as the Mexican bull-fight *corridas* she had seen while at school.

No, she could not tell Bradford about the baby, yet. She had work to do.

Sometime during the night at La Cayuda she had pressed him for the exact date of his return. "Don't really know, Ana. We could finish our work earlier than Captain Frémont figures. My contract with him and my government runs out next July first, and of course I don't know where I'll be by then. But I promise I won't stay with the expedition a day longer. I'll head straight back to Taos from wherever we are. Unless something untoward happens we'll be together again by September first next year."

May first until September first; four more long months. But only four months, hardly any time at all when she thought about what she ultimately faced with Papá. She would have to resolve things with him by the time Bradford came back, when the baby would already be a month or so old, and she could not bear to think of the tiny living thing within her being orphaned, possibly before his father even saw him.

Him? *¡Oh, sí, sí!* It *would* be a boy. Her gift to Bradford.

Unless she had badly misjudged Bradford's character and determination, she knew to an absolute certainty he would race to the *estancia* from Casa Carson, or wherever he came to rest in Taos . . . straight into Barragán guns. She remembered too well the way he had faced her relentless father that day in the *hacienda* study with trembling Luis Aragón looking on, and during the two all-too-short, sweet nights at the *casita* one of the many things she learned about Bradford was that he took her father's words far too lightly.

"I realize I've upset him, Ana, but no one actually *kills* over a thing like this," he had said.

If only she could get in touch with Don Cristóbal. *He* certainly knew the depths of Papá's hatred—and the steel of his determination. Bradford might listen to *him*. She could write Cousin Josefa's husband, of course, but—as she had to remind herself every time she wrote to Bradford—too many eyes would see her letter and know then that she was carrying Bradford's child. For any of a number of reasons having nothing to do with the two of them or their love for each other, even Bradford might want her to keep it a secret for a while. Men could be so strange, so bold one moment, so shy

and secretive the next, and sometimes, for all their rough-
ness, such victims of embarrassment. He probably had yet to
tell his companions anything about her, least of all about
their last night together at La Cayuda. He probably had not
told even Don Cristóbal Carson.

Besides, at this late date, and with his service to Captain
Frémont coming to a close, were he and his friend Don
Cristóbal still together?

No, she could not write to the great scout, either.

Thank *Dios* she had thought to get a promise of silence
from Cousin Josefa until she gave the word. She considered,
but only for a second, asking Señor Carlos Bent, who surely
must have heard of her predicament by now from Doña
Ignacia, to intercede with Papá. But she pushed the idea
away from her as rapidly. Papá hated Señor Bent. He had
once, when she had been too small to understand the reason,
threatened to kill this kindly American, too. Fortunately for
Señor Bent he had only threatened, he had not vowed, as he
had with Bradford.

In all his daughter's memory, Bernardo Barragán, for all
his faults, had never broken a single vow.

She would have to deal with Papá by herself. And time
would run out the moment he knew the truth. She could not
delude herself.

She could indulge herself in no more wishful thinking.
What those *toreros* in Mexico called "the moment of truth"
was at hand.

2

Don Bernardo Barragán arrived from Santa Fe late in the
afternoon on the fourth of May, as promised.

Ana was reading on the patio. She actually felt his eyes on
her before she saw him, and he turned and left the patio

before she got a genuine look at him. It made no difference. She did not have to actually see his eyes to know the terrible, hot accusation they must hold. The dry air seemed to crackle as it sometimes does in the last second before lightning strikes, and for a lingering moment she thought she actually smelled something burning.

It took but five minutes after that . . .

"Don Bernardo awaits you in his study, *mi doña,*" Roberto said.

"Let him wait, Roberto!"

She had not fooled the old *mayordomo* for a long time, either. He had stopped looking at her stomach more than a month ago, but he did stare at it now, the curiosity of his glances of late March giving way here on the patio to a look of abject fear . . . and pity.

Roberto knew what her father wanted her for. But for all his bluster back in November that he might even try to shoot Bradford himself for the bounty his master had placed on the head of the *"yanqui puerco,"* she knew him for a gentle soul, and one whose eyes suddenly whitened with fear for her.

"Don Bernardo is impatient, *mi doña,*" Roberto pleaded now. "Go to him without delay, *por favor. La doña* knows how *inflamado* the *patrón* can get when he thinks we do not obey; if you do not go to him immediately, he might decide Roberto refused to tell you. I fear he already has lost his trust in me, since he knows now I did not tell him that you . . ."

Her heart went out to him. She could not embroil any more people in her troubles. "*Sí, viejo.* I will go to him at once. *Vaya con Dios,* Robert. You need not even announce me. And do not worry, I will not let you come to any grief."

A flash flood of relief washed over the seamed features of the *mayordomo,* and he hurried from the patio, scurrying across the tiles as if his two spindly old legs had become the hundred of a centipede.

She struggled to her feet, leaned back slightly, put her hand to the small of her back, and started for the study.

3

"Who is the father of this monstrosity? And why is your father the last person in the valley to learn of this disgrace to the House of Barragán?"

His voice had not carried anything near the hot, seething fury she expected, but it sent a shaft of ice straight to her heart, and even worse and far more chilling, straight to the beating heart of the child she carried.

"That obscenity, one can presume without any futile doubt," he said, pointing a rigid finger at her stomach, "is the filthy work of that *sucio yanqui* adventurer who lived at the *casa* of Cristóbal Carson last autumn, is it not?

"NO!" She forced herself to look straight into his black eyes. "It was not . . . Señor Stone!"

"You are willing to swear it?"

"*¡Sí!*"

"On your mother's *rosario?*" He held across the desk the onyx rosary she had not seen since childhood.

"*¡Sí, Papá!*"

He pushed the rosary at her. "Take this to your lips and swear again. *¡En el nombre de Dios!* Take it! Swear!"

She reached toward him and he dropped the slim strand into her cupped hands, letting it stream down as if it were a thread of thick, black, hot oil puddling in her palms.

"Swear!" It was the cold dry rattle of a *crótalo*. "But before you do, consider this. To swear to a lie to your father in such circumstances will constitute a mortal sin, *mi hija!*"

She had no choice *but* to lie. God would have to forgive

her, but even if the Diety turned His face away from her and withheld His forgiveness for eternity, it did not matter; that Bradford's life had suddenly become even more endangered did.

She began to bring the strand of beads to her mouth, but he suddenly reached out, closed his hands over hers, and clamped them together as if he would mash them to a pulp. She felt the cord of the rosary snap. Then his fingertips bit into her flesh until she was sure she would bleed.

But she would not look. She would not flinch. She would not cry out. Soon her hands would go numb and the pain would stop. She would swear, *sí*, for Bradford's sake, but she would not beg, not even with God.

"*¡Jura! En el nombre de Dios,*" she whispered, "*en el nombre de Dios, jura . . .*"

He relaxed his grip, and the sudden rush of blood back to her hands brought a terrible, fleeting moment of even greater pain.

"Then . . . who, *puta? ¿Quién es el hombre . . . ?*"

Yes, she had known that would come, too. Oh, dear God, if there were only a name, any name, she could give him.

But even could she think of one, could she put some poor innocent soul in the same danger Bradford faced?

Then something strange happened to Papá.

He leaned back in his big carved chair, tipped back his head, closed his eyes, and pressed the fingers of both hands to his temples. The fierce look of the hunting hawk had left his face, and his features were marked by sickly red, white, and yellow streaks of pain at least as great as hers.

He began to speak, but with neither the burning rage she had expected when she came to the study, nor in the frigid tones he had ultimately used. His voice was low, hollow, pitched not to reach her ears, but only for some inner ear. It was as if he had entered a trance. At this moment she had ceased to exist for him.

Or had she? She had once overheard someone at a party in Santa Fe she and Papá had attended say, "Don Bernardo Barragán there is the most devilishly clever man it has been my misfortune to meet. In his lust to win, pride outweighs principle every time." She had thought it a kind of compliment at the time. Now she was willing to concede that the Devil himself had given Papá this skill. In return for what? she wondered.

"*¡Por el amor del Dios . . . !*" he said now. That sounded strange, too. He had not invoked the name of God—even in commonplace exasperation—five times in all her years. The Church, *sí,* but not God. She must listen with great care now.

"If only she would . . . ," he went on. "I could not forgive . . . but I could forget." Yes, he was talking only to himself. "Do not fool yourself, Bernardo," he said. "It is too much to expect. Women have no understanding at all of what honor means. Does she lie? She does if she will not give me another name . . . the name of someone like us, a man of our own great, ancient race and true religion. Not a barbarous *etranjero,* but a man who would be a faithful *esposo,* and someday a proud master of Estancia Barragán. I would bargain with her. I would break my vow and swallow my pride. I know that even if she tells the truth when she says it is another man, it is the American she wants. I would gladly let *him* live if she married a man who could by granting his name alone keep shame from the House of Barragán. I would swear no vengeance. Such things have been done before in the history of *nuestra familia* . . .

". . . but it cannot work unless there is a marriage within Holy Church to stop all talk."

He was trying to trick her, set a trap. He could not know—or could he?—how willingly she would leap into it to save Bradford. She had a name for him all right, and he probably knew it now, had picked it out himself long before. She felt helpless, but at the same time filled with hope and an odd sense of power.

She felt the child move.

Papá was stirring now, too, coming out of that trancelike state. He fixed her with those hawk's eyes.

"Are you ready yet to tell me what I must know for both our sakes?"

Oh, Dios, but he was devilishly clever, as the Santa Fe man had said.

"*¡Sí, Papá!*"

"And the man's name?"

She drew deep breath, held it until a sudden dizziness made her sway.

"Don Luis Aragón, Papá."

He did not even have the decency to feign surprise.

27

The Order at San Rafael

Monterey, California
July 1846

Brad Stone awoke in the same *posada* he and Colonel—at that time only Brevet Captain—Frémont had stayed in when they called on General Castro in this gleaming gem of a seaport earlier in the year, but this time with his spirits as low as he could ever remember them. He considered all the things which had transpired since the arrival of the expedition at Sonoma.

There would be no visit to General Don José Castro in his daunting, torchlit *fortaleza* office on this occasion. The general had fled to the south three weeks ago in apparent panic, taking his army with him, what remained of it after some minuscule, halfhearted skirmishes with the California Battalion in the Napa country, and the subsequent desertions in this blazing hot July. But that Americans and Castro would meet again someday soon on some battlefield—if Governor Pío Pico at Los Angeles did not overcome Don José politically—seemed fairly certain.

Stone's year-long contract with Frémont and the U.S. Army Corps of Topographical Engineers had actually run out a week ago.

At Klamath Lake, and even before that, he had thought that the first of August, give or take a day, would see him on his way back to Taos and Ana from the Columbia River settlements, and that he would be keeping to the timetable he had given her that night in La Cayuda. Even after they left Oregon, returned to Sutter's, and then marched to Sonoma, he had still hoped to begin his journey back to New Mexico on schedule. But that was impossible now. After the events of the past several days, he had lost hope of leaving Frémont for another month. at least, and for perhaps a great deal longer.

He had not received a letter from Ana in three months. That did not surprise him. Frémont had moved them around so frenetically during that time that he persuaded himself that word from her had to be on the high seas, or on the trail somewhere, and that it would finally track him down when they came more or less permanently to rest. Perhaps when the Pathfinder at last found whatever it was he was after. What that might be, Stone had no more inkling than anyone, beyond some vague apprehension it had to do with the extension of Frémont's "conquest," as everyone here in Monterey called his activities these past five months. But what were the benchmarks of that enterprise?

After their arrival last week in Monterey, and almost as

some careless god's casual afterthought, the news had broken that the United States had gone to war with Mexico—
more than three months before. That the report of an event
of such magnitude could take so long in arriving in the
camps and councils of men and leaders who very well
might have to fight that war here in California sobered
him. And it appalled him to learn that back on May thirty-
first, Commodore John D. Sloat, commanding the naval
forces putting Mazatlán on Mexico's west coast under
blockade, had received a signal telling him of the declaration of war, but had neglected to send the word north to
Larkin.

No one had informed even the commanders of two of the
American vessels now lying at anchor with the newer
arrivals in Monterey's fine, protected harbor: Montgomery
of the navy frigate *Portsmouth* and the merchant-trader
Moscow's Phelps. They had not learned of the war even
when the commodore arrived at Monterey in early July with
three more heavily armed U.S. Navy vessels, the *Congress,*
the *Levant,* and the *Cyane.*

Well, they all knew now what John Sloat had known in
May. Zachary Taylor had won a significant victory at some
place called Resaca de las Palmas, south of the Río Grande.
Kit said he thought *resaca* meant "surf." "It's probably at or
near the mouth of the Río. I ain't never been that far east in
northern Mexico." By now Taylor had probably occupied
that other, differently spelled Monterrey, the capital of the
Mexican state of Nuevo León.

Stone wondered at last if knowing would have made any
real difference in what had happened in Upper California.

Since the taking of Sonoma *Lieutenant* Bradford Ogden
Stone had served as "adjutant." There had not been much of
the work he surmised adjutants did to earn their keep, if he
did not count the barrage of letters Frémont had him send.
The letters went to Senator Benton, Congressman Jakob

Myers, some few other politicians, a number of journalists and newspaper editors in St. Louis, Washington, and New York, and a clutch of apparently important figures in the Navy and War Departments.

Frémont, in a transparent recognition of the assumed influence of Stone's connection with the congressman, had him read and witness the letter to Jake Myers, and doing so brought Stone a flush of hot embarrassment.

The document was a long-winded, flowery litany of self-congratulation on the part of the new colonel, telling the congressman in unblushing, fanciful detail how John C. Frémont had "conquered" Upper California and brought thousands upon uncounted verdant thousands of square miles of the "most fabulous country on the face of the earth" under the flag of the United States.

"Append something to the congressman yourself, Bradford my boy, but it would please me if you would vouchsafe me a look at it before you post it."

It humiliated Stone to add his own carefully trimmed views to those of the Pathfinder, but he did it.

Ultimately, he could not really criticize the Pathfinder for boasting. The man had indeed conquered this territory, even if the "battles" he described in the letter to Jake and the others were largely figments of the flightiest of imaginations. The "capture of a detachment of General Joaquín de la Torre's formidable Mexican army, the main body of which I and my dauntless California Battalion are in hot pursuit of at this very instant. General de la Torre is General Castro's most capable subordinate . . ." had consisted, in plain unadorned fact, of the entirely voluntary surrender of one of de la Torre's dispatch riders to Lucy Maxwell and Dick Owens on the trail between Sonoma and Sutter's Fort.

The letter also recounted "resounding victories in every skirmish undertaken by the Battalion," which Stone could only match with three incidents that did not total a dozen men on a side, and in which only four or five shots were fired, none of them producing so much as a scratch.

The only remotely military action of the "campaign"—as Frémont insisted on calling the mounted peregrinations they made from *rancho* to *rancho* to bask in the cheers of the American settlers—was a foray by Kit and a half a dozen mountain men to appropriate a herd of a couple hundred horses being driven south along the lower Sacramento. The herders had fled without a fight when Kit and his riders appeared.

But the Battalion did cover a bewildering lot of ground, and Stone wished Ed Kern could be with him now to share this and help him put it in perspective.

He supposed he could not dismiss it *all* as the comic opera it had appeared to be earlier.

The dark little drama that played itself out a few weeks ago on the *embarcadero* at San Rafael still haunted him too much for that.

This great "Conquest of the Golden Shore"—Frémont's words—did attack Stone's risibilities. Damn it! It *was* comic opera, if he could only forget San Rafael.

2

In late June Frémont and the Battalion began a leisurely sweep of the Napa and Sacramento Valleys to quell the "widespread armed resistance" the new colonel told his "staff" had broken out like a rash across northern California.

When Owens and Maxwell brought de la Torre's courier into the Battalion's encampment on the lower Sacramento, documents in the man's dispatch case revealed the Mexican general was moving north at that exact time—with the "formidable army" Frémont had described in his long ton of correspondence to the East—to recapture Sonoma from its Bear Flag occupiers.

"Alarums and excursions" ensued. Frémont raced the Battalion back to the "rescue of Sonoma," as he called this newest hurried journey in another letter to Myers. Once there, he ordered "Major" Ted Talbot to deploy the howitzers at the southern approach to the town and sent "Captain" Dick Owens and "Lieutenant" Alexis Godey out with a company-sized force to patrol as far south as the western shore of San Pablo Bay. Stone would probably have to look at San Rafael again.

3

They found everything in the sparsely settled lower valleys leading to the bay in the same state of peace as that which had settled over Sonoma.

The village still looked as flea-bitten, and the Bear Flag still hung as limply at the top of its pole in the bone-littered plaza as on the June day they first rode into town. Until a breeze sprang up and flung out the banner's folds, they would suffer from the same hordes of flying and crawling insects and reel at the same slaughterhouse stench. Sonoma had certainly not improved its appearance since it became the capital of the new Republic.

But no attack came from de la Torre. Frémont occupied himself back at the Vallejo mansion with poring over the Mexican version of ordnance maps spread out on the huge table in the dining room. Talbot had found the maps quite by accident in a desk in Mariano Vallejo's study. The discovery of the maps duly appeared in a report to Washington as "an example of the outstanding intelligence work being done by the Battalion's staff . . ."

Kit delivered de la Torre's rider—a pleasant young corporal named Romero who did not look a bit discomfited by his capture or the prospect of a long confinement—to Kern's new "jail" at Sutter's Fort. The scout rejoined the Battalion at the end of that week, wearing a smile when he reported to Colonel Frémont.

"We been had, Captain." Alone among them Kit had yet to make the switch to calling Frémont "Colonel." Stone had forgotten once, receiving a look from Frémont that smarted as much as a lash from a whip.

" 'Had'?"

"We been taken in, fooled, hoodwinked."

"How so?"

"Romero turned out to be a talkative young buck. The stuff we found in his saddlebag was all a fake. De la Torre only wanted us to think he was coming up this way. He intends to take his men across San Pablo Bay and back down to join Castro at Monterey."

"Preposterous! Your colonel would not be duped that easily, Captain Carson! Remember that. We shall proceed with our defense of the capital. However, we shall take half our force south to intercept General de la Torre before he and his army can board ship. Pick the companies we will take with us and turn them out in battle formation at first light, *Captain* Carson." His emphasis on the "Captain" was obviously meant as a subtle reminder that Kit should call *him* "Colonel." In any event it did not work.

"Just as you say, Captain." Kit's smile had become even broader.

Alone with Stone after his report to Frémont, Kit burst into full-blown laughter. "Beats all hell, don't it, *Lieutenant* Stone? If the captain still believes General de la Torre is on his way here, why the hell are we going to the bay?" Kit's emphasis on Stone's military title was of a different order from that of Frémont on Kit's. He must have figured out at the start how the "lieutenant" embarrassed Stone, and Kit could be a tease at times.

Whether Carson had read Romero's revelation that the plan to attack Sonoma was the planted hoax the youngster said it was or not, the question became moot. Halfway down the road to San Francisco Bay and riding hard after the ephemeral de la Torre, Frémont received a dispatch from Gillespie at Yerba Buena. The enemy had already been ferried across the water with his troops and was returning to Monterey to join his superior, Don José Castro. The marine's message revealed, too, that the Mexican's "formidable army" of the report to Jake Myers consisted in reality of ten infantrymen, half a dozen lancers, a cook wagon, a *remuda* of thirty-some horses, but not a single piece of artillery.

Frémont spent almost all his time in his room at Casa Vallejo. Esteban brought his meals to him. He saw no one, and no one saw him.

4

Another dispatch arrived from Archibald Gillespie. It fell to Stone to take it to Frémont, who read it and looked up, his face suddenly alight.

He handed the message back. "Read this, my boy. It appears as if at least the navy has decided to take me seriously. Pay particular attention to the part at the end."

Gillespie reported that most of the Mexican army had fallen back on Monterey, but there were still isolated units roaming the area around San Jose, pillaging the ranches and threatening the lives of the settlers.

> . . . and perhaps you want to take a hand in quelling these assaults, John, as there is actually some truth in the reports we get here in Yerba Buena. If you agree, my good old seadog friend J. B. Mont-

gomery, captain of the frigate *Portsmouth*, says he'd be glad to dock his vessel at a place on the north side of the bay called Sausalito and take the Battalion aboard and set you down here at Yerba Buena. He can accommodate as many as a hundred men, their mounts, and your three pieces of artillery. It would save you weeks of damned hard marching. J.B. says he'll stay anchored for a week or two to be at your disposal. Let me know.

When Stone finished reading Frémont instructed him to write a note to Gillespie telling him they would be at Sausalito in three days. "Detail one of our fastest riders—I expect it will have to be Godey since I can't spare Carson—to take this message to Lieutenant Gillespie. See that Godey has enough money to hire a boat to take him across the straits from this Sausalito place. He need not return. We'll pick up his horse and join him at Yerba Buena, ready to march on San Jose the moment we disembark. Once you get him on his way have Captain Carson report to me."

He dined with his staff that night. If he had been in one of his down moods before Gillespie's dispatch, he stood proudly on the heights again, the banner of his spirit aloft and rippling.

5

They found no evidence of atrocities around San Jose.

To be sure, some cattle had been spirited away, and a few *haciendas* broken into, but there had been no deaths, no injuries of any consequence, and nothing connected any of these minor depredations to Castro's or de la Torre's Mexican soldiery.

Frémont had only brought a third of the California Battalion, and he voiced a thought at supper one night that they might march on Monterey. In the end he decided against it.

"I still do not know that we are at war with Mexico. We came down here on this humanitarian mission to chase and punish outlaws. The California Republic, as such, has given the Battalion no portfolio south of San Francisco Bay. But we shall stay here in Yerba Buena to keep an eye on things."

Stone had no need of Ed Kern to put the Pathfinder's last remarks in perspective. Besides, a message that same morning from Larkin, still steadfastly at his post in what must have become a very dangerous Monterey, had argued against any move on the seaport until the U.S. naval squadron arrived to support it.

And Consul Larkin said he still had no knowledge a state of war existed between the United States of America and the Republic of Mexico.

Stone himself did not know if Archibald Gillespie—now in some sort of quasi-official position at Yerba Buena, and with his own pipeline to Washington and the Pacific naval forces under Sloat—had received word of war and had passed it on to his now bosom chum, Colonel John C. Frémont, commander of the California Battalion.

6

The next performance of the comic opera, *The Conquest of the Golden Shore,* with Colonel John C. Frémont conducting and Lieutenant Archibald Gillespie, United States Marine Corps, singing the heroic tenor lead, took place after the Battalion's return to Yerba Buena to reembark for the trip across San Francisco Bay and back up to the Sonoma Valley.

Captain J. B. Montgomery had taken the *Portsmouth* out to sea for a short training cruise, and they had to wait in the fishing port for three days until the frigate returned. Bill Leidesdorff had business somewhere on the peninsula, and with Tom Larkin still down in Monterey, Gillespie had sole charge of the consulate. William Hargrave, still on the rolls of the Battalion as a major, but hardly seen since his appointment, had come down from the Napa Valley to take delivery of some trade goods a merchant schooner had left for him weeks before what was now being called the Bear Flag Revolt began.

Gillespie hosted a dinner with Frémont and the staff. Hargrave, to Stone's surprise, sat in. At the end of the meal Gillespie ordered cognac and cigars all around. He leaned back in his chair, and looked at them expansively.

"Did you know, Colonel," he said through a cloud of smoke, "that the Castillo de San Joaquín is situated only a few miles up the coast from Yerba Buena?"

"I do recollect seeing it on one of Mariano Vallejo's old maps. Why do you ask?"

"I reconnoitered the place about a month ago, from a discreet distance, of course. Would you like the Battalion to take a crack at it? I see you still have your three mountain howitzers in tow. To me they look to be stout enough weapons to breach the castle's walls."

To say that the Pathfinder's nostrils flared or that his ears actually quivered would be an exaggeration, but the spark in his eyes made it look that way. For Stone it was almost as if he had said aloud something like, *"At last, at last! An objective worthy of my talents!"*

He turned to Ted Talbot sitting at his right. "What about it, Major? Can your guns handle a fortress wall?"

"I haven't seen a wall in California my guns can't turn to powder, sir!" Even retiring Ted Talbot was beginning to sound like one of Napoleon's marshals.

"Splendid!" Frémont turned to Gillespie again. "Would a lieutenant of marines do the California Battalion the honor of directing our attack?"

"No, sir." Gillespie said. "As senior officer present that honor must be yours, Colonel. However, it would please me mightily if I were granted the privilege of leading the assault on the castle garrison once the walls are breached."

"Granted! Can we do this tomorrow, Archibald?"

"Absolutely, John."

Archibald? John? They seemed like two boys planning a trip to the "ole swimmin' hole" of sacred childhood legend.

Carson looked amused.

Then Hargrave, who had kept silent all through this conversation, said, "May I offer some advice? I have personal knowledge of the *castillo*. I traded there a dozen years ago."

"I think not . . . *Major*. I'm sure Lieutenant Gillespie's knowledge is far more recent. And as a *professional* military man he is in a better position to offer advice."

7

When Talbot's three cannon belched their first fire it was for Brad Stone as if the shoe that dropped at his first sight of the howitzers back at Bent's had thudded down alongside its mate. There had been times when he could not decide if the expedition—almost a memory as such, now that they had become an admitted military unit—was pulling the guns, or if the guns were pushing it.

At any rate, Talbot's faith in the weapons he had shepherded through the mountains and deserts they had crossed proved entirely justified. By the time the echoes of the last of a mere five rounds had died on the coastal wind, the low, gray, seaside wall of Castillo de San Joaquín had indeed become a pile of dust.

On the trip up the beach to the castle, Gillespie had voiced his satisfaction when Frémont ordered his men to "Fix bayonets!"

"In my experience it always comes down to cold steel, Colonel."

Stone wondered where the marine could have acquired that "experience"; there had not been an American war in Archibald Gillespie's lifetime.

The fixing of bayonets had been an awkward operation. The Hawkens and other rifles of the mountain men and their American settler comrades had not been designed to accept the wicked-looking blades issued to them on the trip across the bay. Somehow the men managed, although Stone feared the jury-rigged fastening, made from a leather thong and a short length of wire Kit had found for him somewhere, might not even hold through the first thrust. To make him even more uncertain, Frémont had not held a single drill with the unfamiliar weapons.

Now, with the wall a heap of rubble under a dense cloud of smoke and dust, Stone looked up and down Gillespie's long skirmish line, which of course included what he had begun to think of as the "old guard": Dick Owens, Alexis Godey, Lucy Maxwell, Gus Archambeault, and Carson, of course.

Bugler Tim Howard blew the charge.

Gillespie raised his saber and yelled, "Forward the Battalion!" He had donned his marine blues for this outing and looked every inch the gallant officer. He began the charge at a walk as he had explained he would in his briefing en route on the beach this morning. "Let's tempt them to fire at fairly long range. We will not start to run all-out until after their first volley." His orders made sense to Stone, and when he queried Kit, he found that the scout seemed in full agreement.

"But," Kit had added with an enigmatic smile, "I got a hunch we ain't going to get fired on very quick; we may have to hold ourselves to a walk all the way up to what's left of that wall. Wish to hell we was on horseback. That walk along the beach has got me damn near played-out already."

At that moment Hargrave came up behind them and begged a word with Kit in private. Until then, Stone had not realized that the Napa man had come along.

In response to the bugle call and Gillespie's "Forward!" Stone stepped out and had already taken five paces before he realized that the marine and he were ascending this sandy slope alone. The men in the line behind them had not moved a foot.

They began to move now, but not forward. Some had actually turned around and bent over, some collapsed on the sand. Were they sick?

Another look told him it was not sickness stopping them. They were all convulsed with laughter.

How could this be funny? Flashes of enemy gunfire could blast through the dust cloud at any second.

Frémont's voice, even coming from his position fifteen yards behind the skirmish line, rose like a trumpet above a chorus of chortling and giggling. "Take your men forward, Captain Carson! For God's sake, do not leave Lieutenant Gillespie up there by himself, man!"

Then he heard Kit through the laughter. "But, Captain, there ain't—"

"This is an order, Captain Carson!"

"Yes, sir," Kit said, still grinning broadly.

Now Carson looked to the skirmish line. "All right, men. Let's get up there with them two lieutenants. Take this stuff Lieutenant Gillespie calls cold steel right to the enemy." The line started upward, laughter still ringing up and down and across the length of it.

Even after Frémont's stern treatment of him, Kit still grinned. Up ahead Gillespie had stopped to let the skirmish line catch up with him, but he had not looked back. Apparently he did not want the others to see the humiliation of a sophisticated young officer who had failed to get his troops moving, and that a simple mountaineer had. As Stone watched, Gillespie squared his shoulders, pointed the saber at what remained of the castle wall, and moved upward again, at a brisker pace than before.

Kit, who had reached Stone now, chuckled. "He don't need to be in such a god-awful rush, Brad. There won't be any fire coming from up there today."

"You're sure?"

"Ask Hargrave when you see him."

Stone spotted Hargrave a dozen feet or so to his left and eased toward him. The Napa man was smiling. Stone could not really tell at first if the smile was meant for him or if it had been there all along.

"You would not have made the attack this way, Mr. Hargrave?"

"Wouldn't have made the damned attack at all!"

"Why, sir?"

"Ain't necessary. Nobody up behind that busted wall but rats. At that, they might make good practice for them bayonets. Your mountain men look like they need some."

"You mean the defenders have left the *castillo?*"

"Weren't never no defenders. Not for more than ten years at least. This old heap of adobe ain't been occupied by Mexicans since '35 or '36. Family of Indians lived here for a year along about 1840. They said the place was haunted and skedaddled."

"And that's what you tried to tell Colonel Frémont last night?"

"Yep. The strutting son of a bitch wouldn't listen. I told Carson the castle was empty this morning, and *he* listened."

"How did the men find out?"

"I expect Carson told them. Now, look ye here. I didn't mean for that to happen, I ain't quite the sorehead your commander thinks I am, but I think Carson wanted to teach that other young fool waving his sword up there a lesson."

"Why? Kit's not generally like that."

"I understand Gillespie's stuck in everybody's craw but Frémont's from the day your bunch met him. I know Bill Leidesdorff is plumb sick to death of the way he's taken over the consulate while Tom Larkin's down in Monterey. Well, anyway, he's about to get the biggest shock of his young career. Look at him."

The laughter from the skirmish line on either side of them was blowing full gale now.

8

Gillespie did not show his face once between the time they returned from Castillo de San Joaquín and when Captain Montgomery picked them up on the quay. Frémont stayed in the captain's cabin for most of the trip across the straits.

They left the mountain howitzers on the dock at Yerba Buena. If guns could take on human attributes, then the three constant rearguard companions of the expedition's westward journeys had done so: they looked forlorn.

Halfway across the bay to Sausalito, Frémont called Stone to Montgomery's cabin.

"We must make the most of Lieutenant Gillespie's affair at Castillo de San Joaquín, Lieutenant Stone . . . Bradford."

"Yes, sir."

"I have written a detailed report on the battle to send to Commodore Sloat. I would like you to read and sign it. Once you are done, give it to Captain Montgomery's first officer, Commander Wilson. The commander will see that it gets to the commodore. There's no rush. I simply want my view of that feat of arms to be the one that prevails."

"Yes, sir." Battle? Feat of arms? Was Frémont going to

throw poor Gillespie to the navy's wolves, to be a laughing-stock for the rest of his career? It certainly seemed out of character for the Pathfinder, who for all his faults had never betrayed a friend.

Out on deck, Stone found a capstan coiled with rope and nestled down beside it.

He then read one of the cleverest pieces of writing he had ever laid eyes on. Frémont told no outright, provable lies, but the entire document was phrased so ingeniously that anyone not actually present would have thought a battle had really taken place, with references to "shot and shell" and the "relentless advance against the superior Mexican position, against Lord knew what weapons we could not see, and against a force the strength of which we had no intelligence at all." Carson and even Stone himself came in for praise, Carson for the way he had "steeled and inspired his at-first reluctant troops and led them forward as if he were some rustic Hannibal," and Brad Stone, as Frémont phrased it, for "so quickly, and without regard for his own person, mounting the slope almost in tandem with gallant Lieutenant Archibald Gillespie."

There was a strong suggestion that Colonel John C. Frémont of the California Battalion, formerly Brevet Captain John C. Frémont of the U.S. Army Corps of Topographical Engineers, had planned a flawless action against a formidable enemy. "During the entire assault we lost not a single man, nor did any one of the command receive a wound." He did admit at the end that Gillespie and the Battalion had entered the castle fort to meet "virtually no opposition," but by that time the rhetoric would have dazzled into blindness the kind of reader Frémont intended it for. Even the author himself would eventually come to believe it, if he had not already.

Stone did not want to sign the report, but he wondered how he could point to any single item in it as a reason for his refusal. And something strange had happened to him. He felt a sudden sympathy for his commander. Given much by life, Frémont wanted so much more. There would indeed be more, but there would never be enough. Scourges that men such as Brad Stone and Kit Carson would never feel lacerated the great Pathfinder of the West, harried him day and night.

As he dropped the report in his lap, Carson appeared in front of him.

"What you been reading, *amigo?*"

"A fairy tale. Marvelous piece of work."

"Does it have a happy ending?"

"Depends on what you call happy, Kit."

9

When they disembarked at Sausalito, a message that had come down the river from Ed Kern at Sutter's awaited them. Frémont decided that after the exertions of getting all their animals and gear off the *Portsmouth* they would make one overnight camp, and at supper he read Kern's letter to the staff, including Hargrave.

"Captain Kern has sent me the most troubling news I have received since we left Bent's. I would have expected something like this from the Klamaths or the Horsethieves, but from purportedly civilized people it is unspeakable. Here is what Captain Kern says. . . .

"'Colonel Frémont—

"'Things are in good order here at the fort, but there is one piece of news that I feel I must pass on to you, in the hopes that it catches you before you start back to Sonoma from Sausalito.

"'A patrol found the bodies of two of the American settlers, George Fowler (no relation to John,

apparently) and Tom Cowie—both good Bear
Flaggers—lashed to trees a few miles west of the
junction of the American and Sacramento Rivers,
horribly and indecently mutilated—disemboweled,
and with their genitals excised and stuffed in their
mouths.'"

Frémont stopped reading, and as if it had been a cue, a
swelling growl of disgust came from his listeners. Someone
at the rear called out, "Must be somebody from those villages we hit."

"Hold on a moment," Frémont said. "Captain Kern494
495 considered that." He looked down at the letter and continued reading.

"'At first we thought it the work of Horsethieves,
but we discovered evidence at the site of this atrocity that persuaded me that Californios were to
blame. We tracked what appeared to be seven men
down the Sacramento until the trail split; four of
them, from the sign we cut, heading down into the
Napa country, the three others opting for the eastern
shore of San Pablo Bay. Not having enough men to
give pursuit to both parties, we chose to follow the
Napa lot, and actually succeeded in apprehending
one of them, a boy of sixteen or so, whom it was all
I could do to save from the knives of our men. . . .'"

"Knives?" Gus Archambeault cried out. "That's too goddamned quick and easy. They should have hung the little
bastard or had a pair of mules pull him apart."
Frémont held his hand up and went on.

"'He was terrified enough to give up the names
and places of abode of his six partners in crime.

The three he had been with are now twenty or thirty miles north of Sonoma, but I am taking six men and will begin a hunt for them.

"'According to this lad we now have in custody, the other three, including another boy, by the way, have small holdings in the vicinity of San Rafael on the same side of San Pablo Bay you will traverse on your way back to Sonoma. He says they will lie low for a bit, cross the bay, and then go to ground. I fully intend to go after them so soon as I bring in the three north of Sonoma. With any kind of luck I should have all seven miscreants under lock and key and awaiting you at Sutter's Fort by the time of your return. I will bring them down to Sonoma, of course, should you decide they should be tried there.

"'I must warn you that both Captain Sutter and General Vallejo are of the mind that despite the barbarity of their actions against the two dead settlers, they must be regarded as prisoners of war, and not as murderers. To my surprise, similar sentiments have been voiced by William Ide at Sonoma, if somewhat reluctantly. At any rate, it will be a difficult decision for you at best, Colonel.

> "'Respectfully—
> Edward Kern'"

There had been the first outcries of rage, more gasps and even a shudder or two at Kern's letter, but none of it showed the horror and outrage that had come over Frémont as he read it. It mirrored perfectly the lust for revenge Stone had seen on his face after the attack at Klamath Lake.

It amazed him that Frémont could calm himself as quickly as he did by the time he spoke again.

"Captain Kern has become a model officer," he said. "He demonstrates a splendid sense of initiative, but he never offers his commander advice unless it is sought. I have the utmost confidence that he would also obey an order without question. You are all now dismissed."

Stone glanced at Kit. No flicker of anything came to the scout's boyish face.

Hargrave fell in beside Stone and Carson as they left the meeting.

"That fellow Kern has the right of it. It's a damned hard call. I expect the colonel would do just about anything to avoid making that decision."

"He won't put it off a second, Mr. Hargrave," Kit said, "once he figures out which way he ought to go. The captain's one of the quickest men to set his mind I ever met. And he's sure as hell the smartest. I'll admit I doubted his judgment a time or two in the past, but he sees stuff ordinary men don't see."

10

They began the trek north from under the towering head-lands just west of Sausalito the next morning, with Gus Archambeault and Lucy Maxwell riding point on the high trail to the left of them, and Dick Owens doing the same chore down along the shore, all three a mile or more out ahead of the Battalion. For the better part of an hour Stone lost sight of the bay and their outriders.

The sun bathed the stony path ahead of them in gold, and spirits soared. At breakfast Frémont had promised them a long rest once they reached Sonoma. Alexis Godey whistled incessantly, and Stone guessed the St. Louisan had found a woman there. Now it seemed he would have all the time he needed for such pursuits. For his part, Stone hoped a letter might be waiting for him at Casa Vallejo.

There had evidently been two or three good rains since they went south to Yerba Buena; the trailside grass was green and springy, and the leaves of the oak and live oak of this slight elevation above sea level looked as if they had been scrubbed clean one by one and polished to a gloss.

Except that he could not rid himself of the thought that a letter from Ana might have tracked him down, it was turning out to be an enjoyable ride.

Back along the column where Frémont, riding in the lead as always, could not hear it, there was a good deal of cackling laughter over the grand assault on Castillo de San Joaquín. But *some* of the sounds could not help but reach the Pathfinder. Frémont had to know the cause of the hilarity rolling up the trail. He never looked back, but once or twice his neck stiffened and turned crimson.

Then Dick Owens' horse burst out of the brushwood ahead and on the right of the column's line of march. Owens must have bushwhacked his way up a half mile of scrub-covered slope.

"Colonel!" he shouted as he neared Frémont. "Something I got to tell you and Kit."

"What is it, man?"

"Down on the shore, about half a mile ahead where you can't see it from here, is a little fishing village called San Rafael. The place Ed Kern mentioned if I remember right."

"What about it, Owens? I do not intend stopping the march before Novato."

"This San Rafael's got a funny little *embarcadero*."

"So?"

"There's a small sailing boat coming in toward the dock. It's still fifteen or twenty minutes out in the bay, near as I can figure. I ain't much of a sailor, of course."

"Why should this craft concern us?"

"For one thing, from the tack it's on, it looks to me like it's come straight from the other side of San Pablo Bay, not

up the shoreline." He paused. "And it's carrying three passengers, two men . . . and a boy. . . ."

Frémont turned to Kit, eyes gleaming. "Do you suppose it
could be the men Captain Kern mentioned in his letter, the
ones who eluded him . . . ?"

"No idea, Captain," Kit said. "Sure could be, though. It
would be a hell of a stroke of luck."

The Pathfinder tugged at his beard.

"Captain Carson," he said. "You and Captain Owens get
back down to that *embarcadero*. Take Segundai and two of
his Delawares with you. Apprehend the men in that boat as
soon as they dock, and place them under guard. I'll bring the
column along."

"Yes, sir."

Carson and Owens disappeared through the thick brush,
and Frémont got the column under way again.

In about a quarter of an hour they reached a place where
the trail widened to a broad shelf overlooking the small harbor with its dock. The village itself lay to the south of the
inlet, and presented an appearance similar to that of Sausalito and Yerba Buena, but smaller, with crumbling adobe
huts and fishing shacks, and only a few dogs and chickens
in sight.

Carson, Owens, and the three Delawares were riding a
patch of salt grass toward the *embarcadero,* where the small
boat—to Stone it resembled a Massachusetts sailing
dinghy—was just bumping its nose against the wooden pier.

One of its occupants leaped to the pier with a line in his
hands and looped it around a stanchion. A second figure,
much smaller than the other two, crawled to the stern and
lifted the rudder tiller into the boat itself. They had already
furled the sail, probably had rowed their way to the pier the
last hundred yards or so. Piles of boxes and bags held the little vessel deep in the water. Leaning against the naked,

stubby mast a man in a snow white sombrero watched Carson, Owens, and the three Indians come on.

Frémont's five men rode right out onto the pier, the clatter of their horses' hooves drifting faintly up to Stone and the others.

A good deal of talking took place, or seemed to, and when it ended, Kit looked up the slope to Frémont. The colonel beckoned to him.

Kit rode back the length of the dock and started up toward the high shelf where the column had come to a halt. Behind him, Owens and the Delawares eased themselves from their saddles, while the three boatmen began piling their freight on the pier. The stern of the boat had swung away from the mooring and the boy now jumped into waist-deep water, taking boxes, kegs, and bags the two others handed him and settling them on the dock. Stone became so occupied, looking down at what he had every reason to suspect were the killers described in Kern's letter, that he did not realize Carson had reached the head of the column.

"Report, sir," Frémont said.

"Well, Captain, they *could* be the three men Kern's looking for, but I kind of doubt it."

"Why do you doubt it?"

"They make a pretty good case for themselves, claim they're just farmers out on a little trading run to the other side of the bay. They look like farmers to me."

"Come, come, Captain Carson! You do not truly believe that, do you?"

"I don't know why I shouldn't, Captain."

"Guilty men like these three will always, as you just put it, 'make a pretty good case for themselves.' What did you expect, a confession? Those three killers down there fit in every respect the men described in the report Captain Kern sent us. There can be no possible doubt of their guilt. We must make an example of them. You know what you must do. Do it!"

"You want me to take them prisoner, then?"

"What, precisely, would give you that idea?" Frémont stood in his stirrups. Stone had never seen his eyes quite this wild, unless it was just last night when the colonel had read Ed Kern's report. "What need have I of prisoners?"

"But, Captain, there ain't—"

"This is an order, Captain Carson! Do your duty!"

"Yes, sir."

The words were exactly those used on the slope leading to the blasted wall of the *castillo* the other day. This time Kit did not grin. As a matter of fact Stone had never seen Carson's face so glacial, not even at Pilot Peak.

But then the scout turned his horse and moved rapidly down the hillside.

When he pulled up at the section of the pier where Owens, Segundai, the two other Delawares, and the three Californios stood, he slipped from his horse and pulled his Hawken from the saddle boot. He gestured to Dick and Segundai and the three walked a few feet down the pier together.

Stone swallowed hard. They would not actually . . .

The two mountain men and the Indian now turned back toward the men in the boat and lifted their rifles to their shoulders.

Three reports, two of them close together but clearly distinguishable, and then a third no more than half a second later, echoed from the hillside behind the column.

The man in the white sombrero sagged into the bottom of the boat, the lad in the water fell backward, submerged for an instant, then bobbed up again, and the third now lay sprawled face down on the wooden pier. One of Segundai's two warriors walked to the man who had fallen on the pier, turned him over by pushing at him with the muzzle end of his rifle, and nodded. The other Delaware peered down into the boat and the water at the other two, his rifle ready. He looked up at Carson and Owens and then he, too, nodded. The Indian then appeared to say something to Carson, who shook his head in response.

Smoke curled away from the three rifles and drifted lazily into the sky. Ripples from where the young boy had fallen backward in the water picked up the morning sun and made sparkling semicircles in the bay.

11

Stone had a letter from Jake Myers awaiting him at Casa Vallejo; there was nothing from Ana. It worried him a little until he saw the date the congressman's had been posted from Illinois . . . April third, 1846.

In his letter Myers said he was leaving the next morning for Washington. "I cannot be sure," he said, "but I am fairly confident that the first order of business awaiting me will be a vote on a declaration of war against Mexico. I lament this, of course. There must be more civilized ways to resolve differences, but I believe that at this time, despite the efforts of many men of goodwill, our two nations have now reached an impasse."

He also found a letter from his mother thanking him for at last beginning to write with some regularity. He penned a reply to her before he left the desk in the room he had shared with Kern.

At supper Carson told him he had heard from Josefa.

"How is she, Kit?"

"Just fine."

"Does she by any chance mention Doña Ana?

"Yes . . . she does."

"Did she say Doña Ana is in good health, too?"

"Yes . . . she did. She says Doña Ana is in very good health . . . that she has never looked better in all her eighteen years. She says she glows."

Eighteen years? Yes. They *had* been apart long enough for her to have passed another birthday.

12

The Battalion had been in bivouac at Sonoma again for another week when a new message arrived from Yerba Buena and the irrepressible Archibald Gillespie. Frémont called Stone to Mariano Vallejo's study and showed it to him.

There was no questioning the importance of this dispatch.

Commodore Sloat—not, by Gillespie's report, the swiftest of the United States' West Coast commanders to reach a decision or turn it into action—had finally anchored in the harbor at Monterey. Just in the nick of time, too. Admiral Sir George Seymour of the Royal Navy had moved into the quiet waters of Monterey Bay directly in Sloat's wake with the H.M.S. *Collingwood.* His was easily the most powerful ship of war now operating in the Pacific, a frigate of eighty guns to the twenty of the *Portsmouth,* for instance, and with a full complement of Royal Marines aboard. Apparently the British admiral, whom Tom Larkin had characterized as a renowned fighter and shrewd diplomat and manipulator, had no intention of interfering with Sloat's raising of the American flag over the seaport. He merely wanted to see how things went. "As things are presently constituted here in Monterey, Sir George has every right to show the Union Jack in these waters. There are a number of British subjects living and working here," Larkin said. "Most of them, like that fellow Hartnell I steered you to last spring, are strong backers of the United States. That's why I have never truly feared British intervention."

This view did not square at all with Frémont's frequently voiced fear that Her Majesty's government would try to steal a march on the United States in acquiring California. But Stone remembered the Pathfinder had always relied more on his own *perception* of reality.

After a sluggish start, the American commodore had finally hoisted Old Glory over the town and requested that the Bear Flag Republic center its activities around Monterey as soon as possible.

"Although we all trust and like Admiral Seymour," Gillespie wrote, "Albion could turn perfidious again in the wink of an eye. My personal opinion is that you should bring the entire Battalion down to Monterey forthwith. It seems you have effectively put down any incipient revolt against the Republic in the north, and I think you should play a role in whatever else happens on this coast. You are still the highest-ranking American officer ashore. Big things could be in the offing that will redound to the benefit of our country, and to you personally. Send a courier if you decide to come, and J.B. will have the *Portsmouth* waiting for you at Sausalito. I think I can secure a second ship for transport as well, so your entire force can cross the bay at once."

By the time Stone finished reading Gillespie's letter, Frémont had already summoned Kit. "Captain Carson," he said, "we will march for Monterey tomorrow. This move will occupy us for a great deal more time than any of the others and will keep us out of the north possibly for months, so everything goes—every man, every rifle, every cartridge case, and every horse."

"Yes, sir." Even after San Rafael, Kit still looked at Frémont with that same old eagerness and willingness to serve that Stone had seen back at Bent's.

Stone wondered, as Kern had wondered so many times, if

Gillespie and Frémont had already learned that war had broken out. It would account for a lot that had passed between the two Americans since they met at Klamath Lake.

When Carson left, Stone stood there for a moment, looking expectant, he supposed. Frémont peered at him. "You wanted something, Lieutenant?"

"I would like to remind the colonel that my contract will expire in just a few more days. I plan to return to the United States as soon as you release me."

"Release you, Lieutenant Stone?" Frémont fixed him in his gaze and took several seconds before going on. "Ah, yes. Your obligation to the Corps of Topographical Engineers certainly is about to end, but there is still your sworn oath to the California Battalion when I commissioned you. I cannot possibly release you from that oath so long as the Battalion is a viable entity. We need your fine staff work, my boy."

He wanted to protest, at least mutter something like, "But, Colonel . . ."

The Pathfinder was not through. "One other thing. Find Major Hargrave, Captain Ide, and Captain Merritt, and tell them that they will ride with the Battalion to Monterey."

"Thank you, sir," Stone said.

28

The Drums of Glory

The California Battalion with the Pathfinder and Gillespie at its head—the marine had traveled down to Monterey from Yerba Buena three days earlier, and had come out from town today to meet them for the ride in—entered a very different small city than the one Stone and Frémont had visited back in March, or had it been April? So much had happened.

Monterey became even more different with their arrival. They rode down its main *avenida* two hundred forty-two strong, even the American settler recruits armed to the teeth as were the fifty-some mountain men still left from the original expedition that left Bent's Fort the previous autumn. Not as universally fierce in appearance as the expedition when it rolled to a stop at the foot of Pilot Peak, it still looked impressive. What the homespun-clad rancher and farmer settlers, who now made up the greater part of the Battalion, lacked in warlike mien, they more than made up with a look of grim determination.

Crowds thronged the *avenida,* mostly Mexicans, but with scatterings of American sailors off the vessels lying in the roads, merchant marines for the most part, but more than a few in the bright, trim uniforms of the United States Navy. Cheers and shouts of approval rose in waves from the latter at the sight of Frémont, and now and again a British tar would applaud or tip his cap. American and British navy garb was so nearly identical Stone had to pick the Royal Navy men out by the H.M.S. COLLINGWOOD printed on the band of their brimless caps.

When they reached the *casa de ayuntamiento*—as the citizens called their town hall—the blaring of a brass band, supplemented by guitars and violins and a gigantic drum, almost deafened him. A fat man in a tailcoat emblazoned with a diagonal red silk sash, holding a top hat across it, stood in front of the band, beaming. In a small line behind him what appeared to be a deputation of the citizenry beamed as broadly.

"That's the *alcalde,* the mayor," Stone shouted to Kit, who rode alongside him in the procession. "The colonel and I paid a call on him when we were here. Looks like he's engineered a pretty sincere welcome for us."

"Seems so. I'm a mite curious about it, though. Last I heard, us Americans ain't as popular here as we are in Sonoma. This has been strictly Mexican country until a few weeks ago."

Then the band stopped suddenly. In the lull Stone picked up Frémont talking to Gillespie.

". . . and slip out of the column the first chance you get, Archibald. If you don't pay the money I had promised that fat little fellow and the bandsmen he engaged, they'll follow us right up to the *fortaleza*, where we'll bivouac. And thanks for arranging this reception. Very important. It might even impress the commodore. Do you see him anywhere?"

"I haven't yet, John. At any rate, we may never have to deal with Sloat. He's fallen into bad odor in Washington for acting so slow. I talked with Tom Larkin yesterday. He thinks Stockton will probably take over everything in the Pacific eventually. Sloat has already put him in charge of all land operations in California. You'll like him. He's close to Polk, you know. Once I've finished with the mayor, I'll locate him for you, and the commodore . . . if you still think a conference with old 'Snail' Sloat is necessary."

"No. Just Stockton, if you can work it out that way. I'll pay my respects to Sloat tonight at dinner."

Although Frémont had not lowered his voice after the band stopped playing, Stone knew he and Kit and the others riding directly behind them were not really supposed to have heard any of this, particularly about the payment to be made to the *alcalde*. Stone guessed, too, that none of them were supposed to have heard the intimate "Archibald" and "John" these two usually formal men had used.

The band struck up a new tune, the little Monterey mayor stepped toward Frémont, smiling around a mouthful of gold teeth, and twenty or so of the mountain men let off an exuberant fusillade with their rifles.

The Pathfinder, who had dressed quite plainly for such a

day, except that the eagle feather still quivered jauntily in his hatband, looked every inch the conqueror.

Now he turned in the saddle.

"Captain Carson, after we clear the plaza, turn the column and lead it up to the *fortaleza*. I will see you there at the dinner hour. Lieutenant Gillespie and I have some business to attend to with the commodore and his deputy."

2

Two weeks later Frémont played host at what could have passed for a state dinner.

They dined in the great hall of Monterey's stone fort. Frémont amazed Stone, as he had at Casa Vallejo, at how quickly he could insinuate himself into an unfamiliar new place and make it his own in an instant.

Servants, most of them dressed in what looked to be Mexican army uniforms with the insignia and braid removed, served dinner at a long table facing the *fortaleza*'s huge, gatelike, timber doors, flung wide to catch the evening sea breeze, and affording an unobstructed view of the tile roofs of Monterey and the harbor. From up here, the ships swinging slowly on their anchor chains looked like toys, even the giant H.M.S. *Collingwood*. The slanting sun had turned the water to a sheet of rippling molten gold.

As Stone looked up and down and around the long table, it struck him that this might be the largest gathering of Americans of at least some importance ever convened in the history of California. The English admiral Sir George Seymour sat between Kit and Commodore Sloat, on Frémont's right. Sloat's deputy, the other American commodore in the Pacific, Robert Stockton, was situated to the Pathfinder's immediate left. It was also, Stone supposed, perhaps the largest gathering of influential men of *any* origin in this golden province since Mexico had won its independence from Spain in 1821 and California had followed with its own revolt against the mother country in 1822.

Stone had little doubt who Frémont thought had primacy in this group. He had positioned himself at the head of the table. Hargrave sat at the foot, with William Ide and Ezekiel Merritt on either side of him, as isolated as if they were still back in the barracks at Sonoma.

Stone himself started to settle in somewhere near the middle, but the colonel gestured him to a chair a little closer to him, just below Archibald Gillespie, with Ted Talbot at his right elbow.

From Frémont's appearance it was an exceedingly happy moment, but it must have rankled a little that when Seymour arrived with three of his officers the admiral had asked first to meet Kit. "This remarkable man," he said to one of his aides after he and Kit had shaken hands, "is as famous in Europe as the Duke of Wellington."

Stone took the granite-featured, black-haired Stockton to be in his early fifties, impressive even at a glance, particularly when compared to his retiring commander, Sloat. Stockton must have fought against Admiral Seymour at some point in the War of 1812, both at the time junior officers, but they had greeted each other as affably as brothers when they went to the table, and had engaged each other in smiling conversation as they ate. "If John here"—Seymour nudged Sloat as he said this, but still directed his words to Stockton—"hadn't bestirred himself and finally run up the Stars and Stripes here in Monterey, I assure you I would have claimed this bonnie peninsula for Her Majesty, Robert."

"I know you would have, Sir George," Stockton said. "Glad that didn't happen. I would have felt bad when I took it away from you."

When the meal ended, Frémont whispered something to

Stockton, stood, tapped his empty wineglass with a spoon, and looked up and down the table.

"May I have your attention, gentlemen?" After a dozen different little conversations faded into silence he went on, directing his first remarks to the admiral. "Please excuse me, Sir George, if we do a little Yankee housekeeping."

"Would you like my officers and me to leave, Colonel Frémont? We possibly should not be privy to . . ."

"No, sir. Please stay. I don't intend to reveal any state secrets."

Of course he did not want Seymour to leave. The Frémont Stone had come to know in the last year and a month would never, could he help it, subtract such an illustrious man from any audience he addressed.

Frémont looked down at Commodore Stockton before continuing. Stockton smiled back up at Frémont and nodded. Frémont gazed down the length of the table.

"My first pronouncement concerns my command, the California Battalion," he said. Of all the men of Stone's acquaintance only John Frémont would say "pronouncement," rather than "announcement." "I sincerely regret to inform you that as of this moment, this splendid unit is dissolved as a fighting force with my deepest gratitude and regret. It has with these words ceased to exist."

Groans came from the length of the table, but a sharp cry from Hargrave at the end of it. "Colonel! How about the Republic? And Don José Castro?"

Merritt and Ide echoed him.

"Please, Major," Frémont did not seem at all perturbed at the Napa rancher's interruption. Enjoying himself too much in this glittering assemblage, Stone supposed. Frémont went on. "Allow me to continue. The officers and men of the Battalion can, if they choose, become members of a new elite unit within Commodore R. F. Stockton's command structure, the Navy Battalion of Mounted Riflemen. We shall ride

and fight under the flag of the United States of America.
Any officer or non-commissioned officer of the California
Battalion choosing to join the Mounted Riflemen and swear
allegiance to the United States, its flag, and its constitution,
will be welcome. I must tell you, though, that except for the
lieutenants, each of you will have to be content with one step
down in rank. I will continue in command, of course, but I
will only be a major now. Remember, these will be United
States commissions. As your major I will serve under the
orders of, and will report to, Commodore Stockton here,
whom some of you have met before this evening."

Brad Stone waited for his head to clear.

The breakup of the Battalion would bring about what he
had prayed for every night for a month. It meant he was free,
free to return to Taos and Ana! He had taken no oath to
something called the Mounted Riflemen and he would not.
Ana! He barely registered Frémont's next words. Kit smiled
at him from across the table. He knew.

"To address your concerns about General Castro, Major
Hargrave," Frémont said next, "Commodore Stockton
intends to transport the Mounted Riflemen to southern California by sea within a fortnight. We'll find Don José and
crush him! Now, all of you who are willing to go with us . . .
on your feet!"

Shouts and yells filled the hall. Chairs were turned over as
all of them stood, all save Stockton, four bemused British
naval officers, Tom Larkin, Bill Leidesdorff . . . and Stone.
Even Ide, Hargrave, and Merritt stood. Kit was on his feet,
too, although at a head shorter than the others it was hard to
pick him out.

When the tumult died away, Stone found Frémont looking
straight at him.

3

"I am surprised and disappointed, Lieutenant Stone," the Pathfinder said. "I felt sure that the man who fought so well at Klamath Lake against the Horsethief Indians, and in the recent campaigns, would want to stay a little longer in the company of the men he fought with."

Stone felt every eye in the hall on him now. He stayed in his seat.

"I'm sorry, Major, but as I told you in Sonoma the other day, sir, I have pressing personal business in the East. I have spent more time with the Battalion than I ever intended, and my contract with the topographical expedition was finished weeks ago. Please excuse me from further duty."

Frémont looked at the others. "We want Lieutenant Stone with us, don't we, gentlemen? Let him know!"

The roar gratified him, but, damn it, he was going to stay the course.

"Kit!" Frémont said. "Tell him!"

Kit looked at Stone, but directed his remarks to Frémont. "Can't do it, Captain. Brad's a big boy now. I think he ought to do what he wants to do."

Frémont was counting on Kit to be his ace as he had so often in the past.

Frémont looked at Stone now with a face filled with hurt and seemingly genuine sorrow. "Forgive me, Lieutenant. I have done you a disservice and perhaps a grievous wrong, the way I risked embarrassing you in front of your comrades. There is something I should have told you—" He looked at the others. "—all of you—when the evening began. Had I done so, I feel sure Lieutenant Stone would be standing with us now. I know what a difference it will make to a man of his courage and love of country. . . .

"You see, Commodore Sloat informed me before we sat down to eat that the United States of America and the Republic of Mexico are at war!"

29

Call to Confession

Estancia Barragán

"The *niño pequeño* will come any day now, Doña Ana," Galinda said. "Try not to be impatient. You must feel it yourself; it has kicked hard enough. It will be a strong child."

"I'll thank you not to call my baby 'it,' *vieja!* He is a boy. I have known *that* almost from the beginning. And as for patience, I'm about out of it. He was due more than a week ago."

The *dueña* shrugged. "You never can be sure with the first one. A boy would be *muy bueno, sí* . . . but if it is, Galinda hopes he looks like you, and not like the *yanqui*."

"It no longer matters. Papá knows Bradford is the father. He pretends to think it is Don Luis. He can satisfy his pride that way. And I did not agree to marry Don Luis until Papá gave me his word of honor that Bradford has nothing more to fear from him. Papá has many things wrong with him, but he would never break his word."

True enough. He had already issued orders to Roberto that Bradford was not to be harmed if he returned to the *estancia,* and she could presume he had warned off the Barragán riders as well. It had taken a great weight from her mind, if not from her heart.

"How long will your new husband, Don Luis, be gone, *niña?*"

"Four, five months, perhaps six. He must journey all the way to St. Louis on this trip. He was very sweet. He says it is just as well that he is gone, that it will be better if the baby is a little older and I feel fully recovered from the birth before we . . . you know. The poor dear couldn't say it. This is all very hard for him and of course it is all my fault."

"You will become a real *esposa* to Don Luis when he returns, *querida?*"

"We'll see!" She had asked herself that often enough without Galinda bringing it up.

"He can insist." Galinda did not look at her. "It is his right."

. "I know . . . but when Bradford comes back . . . ?" How could she face *him* now? How could she tell him of her wedding to Luis in Mamá's tiny chapel with only Papá, Galinda, Roberto, Luis's highly suspicious mother, and an altar boy brought up from Santa Fe looking on while Padre Martínez read the nuptial Mass? Papá had barred the chapel to the other servants, the *vaqueros,* and the families of the sheepherders until the ceremony had been concluded. He did not even allow Cousins Josefa and Ignacia to come out from town to be with her.

She had not been able to bring herself to write to Bradford since. He still could not know what had happened unless Cousin Josefa mentioned it in a letter to Don Cristóbal, and she had begged her not to. No worry about that; Josefa would not betray her trust. Josefa said she had not even told her husband, Kit, about the child, and Ana believed her.

"You should not think about the *yanqui* at all," Galinda said now. "You are a married woman, even if you have not shared a bed with your husband."

"I know. But I cannot help it. That is what makes this so difficult. And as for Don Luis insisting, he would never insist. He is so patient about that I sometimes wonder if he has any blood in him. It would be so easy, Galinda, and so much better for everybody, if I could only love him as I do Bradford. I can take care of some of that when Padre Martínez returns and I can make my confession and take communion."

"That's another thing. As close as you are to going into labor, you should forget about making a hard trip into Ranchos for something so ridiculous."

"You wouldn't understand, Galinda. You're not a Catholic. If I do not make confession something terrible could happen."

"What do you have to confess? Everybody who counts in your life already knows what you have done."

"Padre Martínez doesn't . . . nor does Bradford."

"Galinda thinks it is more important that you tell the *yanqui* than the *padre*. You should write to him. When do you expect him to return to Taos?"

"He said he would be back September first, but with this war now, I don't think he will. Señor Bent says Bradford and Don Cristóbal will probably be caught up in the fighting in California. Now I must fear for Bradford's life for other reasons than what Papá would have done."

"The war has not been so bad here in Nuevo Méjico, *niña.*"

"Only because Don Manuel Armijo is such a coward. Papá is furious with him."

"Maybe *el gobernador* in California will be a coward, too, and there will be as little fighting there as there has been here. Galinda cannot call it war when no warriors die, and no women weep."

It was true. Ana had heard of no amount of bloodletting yet, in California or here in New Mexico, and they had yet to see one of the *soldados norteamericanos* in the streets of Taos. The Americans had been in the province for two weeks or more and were now close to Santa Fe, perhaps there already, since Governor Manuel Armijo—with Don Bernardo Barragán trying to help him—had failed to stop them.

Papá had ridden to Cañon del Apache east of Santa Fe a week ago, where Governor Armijo's three hundred dragoons and a few volunteers from Albuquerque and the Río villages were reported to be lying in wait for the American invaders. Before he left the *estancia* he had filled the air with praise for Don Manuel's brave stand, so excited he abandoned the daily critical, accusing looks he had given her since her pregnancy really began to show.

If no one else from Taos would, Don Bernardo Barragán meant to fight the Americans, no matter how strong their army was, or no matter how peaceable they claimed or seemed to be.

"That *yanqui* general, Kearny, is a *bufón*, a fool! He must think he can have everything his own way without a fight. It will not be that easy! He has come down over El Paso del Raton from Bent's in one long march. His men and animals must be exhausted. He should have rested and refitted on the Río Mora before he entered Cañon del Apache. Don Manuel can now crush him easily. And Bernardo Barragán will be there to help him do it."

Papá had taken with him twelve of Estancia Barragán's fiercest *vaqueros,* the same ones he had assigned earlier to kill Bradford if he came this way, all of them armed to the teeth. Watching them ride off, she had felt a throb of guilt at some very dark thoughts. They surfaced when it occurred to her that if anything happened to her father, she would be free to ask Padre Martínez to set in motion the annulment of her marriage to Luis. The priest should do that, since there had been no consummation of it.

Would he take issue with her, though, about the baby, whether or not it had arrived by then? When she confessed, he would know that Bradford—a *norteamericano* and worse, a non-Catholic—and not Luis Aragón, was the father. Padre Martínez's feelings toward Americans had always been every bit as strong as Don Bernardo's.

But the padre would listen to her for one compelling reason. If Papá died, she would become the *hacendada* at Estancia Barragán and the padre's richest parishioner. From watching him with Papá over the years, she knew that even if Padre Antonio Martínez feared no man in the valley, he did stand in respectful awe of her father and his lands, his cattle, and his sheep. He would make almost any concession to keep Estancia Barragán and its thirty-six or thirty-seven souls within his purview and helping to fill the coffers of his church.

The padre had once refused to allow the burial of an old, non-Christian Navajo shepherd in the consecrated Barragán burial ground near the gate. Papá, whose father had brought old Juan from Cañon de Chelly as a boy to work with the Barragán flock, had threatened to install his own private priest in the chapel at the *hacienda* if he did not get his way. Padre Martínez had capitulated in a hurry. Juan now rested not fifty feet from Mamá.

In any event, despite the horrid thoughts that to her shame nearly became wishes, nothing physically bad happened to Papá in Apache Canyon.

He rode back to the *estancia* in a mere three days without having fired a shot at the Americans, raging against "that cowardly tub of fat, Armijo," with spittle flying from his lips and his iron-gray hair in wild disarray. The governor would never be "*Don* Manuel" to Bernardo Barragán again. No one could ever call Papá an inconstant man, especially in his hatreds.

She had finally been able to deduce from his ravings that Governor Armijo, after much drunken boasting about what he would do to the Americans when they arrived, had fled

Apache Canyon with his three hundred soldiers and shaky volunteers before the enemy ever came in sight. Armijo led his dragoons at a hard gallop back down the river to Albuquerque. The volunteers had sped past the regular militia in panic. Some said Armijo was already seeking safety in Mexico.

A disgusted, fuming Don Bernardo, left behind with his handful of men in the narrow canyon, finally recognized the folly of facing an army with field artillery with only a dozen riders, took his *vaqueros* back north, and now nothing stood between General Stephen Watts Kearny and the capital of the province of New Mexico except a few tiny adobe villages defended mostly by pigs and chickens.

2

Then, only a day after Papá's return, some aspects of life at the *hacienda* changed.

A stream of visitors flowed through the gate of the *estancia:* local *rancheros* and tradesmen, blanket-wrapped Indians from the Pueblo north of Taos—she could not remember a Taoseño ever coming to Estancia Barragán before—and a few other New Mexicans who looked like highwaymen or ne'er-do-wells. Papá saw them all in his study. He never told her what took place behind its thick door, nor did he introduce her to any of his visitors.

Something odd was going on between Papá and the strangers, who spoke to no one in the *hacienda*. She did not ask about it.

She did not *care* much about what was going on, either.

What was happening inside her was all she could think about—and all she wanted to think about.

For all her bravado and talk with Galinda this morning about how she wished the birth would come about quickly and be done with, she feared it. Galinda could talk herself blue in the face about how easy and natural having a baby was; the old Navajo had never borne a child herself, or had kept it a secret all these years if there was one back in Dinetah. Besides, she was an Indian. It *was* easy for Indian women, or at least it had seemed so on the trading trips Ana had made over the years to Cañon de Chelly with Papá. Although she had never actually seen a birth there, she had even as a child been close enough to several to hear a newborn's first cries, and in the *hogan* she shared with Galinda and at the cooking fires of Galinda's sisters she had listened to a lot of talk about giving birth.

In the last two months she had heard a different kind of talk from Ignacia Bent. Ana did not know whom the older of her two Jaramillo cousins frightened more with her tales, Ana herself or Josefa Carson, who like Ana had yet to bear a child, but who confided to Ana shyly that she was going to try once Kit returned.

Actually, Ignacia's forecasts of the physical pain she would shortly undergo did not trouble her nearly as much as the way her cousin looked at her.

3

On one afternoon visit to the Bent home just last week, right after Papá's return from Apache Canyon, Ignacia spirited her away from Josefa and into her sewing room, saying she wanted to show her the christening dress she had half finished. Ana puzzled over this as she followed her through the parlor; Ignacia could have more easily brought the delicate, white gown out to the patio where the three of them were having tea.

"I fear for you, *mi prima*," Ignacia said when they were alone. "I see something in your eyes I do not like. Is that

Dineh woman, Galinda, looking after you and the baby you are carrying the way she should?"

"*Sí.* Certainly. Why would you think she would not?"

"She is an Indian. A Navajo. Who knows what secret hate she could have for people like us? Galinda's people in Dinetah do not keep their hate a secret. They steal from us constantly and try often enough to kill us. They succeed, too. Just last week Navajos raided the Emiliano Gutiérrez *rancho* on the west side of the gorge. They ran off more than a hundred of Don Emiliano's sheep and killed two shepherds, boys—smashed their heads flat with rocks."

Anger shook Ana as if she were a rag doll. She had heard too much talk like this in Taos since she was a child. Always the Navajo! Galinda's people. It was terrible for Don Emiliano and Doña María and their two dead shepherds, of course, but . . . the government in Santa Fe had sent its own raiders into the west to punish the Dineh often enough. If they had not done so this time it was only because of the advancing Americano army.

"The Dineh would never attack Estancia Barragán! Papá is the only *hacendado* in the valley who has befriended Navajos and let them work for him. And whatever that raid across the gorge was like, it has nothing to do with Galinda. She has cared for me since I was born. She is no more a Navajo now than I am, and the only thing close to a mother I have ever had."

"I suppose you are right. Perhaps it has nothing to do with Indians after all, but I still have this feeling when I look in your eyes, *querida.* I do not see death so much, although there is a little of it there, but I do see some disaster looming. I see . . ." *¡Dios!* She actually looked distraught. Then she went on. "*Por favor,* be careful, Ana. Would you like me to read the tea leaves for you when we rejoin Josefa? Perhaps the future will be clearer if I do."

"*No, muchísimas gracias, Doña Ignacia, pero no.*"

"Then please, Ana, for the baby's sake if not for your own, at least go to confession—and pray every chance you get. I sometimes fear you are not the best Catholic you could be."

The anger flared again. What right did comfortable Ignacia, who lived little more than a hundred meters from a church, have to criticize her?

But the anger ebbed, and in its place she felt a bone-deep chill. She remembered that a few years back a few of the Taos villagers had looked on Ignacia Bent as a *bruja* for a while, even though Ignacia attended Mass as faithfully as anyone in town. Ana did not believe very strongly in sorcery herself, did not credit her cousin with any special powers, but it could not hurt to take the care Ignacia urged on her. If she had not remembered the talk about Ignacia being a *bruja,* Galinda would have reminded her of it. There seemed to be a sudden intense rivalry between the two of them over the management of Ana's lying-in. "I have no objection to Galinda looking after you, *Dios* knows," Ignacia said now, "but I am, after all, a Jaramillo, and the same blood runs through your veins as through mine."

Ana very pointedly did not ask the size or shape of the disaster Ignacia thought she saw, or hinted she might find, in the tea leaves. Disaster could only take one form for Ana Barragán.

Something might have happened to Bradford.

If she had heard anything even resembling such a possibility from her cousin, it would have been more than her soul could stand in these final long days of waiting. She vowed to shut every last thing from her mind but the birth. She did not tell Galinda of the talk with Ignacia, but Ignacia's insistence that she confess did fasten itself to her mind.

4

Roberto had driven her to Taos the day of that conversation with Ignacia Bent. On the way back to the *estancia* she suddenly realized she had not made a confession or taken communion since before the night spent at La Cayuda with Bradford. How could she have let an important thing like this drift so long?

She had always considered herself devout enough, no matter what Cousin Ignacia said, but she had been a little indifferent to the needs of her mortal soul at times. Papá had always been there to insist on her performing her religious duties, and since her first communion he had been unfailingly strict. But she had seen little of him during those first months before he knew about her condition, and Padre Martínez was not one of those priests who constantly track down their truant communicants to bully them into attendance at Mass or in the confessional. The bullying awaited them only when they finally showed up, and not always then.

Probably because Papá was there for the ceremony the day she married Luis, Padre Martínez had not even asked her to enter the booth in Mamá's chapel. Luis, immediately on his arrival, had confessed in the rickety box, where Padre Martínez had heard Barragán confessions for more than a generation. As low as she felt that day—wishing it were Bradford at the altar with her—it had amused her for a moment to wonder what sweet, decent, honorable Don Luis Aragón oould ever have to confess.

That was the last time she had been inside the church, if she could call the tiny chapel one.

Cousin Ignacia had said today that she should pray. Well, she had prayed. Incessantly. She had prayed for Bradford, for the baby, and a little for herself, every night since Bradford left; but now, as Roberto drove her away from Taos in the carriage, she felt a sudden, hungry need to enlist a stronger, more persuasive voice than hers to plead for divine intercession on his behalf.

And after she had asked the Virgin's help for *him,* she would make that overdue confession. That had suddenly, just on the short ride out from Taos, become even *more* important.

She did not want her baby entering this world when she herself was not in as perfect a "state of grace" as she could be, utterly absolved of the sin that, brought the baby about. Some secret inner voice was now warning her that without this absolution she could be doomed and damned. It could not touch the child . . . or could it? She would have to ask the padre about that when she confessed.

When she and Roberto reached the huge old church in Ranchos de Taos on the way home, she directed the *mayordomo* to turn into the churchyard and stop. She climbed out of the carriage, borrowed some coins from Roberto to buy a candle, and walked toward the silent church.

Old Porfirio, the gardener who also served Padre Martínez as sacristan, was on his knees, puttering in the rosebushes on the north side of the crushed-stone walkway that led to the church door. He looked up and smiled as she reached him.

"I will need a candle, Porfirio," she said. "I will leave the *dinero* on the little table in the foyer."

"*Muchas gracias, Doña Ana.*" He began to struggle to his feet.

"Do not get up, *viejo,* I beg you."

She entered the church. There was no one else in it, all to the good as far as she was concerned. The dark coolness of the nave pleased her as much as when she had been a child, and the desire to kick off her *huaraches* and feel the cool hard earth as she had on every visit back then overwhelmed her, but she knew what a struggle it would be to get them on again with her new girth. Even the thin soles of the sandals between her feet and the packed floor of the church would take away some of the intimacy she had always delighted in when she came to Mass or confession here at San Francisco de Asis back in those lost days. It could not be helped. It was going to be hard enough for her to kneel, harder still to stand up again.

She lighted the candle, leaned over the altar rail, placed the candle in an empty candlestick holder at the feet of the *estatua* of the Virgin, and knelt. The tiny stones embedded in the earthen floor pressed into her knees painfully.

The prayers did not come nearly as easily—not for any of them, Bradford, Don Luis, the baby, not for her, least of all for her—as they did in her bed at night.

Well, her confession would have much more substance than her prayers.

She grasped the altar rail and pulled herself upright, more conscious suddenly of her swollen belly than when she had walked past the Taos plaza earlier today on the way from Cousin Josefa's to Ignacia Bent's. In that short trip she had passed a dozen people she knew by name and reputation as shameless gossips. They had peered at her with undisguised curiosity. It was obvious Josefa and Ignacia had not told their neighbors or any of the other villagers of her marriage to Luis Aragón, and getting married at the chapel meant that banns had not been posted at the *iglesia* in Taos or here in the dark vault of San Francisco.

After one more wistful look at the *Virgen* and the burning candle she walked to the confessional. The door on the confessor's side gaped open. She picked up the shepherd's crook that leaned against the wall, lifted it by the shaft, and caught the cord that ran through a hole in the adobe all the way to the bell in Padre Martínez's *casa*. She jerked on the cord three times, heard the faint tinkling of the silver *campanita* in the padre's living quarters, and sank onto the bench on the supplicant's side of the booth. She pulled the door shut and stared at the grille. How many times had she sat here as a terrified child? How Padre Martínez must have laughed inwardly at the things she considered sins . . . in her young mind, mortal sins: coins withheld from the offering to be spent on sweets; fits of black temper with poor Galinda; lying to Papá; Manuel kissing her at Cañon de Chelly and her not struggling against the kiss; disobeying Papá in some small way almost every time he left the *hacienda*.

Well, she would confess a genuine sin today, if only venial and not mortal, but genuine and serious in the padre's lexicon . . . and in hers. She had never tried to delude herself into thinking that the passionate coupling of the night in the *casita* with Bradford was other than a sin, one made worse because the act had been so deliberate on her part. She could not even claim Bradford had seduced her.

In the matter of penance it would not surprise her if things went hard for her. Padre Martínez, while not as inhumane a priest as the ones she had known at school, could not be called the easiest of confessors, particularly for women. He hated it particularly when a sin like Ana's went unconfessed as long as this one had. He terrified those women in the district such as her Jaramillo cousins when they went to confession, and they certainly had never had to answer for anything like this. For their confessions Josefa and Ignacia generally sought out the more lenient Padre Gómez, who presided at the much smaller San Fernando just off the plaza. But if she were to accomplish what she wanted, she would welcome the harshest penance, almost beg for it, and she would receive it from this priest.

Strangely though, she probably would be assigned no penance whatsoever for what she regarded as the much more serious sins she had committed and in a sense was still committing, those bordering on the mortal in her conscience at least: first, the wicked thing she had done to poor Luis Aragón by marrying him without loving him, and secondly, what she secretly intended doing when Bradford returned, abandoning Luis for the man she truly loved almost the moment she and Bradford were together again. Those sins would probably not even elicit criticism, the former because the padre could never bring himself to deem holy matrimony sinful no matter how wanton the bride had been, the latter because she had not actually done it yet. . . .

She jumped at the tap on the door. No one had appeared in the shadows beyond the grille.

"*¿Padre?*" she whispered. Until she heard her own thin, quavering voice she had not realized how tightly her thoughts had stretched her nerves.

"*¡No, no, mi doña! Soy Porfirio.*"

She opened the door on the old gardener-sacristan.

"*¿Sí, Porfirio?*"

"Forgive me, *por favor.* Porfirio did not know *la doña* wanted to make confession until he heard her ring the *campanita.* Padre Martínez is not here today. He has ridden down the gorge to Embudo to give Rudolfo Ramírez's *abuela* the last rites."

"When will he return?"

"One does not know how long it will take for Rudolfo's grandmother to die, of course, but I expect the padre back late Saturday. I do not think he will miss Sunday's Mass."

It was Monday. Would her taut nerves hold until Saturday or Sunday? Could she get back here before the baby came? Now that she had decided on the confession, every moment made it more imperative. "If he should return before then, Porfirio, please have him send word to the *estancia.* I *must* make my confession. Tell the padre it's a matter of life and death. I don't expect him to make a special trip out to the *estancia* for me. Tell him I will come into Ranchos at *any* hour of the day or night that he will hear it. Do not fail me, Porfirio. *¡Por favor!"*

"Porfirio will come for you himself on old Imelda there, Doña Ana." He pointed to a small, stone-gray burro grazing fifteen feet away in a patch of goathead weeds. *"Lo prometo."*

Wonderful old man! To ride that tired-looking little animal the sixteen or seventeen kilometers to the *estancia* at his age, possibly in the dark of night, and for the daughter of a proud, overbearing man who probably had never so much as spoken to him once. *"Muchas gracias, viejo."*

"De nada, mi doña. Your mother, may she rest in peace, did many kindnesses for Porfirio in her time."

¡Mamá, sí! What kind of daughter had she become? A long time had passed since she prayed for Mamá's soul. Before she left the church today she had better light another candle for the woman who had died giving birth to her. Pray for Mamá's soul, and pray, too, that history did not repeat itself. . . .

30
Storm and Silence

By Friday evening there had been no word yet from Padre Martínez, and no sight of Porfirio and his burro on the white road leading from the gate.

Her talk with Galinda this morning had reassured her some, until she remembered the *dueña*'s remarks about Luis's right to come to her bed now that she had married him. The confession was assuming more importance for her by the minute. The thought of moving to Ranchos and having the baby there crossed her mind. She would not even have to consult Papá; he had left this morning to "see some men" in Rayado, and would not be back until sometime Sunday afternoon or Monday morning. Perhaps she would make the move tomorrow.

She retired early, exhausted, but found she could not sleep. Since childhood she had always slept on her stomach, but in this last month she had found herself seeking sleep curled up on her side more often than not. She settled in that way now. It eased the heavy fullness of the child inside her a little, but not entirely. In this last month she had become a human cocoon whose only purpose on this earth was to give birth to this baby. He was part of her, but separate, too, and already making demands with his kicks and stirrings.

What would they call him? They? She would have to make that decision on her own. Padre Martínez would insist that a name be chosen before the christening, and it now seemed all hope had fled that Bradford would be back before that happened. Josefa had not had recent word from Don Cristóbal, either. Papá would absolutely forbid her to name him after Bradford. The baby's last name, of course, would be Aragón, and there was something to be said for letting Luis pick a Christian name for him, as a sort of reward for his generous self-sacrifice.

She finally fell into a sleep where dreams found her.

2

"Wake up, wake up, *por favor,* Doña Ana!" Galinda's brown hand felt almost rudely insistent on her shoulder. She had already lighted and turned up the oil lamp. "That old *jardinero* Porfirio from the big church in Ranchos is here. He says the padre is back from Embudo and will see you now, tonight. Get dressed, *querida,* while I get Roberto up and have him hitch the carriage. We will wait for you under the *portal*. But perhaps you wish Galinda to send him away. This is no hour to travel."

"No, no, Galinda. I will see him."

She had not once mentioned to Galinda her intent to make confession before the baby came. But the urgency in the *dueña*'s voice and the determined firmness of her hands told Ana the old woman knew all about it, and how important it was to her. A glance also told her Galinda had laid out her clothes. She must have done that while Ana still slept, but right after Porfirio lifted the knocker on the great, carved door of the *hacienda*. Ana smiled. She knew the Navajo woman would claim it as still another proof of her "second sight."

Ana dressed, trying to recall the dream the *dueña* had interrupted. Nothing came, except the feeling that the dream had been a bad one, and she had better forget about it, keep her mind firmly on the confession she would make when she reached San Francisco de Asis and the padre. But perhaps the dream and the confession were essentially the same. *¿Quién sabe?*

At the door to the *portal* she found Galinda holding a lantern whose yellow beams bathed the kindly face of old Porfirio. In moments she heard the rattle of the carriage. Thank God she had these good friends and servants to help her.

Instead of the carriage she expected, Roberto had brought around one of the light wagons, hitched to a team of mules.

"I am sorry, *mi doña*," the *mayordomo* said. "Tibo has taken the good carriage apart for repairs."

"It doesn't matter, Roberto." Actually, it did matter. She knew this small wagon well; it was the one she and Galinda had taken to La Cayuda to meet Bradford that night. A crude affair with no springs, it was little more than a *carreta*, a narrow box on wheels, and it rode like a miner's cart. It would jolt and jar her all the way to Ranchos, hardly a journey she should be making in her condition.

Galinda looked consumed by massive doubts, too, but she helped Ana toward the wagon. "You will ride in the wagon bed, *mi niña,* where you can lie down. Galinda will go into the *hacienda* and bring out a featherbed, pillows, and some blankets. If only this *estúpido* Roberto had told her about the broken carriage, she would have had them here already."

"I will not need them, *vieja.* It is a warm night."

"They are not for warmth. This ride will be hard on you and the baby, but we can pad that hard wagon bed."

"All right, all right! Go and get them, but hurry. As it is we will keep the padre waiting longer than I want to."

Galinda started for the door, turned back. "You should not be doing this, Doña Ana. You are too close to—"

"I *must* do it." Ana broke in.

"But if you begin—"

"*¡Basta, Galinda!* Go! Or we will leave without you."

3

At last Galinda settled her in the bed of the wagon. Ana lay on a thick pile of *colchas* and blankets, with four pillows jammed in at her sides and two more beneath her head. The narrow wagon with its high wooden sides only permitted her to look straight up at a field of stars. Held in tightly by the blankets, robes, and pillows Galinda had wedged around her to keep her from rolling, and to ease her through the bumps and bounces that were sure to come, she felt as if she were lying in a coffin. Even as tightly bundled as she was, she shuddered.

Galinda climbed in at the rear of the wagon and took a seat.

"Where did you find all this bedding? I do not recognize any of it."

"From the *recámara de su madre,*" Galinda said.

"My mother's bedroom? Why?"

"It is the bedchamber closest to *el portal,* as you know, *mi doña.* And you were in a hurry."

"Is it . . . ?"

"*Sí, querida.* By the orders of Don Bernardo her room has not been touched since . . ." She stopped, remained silent for a moment. "I had to strip the bed itself to find enough."

What courage Galinda had shown in defying Papá's orders about Mamá's bedroom. "My mother died in these robes and blankets, is that not so?"

"*¡Sí!* But *por favor,* remember that you were born in them."

All she could do was gaze up at the stars. She thought she found the one Papá had called Sirius, the Dog Star, on one of the early trips to Cañon de Chelly.

"Are we ready, *señoras?*" Roberto asked from the driver's seat.

"*Sí, Roberto,*" Galinda said. "Drive with great care, *viejo!* If anything should happen to *mi doña* or her baby, Galinda will have your heart for *almuerzo!*"

"*¡Vamonos!*" the old *mayordomo* cried out as he cracked his whip. If mules can be said to leap, this pair leaped. The driver-side mule trumpeted his displeasure.

Galinda screamed. "*¡Bufón!* Take care!"

With the mule's braying and Galinda's scream, no one heard Ana's faint cry at the first hard, clamping grip of pain.

She gathered the edge of a quilt, pushed it into her mouth, and bit down hard. If the pain came again Galinda must not hear the cry it provoked, no matter how faint. The tough old Navajo woman was in full cry of command, and neither Porfirio nor Roberto or the two of them together could stop her from returning Ana to her room if she thought labor was under way.

She had to get to Ranchos and make that confession. Her life—in this world and the next—turned on it. Besides, there was a chance that she had not begun her labor. Ignacia Bent had said she had gone into false labor with two of her pregnancies. It made up a good part of the horror story Cousin Ignacia had told repeatedly the last three months.

If Ana were to get to Ranchos and make her confession before things got critical, she would have to muffle any outcry, any moan or groan, no matter if the pain threatened to cut her in two.

Almost twenty minutes, at a guess, passed before the next pain came, and although it was sharper and deeper—like the cramps she sometimes got when her monthly time came, only much, much worse—she somehow managed to keep from uttering a sound. If she remembered what Cousin Ignacia had said—this at least validated by Galinda—the *espasmos* would have to come at much smaller intervals than that before things began to happen.

Above her head the stars winked out as a high cloud moved under them.

Nine kilometers stretched between the *hacienda* and the gate, and they would have to travel still another eight before they reached San Francisco. At the rate they were going it would be the better part of two hours before they got there. Dawn. The worst of it was that with her pendant watch left behind when she dressed in such haste she had no way of telling how many minutes elapsed between the pains. Roberto carried a watch in his vest pocket, but if she kept asking the *mayordomo* for the time, Galinda was sure to guess what was going on.

Then, in a sudden drowning rush, her water came. The flesh of her inner thighs shrank from it, and it flooded between her legs. It soaked the bedding, and for an instant she feared it might reach Galinda where she sat, but her fears subsided when the Navajo woman did not so much as look at her.

The pains began again, and even without a watch she knew that her *contracciones* were coming considerably less than ten minutes apart. In a dark distortion of time they came right on top of each other, and yet with an eternity between them.

Do not let it rain, por favor, Dios, *do not let it rain.*

She could not hold back a small, bitter laugh.

"*¿Qué pasa, querida?*" Galinda asked.

"*Es nada, vieja, nada.*" She could not tell the *dueña* of the image which had just appeared in her mind's eye: the confessional with the padre pressing his ear against the grille as he tried to listen to a bedraggled, rain-soaked woman moaning and groaning and thrashing about in the throes of labor, and all the while mumbling some gibberish about her sins. Under those circumstances, would she be able to confess? The padre, even could he comprehend her frenzied, blurted words, would never absolve her of anything if she actually gave birth in his confessional.

Then came a convulsion so vicious she could not hide it, could not muffle the scream.

"*¿Qué pasa?*" Galinda called. Ana felt the *dueña* begin to crawl forward in the wagon bed, felt her hand touch the soaked bedding below her waist and then withdraw. "*¡Su agua!* Your water has broken, *niña!* When?"

Ana shook her head. "I do not really know."

"When the pains came that you have hidden from Galinda?"

"Before that."

"The *contracciones*—they are coming close together, no?"

"*Sí.* Two or three minutes apart perhaps."

Rain began to fall, only a drizzle at first, but with the sure promise of a coming torrent.

"We cannot go on," Galinda said.

"We must!" Ana drew a breath. "I order it!" She sounded just like Papá, and hated herself for it.

"Galinda cannot obey, *querida*. She is truly sorry. Dawn tried to break a moment ago and then the sky in the east turned black again. The storm has surely reached Ranchos de Taos by now. The arroyo will be running full. We could never cross it before the baby came."

She wanted to make one last fight, but knew in her heart fate had already defeated her.

"Where are we?"

"Half a kilometer from the graveyard of *su familia*. There is an old *jacal* there. It is not much, hardly more than a leaky hut of sticks and branches, but it will give us a little shelter against the rain. Galinda thinks you will have your baby there. There will be no time to return to the *hacienda*."

For the first time in all the years Galinda had cared for her, Ana Barragán heard fear in the Navajo woman's voice, dark fear—and something close to panic.

She made no argument as the *dueña* gave Roberto his new instructions.

In ten minutes or so Roberto turned the mule team onto the narrow sagebrush-lined trace leading to the graveyard, and although she could not see it from the depth of her "coffin," she knew in her heart the moment they passed Mamá's grave.

Some probably long-dead Barragán servant had erected the *jacal* at the far side of the *cemetario* and Roberto had a difficult time guiding the wagon, small as it was, through the grave markers and the sage.

By the time Galinda helped her from the wagon bed, pulled the soaked bedding after them, and laid her down on top of it under the dripping roof of the hut, old Porfirio had caught up with them with his burro and his lantern. Galinda took the lantern from him and set it down by Ana's side.

"*Perdoname, mi doña*," she said, "but now Galinda must have a look to see if he is ready to be born."

The drenching rain beat heavily on the roof of the *jacal*, as if it were trying to hammer flat her very soul.

Galinda whispered, "We have work to do, Doña Ana."

She had failed. Her perception about the need for the confession might be only that, a perception, but . . .

. . . it would be better for all of them, Bradford too, if she were to die, now that she could not make it.

"Bradford!" she called out. None of the other three gave the slightest sign that they had heard her.

The sky broke open now. She felt as if the torrent might wash the *jacal*, the wagon, Porfirio's burro, the mules, and all of them away.

31

City of the Angels

Los Angeles
August 1846

The luck of John C. Frémont continued to hold, held so well, in fact, that even Brad Stone began to think it might not be luck at all, but a manifestation of some mystic, unwitting, unconscious genius. From the very beginning, even before the Bear Flag Revolt began, Frémont and his band of mountaineers and adventurers had seemed to be in the right place at the right time—at least for what Stone presumed to be Major Johnny's purposes.

Except for the disaster at Klamath Lake, everything for the Pathfinder had gone as if he had planned it to the last small detail. Of course, with the frantic, spur-of-the-moment moves and marches they had made since crossing the Sierras last fall, they had been in so many places, and at such different times, that the odds favored something good happening somewhere along the line.

The trip down the California coast from Monterey to San Diego, and now back up to Los Angeles, had been a repetition of sorts of everything else they had done, with only some minor "variations on a theme" to set it apart from the other journeys. Even a determined enemy—and Stone had not yet persuaded himself there *were* any—would have been hard put to even find Frémont, when at times during the last six months he hardly seemed to know where he was himself.

One of the "variations" had been the voyage south aboard Commodore Robert Stockton's warship, the *Cyane*.

2

Small storms plagued them from the moment they sailed out of Monterey's priceless harbor into the moaning swells and surly, snapping whitecaps of the Pacific. The result was that most of the mountain men, Kit among them, fell prey to a siege of seasickness that laid them low the entire time at sea, except when they dragged themselves to the gunwales. The scout—who suffered perhaps more than anyone else on board—swore he would never set foot on an oceangoing vessel again.

"Not even if my life depended on it. I'd rather ride a cross-eyed, lamed-up mule clear across the Rockies. I ain't going out in any water deeper than the Big Muddy ever again. You got my word on that, *amigo*."

Brad Stone escaped his shipmates' ordeal. Perhaps his Harvard College weekend in the schooner off Martha's Vineyard facing a genuine Atlantic storm had toughened

him. Although filled with sympathy for pale, retching Kit, it
secretly pleased him to be able to take care of *him* for a
change, insofar as the scout would let him. He ferried bowls
of watery barley soup to him, and for two days the thin liquid was all Kit could keep down, and that only after a number of abortive tries. He lay curled up on deck beside a
vacant gunport where he only had to lift his head a few agonizing inches to vomit into the ocean.

The *Cyane*'s old-salt crew, and most of the fifty U.S.
Marines who boarded with the mountain men and the settlers at Monterey, seemed as impervious as Stone to the nausea attacking the men of the Battalion. They poked a good
deal of cruel fun at the sufferers who lined the rails at the
leeward side of the *Cyane,* gagging and heaving until Stone
feared the poor devils might lose their entrails.

All through the voyage, Frémont—who like Stone, the
ship's crew, and the marines, had gone unaffected by the virtual epidemic of mal de mer—appeared in the midst of all
this misery superbly elated, the "conquering hero" in every
respect. He dined with Commodore Stockton and his ships'
officers every night. Stockton apologized to the staff of the
Battalion that he could not include them in the dinners for
lack of space, but it certainly made little difference to poor,
suffering Kit.

With Carson and two or three others of the "old guard,"
such as Dick Owens and Gus Archambeault, laid up and
wasted, the Pathfinder called no meetings of his own.

Even before they docked at San Diego, and the bedraggled, smelly Battalion staggered down the gangplank,
Stockton had already emerged as the principal figure and
guiding force in whatever struggle remained for the complete control and pacification of California. He seemed to
have eclipsed Commodore Sloat totally. No one mourned
"Snail" Sloat's passing from the scene. Stockton was a
genial, vigorous Irish-American with a penchant for swift

action lacking in his predecessor, and whose only fault in Stone's eyes was that he was even more given to flamboyance and rhetorical bombast than was Frémont.

Rumors, not just among the mountain men, but among the crew and officers of the *Cyane,* flew like loose chaff above a heaving threshing floor: Stockton would replace Sloat as commander-in-chief of all the West Coast operations, not just the naval ones. He would form a new civil government and possibly serve in it himself, at its head, of course. He would shortly leave the province, make rendezvous with a new American army already on the high seas and well around the Horn into the Pacific and on its way to join in the war against Mexico, and take it ashore at Mazatlán or Acapulco with an eye to attacking the Mexican capital from the west. It sounded wonderfully heroic and daring, just Stockton's cup of tea, but even some of the commodore's closest lieutenants, while wistfully hoping it might happen, scoffed at that last idea.

Stockton did call one meeting of not only his own officers, but including the commanders of the marine detachment and those few of the Battalion such as Frémont, Stone, and Alexis Godey who were not completely *hors de combat.*

"This is the plan for the next few weeks, gentlemen. Our spies in Los Angeles tell us that General Castro has assembled a formidable army, perhaps five hundred men, lancers and infantry, and with as many as eight pieces of field artillery. The *Cyane* will land Major Frémont's Battalion and the marine unit at San Diego and return to Monterey to bring down the reinforcements the navy is recruiting and training there. Lieutenant Archibald Gillespie of the U.S. Marine Corps, with whom many of you are acquainted, will command this new force. He will by then hold the rank of captain—"

"There'll be no living with the little bastard!" Alexis

Godey cried. Frémont's look of rebuke at the St. Louisan was incendiary, but Stockton merely smiled before going on.

"We should be able to get Captain Gillespie and his men ashore at a harbor called San Pedro just a few miles south of Los Angeles by the time you reach that point on your northward march. Castro will have his scouts watching you, and you alone, from the time you start out from San Diego, and we feel we can get the new military units in position without their presence being detected until it is too late for the general to change his battle plan or rally more men to his side. We will be outnumbered slightly at the outset, but we think the quality of our troops and arms to be far superior to those of the Mexicans'."

"My men will be up to it, I assure you, Commodore," Frémont interjected.

"I have every confidence, sir," Stockton said. "When you, Major Frémont, and Captain Gillespie join forces at San Pedro you will move immediately to the attack on Los Angeles."

Gillespie must be beside himself with joy back in Monterey, and fairly quivering in his eagerness to get into action, Stone thought. The proposed attack on an enemy city with legitimate defenders would give him a chance to redeem himself after the farcical "victory" at Castillo de San Joaquín. Actually, a few chuckles at Stockton's first mention of the marine's name had come from the mountain men who had walked up the slope behind the saber-wielding young officer that comic day.

Stone decided Stockton's battle plan was sound, worthy of a Napoleon—or a Kit Carson. He chuckled; one would think he had now become a strategist himself. Everyone began to think like that when they were around the military too long.

3

Once ashore at San Diego, and with the Battalion moved far enough inland for a temporary bivouac, Stone returned to the waterfront to meet each arriving supply vessel, seeking in vain for a letter from Ana. Was one even now arriving at Monterey? If so, perhaps Gillespie would bring it with him to San Pedro. The marine had been very good about forwarding mail when stationed at Yerba Buena, and when the expedition was still in camp at Oak Bend or Sonoma. Kit had not received word from Josefa in some time, either, and none arrived on any of the packet ships putting in at San Diego's wharf.

But stacks of newspapers, dispatches, and intelligence reports addressed to Stockton did come down from navy headquarters in Monterey. The commodore proved generous with the newspapers, and it delighted Stone when Frémont passed along a dog-eared copy of *The New York Times*. He found he was occupying a ringside seat at some of the most portentous, dramatic events in his country's history since 1812, in a few of which he had played a minor role himself.

Zachary Taylor had pressed the war deep into Mexico. The capital of the state of Nuevo León had fallen to American arms, and Old Rough and Ready was now pushing on to Coahuila's capital, Saltillo. President James Polk had appointed Winfield Scott the commanding general for the entire war effort in Mexico. In what Stone thought a lamentable breach of security, the first American newspaper he had seen since leaving Independence on the way west last year announced Scott's strategy. The American general had made it no secret that he intended to land a large army at Vera Cruz and strike straight for the heart of Mexico while

Taylor was driving down from the north through the center of the country.

Stone picked a secluded spot well away from the main encampment and read the *Times* articles to Kit. Frémont and the mountain men knew Carson could not read, but Stone wanted to spare the scout any embarrassment in revealing it to Stockton or the naval and marine officers who had come ashore with them.

Stone discovered as he read to Kit that Frémont and his men had not been working in the total vacuum he had thought as they made the great trek from Bent's to Sutter's, to Monterey, San Diego, and now here to the City of the Angels. The East, almost forgotten for more than a year, had watched every step of their journey with fascination.

The paper devoted a lot of space to "Brevet Captain John C. Frémont's Conquest of Northern California," and although both Stone and the scout shook with mirth at a story headlined "Intrepid Engineer Officer Storms and Captures Formidable Enemy Castle of San Joaquín, a Tale of Daring," both of them confessed to their pride that the Pathfinder was finding himself almost buried under an avalanche of journalistic praise and attention. As Ed Kern might have said— "He's a bastard, but he's *our* bastard!" At that it was no "confession" on the part of Kit. As much as the tragic disturbances at Pilot Peak and San Rafael must have wracked Carson's soul, he never wavered in his affection for, and at least myopic if not utterly blind loyalty to "the captain."*

One tiny thing amused both of them. The story about Castillo de San Joaquín placed the ruined fortress "a few miles from the seaport of San Francisco, formerly Yerba Buena, a minor appendage on the California commercial structure centered in Monterey." The story ran on for a few more lines. "Losing its castle will probably cost this obscure, infant 'City of San Francisco' whatever importance it might ultimately have had."

"Don't that beat all hell?" Carson said. "Didn't you tell me once that the captain told the villagers they ought to change Yerba Buena's name?"

"He virtually insisted on it."

The biggest news for the two, however, came on the second page. A general named Stephen Watts Kearny had made a tough, forced march across the grueling prairie trail from Fort Leavenworth to Bent's Fort, then down over Raton Pass to Santa Fe with the newly formed Army of the West— composed in part of the famed First Dragoons. The reason the story had been relegated to the second page soon became obvious. There had been no actual fighting when Kearny's army reached the capital of New Mexico, nothing to titillate the *Times'* readers in the way the supposed martial triumphs of Frémont in California had. Kearny had conquered New Mexico without his dragoons lowering a lance and without his foot soldiers firing a shot or fixing a bayonet.

A box next to the news story enclosed a copy of the proclamation Kearny had read to the Mexican populace in the plaza of Santa Fe the day after his troops took possession of the city.

The pronouncement sounded warm and surprisingly conciliatory for one delivered to a "conquered" people. It promised to extend the democratic rule of law over the territory, and pledged the honor of the United States of America that there would be no intrusion into the indigenous culture. The document included an especially emphasized guarantee of freedom of religion. The story went on to state that as soon as a civilian government had been put in place, General Kearny would march the Army of the West to California to join in the war against Mexico. It ended with a list of appointees to that new government, and it surprised Stone to find a number of Spanish surnames on the list.

"Smart move on Kearny's part," Kit said. The name of the new governor replacing Don Manuel Armijo was a familiar one and at first even more surprising: Charles Bent of Taos. Kit went on. "That's even smarter."

Other than that, the article made no mention of Taos, but Stone knew as he read aloud to Kit that the tiny village near the great gorge of the Río del Norte loomed uppermost in his friend's mind—as it did in his.

Sure enough, Kit interrupted Stone's reading. "Wish we'd hear from the folk in Taos . . . now in particular," he said. "Although I figure maybe the 'no news' you just read me is good news. Whatever we get straight from Josefa and Ana will be at least two, maybe three months old, anyway. From long before Kearny reached Santa Fe. By the way, I know Kearny."

"How?"

"The captain and me bumped into him a couple of times at army cantonments in the High Plains. I got the idea he don't care much for our leader. If he reads these stories, he'll like him even less. Maybe he's changed. That speech in Santa Fe don't sound much like the man I met. He's a hard, tough soldier. All spit-and-polish and by the book. Sees everything in black and white, and that's made him some enemies. Got to admit he done one or two things right this time, though."

"And they are?" Stone asked.

"Number one: he didn't come down into New Mexico spoiling for a fight. And Don Manuel's running like the weasel he is don't surprise me one little bit. But the smartest thing Kearny's done was appointing Charlie governor, but only if he listens to him."

"About what in particular?"

"Well . . . from what this newspaper fellow said"—he pointed at the *Times*—"it looks like the Nuevo Méjicanos welcomed Kearny with open arms. With most of them it's probably true. They ain't been happy with Mexico City for a long time, same as we found the Mexicans here in California, and they'd already been trading with the United States for a hell of a while."

"The main thing is that Taos seems safe enough," Stone said.

"Yes. Folk in Taos won't cause no trouble. They figure they know Americans and that we ain't all animals. Sometimes I think money binds people even tighter than laws or blood. In the main they like us, all right, but there's always a few around like Don Bernardo Barragán who will always hate our guts, no matter how we behave. Hope I ain't stepping on your toes by talking like this about the man you want for a father-in-law. You knew I doped that out, didn't you? Or are you trying to keep it a secret?"

Stone laughed. "No, no secret, Kit. Not anymore, and least of all from you. I think maybe you 'doped that out' even before I did, when we first got to Taos."

Kit resumed. "Don Bernardo feels about Mexico the same way the captain does about the United States, maybe even a mite stronger. And there're a hell of a lot more firebrands like him in the hills and *llanos* around Taos. They could cause a lot of trouble. Unlike the folk in town, most of *them* got a number of people working for them, damned good men who know how to handle rifles. They're as proud and cantankerous as Don Bernardo."

"I thought you said the Taos people wouldn't cause any trouble for Kearny."

"I did. And in the main I believe it, but I like to consider everything. Charlie Bent knows who the troublemakers are, but being an appointed governor of a military territory ain't like getting elected back in Illinois. Charlie will have to follow whatever orders Kearny gives him, but if Kearny's gotten as smart as it sounds from what you read me, he'll let his new governor call most of the shots, at least those that have to be fired in *our* part of the country, north of Santa Fe."

Stone noted the slight emphasis on "our." It pleased him,

and he would have said something, but Carson was continuing. "If I was Kearny, I wouldn't be in no hurry to leave Santa Fe with my army, either. Charlie may need some guns behind him until he settles in and starts up a militia or something like a police force of his own."

Stone's stomach tightened.

Kit Carson was no garden-variety alarmist.

But Kit's wish that they would hear from Taos left Brad Stone twisting in another agony of longing.

4

Frémont and the battalion met the three well-equipped companies Stockton disgorged on the waterfront at San Pedro, together with Captain Archibald Gillespie. The marine sparked with such energy he seemed capable of setting everyone he talked to on fire, as they began the last leg of the march on Pueblo de Los Angeles.

Gillespie's sparks were quenched with hardly a sizzle when one of Stockton's agents in the city met them on the road with news: General Castro had abandoned all his defensive positions in the city and had dispersed his army into the hills behind it. There would be no battle. The marine looked so crestfallen Stone felt tempted to ask Frémont to let the poor devil have a battery of mountain guns and fire off a barrage or two.

Somehow Frémont had found twenty-two brass and string musicians to form a band to lead them into the city. Except that there were far more men under his command this time, the Pathfinder's grand advance became exactly the same tatterdemalion parade as his entrance at Sonoma and again at Monterey.

At this stage of their acquaintance, Stone almost whistled his admiration for "Captain Johnny" as they rode to the city's plaza between ranks of smiling, but wary, Californios.

The conquest of California now seemed complete, and Frémont could rightly be called "the Conqueror."

Old Glory flew from flagstaffs as far apart as Sutter's Fort in the north and San Diego at the very southern end of the province. Except for a score or so isolated Indian villages, every inch of California soil had become American. The navy ruled every Pacific wave from the mouth of the Columbia to the beach at Mazatlán, and its ships dipped their colors to no one but Admiral Sir George Seymour aboard the *Collingwood,* and that only in a courteous, if faintly contemptuous "tip of the hat" whenever Sir George put into Monterey for supplies. The British admiral was said to have actually fired a seven-gun salute for Commodore Sloat when he sailed off to the obscurity of retirement.

Certainly the support former Brevet Captain Frémont received from other Americans had been important, but it had not been vital.

Leading at the most sixty largely undisciplined mountain men, Frémont had added to his country's sovereign territory an incomparably rich and breathtakingly beautiful land almost as large as the thirteen original colonies. He had given his nation a frontage on the world's mightiest ocean, fulfilling his father-in-law's dream of "Manifest Destiny" well in advance of the time the senator had set for that fulfillment.

And all this without fighting a major battle, and with the loss of less than a score of Californio and American lives.

No one thought to count the nearly two hundred former mission Indians who died in their villages along the northern riverbanks.

5

Stockton, if not precisely a genius at organization, proved a whirlwind of official activity as he set the governance of California in order.

Within a week he issued proclamations putting California from top to bottom under martial law. He divided the territory into three military districts, the most southern stretching from Santa Barbara to Old Mexico under the command of Archibald Gillespie, now suddenly a major after basking in·the warmth of his captaincy a mere two weeks.

Stockton himself retained command of the middle district—all the land from Santa Barbara north to Yerba Buena, the forlorn seaport newly christened San Francisco.

After making Frémont a colonel for a second—and now more official—time, Stockton assigned him the highest military post in the northern district, a command that stretched from San Francisco to the Oregon border. At a staff meeting in the office he had commandeered in the *ayuntamiento,* Los Angeles's graceful Spanish-style city hall, he announced the Pathfinder's promotion and new assignment. Stone saw the grim look on the face of the brand-new colonel and could guess the reason for it. Stockton apparently had come to an identical conclusion.

"Don't be put out, Colonel Frémont. I know you have no wish to be posted so far from what you correctly see as the center of things. You will not be in exile in the north very long. When I am back at sea, and, I hope, on my way to Mexico, you will become governor of the entire United States Territory of California, with the power to decide where the seat of your government will be."

As he listened to the cheers and applause that greeted Stockton's words, even Stone thought the promised appointment somehow fitting, and with his own quiet smile, and a nod he could not stop, he must have shown it, at least to Kit. The scout smiled back at him, perhaps pleased that Stone seemed to be becoming more of a Frémont man every day.

6

The next morning Frémont sent word that he wanted to see Stone in his own office, next door to Stockton's.

When Stone entered, he found Frémont at his desk with Kit sitting across from him.

"Ah, Bradford, my boy. Sit down, sit down. We have a few odds and ends to clean up before Kit leaves for the East." Frémont must have seen the perplexed look on Stone's face. He hurried on. "But of course! You have not yet heard that I am sending Captain Carson to Washington." He paused, obviously waiting for the effect he intended with his news. "He will be carrying important dispatches, articles for publication, letters to my wife and her father, and special reports solely for the eyes of President Polk from the commodore and me." At that last, Stone's eyes did widen. Frémont smiled his satisfaction. "There are some sections of *my* report to the president on which I would like your signature. I've marked them lightly in pencil to permit erasure. Look them over, please, while Kit and I finish planning his trip." He pushed a leather case across the desk.

Stone pulled a sheaf of loose papers from the case. They looked to be the same sort of documents he had validated when the *Portsmouth* took the Battalion back to Sausalito after the "fall" of Castillo de San Joaquín, and for a moment it irritated him. Ed Kern's voice seemed to whisper in his ear, *"He's using you again."* But he figured he might as well sign the damned things and get it over with.

He was happy for Kit. The scout's mission to the nation's

capital would be the sort of trip most western Americans could only dream about.

He leafed through the pages and found the half dozen on which Frémont wanted his signature. He sighed. It was not as if these fictions would cause any great harm to anyone. As he signed them, he could not help listening to Frémont and Kit.

". . . no more than fifteen men," Frémont was saying. "All the livestock, weapons, ammunition, and provender you think you'll need, of course."

"Fifteen men?" Kit asked.

"Fifteen should do it. Any of them you want except Captain Owens, Lieutenant Godey, Segundai, and Sergeant Gus Archambeault. Even with the worst of the war here in California probably in the past, I want most of my most capable fighting men, except you, of course, with me."

"Can I have Lucy Maxwell? We might need an experienced scout if anything happens to me. A tracker, too. Swanok, maybe?"

"Yes, take Sergeant Maxwell and the Delaware. Now, about your route. Going north to Sutter's before you cross the Sierras is clearly out of the question. I think you ought to strike out on whatever acceptable southern trail you find, straight across the Colorado."

"Pretty dry, hot country across the Colorado, Captain. I ain't been there myself, but old Southwest hands have told me it can be pure misery."

"I know. It will be a hellish journey, but you've never shied from that sort of thing. I wouldn't even suggest it, but it's a lot shorter than the Santa Fe Trail. After you reach Socorro in New Mexico use your own judgment, but crossing Texas on a straight west-to-east line looks to be the best route to me. We do need up-to-date information on the southern route, anyway."

There came a long silence before Kit spoke again. "Begging your pardon, sir, but do you have any objection if instead of going through Texas I turn north at Socorro and take the Cimarron Cutoff from Santa Fe? I got a hunch I'll reach the railroad quicker by going east through Kansas than through Texas. Easier to find remounts that way, too, if I need them, and I expect I will. And last time I heard, near six months ago, they'd already laid railroad track halfway across Missouri. They may be almost to Independence now." He paused before going on. "Got to be honest with you, Captain, if I go through Missouri I'd get to see my daughter Adaline. She's in school there. I guess you already knew that."

Frémont tipped his head back and snorted laughter. "No one but me knows how clever you can be, Kit. I do believe you want to see your daughter, and yes I did remember her. But if you go through Santa Fe to the cutoff, it also means you can make a quick side trip up to Taos, and rejoin your men well before they reach Council Grove, doesn't it? I don't suppose they would even miss you."

"The captain sure remembers the lay of the land, all right. Yes, sir. I did have something like that in mind."

"And you will consequently be able to spend a couple of days with Mrs. Carson, is that not so?"

"You sure can read me like a book, Captain."

"Even after all these years it's still a fascinating text, Kit. Go east the way you best see fit, then. Keep this dispatch case by your side every moment. Sleep with it. You don't have to actually padlock it to your wrist, of course, until you reach what for some reason I cannot fathom is called 'civilization.' Does Taos answer that description? I would never demand that you greet Mrs. Carson chained to a leather bag. Give her my best."

Stone looked at two supremely happy men. He wished he could share their delight.

Then a wild hope—why had it taken so long in coming? He knew suddenly that he had to make this ride with Kit.

A journey twenty times as long and a hundred times as "hellish," as Frémont had pictured it would be worth it for two days with Ana.

But damn it! He could not ask. He should swallow his pride, blurt out a plea, go to his knees if necessary. He could not.

He had begun to fit the letters and reports back into the case when Kit spoke again.

"Captain . . . ," he said, "could you see your way clear to letting Brad Stone here tag along with me?"

God bless Kit! He should have known the scout would read his mind. More to the point, he should have known he would not let him down!

Frémont looked at him and then back at Kit. "I'm afraid not. I will need Lieutenant Stone's administrative skills here in California more than ever in the weeks and months ahead."

So much for that wild hope.

But he had forgotten that Kit could exhibit a stubborn persistence to match Frémont's. "No offense, sir," the scout said next, "but them same skills you just now mentioned could come in mighty handy for *me*. You know I can't read or write. I'll look a plumb fool in Washington trying to deal with all those school-learned politicians and the president of the United States himself if . . ."

Frémont held up his hand.

Stone held his breath.

"I'm still reading you quite well, Captain Carson," Frémont said. "I'm not even having trouble with the fine print I detect. Does it surprise you to learn that I know of Lieutenant Stone's romantic involvement with some young lady in your neighborhood? I've been told she is a cousin to Mrs. Carson. While I am in sympathy with his quite natural, human desires, I cannot permit him to play fast and loose with his duties in the governing of this territory to indulge in the calls of love. . . ."

Stone fastened the clasp on the case. It snapped shut with sickening finality. A simple no from Frémont would have been quite enough.

"But . . . ," Frémont went on, ". . . it might be of some slight use to his government were he to, as you put it, Captain, 'tag along,' and do some of the work he originally signed on to do. We do need good new maps of the country you will travel through between here and Socorro, and with me engaged in my duties here and Captain Kern still up at Sutter's, Lieutenant Stone is the only cartographer available, should I decide . . ."

Here the Pathfinder indulged himself in another of his pet pregnant pauses. Stone did not let himself even *begin* to hope again.

"All right, Kit," Frémont said at last. "You can enroll Lieutenant Stone in your party. He can do some mapping, but he must remember at all times that your mission takes priority over any topographical work he may want to do, no matter how important it may seem. Now . . . when can you leave?"

"If we start getting things together right this minute," Carson said, "we can hit the trail to the east at first light. I'll set Lucy Maxwell to gathering the gear, supplies, and animals we'll need, while I start picking out my men."

Frémont turned to Stone. He favored him then with the winningest smile he had ever bestowed on him. "*Buena suerte,* Lieutenant Stone," he said. "The best of luck in everything. Give my regards to the lady at Taos and tell her I hope to meet her some day soon."

Brad Stone probably slept some that night, but it seemed as if he did not even close his eyes.

Ana!

7

"Time to catch up!"

There had been mornings in the past when Kit's familiar old wake-up cry, jolting Stone out of a pleasant dream into a freezing, gray dawn, had brought a foul-tempered growl. Not so today.

Of course, he had also known scores of mornings when the sun rose on his eager anticipation of the coming day in the mountains or the deserts. Once or twice he actually had broken into song back then, until Gus or Basil or Lucy Maxwell or Ed Kern had hooted him to silence. But he had never faced life with quite the buoyancy he felt as Kit and his team began the journey back to New Mexico. His nerves tingled and his step turned immeasurably springier. Even Lucy Maxwell's execrable coffee seemed like nectar.

Tenderfoot no longer, he had even gotten the diamond hitch on at least the first of his two mules as tight and right this morning as had any of the older hands.

Of course it was the prospect of seeing Ana Barragán that sent him bounding from his bedroll at Kit's awakening shout, but there was something more than that.

He would have been happy to get on the road again with his mountaineer friends even had Ana not been waiting for him at the end of it. This party resembled in many ways the smaller one of last fall that split off from Joe Walker, Ed Kern, Ted Talbot, and the main body of the expedition at Walker Lake and climbed the eastern foothills of the Sierras on its way to Sutter's. The only significant difference between the two teams was that Frémont himself did not lead this one.

Damned if he did not miss the Pathfinder, even on this first day out. He missed Godey, Owens, Archambeault, some few of the other mountain men, and the Delawares—silent, intelligent Segundai in particular—with whom he had ridden from Bent's. And he would miss marvelous old Basil Lajeunesse to the end of his days. But when he found himself peering constantly at the head of the column, he knew he was looking for the eagle feather that had bobbed and darted out in front of them for so many months.

He realized now how close the expedition had come in recent days to losing the special identity it had had when it spilled over the Sierras and crisscrossed California in that frenetic winter, spring, and early summer.

Picturesque and outlandish as Kit's friends—*his* now—had continued to appear, the sixty-odd former trappers, voyageurs, hunters, and scouts who had left the Arkansas last year had been almost swallowed whole when they reached the Monterey Peninsula. They had been absorbed by the other Americans they had been thrown together with, consumed by the great maw of officialdom as seen in men such as Gillespie, Stockton, and even Tom Larkin. They had still been wild, but in too many ways they no longer had been entirely free. By the time they rode into Monterey under the flag of the California Republic in the company of their new allies, the American settlers of the Napa and Sonoma Valleys, it had struck him that they had almost become fur-clad anachronisms. Even—and this weighed him down with a terrible sense of loss—even Kit. Yes, sadly, even Kit.

The feeling had grown stronger day by day once they reached Los Angeles.

Then it had vanished miraculously the moment Kit called out, *"Time to catch up!"* this morning, before they took the trail that would take them out of California at Las Agujas, which Americans had begun to call The Needles.

With every mile they put behind them they seemed to tack a page back on the calendar. They became the fabled mountain men again, brave, beastlike but all-too-human animals seeking the unknown. And he, Brad Stone, seemed well along a return path to the innocence he had known before the fight with the Comanches on the upper Cimarron.

He would never, of course, be able to retrace his steps along that path completely, would not want to. He wanted only to take it back as far as the sharp, breathtaking bend of the Río Grande del Norte that had first brought him to Ana Barragán.

32

Passage to Socorro

Three days out. Frémont had been absolutely right about the trip being a hellish one. The journey was already taking a toll on the party, experienced as they were; except for Kit, goaded along by his sense of mission, none of them had the lodestone Brad Stone had.

He would see Ana soon!

The last time he had crossed a desert of this magnitude had been when he had made that ride with Kit across the alkali flats between the Great Salt Lake and Pilot Peak. That journey had been accomplished entirely in the clamping cold of night. Although they did a great deal of riding by starlight this time, too, Carson kept them in the saddle until almost every noon, when they stopped to eat and then sleep until sundown, if the heat would let them. Some made makeshift tents from blankets and oilskins propped up with sticks and even rifles. Some, the Delaware Swanok for one, simply collapsed into heaps, and cooked in their own rank juices.

From the first day after passing through The Needles the sun beat down on this rock-hard desert almost audibly, a giant, glowing sledge that hammered them deep into their saddles, running burning sweat down into their eyes and soaking their shirts to the skin. It would not have surprised Stone if its rays suddenly raised blisters on their leather tack. Although their chests and backs were wringing wet, their mouths were still parched dry as emery cloth, their tongues as rough. The superheated air they breathed seared their gullets, leaving them aching for as little as a single drop of water. They hardly spoke; when they did they had to make an herculean effort not to reach for the canteens and water bottles.

The spans between springs and barely inch-deep sinks with scummy, greenish yellow edges dictated how many miles they made each day, sometimes as little as fifteen, often as many as fifty, and even eighty once. They rode out every evening fully aware of the danger they would face when the sun came up. Not one member of the party, not even Kit, had traversed this exact route ever before, and consequently no one had any knowledge of how far away the next water was. They found some every day, but to a man they knew the day could dawn when it could be miles beyond their reach. On such a day they would begin to die. No one talked about it.

They drowsed as they rode, all save Kit.

Whenever Stone forced open eyelids gummed shut by powdery sand drifting up from the hardpan, he saw the scout well out ahead of the column, rifle half out of the scabbard or cradled across his chest, his head moving slowly from side to side as he viewed through those remarkable eyes the distant low hills shimmering on the horizon. Impossible to believe that Kit's head never drooped from the exhaustion he surely must be sharing with the rest of them, but Stone never once caught him in any attitude but one of keen alertness.

Mirages. They came and went almost on the hour: trees; forests; maddeningly real gardens with tinkling fountains;

soft, seductive fields filled with grazing sheep; but most of all . . . lakes. No one else talked of them, if they saw them too. And he certainly talked to no one about the one all-too-realistic vision he knew to be peculiarly his own, when he saw Ana once, riding through the great gate of Estancia Barragán and beckoning to him. In his drowsy, semi-comatose state he almost set the spurs to his horse and took his quirt to it to chase after her.

2

At high noon on the fourth day after leaving California they met a party of almost twenty Mexican mule traders up from Chihuahua and heading for San Diego with a string of perhaps a hundred noisy animals in tow.

The Mexicans halted their caravan about a quarter mile away from the party's midday camp, and two men who appeared to be the leaders of this party rode to where the mountain men had already started a fire and were settling down to cook and eat.

Stone fidgeted as he thought about the outcome of this encounter. After all, Mexico and the United States had now gone to war. Could this turn out to be a tiny, unnoticed battle in that war? The thought must have occurred to the others in the Carson party, too; several of them checked their weapons carefully as the Mexicans rode up.

Kit gestured to the pair to dismount, and with wary smiles he and Lucy Maxwell engaged them in conversation.

Stone's Spanish had come along well the past few months, but he could catch no more than half of the rapid-fire exchange. Friendly as the talk seemed, Maxwell and Carson sat with their rifles in their laps, cocked. Through it all, the Mexicans' eyes wandered repeatedly to the cooking fire with eloquently hungry looks.

Carson and his men had scared up no game for more than two days, and the larder was running low. Nevertheless, when it turned out the Mexicans were in even worse shape for food than they were, Kit asked them to share the column's noonday meal of California jerky and soupy, almost tasteless cornmeal *atole*.

Beadle Jimson, a sour-faced, older mountain man whom Stone knew only by sight and name, had lagged a little behind the rest of them on the morning march, and he had now ridden up to where Carson, Stone, and Maxwell sat next to the two trader leaders, just in time to hear Kit make the offer.

"Goddamn it, Kit!" he roared. "We ain't got enough vittles to feed our own selves. I say *no!*"

"You can say it till you're blue in the face, Beadle," Kit said softly, "but that's the way it's going to be."

Jimson unlimbered his Hawken. Kit did not move his own weapon a millimeter, but he slid his finger inside the trigger guard.

"Please don't, Beadle," Kit said. "We knowed each other a long time, but you'll just plain have to die right where you are if you do something foolish. We're getting ready to ask help from these *hombres*." His voice was so low and level he could have been giving the bristling mountain man the time of day. Jimson must have seen where Carson had placed his trigger finger: he jammed his rifle back in the saddle scabbard, and with a smoldering glare, turned his horse and mule away.

Stone breathed easier.

Maxwell chuckled. "Don't get the idea Beadle was scared, Brad. He's just practical."

"Will he brood about this and try again?"

"Nah. This heat just got to him a little. He's had his say now. That's all he really wanted. It's kind of like when old Bass stopped me from doing something just as silly back at

Oak Bend that night when I started toward the captain's tent. I still thank Bass for that. Beadle there will come to thank Kit the same way when he thinks it over."

"Something you want to say, Brad?"

Stone had caught Carson's eye, and nodded toward the Mexicans. He had to take the chance their guests did not understand English. "Do these people know our countries are at war, Kit?"

"It came up, kind of. They said it don't make no never mind to them, and I believe them. I don't think they got the same notions about 'country' we got, Brad. They just live from one meal and one payday to the next. If they got any loyalties, they'll be to their villages and their families. Bet my last dollar not one of them could name the president of Mexico."

He turned to the mountain men who had crowded around them while all this was going on. "If any of the rest of you agree with Beadle Jimson, say so. But hear this first. We got us a fair trade going with these *amigos*. We maybe even got the best of it. Señor Gonzales sitting here next to me just told me about a rock spring that's fifteen, sixteen miles ahead of us, but two miles south of the course I meant to take. There ain't no *bosque* or brushwood to call our attention to it, and we would have missed it completely on the track I picked. If we *did* miss it, our *amigo* here says that going the way we were going, the next water is at least another twenty-five or thirty *leguas*, way more than a hundred miles American. I ain't real sure we would have made it with the water we got left."

"How the hell do we find it, then?" Maxwell said.

"After we eat, Señor Gonzales is going to help Brad here lay out a map. From the rock spring it will take us clear to the Gila River with a water hole every fifteen miles or so along the way. As for vittles, we'll just have to tighten our belts for a day or two. Gonzales says that although he ain't been up that way for a year or two, there's plenty of game once we hit Chiricahua country, and once we reach the Gila it's only a hop, skip, and jump to the Río Grande."

After the scanty meal ended, Stone worked with the Mexican Gonzales on a crude map, with Maxwell serving as an interpreter, a service it pleased him to find he only needed once. His Spanish *had* improved.

Before the traders got under way to the west again, Kit bought three mules from them to replace a trio of the party's own pack animals that seemed about ready to come down with the staggers. Most of the payment Carson made took the form of powder and balls. "Don't know how they figured on getting to the coast and back with so little ammunition," Kit said. "Times must be tough down Sonora way for them to risk their lives like this."

Stone tried to sleep after the Mexicans faded into the hazy western distance, but the ungodly weather had turned even hotter. He had draped a poncho between his transit tripod and his plane table and he now huddled under it and gazed out over the desert.

Under the circumstances, he and Señor Gonzales had created a fairly good map, one he could use in place of field notes to make a finished projection at some later date. The Mexican showed a surprising knowledge of the territory between where they were and Santa Fe. But drawing the map with the Mexican's help reminded him he had done no other mapping at all since they left Los Angeles, and he mentioned this to Kit when they saddled up again after the sun went down.

The scout reassured him. "You just *made* a map, Brad. As for any others you think you should have made, it ain't your fault, and don't fret about it. I don't actually think the captain was too serious about you doing a whole hell of a lot of map work, anyways."

"I guess you're right."

"It may not seem like it, but we're moving a lot faster than we did when we crossed the Sierras, or when we went north to Oregon. And with us riding out at sunset now you can't get far enough ahead of us early enough to take your sightings before dark sets in. Anyway, with the water situation what it is, I would kind of like you to stay close to camp."

Brad laughed. "Don't worry. I'm not about to go exploring on my own."

"It ain't no secret I don't really know this country," Kit said. "Any Indians we meet are going to be Apaches, and I rightly ain't sure just how they'll behave. By the way, I think you ought to leave your gear in Santa Fe before we go north to Taos and then push on to Washington. When we go back to California we'll come by way of Taos again and we'll probably be traveling a lot slower than we are now, you and I. Maybe you can do some mapping then."

On to Washington? Back to California? He had been so caught up with getting to Taos and Ana he had given no thought at all to what would happen after that. Two days with Ana would be far from enough time, but so would twenty or a thousand. Now he found he looked forward to watching his friend Carson cope with the unfamiliar world of the nation's capital. That this surprising little man could do it splendidly he had no doubt, but he could find himself at a disadvantage with some of the sophisticated politicians he would meet. Stone could help him there. He could be Carson's scout and guide through the nation's labyrinthine tunnels of power.

What had Kit said about the Mexican traders? *"I don't think they got the same notions about 'country' we got."*

When it came right down to it, he could only guess at Kit's notions about "country"; he could not even do that about his own. Whatever his America had been when he left Illinois a year and a half ago, it was a different country now. Something strange had happened to it when it reached the

Pacific Coast, and it had happened by the mere fact of reaching it.

All through his childhood, he and most other boys he knew had held fast to the dream of the "possible," the constant if unspoken promise that if everything did not go right where you were, the expanding and limitless West always beckoned. Now that Old Glory flew above the great headlands that looked down on San Francisco Bay, an outer limit had been reached. He consoled himself now that although there could be no further expansion, no one could impose *inner* limits on his country. Not while capable, dedicated, fearless men like Carson—and yes, even Frémont—served it the way they did.

When Jake Myers had put him on the train in Chicago, men of the stamp of Carson and Frémont were still opening the West. He did not know how historians would ultimately view what had happened in the past two years, but it seemed to Stone that he had been present at its closing. Ironically, it might have closed on the ridiculous day they hoisted the flag over the piles of dust and debris that had once been the Castillo de San Joaquín. It certainly had closed tightly when they completed the loop at Los Angeles. From now on, the settling of Brad Stone's America would be only backfill, if of a very complex order. It would require the devotion, strength, and courage of countless other men such as Kit Carson . . . and Colonel Johnny Frémont . . . and women, the long-suffering but always resourceful Yankee counterparts of Josefa Carson and Ana Barragán.

Every square inch of the land that mattered, and even some that seemed not to, such as this trackless, burning desert they were crossing now, would someday feel the possibly devastating imprint of the "civilization" he no longer trusted quite as completely as when he'd left it. Of course it was too far-fetched to think that *these* particular "*lone and level sands*" would ever feel the blade of a plow. Nothing would ever grow in this desolation but the cacti and the other tortured, thorny growth he looked at now.

Funny, the last time that Percy Shelley's sonnet "Ozymandias" had come to mind was when he'd first gazed at the awesome gate of Estancia Barragán. How many days would pass before he looked at that gate again, and would it still wear that clearly visible "*sneer of cold command*"?

He had to keep in mind that when he saw Ana again he would also be forced to deal with Don Bernardo.

3

The night following the meeting with the traders, they rode into high sandy country holding the strangest living things Brad Stone had ever seen.

When first sighted in full moonlight from two or three miles away, he had thought them something made of stone or wood, perhaps the artifacts of a long-extinct primitive people.

At a distance of half a mile he realized he was looking at some sort of titanic plant life, the same fantastic vegetation he had seen in the work of some turn-of-the-century artist whose name he could not recall. At the time, viewed in a sedate Boston gallery dedicated for the most part to portraiture, he had thought the monstrosities on the canvases entirely the figment of the painter's imagination.

He gawked as the column rode through them. In the light of the full moon their silver-and-olive-green corrugated trunks were as round and bare, and as tall and dead, as the telegraph poles near the railroad tracks in Chicago, but with branches that extended a foot or two away from the main upright growth before bending skyward again. It made some of them look as if they were abstract human figures holding their arms overhead at gunpoint.

"*Saguaro*," Kit said. "They're a kind of cactus. I ain't sure, but I don't think they grow anywheres else, except maybe Mexico. In a bad pinch you can take a chunk out of one of them with an ax and actually squeeze out a little moisture. Friends of mine swear they stayed alive that way. Never had to try it myself. Didn't taste too damned good, they said. Ain't got much use. They tell me the Mexicans make that firewater they call *tequila* out of a cactus called *agave*, but it never worked with this one." The scout scowled as they rode through the ghostly forms. "Ridiculous-looking things, ain't they? Like something a kid might draw on a slate. They ruin the looks of this country. Still, they take more than a hundred years to grow, and I don't want to be the son of a bitch who hacks them down."

To find in the uneducated little mountain man something marvelously close to an aesthetic, pleased Stone enormously.

4

On the trek across the flattest part of the desert, where the visibility, even through the haze, was limitless, they had traveled without a point guard or a single outrider on either side of them. Once past the biggest stands of the giant *saguaros*, they entered a range of low mountains blanketed in ponderosa forests, where cool breezes whispered through shallow canyons. The journey turned immeasurably better after the desert, but the game the Mexican traders promised failed to appear. They tightened their belts another notch.

"Apache country," Kit said.

Carson ordered Maxwell and Swanok to share the chores of riding point, and the column itself now traveled only in the daytime. Kit also assigned a picket detail for the mules and horses every night.

The third morning in the mountains, Maxwell started fifteen minutes before the rest of the party, to get out on point. They watched him disappear where some great, rounded rocks bordered a trail above a small river forty or fifty feet below and dry in most places. Actually, Stone could not detect any trail at all, but Carson, Maxwell, and the Delaware apparently had no difficulty making one out.

"Bad year for water in these parts," Kit said, pointing at the stony riverbed. "That's why we ain't seen game. We can't waste time in these mountains. Besides there being nothing to hunt, them slopes look like they could go up in flames any second. Wouldn't want to be caught in a fire here."

Stone, Kit, and the others had hardly rounded the first bend above the intermittent stream before they came upon Maxwell again, dismounted and kneeling in the trail where it joined a larger one leading up from the little river, a trail Stone had no trouble making out.

When they reached Maxwell he was brushing his tough hand across some bent grass sprouting between the pebbles. It caught on something.

"This could be a Chiricahua trail, Kit," he said. He held something up to the scout. It looked like a long, skinny strand of jerky painted a dull vermillion.

"Wrapping that's worked off a lance," Kit said. "It ain't Chiricahua, though, Lucy. I think maybe we run in behind a Mimbreño hunting party. You don't see that particular color on any Apache gear except the lances the Red Paint warriors tote."

"Chiricahua . . . Mimbreño . . . who gives a shit? They're all murderous Apache bastards as far as I'm concerned."

"We may be fretting for nothing," Carson said. "This don't exactly tell us how long ago they came this way. Take a closer look." He twisted in the saddle. "The rest of you stay where you are, except Swanok. Don't want any of you messing up sign before Lucy even cuts it."

Maxwell walked ahead a dozen paces, trailing his horse and peering at the ground. Swanok urged his animal forward and slipped silently from the saddle to join the mountain man. They walked together a few more feet before Swanok bent to pick something up. He turned and held it above his head where Kit could see it.

"It's horseshit, Kit!" Maxwell called out. "There's more up here. Twelve to fifteen animals came through here, I figure. And you were right. We're behind them. They're heading uptrail. East."

"How long ago?"

"Less than half an hour. Some of the shit's still smoking."

"All right. You and Swanok get on after them. We'll wait here for an hour."

While they were gone, Stone reflected on Maxwell's characterization of the party that left the signs as "murderous Apache bastards." His voice had not revealed any particular hatred as he'd shouted back to Kit, and in this, as in his other uses of unflattering euphemisms for Indians, the former trapper had differed little from most of the other mountain men who had been Stone's companions for more than a year. Basil Lajeunesse had professed an out-and-out liking for Indians, but even that sweet, tolerant old giant was given now and again to expletives when he referred to the indigenous peoples they met. To Basil, too, they were "polecats," "red devils," "savages," "varmints," "redskins," and a lot of other names of even less gentility.

But never once had he heard Carson use any of these or *any* terms that would suggest that Indians were less than human. As a matter of fact, to Kit they were seldom just "Indians"; they were Utes, the Dineh, Bannocks, Arapahos, Klamaths, and Apache.

Maxwell and the Delaware returned in forty-five minutes.

"That bunch that came along here is only part of what's up ahead, Kit," Lucy said. "They're in a *ranchería* that's two, two and a half miles up this trail. Swanny and I got a real good look at it. Must be near a hundred of them, and most of them are men. A war party, I reckon. Looks like maybe half a dozen small parties have gotten together to make some real big mischief in the ranches along the Río. They look starved."

"Is there another trail that will take us past them without them seeing us?" Kit asked.

"Not that Swanny or I could find."

"Do we have a chance in a fight? Could we rush them tonight, bring down a bunch, and get out the other side of the *ranchería* before they know what hit them?"

"No chance," Maxwell said. "We'd never kill enough of them to stop the rest from coming after us. They're in a hell of a good position, about a hundred feet above this trail. Big rocks. They could hold off an army. No *way* we could rush them. We'd be lucky if even one of us made it through. There's one more thing, Kit. This outfit up ahead has got a sight more rifles than any redskins I ever saw."

"I ain't surprised. The northern tribes don't get the chances to get rifles the Mimbreños and Chiricahuas do," Kit said. "Them and other Apaches been taking firearms away from the Mexicans for a couple of hundred years, I guess." He turned to Stone. "Let me have a look at that map you and Señor Gonzales put together, *amigo*."

Carson took it and laid it across his horse's neck. After Stone oriented the map for him, and showed him where he believed the party to be at the moment, the scout studied it in silence for the better part of a minute.

Then he folded the map, handed it back, and turned his horse around in order that he could face the entire party.

"Here's what we're looking at. Lucy says we can't get past these Mimbreños, and that if we try to shoot it out, we got no chance. I've fought with Lucy Maxwell for never mind how many years, and I trust his judgment on this. If we turn around here and look for another pass into the Río country it will add four or five days, maybe a week, in getting to Santa Fe." He paused for a moment and looked straight at Stone. He continued. "Some of us can't abide the thought of that. Now it ain't no secret that I'm carrying letters from the captain back in Los Angeles to President Polk in Washington. I mean to get them there before the century runs out. What this all boils down to is that I'm going right through that Mimbreño *ranchería*. Any of you who ain't in the rush I'm in, and who wants to go back out of this canyon and look for another way can do that. Sure would like to have a few of you come with me, though. I guess misery does love company. Bear in mind that if you do stay with me, you got to trust me completely." He stopped. Half a minute went by before he spoke again. "How many of you can I count on? Raise your hands."

Stone raised his. He did not even have to look behind him. No one spoke. No one needed to.

"All right, we'll ride," Kit said. "Stay back here with us from here on out, Lucy. We don't need no point rider now. You know as well as I do they'd get the point man no matter what else might happen. We'll pull up and make a short halt for an adjustment or two when we come in sight of the *ranchería*, maybe when we're about a quarter of a mile away. I'll give my only orders there." He stood in the stirrups and pumped his arm in the air.

"Time to catch up!"

As they rode, Stone wondered if he had made the right choice. Four or five days more before reaching Santa Fe and then racing on to Ana would not really have been the eternity it seemed from here. Going with Kit and these other desperate men might mean he would never see her again at all. In truth he had no choice.

After a ride of no more than half an hour the trail widened unexpectedly, and there ahead of them the Apache *ranchería* loomed above a rocky slope. It looked like the approach to the Ute camp at Pilot Peak in miniature. The only way past it was a narrow trail on a precipice above the stream, and even here the Indian encampment hung over it for an eighth of a mile or so. It would make a horrible, bloody gauntlet if they were forced to run it.

Carson called his halt.

"They've seen us," he said.

As if to punctuate his words, a strand of white smoke curled over one of the huge rocks at the edge of the Apache camp. The report of the rifle followed fairly quickly, and then came the spurt of dust ten yards or so ahead of the scout's horse.

"Weren't nothing personal in that," Kit said. "Mimbreños don't shoot all that bad. Somebody up there just wanted to make sure we knew they was there. They won't fire again unless we move. We can figure a way to get around that, too."

Apache heads began to appear above the rocks and boulders.

"Should we just pick targets our own selves, Kit?" Maxwell asked. "Or do you want to lay out a firing pattern?"

"Ain't going to be no targets, Lucy." He turned in the saddle. "Get off your animals, every one of you. Put any sidearms or small weapons you're carrying in your saddlebags and take your rifles out of the scabbards and stuff them in your mule packs. That goes for knives, too. Don't even try to hide what you're up to. I don't want anything that even looks like a weapon anywhere in sight."

In less than a minute every firearm in the party had disappeared and every one of the men was back in the saddle. Stone had expected at least a little growling, but it was all done in deadly silence. Stone could not decide whether it was trust—or resignation.

"Beadle Jimson!" Kit called out.

"Yeah, Kit?" Jimson answered from the rear of the column.

"Cut out the three fattest mules we got left in the string and bring them up to me."

That took another minute. When Jimson had moved the three mules up even with Carson, the scout went on. "We'll just ease up that slope now. Slow. I don't want one horse or mule skittering around. We'll find out right quick—in the next ten seconds or so—if the first part of this is going to work at all." He eased his horse forward with only a gentle pressure from his knees. "Let's go."

Now came a different kind of fear than any Stone had known. He felt no urge to turn his horse and bolt, was not at all sure he could have done so had he wanted to. Something had turned his arms and legs to water. There was nothing left to do but make this short ride with Kit. Mounting the steps of a gallows must be very much like this.

5

"So far, so good," Kit whispered when they were halfway up the slope. "They don't quite know what to make of what we're doing. They may want to take us only when we're inside the stronghold, where they'll be on all sides of us, and where the women can get at us. They'd want us alive for that."

By the time they reached the break in the rocks that Lucy had said was the gateway to the camp, the Apaches began standing up. All of them were armed, and all of them had trained their rifles on someone in the column.

Stone did not even try to pick out the one whose sights were fixed on him.

The Mimbreños who had been in the rocks had fallen in behind the party, and it was as if they were now shepherding

Carson and his men along. Stone wanted to look back at them, but something told him he should not. He wanted even more to keep his attention on whatever might happen in front of them.

A dished, hardpan plaza of sorts, again reminiscent of the campground at Pilot Peak, held a score or more low, rounded bark-and-hide huts, and women and children stood in front of them with bright, black eyes sunk in sullen, hollow faces. Lucy had been right. These poor wretches were starving.

"There's the man we want to talk to," Kit said.

Stone followed Kit's gaze to where an incredibly tall, black-haired Indian, taller than Stone by half a foot, stood in front of one of the huts. Tall as he was, the most arresting thing about this Apache was his enormous head, much too big for even his big body. The easy, confident way he held himself and the thread of a smile on his lips left no question he was the leader here.

"A lot depends on this conversation," Carson said, "and how well I handle my end of it. Wish us luck!"

"Do you speak Apache, too?"

"Not exactly. I've got more than a smattering of Navajo, though, and the two lingos are a lot alike. Actually, we'll probably do most of our palavering in Spanish. Apaches use Spanish about as much as they do their own tongue. They've had a lot to do with Mexicans, one bloody way or another."

He urged his horse toward the tall Apache, the others following close behind, but stopping when Kit held up his hand when they were still twenty or thirty feet away. Once his men had come to a stop, the scout moved in closer by himself. He signaled Beadle Jimson to bring the three mules forward. The Apache leader made no move to take the offered lead. Jimson, who had brought the pair up on foot, let the *reata* drop to the ground at the Indian's feet, then retired to the line of mountain men.

Kit, pointing first to the mules and then to the north and west, began to utter a stream of aspirates and glottal stops in some totally strange dialect Stone assumed must be Navajo-Apache. He went on at some length.

The Indian replied readily enough during the breaks in Kit's little speech, opening his long arms wide in the direction of Stone and the mountain men as he did, ending a couple of what could be sentences with short, barking laughs. Then the words flew back and forth between Kit and the Apache like balls between jugglers at a carnival. The laughs came again from the Mimbreño, but so did a scowl now and then.

Carson and the Apache made as strange a pair as any Stone could recall: the gigantic Indian with the improbably large head and the trim, quiet little mountain man.

Maxwell had come to a stop beside Stone, and Stone turned to him. "Can you understand them, Lucy? I caught some of the Spanish, but the other . . ."

"Not too damned good. Like you, I'm all right when they use Spanish, but I ain't got Kit's moxie with Apache talk. I did kind of get the drift of it. This ungodly big Mimbreño just pointed out that his warriors could have killed every one of us, and he ain't sure but what he'll let them do just that before this is over. He don't mince words."

"But he seems in a pretty good mood, what with the way Kit made him laugh, Lucy."

"I ain't sure you want to know what Kit made him laugh about. He offered to let him pick a slave or two. It was a joke, of course, but it might give Bighead there some ideas. And hell! An Apache is always in a good mood when he's thinking about killing somebody. Only time it gets any better is when he's actually doing it. You saw Kit offer him the mules. Bighead said that if he wanted he could take and eat *all* our mules, and our horses, too, because after his women got through with us we wouldn't need any of them for anything. Then he asked Kit if he wouldn't do just that if he was in Bighead's moccasins."

"And . . . ?"

"Kit allowed as how he sure would. Said he'd do it in a second. But only if he was a Mexican. Kit's good. I would have lost my temper and messed it up by now. He's playing on the way Apaches despise Mexicans. Kit went on to say that the great warriors and chiefs of the North and East would never kill a guest like a Mexican would. Right off, the chief reminded Kit that nobody had invited us. Kit told him he ought to. Bighead ain't answered that yet."

Carson and the Apache had fallen silent. It gave Stone a chance to look around. They were hemmed in on all sides by Apaches with rifles. He had no personal knowledge of these things, but from grisly stories heard back at Bent's and around the old expedition's fires, he knew they would be far better off if Kit's oversized nemesis there turned them over to these warriors for immediate slaughter than if he let the women have them.

Finally Carson turned back toward Stone, Maxwell, and the rest of his men.

"I wish I could tell you what's going on here, but I can't. This *jefe* won't give me an answer one way or the other. I just plain can't figure him out." He turned his horse back to the party. "Let's just turn around and mosey on out of here as if he said we could go. If we rode slow coming up here, I want us hardly moving at all when we ride back down to the trail. It just might be that their pride wants us out of here before they start eating them three mules. It ain't going to be a pretty sight."

He started back toward the opening in the rocks and the column turned and followed him. The Apaches with rifles stepped aside and let them pass.

"He could be playing cat-and-mouse with us," Maxwell said. "Apaches can be like that."

If the ride up had stretched Stone's nerves thin, the slow procession along the trail spun them out to tingling gossamer. Apaches hung over the rocks, rifles trained on their backs again.

"Just thought of something, Kit . . ," Maxwell said when they reached the end of the encampment where the woods began. "That Apache with the big head. I seem to recollect hearing somewheres about a Mimbreño that looks like that. Do you suppose . . . ?"

"That was Mangas, all right."

"Who, Kit?" Stone asked.

"Mangas Coloradas. Red Sleeves. He's the craftiest and easily the best of the great Apache chiefs. No one else has ever held more than fifteen or twenty Apaches together at one time. I think he could raise a whole army of them if the stakes was high enough." He turned to Maxwell. "You're wrong about one thing, Lucy. Mangas won't play cat to our mouse. I'll be glad to apologize if I'm wrong, but I think we'll get out of here alive."

As slow as they kept it, they had ridden well clear of the camp by now, but even Stone knew that unseen warriors were flitting through the woods above the trail, shadows within shadows. After a quarter of a mile or so the feeling diminished to nothing. Still, more than twenty minutes went by before Carson gave the order to quicken their pace.

With all the fights he had now made with Carson, and with all those he might make with the scout in whatever time they still had together, Stone would always think back on this as Kit's greatest victory.

33

Dragooned

On the fifth of October, 1846, they reached the banks of the Río Grande, and early in the morning of the sixth, rode into the New Mexican village of Socorro, a few hundred yards west of the river and one hundred forty miles south of Santa Fe.

Stone had expected to see just another sleepy, riverside cluster of adobe homes with the usual weedy garden plots and sunbaked empty streets and fields. He saw the adobes, sure enough, and a full, hot sun did beat down on Socorro's dirt streets and fields, but they were far from empty.

General Stephen Watts Kearny and the United States Army of the West, on its way to fight the "war" in southern California, had come to town.

Carson and his men rode up to the plaza from the Río through a bright yellow cottonwood *bosque* where parts of uniforms, fresh from laundering in the nearby river, had been hung out to dry on the lower branches of the old trees. Thirty or forty naked men were splashing and hollering in the water.

Not a soul challenged the Carson party as it reached and rode on through the first picket line.

"We could take this place as easy as Bill Ide and his farmer friends took Sonoma," Maxwell said.

Rifles were stacked everywhere in the cottonwood grove, and horses were tethered singly and in groups of two or three at intervals throughout it. Men in varying degrees of undress, some of them still bare-naked and dripping water from the river, gawked at Carson and his party as they rode by. Stone chuckled. Sweat-stained, trail-worn, and filthy as they were, they hardly presented a prepossessing sight. One soldier, struggling into his tunic, grinned and held his nose with the thumb and forefinger of his free hand.

"Where the hell you bums come from, mister?" a man clad only in long underwear yelled at Kit.

Carson merely smiled and pointed to the west.

"Come to join the army?"

Kit shook his head.

"Don't know as the general would take you if you wanted to," the man said. "Looks like you ain't had a square meal in years. Maybe you can talk the general out of last night's slops."

How would this man react if someone were to tell him that he was addressing *Kit Carson?*

"Just who is this general?" Kit asked.

"Stephen Watts Kearny."

"Then you men must be the First Dragoons."

"None other, mister."

"If it ain't asking too much, where do we *find* the general?"

"He's headquartered in one of them mud huts smack in the center of this sorry town. Up the hill a piece. Place has got a flag out in front of it. Don't waste your time, though. General Kearny won't see you. Him and his officers is too busy planning our move out of here tomorrow."

"Move? Where to?"

"California!" The man in the underwear grinned broadly.

"Thanks, friend," Kit said. He turned to Stone and Maxwell. "Let's get to the plaza. If the general won't see us, it sure as hell is all right with me. I hadn't planned to stop here anyways, but we ought to at least pay our respects before we head on north."

Stone did not relish even the tiny delay a sociable visit

and a chance to meet an important American general would take. Almost two hundred miles still stretched between him and Ana. The faster they began to put some of those miles behind them the better.

2

In the plaza, seven or eight pieces of field artillery of a little more recent vintage than that of the three mountain howitzers abandoned on the wharf at Yerba Buena had been parked under the roof of a shed. The American flag was cocked from the doorjamb in one of the adobes on the north side, and a long hitchrail in front of the door held three horses with military saddles and one with leather tack indistinguishable from that Stone rode with at the moment, including a fringed, buckskin saddle-scabbard holding a Hawken gun.

Just as Kit in the lead reached the rail, a rangy, rawboned, powerful-looking man with a scraggly beard and wearing buckskin as unkempt, tattered, and greasy as that of any of the mountain men in Carson's party emerged through the small door.

The man took one look at the scout, blinked as if he could not believe his eyes, and yelled, "Kit!"

"Tom!" Kit shouted back. "Tom Fitzpatrick!"

Stone knew that name. Horace Trevelyan had written about Tom "Broken Hand" Fitzpatrick in his book about Kit. Charlie Bent had mentioned him. Fitzpatrick had trapped, hunted, and fought with Kit for the better part of twenty years, and he had been out with Frémont a couple of expeditions ago, too.

Kit almost jumped from the saddle, raced to the tall man, shook his hand, and embraced him, his small body almost lost in the man's long arms. They broke apart. "Lucy

Maxwell's with me, Tom," Carson said. He pointed to Maxwell, who waved, grinning. "The young buck next to him is a good new friend . . . Brad Stone. You know most of these other old coots, too. Brad, this here's Tom Fitzpatrick, one of the best mountain men who ever laid out a line of traps or robbed a buddy of his plews." He turned back to Fitzpatrick, grinning. "What the hell you doing here?"

"I'm chief scout for General Kearny. He picked me up at Bent's. I'm supposed to take him and his dragoons to California to get them into the war."

"Ain't no war going on there. It's over with."

"Suits me. We left Santa Fe three days ago, so you can see we're not getting anywhere very fast. Armies don't cover ground like *voyageurs*. Where in tarnation did you come from? I heard you was in California. Hoped to see you when we got there."

"I left Los Angeles two weeks ago."

"You come east through the Mojave?"

"South of it."

Fitzpatrick pursed his lips and whistled. "Bet that took some doing. No wonder the bunch of you look the way you do. The general wants me to take him to San Diego by going that way, and I weren't able to talk him out of it. How is that trail, Kit? I never set foot on it before."

"Neither did I until this trip. It's bad, Tom—where it ain't impossible. Damned little good water. We got a map that could help you out, if Brad here will part with it. The fifteen of us had hell's own time getting here. . . . You're taking an *army* to California across that desert?"

"That's what this Kearny says," Fitzpatrick said.

"I don't know about that. What we saw of your dragoons coming up through the *bosque*, them soldier boys ain't the *voyageurs* you just talked about. I'm sure glad it's you scouting for Kearny instead of me."

"They're willing, Kit. That's the best I can say for them."

"How you getting along with the general? I met him once, with Captain Frémont."

Fitzpatrick's smile disappeared. "Well . . . he ain't the easiest army officer I ever worked for. Demanding son of a bitch! Everything by the goddamned book. Makes his people dot every *i* and cross every *t*. But I got to live and work for him awhile. At least the pay is good. You just told me where you been, Kit. Where the hell you bound?"

"Santa Fe and Taos first. I'm taking dispatches and stuff on to Washington, to the president of the United States."

Fitzpatrick tilted his head back and actually howled at the sky. "Washington, D.C.? You lucky little devil! I'd sure admire to make that trip myself. Ain't apt to happen in this life, I reckon. How's Captain Johnny?"

"Tip-top when we left him in Los Angeles. He's a really important man now. Commodore Stockton, the U.S. Navy big shot out there, allows he'll make the captain territorial governor pretty soon. Maybe by now, in fact. By the time you get Kearny to California, you both will have to report to the captain."

"Kearny won't be happy about that. He hates Johnny's guts. Guess it goes back to when they both came west, but you know all that as well as I do. The way the papers played up what Frémont did in California—all but ignoring what Kearny did here in New Mexico—has made it a sight worse. He's got a journalist from *The New York Times* traveling with the army, and another from some paper in Chicago."

"How do *you* feel about the captain's good luck, Tom?"

"It may surprise you, but I'm glad to hear it."

"It does surprise me. I never mistook you for one of the captain's admirers. As I recall, you didn't cotton to him near as much as I did when we all rode together."

"That was before spending the last two months with this fussbudget asshole of a general. I damned near quit him yesterday and headed back to Bent's. After what you just told me, I'll be glad when we reach California and I get to take my orders from Johnny Frémont again. He's looking better to me all the time. . . ." Fitzpatrick broke off as three blue-uniformed men stepped through the door. One took a position slightly in advance of the other two.

3

No two ways about it, Stone decided at a glance, Stephen Watts Kearny was an imposing man.

Tall, stiff as a lightning rod, his head and features under his uniform cap were well formed and regular. His immaculately clean-shaven face, handsome enough, would have been pleasant as well, but for a petulant lower lip that did not seem to go with the firm jaw. It made him appear as if he were pouting.

"General," Fitzpatrick said, "this here scruffy little gent is—"

"No need for an introduction, Mr. Fitzpatrick," Kearny broke in. "I made the acquaintance of the celebrated Mr. Carson some years back." He held his hand out to Kit. "I said *Mr.* Carson, but that is not quite correct, is it, sir? Recent dispatches inform me that you are now Captain Carson, even though you are not at present in the uniform of an officer of the U.S. Army."

"We don't run to uniforms where I been lately, General."

"You must rectify this at your first opportunity. How have you been since last we met, Captain?"

"No complaints, sir."

"From the . . . condition . . . of your attire, may I assume you've been traveling?"

"Yes, sir."

"You must just have arrived from California, then."

"Yes, sir."

"And how did you leave things there?"

From this touchy point the conversation proceeded along the same path Kit had taken Fitzpatrick down, complete with the news that the war in California seemed over. Kit introduced Kearny to Stone, Maxwell, and a few of the mountain men, but Stone knew the general had not caught the names. He did look at Stone for a moment. Kearny's eyes were far and away his most arresting feature. John C. Frémont's eyes, before Stone got used to them, had always pierced him to some degree; the eyes of Stephen Kearny bored into him.

Carson, no doubt on his guard after Fitzpatrick's remarks about the general, did not mention Frémont, nor had he told Kearny of the mission to Washington; perhaps he did not intend to. It suddenly became clear from the scout's uncharacteristically uneasy manner that all he wanted was to get this meeting over with so they could be on their way. That suited Stone, but he saw irritation and impatience building in the general.

"Captain Carson," Kearny said when Kit finished, "I would like you and one or two of your most important men to take mess with me and my officers tonight. There are matters we must discuss. For one thing, I want a fuller, more detailed report on the military and political situation in California."

"I'd like to beg off, General. We'd figured on making half the distance between here and Albuquerque before the sun went down today. We got important business."

"Business more important than being a guest at my table?"

"With all due respect, I think so, General."

"Please enlighten me, Captain."

"Well . . . I'm carrying dispatches from Colonel Frémont to the president of the United States."

"What?" Kearny turned white.

"I'm under orders to deliver Colonel Frémont's letters and documents to the president in Washington—personally."

In the silence that followed, Stone picked up the heavy beat of booted feet tramping behind the adobe building, and a gruff voice barking orders . . . a drill squad, obviously. Kearny did not speak again or try to until the sound of the marchers died away.

"The men of your command, sir," Kearny said next, "look ragged and hungry. A day of rest in my camp would do them a world of good. I *insist* you stay."

"Begging the general's pardon, Colonel Frémont and Commodore Stockton would not want me to delay at this—"

"Enough!" Impatience and irritation had shredded the last of Kearny's self-control, making his martinet voice tremble. "Perhaps, Captain Carson, you are not yet enough of a soldier to know that a general officer's insistence, indeed his mere wish, is tantamount to a command. You *will* dine with me . . . but not in your present disgusting state. Mr. Fitzpatrick will see to your animals and show you where you can shave and bathe. We have separate sections of the river cordoned off for officers and men. As difficult as you may find the task, sir, *try* to make your person, and the persons of the men you bring to my mess, at least minimally presentable. Two members of the Fourth Estate who are traveling with my army will be dining with us tonight. I suppose they will want to interview the great Kit Carson."

"I could do without that, sir."

"So could I! Dismissed!"

With that Kearny spun on his heels and started for the adobe building's door, the two other officers scurrying ahead of him and rushing through the door in a manic effort to get out of his way. Before the general entered himself, he turned back to Kit again. His face had gone chalk white earlier; it had now turned livid, but he did seem to have regained his composure.

"I've changed my mind, Captain Carson. Forget about joining me at mess tonight. But we might as well get something straight this very moment. . . .

"You will not be going on to Washington, sir. You are herewith relieved of that duty. I am ordering you, along with every member of your party, to guide my Army of the West to California along the same route you just traveled to reach Socorro. Report here to my headquarters immediately after you hear the bugler sound retreat in order that you and I may discuss this new assignment. Bring the dispatches you are carrying. I shall assign a military courier to take them on to Washington and the president."

4

"You *can't* just run up to Taos and hide, Kit!" Maxwell came close to screaming. "This son-of-a-bitching tin soldier will crucify you! Even Charlie Bent won't be able to lift a finger to help, and Colonel Johnny, the only one who *might* be able to help, is way to hell and gone out in California. This country's at *war*, for Christ's sake! Kearny can court-martial you for insubordination, even desertion. The bastard could actually have you shot."

As he had done since his startling announcement that he intended quitting the army and starting for Taos immediately, Kit remained silent.

Stone had almost staggered at Kearny's cavalier destruction of Carson's mission. Carson had hardly spoken of it since they'd left Frémont's office in Los Angeles, but so many things had happened as they trekked across the desert, he could make a pretty good guess about how much going to Washington meant to his friend.

The party had made a camp just inside the edge of the cottonwood grove by the time Tom Fitzpatrick, looking glum and apologetic, arrived with a squad of soldiers with bayonets fixed to their rifles.

"Sorry, Kit," he said, "I got to take your horses. The general says you're under house arrest, even if you ain't exactly in a house. You can go as far as the river to wash up, I guess. And the general's ordered vittles for you." He stayed long enough to hear Kit's threat to go home, and like Maxwell, now implored the scout not to do anything so rash.

"I can't figure out why this general's so down on me, Tom. He really don't know me well enough," Kit said.

"It ain't *you!* You're Johnny Frémont's man, and the mere mention of Johnny almost makes Kearny puke."

Despite Kearny's saying, *"I am ordering you, along with every member of your party, to guide my Army . . . ,"* it was not until a smart-looking young lieutenant whose nerves were getting the better of him at meeting the fabulous Kit Carson rode into their bivouac with more orders from the general that Stone finally realized how this sudden turn of events would affect *him.*

Kearny's *"you, along with every member of your party"* meant Brad Stone as well as the rest of them. The dream whose promise had inured him against much of the rigor of the trip across the desert went glimmering. If he had to return to California with Kit and Kearny, he might not be able to get to Taos until long after the war was over.

His first impulse, and he very nearly yielded to it, was to blurt out encouragement to Kit and beg him to take him north with him and damn the consequences. He held his tongue until the lieutenant finally saluted Carson and rode back up the slope to the village.

"Kit . . . ," Stone began. He stopped when Carson looked at him. He simply could not do it. He could not let his own selfish concerns contribute to what could turn out to be the ruin of the finest man he had ever known. "I think . . ." He went on. "I *beg* you not to do this. You've worked too hard and too long to earn the reputation you have to throw it away like this. There will be other chances for the kind of thing Colonel Frémont asked you to do."

"It ain't just the trip to Washington, Brad. Actually, that's the least of it. It's the trust the captain placed in me. I've never let him down before. It kills me to do it now."

"But you're not letting him down. How do you think he would feel if Kearny court-martialed you? The whole country knows you've been Frémont's right-hand man for years. Your names have been so closely linked the two of you are looked on almost as brothers. This kind of trouble and the disgrace that might come with it would be bound to reflect on *him.*"

"I'll think about it, Brad," Carson said. "But right now I want to do that thinking by myself. No offense."

He slumped down at the base of a cottonwood, laid his head back against the trunk, and closed his eyes.

Stone tried his best not to watch him for the rest of the afternoon. He hiked to the river, stripped to the skin, and bathed himself thoroughly for the first time since he had left Los Angeles. As he walked back through the *bosque,* he saw that Kit had left the tree and was making his way to the water. The little man's customary quiet confidence and energy had gone in hiding. His steps looked tentative and listless.

Kearny had ambushed Kit more successfully than the wiliest Comanche could ever have. He had no defense against this sort of thing.

5

At five o'clock the notes of the bugle floated into the cottonwood grove, and Kit, who had settled into the same deep silence against the tree again after his return from the riverbank, got to his feet and walked to where Stone was inking in the penciling on the map he had made with the Mexican trader Gonzales. Through the long afternoon he had nurtured the vague hope that somehow Kit could persuade Kearny to make do with the map instead of him. As Kit had said about the first rough draft back in the desert, it was a *good* map.

"I'd like for you to come with me when I meet with the general, *amigo*," Carson said now. "Bring the map. Maybe Kearny will at least take some advice."

"Sure, Kit. But I don't know what possible use I can be to you when you talk with him."

"Ain't a matter of being of 'use' to me. But what I got to say to him will concern you more than a little."

Neither of them spoke as they walked up the hill to the plaza, but Stone's mind churned.

6

In the tiny, airless room with sagging *vigas* that the general used for an office, Carson nodded toward the young officer who had visited the party in the afternoon. Kearny, who was toying with a riding crop, tapping it lightly on the table in front of him, did not bother to introduce them, nor had he so much as acknowledged Stone's presence.

"I got nothing against this young lieutenant, General," Kit said. "But I would appreciate it if you would excuse him while we talk. It feels a touch crowded in here."

"How about your man there, Captain? Should I not excuse him as well and thin the 'crowd' even more?"

"Lieutenant Stone will figure in our talk, sir."

"*Lieutenant* Stone? I don't recall you mentioning this morning that he is an officer."

"Didn't mean to hide it. Like it is with that uniform I

ought to wear, we don't pay much mind to rank in the desert. I keep forgetting Brad's an officer."

"From the look of him, apparently he does, too. What is Lieutenant Stone's military specialty?"

"He's a mapmaker, what I think they call a cartographer."

Kearny's eyebrows shot up. "One of Johnny Frémont's clever young men? Perhaps we can make some use of him on the way west."

From the tone of his voice, a total stranger to the mutual history of John C. Frémont and Stephen Watts Kearny would have guessed at the general's hatred for the Pathfinder. That, however, was not what was uppermost in the mind of Brad Stone at the moment.

"All right." Kearny nodded at the uniformed youth, whose face fell in disappointment as he got to his feet and left the room. He had stared as worshipfully at Kit as Stone himself must have stared at him those first days back at Bent's. "Now," Kearny went on, "let's get to the business at hand. How many days will it take you to get us to California?"

"Don't recall I *agreed* to take you to California, General."

Kearny reddened. A vein in his forehead throbbed.

"What?"

He snapped the riding crop down on the table. It sounded like the crack of a pistol. Stone flinched; Kit did not. "Where did you get the preposterous idea that your *agreement* is necessary or even desired, Captain? I have *ordered* you to guide me! That will suffice."

"I don't think it's going to work quite that way, General Kearny. I *might* serve as your chief scout and take your army west—but only under certain conditions."

"Might? Conditions? How dare you!" Kearny stood up, and the chair he had been sitting in fell away and thudded on the earthen floor behind him. "I will have you court-martialed before the sun goes down, sir, and I'll see you in shackles before it comes up again!"

"Begging the general's pardon, I don't think either of those things will happen. I figure you as being too smart for that. First off, you've got no witnesses to what I just said."

Kearny looked at Stone for the first time.

"I wouldn't count on *mi amigo*, General," Kit went on. "Now, I ain't quite the fool I look, either. While I recognize that you probably can make a court-martial stick, I don't think it would be in your best interests to go ahead with one. Have you told the two newspapermen traveling with you that you've put me and my men under 'house arrest'?" He paused. "I thought not. I bet they don't even know I'm in Socorro. I don't want to brag none, but neither one of them has looked me up, and that ain't usual. . . ."

From the look of Kearny, Kit's shot was as sure as any he had ever made on any target.

"Now . . . ," he said, ". . . it wouldn't surprise me if one or both of them are acquainted with Senator Benton of Missouri or his daughter, Jessie Frémont. It ain't very modest of me to point this out, I admit, but they probably also know a hell of a lot about *me*. And it might also interest you to know that Lieutenant Stone here is a friend of Congressman Jakob Myers of Illinois. If I recollect right, the committee Myers heads up kind of looks over President Polk's promotion list. A word from him—"

Kearny leaped to his feet. "This is extortion, Captain Carson!" He had tried to keep his voice low, but it threatened to soar out of his control.

"Yes, I expect it *is*, General. Ain't it kind of nice there's a way out of this for both of us?"

"Explain yourself."

"I know you got all the right in the world to order me to California, and I reckon I want to be as good a soldier as the next man. It's them conditions you still ain't let me tell you about. I'll skip out of here and take the court-martial if they ain't met."

"All *right,* man! Name them, if you must."

"First off, there just ain't going to be no *military* courier taking these dispatches to Washington. I want somebody I can trust, somebody Captain Frémont would trust if he was here. Tom Fitzpatrick will fill the bill. Captain Frémont knows him near as well as he knows me. Tom's been out in the wilderness with the captain a time or two. If you've got me to guide you, you won't need him. Second—and maybe this is the most important thing—I want you to send my friend Lieutenant Stone here on to Santa Fe with a letter to Charlie Bent. I understand you just made Charlie governor."

Stone snapped his head toward Kit. What the devil was he up to? Carson did not return his look.

"*What* letter to Governor Bent?" Kearny asked, his voice sharp with suspicion. "And who is this letter from?"

"You, sir."

"Me? Why would I . . ." Kearny narrowed his eyes. The pout became more prominent. "What will be the gist of this letter?"

"You will suggest that Charlie Bent . . . Wait, you won't just *suggest.* Since you're so all-fired set on giving orders—and that's sure all right with me—you're the general—you will *order* Charlie to make a place for Lieutenant Stone on his staff at the Palace. It ain't like he ain't qualified. He's done this kind of work for Colonel Frémont for a year."

Stone almost gasped. Something like this could mean . . .

The rest of the thought was lost when Kearny spoke again. "And if I do not do these things, Captain Carson."

"Then I suppose you'd better get your court-martial under way. . . ."

Part Three

THE
MAPMAKER

34

Break in the Ride

Santa Fe!

The plaza teemed with at least three times as many people as he had seen when he first saw it last year. Throngs crisscrossed it almost at a trot, Mexicans, Americans—not as many Indians as last year, though—all of them, it seemed, at the point of shouting out their own importance or the urgency of their business. With the brilliant sunlight and not a cloud in the turquoise sky, the air seemed to crackle.

Brad Stone entered the capital of the new U.S. Territory of New Mexico in an entirely different frame of mind from that of his first visit to the small city on the Río Grande del Norte a year and a half ago.

In the first place, while Tom Fitzpatrick had provided good company on the two-day ride up the Río, particularly with his tales of "the olden times" on the dark traplines of the Rockies with "good old Kit," he and his stories could never begin to take the place of the scout himself. Save for the trip from Sutter's down to Monterey with Frémont to see General Castro and Tom Larkin, this was the longest time Stone had been apart from Carson since they'd met.

There was, of course, no way he could ever thank Kit adequately for generating the letter from Kearny to Charlie Bent he carried now. He could say this much for the autocratic general: Once he realized how skillfully and completely Kit had outmaneuvered him, he put a decent, sporting face on the proceedings. He showed Stone the letter he wrote Charlie, insisted he read it aloud, so Kit could hear it. It glowed with praise for skills Stone felt he had not even begun to possess.

But what a godsend! Only a posting in Taos itself would have been better. Even if he had to work out of the Palace of the Governors here in Santa Fe, the capital was hardly more than a hard day's ride from Estancia Barragán.

2

Before checking into the hotel he had stayed in with Kit last year, he reported to the Palace and asked for Mr. Bent. A pretty young Mexican girl who served as some sort of clerk-receptionist told him that *"Gobernador Bent no está aquí, señor. Está en Taos con su familia."* She wrinkled her nose as she spoke, and stared furtively, but with unmistakable disapproval, at his greasy buckskins. She looked doubtful when he told her he held a commission as an officer in the U.S. Army, but actually—and cheerfully—walked him to the bursar's office down a long adobe corridor when he told her he had back pay to collect.

That operation took three-quarters of an hour and nearly thirty signatures. It finally netted him fifty U.S. dollars of the several hundred that a decent, helpful if slightly bored sergeant agreed he probably had coming, not as an officer— the sergeant showed no record of his being one yet—but under the terms of his now expired civilian contract with the Corps of Topographical Engineers. As far back as Bent's he had learned that Frémont had gone to great lengths to see that his men's records and accounts had been forwarded to every government financial office west of the Mississippi. Now that he had parted company with the Pathfinder he seemed to be finding more and more things about him to prompt admiration.

"Sorry I can't give you more, Lieutenant," the sergeant

said, "but we're dead busted here for another week, when a pay wagon is due in from Bent's. You'll get a bigger advance from that gambler woman at Casa Tules."

"Señora Barceló?"

"Yes, sir."

"What has she to do with paying Americans?"

"She's been taking chits from the army ever since we got here. Crazy as it sounds, General Kearny even hit her up for enough to meet his entire payroll last month, when money didn't arrive from Leavenworth. Can you imagine a Mexican woman who's really not much more than a fancy madam and monte dealer having enough money to bankroll the government of the United States?"

Stone could not think of anything he needed that the fifty dollars would not cover until he found a regular bank to handle his money, either here in Santa Fe or in Taos.

He was not truly disappointed that Charlie Bent was out of his office on this first call. While in the hustle and bustle of *el palacio,* he had felt a tiny prod of fear that the new governor might put him to work immediately and delay his getting north. Now he could see his old friend and prospective employer at both their leisures in Taos, and he certainly could devote himself more wholeheartedly to any task Charlie set to him after he set eyes on Ana again.

He wondered where he and Ana would meet. Josefa Carson's? Most likely. Certainly not at the *estancia,* not before he had had a chance to take the emotional temperature of Don Bernardo. It was far too much to hope it would be at the *casita* on the edge of the gorge, with or without discreet old Galinda.

He had ridden into Santa Fe with Carson last year soaked to the skin, bone weary, and still shaking from the encounter with the Comanches on the upper Cimarron. He had not at that time met Ana Barragán.

Everything about today's *entrada* seemed new and different, and it was not due solely to the bright, beaming sun, the dry, crisp, stimulating autumn weather, or even to the city's new air of urgency and uproar, or to the sight of so many American army uniforms in the plaza. The change must have occurred in Brad Stone.

3

Through with his little bit of business at the Palace, he led his horse and his two mules across the plaza to La Fonda.

A brand-new sign—white, with blue-bordered red letters—hung from the *portal:* THE UNITED STATES HOTEL.

The change in the inn's name seemed to stand for all the other changes he saw around him, as well as those within himself. But once inside, he discovered one thing that had not changed.

Fabiano Minjárez still reigned at his high desk in the foyer. As Stone walked in, the innkeeper looked up from his ledger.

"Señor Stone!" Minjárez dropped his quill and slammed the ledger shut, his earnest brown face opening in a broad smile. *"¡Bienvenido!"* Flattering that he would remember Stone after more than a year, but perhaps he never forgot anyone who came through his front door with Kit Carson. "How is Don Cristóbal, *por favor*?" Minjárez asked.

"Splendid, Señor Minjárez." Stone hoped that was still true. Carson and General Kearny were now nearly two days into that terrible return journey to California. It would turn bad from wherever they were now on out, much worse than when they had come east. The scout, after agreeing to guide the general, had been unable to talk Kearny out of taking the merciless southern route. Its endless dry stretches would play a hell of a lot more havoc with an army and its gargantuan thirst than it had with Carson's party of fifteen self-sufficient mountain men.

"Will the room you occupied when you were here last year with Señor Carson be acceptable, Señor Stone?"

"Perfectly."

"I will have *mi mozo de camas* prepare a tub for you."

"That would be marvelous, *señor* . . . but wait—" He suddenly rebelled at the thought of scrubbing himself clean and then putting on the same filthy clothes. His saddlebags and the packs on the mules contained not a single item of apparel that did not reek from weeks of wearing it plastered to his chest and back and drenched with sweat. Had he been foolish enough to try to launder them at one of those stingy, shallow desert water holes, one of the old-timers would have shot him without blinking an eye.

Having someone here at the hotel do a wash for him would not work, either; it would take hours, perhaps overnight, and he wanted to be on the road north bright and early.

"Señor Minjárez," he said, "where can I buy some new clothes in Santa Fe? A suit . . . shirts and linens and the like?"

"Ah, *señor,* there is a most excellent *sastre*—I think in English you would call Octavio Talamantes a tailor—not two hundred meters west of the hotel in La Calle de los Burros. He speaks your language with great fluency, too."

"*Lo siento, Don Fabiano.* I do not have time to wait for things that must be tailored."

"Señor Talamantes sells some ready-made apparel, *también.* A full suit would take some time, of course, but shirts and undergarments he should have on hand. *Por favor,* tell *mi amigo* Octavio if he does not outfit you speedily and to your complete satisfaction, he will have to answer to Fabiano Minjárez."

"*Muchísimas gracias, Don Fabiano.* I will go there now, and when I return I will welcome the bath you offered." ·

"*De nada, señor.* Will you dine here at the United States tonight, Don Bradford?"

It was the first time anyone had called him "Don Bradford" since Ana Barragán had. It felt good. "*Sí.* And I believe I will retire immediately after dinner. I intend leaving Santa Fe before sunrise tomorrow morning."

4

He found tiny, hunchbacked Octavio Talamantes sitting cross-legged on top of his cutting table, a pair of half-finished woolen trousers draped across his lap, needle poised in a hand that seemed too large for the twisted little body and far too large for the seemingly delicate stitchery engaging him.

Stone told the little man what he wanted and how quickly he had to have it, and Talamantes hopped down from the table. "*¡Sí, ciertamente, señor!*" he said. "Time, one can see, is of great importance. Perhaps Talamantes can help."

Shirts, linen underdrawers, and stockings presented no problem; they were already in stock as Minjárez had surmised, laid out neatly on shelves behind the table, each garment of a design that seemed to promise "one size fits all." The workmanship, however, seemed superb. Stone bought the first three of each that Talamantes showed him. Then the tailor brought out one more shirt, a dazzling, fancy, richly ruffled white one cut as full as a woman's blouse.

"A wedding shirt, *señor,*" the little tailor said. "A man should keep at least one such *camisa de hombre* in his wardrobe all the time. One can never tell. . . ."

Something stirred inside Brad Stone. "I will take it, Don Octavio."

"There is one more thing, *señor*," Talamantes said. "In the back room I have a suit I tailored a month ago for a man who will not now be calling for it. I think it will fit the *señor* to perfection. If any small alterations are needed, Talamantes can do them within half an hour, even while you wait. And he will make you an excellent price for taking it off his hands. The man who ordered it was a very stylish gentleman."

The black tailcoat suit Talamantes brought out looked more elegant than anything Stone had ever worn, including the evening outfit he had rented for the opera once in Boston. With his plain, Illinois-nurtured tastes, which ran as much to homespun ready-mades as anything, he would have turned it away immediately. But he suddenly felt he owed it to the earnest, helpful little man holding it aloft with pride gleaming in his black eyes to at least . . .

He tried the suit on.

One glance in the full-length mirror Talamantes wheeled in front of him persuaded him.

Ana would like this suit. Damned if he did not look passably handsome in it.

"Why didn't the man who ordered this call for it, *señor?*" he asked.

"*No puede, señor.* He cannot. He is a dead man, *un muerto.* He died in a knife fight over monte at Casa Tules."

"He was a gambler?"

"*¡Sí!*"

He waited while the tailor repositioned one button on the waistcoat. When he paid Talamantes for the linens, shirts, and the suit, he discovered that his fifty dollars, plus the little bit of money he had with him when he arrived in Santa Fe this morning, had dwindled to seven dollars American and half a handful of Mexican coins whose value he did not know. Surely not enough in toto to eat for more than a week in Taos or rent a room for more than a single night.

He would have to pay a call at Casa Tules.

He would not stay longer than it would take to get some money and have a courteous but brief conversation with Doña Gertrudes. His early departure would still be a certainty.

He would now get that tub and Fabiano Minjárez's dinner . . .

. . . and, for luck, wear the new suit for his visit at Casa Tules.

5

When he finished bathing and dressing he went down to Don Fabiano's dining room.

"Would Don Bradford mind too much sharing a table with two other guests. My small room is almost filled tonight," Fabiano Minjárez said. "Like you, *señor*, they are Americanos, but newly arrived in Santa Fe."

"Perfectly all right, Don Fabiano. I'll be glad to share a table."

Minjárez led him across the room to a corner table, where a tall, striking-looking man had risen to his feet. But it was not the man who claimed the bigger part of Stone's attention. One look at the man's companion, still seated, did. The seated figure was that of a young American woman. He had not seen an American woman since Council Grove, almost a year and three months ago, and not one of the last few poke-bonneted, weathered settler women bound for Oregon had been the stunning creature this one was. Light brown hair, tied back in a loose bun—but not a sedate coiffure by any means—framed a classically beautiful face. She smiled, revealing even white teeth flawed only by one of them being ever so slightly out of line. If anything it added something to the smile.

"Permit me, sir," the man said, putting out his hand. "I am Morton Bailey. May I present my sister, Miss Elizabeth Tapper Bailey? She has graciously come to New Mexico to run my household for me." Bailey's grip was rock solid.

Stone turned to the woman then and bowed. "A pleasure, Miss Bailey," he said. The young woman surprised him by sticking out her hand every bit as forthrightly as her brother had, and her handclasp was every bit as firm.

"And you, sir, are . . . ?" Bailey asked.

"My name is Bradford Stone, Mr. Bailey."

The man's eyebrows lifted. "Not the young mapmaker and painter who accompanied Captain Frémont and Kit Carson to California?"

"Yes, sir." How on earth had this newcomer heard of one of "Captain" Johnny's lesser hands?

"I see you are surprised that I know of you, Mr. Stone. I was privileged to read a good deal about you in the notes that came with the reports Captain Frémont made to President Polk. Glowing with praise for you, I might add. My sister knows the gist of those notes as well. I warn you, sir, she is likely to pump you for every bit of information you might pass on to her about the legendary Mr. Carson."

"Thank you, sir, but how . . . ?"

Bailey chuckled. "How did I get to read them? Well . . . I am an assistant attorney general of the United States. Don't be too impressed by that. I am in fact but a simple country lawyer who has been very lucky. President Polk has breveted me to Governor Bent to assist him in forming his new government in the territory. I am proud to make your acquaintance. You and your fellow expedition members did a splendid job in California."

Stone decided that he had better pay close attention. Bailey was breveted to Charlie Bent? Stone might find himself working with this man—or for him.

He sat in the chair Bailey motioned him to. He had not yet heard the young woman's voice. He did now.

"To begin with Mr. Stone," she said, "let us dispense with that 'Elizabeth Tapper Bailey' nonsense. Please call me Liz."

"You must be the first American woman to come to Santa Fe, Miss . . . Liz."

Her laugh was warm, musical. "Not so, Mr. Stone.˙. . . May I call you Bradford? The honor of being first belongs to an old friend of mine, Susan Shelby. Susan Shelby Magoffin now. She married the noted trader James Magoffin just last year. She came through Santa Fe on her way to Chihuahua last August, I believe."

"First, second, or whatever . . . it took a great deal of courage to make the trip you made."

Minjárez himself served their dinner.

The Baileys might be new in Santa Fe, but they seemed to already have accustomed themselves to New Mexican food. Brother and sister alike set to work with obvious relish on the *carne asada* and rice Minjárez served them. They ate in dedicated silence as the curious hotelier fussed around them.

Liz Bailey kept her hazel eyes on her plate for the most part, but she blushed once when her eyes met his full-on.

His mind ran back to what Bailey had said at the outset, that Frémont had made glowing remarks about him in his reports to President Polk. If true, and he had no right to doubt the United States assistant attorney general, they had to have been written before Pilot Peak or Walker Lake, back when he was convinced his employer held him in mild contempt. Stone had been privy to almost every one of the Pathfinder's dispatches since. As his mother would say, "Miracles never cease."

It was turning into an altogether too pleasant evening. At this rate it would be nearly ten before he got to Casa Tules. Dawn would come all too quickly after that.

He hated to, but he had to excuse himself.

"We'll see each other again soon, I trust . . . Bradford," Liz Bailey said when he did.

"Indeed, ma'am."

"Liz."

"Yes, Liz."

6

"*¿Cómo estás, Señor Stone?*" The eyes of La Tules sparkled in the light from the wrought-iron chandelier suspended above her monte table.

"*Muy bien, Doña Gertrudes.* And you?"

"You have eyes, *querido.* How does La Tules *appear* to you?"

"As beautiful as ever, *mi doña.* I sincerely hope your health is in the same state of excellence as is your appearance."

"Ah, *señor! Tu eres un tesoro*—a treasure. You are every bit the gallant *caballero* you were when you were here before, perhaps more so. You have had practice talking to the heart of a woman since I saw you last, no?"

"I have been too hard at work for that."

"*¡Sí!* I forget. It shames me. And how did the great expedition of Captain Johnny Frémont go? I *have* heard amazing reports of the spectacular events in California."

"It went perhaps even better than expected, *señora.*"

"Tell La Tules all about it. I insist."

So much for the intended "courteous but brief conversation." Not only was she not letting him keep it brief, he found suddenly that he really did not want her to. He was enjoying every moment. He would stay awhile longer, sip a second, perhaps a third glass of *aguardiente.* If he went back to his hotel right this minute, he probably could not sleep, anyway. It would be a long wait until dawn and the start toward Taos.

He did not delude himself about La Tules' welcome. Diplomat and probably shrewd businessman as Fabiano Minjárez was, when it came to more subtle flattery the innkeeper could not hold a candle to this magnificently upholstered woman. She seemed genuinely pleased to see him, and she had recognized him instantly, but he knew that it was due to his connection with Carson, even though she had not so much as mentioned the scout. For La Tules of Santa Fe, and for this moment at least, she maintained the fiction, without a slip or flaw, that no one on the planet existed except Brad Stone.

"You have not yet inquired about our mutual friend Kit Carson, *mi doña*," he said.

"I will inquire about Don Cristóbal *from* him—when I see him." She tapped him on the shoulder with the folded black fan she carried. "Now . . . let us retire to my *sanctum sanctorum*, Señor Stone . . . or may La Tules call you Don Bradford?"

"By all means, Doña Gertrudes."

They walked to the same alcove she, Kit, and he had shared last year, and the same crystal decanter and brandy glasses appeared at their same small oval table, placed there by the same servant who had brought them the last time.

"And now, Don Bradford . . . ," she said after she had filled his glass with *aguardiente*, "The story of your adventures, *por favor*, the whole story, with not a thing omitted, not the tiniest detail. And I do not want you to give Don Cristóbal and Johnny Frémont all the credit for everything the expedition did since I saw you last."

It took nearly an hour just to get to where Kit, Lucy Maxwell, the other mountain men, and he left Los Angeles with the Pathfinder's messages. He told it well, deciding it was a needed rehearsal for when he told it again to another woman. When would that be? Not tomorrow, probably. There remained the long ride up the Río del Norte and the settling in at Taos. The day after, then? Not likely, either. Days could pass before he got a message to her at the *estancia,* days more before Ana could make arrangements for the two of them to be together. For now, all he could do was hope. Being so close to her and still so far away was worse than the longing he had known in the deserts and the mountains. Those great distances had enforced a fragile patience he could not look for any longer. But as impatient as he was, he could not remember ever having felt better— about himself, his prospects, or about this suddenly glistening capital, or the quieter, and to him even lovelier town he would see tomorrow night.

He told La Tules about the meeting with General Kearny at Socorro and of Kit's verbal legerdemain in getting him posted to the staff of Governor Charlie Bent.

"I could not have heard better news, Don Bradford . . . for me, my city, or for all of Nuevo Méjico. Even though no New Mexicans tried to resist General Kearny's *entrada,* and although most of my *paisanos* welcome you Americans, there are a few, like Don Manuel Armijo, who are afraid they will not be able to go on stealing from the poor the way they always have. There is some small unrest in the territory and such men as Don Manuel will try to feed on it. *El gobernador* Bent will need young men like you. Don Cristóbal Carson should come back and help him, too."

He tucked that away in his mind. Charlie Bent would be his most reliable source on conditions in New Mexico, not the mistress of a gambling hall. Wait. He should not underestimate a woman who financed an invading army. And that brought his purpose for this visit to mind. "I need *your* help, Doña Gertrudes." He hated this. "I have been told you have become the de facto treasurer of the United States of America since General Kearny arrived in Santa Fe. Would it be . . . possible . . . to get a small advance on my salary?"

"*¡Ciertamente!* How much would you like?"

"A hundred dollars American would do me nicely."

"Done!" She beckoned to the servant. "Geraldo, *por favor.* Bring me the money box from my *oficio.*"

Geraldo returned with a sizable, padlocked metal box while Stone was still blinking at her readiness to help him out. She reached inside her bodice, extracted a brass key, and opened it.

Stone nearly whistled in his amazement at what he saw. The box was stuffed to overflowing with U.S. currency, mostly notes of the larger denominations—twenties, fifties, hundreds, and at least one of them a thousand-dollar bill, the first he had ever seen—and a neatly tied packet of slips of paper, obviously the "chits" the sergeant at the Palace had spoken of. There were a number of squares of loose note paper, too. She slipped one across the table to him. *"Por favor,* Don Bradford. A formality."

The chit already bore the amount of the advance. He signed it, all the while marveling at the supreme confidence of this woman. She was displaying a tremendous amount of cash in a room that probably contained any number of shady characters not averse to thievery. And she kept this small fortune in her office where her servant Geraldo and many others could see it every day.

As he pocketed his money, La Tules began to speak again, not giving him a chance to thank her. "You will do well here in Santa Fe, Don Bradford. With your engaging manner, it will not be difficult for you to make friends other than La Tules."

"I already have one good friend here, Doña Gertrudes, although I've not seen him since Kit and I left Taos for Bent's Fort over a year ago."

"¿Quién es?"

"A trader named Luis Aragón."

"Don Luis? *¡Magnífico!* He is a dear friend of mine as well. He was here the same night you first came here."

He had forgotten. Luis had talked of Ana, then, when she was no more than a name. "Is he in Santa Fe at the moment?" Much as he would like to see Luis, there would be no opportunity to do so before he set out for Taos in the morning. Nothing could interfere with that.

"As a matter of fact he *is* in town," she said. "He did much traveling in the early part of the year, to Independence and St. Louis, I have been told. I understand he has been back here for about a month. Now that you have mentioned him and I think about it, it makes me wonder why he has not come to Casa Tules even once since his return. He used to show up here as many as two and three times a week to separate La Tules from her hard-earned *dinero*. He is a fine young *hombre*."

"Indeed he is. Kit thinks highly of him, too."

"Don Luis is fortunate in that. Don Cristóbal's good opinion is all the recommendation *any* man needs in Nuevo Méjico—and many other places. But it occurs to La Tules that there is something even stranger at work here. *Muy misterioso.* I wonder why Don Luis spends his time here instead of Taos."

"Why should that be so strange, Doña Gertrudes?"

"Ah, perhaps you do not know . . . but of course you could not; you have been traveling, too, and out of reach of news of what goes on here. Two months or so ago, your *amigo* Don Luis took an *esposa*. He is married now . . . to the daughter of an important *hacendado* in the north . . . Doña Ana Barragán."

A heavy door closed on the instantly empty chamber of Brad Stone's mind.

La Tules went right on talking, but he heard not one intelligible word beyond that *"Doña Ana Barragán."*

". . . why would he spend so much time away from his lovely bride so early in their marriage? They should be busy making the first of many children. . . ." Her voice was that of

some distant mountain brook, its liquid babbling muffled by the undergrowth. *"I have not heard much from Taos this past month, and there has certainly been no gossip that the union of Don Luis and Doña Ana ..."* Then even the clattering noises of the casino fell away to nothing. *"... is not going well, and trust me, I would have heard if there had been the slightest hint of trouble."* He tried with all his soul to pull himself back to La Tules and her unabated stream of words, but could not. *"But I do wonder. Doña Ana is a fiery, headstrong little beauty. ..."*

Then he tried to isolate his own thoughts, but had no luck there, either.

"... and Dios knows she would not be the easiest woman for any man to live with. Do you know her, Don Bradford? Doña Josefa Carson is Doña Ana's cousin. Perhaps you and she met when you were in Taos with Don Cristóbal last year. ..."

It finally broke through the cloud of his sudden lapse from consciousness that she had asked him something.

"Do you know her, Don Bradford?"

He fought his way out of the silence. "I thought I did, *señora.*"

7

He left Casa Tules and returned to the hotel as if he were walking in his sleep. He did not sleep after he reached his bed. He spent the entire night turning over and over in his mind the wild notions that had attacked him as he sought desperately for a way to deal with this crippling news.

Was there a way? If one could be found, he would have to begin the search by seeing Luis Aragón. ...

35
Echo of the Storm

Bradford Stone told himself grimly that if he had any sense at all, he would abort this short ride down to the Río and the cottonwood-shaded trading compound of Héctor Aragón e Hijo.

During the long night he had no trouble at all abandoning the trip north to Taos he was to have begun at first light this morning. He would not ride for Taos now. In all likelihood he never would.

In the wake of La Tules' paralyzing news the night before, Estancia Barragán had become the last stretch of earth he wanted to see again—or so he had persuaded himself during the unending night. He should give up on seeing Luis, too, recognize and cut his losses, and get on with his life any way he could.

Yes, he should turn his horse around, go back to the hotel, and then leave word at the Palacio that Charlie Bent could burn Kearny's letter. Such a course would prove best for everyone concerned.

Besides, one other troubling thought remained. If La Tules had it wrong, and if Ana had in fact come down from Taos and was living here at Casa Aragón, he would not want to see her. For his sake, as well as hers. Although it would hurt, he *could* face an Ana Barragán who had turned him away, but a *Señora Aragón?* The least he could do would be to save her the embarrassment a meeting now would bring.

His first impulse when he arose this morning had been one of anger and humiliation. He wanted to fight back, have it out with Luis. It ripped him to the bone that Luis had taken some unfair advantage of Stone's long absence from Ana and had moved in like a thief in the night. But his rage did not last. When he finally reached something resembling sense, he knew he had no right to rage.

Whatever black arts of persuasion Luis might have used to take her from him could be no more unfair than what Brad Stone had done to *him* when he first came to Casa Carson in Taos last year.

He smiled ruefully. He should, after all, consider himself lucky that Luis Aragón had not acted back then on what had almost been a demand by Don Bernardo, that as a man of honor he should "call him out."

"All's fair in love and war."

Luis's claim on the woman they both loved—while seemingly doomed to dismissal after the night in the *casita*—certainly predated his, and the decent little merchant trader had every right to look out for himself.

He had too much regard for Luis to yield to the baser side of his nature.

But in the end he knew he had to see him.

And . . .

There remained the one wispy straw for him to try to grasp. La Tules had said, *"There has been no gossip that the union of Don Luis Aragón and Doña Ana Barragán is not going well . . . but I do wonder. . . ."* This was hardly enough of a straw to pick up and try to rebuild his shattered dream. Forgetfulness, no matter how long it took to reach it, was his only realistic goal.

But . . . Luis might reveal, perhaps unwittingly, what had caused her to change her mind. Perhaps Stone had deluded himself about her love for him from the very start. For his own inner peace, he had to know. Even in the all-too-short time he had known her, he had discovered what a creature of incendiary impulse Ana Barragán could be.

Her marriage to Luis explained, of course, why he had gotten no letters from her for so many months; although she certainly would not lack the courage, she probably did not have the heart to tell him that it was finished between the two of them.

Had he been all along only a convenient instrument to get Luis—a man completely acceptable as a son-in-law to Don Bernardo—to propose to her? He would not allow himself to believe that. She had too great a heart to play him false.

Last night at the casino, before La Tules had pulled the earth from beneath his feet with what she doubtless thought a casual, innocent comment, he had been borne aloft by a euphoria such as he had never known. This morning the world—for all that a blinding-hot sun burned him through his jacket—had turned dark, empty, cold, and as silent as the casino had seemed to be last night as he said good-bye to a bewildered-looking Doña Gertrudes Barceló. He felt some shame now when he remembered how he had brushed away her hand when she tried to take his for a moment and had said, "¿Qué pasa, mí amigo?" He had not answered her.

If he had felt on top of the world last night before her revelation about Ana, he was drowning now in a deep well of despair. His only consolation: It could get no *worse* than this.

2

As he rode through the gate of a rambling, piñon-post corral that stretched between him and the Río he remembered the letter from Kit he was carrying to Doña Josefa. Since he would not be going to Taos it would have to be delivered by other hands, those of Luis Aragón, perhaps. Luis could also deliver the other letter, the one he had written this morning after he found he could not eat so much as a morsel of the breakfast Don Fabiano's *mozo de camas* had served him. The letter wished Doña Ana Barragán y Aragón every happiness.

The good-hearted Mexican would not deny him that. And he would not refuse the silver platter Stone had bought the happy couple for a wedding gift before he started for the Río.

A number of adobe buildings clustered on the east bank of the river made up the Aragón and Son trading post. One, much larger than the rest, and with a huge *portal,* seemed to hold the main place of business and the living quarters. An older Mexican woman stood in the shadows of the overhang, looking at him as he turned his horse to the hitchrail in front of the *portal.* The woman disappeared through an open door with carved lintels and a brightly painted jamb.

He tied the reins off at the hitchrail and looked toward the door again. It framed the slight figure of Luis Aragón.

"I have been expecting you, Don Bradford," Luis said. "I did not know exactly when you would come, but I knew with certainty you would."

A tiny echoing tremor of that first fine rage shook Stone.

"Look, Luis. . . ," he began.

He stopped when he got his first clear, full look at the trader's face.

3

This could not be the Luis Aragón of that night on the Cimarron, or even the painfully ravaged, deeply wounded Luis Aragón of the dance in the Taos plaza when Ana turned him aside so summarily. This face looked back at him as blank and forbidding as a gravestone.

"Luis . . . ," Stone began again, "how is Doña . . ."

He stopped. Had the trader's face darkened even more?

For no apparent reason Brad Stone felt as if he had been struck.

He could not go on.

He suddenly *knew,* as well he had ever known anything in all his life, that the question on his lips would bring an answer he did not want to hear, that the question would dig at the earth beneath the gravestone. Fear clamped icy fingers around his heart.

"Doña Ana is . . . ," Luis Aragón said. He stopped, took a trembling breath, choked, and began again. "Doña Ana is dead." A sob shook his slight body. "And so is the son *mi doña* bore you, *mi amigo. . . .*"

36
No "Child of God"

The longest and most desolate month in the life of Bradford Stone began predictably enough with his longest and most desolate ride, the one to Taos with Luis Aragón.

He had thought the trip up the Río—with every imprint of his and Luis's horses' hooves and those of the two mules Stone trailed bringing them closer to the great *estancia* where Ana and the child had died—actually took less time than when he and Luis, in company with Kit, had ridden up the valley of the Río del Norte more than a year ago. It seemed to stretch out interminably.

Twice Luis had tried to tell him of the particulars of Ana's death—and the child's. And once—marked not so much by what the Santa Féan said, but by the way he stammered as he said it—Luis tried to make an explanation, and an apology, Stone presumed, for his marriage to Ana. Stone turned a deaf ear on all three occasions. The only thing that registered was that Luis himself had not known of Ana's and the infant's deaths for more than a month, learning about it when he rode to the *hacienda* after his return from a long trading mission to St. Louis.

Some day he would want to know every detail, but not now.

But he did not doubt for a second that the child was his. Luis Aragón had said, ". . . *the child* mi doña *bore you. . . .*" The little trader would never lie about a thing like that.

It was almost sundown when they reached the gate.

2

"I'm going in to see the graves, Luis," he said. Except for the trader's feeble efforts to tell him about what had happened, not twenty words had passed between them since they rode away from the northern outskirts of Santa Fe.

"*Sí.* I knew you would."

"Will you wait here for me, or ride on into Taos? Dark will settle in pretty soon."

"Wait? I shall go in with you, of course. . . ." He paused. "Unless you would rather I did not. I would understand."

"I welcome your company, my friend. I will want some time alone with the graves. I was only thinking that if Don Bernardo's order about me still holds, I would not want you caught up in it."

"You need not worry about that, Bradford. I do not believe the Don's threats should worry you now."

"No?"

"Perhaps. I am not *absolutely* sure, but it is not that alone. Even if Don Bernardo still wanted to kill you, he cannot do so tonight. He is not in residence at the *estancia* now. He has not been seen here since a week after Doña

Ana died. All of the servants and the *vaqueros* are gone as well."

"Even Galinda and Roberto?"

"*Sí*. They were the first to go. There is not a *living* soul there now. The whole place is empty from this gate to the gorge on the Río."

"If the *vaqueros* are gone, who looks after the stock?"

"The Navajos will look after it soon, if it goes unattended."

"Where has Don Bernardo gone?"

"No one knows. I have not seen him since I returned and discovered what had happened. My first thought, of course, was to hear from Don Bernardo about . . ." He stopped. "I have asked about him and looked for him everywhere . . . to no avail. He has disappeared completely."

"Let's go, Luis." Stone put the spurs to his horse and rode through the gate.

He reined in at the roadside entrance to the graveyard and began to dismount.

"Don't stop here, *mi amígo*," Aragón said. "We can reach the two graves more quickly if we ride around to the northwest corner, to the old *jacal*. We should proceed on foot from there."

It seemed to Stone that it would have been easier if Luis had taken the lead, but he knew the man would never push himself to the fore that way. That gentle *cortesía* again. It seemed doubly touching now. No matter what they said to each other today and tonight, Stone had to keep in mind that except for the child, his loss was hardly greater than Luis's . . . in Luis's mind at least.

3

They tied off their mounts at the rickety, windswept old hut.

"This *jacal* is where your son was born, Bradford," Luis

said. "Doña Ana, Galinda, and Fra Porfirio, the sacristan at San Francisco de Asis in Ranchos de Taos, were on their way to the *iglesia* for *mi doña* to make her last confession to Padre Martínez before the *niño* came. A big storm stopped them here. They took shelter in the *jacal* just before the baby's time."

"Is this where they died?"

"No. Right after the birth Galinda and Roberto took her and the *niño* back to the *hacienda*. Fra Porfirio waited for the storm to go away and came to San Francisco de Asis. They died two days later, Fra Porfirio told me. Only Galinda, Roberto, and the Don were present then. Padre Martínez did not reach the *hacienda* in time to administer the last rites. Another great storm stopped him. I, of course, was still returning from St. Louis. We could go to Fra Porfirio if you like, but you will find him quite confused."

Stone looked down the line of markers toward the road. None of them appeared as if they had just been set in place. The graveyard did not look as if it had changed by as much as one solitary clump of weeds since he saw it last.

"The two new graves are not with those of the other Barragáns, Luis?"

"No."

"Why not? Do you know?"

"I think you will know when you look at them. . . ."

Luis pointed away from the graveyard and up a path, obviously new, but with young, pale green and dead white shoots of sage already beginning to close it up. Another few weeks and even someone who knew it was there would have difficulty finding it. The path led off to the northwest and away from the graveyard itself.

"But that's not even in the cemetery," Stone said.

"No, Bradford. It is not. It wounds me deeply, but apparently Don Bernardo would not listen to Padre Martínez. The padre is a stern priest, but he said that in this case he would gladly have Doña Ana buried in consecrated ground. The Don would not hear of it."

"He denied this to his own daughter?"

"I was as mystified as you . . . until I saw the gravestones."

The Santa Féan hung back again until some moments after Stone set off up the path, then he swung in behind him. A hundred feet from the *jacal* a large *chamisa* partially hid the two stones.

He read the first.

Ana María Barragán y Aragón
A.D. 1827–A.D. 1846

No "Wife and Mother," no "Child of God," no "Requiescat in Pace," just the bare, emotionless notation of Ana's nineteen vanished years . . . not even the month and day.

The smaller marker shocked him even more. He knew why Luis had said, ". . . *you will know when you look at them. . . .*"

Bradford Luis Cristóbal Aragón
A.D. 1846

Naming the child for him must have been the last impulse to which impulsive Ana María Barragán y Aragón ever yielded.

He could only guess at the rage that drove Don Bernardo Barragán to bury his daughter on godless ground.

He turned away from the stones. He and Luis looked at each other for a moment, then the Santa Féan stepped forward and took Brad Stone into his embrace, an awkward movement for the smaller man. Strangely, it was less so for Brad Stone.

"Do you wish your time alone now, Bradford?" Luis said.

"I do not think I do after all, Luis."

He cried. Sobs shook him, their regular, deep rhythm interrupted by those he heard coming from Luis Aragón.

37
Through Carson's Eyes

Brad Stone's third day in Taos had ended by the time he remembered he should by rights report to Governor Charlie Bent.

Actually, he could think of no reason to rush a meeting with Bent, except that he would sooner or later have to tell that good man he would be leaving his service at the Palace in Santa Fe even before he entered it. General Kearny's letter specified no date either for reporting to the governor or beginning a tour of duty with him. When he had ridden north from Socorro to Santa Fe with Tom Fitzpatrick he had smiled at the latitude afforded him by these convenient omissions. Without any particular pangs of guilt he had, since Socorro, planned several days, perhaps a week, with Ana before he saw Bent. His intent had firmed when he failed to find the governor at the Palace.

But now he recognized that he not only had to answer the call of duty where it concerned Charlie, but that he was even deeper in debt to Kit. Had it not been for Stone talking him out of coming north before they met with Kearny, Kit might well be in Taos at the moment, too, and with Josefa. But the scout's presence in Taos now would have laid Kit open to charges of desertion and would have posed grave risks for Stone's friend. Stone's being on the scene at Socorro had surely denied Carson any option for himself, but it had given

Stone everything he wanted. Yes, he owed Kit. Nothing new or different in that.

He decided with some reluctance to give Taos until Christmas. The decision was a painful one, but not, when all was said and done, a difficult one to make. Luis told him that no wagons were leaving for Bent's Fort or the Cimarron Cutoff until sometime in late January. Perhaps he would get lucky. Charlie might want to send him back down to Santa Fe to work. But did he want to stay in the capital any more than he wanted to stay in Taos?

He knew he could not afford to keep his room on the plaza very long. And buying all his meals singly, inexpensive as it was here compared to Santa Fe, would deplete his money all too soon, particularly if that good sergeant down at the Palace had not yet figured out a way to get him at least a little more of his back pay.

Luis helped him rent an adobe *casa* at the southern edge of town that belonged to Ceran St. Vrain, who set Luis a ridiculously low price. "I would have let Brad have it gratis, *mi amigo*," St. Vrain said, "but I have a reputation as a shrewd businessman to maintain."

The little dwelling boasted a postage stamp–sized corral and a *jacal* that to Stone's mild revulsion looked a disturbing twin of the hut at the burial ground where Ana had given birth to Bradford Luis Cristóbal that night.

He hated the *jacal*.

During those first three days, whenever he rode to the small *mercado* in the plaza to buy food, or when he returned from the two trips he made to the graveyard by himself, he just turned his horse loose in the corral with the two mules rather than lead it across the straw, caliche, and manure, and into the piñon-post shelter. He had not entered the *jacal* at the graveyard. And he would not have entered this one, either, even once. But the close quarters of the *casa* itself demanded that he use the shed to store his mapping and painting gear. There was a lot of it: the theodolite and plane table, leather map cases. His sketchbooks and the finished and partly finished canvases now filled three wooden crates. He wondered if he would ever again find the strength to return to the field sketches and unfinished paintings.

The *jacal* had been laid out poorly; its open side faced the north and the worst of the weather. He did not let it worry him. He had not refined his plans, but they definitely did not include a stay of any length in Taos. Christmas, he had told himself, but perhaps not even that long.

He draped a tarpaulin from the ridge line to protect his goods, and once he'd lashed the tarp in place he grimaced at how little the work looked like the diamond hitch he had finally learned to tie. Some of the unfinished pictures lay on top of the plane table. He forgot about them. Or thought he did.

2

His fourth full day in Taos, a rare cloudy one, he spent almost entirely within the four walls of the *casa*, staring at the remains of a neglected fire. He could not rouse himself to stir the ashes or rekindle it. He kept his two tiny windows shuttered and the front door barred.

His mind turned again as to what he would do once he left Taos. A return to Illinois for a few days at least, but then what? He would think about it again tonight. Being left alone like this had its compensations. Even the company of Luis Aragón would have been excessive.

But when five o'clock rolled around and Luis knocked at his door to ask him to supper, he found he was glad to see the Santa Féan again.

3

"Señora Carson has asked about you, Bradford," Aragón said when they looked at each other across the table in the tiny cantina on the south side of the plaza, right in back of the *portal* where he had taken wine with Ana at the dance that night. Luis had been there at the time, too, he remembered. "Doña Josefa is concerned about you. You must call upon her and set her mind at ease. I think, too, that she wants news of Don Cristóbal."

"She knows I am in Taos?"

"*¡Sí!* Everyone knows you are here. Not only Doña Josefa, but Don Carlos Bent, Doña Ignacia, Señor St. Vrain, of course, Señor Turley . . . all of Don Cristóbal's friends . . . and yours. They are *all* worried about you."

"None of them have called on me. Not that I blame them. I'm poor company these days. And they probably think me responsible for what happened at the *estancia*." He thought that over. "At that . . . I cannot deny I am responsible."

"*¡No, no, no, Don Bradford!* It is not so! And they would never think it was. They only wish to leave you alone with your grief . . . for as long as it will take."

"*¿Y tú, también, Luis?* Do they leave *you* alone?"

Luis shrugged, a small, failed attempt to rid himself of pain. "*¿Quién sabe?* They grieve some for me, of course. But for all that Doña Ana and I were man and . . ." He broke off, flustered, controlled himself with an effort that left him trembling. "I do not think they ever really put Doña Ana and me together in their minds. It was always you, Bradford, from the first day you rode into Taos with Don Cristóbal and me and met her at Casa Carson."

This grief-stricken man, for all his decency, must rue that day deeply. "Well . . . ," Stone said, "I do have a letter from

Kit to Doña Josefa to deliver. I realize now I should have done it sooner. I'll see her tomorrow morning, and Señor and Señora Bent in the afternoon."

"*¡Bueno!*" Luis's smile was one of unbridled delight, but then it subsided. "*Por favor*, Bradford . . . I . . ." He could not seem to get underway again.

"Go on, Luis."

"On the ride up from Santa Fe . . . I tried to tell you some things. I beg you to listen to me now."

"Go ahead, *amigo*."

"I must assure you . . ." There was no mistaking the blush that came to Luis's face now for the reflection of a red sky. "Please . . . it is important for the memory of Doña Ana that you believe me about this. She and I . . . never . . ."

Stone saw at once where this was leading. He wanted to stop Luis, but he knew the man had to get this out.

Luis continued. "We never once . . . lived as man and wife. Had she not died, I do not know whether or not we ever would have. . . . She only married me to wring a promise from Don Bernardo. She had no love for me such as she had for you. I do not delude myself."

"You did not have to tell me this, Luis."

"I do not know about *yanquis,* but here in Nuevo Méjico, men feel very strongly about such things."

Then it all gushed out, as if Luis Aragón were a suddenly opened genie's flagon that had been stoppered for an eternity.

Stone heard it all, saw it all clearly, felt every pang as if every bit of it had happened to him.

Tiny, impish Ana Barragán at the age of nine, sitting with her black head bowed in not entirely convincing piety in the cathedral at Santa Fe when her widowed father took her to the provincial capital for Easter Mass. Sober, slim, sad-eyed, sixteen-year-old Luis Aragón, full of adolescent dignity in the row behind her, trying to catch her black eyes and somehow persuading himself he could do it without her knowing how hard he was working at it. Luis at nineteen, on a visit to Estancia Barragán with his trader father, with a rage in his loins when he caught sight of her that shamed and delighted him all at once, and getting himself sadly beaten in a horse race against a twelve-year-old Ana who had already ridden like the wind when only half that age. Twenty-two-year-old Luis writing a dozen impassioned letters to her in as many days—without posting a single one of them to the budding chatelaine in the grand *estancia* up the Río, for fear that she might laugh. Clumsy Luis carrying a flute of champagne to Ana at a party at the Palace in the days when Manuel Armijo governed New Mexico, only to trip and spill it over her black-lace tea gown when he reached her.

Worse still was the scene in which Stone himself played a part. The fandango in the Taos plaza. Luis did not mention it in his heavy, aching litany, but Stone remembered it, too well for comfort now. He remembered, too, his own misconceptions at the time.

At the dance he had been sure he had made an enemy, and felt that way until the night Luis helped him find La Cayuda.

Oh, yes, he remembered it. Crushed, lonely, forsaken Luis facing Stone and Ana that first night, when she said, "*Lo siento, Don Luis. . . .* I am sorry, but I have promised every dance to Don Bradford here," and then turned from him without so much as another glance.

So much for comparing losses. Brad Stone had known Ana a mere two weeks. Until this moment he'd had no conception of what torment loving Ana must have been for Luis, who had held the dream for more than ten years, had at long last won the prize he sought—if one could *call* it winning—only to have it ripped from his grasp before he could take a firm hold on it.

"*Muchísimas gracias, Luis,*" Stone said as they parted. "I am much in your debt, *amigo.*"

"¿*Por qué?* For this pitiful little dinner and that execrable *aguardiente? De nada.*"

4

"Don't apologize, Brad," Charlie Bent said. "But I *am* glad you saw Josefa Carson first. She's been worried sick about you. Ignacia and I didn't mind the wait."

"Thanks for understanding, Mr. Bent." Stone smiled for the first time in a week.

Dressed in what was probably her Sunday best, Doña Ignacia looked ready to swarm on him, too much like Aunt Flossie back in Groverton, who was never completely happy unless she got a chance to mother someone violently. When Stone came through the door three minutes earlier, Ignacia had hugged him with every bit of the force the giant Basil Lajeunesse might have used, and when she released him, flooded her lace handkerchief with tears.

"I believe I persuaded Mrs. Carson that at least I was in the land of the living," he said.

"Now look, son . . . ," Charlie said, his discomfort all too apparent. "If you don't want to talk about what happened at Estancia Barragán, we'll understand that." He cast a stern if loving look at his wife.

"Thank you again, sir. I guess I don't want to talk about it. Not yet, at any rate. What I suppose we *have* to talk about is General Kearny's letter. I hope you didn't mind my having it delivered this morning instead of bringing it around myself. I wanted you to have time to digest it before we met. I'm not sure I could have watched you read it without bolting. And I had Mrs. Carson's letter from Kit to deliver, too."

"I didn't mind at all. I sure didn't expect to hear from Kearny about you, of course, but I must say that few pieces of correspondence in all my life have made me happier."

"It was Kit's idea, Mr. Bent."

"No surprise. It was too damned delicately phrased for the Stephen Watts Kearny I worked with in the early days of the American occupation, and entirely too reasonable. Yes, I smelled Kit's horny little mountain-man hand all over that letter. That said, and now that you know how welcome you are here . . . when can you start to work for me—for me and New Mexico?"

Stone wondered if he had steeled himself sufficiently for this. "That's what I want to talk about, sir. I . . ." He had to cast the die. "I wish to resign my commission and return to my home in Illinois."

A thunderclap could not have frozen Charles Bent more.

"Don't . . . don't say that, Brad," he stammered when he recovered. "Your country needs you . . . we need you . . . here."

"I *will* be serving my country, Mr. Bent." In the past few seconds he had reached a decision. "I intend to find one of the regiments still forming for duty in Mexico, and enlist, right after I've seen my family. I'm sure Kit would agree it's what I have to do. I would rejoin him rather than go east, but I'm not sure I could get back to California by myself. Besides, the war seems to be finished there."

"There's a lot more to serving your country than just picking up a gun. This territory has a desperate need of capable, educated young men like you."

"But now that it's part of the United States there will be hundreds of such men coming out from the East . . . lawyers, doctors, engineers . . . solid professionals with much more to recommend them than is the case with me, Mr. Bent."

"That's only partly true. Each of them will have one big thing missing in their makeup."

"What's that, sir?"

"Not one of them will just have finished more than a year of working, exploring, and fighting with Kit Carson, as you have." Charlie smiled. "You know . . . I could just plain order you to join my staff. I would, if I thought I could get the same kind of good work out of you I would get if you joined it willingly. Tell you what. Take a week to think it over. Give me your decision then."

"All right, Mr. Bent. I've got time. Luis Aragón says there are no outfits leaving Santa Fe for the East for at least another month, anyway. But I don't want to hold out any false hopes to you in the interim."

Doña Ignacia burst into another short session of weeping just before he made his good-bye.

5

He met with Charlie the next morning in the governor's Taos "office," a dingy, lamplit alcove in the same cantina where Stone and Aragón had dined a few nights before.

A line of villagers, mostly women, stretched from the table to the door. It became clear at the start that the day's business would consist of listening to complaints. Someone's goat had ravaged someone else's vegetable plot, the headgate on an irrigation ditch had been closed an hour before it should have been. With the latter grievance played out like a miniature trial—no lawyers, but with testimony from a variety of voluble witnesses—Stone began to understand something of the relatively awesome power over village life held by an *acéquia mayordomo,* a "ditch boss." If he had not known it before leaving Groverton, the last year and a half in the West had taught him that there was only one thing that counted for more than a tin of beans out here west of the 100th Principal Meridian: water.

"This kind of thing used to be handled by the Taos *alcalde*," Charlie said during a short break in the morning's proceedings. "We ain't had an *alcalde* since Kearny marched into Santa Fe. The old mayor was an Armijo man and he just picked up and left."

"But isn't there some village government in place?"

"Not much. That lawbook Kearny had his Colonel Doniphan write ain't too clear about how some of the smaller places like Taos ought to be run. I'd like you to take over this chore for me, Brad, whenever I'm down in Santa Fe. I hold it to one of these sessions a week. I'll bring you down to the capital with me as soon as we get a new *alcalde* or somebody like him here. You'll stand in for him till then. You'll have to find other ways to occupy your time. It ain't exactly a full-time job."

It did not look hard. But if it were not "exactly a full-time job," why did not Charlie turn it over to someone like Ceran St. Vrain, or Simeon Turley? They knew these people far better than Stone ever would, knew their needs and desires, and at least something of what they might consider justice. He had to admit to a deep satisfaction that Charlie Bent wanted him to stay so badly.

The small items of business Charlie discussed with his petitioners sounded serious enough, but the alcove resounded with a lot of high good humor, too. It there was any of the unrest La Tules had spoken of here in Taos, Stone failed to detect it in the conversations and comments that emanated from the patient line which at times stretched clear into the plaza.

He had dinner again that night with Aragón and discussed La Tules' faintly troubling views with the trader. It occurred to him that he might perhaps be taking a mild risk. He knew nothing of Luis's politics. For all Stone knew, he could be part of the unrest, if there were any.

"Perhaps there's some discontent down around Santa Fe, but not up here, Bradford," Luis said in answer to his question. "Most of our ties with Mexico were frayed or broken years ago. I do not suppose it would be wise for your government to try to make us into *yanquis* too quickly, but most of us look for better times now that you and your army are here. Not the least of the 'better times' will be a chance for more freedom than we have ever had under Mexico. *Pero* . . . much like *aguardiente* on an empty *estómago* . . . some of freedom's blessings can be heady stuff for a people who have always looked at their rulers as *los papás grandes*. We might not all be ready for too much freedom all at once."

"Then you think if there was to be trouble it would happen in Santa Fe rather than here?"

"*¡Sí!* In Santa Fe it would not surprise me greatly."

"How long are you going to stay in Taos, Luis? You do have a business to run in Santa Fe, don't you?"

The Mexican cast his eyes down into his plate. "I will stay here until I see Don Bernardo. I will keep my room at La Posada."

"Oh?"

"You will soon be gone from this country, Bradford. Someone must look after Doña Ana's grave . . . and that of the child. If Don Bernardo brings the servants back, only Galinda would dare to tend a grave in unsanctified ground. I want his permission to come and go on Barragán land freely." He looked up and straight into Stone's eyes. "You must understand, Don Bradford, that even if the Don does not allow this, I will do it anyway. After all, Doña Ana is . . . was . . . my wife . . . and the boy bore my name. But I do wish Don Bernardo's blessing."

When Aragón had said, *"You will soon be gone . . ."* Stone had not heard the faintest hint of criticism. Perhaps it pleased Luis to be the sole guardian of that tiny, lost stretch of earth. More likely, knowing the man as he had come to know him, Luis was just giving his assurance that Stone need not worry.

6

Ignacia Bent invited him to dinner, and when he arrived he found the expected assortment of other guests: Josefa Carson; Ceran St. Vrain, minus his wife who had pleaded illness; Simeon Turley, the mill owner from Arroyo Hondo north of town; and Mrs. Turley, whose first name did not register. Aragón's presence was a minor surprise.

He found his place at the table next to Ignacia and directly across the table from still another guest, a dark-eyed young woman whose beauty was slightly marred by what appeared to be a perpetual sulk. Other than that, she looked so much like Josefa Carson he would have bet his last dime she was a Jaramillo. Yes, she looked like Josefa, but another, closer look revealed an even more remarkable resemblance to Ana Barragán.

He was not the only one at the table who felt that way. Luis, from his wounded, utterly sick stare at the girl, who was two places from him, must have been struck hard by the resemblance, too. If Stone had not already sized up Ignacia Bent and made allowances for her as another of those obsessively mothering, "Lady Bountiful" types, he would have thought the presence of the young woman a cruel joke, one played on Aragón as well.

Ignacia sat at the foot of the table with the young woman on her left and Stone on her right. She beamed first on one and then the other, making faint clucking sounds which Stone tried not to feel uncharitable about. "Señor Stone," she had said as they all sat down, "allow me to present *mi prima Señorita Ángela Peralta Jaramillo. Doña Ángela, te presento Don Bradford Stone, un amigo norteamericano de mi esposo.*"

Yes, she was another Jaramillo cousin. He smiled at the girl.

Ignacia turned back to him. "Doña Ángela is an unmarried lady, Don Bradford."

It struck him squarely between the eyes. How could he have been so stupid? Ignacia had no thought of cruelty. She was matchmaking!

He had little to worry about. Doña Ángela obviously had tumbled to what her cousin was up to well before Stone had himself, and was even more put out at the attempt at pairing the two of them than he was. She sat as mute and unresponsive as an adobe brick.

When they had finished eating and had moved into the parlor, Bent fell in beside him. "Sorry about that, Brad. I tried to stop her, but Ignacia is a very determined woman. However, she won't throw Cousin Ángela at you again. She does learn. But don't look so relieved. You're not out of the woods yet. There are more than a dozen other unmarried Jaramillo *primas* in the valley. There will be a parade of them when you are here."

The talk over coffee, *cigarros*, and *aguardiente* soon ran to the war with Mexico and the situation in California.

"Do we control the whole coast now, Brad?" St. Vrain asked.

"We did when I left, sir. Colonel Frémont must be governor by now." He noticed that he had said the last with more than a little pride. Well, he and Kit had been through a lot with Johnny Frémont. "I guess the situation is much as it is here. The native Californios have gotten tired of being Mexicans. Like *New* Mexicans, they've pretty much turned in favor of the United States after years of dealing with our traders and settlers. There are times, though, when I do think they might want to have their own little country instead of joining us, and that alone could lead to trouble. I'm no strategist, but from what I saw in Los Angeles, our commanders on the scene, Colonel Frémont and Commodore Stockton, are ready for it if it comes."

St. Vrain turned to Aragón. "*Are* Nuevo Méjicanos and Californios alike in the respect Mr. Stone just spoke of, Don Luis? Do your people here want to throw us Americans out so they can have their own country?"

Poor Luis. He looked as if St. Vrain had just slapped him. "I am not a political *hombre, señor*," he stammered. "I am only a man of business. Surely you know that."

Stone saw a small ripple of doubt or trouble or something like both of them pass over the trader's features before St. Vrain spoke again.

"Of course, Luis. Forgive me. It was unfair of me to ask. We have absolutely nothing to fear here in Taos. Not with so many New Mexican friends like you." St. Vrain turned back to Stone. "How does Kit feel about things in California?"

The question shocked Stone, not so much by its content, but by the fact that after more than a year of close, at times intimate, contact with the great scout, he found—even at this moment—that he had no deeper understanding of Carson than he had had that day when he sent him sprawling in the mess hall doorway of Bent's Fort.

"Kit doesn't give much away, Mr. St. Vrain."

"No, he doesn't." That seemed to close the subject for the Taos merchant. He turned to Charlie Bent. "When are you heading down to the capital, Charlie?"

"Next week. Soon as I get Brad here set for his duties as my deputy in Taos. I'll be back the second week in January."

"Just about the time I leave for Santa Fe."

"Hate to miss Christmas with Ignacia and her family, but it can't be helped," Bent went on. "Maybe Brad can fill in for me there, too, provided I get Ignacia's word that she won't marry him off by New Year's Day." The laughter that followed told Stone that no one had missed the byplay at the table.

The evening ended shortly afterward, and Stone walked Luis Aragón back to his inn on the way to his own tiny adobe house. A blind and deaf man would have seen and heard the trouble besetting the Santa Féan, even though he had not uttered a word by the time they reached the empty, silent plaza.

As they neared the weathered old gazebo, Stone pointed to its steps. "Let's sit down and talk for a moment, Luis. Something's bothering you."

"No hay problema, mí amigo. But perhaps it would be better if I did unburden myself. I feel a little ashamed that I did not feel I could do so with those two fine men back there, even though I am firmly in their camp when it comes to the future of New Mexico. Most of my people have no desire to remain under the rule of Mexico City, but in this day and age it would be futile to try and become a nation on our own. We are astride the most logical trade route to California and that alone would bring difficulties. There are, I fear, some who think we could manage our own affairs successfully. I am not one of them." He fell silent. His slight body seemed to quiver a little, as if wracked by inaudible sobs. "It shocked me to find that Señor St. Vrain feels there is nothing to worry about here in Taos. In the main I agree, but the easy conquest General Kearny made when he reached Santa Fe has, I am afraid, lulled the *señor* far too much. I don't know about Señor Bent."

"I noticed your uneasiness, Luis. Do you know something that . . . they don't?"

"Not really, Bradford. It is just a feeling. If I had any facts at my disposal, I would have spoken. But the feeling is a powerful one. The extended absence of Don Bernardo still troubles me. Perhaps he has just gone to Cañon de Chelly to trade with the Navajo, but if that is the case, why did he take his *vaqueros* with him? He is welcome in Dinetah, but his riders aren't. Of course there is no evidence that he took them anywhere. He might just have let them go. I myself might well have abandoned my own life and property—and certainly my work—if I had lost a daughter in the terrible way . . ." His voice trailed off.

"I know it sounds ridiculous," Stone said, "but when Señor Bent goes down to Santa Fe next week, I will more or less be in charge here. I'm not sure I'm up to it. Please help me. Stay on in Taos until Señor Bent returns, *por favor.*"

"I will be glad to help in every way I can, *amigo.* It will not at all be hard for me to do. I hope you will stay many years in New Mexico."

"I won't stay in New Mexico, Luis, and particularly not in Taos. I can't. Not after . . ."

"I am staying."

"But this is your home. Or close enough."

"I hoped by now it would be yours as well. Your heart will always be here, Bradford. And you are exactly the kind of man we need, even more than we need Señor Carson."

"That's flattering, my friend, but no one could ever take Kit's place."

"I suppose not . . . but if there were someone—it would be Don Bradford Stone."

7

The next morning Stone became aware that something disturbing had been happening to him.

Try as he might, he had difficulty recalling exactly what Ana Barragán looked like. The worst of it was that he could safely bet any amount of money that nothing of this sort had happened to Aragón—and never would.

Through all the waking hours of the next three days he conjured up her image only to have it fragment like a struck pane of glass whose shards, lighter than air, fluttered to the earth.

Could this possibly mean that he had not truly loved her?

He could not, *would* not believe that.

If he lived a thousand years the void inside him would never fill.

But he had to get her back, had to at least see her loved face again, if only in sorrowing memory.

It would have to begin with getting over the fear of the dilapidated *jacal* where she had given birth to his son. It would be easier to enter it now that he knew that she and the child had not actually died there.

He rode to the Barragán graveyard on the third afternoon, stood bareheaded in front of her headstone, and went through the same exercise—with no more success than he had known in the seclusion of his room. He nearly panicked when her face flickered into sight and then faded before he could fix it again in his mind.

He walked to the *jacal* and stepped inside.

He found nothing but errant weeds. The weak, late December afternoon sunlight sifting through the flimsy, latticed roof of the *jacal* made pale hieroglyphics on the dark floor, and the shadows it formed were impossible to separate from substance.

Then a glint of reflected sunlight on the floor of the *jacal* caught his eye. He went to his knees to look at it. Something was half buried in the weeds and dirt. He pulled it free from the grip of the caliche and held it up to a shaft of light.

It took a moment for him to realize he was looking at the silver pin Ana had worn at her neck the day he'd met her at Kit and Josefa Carson's.

He struggled to his feet and jammed the pin in his pocket.

One more thing remained to be done while he was here. Luis could be wrong, of course, when he said the Don and his servants had deserted the *estancia,* but he had to chance it. He had to get closer to where Ana and his son had died.

He mounted, eased his horse back to the white road, and turned it toward the *hacienda.*

On the southern side of the road a small herd of Mexican cattle pushed their way through the sage, perhaps twenty animals in all, and nowhere near as fat or ponderously lively as he remembered the Barragán stock. One or two actually looked gaunt, close to starving. They paralleled his ride nervously for perhaps half a mile, then turned back into the sage as if giving up on something. *"This hombre who rides so carefully,"* they seemed to say, *"will not bring us salt, or move us to a lusher pasture. He is of no further use to us."* They sent baleful, reproachful looks back at him just before they vanished.

The mammoth old brick-and-adobe mansion indeed looked forlornly empty when he neared it, the gates in the stockpen fences gaping wide and with no slavering wolfhounds raging at him from the *portal* this time, either.

He made a full circuit of the *hacienda*, looking for signs of occupancy. He found none. He had to guess at which of the small dark windows opened into the room where Ana and their baby died. *Their* baby? He had been so shattered by the loss of her he had not considered his other loss sufficiently. When he settled on the most likely window, he stared up at it for long minutes. There could be no rushing this, and little need.

No Don Bernardo Barragán nor any of his ruthless *vaqueros* lurked behind the columns or in the covered walkways to threaten him.

And yet . . .

Perhaps it was only because his horse suddenly reared without warning and whinnied apprehensively, but he could not have felt a greater sense of menace had he faced a dozen rifles aimed squarely at his head. It lasted but a second.

He would leave now. The trip had solved absolutely nothing, had brought no answers.

He rode out through the gate without one backward glance at the wrought-iron sign whose black arch had lost none of its searing insolence. It did not matter. This might be the last time he ever came to Estancia Barragán.

But as he passed the massive bulk of San Francisco at Ranchos de Taos, he remembered something and his heart leaped.

He dug his spurs into his horse mercilessly, and used the free ends of the reins on its flank harder than he ever had.

Back at his little adobe *casa* he turned the poor flagging animal loose in the corral before unsaddling it or wiping it down, and sprinted for the *jacal*.

He found what he was looking for quickly enough; the sketches he had made of Ana at the *casita*. As he studied them he knew—even in the waning light—that now he would never forget her face again.

He would begin tomorrow morning, turning the sketches into the oils he had always planned. If the mild weather of the past month held for as much as one more week, he could use the open-sided *jacal* as a studio and accomplish miracles. The careless situating of that open side would now work to his advantage. It would provide him with all the north light he needed.

He did not even have to make a conscious decision about the style of Ana's portraits. The technique he used would be the one Ed Kern had been so ecstatic about in the shade of Lassen Peak. Estancia Barragán, the graveyard, the great *hacienda* itself, and the *jacal* at the northwest corner of it, would find their ways into the backgrounds. If his work was fearless and truthful enough, so would the gate and its hateful sign. Ana's face and figure in the foregrounds would counter any threat he felt.

He could almost hear Kit's voice prompting him to his duties.

8

By the time Charlie Bent left for Santa Fe on the following Monday, Stone had already done three paintings that pleased him, and brushed in the underpaintings for half a dozen more, including one from the nude charcoal study he had made of her just before they parted. For that he had used up the last of the canvases he had trailed the better part of five thousand miles around the West. He had also managed to find time to log in three sessions with the governor at the alcove table in the cantina.

9

Bent raised no objections when Stone suggested that Luis sit in with them. As a matter of fact he welcomed the idea, and gave his full approval when Stone asked if he could employ the trader as an assistant "at least until my feet are on the ground, Mr. Bent."

"Absolutely," Bent said. "I can't pay him, though, until my government stops relying on La Tules' charity. But by the way, Brad, ain't you going to get around to calling me Charlie even once before I die?"

His intentions for the long haul notwithstanding, he did feel at home in this sweet little village. And the feeling would intensify when Kit returned to it. That, of course, was unlikely to happen until long after Stone packed his bags and left for Illinois, something he had better get straight with the governor without delay.

"I'll stay on the job until you come back up from the capital, Charlie."

"Nothing can persuade you to settle in Taos permanently?"

"No, sir."

"You won't wait for Kit?"

It hurt Stone a little when he said, "I'm sorry."

10

With his mind made up to leave as soon as Charlie Bent returned, he actually turned his energies quite willingly, and certainly with industry, to doing the work Bent had assigned him. Fastening his attention on the problems a steady stream of villagers and farmers brought to the alcove table kept him from agonizing over his own predicament . . . some. It seemed to do Luis a world of good, too.

Aragón proved invaluable. Stone needed him for his Spanish, but the trader surprised him with the close way in which he identified with the wishes of the petitioners. Vastly more educated, certainly separated by wealth and background from the humble people who came to the table, Luis demonstrated an almost uncanny ability to become one of them in the blink of an eye.

But however much the Santa Féan's empathy gave birth to a clear, sensible solution to a vexing problem about grazing rights or water distribution through the *acéqias,* he discreetly deferred to Stone in every decision. Those decisions for the most part proved easy and obvious, made so by the information Luis elicited from the cotton-clad would-be litigants. Most were merely suggestions, agreed to readily enough by both sides of a dispute. These peasants and townsfolk wanted more than anything to just be heard, and more frequently than not a sympathetic hearing was all it took.

"You have a genius for this, Bradford," Luis said at the

end of one session. "Governor Bent is fortunate to have your services."

"Nonsense. You do far more than I."

"*Por favor*—listen to a friend. You should stay in New Mexico."

"Don't start that again, *amigo*. I'll be on my way east as soon as Charlie Bent comes back."

11

He spent a quiet Christmas Day with Ignacia Bent, Josefa Carson, and Aragón. The Jaramillo sisters tried valiantly to make their Christmas dinner a festive one, but without Kit or Charlie present, their efforts succeeded only in part.

Ignacia must have heeded some warning from Charlie. Stone had more or less expected to see another young Jaramillo woman—perhaps two of them, since highly eligible bachelor-widower Luis probably figured in Ignacia's matchmaking schemes as much as he did—but none appeared.

In the shop next door to the cantina he had bought a pair of fine woolen *rebozos* for the two women, who donned the shawls immediately with a sincere show of gratitude, despite the fact that a blazing fire in the beehive fireplace had turned the sitting room almost uncomfortably warm.

He decided he would never really know how his gift for Luis—one of the smaller paintings of Ana, a quite traditional head study—had been received. He had pondered long and hard over whether to give it to his friend or not, had finally decided he wanted to do it so much that he had to take the chance.

"*Muchísimas gracias, Don Bradford,*" Luis muttered in dead, flat tones when he peeled the wrapping from the small canvas.

He stared at the painting in silence.

"You'll have to get it framed when you return to Santa Fe, Don Luis. I found a brilliant woodcarver here in Taos, what I believe you call a *santero*, but he has never done picture framing."

Luis excused himself, saying he wished to step outside to smoke a *cigarro*. He did not ask Stone to accompany him. Ignacia opened her mouth, probably to tell the Santa Féan he could smoke inside if he wished, but Josefa held up her hand and hushed her. Sensitive woman, as well as beautiful. No wonder Kit loved her so .

Brad caught a glimpse of Luis through the front window, but turned his eyes away. Even *looking* at him now would be an intrusion.

12

He excused himself from his *"alcalde"* duties for the week between Christmas and New Year's and finished the rest of the Ana paintings. They pleased him immensely, but he idly wished he had a good critic at hand to give him an honest opinion. He would have to send them east, and for right now he was not inclined to do so.

He opened his "office" at the table in the cantina on the second day of January 1847. A muscular *carretero* from a Río village wanted a license to freight goods in and out of Taos. Charlie had not mentioned this sort of thing specifically, but Stone wrote the man a letter and charged him one American dollar for the privilege of doing business with the local merchants. He was not quite sure what he should do with the money. The burly teamster seemed to think the arrangement fair.

Stone had not looked at the man waiting so patiently in line behind the *carretero*. He began an apology in Spanish for the length of the previous transaction without looking up from his paperwork.

The man in line interrupted. "Don't apologize, Brad. We all have our cross to bear," he said.

Stone looked up, straight into the grinning face of Edward Kern.

"Good Lord, Ed! What on earth—"

"I'm on my way to Bent's," Kern said. "I'll be heading back to California with a trainload of ammunition and supplies I'm to escort across the mountains once it gets to the Arkansas, about the first of February. I came east on the old Spanish Trail and it gave me a chance to stop in Taos and have a cup of coffee with you. Finish up your business. Don't rush on my account. I'll be at the bar."

There were only three more locals in the line, and Stone heard their pleas and settled with them in a hurry. He put Luis in charge of dealing with any stragglers or latecomers and joined the Philadelphian.

"How are things in California?" Stone said.

"We've had to put down a full-scale rebellion."

"What?"

"It produced the heaviest fighting since we reached the coast last year, but maybe you already know about it."

"I haven't heard a word. There hasn't been a peep out of Santa Fe either. I thought the war in California was over."

"So did we. But Don José Castro had other notions. He surprised Kearny at a place called San Pasqual, soon after he reached California, and gave him an awful beating. His lancers absolutely decimated Kearny's famous First Dragoons."

An alarm bell rang in Stone's head. "How's Kit?"

"Fine . . . now."

"Now? He's not been hurt or wounded, has he?"

"No, not a scratch. He came close enough. Anybody else would sure as hell have died. What he did do was to save Kearny's pompous military ass."

"How?"

"There's a whole lot of stuff I'll have to tell you first. Incidentally, I'm carrying a letter from Kit to Mrs. Carson."

"Let's get that done right away, then. Look, I'll try to be patient about that 'whole lot of stuff,' but I want to hear all of it. How long can you stay?"

"Just a night or two. Do you have a place I can scrub off some of this trail muck before I meet Mrs. Carson?"

"We'll go to my house. It will take an hour to start a fire and get enough water heated for a decent bath, though."

"I'll wait. I can use that coffee I spoke about, too."

"How did you know I was in Taos, Ed?"

"Kit said you wouldn't be anywhere else. He mentioned a young woman. . . ."

"Luis," Stone called out, "please take over for me. Send for me at *mi casa* if you really need me."

13

As they walked the half mile to the adobe with Kern leading his horse, and Stone his friend's packhorse, Stone began to get some of the particulars of Ed's present trip to Bent's and of the events in California since he left it.

"Did you ride east alone?" he asked.

"Hell no! I'm not Kit. I've got six men here in town."

"Anyone I know?"

"Don't think so. They're all Californians, three of them Hargrave's people. Good bunch."

"Do they need food or anything?"

"They've already started to trade with the villagers. This is a mighty friendly town. Carson said you'd be here, but you could have knocked me over with a feather when I found out you were working for the governor. By the way, those of your new friends I talked with this morning think the world of you. If they held an election tomorrow you just might give Charlie a run for his money."

Stone decided to pass on that for the moment. "It's good to see you, *amigo*. Now, bring me up to date on things on the coast."

"Well, about three weeks after you and Kit came east, Castro began his revolt. Took us completely by surprise. You might get your friend Charlie Bent to stay on his toes here in New Mexico."

"We don't expect any trouble."

"Nor did we. Maybe it's different here. I guess after Gavilán Peak and the way he abandoned Los Angeles last summer, Frémont and Stockton didn't think Castro would ever fight."

"I sure thought that way myself," Stone said.

"Well . . . he gathered nearly eight hundred men, mostly those deadly lancers, and pushed Commodore Stockton and Colonel Johnny out of Los Angeles after some pretty heavy fighting. I was still in the north at Sutter's when all this happened, so most of what I'm telling you is hearsay."

"No matter."

"Anyway, Stockton regrouped at San Diego, Frémont raced north to Monterey for reinforcements, and when Kearny got to California with Kit, Castro moved out of the city and fell on him. Kearny then turned for San Diego to link up with the rest of our forces, but Castro cut him off at San Pasqual. After crossing the Arizona deserts, Kearny's Dragoons were in no shape to fight, and those damned lancers skewered them right and left in a whole series of small skirmishes. I don't even know how many men Kearny lost, but it was more than a hundred."

"What about Kit?"

"He damned near got killed himself. He had his horse shot out from under him and he only escaped by playing dead. Once the lancers passed him, he was up on his feet again and using that Hawken as only Kit can use one. A night later, Kearny, after pulling his troops into a defensive position completely surrounded by Castro's army, asked for a volunteer to sneak through the enemy lines to San Diego to bring relief. A navy lieutenant named Ned Beale—who had come out as a liaison officer from Stockton's command headquarters in San Diego—stepped right up and said he and his Indian servant would take a message through."

"I'm surprised it wasn't Kit."

"Oh, he got into it quick enough. He sized Beale up right away and liked what he saw. Said he would go, too."

"And he did?"

"Kearny didn't want to let him go, figuring—with a hell of lot of justification—that he needed Carson with him. He gave in after a talk with Kit nobody overheard, and the three of them slipped out of camp in the dark with a handful of mule meat and dried beans and with their shoes stuffed in their belts. They had to crawl two or more miles through Castro's line of sentries, one time so close to the enemy Kit got a little burn when one of them flipped a *cigarro* away. They all three lost their shoes sliding into an arroyo once when they damned near got caught."

"Without knowing the exact particulars I'll bet it was Kit who got them through."

"Seems true enough. The next day they had to negotiate thirty miles under a blazing sun with no water, *barefoot*, and then make another crawl that night through the Mexicans facing Stockton at San Diego. They split up there. Kit deliberately showed himself to the Mexicans to draw them off and give the other two a better chance, and the Indian actually reached Stockton first."

"Typical Carson," Stone said.

"Kit got to San Diego last, but in far better shape than Beale or his Indian. I heard Beale won't be fit for months. We probably won't ever know how Kit escaped capture; you know how he is about talking about his exploits. Well, he *might* someday tell Jessie Frémont. Colonel Johnny's wife has ways to pry things out of Kit the rest of us just plain don't have."

Yes, and perhaps that held for the earlier part of Ed's narrative, too. Stone pined to know exactly what had been said in Kearny's *"talk with Kit nobody overheard."* Based on the clever "extortion" in Socorro, as Kearny had called it, he could make a shrewd guess.

"Anyway," Kern continued, "Stockton moved to the relief of Kearny, and as it turned out, Castro then found himself caught between two armies. A week later Frémont stormed down from Monterey and defeated Pico at Los Angeles. The second 'Conquest of California' was over with."

When they reached the *casa* Stone opened the door and gestured Kern in ahead of him. Half a step inside, the Philadelphian stopped suddenly and Stone overran him.

"My God!" Kern whispered hoarsely.

In his total absorption with his friend's tale Stone had forgotten that for fear of inclement weather winging in from the north while he was at work at the cantina, he had moved the paintings of Ana inside the little house. Two of them he had hung on the far wall; three others leaned against chairs and the table, and one—the nude—rested at the foot of the bed.

He tried to get around Kern, looking frantically for a sheet or something with which to drape the nude, but he stopped. Hell . . . Ed Kern was an artist, too, not some pitiful Peeping Tom.

"All right, Bradford, my lad," Kern said softly. "Fix me that coffee, start my bathwater . . . and don't say a word for half an hour. I want to study these."

While Stone busied himself with the chores, Kern drifted from canvas to canvas, doubling back, peering at each of them several times with his nose a mere foot away, and then from as great a distance as the cramped room would allow. Once or twice he grunted. He lifted the one of Ana in her black costume astride Soberano Negro—the Barragán gate in the middle distance—carried it to the door, and held it to the light. He sighed.

But he did not utter a word until he stripped to the skin and settled himself in the tub. Stone handed him a cup of coffee. "Jesus! It's as bad as any Bass Lajeunesse ever made. Do you have a drop of honest whiskey?"

"The stuff they call Taos Lightning. You drank it at Bent's last year. It's distilled right up the road at Turley's Mill."

"Great. I remember it. Who wouldn't? I may need a belt or two for what I've got to say. And reach in my saddlebag and dig me out a *cigarro*. Have one yourself if you've a mind to."

Stone took the cup from him, dumped what coffee Kern had left into the slop bucket, got the whiskey down from a shelf over the fireplace, and poured two inches of it into the cup. After handing the cup over he found the cigar, used the tongs to pull a coal from the fire, and lighted it. Once it was going well he handed it to Kern.

His hand trembled. He did not have to ask Kern if the paintings were good. The Philadelphian's stunned look when he first sighted them had already made that clear. Something else hung in the balance.

"Let's talk, my friend," Kern said, "or rather, let *me* talk. You just listen. Maybe answer a question or two." He jabbed the *cigarro* toward the paintings on the wall, then waved it at the others. "That's the young Barragán woman, isn't it?"

"Yes."

"Where is she now?"

"She's dead."

Silence, but not a long one. "I'm sorry, but I'm not terribly surprised. I can see the seeds of death germinating in her in the paintings." He looked properly sympathetic, but no more than that. Something else showed in his face. He waved at the portraits again. "These were all done after her death? Never mind, I know they were. They all show that same sense of utter loss. They're wonderful, of course. I shouldn't need to tell you that." His eyes pinned Stone.

"Now . . . pay attention," he said. "Forget about acting like some damned colonial bureaucrat tomorrow—hell, this afternoon. Use the time to get these canvases crated up. There must be a local carpenter or handyman who can do it for you. I'll take them with me to Bent's when I leave Taos day after tomorrow, and I'll see that they get sent to that gallery in New York I told you about back at Lassen Peak." He paused. "I suppose you'll want to keep one here, and I can understand that. Make it the nude, though. I wouldn't give it house room myself."

"Hey! What's so—"

"Don't get your feelings hurt. It's not all that bad, but it's not art—it's a love letter, and a pretty mushy, sentimental one at that. The others all go with me. Find the one you did of me at Lassen's, as well as those of Kit and Frémont painted at about the same time. There's one of Segundai and another of Lajeunesse, too, if I remember right. Find them. If there are any more in that Renaissance style you used when you did them, I want them, too. Every one of them."

Stone nodded dumbly at everything Kern said.

"Resign your commission," Ed said next. "The way you've fought, you needn't fear anyone calling you anything less than a patriot. Then tell Bent to find himself another clerk."

"I had planned to do that, anyway. Right after the governor returns from the capital. I'll be leaving for Illinois before the month is out."

"Good idea. See your family and take a well earned rest. Then hop it back here and get to work. You've got a lot of it to do."

"I can't come back, Ed."

"What . . . ?"

"I can't come back, not to Taos or anywhere else out here. I'm finished with the West."

"You can't mean that."

"But I do. Never meant anything more in my entire life."

"Because of her?"

"Yes. I won't find peace or have any chance of forgetting her until I cross the hundredth meridian . . . heading east."

Kern took a deep pull at the *cigarro*. He sat motionless in the tub for another few seconds before he waved a cloud of smoke away. "You're a big boy, Brad, and I'm certainly not going to tell you what to do—except about these paintings—but there are still one or two things I have to point out to you."

"It won't do any good. My mind's made up."

Kern did not look as if he had heard him. He began speaking again. "You apparently haven't the slightest idea of how right you look here in Taos. And you don't seem to know how right Taos looks in the larger scheme of things. The entire West for that matter. The tragedy is that in twenty years a good deal of it aside from the rivers, the mountains, and the deserts will be unrecognizable, the people most of all."

"I can't help that."

"Yes, you can. You have a unique gift, and absolutely no right to keep it to yourself. Writers, businessmen, and politicians are all going to take a stab at capturing the West before it's gone, and some of them even with decent motives, but no one working today can give America a *look* at what it fell heir to, stumbled into—and yes, at times even stole, the way I personally think we're doing now with Mexico—the way you can." He stopped for a moment. "There's something else. You have your own artistic vision, but this year you have also looked through Kit Carson's eyes. Not many men get that chance. You now have a bounden duty to record it with *your* hand." He doused the *cigarro* in the bathwater and threw it toward the fireplace. "Now, for God's sake get me some more hot water before I catch my death."

14

Kern and St. Vrain left Taos at the same early hour two mornings later, the one for Bent's Fort on the Arkansas, the other for the capital.

Brad Stone did get his paintings, nineteen in all, packed to accompany Kern. He found a funny, sullen little *carpintero* named Jaime Carbajal to crate them for him. Kern said no more about Stone staying in the West, it was Stone who brought it up himself, to underline once and for all the firmness of his intention to go back to Illinois permanently once the governor returned.

"I can't do any more painting, anyway, Ed. I'm out of canvases. Oils are running low, too. Might as well go home."

Kern merely grunted, shook Stone's hand, and rode off, heading north to Turley's Mill to lay in a stock of Taos Lightning. It seemed, on the surface at least, as casual a farewell as the one Stone had gotten from Caleb Miller when he and the trader parted company at the cutoff an eternity ago.

15

Charlie Bent came up from Santa Fe the evening of the fifteenth of January full of warmth and good cheer at being with his family again. Stone met him at the Bent home, and filled him in on the last two weeks' deliberations and the decisions he had made at the cantina "office."

"Sounds as if you've done the fine job I expected," Bent said. "My compliments and gratitude to both you and Don Luis."

For all the bonhomie in his comportment, Bent brought slightly troubling news. Army intelligence in Santa Fe had intercepted signals from New Mexican malcontents to the effect that they planned an uprising, together with the assassinations of American military and political chiefs.

"We were able to thwart it with a dozen arrests," Charlie said, "but I fear the two top leaders of the insurrectionist *junta* have fled the territory. But this should put an end to any other secret attempts on the government."

Stone wanted to delve into the abortive rebellion a bit deeper, but Charlie turned the talk to *him:* "Are you still so set on leaving Taos?"

"More so than ever, Charlie."

"When?"

"Just as soon as I can turn things back over to you, sir."

"Well . . . we'll have you until at least the twentieth, then. I don't even plan on showing my face in the cantina until the morning of the nineteenth. Damn it, my boy! New Mexico *needs* you. At least stay until Kit gets back."

38

The Head of Charlie Bent

Taos
January 19, 1847

"Don Bradford! Wake up! *¡Por favor!*"

Luis Aragón's voice rang with more alarm than Stone had

ever heard from him. Luis's fists beat against the door of the *casa* as if he would break it down.

Stone rubbed his eyes; through the one tiny window he could see nothing but blackness. Dawn had not broken yet.

Something serious must have gone wrong for the trader. Stone kicked the covers off, sat up, and began to pull his trousers on.

"Bradford! *¡Por favor!*" The Santa Féan's voice now verged on hysteria.

"Hold on, Luis!" he called out.

The banked fire gave off just enough light for him to stumble to the door without mishap, and to then illuminate Aragón's features when he opened it.

He had not seen his friend look this unraveled since the Cimarron.

"*¿Qué pasa, amigo?*" Stone asked.

"Nothing yet, *mi amigo*, but I fear . . . I fear greatly."

"Spit it out, man! Exactly what do you fear?"

"Armed men, many of them, have ridden into town."

"So?"

"Hurry! We have no time to waste. I will tell you what I have seen as we ride to the plaza. Let me saddle your horse for you while you dress." Aragón's breath hung in the frozen air. He spun about and sprinted for the corral, where his own mount nodded at the rail.

Stone finished dressing quickly, raced back to the door, stopped there at the sight of his Hawken gun in its rack above the doorway. He pulled it down and stepped into the frigid, predawn silence. Luis, mounted, was already moving toward the *casa* trailing Stone's horse. Stone swung into the saddle and Aragón led them away from the *casa* at a fairly rapid trot.

"Now . . . tell me!" Stone shouted when he pulled even with his friend.

"I awakened very early this morning at the sound of many

horses in the plaza." He stopped for breath. Hard for him to talk as they rode. Stone could not be sure he caught every word as Luis spoke in bits and pieces. "Men on horseback and carrying torches . . . filling the plaza. Thirty of them . . . no, many more. Not . . . not ordinary travelers. *De veras,* I recognized two of them. . . . Pablo Montoya . . . I have done business with him . . . an Indian named Tomacito . . . wicked, dangerous *hombres* both . . . no love for Americans. Many in this mob were Indians, Taoseños from the big pueblo north of the village. They seldom come into town, and never at such an hour."

"And you say they're armed?"

"*¡Sí!* All of them . . . most carry rifles . . . a few machetes, and some of the Taoseños only bows, arrows, war clubs . . . and stone axes, but *sí,* they all are armed in some fashion."

"What do you think they're up to, Luis?"

Aragón reined his horse to a stop and turned in the saddle when Stone pulled in beside him.

"It looks to me like a rising, the rebellion Señor Bent and Señor St. Vrain said . . . could not happen here."

"Let's not panic. Even if you're right, Charlie can still stop it. He's probably the only man in Taos, or New Mexico for that matter, who could."

"I do not think so, Bradford," Aragón said. "This Tomacito worked once for Don Bernardo, perhaps still does."

This startled Stone. Bernardo Barragán? Would that proud man involve himself in a *rising?*

"We'll have to get to Charlie's," Stone said.

"*Sí.* But I do not think it wise to go directly there. The way to Señor Bent's may be blocked already."

Stone had stuffed the Hawken in his saddle boot when he mounted. He had not so much as looked at it since his arrival in Taos three months ago, and he now reached down and pulled it out to make sure it was dry and loaded.

"What are you doing with that rifle?" Aragon asked.

"I guess I'm getting a little like Kit. I'm so used to having it with me when things get even a *mite* touchy I took it from its rack without even thinking."

"We must get rid of it. If these men see an armed *yanqui*, I do not know what they might do to him. From my room they looked quite threatening, desperate."

Perhaps Aragón had it right. "I can hide it somewhere off the plaza before we get there. I have a key to the cantina."

"We must not go anywhere near the cantina, either. Let me have it, and I will take it as far as the alley door to La Posada. We can decide about it then."

Stone handed the Hawken to Aragón, who slipped it into his own empty saddle scabbard.

Aragón dug his spurs in savagely. *"¡Vamos!"*

2

They turned into the narrow *calle* a hundred yards or so south of the plaza. At the rear door of La Posada they found a large wooden dustbin and Luis lifted the lid and placed the rifle in it. "We can tie our horses here, and go to the plaza through the hotel," he said. "It will give us a chance to stay out of sight and observe for a bit before we proceed to Señor Bent's."

Stone followed the trader through a dark, narrow corridor that opened on the inn's small foyer. There was no one at the desk and Aragón, with Stone following, mounted a bench under a high, slit window on the plaza side of the room.

The sun's first rays had just touched the roof of the gazebo, and two mangy dogs were nosing at the steps. Except for them, the plaza itself appeared completely empty and silent. For a moment Stone wondered if it were possible that his friend had only dreamed what he had told him, but then he saw smoke rising from torches apparently tossed away when the sun rose.

They walked outside.

"Where do you suppose they've gone?" Stone said.

"I am afraid to think about it, Bradford," Aragón said.

Then a *pop-pop-pop* of rifle shots rang out from somewhere north of the plaza, the reports muffled slightly by the line of adobes on the other side. Shouts followed on the echoes of the shots, shrill screeches of anger, then something like whoops and howls. The sounds seemed to come from every part of the village. Looking down the dark *calles* that radiated from the plaza Stone made out small bands of horsemen riding through the shadows, and many more men on foot, running helter-skelter, as if they were following some crazed orders.

"We had better get back inside, Bradford," Aragón said.

Two . . . three more muffled shots sounded from much closer to where they stood.

"Those came from Charlie's place!" Stone said.

Without a thought or a look at Aragón, Stone began to run, exploding into motion and racing across the plaza. Behind him, Aragón screamed, "No, no, *no!*"

Aragón caught him just as he ran under a *portal* fronting the *calle* that led up to the Bent home. He threw his arms around Stone's waist and somehow brought him to a halt. "No!" he shouted. "You cannot go there, *mi amigo,* no matter how much you want to help. You are the *yanqui* who works for Señor Bent . . . remember. If what I think is true, they will harm you as quickly as they will Don Carlos or any other Americano. They might even kill you."

"We've got to *do* something, Luis!"

"We must plan. We can get a little closer without being seen, but as for stopping anything—it is impossible. Perhaps there will be nothing but talk. We must pray for that."

They slipped through the dark blue early morning shadows in the *portales,* hugging the walls, and from time to time sheltering themselves behind barrels and crates, stopping to listen for a moment, and then moving on.

Then, up ahead, Stone saw that a crowd had gathered at the Bent house. Two men on the roof hacked at it with axes.

At last, hidden behind an enormous pile of hides on the *portal* of the harness maker's adobe *casa* across the *calle* from it, they faced Charlie's house directly.

At least two dozen men crowded the front patio of the *casa*, pushing each other toward the door, all of them, it seemed, shrieking and gesturing. Wild, obscene laughter broke from some of them.

They saw Charlie Bent, too, and Stone shuddered at the sight of that good man.

The governor stood in the doorway of his home, clad only in his trousers, his hands braced hard against the jambs, his thick, powerful arms now barely able to support him. Blood spilled in a red stream from his chin, and a crimson cascade gushed from a gaping wound in his stomach. He looked as if he were trying desperately to talk, but more blood bubbled at his mouth.

Half of the men who faced Charlie Bent were Mexicans from the look of them, brandishing rifles, but closer to him a number of Indians waved bows. Stone stood transfixed as four of these Taoseños fitted arrows to their bowstrings, and let fly at Bent from no more than ten feet away. One of the arrows lodged deep in the governor's right cheek, one found the roll of fat between his neck and shoulder, and a third his chest. The fourth tore through his trouser leg. Bent's hands slipped slowly down the doorjamb, and he collapsed backward into the house, rolled over on his hands and knees, and began to crawl away, his hands slipping in his own blood, his big gray head dropping and scraping repeatedly against the floor as he tried to lift it, the arrow in his cheek bobbing and twisting hideously. He sat back on his naked heels and pulled the arrow free, tearing the flesh of his face to bloody tatters. He began to crawl again, and moved out of sight in the darkness inside the house.

The four Indians, joined by two rifle-carrying Mexicans, now crowded through the doorway. Another Mexican, wielding what appeared to be a Bowie knife, followed on their heels. Bent and his attackers had now completely disappeared inside the dark room. Then a light flared, and someone inside screamed . . . a woman.

In only seconds, the man with the knife appeared in the doorway again. In his right hand he waved a gray thatch of scalp, shook it. Bent's blood spattered the man's *sarape* when he tossed the scalp to grasping hands amidst a great throbbing roar.

A strangled, wounded cry came from Aragón.

The marauders had not yet finished.

One of the Indians came to the door. He held something out to the crowd in two bloodstained hands.

The head of Charlie Bent.

Even from more than fifty or sixty feet away Stone could make out Charlie's dead eyes.

Stone felt absolutely nothing. This moment went far beyond any *feeling*.

"Let us return to La Posada, *por favor*, Bradford," Aragón said in a flat and hollow whisper. "There is nothing we can do here. If we attempt to interfere, we will die just like that."

"But Mrs. Bent . . . and Charlie's children . . ."

Stone stepped out from behind the pile of hides, but Aragón reached up and gripped his arm hard.

"No! We can only hope they have escaped somehow."

"We have to find them!"

"No. Do not make a move, *mi amigo. En el nombre de Dios*, do not let them see us! Perhaps Señor Bent somehow got them out. And as horrible as this has been, I do not think even these filthy monsters would harm a woman or a child."

"But—"

"Listen to me, *please!* Señor Bent is gone. We must look to ourselves now, and only then think about the others. We cannot help them if we die, too."

Stone knew he could not argue about this, but he could not check the wave of guilt that engulfed him at the thought of doing nothing. Luis was right. There was absolutely *nothing* they could do. They would not last a minute if the killers in the front yard of the Bent house saw them. What could even Kit have done?

"We must get back to the hotel and hide in my room while we make a plan, Bradford," Aragón said.

They moved together through the shadows. Behind them the cries and shouts of the mob went on unabated.

As they were about to start across the plaza, a group of riders burst out of the *calle* at the southeastern corner, and they dropped prone on the ground, their faces down hard in the frozen caliche.

Stone raised his head only after the horsemen rounded the gazebo at a gallop. They looked vaguely familiar, and then his eye found the man leading them.

Don Bernardo Barragán was lashing the flanks of Ana's black horse, Soberano Negro. The men following him were the *vaqueros* of Estancia Barragán.

"*¡Nombre de Dios!*" Aragón whispered bitterly. "I could not have foretold this, *mi amigo,*" he said when Barragán and his *vaqueros* rode on out of sight, "but now that I have seen Don Bernardo, I am not surprised. *¡Ahora!* We must go fast across the plaza to my *posada* before more of them come upon us. It is important we get you hidden. My room is your only chance for a while. You dare not go back to your *casita* now."

Important that they get *him* hidden? What about Aragón himself?

Aragón did not explain himself as he virtually pushed

Stone inside the room on the second floor. "Do not leave here for any reason, Bradford. We are fortunate the innkeeper was not at his post, but that might also mean he is out with the rebels. I must go now. There are things that I must find out—and things that I must see to."

Was the small man planning something desperate that did not include Brad Stone?

"Aren't you putting yourself in danger, Luis?"

"Possibly. But I am Mexican. I shall have to rely on that." He went to the door, opened it, turned back. "I would not walk about too much. My host, Señor Morález, has sharp ears, and this old floor squeaks. He must at all costs think my room empty." He suddenly looked embarrassed. "Forgive me for presuming to give you orders, Bradford. It is not my place. *¡Hasta la vista!*"

3

Aragón's room appeared more lived-in than most hotel rooms. His suits, several of them, including the black one he had worn to that dance down in the plaza, hung neatly inside an open armoire. On a small, delicate table at the window, magazines and newspapers made a tidy pile alongside a crystal decanter of what looked like *aguardiente*. Tellingly, only one gold-rimmed glass stood beside it. A bachelor's room.

This must have been the Santa Féan's home away from home all those years he had made that fruitless pursuit of Ana, when it seemed he would be a bachelor for life.

A graceful mahogany crucifix adorned the wall above the headboard of a high, narrow bed with a featherbed rolled up at one end of it. On the opposite wall, placed there perhaps so it would be the last thing he saw at night, Luis had fastened the small portrait of Ana which Stone had given him for Christmas. A broad shelf below the picture held burned-down candles with twisted, blackened wicks, eight or ten of them.

Yes, Ana Barragán's face was the last thing Luis Aragón saw each night.

. Had Luis seen the nude of Ana when he stood in the door-way of the *casita* this morning? In the darkness perhaps not, and Stone hoped that was the case.

Another object caught Stone's eye, a carved wooden *santo*. Saint Sebastian. The arrow shafts protruding from the saint's tortured body destroyed any hope that he could for-get Charlie Bent, even for a second.

4

The bright day dissolved to black night hours before Aragón returned, bringing with him a gunny sack of food, Stone's rifle, and the ammunition case from his saddlebag. "The horses are safe," he said. "I moved them to my stables when I left here. Fortunately, you have done so little riding about the village these past three months no one knows your ani-mal, Bradford. As a trader I bring many different horses to that stable, so yours raised no suspicion."

Strange how good it felt to have the Hawken back in his hands. He had not missed carrying the weapon here in Taos, but with danger breathing on him now, and on Aragón as well, the solid, familiar weight of it reassured him, even though he realized that if someone found them, the rifle could probably not delay death more than a few seconds, for either of them.

Until he started in greedily on the spiced pork and cold beans Luis brought, he had not realized that more than twenty-seven hours had gone by since he had eaten. While he ate, Aragón spoke.

The situation in the village, according to his friend, had turned even worse through the morning, the long, interminable afternoon, and the early evening.

"There have been many more killings, Bradford: *el abogado* Señor Leal, whom they ran naked through the *calles* before they filled him full of arrows; Sheriff Stephen Lee; Doña Ignacia's and Doña Josefa's young brother, Pablo Jaramillo, and his even younger *amigo*, Narciso Beaubien; the Taos prefect Don Cornelio Vigil, who rebuked and cursed his assailants all the while they hacked him to pieces with machetes. They are searching everywhere for Americans and the villagers who have worked for them since the conquest. It is so far only a rumor, but they are said to have killed Señor Simeon Turley and eight of his friends at the mill on the Río Hondo. One band has ridden to attack the American *estancias* near Mora. Two have been killed on the Río Colorado, the next little stream north of Turley's Mill. Here, I fear, the killing may not be finished yet."

"Doña Ignacia and her children . . . ?"

"All alive and safe—if suffering greatly, as is Doña Rumalda Boggs, Doña Ignacia's married daughter. She spent last night with her mother and stepfather at Don Carlos's house at the governor's request. He must have suspected something, but apparently not enough. Señora Carson is safe and sound, too. She was staying with the Bent *familia,* too."

"How on earth did you get to them?"

"I found them in the courtyard of the house next door. Señora Bent and Señora Carson dug their way through the adobe wall and escaped, *por el momento*. They pulled the body of *el gobernador* through after them."

"Josefa was at Charlie's? Then you were right, Luis. Charlie must have at least had an inkling of the danger facing him. He should have run for it, but I guess that was simply not the way of Charles Bent."

Good thing Stone had not known that Josefa was in the

house this morning. Luis might not have been able to hold him back at all. "How were they when you left them?"

"They are tired, cold, hungry, and still mortally terrified, but they are all alive and physically unharmed. Señor Bent's daughter, Teresina, weeps continuously. I was able to comfort her a little before I left them. Within an hour the rebels found them and put them under arrest, I have learned since I was there, but *gracias a Dios* they did not molest them. It must have been ghastly for them to spend all day with Don Carlos's body. After dark, kind, brave friends came and took him away and buried him. His enemies will not find him— *lo prometo.*"

"You were one of those friends, weren't you, Luis?"

Aragón said nothing.

"Has anyone set out for Santa Fe with the news of what has happened here?"

"I do not think so, Bradford. The few I could trust enough to ask feel the trail through the lower gorge of the Río will be under heavy guard, probably where the Río flattens out at Estación Embudo. It would be near impossible for a man to get through there."

"Kit would probably say it would be even harder with ten men. I wonder . . ."

"What are you thinking, Bradford?"

"Nothing."

"You want to try it, don't you?"

"Yes."

"I cannot allow it."

"Ah . . . Don Luis." God bless his small friend. "Not so fast, *por favor, mi amigo.* I took your orders gladly this morning. Now I must decide for myself."

"You will go, then, no matter how much I entreat you not to?"

"Yes."

Stone would have felt more confidence had he not seen

the look of shivering fright in Aragón's eyes. What a remarkable man the Santa Féan had turned out to be. He had totally risked his own safety by openly roaming Taos during the long, dangerous day and a good part of the night . . . and yet now he was terrified for Stone.

"Take me with you, *mi amigo*."

"I cannot. You may be needed by those women and children. They are not out of danger yet."

"Then let me give just some advice if you insist on going, Bradford," he said. "Do not leave before the small hours of the morning . . . three or four o'clock. The rebels have broken into the cantina, and by then they will probably be drunk. Take my horse, as well as yours."

"You will not need it?"

"I can do what I can do better on foot. I will bring the horses to the alley, together with feed for them on your journey. We cannot risk you going to the stable. Take what is left of your supper along with you. Be especially careful when you enter the lower gorge. You should see nothing of the enemy until then, but be on your guard. For now, you must sleep. You will need all your strength to make this ride."

39

The Gift Horse

At Estación Embudo he found armed men guarding the trail just as Aragón had predicted.

He might have ridden right into them, but the smoke from their breakfast fire had caught his eye half a mile before they came in view.

When he had narrowed the distance between them to a

quarter of a mile he left the trail and turned his two horses up in the scrub piñon on the sloping canyon side above the Río. Below him the great river had broadened just enough to calm it, but the roar of the white water behind him still echoed from the canyon walls. On this side the trail had narrowed, pinched in by the river itself and the rock outcroppings on his left.

Actually, the trail forked here, one fork running out over a plank bridge and fading into a broad meadow on the other side of the river, but with the narrow main thoroughfare heading south toward the canyon mouth. A traveler unfamiliar with the road to Santa Fe, and riding down at river level, might have easily taken the wrong fork, over into the meadow; it looked the more logical route. Stone might have done so himself had he not decided to get a better look at the trail by leaving it for a bit, and riding up to this high vantage point.

Aragón had been right in every other respect, too. He had not encountered a single rider or sign of danger since Ranchos de Taos, but the nine men bivouacked on his side of the river, blocking the trail, changed all that. They were not all riders. Not today. There were only two horses in the camp. Perhaps the great rebellion still raging behind him was short of horseflesh for tasks such as the one these men had been set.

They had thrown a formidable-looking barricade across the trail not two feet past where the southern fork began: piled it high with boxes; piñon trees uprooted and dragged down from the mountainside; crude, rusty remains of farm equipment of some sort; and a tangle of other junk. It looked impenetrable from where he sat on his horse. The only possible gap seemed to be a narrow opening, hardly more than a yard wide, near the river. A rider could make it through there, but not with nine armed and probably nervously alert men barring the way.

The way the barricade snugged against the canyon wall also furthered the illusion that the road across the plank bridge was the right one to take.

He had no worries about his two horses making any noise that would give him away as he planned his next move, which probably would turn out to be one of desperation. A slight north wind was carrying the sound of the rapids right down the canyon. He was well hidden here in the piñon, too. Yes, he could take his time.

But waiting too long would demand its own steep payment. The camp below him looked permanent, and for all he knew, even more men could now be on their way to join the ones he saw. And in any event, if he waited until nightfall more ugly things could be occurring in the north. More friends could die. Time was everything. Sooner or later the men at the fork of the road would get reinforcements. Their fellow marauders back up the river had already decimated Taos; they would probably turn next to attacking the river towns along the route south to the capital.

Sooner or later, whether he made it through today or not, word would reach the Army of the West of the tragedy in Taos, and sooner or later the army would march north for rescue and revenge . . . right through the lower gorge here. The rebels had to count on that. They could not have found a finer place to meet their enemy than this narrow point in the rocky gorge, and the longer the army took before marching north, the more fortified the *estación* would become.

Although he could probably remain hidden from the men down at the barricade, he would quickly and easily be discovered by anyone coming down the canyon from behind him. That thought took away his only other option. He could not retrace his steps up through the gorge and find a trail over the mountains to the east of here for fear of riders who might this instant be coming down from Taos.

2

He studied the fork, the bridge, and the rebel guards again, paying even more attention this time to the way the road forked and led to the bridge.

One of the nine men walked to the water's edge and urinated. Two others kept themselves busy at the fire. Three more, apparently just coming off night duty at the barricade, were laying out bedrolls. Several more checked their weapons. No reliance on machetes in this crowd; all had rifles. Actually, it brought him a little weird comfort.

Then one of the horses tethered to the barricade suddenly broke free. It bounded off, straight for the bridge. Weapons dropped from the men's hands, and the would-be sleepers left their bedrolls.

The horse stopped to graze in the first of the winter-withered grama grass in the meadow, and was taken in hand fairly quickly and brought back across the bridge to the bivouac, to angry shouts in Spanish.

Yes . . . riding stock was much more precious to men such as these down below him than it was to the sedentary merchants back up in Taos. He should know. He had lived in the wild for more than a year as utterly dependent on horses as a man could be.

But . . .

What had suddenly come to mind would not work one time in a thousand. He had to do *something*. The sun would climb above the top of the canyon wall in minutes, and even in January it could turn this rocky, piñon-studded slope into a griddle.

He slipped from the saddle and hitched his and Aragón's horses to one of the sturdier piñon trees. Disaster would result if one of the two got away from him now and the men at the barricade saw it. He unbuckled his saddle, took it off, stripped the blanket from the animal's back, and threw the gear, rifle, saddlebags, and all on Aragón's lighter, smaller, and, he hoped, swifter horse, unhitched it and climbed into the saddle.

With his eye hard on the men at the bridge, he eased himself and the two horses down the steep slope almost to the trail, finally taking up a position in the cover of a large, well-needled piñon. He dismounted again, tied Aragón's mount loosely to the tree, took the lead rein of his old horse, and led it out into the middle of the trail.

Once there, he headed the horse toward the bridge and the barricade, and stripped away the halter he had put on it when he made the switch. He took a tight grip on the leather in his hands, a deep breath, and swung the halter against the horse's rump with all his strength.

The horse bolted down the trail as he had prayed it would, and he took two steps back behind the tree and mounted Aragón's. He pulled the Hawken from the holster and used the barrel to part the piñon's branches so he could see the barricade and the bridge.

His horse had reached a point halfway to the bivouac. The men at the barricade had not seen it yet. Nothing looked changed. Then one of them stood up. This one heard something. He looked back up the trail and started shouting.

But before he could react, the horse was on him. The man made a grab for the mane, caught it, and Stone's heart stopped until he saw the animal break free and thunder out across the bridge.

Don't stop to eat, old friend. Move out into that meadow. Lead them away from here.

Running free, the big horse tossed its head as if in answer, and moved into the grass on the other side of the river.

Pandemonium broke loose at the barricade and at the fire. The men who had laid out their bedrolls were on their feet and racing for the bridge. The lone man who had urinated into the Río had already started across it in pursuit, and one by one the others followed. Three were shaking out *reatas* as they ran.

He had to wait. They had to get far enough into the meadow to give him time to ride to the barricade, take care of the one thing he had to do there, and move on through the opening.

The horse was doing its part. Frisky as a colt, it shied from every man who neared it, moving closer to the mountain wall every time one of its would-be captors came close to it. One of the men, a fat, waddling ruffian in a big sombrero, and with perhaps less liking for the chase than any of the others, had lagged considerably behind.

Stone forced himself to wait until the horse and its closest pursuers were a full quarter of a mile out into the longer grasses. The loner marched along lackadaisically, at least half the distance between the river and his companions.

Stone set the spurs to Aragón's horse, shook up the reins, and rode hard down the trail, straight for the two animals hitched to the barricade. Only one of them was saddled. He rode right up to it, placed the muzzle of the Hawken under its eye, and pulled the trigger. He had to rein sharply to the left to get his own mount out of the way of the other horse as it fell.

Then he steered quickly to the unsaddled horse, unhitched it, trailed it behind him, and took his new little cavalcade through the opening. Good. He might need another horse for the ride he had yet to make.

One glance told him the nine men had stopped in their tracks at the sound of the Hawken. The fat man nearest him surprised him by moving first. Stone knew he could afford no more glances. He guessed he had a minute . . . maybe.

Up ahead the trail rounded a shoulder of craggy rock. If he could get to that turn he would be safe for a while. It would take at least thirty-five or forty seconds before the laggard in the meadow reached a rifle, even at a dead run.

Sooner or later the other eight would return to chasing down his horse, and perhaps they would eventually catch it. But by the time they did, he would have released the one he trailed, far enough along the river road that it would no longer be of use to them. Perhaps they would not try to run him down with only the one animal then in their possession.

The trail climbed steadily toward the point of rock. It soon became all he could do to keep from whipping up Aragón's horse. The smaller mount seemed willing enough, perhaps too willing. He did not want to wear it out now, with the last and most vital part of the ride still ahead of him.

Then, with the rock outcropping a mere five yards away, the bullet tore through his left shoulder.

The sharp report of the rifle followed an instant later, and an instant after *that* the pain bolted down to the soles of his boots and almost took him from the saddle.

3

Fever and red delirium had claimed him by the time he rode into the dark plaza at Santa Fe.

The Palacio, silent and with no light showing, looked locked and barred, but across the plaza a glowing oil lamp cast its beams out through the open door of the old hotel.

40

Return to Taos

"You're awake, Mr. Stone. Thank God!"

He would never be able to claim he had recognized the woman's voice, and from the bed he found himself lying in, he could only barely make out her form in the dim light. He did recognize the room; he had occupied it before in his two other stays in Fabiano Minjárez's United States Hotel, but how he had gotten here eluded him.

The woman got up from a rocking chair and moved to the window he remembered overlooked the plaza. The chair creaked a time or two. She opened the drapery and warm, deep old-gold light filled the room. It must be late afternoon. How long had he been lying in this bed? And what was he doing here? The last thing he remembered was slipping from Luis's horse and collapsing in a heap on the brick floor of the hotel's *portal*. All else was a blank.

Now the woman stepped away from the window, and in the sudden full rush of light he saw her clearly.

He had met her with her lawyer brother right here in the hotel before he went north to Taos in October. Bailey, he remembered, Elizabeth and some unusual middle name. Why would she be in his room?

"What happened to me, Miss Bailey?"

"You remember me! I feared you might not. You rode in late last night . . . Brad. You did once say I could call you that." She walked toward the bed. "I thought you were at death's door when Señor Minjárez called me down to the foyer. We'll never know how much blood you lost. Now . . .

let me have a look at that wound. Please forgive me if this hurts a little. I've not had a lot of experience taking care of wounded men . . . although I did nurse Morton through a broken arm once, or he pretended that I did." She did not exactly laugh, but something bubbled pleasantly in her voice. "I was twelve then. I must have been insufferable as a nurse."

Had she said "wound"? He felt then for the first time the dull, hot ache in his shoulder, and found that someone had bound it tightly with bandages, and strapped his left upper arm against the side of his naked chest.

Her hands were soft but insistent as she undid the fastenings of the bulky dressing. Some of it had gotten wadded up as he slept. "Although we managed to get you out of your sheepskin jacket fairly easily, Don Fabiano and I had to cut away your shirt. Some of it was stuck in the wound." While she worked, he made the discovery that he was not wearing a stitch of clothing, and with his right hand he pulled the coverlet about him as high as it would go. She noticed, and smiled.

Had this slim young creature with the guileless look undressed him?

"It looks good, to me at least," she said when she replaced the bandages and bound them up again. "Clean. Not a trace of infection I can see, but to be really sure I suppose we'll have to wait until Señor Quiñones, the doctor Don Fabiano brought to see you, comes back again—probably tomorrow morning. He said you were extremely fortunate the bullet went right on through your shoulder. And although it probably tore up the muscle, it apparently did *not* strike bone. He was about to dose you with laudanum when you passed out. He left it with me in case you need it. Do you?"

He shook his head.

"Tell me, Miss Bailey. Did I say anything before I lost consciousness?"

"Quite a lot. You frightened poor Señor Minjárez right out of his skin. Even though it was the middle of the night, he sent one of his *mozos* for Colonel Price. You talked even more after the colonel got here."

"Did I make any sense?"

"Yes, indeed. Oh, you raved some, but then you pulled yourself together amazingly. Your fever must have broken then. You told Colonel Price quite clearly about what happened up in Taos. It horrified me."

He breathed more easily. Thank God he had at least managed to get his message across to this Colonel Price. They had not, then, lost any *more* precious time. "When can I see Colonel Price?"

"He is very busy getting his soldiers ready to march north because of your news, but he said he will come back to see you this evening. A Mr. St. Vrain of Taos is waiting downstairs in Señor Minjárez's office. He wanted to see you immediately, but I could not let him come up while you were sleeping, and I fear I vexed him. He is very concerned about you. . . ." She paused. "As we all are."

"Could you bring him up now, Miss Bailey?"

"I thought we had settled when we first met that it was to be 'Liz' as well as 'Brad'. Yes, I'll go down and get him. I will not, however, permit him to stay very long. I would like you to rest again. In fact, I insist you rest."

"How about you . . . Liz?" He took a shot in the dark. "You've been up all night tending to me, haven't you?"

Even with the glow of sunset now reaching to every corner, the room had not become light enough to determine if what passed across her face was a blush or not. "As a matter of fact, I have," she said. "But don't worry about me. Anyone would have done the little I did. I may not look it, but I'm quite strong."

She went to the door, opened it, and looked back at him. "I'll send Mr. St. Vrain up. Mind you now, I'll give him ten

minutes. I'll be along with your supper directly afterward."
He continued to stare even after she pulled the door shut
behind her.

Only once before had anyone bound a wound he had suffered or looked after him in any fashion: Kit at Klamath
Lake.

2

Ceran St. Vrain looked to be a man in deep shock. When he
entered the room he dutifully and sincerely asked about
Stone's wound, but clearly that was not foremost in his
mind. "Tell me about Charlie," he said. "Please don't try to
spare me."

"I'd rather not tell you, sir, but I suppose I'll have to,"
Stone said.

He recounted as simply as he could the horrible things he
and Aragón had witnessed from the *portal* across the *calle*
from the Bent home. The grisly tale must have served as a
catharsis of a sort; the deeper Stone got into the story of the
murder, the more St. Vrain's look of shock faded, replaced
by one of grim determination. A long, long time would have
to pass, Stone suspected, before the familiar, genial, light-
hearted Ceran St. Vrain reappeared.

"Sterling Price will start north in just two or three days
with as many units of his Second Missouri Volunteers as he
feels he can take without weakening the defense of the capital," St. Vrain said when Stone finished. "I've already had a
talk with Donaciano Vigil, who has become acting governor
since Charlie's death. I persuaded him to let me raise a company of irregulars from among the civilians here in Santa Fe.
I've gathered more than thirty men already. In case you're
wondering, many of them are Mexicans, which wouldn't
have surprised old Charlie."

"How long will it take you to assemble your force, sir?"

"Not long. We won't be more than half a day behind Colonel Price when we leave Santa Fe, and we'll catch up with him right quick. The available companies of Sterling's Second Missouri are composed entirely of infantry. He does have field artillery. My men will all be mounted."

"Enlist me, sir . . . please."

St. Vrain smiled a bit at that. "You won't be fit to ride for at least another week, my friend. I've got to leave Santa Fe before then. I must turn you down. You've already done enough. Stay here and get well. That's all any of us would ask of you now."

"Please don't count me out, sir. I *have* to get back north, if only to see how Luis Aragón has fared. He's pretty much alone up there. As for me, Miss . . . well, people here seem to be taking excellent care of me. I recover pretty quickly."

"I suppose you do. You're a tough man for an easterner. I keep forgetting about all the time you've put in with Kit. He'll be proud as a peacock of you when he hears about the ride you made to bring the news to us. He couldn't have done it any better himself. But Kit would never forgive me if I let you ride with me in the shape you're in and something happened to you."

Stone finished telling St. Vrain of the rest of the tragedy in Taos as he had learned it from Aragón: of the deaths of the lawyer Jim Leal and the prefect Cornelio Vigil, the betrayal and murders of Pablo Jaramillo and Narciso Beaubien. The merchant blanched as he heard Aragón's description of how the rebels had butchered Sheriff Lee. "I can't vouch for this myself, sir," Stone said, "but Don Luis told me he learned that the revolt spread through all the northern parishes even the first day, beginning with the attacks at Simeon Turley's mill and distillery on the Hondo, and the American settlements at Mora and the Río Colorado."

"Damn!" St. Vrain said. "It's not as though we had no

warning. Trouble is that Charlie Bent would trust the devil himself." He got up from his chair. "I'll have to get back to my recruiting now. Besides, I have no wish to answer to Miss Bailey if I stay longer than the time she allotted me. Capable young woman. Very decorative, too, if an old man may say so. I'll check back first thing tomorrow morning, if I haven't already started north."

"Please, Mr. St. Vrain . . . before you leave," Stone said. "Could you fish around in that armoire, find my trousers, and help me put them on?"

"You're not going anyplace."

"Please, sir. Before Miss Bailey comes in again."

3

In an instant after St. Vrain left, Liz Bailey did return. She led one of Fabiano Minjárez's waiters carrying an enormous platter heaped with steak and beans. She herself placed a huge, steaming water pitcher and a basin on the table at the window, and unburdened herself of a stack of plump white towels.

"We'll feed you your supper first," she said, "and then we'll get you bathed. You'll feel much better after that, I assure you. And I expect you'll be ready for that rest about then. Colonel Price sent word he could not see you until tomorrow."

After St. Vrain had helped him get his trousers on he had not bothered to pull the coverlet over him. When Liz Bailey turned from the table at the window she looked, put her hand to her mouth for a second, and stared directly into Stone's eyes.

"How on earth did you . . . ? You didn't get out of bed, did you?"

"Mr. St. Vrain helped me."

"The nerve of him! I should never have left the two of you alone. The moving around you did could have disturbed that wound. And what are you trying to do now?"

He had swung his feet over the side of the bed and was struggling to sit up as she talked. "I'm most certainly not going to eat lying down, Miss Bailey!" He could have kicked himself for sounding as if he were a sulky ten-year-old.

"Still can't manage Liz, can you? Are you afraid . . . ? Never mind answering that. I have no right to ask such questions. Please move carefully."

To his further discomfort, she had to help him eat, cutting his meat and helping him get the beans on his fork. And although he made small, futile attempts to pull his head away, she even wiped his mouth with a serviette between bites. He supposed he should be grateful.

The bath she had mentioned would definitely be another matter. He would fight her like a bobcat rather than submit to any such humiliation.

Neither of them had spoken while he ate, but sure enough the subject of the bath came up almost the moment she removed the tray from his lap.

"You've been awfully fidgety, Brad." She laughed. "I think I can guess why. Let me put your mind at ease. I have no intention of bathing you myself, or even helping you. I'll send Señor Minjárez's nice young *mozo,* Ricardo, in for that, and I promise I'll see to it that *he* is discreet. I would not have your privacy violated for the world." She laughed musically, but then her fine, arched eyebrows suddenly knitted themselves together. "Forgive my pitiful attempts at humor. Are you in pain? I should have asked long before now. Do you need the laudanum?"

"I'll manage without it," he said. Suddenly, he would have welcomed the drug, but there was no way he was going to let this earnest young woman think him a weakling.

"Then I'll leave now," she said. "I'll send Ricardo in, and when the two of you are through I want you to sleep. I'll look in on you in the middle of the night to see if the fever has returned and if you've changed your mind about the laudanum."

"I won't have."

"I'll say good night, then. Pleasant dreams."

Pleasant dreams? This handsome, earnest young lady—astute as she seemed—could not know that the last pleasant dreams he could ever expect in this lifetime had come and gone, long before tonight.

"Good night . . . Liz."

4

By the time he awoke in the morning the shoulder had stiffened to immobility, but his head had become immeasurably clearer.

St. Vrain had been absolutely right in his glum outlook yesterday. Stone knew he would be nowhere near fit to ride when the Taos merchant, suddenly turned military commander, led his irregular cavalry north. Except for Ana's death nothing had depressed him so since Basil Lajeunesse died and Carson had kept him out of the next day's fight against the Klamaths.

Ricardo brought him breakfast at eight o'clock, together with a chamber pot Stone found he needed badly. He turned his attention to the latter chore first. It was not an easy task with his arm still bound to his chest, and his left hand immobilized, but he wanted it over with before Liz Bailey showed up again, possibly even walked in on him. The *mozo,* at his direction, posted himself outside the door to his room. Good thing he had thought of that. He had not quite finished when he heard her talking to Ricardo in the hall. He hurried the chamber pot to the armoire, shoved it in the bottom, and covered it with some extra bedding he found, a far cry from the way he took care of bodily functions in his days in the wilderness with the mountain men of "Captain Johnny's" expedition. Not for the first time he wondered if somewhere on his journey through the deserts and mountains, in the company of some of the world's roughest men, he had unwittingly abandoned all the uses of polite society.

He dragged a straight-backed chair to the table by the window where Ricardo had set his tray.

"May I come in?"

When he said yes and she entered, he realized that last night when he first opened his eyes in this room, he must still have been feverish and more than a little disoriented. He had not really seen her then. He remembered he had thought her attractive, but this morning she looked truly beautiful. She carried herself as straight as an arrow, with her head held appealingly erect, her eyes, a deep blue he saw now, seemingly alert to everything, and—if he did not give himself too much credit—particularly to him. He had not remarked to himself on her beauty when he'd first met her with her brother before he went north to Taos more than three months before, but he had been a different man then, totally uninterested in any woman in the world but Ana Barragán. But that still held true, did it not?

She dragged the rocker to the table and sat down opposite him. "I should be vexed at finding you out of bed, but I will admit you seemed to have managed it pretty nicely. I'll inspect that wound again when you've finished breakfast," she said.

"I don't think you need to, Liz. I've got to get back to Taos. I can't lie around here much longer."

"Yes, you can!" Her blue eyes seemed to actually spark. "You're in no condition to even leave this room yet, never mind go back to Taos. You won't be able to for several more days, perhaps a week or two. Mr. St. Vrain told me how much you want to ride with him, and he agrees with me that while that's laudable, it's also absolutely out of the question. Colonel Price asked me to take care of you, and see that you get well. Although I did not ask for the job, I have every intention of doing it as best I can. And that includes keeping you right where you are."

Something told him that the peculiar discretion that was in this case "the better part of valor" would best be served by his saying nothing.

"Tell me about yourself." That seemed safe enough.

She leaned back in the rocker. "All right, but when I begin to bore you, kindly remember that you asked for it."

New York, she said, born in Albany. Her middle name, Tapper, had been her mother's maiden name. Morton was her senior by seven years. He had taken care of both of them since their mother and father died in the same year, when she was twelve, fortunately leaving enough money for him to educate her while he began practicing law after Yale. "I had no desire at all to come west with Morton. This horrible thing up in Taos is just the sort of ghastly business I feared might go on out here, but when President Polk appointed him to Governor Bent's staff, I decided I could pay him back a little by keeping house for him while he is posted to Santa Fe, and I will, once we find a place to buy, or rent for a while."

"Hasn't this rebellion changed your mind?"

"No . . . to my surprise. Houses in this town are hard to find what with all of the Americans flooding in to help organize the new territory. When I first got here I thought Morton was condemning me to purgatory, but now . . . well, I don't think I could live anywhere but here. I have already come to love this country every bit as much as you do."

"You think I love it?"

"Don't you? That night we first met . . ." *

"I was a different man then. I wouldn't characterize my feelings about New Mexico quite that way now." Did she detect the bitterness he heard in his own voice?

If she did detect it, she ignored it. The other question was apparently going to remain unanswered.

"Your turn," she said. "I particularly want to hear something of your adventures with Mr. Carson and Colonel Frémont this past year. I heard a little about them when our wagon train reached Bent's Fort. That was where your expedition set out from, wasn't it?"

He told her then the story of his year, carefully dulling some of the more sharply painful edges.

Nor did he mention Ana Barragán, or her death. She had no need to know anything of that.

She listened wide-eyed through it all, but at the end her eyes narrowed. "Fascinating. Exciting, too. You have a gift for this sort of narrative. You should reduce all these memories to writing someday. There are not nearly enough first-hand reports of the way things really happen in the West." She paused. "One thing, though . . . there seemed to be one major character missing from your account."

"Oh?"

"I heard so much about Kit Carson, Colonel Frémont, someone I think you called Alex Godey, or something like that, a certain Mr. Kern, and at least a dozen others, including the famous Captain Sutter. All marvelous, courageous, capable men, I am sure, but . . . I did not hear one word about Bradford Stone!"

Before he could answer there came a sharp knock at his door. "Sterling Price here, Mr. Stone. May I see you?"

Colonel Sterling Price, commander of the Second Missouri Volunteers, turned out to be a tall, well-set-up, handsome man of about Frémont's age, with an odd little cupid's-bow mouth, but also with a look of bright steel in his eyes.

"Please forgive the brevity of this visit, Mr. Stone," he

said with a smile, motioning Liz back down into the rocker she vacated and offered him. "As you might have guessed, I am heavily engaged in preparing my command to move north. But I simply had to meet and personally thank the brave man who rode down from Taos with the news of the insurrection. I am proud to know you, sir." Brusque perhaps, but genuinely sincere. Price seemed no Archibald Gillespie or Stephen Watts Kearny.

"Thank you, Colonel," Stone said. "May I inquire as to exactly when you will move north . . . . unless it's confidential information?"

"No secret. There are probably a hundred spies here in the capital. We'll march out by sundown the day after tomorrow. That will be the twenty-third. Mr. St. Vrain and his volunteer cavalry will leave Santa Fe on the morning of the twenty-fourth. They will join us a few miles south of La Cañada. We now have intelligence that the enemy has fortified that village."

Why the delay? Kit Carson could have had an entire division of the most individualistic, sometimes mutinous men on the face of the earth ready to ride out and meet the most unexpected emergency within an hour. A military force occupying what had suddenly turned into enemy country again should have been prepared to counterattack in minutes.

Would Luis Aragón still be alive when Price and his men reached Taos, particularly if the Second Missouri and St. Vrain's irregulars had to fight their way into the village?

As Stone had expected, Price left after no more than half a dozen more inconsequential words, a farewell handshake, and a smart salute.

"You seemed distressed by what Colonel Price had to say," Liz Bailey said when the officer had gone. "Even a little angry."

"I'm sorry. It had little to do with the colonel, I assure

you. I was thinking about a friend of mine. I've got to get to Taos and find out what's happened to him."

"Not today. Or tomorrow . . . or when Colonel Price and his soldiers leave. Now . . . please get back in bed and get some rest. You still look tired. I'll be back at lunchtime."

He felt rested and energetic, and he would have told her so, but he had pretty much worked out in his mind what he would eventually have to do, and it was a foregone conclusion she would disapprove. He had not asked Price if he could go north with him; he was sure the colonel's response would be the same as St. Vrain's. He was going to have to persuade someone that he was fit to ride, or would be soon, and the first persuasion could not come about with the lady who was looking after him.

"You could do me a mighty big favor, Liz."

"Yes?"

"Would you go to the tailor Señor Octavio Talamantes and buy me some clothes? His little shop is no more than a couple of blocks from here. Don Fabiano will direct you. All I have to wear is what I rode down from Taos in, and you told me you've already cut up part of that."

She regarded him closely. "You won't need any clothing for a while," she said.

He tried his damnedest to assume a look of innocence. "I know, but I'll feel better just knowing it is hanging in the armoire." He had almost asked her to get his wallet from his sheepskin jacket, but remembered that he would have to tell Ricardo to take the chamber pot away. "Ask Señor Minjárez to advance me some money and put it on my bill."

"You aren't planning on sneaking out of here behind my back, are you?"

"No," he said.

"All right, Brad." She still looked doubtful. He had to allay any doubts she still harbored.

"I will rest now. Could you please help me to the bed? You're right. I'm suddenly exhausted."

He felt guilty. Beyond his natural regard for her as a new-found, caring friend, he would not allow her to mean anything special to him, not with the grave at Estancia Barragán so fresh in memory—and fairly so in reality.

But Liz Tapper Bailey had in just this moment become someone with whom he did not want to even approximate a lie. And he was lying to her in a way, even though it was in the service of what he deemed the best of causes.

After she helped him into bed, she went to the door and looked back at him for what must have been a full minute before she stepped through it and closed it behind her.

5

The *mozo* Ricardo, once Stone had managed to evade Liz Bailey's watchful eye long enough to get to the armoire to retrieve his money, proved a willing and skillful coconspirator. The young Mexican promised to have Aragón's horse at the back door of the hotel two hours after St. Vrain's volunteers started north. He would have the well-rested animal fed, provisioned, and place the Hawken back in the saddle scabbard, and load food for its rider in the saddlebags. Stone had figured out that he could not very well start back for Taos in advance of the irregulars. The same insurgents, probably heavily reinforced by now, would be waiting at Estación Embudo. He could never fool them twice.

There only remained now the agony of impatience he knew would plague him in the next two days.

41

No Wall Too Strong

Taos
February 3, 1847

"Colonel Price will move to the attack on the pueblo this afternoon, Luis. He isn't wasting any time," Stone told Aragón when he found the Santa Féan in his room at La Posada, alive, if not exactly well.

Stone had ridden into the plaza with St. Vrain's Volunteers that morning.

Aragón explained what had happened to him through swollen lips.

Some of the insurrectionists had remembered that he had worked with Stone and Charlie Bent at the cantina, and after deliberating on whether or not to kill him, had settled for giving the poor devil a thorough beating. They had mashed his handsome, brown face to a purple-and-yellow pulp, and administered a *bastinado* that left him unable to walk. When he entered the room Stone found him trying to daub some native medicine on a back striated with the marks of whips. Stone could not suppress a faint cry of anger as he took the job over.

"I think they eventually would have killed me, Bradford," Aragón said. "But one of their leaders ordered them to let me go, and had three of them carry me up here to my room. You know this leader."

"I do?"

"It was Don Bernardo Barragán."

Stone's heart doubled its beat. "He stayed in Taos?"

"Yes. Until Colonel Price and his army came in this morning. He has been quite a presence among these revolutionaries, at least since that morning we saw him ride through the plaza. They listen to him. I wanted to get some time alone with him, to ask him about the last days and moments of Doña Ana. . . ."

"And did you?"

"No. He did not speak after he called the others off, and although I begged him, he refused to come and visit me."

"Is he still with the enemy?"

"I do not know."

"He might have changed his mind about protecting you. We ought to get you to a safer place. I have time before we move against the pueblo."

"The town is safe enough now. I'll stay here, Bradford." Aragón fell silent, but then began again. "Enough of that. I do not wish to talk about the don. Look . . . I believe I can ride if you help me into the saddle. And I most assuredly can shoot if we can find a weapon for me."

"St. Vrain would hit the roof if he found you riding with his men. As it is, he's trying to hold *me* back, and I'm a good deal more fit than you are. You have no need to prove your loyalty, *amigo*. He's aware of what you've done since Charlie's death."

"But there is something I must do."

"What?"

"It is personal, Bradford. *Lo siento.*"

Damned if the little beggar did not look secretive. "All right, I won't pry. But I beg you to forget it. Get well."

Stone knew he should have argued more with the battered Aragón, but he only shook his head and left him with a promise to return.

2

It had taken eleven days for the combined forces of Ceran St. Vrain and Colonel Price to reach Taos. They had already fought and won two sizable battles on their way up the trails paralleling the Río.

Stone had planned to follow St. Vrain and his men, keeping out of sight—not hard to do with St. Vrain's scouts watching only the road ahead of them—and perhaps catching up with them at Ranchos de Taos, when it would be too late to turn him back toward Santa Fe, and too dangerous for him to ride back alone.

Actually he caught them, and the Second Missouri, when they had just reached La Cañada and found an enemy force that could have numbered over a thousand men defending the little town. He witnessed the battle they fought there from a distance, but close enough that he could smell the powder and hear the screams of the wounded. He wanted to get into the fight himself, but he feared if St. Vrain saw him when they were still this far south, he would send him back, and perhaps with an escort the Taos man would be loath to spare.

Much the same thing happened at Estación Embudo, where another army of insurgents awaited Price and St. Vrain. By that time two squadrons of dragoons had arrived from Albuquerque as reinforcements. St. Vrain, a captain now, and his mounted volunteers, caught escaping insurrectionists in a deadly cross fire that sealed the victory.

St. Vrain finally cornered Stone in the aftermath of the second battle, cursed roundly, but reluctantly permitted him to journey north with his column when Stone pointed out that despite his men's efforts, numbers of the enemy had escaped to the south and could block his way.

Stone apologized, but also told the erstwhile merchant that he thought "it only fair to warn you, sir, but in any hostilities at Taos itself, or anywhere else from here on out, I *will* fight."

Scouts rode back from reconnoitering the arroyos and sage prairies past Ranchos and San Francisco de Asis. They reported no sign of resistance or enemy patrols on the southern approaches to Taos, and moments later more scouts brought the news that enemy forces had vacated the village. They now occupied the fortresslike pueblo of their Indian allies.

As they rode into Taos, the column of irregulars passed Stone's *casita*. It looked untouched. The mules seemed at the point of starvation, however, and Stone broke away from his companions long enough to feed them. There had evidently been a couple of good rains or snows in the two weeks he had been gone; the watering troughs were running over.

When he reached the plaza, it amazed him that Price had already given orders that they would move to the attack directly after lunch. "No rest," the colonel said. "The enemy won't be resting as they prepare to meet our attack. The more time we grant them, the harder they will be to dislodge."

It left Stone an hour to look for Aragón; he did not need it. He found the trader sitting by the window in his room at La Posada, nursing his injuries.

"Bradford!" Luis had cried when Stone came through the door. "I had all but given up hope of ever seeing you again. I tried to attract the attention of the *soldados* down in the plaza so I could ask about you, but I fear my voice was too weak to be heard above the noise they made. What are you doing here?"

"I owed you a horse, *amigo,* remember?"

Aragón ignored that, and pointed to the bandages at Stone's shoulder, now filthy gray and tattered. Even lifting his arm to point brought pain to his dark eyes.

"*¿Qué pasa?* What has happened to you, my friend?"

Stone told him of his frightening misadventure at Estación Embudo on the ride down to Santa Fe.

"Give me a moment to get some clean cloth from my host downstairs and I will change that dressing. I do not know if Manuel Cardoza, the *médico* here in Taos, is still alive, but I will try to find him."

"Sit still, Luis! I don't need a doctor, and I don't want you moving around. My shoulder is almost healed now, anyway." That was far from the truth, but he certainly could not complain about his own pain when he looked at Luis's misshapen face. "We're a fine pair, aren't we? Perhaps we'll always need Kit to look after us. As I recall, neither of us got a scratch on the Cimarron."

"I must confess that there have been a time or two these past two weeks when I would have welcomed the presence of Don Cristóbal and his rifle. But no more than I would have welcomed *your* presence, Bradford."

Before Stone left to rejoin St. Vrain in the plaza, he glanced at the small portrait of Ana Barragán. The shelf beneath it held the waxy remains of four more candles.

3

At two o'clock in the afternoon of the third of February the final major battle of the Taos Rebellion began with barrages from the field howitzers and mortars of the Second Missouri Volunteers. The guns' principal target was the pueblo's adobe church with its twin bell towers.

Scouts had estimated that the Taos pueblo harbored more than seven hundred New Mexican rebels and their Indian allies. The defenders faced about three hundred fifty Americans, and some sixty or seventy other New Mexicans. These latter professed an entirely different political persuasion from that of the ones inside the church and those sniping at the attackers from the tiered stone-and-adobe buildings looking down on the pueblo's *plaza mayor.*

Stone certainly had ideas about the matters which had ranged these men against each other, and had reduced it all to a simple equation—for him, anyway.

Men inside these walls had murdered and beaten friends of his—and theirs. Someone had to stop the killers behind those mud walls, kill them if it had to be done, even if some slightly less culpable men died with them. His attitude resembled the attitude he felt sure would be that of his friend Christopher Houston Carson in similar circumstances.

The attack on the church and the walls adjacent to it now began in earnest, but Price held his infantry and the mounted volunteers out of the battle that first afternoon, and left the first day's entire effort to his artillery.

From time to time a head would appear briefly above one of the pueblo walls, but too far from where St. Vrain and his men sat their horses to chance a shot. Stone looked in vain for the face of the man whose name had dropped into Luis's story with the impact of one of the cannonballs striking the side of the church. Although he did not see him, he felt in his bones that Don Bernardo Barragán was somewhere inside the compound.

He looked at the riders closest to him. They all carried rifles in saddle holsters, but a number of them had sabers belted at their waists, and one or two displayed lances such as he had seen in California. He wondered how much he could contribute to any attack. He certainly did not consider himself skilled at reloading the Hawken in the saddle, and the bad shoulder severely limited movements of his arm. One shot from his old Hawken and he could well be through for the day. He longed to have Carson's Paterson Colts jammed in his belt.

The field howitzers, and a battery of six-pounder cannons, fired round after round at the surprisingly strong buildings and thick adobe walls. Stone could discern no visible effect from the countless barrages, which hammered at the old church right up to sundown.

"That adobe is the strangest shit I ever turned my guns on," Price's artillery officer, Captain Woldemar Fischer, said when the colonel ordered a cessation of the day's hostilities. "It doesn't really resist the shells at all. It just swallows them, slows them down, and closes behind them the way a wound heals, only faster. I feel like I'm just making those damned walls stronger."

As darkness approached, Price called for a complete withdrawal, and marched his cold, hungry men the three miles back to the plaza.

Crippled as he was, Aragón had somehow struggled down to street level to meet them. He sat in a buckboard with a mule hitched to it. "You stubborn little bastard. What are you doing out of bed?" Stone said.

Luis ignored the question. "Were you in grave danger at any time today, Bradford?" he asked.

"Not a bit. Although Colonel Price does not waste time, he does not rush things, either. It has been a very careful assault so far. I think tomorrow he will press the attack more closely. I am impressed with him. I think Kit would be, too."

"¡Bueno! His being careful may save some lives. Not all the men at the pueblo are evil *hombres*." The trader looked Stone over carefully. "I rented this wagon with the thought that if you are not too tired, and if your shoulder gives you no more trouble than it seems to be giving you now, we might pay a call on Doña Ignacia and Señora Carson. They are both living at Casa Carson. I fear I could not walk that far."

"I'd be glad to drive us there."

4

The thought of visiting Ignacia and Josefa had occurred to someone else. Ceran St. Vrain and his wife were paying a call when Stone and Luis arrived. Stone had forgotten that Mrs. St. Vrain had stayed in Taos through all the troubles. St. Vrain had not once mentioned her when Stone saw him in Santa Fe, but her safety must have weighed heavily on the affable Taos merchant's mind. Ever since the revolt began on the nineteenth of last month, and particularly during the eleven-day march north, he could have had no inkling of what he might find in Taos. Tonight he looked less the vengeful military man and more the old St. Vrain of Stone's first acquaintance with him, chatting amiably with the sisters and Ignacia's two daughters, Rumalda Boggs and Teresina Bent.

But the amiability was all on St. Vrain's side. Ignacia and Josefa still looked gray and stricken. The young girl Teresina's face remained as blank as a sheet of new sketching paper throughout the evening, and as barren of emotion.

If Stone had felt any doubt about the rightness of the battle they would fight in the morning, it left him now.

"*Por favor,* Don Bradford," Josefa Carson said as Stone and Luis left. She stood on tiptoe to kiss his cheek. "Do not let any harm come to you tomorrow. Although Cristóbal has more friends than he can count, he cannot afford to lose one such as you. Except possibly for Colonel Frémont, he speaks more highly of you than he does of any man he knows. *¡Hasta la vista y vaya con Dios!*"

42
The Vows

The first two hours of the next morning's resumed attack seemed a frustrating repetition of that of the day before; barrage after barrage of artillery failed to make a breach in the thick walls. The artillery captain Fischer cursed incessantly.

At about eleven o'clock Captain I. H. K. Burgwin and two companies of dragoons charged the west wall of the church, while a captain of the Missouri Volunteers, whose name Stone had not caught, led his infantry in from the north. Both contingents hacked away at the adobe brick, while another party of infantry brought up a scaling ladder, climbed the walls with torches in their hands, and set a series of small fires on the roof and in the belfries. Someone passed the word along to St. Vrain's mounted Volunteers—Stone among them and still riding Aragón's horse—that Captain Burgwin had been killed by enemy rifle fire.

St. Vrain decided to ride to Colonel Price's command post to complain that his irregular cavalry had nothing to do, and asked Stone to accompany him. They found the colonel in a small grove of cottonwoods, calmly eating from a plate of stew, and still on horseback.

"My men are chafing at the bit, Colonel. Ask Brad here, who will lead the attack with me. He's just finished a year of riding with Kit Carson and John Frémont," St. Vrain said. "At least let us go after the domiciles to the east. We'll have to face them there sooner or later, anyway."

"Hold your ground, Captain," Price said. "When we drive the defenders from the church, you will find more than enough cavalry work to do. If I turn you loose to cross that compound before we clear the enemy from this position, you will expose your men to heavy fire from the left flank and the rear. I simply will not be hurried into losing men I need not lose. But when the enemy leaves the church—attack!"

If St. Vrain did not, Stone saw the hard, cold intelligence—and the humanity—of the colonel's tactical decision, and his confidence in the commander rose even higher. Price seemed no more willing to accept big losses for the sake of glory than Carson would have been. To St. Vrain's credit, he put up no argument. They rode back to the edge of the compound.

A six-pounder cannon off to the left of St. Vrain's command now spewed enormous amounts of grapeshot into the main part of the Indian village. It had no effect other than to keep the enemy pinned down in the buildings at the east of the pueblo—St. Vrain's "domiciles."

But now the gunners wheeled the big cannon to within sixty yards of the church. Some of dead Captain Burgwin's infantry had managed to cut several small holes in the walls, and the six-pounder's crew brought the field piece's shattering fire directly to bear on one after another of them.

Stone was astonished when foot soldiers dashed to the holes between rounds and threw fused artillery shells through by hand. Stone saw three of the Missourians fall, apparently cut down by rifle fire from inside the church. One other man was blown apart when the shell he had carried to the wall detonated before he reached it.

The men at the six-pounder moved the gun again, this time to within half a dozen yards, losing two more men in the process. It took only three more rounds to make a breach large enough that Stone felt sure he could get through it mounted if he had to.

The infantry poured through the enlarged breach two

abreast, and the cannonade stopped. From inside the church the racket of small-arms fire grew to deafening proportions. It did not abate for fifteen minutes.

Then flames engulfed the southernmost of the twin belfries, and as Stone watched, one of the structure's four main supporting timbers burned completely through, dropping the huge bronze bell to the hardpan at the church's entrance.

The great dull clang that echoed from the high buildings at the northern and eastern perimeters of the pueblo as the bell struck the ground could have been a signal. The church doors burst open and a tide of men spilled out into the compound. Only one out of three of them carried rifles.

"Let's get at them!" St. Vrain shouted.

Sabers flashed, lances stretched level with the ground, two or three rifles waved in the air, and St. Vrain's horsemen swept out across the flat, rock-hard, frozen caliche of the compound, riding fleeing runners down across a broad, confused front as they raced for the buildings on the east, the riders slashing them, driving the lances home with now and again a near disastrous accident. An occasional lance would not pull free and twice he saw riders tumble to the ground.

Ahead of him he spied a lone man lagging behind the other racing figures. His pace looked more limp than run, but unlike so many of the others, he did carry a firearm, an ancient muzzle-loader. The man stopped in his tracks, and grounded the stock of his bulky old weapon in the caliche, preparing to reload. He looked up at Stone, fear seeming to paralyze him.

Stone looked squarely into the haunted eyes of Jaime Carbajal, the comically grouchy little *santero* who had packed the paintings for Ed Kern to take to Bent's Fort.

Stone veered his horse away and kept on riding. Someone else would have to account for Jaime.

Ahead of him another man knelt, facing him. He had fixed his sights on Stone, and this time there would be no time for a moral choice. Stone lifted the Hawken to his good shoulder and pulled the trigger. The man rolled over on his side, and as he did his rifle discharged harmlessly into the air.

But now Stone's one precious load was spent.

He had reached the line of the eastern buildings, and a brief survey revealed a narrow alleyway. Just inside its opening he found a hitchrail, reined in his horse, slipped from the saddle, hitched the animal loosely to the rail, and began to reload his rifle.

"*¡Yanqui!*"

For a moment he could not tell from where the voice had come. But he knew the voice. Knew it well. The last time he had heard that voice, it had quivered in rage with a promise to kill Stone or have him killed.

When he looked toward the end of the alley, he found the speaker.

It was Don Bernardo Barragán, all right, not twenty feet away from him.

The master of Estancia Barragán held a pistol leveled on him. The look on his hawk face was one of hatred so pure it was almost a thing of beauty. Stone's heart turned to ice.

He could not, would not turn and run. He steeled himself. It would be over soon enough.

Then . . .

Barragán lowered the pistol and fired it into the ground at his feet. He raised the now empty weapon again.

And another shot rang out behind Brad Stone. A great blotch of blood spread like spilled wine across the chest of Bernardo Barragán. He crumpled to the caliche.

Stone turned to find that another mounted man had ridden into the entrance of the alleyway.

Luis Aragón.

A pistol in the trader's fine-boned hand still smoked. How had he . . . ? Stone could not take time to think.

He moved quickly then to the fallen man at the end of the alley. Don Bernardo was trying to talk. Stone knelt beside him. Pinkish yellow foam bubbled through the blood soaking Barragán's ruffled shirt.

"Why did you not kill me when you had the chance, Don Bernardo?"

Barragán stared at him through black eyes that had begun to glaze. "I promised someone once . . . that I would not." Blood bubbled through the hard mouth. "I have kept that promise." He coughed. More blood gushed. "But do not think for a moment, *yanqui* . . . that anything has changed between us. I . . . will hate and curse you . . . through all eternity. . . ."

He closed his eyes and died.

2

Sterling Price decided they would not attack again that day. Bodies littered the compound, more than a hundred of them, Stone guessed, when he examined the battleground after the Second Missouri's bugler blew the recall. "We shall give them until tomorrow to strike their colors and accept our terms," the colonel said. "Surely there has been enough killing, even for them, and surely whoever commands them will have the sense to see their cause is lost."

3

"I did not know you were no longer in danger when I found you in the *calle*, Bradford. I thought I was about to save your life," Luis Aragón said after Stone had helped him up the stairs to his room. "But now . . . I must tell you the truth. . . . I would have killed Don Bernardo anyway, even had I known his pistol was not loaded. You see, like the Don, I, too, made a vow."

"Why? He was my enemy, not yours." On the agonizing ride back to the plaza from the pueblo and its ruined, smoking church, with Luis almost slipping from the saddle once, and still in great pain from the beating, Stone had told him of Don Bernardo's strange forbearance when he had the *"yanqui puerco"* in his sights. "After he only fired at the ground, I would have asked for his surrender. But perhaps it's better this way. I shudder at the thought that he could have gone to the gallows for his part in this."

"And so do I. . . ." Aragón grimaced as Stone eased him onto the bed, but his face turned placid when he looked up at Ana's portrait above the miniature mountain range of melted wax. Then he spoke again. "But it is not because I have the forgiveness in my heart you have always shown, *mi amigo*. Letting Don Bernardo go to the hangman would have cheated me."

"How so . . . ?"

"I had another talk with Fra Porfirio while you were in Santa Fe. It was then I made *my* vow."

"Oh?"

"I am not entirely sure I should tell you this, even now that Don Bernardo is dead. . . ."

"Please don't hold back, Luis."

"Porfirio, good man that he is, told me something that ate at my heart for days. . . ."

"For God's sake, what?"

"He crossed himself and said . . . that Doña Ana and the *niño* were both in excellent health when Roberto drove them back to the *hacienda* that night. He says he could hardly believe it when Padre Martínez returned to Ranchos from Estancia Barragán a week later and told him that Don Bernardo said they both had died. The padre never saw Galinda or Roberto. They were gone by then. Only the Don himself was still living at the *hacienda*." He stopped, took a breath that wracked his slim body before he went on. "Would you get a candle from the chest, Bradford, light it, and place it on the shelf, *por favor?*"

When Stone lit it, the candle sputtered and flared as if a cold draft were moving through the room.

"Don Bernardo," Aragón said now, "killed Doña Ana and your son."

"*What?*"

"He killed them."

"Luis! I cannot believe that. Not even Don Bernardo could—"

"*Un momento, mi amigo, por favor.* I do not mean he actually took a knife and cut their throats, although knowing Don Bernardo as I do, he could have . . . but he did *something*. Something terrible. He drove them off into the desert to die, or made Doña Ana bring it on herself. Whatever he did, *he killed them!* Nothing will ever persuade me differently."

The flame of the candle on the shelf guttered once and expired.

"Why did you not tell me of this before, Luis?"

"You would have tried to kill Don Bernardo yourself, Bradford, if you ever talked with Fra Porfirio. And no matter where or when you found him, he would have been ready for you. I knew he would never think *I* would try. He once doubted that I had honor or *cojones,* remember? If you do not, I do. Remembering that made it much easier for me."

"But why *you?* It was after all, my love and *my* son you say he . . ."

"*Ah, sí . . . pero . . . lo siento. . . .*" There came a longer pause this time. ". . . Doña Ana was my wife . . . and *joven* Bradford Luis would have become my son, *también. . . .*"

43

Until You Are Dead . . .

"Then I will see you in Santa Fe, Bradford?" Aragón said. "I would wait and ride down the Río with you, but my father has sent word that I am neglecting our business. We have two big shipments coming in from Independence in another week or so, and he needs my help."

"I'll be fine. My shoulder is finally as good as new, and at any rate, when I go south this time I will have no trouble getting past Estación Embudo. If Colonel Price has not yet rounded up all the rebels, the few who remain at large have either left the territory or are lying low."

"Do not leave Santa Fe without saying *adios* to me, *mi amigo,* or rather *hasta la vista.* Nothing will change your mind about leaving New Mexico?"

"I'm afraid not, Luis. I've already stayed six months longer than I intended."

"*Por favor, Don Bradford,*" Luis said, "we Nuevo Méjicanos need you here. Not only do we need you; your own country needs you here as well."

2

The end of the battle at the pueblo, the surrender of the ringleaders of the revolt, the trials that followed swiftly, and the hangings of the last week, had only strengthened his determination to leave a land that seemed crueler by the day.

In the middle two weeks of April the court presided over

by Charles Beaubien sentenced at least one man to death a day. For the rest of Stone's life the hollow voice of grim-faced Beaubien chanting, *"Muerto . . . muerto . . . muerto . . ."* would echo through his corridors of conscience.

Neither he nor Aragón had watched the executions. They did attend the trials.

Stone sat in dumb shock through most of the proceedings, only speaking to Aragón when the court recessed, something that did not happen too frequently, since Beaubien, judicial and calculating enough in appearance, voice, and manner, seemed in an ungodly hurry to get things over with. Seldom did one of the trials last as long as half an hour. Never did the jury deliberate as much as fifteen minutes.

"I am troubled by all of this," Stone said once as he and Aragón ate lunch in the gazebo in the plaza. "In the first place I question the choice of Charles Beaubien as judge. He seems a capable jurist, certainly an efficient one, but did you not tell me, Luis, that one of the victims of the rising's first day—if it can be called a 'rising'—was his own son Narciso? I do not think that makes for complete impartiality. I find it even more troubling that Beaubien's brother George is foreman of the jury."

"You do not consider the revolt a 'rising,' Bradford?"

"Hardly. We're still at war with Mexico. Some people might claim these rebels were only defending their home-land, that they are in no wise criminals, but soldiers, prison-ers of war. They're being tried for *murder* . . . and treason. I know how ghastly their behavior was, and possibly some of them could be tried for 'war crimes'—if the law recognized any such things—particularly those who butchered Charlie."

"I like and admire you *americanos,* Bradford," Aragón said, "but I sometimes despair of ever understanding you. Those fiends deserved to die. You saw them yourself. I can-not trouble myself about how we get them to the gallows."

"There are other things, too," Stone went on. "Assigning

army privates as defense attorneys, for one. I understand they've had some legal training, but they must be aware at every moment how much their army superiors want convictions. It's disgraceful that there will be no appeals. So far as I know, there has not been one single transcript written yet of any of these trials."

"You sound like an *abogado,* Bradford," Aragón broke in. "Why are you so upset today?"

"That defendant this morning."

"Pablo Muñoz?"

"Yes."

"Did *you* see him at Charlie's when you and I were there on the nineteenth, Luis?"

Aragón wrinkled his brow. "No . . . I did not!"

"I didn't, either. Come on, then! We have to have a word with Judge Beaubien before court reconvenes. We don't have a hell of a lot of time."

3

"No, Mr. Stone," Charles Beaubien said, "I cannot retry Señor Muñoz. May I point out, he made no attempt at a defense on his own behalf. He may very well have taken part in Governor Bent's murder without your seeing him. He most certainly took a large part in this criminal revolt. Some of the witnesses against him are his own people. I suggest you let that thought comfort you. The same holds true, of course, for you, Señor Aragón."

4

The morning wore a coat of gray clouds when Stone waved the Santa Fe–bound Luis Aragón on down the road at Ranchos de Taos. He would have ridden farther with his friend, but he knew Aragón would turn in at the Estancia Barragán gate and pay a visit to the graveyard. Stone wanted to go there alone himself, and would, but he knew that with Luis it was much more than a mere want; it was an imperative.

He returned to town. As soon as temporary governor Donaciano Vigil arrived in Taos the day after tomorrow and relieved him of the civil duties he had resumed at the cantina after the surrender at the pueblo, he would leave. There remained a few things to be attended to before he packed.

5

When he saw Ceran about the last of the rent for his little house, the merchant would not accept a penny.

"I have no wish to leave New Mexico owing anyone anything, Mr. St. Vrain."

"Nonsense. This territory and every soul in it is in debt to you, Brad. Even some who aren't here at the moment, Kit for instance. I only wish you could see your way clear to—"

"Please, sir. It is difficult enough to say good-bye as it is."

When he bade Josefa Carson and Ignacia Bent farewell, much the same thing happened, and he turned their pleas aside as gently as he could. They, too, invoked Carson and his high regard for Stone as a reason he should stay. Although he longed to see the scout once more, he decided fortune had smiled on him by keeping Kit in California. It would be a good deal more difficult saying no to Carson, should he ask Stone to stay, than to anyone else.

Back at the adobe *casa* he began his packing.

What to take and what to leave? With the purchases Liz Tapper Bailey had made for him during his convalescence, he now had a far larger wardrobe than he needed for the return trip to Independence and on to Groverton. He discarded his stained old buckskins and all other trail clothes, saving only enough of the latter for the arduous trip across the Great Plains. The Hawken would go back with him, if only to hang over the mantel in his parents' home and never be fired again. He would need his surveying equipment. His money would last nicely on the homeward journey, but he would have to get back to work soon after reaching Illinois. He packed scores of the field sketches made in the mountains and the deserts. He would not quit painting; he would only quit the West.

After looking long at the nude of Ana, he packed it, too.

His thoughts about money reminded him of one stop he had to make in Santa Fe before moving on. Casa Tules. He had to reclaim the chit Doña Gertrudes had taken for the money she advanced him. Doubtless she would add her rich contralto to the chorus clamoring for him to change his mind.

Clever as La Tules was, she would meet with failure, too, as would all the others.

6

At Ana's grave he found that Aragón, sure enough, had stopped here on his way south. When they said good-bye three days ago, how had the trader managed to hide from him the bouquet now atop the mound? It was only the newest among five others. Aragón must have come out here once a week since Brad Stone himself had been here last. He must have resumed his visits when he was still recovering from the beating he received. Stone added his flowers to the others.

He looked down at the grave for a long time, made one quick excursion through the *jacal* where Ana had borne his son, and then mounted, took his two mules in tow, and left the graveyard and Estancia Barragán for the last time.

Once he passed under the high, arched, wrought-iron at the gate, he did not look back. Had not this happened once before?

7

Unlike the morning three days earlier, when he had set Aragón on the road at Ranchos, the first light cracking above the deep blue Sangre de Cristos in the east promised a brilliant, cloud-free morning.

Stone and his small cavalcade moved slowly but steadily upward through the sage for an hour, until they reached the top of the hill where Aragón, Carson, and he had stopped the morning he first came to Taos.

Was the gorge even deeper, blacker, emptier, and more forbidding than when he had first seen it?

Or was the great, yawning void only expanding to match the one inside him?

He turned his horse and the mules toward the trail south.

"Goddamn it!" He hurled the words against the mountainside.

"Time to catch up!" he yelled up at the peerless sky.

44

The Road Back

He registered at the United States Hotel under the gratified eye of that nonpareil boniface, Fabiano Minjárez.

"I'll be staying only about a week, Don Fabiano," Stone said. "Don Luis Aragón is trying to find a trading party for me to ride east with."

"*Ah, sí,*" the innkeeper said. "Don Luis stopped by here last night with a message for you to see him as quickly as you can, *señor.* Perhaps it is about your trip . . . which I still hope you will abandon. *Por favor, Don Bradford.* I beg of you. Stay here in New Mexico."

Fabiano, too? Well . . . with Minjárez it was probably only that *cortesía* he had found so often in New Mexico. The innkeeper could not know how sick Stone was of hearing it.

"*Muchísimas gracias, Don Fabiano.*" The *mozo* Ricardo had picked up his saddlebags. Stone prepared to follow the boy to the room, but turned back to Minjárez. "Is Señor Morton Bailey still staying with you?" Why had he not asked about Liz outright?

"No, regrettably," Minjárez said. "Señor Bailey and his sister have bought a house on the Alameda. They still dine with me here at the United States, however."

2

"When Don Fabiano said you were anxious to see me, Luis, I really hoped you wanted to tell me I could leave for the East earlier than you first expected."

"I am sorry, Bradford, *pero no*. It will be ten days before I can place you with a wagon train. Something else has come up. A shipment for you, half a wagon load, came in from St. Louis by way of the Cimarron Cutoff just yesterday."

"A shipment for me . . . ?"

"*Sí*. Follow me, *por favor*."

Aragón led the way past the corrals to where an unhitched Murphy wagon stood, its canvas top rolled back. The wagon bulged with boxes and crates, all marked in huge black letters: MR. BRADFORD STONE, ESQ., TAOS, NEW MEXICO TERRITORY.

"Who's it from?"

Aragón reached up into the wagon and pulled an oilskin pouch from under the seat. "Here is the waybill and a letter."

According to papers in the oilskin, the shipment came from a company in St. Louis called Emile Girardeaux and Sons. A brief note on the firm's letterhead read:

> Dear Mr. Bradford Stone, Esquire,
>
> Mr. Edward Kern of Sutter's Mill, California Territory, has requested us to consign this shipment to you. It comes to you with no charge whatsoever, as Mr. Kern has paid for it in full.
>
> Should any of the materials be damaged or defective, Emile Girardeaux and Sons of St. Louis,

Missouri, will replace them—also entirely free of charge.

Yr. Obt. Svt.
Phillipe Girardeaux

Stone climbed up into the bed of the wagon. There must have been three or four dozen canvases of assorted sizes and shapes, some on stretchers and crated, still others piled loosely and in rolls. Box after countless box held tubes of paint, brushes, among them sables and brights far better than anything he owned, plus painting knives, two new palettes, stacks of sketchpads, and a much larger easel than his old one, which at least twenty different packhorses and mules had lugged across half the continent.

Enough stuff filled the bottom of the Murphy to keep the most industrious painter in Christendom in his studio for years.

"Luis!" he said. "Return this stuff to the shipper. Immediately!"

"But, Bradford," the trader stammered, "if you should change your—"

"Luis!"

3

When he returned to the hotel he found that the Territorial Postal Service in the Palace of the Governors across the plaza had discovered he was in Santa Fe and had delivered another letter for him.

ORPHEUS GALLERIES, LTD.
127 Fifth Avenue
New York, New York

April 14, 1847

Mr. Bradford Stone, Esq.
Taos, New Mexico Territory

Dear Mr. Stone:

On March 28th last, we received nineteen oils-on-canvas bearing your signature. These paintings were consigned to us by Mr. Edward Kern, Esq., formerly of Philadelphia, Pennsylvania, and now of Sutter's Mill, California Territory, who has been a client of this gallery for seven years. He represents that you are interested in showing with us, and we would be honored indeed if such is the case. You, we are sure, will fully understand that we must hear that this is so directly from you. We are enclosing a copy of our standard contract for you to study.

Ed Kern had connections, sure enough. Stone went on reading.

Please note that we ordinarily only accept works of relatively unknown artists on a consignment basis. In your case we are so certain of your ultimate success we will be glad to purchase your paintings outright. Please ask your friend Mr. Kern about what this means in the way of expressing the confidence we repose in your future as an American artist.

In the event that we come to mutually acceptable terms, we will want more than the nineteen canvases currently in our possession, and we will want them as quickly as you can send them. We would want more of those splendid portraits, of course, but we would also like many more landscapes in

the style of the two done at Monterey. Mr. Kern
says that you are even better positioned now to do
this sort of thing since you have relocated to northern New Mexico.

Damn Ed Kern. He must have told the Orpheus people
that he, Stone, was staying on.

Suffice it to say for the moment that we agree
with Mr. Kern that no painter at work today pos-
sesses your genius for portraying the American
West. The American public hungers for just this
sort of work. Yours is among the finest we have
seen. This opinion is that of a gallery director who
once showed Catlin.

Yr. Obt. Svt.
Jasper Abernathy, Director

Ed Kern was clever, but not subtle. It would avail him
nothing. Stone could paint the things this Jasper Abernathy
wanted every bit as well in Groverton as he could in Taos.
And if, in the event he could not, so be it.

4

When he came downstairs for supper he found Liz Bailey
and her brother Morton at the same table where he had first
met them. He almost yielded to an impulse to back out
through the door and seek another place to eat, but Morton
beckoned to him.

"Please join us, Mr. Stone," Bailey said.

"I'd be intruding."

"Not at all. Would he, Elizabeth?"

"Of course not." She had not looked at him, but now she did. "Sit down, Brad. How's that shoulder?"

"As good as new, due in no small part to you."

"That's right," Morton Bailey said. "Forgive me. I'd forgotten you were wounded. And forgive me, too, that I've never told you how much I admired your courage when you made that ride down from Taos."

"Someone else would have done it, sir."

"But no one did. And another rider might have taken much, much longer. More innocent people could have died."

Liz looked up and squarely at him. "Señor Minjárez tells me you're leaving in a week."

"Yes."

"Pity," was all she said. It seemed there would be no entreaty from *her*, at least. Funny, he almost wished there had been one. Not that it would have made a particle of difference.

As before, Minjárez served them himself.

"When we first met," Bailey said when soup arrived, "I got the impression that you were going to make your life here in the West."

"Things have changed, sir."

"I know you fought in that last battle," Bailey said now. "Did you, by chance, attend the trials?"

"Yes, sir."

"I am a little disturbed by what I heard about them."

Without meaning to, Stone let some of the things he had told Luis Aragón slip out. During his accounting of them, Liz Bailey kept her blue eyes on him, but she said nothing. Yes, she certainly was marvelously attractive. In some other time . . . in some other place . . .

He had better stop that sort of thinking, now.

"You know," Bailey said when Stone finished, "we promised the people in this territory we would bring them the American rule of law. It seems you agree with me that this was hardly the way to start. I hope the right sort of my countrymen can come in here and begin to make things right. Men such as you, for instance. But I forget. You are leaving."

They consumed the rest of the meal largely in silence, and after coffee Stone excused himself. "I'm sorry I must leave. I have to pay a call on an old friend."

Life's tiny coincidences. The first time he met them he had left them sitting at this table to get money from La Tules, now he would do the same to pay Doña Gertrudes back.

At the door of the dining room he paused and looked back. He could not tell for a moment if she was looking at him. Yes, she was. But . . . her face told him nothing.

5

True to form, Doña Gertrudes Barceló made her own strong plea for him to stay in the territory. He found it difficult to credit what she said about the number of people in Santa Fe who felt as she did, from Donaciano Vigil in the Palace, who had returned from Taos the day after Stone came down himself, down through his host at the hotel, Fabiano Minjárez, and his tailor, Octavio Talamantes.

At the end she gave him a crushing *abrazo,* and he walked back to the hotel feeling himself a fugitive, thankful that it was dark enough that almost no one saw him.

The diminutive man sitting on the bench at the door of the United States Hotel saw him, though.

45

A Lion Remembered

"I'm on my way to Washington for the captain and Commodore Stockton again. Without no General Kearny to turn me around this time, maybe I'll make it," Kit said in answer to Stone's question. "I ain't going near that Colonel Price, just in case. I got to get a bite now. I ain't ate nothing but some jerky since I left Taos." Minjárez had apparently opened the *cocina* and the dining room just for his famous guest.

"But how . . . ?" Stone said when they settled into the same table he had shared earlier in the evening with Liz and Morton Bailey. "You came down from Taos, Kit? How on earth did you get there?"

"I rode from Los Angeles over the Spanish Trail. It's still quicker than the route we took last October. I got to Taos late in the afternoon of the same day you left."

"Why didn't you go straight north over the Sangres, instead of coming down here to the capital?"

"I wanted to thank you and Luis Aragón for what you done for my town, and for Josefa in particular. Cerrie St. Vrain filled me in on everything."

"It was a damn sight more Luis than me."

"Maybe."

"When will you leave Santa Fe?"

"Tomorrow morning. I already seen Luis about horses and new gear."

Carson fell silent, but to Stone it seemed as if the other shoe was about to fall. With Kit making that stop in Taos and talking with St. Vrain, there could be no doubt that the scout knew he was leaving New Mexico.

It would be far more difficult when his friend added his voice to all those others begging him to stay. He was lucky. It might have been even more difficult telling his old comrade no if he had done so on the very ground he, Brad Stone, had once adored.

But, without expecting this meeting to take place before he left, he knew now that he had been readying himself for it for more than six months. Not even Kit Carson could change his mind, no matter how compelling his arguments.

"Cerrie tells me," Kit said, "that you're leaving New Mexico for good. Is that true?"

"Yes."

"Brad . . . ," Kit said.

Now it would come.

"Yes, Kit?"

"Oh, nothing, I guess."

Might as well let it come. "Come on, Kit. Out with it."

"It ain't anything, really. Don't know why, but I was just thinking about that catamount we saw up on Raton Pass when we first came down to Taos. Remember it?"

"Yes." Surely it would come now.

It did not.

Kit said nothing. A full minute passed. Stone tried to read those innocent blue eyes, found nothing.

Two or three more minutes were lost forever before Kit spoke again.

"Why don't you get your gear together and ride out with me tomorrow, Brad? We could keep each other company as far as St. Louis, maybe. I'd admire that a lot."

It was Brad Stone's turn for silence, but at last he said, "Sure, Kit . . . I'll be ready."

"¡*Bueno!* I'll say good night, then. It's going to be 'time to catch up' before we know it."

He tossed and turned all through the long night. Every time he seemed to find sleep, a mountain lion bounded through the fragments of a dream and each time distant voices awakened him. . . .

Once it was his own.

"*Kit . . . ,*" it said. "*I don't think I could ever leave this country now that I've seen it. I belong here.*"

And then another voice.

"*Someday, when you feel like throwing it all away, when things are at rock bottom, think about that lion and how you felt today. Amazing how a little thing like that can see you through.*"

And then—

"*. . . Time to catch up! . . . Time to catch up! . . . Time to catch up!*"

46
Meridian

They met again at breakfast.

"You ain't wearing trail clothes," Carson said.

"No."

"How come? You know what traveling with me is like."

"Yes, but I won't be traveling with you."

"Rather go by yourself?"

"On this trip, yes. I going back up to Taos for a bit."

"Oh?"

"I've got some pictures I've got to paint."

"Maybe I can wait here for you a couple of days or a week. How long will painting these pictures take?"

"Don't really know, Kit." He grinned. "Ten, fifteen years. Hell! Maybe thirty."

The sly smile and sparkling eyes of Christopher Houston Carson suddenly became a work of art.

Available by mail from

TOR
FORGE

1812 • David Nevin
The War of 1812 would either make America a global power sweeping to the pacific or break it into small pieces bound to mighty England. Only the courage of James Madison, Andrew Jackson, and their wives could determine the nation's fate.

PRIDE OF LIONS • Morgan Llywelyn
Pride of Lions, the sequel to the immensely popular *Lion of Ireland,* is a stunningly realistic novel of the dreams and bloodshed, passion and treachery, of eleventh-century Ireland and its lusty people.

WALTZING IN RAGTIME • Eileen Charbonneau
The daughter of a lumber baron is struggling to make it as a journalist in turn-of-the-century San Francisco when she meets ranger Matthew Hart, whose passion for nature challenges her deepest held beliefs.

BUFFALO SOLDIERS • Tom Willard
Former slaves had proven they could fight valiantly for their freedom, but in the West they were to fight for the freedom and security of the white settlers who often despised them.

THIN MOON AND COLD MIST • Kathleen O'Neal Gear
Robin Heatherton, a spy for the Confederacy, flees with her son to the Colorado Territory, hoping to escape from Union Army Major Corley, obsessed with her ever since her espionage work led to the death of his brother.

SEMINOLE SONG • Vella Munn
"As the U.S. Army surrounds their reservation in the Florida Everglades, a Seminole warrior chief clings to the slave girl who once saved his life after fleeing from her master, a wife-murderer who is out for blood." —*Hot Picks*

THE OVERLAND TRAIL • Wendi Lee
Based on the authentic diaries of the women who crossed the country in the late 1840s. America, a widowed pioneer, and Dancing Feather, a young Paiute, set out to recover America's kidnapped infant daughter—and to forge a bridge between their two worlds.

Call toll-free 1-800-288-2131 to use your major credit card or clip and send this form below to order by mail

- -

Send to: Publishers Book and Audio Mailing Service
        PO Box 120159, Staten Island, NY 10312-0004

❑ 52471-3	1812 . . . . $6.99/$8.99	❑ 53657-6	Thin Moon and Cold Mist . . . . $6.99/$8.99
❑ 53650-9	Pride of Lions . . . . $6.99/$8.99	❑ 53883-8	Seminole Song . . . . $5.99/$7.99
❑ 54468-4	Waltzing in Ragtime . . . . $6.99/$8.99	❑ 55528-7	The Overland Trail . . . . $5.99/$7.99
❑ 55105-2	Buffalo Soldiers . . . . $5.99/$7.99		

Please send me the following books checked above. I am enclosing $_____. (Please add $1.50 for the first book, and 50¢ for each additional book to cover postage and handling. Send check or money order only—no CODs).

Name _____

Address _____ City _____ State _____ Zip_____

Available by mail from

TOR FORGE

THIN MOON AND COLD MIST • Kathleen O'Neal Gear

Robin Heatherton, a spy for the Confederacy, flees with her son to the Colorado Territory, hoping to escape from Union Army Major Corley, obsessed with her ever since her espionage work led to the death of his brother.

SOFIA • Ann Chamberlin

Sofia, the daughter of a Venetian nobleman, is kidnapped and sold into captivity of the great Ottoman Empire. Manipulative and ambitious, Sofia vows that her future will hold more than sexual slavery in the Sultan's harem. A novel rich in passion, history, humor, and human experience, *Sofia* transports the reader to sixteenth-century Turkish harem life.

MIRAGE • Soheir Khashoggi

"A riveting first novel.... Exotic settings, glamorous characters, and a fast-moving plot. Like a modern Scheherazade, Khashoggi spins an irresistible tale.... An intelligent page-turner." —*Kirkus Reviews*

DEATH COMES AS EPIPHANY • Sharan Newman

In medieval Paris, amid stolen gems, mad monks, and dead bodies, Catherine LeVendeur will strive to unlock a puzzle that threatens all she holds dear. "Breathtakingly exciting." —*Los Angeles Times*

SHARDS OF EMPIRE • Susan Shwartz

A rich tale of madness and magic—"*Shards of Empire* is a beautifully written historical.... An original and witty delight!" —*Locus*

SCANDAL • Joanna Elm

When former talk show diva Marina Dee Haley is found dead, TV tabloid reporter Kitty Fitzgerald is compelled to break open the "Murder of the Century," even if it means exposing her own dubious past.

BILLY THE KID • Elizabeth Fackler

Billy's story, epic in scope, echoes the vast grandeur of the magnificent country in which he lived. It traces the chain of events that inexorably shaped this legendary outlaw and pitted him against a treacherous society that threatened those he loved."

Call toll-free 1-800-288-2131 to use your major credit card or clip and send this form below to order by mail

- -

Send to: Publishers Book and Audio Mailing Service
PO Box 120159, Staten Island, NY 10312-0004

☐ 53657-6	Thin Moon and Cold Mist	$6.99/$7.99	☐ 54817-5	Shards of Empire	$5.99/$7.99
☐ 55386-1	Sofia	$6.99/$8.99	☐ 54471-4	Scandal	$6.99/$7.99
☐ 55094-3	Mirage	$6.99/$8.99	☐ 53340-2	Billy the Kid	$6.99/$8.99
☐ 52293-1	Death Comes as Epiphany	$4.99/$5.99			

Please send me the following books checked above. I am enclosing $_____. (Please add $1.50 for the first book, and 50¢ for each additional book to cover postage and handling. Send check or money order only—no CODs).

Name _____

Address _____ City _____ State _____ Zip_____